Reeta Chakrabarti
Finding Belle

Reeta Chakrabarti is a journalist and broadcaster who is a Chief Presenter for BBC News and has also reported extensively at home and abroad for the BBC. Born in London, she was brought up in Birmingham, lived in Calcutta, India, as a teenager where she attended Calcutta International School, and returned to the UK for university. She began working for the BBC in 1992 and has been there in various roles for over 30 years. She has previously been a judge for the 2021 David Cohen Prize for Literature; she was the chair of the 2021 Costa Book of the Year; and in 2023 chair of the BBC National Short Story Award.

She lives in London with her husband and has three children.

@reetacbbc

Reeta Chakrabarti
Finding Belle

HarperCollins*Publishers*

HarperCollins*Publishers* Ltd
1 London Bridge Street
London SE1 9GF

www.harpercollins.co.uk

HarperCollins*Publishers*
Macken House, 39/40 Mayor Street Upper,
Dublin 1, D01 C9W8, Ireland

First published by HarperCollins*Publishers* Ltd 2025

1

Copyright © Reeta Chakrabarti 2025

Extract from 'Mad Girl's Love Song' by Sylvia Plath. From the book
The Poems of Sylvia Plath by Sylvia Plath. Copyright © Faber and Faber Ltd
From the book *The Bell Jar* by Sylvia Plath. Copyright © 1971 by Harper & Row,
Publishers, Inc. Used by permission of HarperCollins Publishers.

Reeta Chakrabarti asserts the moral right to
be identified as the author of this work.

A catalogue record for this book is available from the British Library.

ISBN: 978-0-00-855305-0 (HB)
ISBN: 978-0-00-855306-7 (TPB)

This novel is entirely a work of fiction.
The names, characters and incidents portrayed in it are the work of
the author's imagination. Any resemblance to actual persons,
living or dead, events or localities is entirely coincidental.

Set in Adobe Caslon Pro by HarperCollins*Publishers* India

Printed and bound in the UK using 100% Renewable
Electricity at CPI Group (UK) Ltd

All rights reserved. No part of this publication may be r̶e̶p̶r̶o̶d̶u̶c̶e̶d,
stored in a retrieval system, or transmitted, in any form or ̶b̶y̶ ̶a̶n̶y̶ ̶m̶eans,
electronic, mechanical, photocopying, recording o̶r̶ ̶o̶t̶h̶e̶r̶w̶i̶s̶e,
without the prior permission of the publ̶i̶s̶h̶e̶r̶s̶.

This book contains FSC™ certified paper and other controlled
sources to ensure responsible forest management.

For more information visit: www.harpercollins.co.uk/green

To Paul, Daniel, Roxana and Leon

I dreamed that you bewitched me into bed
And sung me moon-struck, kissed me quite insane.
(I think I made you up inside my head.)

'Mad Girl's Love Song', Sylvia Plath

PROLOGUE

After Mama lost the baby and then lost her self, I had a vivid and terrifying dream.

It was night-time, and she was in a boat, being rowed by men I didn't recognise. The men were not sinister, but their silence was eerie as they rowed in unison, their oars rising and dipping in perfect rhythm.

The water around them was on fire, great gusts of blaze lighting up the sky, and I was in another boat while Mama was rowed further and further away from me.

'Mama, Mama!' I screamed, my panic rising as Mama slowly grew smaller and more distant.

She made no reply, and sat passively in the boat as I screamed and screamed again.

I woke myself up, sweating with terror, and rushed next door for comfort, even though Mama was in no fit state to help me.

For years, even deep into adulthood, I remembered the nightmare vividly, as a warning and a premonition.

PART 1 – 1979

CHAPTER 1

The voices down below began as a distant rumble, like a drum roll of approaching thunder. Mama's voice grew louder and louder and then hit a peak that was shrill and sharp, letting out a stream of curses and insults. In fact, it was the opposite of a storm: the thunder first and then the strikes of lightning.

Daddy responded with a steady murmur, too low to be distinct. I strained to hear him, leaning forward, close to the banister, mindful of the loose spindle that he hadn't mended, hugging my knees tightly. I sat halfway down the stairs, where I could follow most of the row, but then beat a hasty retreat if either of them emerged.

The naked light bulb in the hall shone harsh and white. Adèle was propped up stiffly next to me, her blue eyes fixed and staring, the two of us partners in this illicit listening in.

Mama's voice rose again sharply. 'You are completely free of duty!' She was yelling. 'No duty, no care! You parade yourself, and shut me up, and cut me off!' More words followed in that funny language she would use sometimes. '*Saitan! Badmaash!* You flaunt yourself, and shut me up here, with no love, no care!' She seemed to be crying. 'I was a famous beauty, you know, and I have no value to you, you *Saitan*, you bastard!'

I didn't know what bastard meant either, but I quickly covered Adèle's ears.

Daddy's grave, gravelly tones came through the door. It was frustrating that I couldn't fully hear him, but I knew he must be saying the right thing.

I could feel my heart beating fast with worry – and excitement. The row was alarming but also, at some level, thrilling. Naturally, I would have preferred family harmony, but I found other people's fights compelling, even if they were my own parents'.

Besides, this was becoming a regular event.

Mama's voice rose again, so shrill that I covered my own ears for protection. 'Why do you strut and phut like that, like a peacock! You think you are so big! Shameless man, always "look this way, look at me!" And no duty for your wife! No duty to me!'

I clutched Adèle and tried to cuddle her unyielding limbs. Her stiff hair still smelt of the factory, but I found it comforting. Everything familiar was comforting at this moment: the worn brown carpet on the step, the hot smell of my knees as I hugged myself, even the large cobweb in the corner. All these things were in their place, even if Mama was beside herself.

I heard a movement below, a signal that the fight had run its course, and I slipped soundlessly upstairs, mindful not to knock Adèle against the wall and give us away. I got into bed and arranged myself and my doll in an attitude of sweet sleepiness. Daddy would probably be in soon.

Sure enough, a few minutes later, a light went on in the hallway, and he put his head around the door. He was still in his suit from work, his tiepin glinting in the light. He must have caught sight of himself in my little mirror as he padded in, because I sensed that involuntary sweep of his hand over his hair. Daddy hated to have a hair out of place.

I felt the warmth of his face over mine, and I stirred as if out of a deep slumber.

He pushed a curl from my cheek, and gave me a soft kiss. 'Goodnight, Mivvi, my little Sweet Pea, sleep well.'

I mumbled sleepily in assent, and as he quietly left the room, I turned over to contemplate the evening's fight, before slipping into the effortless sleep of a child.

*

In the morning, Mama was contrite. She could be like that, full sails on a stormy, raging sea, and then becalmed and deflated the next day.

Daddy was stern. 'No more, Belle,' he said tersely, as he straightened his tie. 'This has got to stop.'

Mama looked meek and mumbled something that sounded like agreement. Daddy bent down to kiss me goodbye, but then left without embracing Mama.

'Fairfax,' she said weakly, as he went out the door, but he didn't respond.

Mama turned back, looking crumpled, and I felt a strong tug of pity and love. Adult rows were fascinating, but the aftermath unnerved me. I was on Daddy's side in most things, but at that moment I felt sorry for my bewildered mother.

'There's no school today, Mama, remember? It's teacher training.'

Mama hadn't remembered, and she stood in the kitchen as if uncertain what to do next. Her thick black hair was unbrushed, and her large, long-lashed eyes, which must have flashed white hot the previous night, were dimmed and red. Her new housecoat, with its jaunty pink flowers, looked at odds with her diminished self.

'Will you tell me a story?' I asked. 'And we can look at the photos?'

Even at 7 years old, I knew how to take charge, and Mama followed me to the sofa. When she was soft and docile as she was now, looking at the photographs and hearing some of the old stories was what I liked best. Her lap was big and warm, and her familiar scent of powder and face-cream and a hint of night sweat was comforting.

I arranged myself against her soft body, even though I was now really too big, and Mama turned the pages of the well-thumbed album. There were pictures of a long stretch of golden beach, with a sandstone castle – which she said was really a fort – right up against the crashing waves. The sky and sea were an impossible blue, and the whole image ablaze with heat.

This was Mombasa, a name that I would chew in my mouth; it tasted of sweet spices and oranges and mangoes. It was where Mama had grown up, although as she would remind me, her family was from further east. Mombasa was where she had met Daddy. Their fathers had been friends, and when he had arrived by boat to visit, he had swept Mama off her feet.

I hugged Mama gleefully, happy that the story always stayed the same, whatever the scenes of the night before.

There was a grainy shot of Mama and Daddy on the glowing sand, she in a floaty, thin dress, her hand resting in his. Over the page were pictures of them on their engagement: Daddy was dashing, with blond, classic film-star looks, and Mama was dark-skinned and slender. He looked directly and confidently into the lens, but long-necked Mama's sloping gaze was turned inwards, like a swan feeding upon its own beauty.

'Why did you leave Mombasa, Mama?' I had asked this question before, but these photos, these moments together, always made Mama talkative.

'Your daddy lived here – this is where his work was, and his life. Why would we stay in Mombasa? There was nothing for us there.'

'What about your parents?' I studied the formal black and white portrait I had seen so often before: my grandfather upright and dignified, and my grandmother frowning, as if something had displeased her.

Mama stayed silent.

But I persisted. 'Weren't they sad when you went?'

Mama's eyes flickered. 'They wanted me to make a good marriage. That's what they expected of me – well, Ma did anyway. I was good in school, but Ma didn't want me to be too good. Just be average, she would say, just average.'

I couldn't understand this. I was top of the class, and it gave me a warm glow. I wanted to shift the conversation onto safer territory, but Mama went on.

'My ma wanted also to leave Mombasa, but my baba said no, they should stay. It was his home; he went there to make his life.'

'Why did she want to leave?'

'She was not so attached to the place.' Mama's expression turned sad. 'And they didn't want us there.'

'Who? Why not?'

'The people of the country,' Mama replied with a sigh. 'I do not understand these things. We were happy, but they turned against people like us.'

I also didn't understand, but I could hear the trouble in her voice and tried to comfort her.

'But then you had me,' I declared, 'and you were happy!'
Mama's face softened.

'Were they happy? Your baba and ma?'

'Were they happy? I don't know.' For a moment, Mama looked confused. 'I think they wanted me to have a boy. That's what they were like. Well, Ma was anyway.'

'Silly!' I said confidently, picking up Adèle for confirmation. 'Girls are good – especially girls called Mivvi.'

'You know that is not your real name,' said Mama, smiling.

I did know, but Mivvi was the one which had stuck. I liked it; it made me think of an ice-cream, cool and sweet.

'Were they sad that you came here?'

Mama looked thoughtful. 'My baba was sad, yes. But he wanted good things for me, and he said that would be here.'

'And your ma?'

'I don't know.'

'You've got a brother, too, haven't you?'

She nodded.

'Will I have a brother or a sister, Mummy? Katie's getting one.'

'I don't know, Mivvi,' said Mama again.

'Is your brother nice?'

Mama considered the question. 'I do not know if he is nice. Little brothers can be painful. But anyway, he is my brother.'

'Is Daddy painful sometimes?'

Mama started. 'What sort of question is that?'

I realised I had overstepped the mark and did my best to look innocent, but it was too late. Mama looked suddenly tired. 'Go and play now,' she said. 'No more speaking.'

Mama could never talk very much, but her presence was always a comfort, and her lap a place of safety. I knew I had to be satisfied with these short spurts of engagement, and the well-loved stories were food for play.

I went to sit under the kitchen table with Adèle, pretending we were on the Mombasa beach, while Mama trailed off to her bedroom. When I crept up briefly to check, Mama was sitting on the edge of her bed as usual, rocking herself gently. It was her favourite place, and she had a dreamy look on her face. Perhaps she was thinking about Mombasa too.

I quietly went back downstairs.

I knew it was one of Mama's good days because much later, in the early evening and just before Daddy got home, she changed out of her pink and white housecoat into a crisp pale-blue cotton sari and sat at her dressing table to make herself up. Many days this didn't happen. I knew that this was the time they got ready in Mombasa, where the evening promenade was the day's main event.

I sat watching as she dabbed her dark skin with white powder, and painted her lips a crimson red. The powder was stark on her brown face, but I wasn't critical and only saw Mama taking care of herself. She finished with a streak of vermilion powder in the parting of her hair – 'to show I am married,' she explained.

After she put the stew on for dinner, we sat at the blackboard, tracing words with yellow chalk. Mama had taught me the alphabet when I was only three, and I was proud to be able to read and write easily. Even now I was at school, Mama still liked to give me these homely lessons, sometimes.

When we were tired, I played on my rocking horse, listening to it creak under my weight. Mama began to sing, her pure clear voice soaring with a song from home. It sounded dull and mournful, so after a few minutes, I badgered her to put on a tape of songs from musicals.

I dashed upstairs to change into my favourite party dress, which was yellow and white, and made of lace, and while Mama sang sweetly along with Doris Day, I twirled and spun in front of her, feeling golden like the sun.

In the seconds before I began to feel dizzy, there was complete unity between me and the music and Mama.

Nothing was really wrong between the two of us. A more consistent attentiveness is all I would have asked for, if I had known how; but the fact of Mama's distant nature seemed to me immutable – like sunrise, or bedtime.

But when Daddy came home that night, his face was dark and brooding. Perhaps he was still angry about the night before. He looked balefully at Mama as he walked into the kitchen and smelt the dinner.

'What, stew again?'

'We didn't have much, Fairfax,' Mama replied, mildly.

'But this is the third night running!' he exclaimed. 'Belle, did you not get out of the house today?'

'Mivvi didn't have school. It was teacher training.'

I nodded silently in support.

'Still, you could have gone out for some food,' he said. 'You do so little – you just sit around brooding.'

I wanted to tell him that people looked at Mama differently outside, but the words wouldn't come.

'What is it to you, Fairfax?' she replied. 'I am quite content at home.'

I saw Daddy glance down at me, and I quickly busied myself at the blackboard, pretending not to listen.

'Belle, you should do something, get out more. I don't think it's healthy being shut up in here on your own all the time.'

Mama frowned. 'Well, you are so busy, you cannot be at home. I am alright. Nothing else has worked for me. I am okay here.'

'It just proves I was right that you should learn to drive. Impossible to live here without a car!'

New town, new project, I mouthed silently. It was what Daddy usually said about us living in Milton Keynes. But this time he didn't.

He went on, not seeing Mama's sad expression. 'You should try and work, Belle – I keep telling you. It would be good for you. What do you think, Mivvi? Your mama should get a job, right?'

I smiled up at him uncertainly. Mama's care was uneven, but who would look after me if she didn't?

'Oh, Fairfax, stop please. Just leave it alone.'

I knew, because Daddy had told me, that he had been trying for years – before I was even born – to persuade Mama to get a job. She had started a typing course to learn to be a secretary, but Daddy said she had given up because the people were unfriendly. Then she began learning to be a special kind of teacher – Monty Soary, he said – but she had abandoned that, too.

'We could do with the money,' Daddy said to her curtly. 'Well, you know that.' The tips of his ears were turning pink, a sure sign he was warming to his theme. Mama had turned her back on him to wash some pans, but he wouldn't stop. 'How far do you think your five grand goes, eh? Forever and ever?'

'Fairfax!' she spun round. 'That is very low! Don't speak that way! Baba did everything he could. Everything! It is not my fault what happened, to Baba's money – to your father!'

Daddy glanced down at me again, as if only now registering that I was listening. He seemed about to speak but checked himself and, with a ruffle of my hair, he went upstairs.

I followed him up into the bedroom, trailing Adèle along on the floor. He was changing out of his suit into the old grey trousers and jumper he always wore at home. I sat down on the floor, wondering if he might say something. Sometimes he told me things about Mama that were most interesting.

'Your mother should do something. I kept trying to persuade her, but she could never hold down a job.'

It felt like he was speaking to himself, but I nodded wisely. Tabitha's mother went to work – 'a social worker,' Tabitha once told me snootily – and part of me felt that Mama should work too.

'She thought people were talking about her,' said Daddy.

I understood that this was not in a good way.

'Daddy,' I said as sweetly as possible, to avoid making him disgruntled again, 'why does Mama get so unhappy?'

Daddy was looking at himself in the mirror, smoothing his blond hair. He looked down at me reflectively. 'It's a good question, Sweet Pea. She has no reason to. She has you and me, and everything she needs. Sometimes I think it's just ... self-inflicted.'

'What does that mean?'

'It means she does it to herself.'

'That doesn't make any sense.'

'No,' he said, 'it doesn't.' Then he turned his huge smile on me and held out his arms.

I nestled against him, basking in the comfort of his certitude.

*

There was no row that night, and I went back to school the next day after a deep and uninterrupted sleep. My best friend Katie and I were engrossed in an elaborate game, a fantasy we played every lunchtime at the end of the field, darting in and out of the tall heather which we called the Pinkish Jungle, escaping an unnamed menace. I forgot about home, and Mama's problems, and Daddy's anger, until it was time for the bell.

Mama had come to pick me up. She stood apart from the other mothers. They were dressed in jeans and boots, but she shivered in her sandals, her thick socks incongruous with her footwear, her yellow sari defenceless in the grey drizzle.

A battered old car drew up, and Tabitha's mother got out. I was in awe of the outspoken, strong-minded Tabitha, and any potential encounter with her made me tense. But her mother greeted us warmly, and I was relieved that Mama, who could be awkward, was charming in return. Tabitha came out and stood there appraisingly, and I desperately wanted the two of us – me and Mama – to make a good impression.

'You look so elegant, Belle,' said Tabitha's mother. She wore faded jeans with leather boots and a weathered sheepskin coat, and looked too cool to be a mother.

'Thank you, but I am cold!' shuddered Mama, with a laugh. 'Well, well, I have to put up with it.'

'You look like the sunshine we all need,' said Tabitha's mother warmly, before flashing us a smile and ushering Tabitha into the car.

I heaved a sigh of relief when they were gone.

On the way home, we went down an underpass to get to a newsagent, so that Mama could buy a magazine.

'A *Woman's Journal* please,' she bellowed to the woman behind the counter, and I winced at her voice; it was always too loud and sharp when she was outside.

'What?' asked the assistant, who had straw-coloured hair and freckles like Katie.

'A *Woman's Journal*!' said Mama, even more loudly.

'I can't get what you're saying,' said the younger woman, barely looking up.

Mama always said 'woman' in a funny way, without the w, so that it came out as 'oman'. I thought it was perfectly clear, but the shop assistant was obviously having trouble, so I stepped in.

'She wants a *Woman's Journal*,' I said, with a helpful smile.

'Oh, I see,' said the assistant. She turned around to fetch one from the shelf behind her, and I thought I heard her muttering, 'Should have said so, then.' She sulkily took the money Mama offered her.

Mama was always quiet, but as we walked home, she seemed particularly flat and low. I trailed along behind her, hoping there wouldn't be another late-night thunder-and-lightning row. These difficult moments were not Daddy's fault, but I had a feeling that in Mama's head, they were somehow linked.

When we got home, Mama had a familiar crushed look about her. I wanted to go and watch TV with a sandwich, but I felt uneasy about Mama.

'Shall we look at the photographs, Mama?' I asked valiantly, although really I didn't want to.

'No, I am tired now. You go and play.'

'You could tell me stories about Mombasa? You used to go out a lot then. You could tell me about your college days, and going out for soda and ice-cream with your friends!'

I tried to climb onto Mama's lap, but she gently brushed me off.

'No, Mivvi, not now. Anyway, that was a long time ago. Now I am here, with these chilly people.'

I laughed, scooping up Adèle to laugh with me. 'People can't be chilly!'

'They need defrosting,' said Mama gloomily.

Like fish fingers, I thought, and seized the moment to slip out and turn on the television.

But I was hungry, and a few minutes later, I ventured back into the kitchen. Mama usually made me a snack after school for tea, but sometimes she forgot. She was sitting at the kitchen table, a red shawl wrapped around her shoulders, rocking herself gently backwards and forwards, lost in her thoughts.

I didn't want to disturb her, so I tried to sidle past to the cupboard – but she suddenly looked up.

'What did you say?' she asked, sharply.

'Me? Nothing,' I said, surprised. 'I didn't say anything. I'm just getting some biscuits.'

Mama gazed at me blankly for several seconds, long enough for me to start to feel uncomfortable. I wanted to go back to the TV and began to edge out of the room.

'Are you alright, Mama?' I managed, from the doorway.

It seemed to shake her out of her state. 'Yes, yes,' she said. 'Sorry. I thought you said something. I thought I heard somebody's voice. But there was nobody there.'

REETA CHAKRABARTI

December 1st 1979

F is now in the open laughing at me. In front of our own little girl. Today again he started to mock: why do you never do work, why don't you learn driving? How he loves to criticise here and there. He thinks he is big man, making me small. It is difficult. I don't know why. I am not small but I cannot pick up things here. The instructor, he showed me steering and gear change for many lessons, and then he said Madam, I'm afraid you'll never learn.

'Madam, I'm afraid you'll never learn' — these words F uses now against me, puffing up his chest for the little one, putting on a big man's voice to make her laugh. I do not care! I do not like it but I do not care!

What need is there for cars and driving and always dashing about? At least the instructor did no insulting of me. That badmaash shop girl today, so rude! Pretence of not understanding me! A lowlife girl! At home, no one would be daring to behave this way to me.

Ma said to me, no servants in UK, Bela — you have to do everything yourself. But servants themselves here are rude to me. Ma said life is different over here. But Ma so much wanted to come here too. So angry she was, not to leave! It makes no sense.

It is okay. I must manage. I need nothing much. I can take to school and fetch my girl. I can do cooking. This quiet life is enough.

When F is gentle as before, it is also enough. I was his dream, he said, his beautiful Belle dream. Our life will be so good, he said. But he is never here, always working working working, and I am all alone.

Today he is taunting about the money which Baba scraped together from here and there, getting every penny he could for the Sahib son. So cruel is F to laugh. And Ma's voice is always sharp and mocking — you cannot manage, you cannot do it, I told you so, I told you so. But she was as desperate for this marriage as me! Always, she was judging me, do this, do that, always finding fault. Today she speaks to me, her harsh tongue just behind me, stab stab stab. But when I turn around, there is nobody there.

I wish Meera were here.

Perhaps no more writing for me. Of what use is it? My pen no longer flows as before. What is happening? Words are more difficult. Words come in my head but not on the page.

My lovely baby looked at me in fear when Ma spoke. But she did not speak. It was words but no words. Sound but no sound.

CHAPTER 2

I tried to banish thoughts of Mama's strange behaviour, and I didn't tell Daddy. How would I explain it to him when I couldn't make any sense of it myself? It was a passing moment, and in my mind the incident quickly became blurred and half-forgotten. But I was left with a nagging sense that Mama wasn't like other people, and I feared that her strangeness might spill over into the outside world too.

It was different when Daddy picked me up from school, which he did when Mama was low, when he could get away from the office. He was a solicitor, a word that I didn't understand, but I was convinced it was better than a social worker – not that I would have dared say so to Tabitha. Sometimes his soliciting allowed him to get away for half an hour at home time.

My teacher behaved oddly whenever Daddy came: her cheeks went red and she started to flutter and bob. I had come to realise that Daddy had this effect on many people.

'Well, you must be very proud,' Miss Jenkins gabbled, her eyelashes rising and dipping as she spoke. 'How very lucky you are to have such a bright daughter! I wonder who she gets it from?'

I smiled shyly. Mama had taught me reading and writing, and Daddy had taught me maths, and I knew I was clever, although I had never seen Miss Jenkins react this way to Mama.

Daddy smoothed down his blond hair. I sensed that he had been expecting this sort of reaction, knowing somewhere in my young soul that he was not a modest man. And really, how could he be, when he was so appreciated?

Even now, as we walked out of the school gate together, I was aware of the other mothers stealing a glance at him. It must have been because his hair was so blond. Katie's mama had said once that he looked like a fair version of someone called Cary Grant, which could only have been a compliment.

Sometimes, he came to fetch me in the car, which was silver and shiny – 'a Ford Capri', he boasted – but this time he had come on foot. We walked home together, his shoes loudly tip-tapping on the pavement, because he had stuck little metal attachments at the back of his heels, to alert everyone to his arrival. He glanced at his reflection in the shop windows as we went past, and I noticed the *Woman's Journal* assistant looking at him. He didn't see her, but I caught sight of my own small self, my hand upstretched in his, and I felt safe and secure as I trotted along beside him.

'We're going out tonight, Sweet Pea,' he said. 'Remember I told you? It's a special Lawyers' Guild dinner for Christmas.'

My heart leapt. That meant Mama and Daddy would be happy all evening, and it meant Céline would come too.

'That means I get Céline!'

Daddy nodded down at me and smiled. I loved Céline and I knew that Daddy liked her too.

Céline often came to the school gates to collect Tabitha. 'Céline is our O pair,' Tabitha had told the whole class, and I nodded as knowingly as I could, thinking how fortunate Tabitha was to have one.

*

Mama always glowed on the rare evenings when Daddy took her out, and tonight she dressed herself in purple silk, which offset the whiteness of her powdered face, and gave her a queenly air. I sat and watched her getting ready, excited at the transformation of Mama into Belle.

'The Belle of the ball,' Daddy called her when they were getting on well, which they were tonight. 'I used to call her my Mombasa Marvel, you know,' he said to me with a wink, which prompted a tut-tutting from Mama. She didn't like it when Daddy became soppy.

The doorbell rang, and I rushed down the stairs to let Céline in. A rush of sweet, flowery perfume filled the air as she bent down to give me a fond kiss.

'How is my little Adèle getting on?' asked Céline. It was she who had given me the doll, brought back from one of her trips home to France. Adèle had blue eyes and chalky white skin, with flowing hair and a fancy frock, and I had given her the most French-sounding name I could think of.

I showed her to Céline now for approval.

'Very good,' she said, 'you are looking after her well! Adèle has a very good mummy!'

I beamed with pride.

Daddy came downstairs dressed in a three-piece suit, a little square of silk peeking out from the breast pocket of his jacket. His aftershave was strong, and his hair shiny with a special cream. He gave Céline's arm a squeeze, and I watched curiously as Céline brushed his lips with her fingertips. There must have been a crumb sticking there.

'I've left you sandwiches, Céline, and there's a little bit of gin,' he said, and then added playfully, 'but not too much now!'

All three of us laughed loudly. Céline would always help herself to more gin, but it made her jolly and funny, so I didn't care. She had an angular face like a Punch and Judy puppet, and I knew I could look forward to playing with her well beyond my bedtime, perhaps improvised tennis with my old soft toys. The last time she came, Céline's jumble of scarves and bangles and long earrings got tangled up, and she fell over herself and collapsed in a heap while trying to get the ball.

Mama swept down, her purple silk sari like a train on the stairs. She never talked much to Céline, although Daddy was always pleased to see her.

'Hello, Céline,' said Mama, quite stiffly. She got the emphasis of her name wrong. 'How is Tabitha and her family?'

'They are fine, Belle,' said Céline pleasantly. 'Have a good evening now!'

'What shall we do?' I asked, once they had gone. 'Shall we play tennis in the hall? Or will you teach me some more French?'

I enjoyed copying Céline's clipped accent and trying to imitate the funny sounds.

Céline gave a small yawn. 'Mivvi, I am a bit tired today. Shall we watch television? There is a nice movie – I saw it at Noel. Yes? Let me just get a drink.'

We settled down to watch a film about some children who had a lovely nanny who fell in love with their father. I didn't understand the story, although I liked the songs, but Céline enjoyed it all immensely. She cooed at the scenes where there was kissing, and laughed affectionately at my disgust.

'You are funny,' she said, pulling me close to her and kissing me on the head. 'It's romantic!'

'Yukky yuk,' I said, pulling an exaggerated face. As I rested my head against Céline's shoulder, I took in her flowery perfume and her hair that smelt fresh like a meadow. Her long thin legs were smooth and tanned, but her skirt didn't cover them much, and I wondered if she was cold.

When the film finished, it was long past bedtime, but we knew that Daddy and Mama would be out for a while still, so Céline helped herself to another small glass from Daddy's bottle, and then sat down to paint her nails. I enjoyed the sharp smell of the varnish and watched her curiously.

'Shall I do yours too?' she asked. 'Pale pink will look very pretty.'

I hesitated. It was so tempting; the varnish made Céline's nails look sugar-coated. 'Daddy might be angry,' I said.

Céline laughed in surprise. 'Why would he be angry?'

'Mama did them once, and he said I was too young.'

'Ah,' said Céline lightly. 'We won't then. I don't want to get you into trouble. Maybe it's time for your bed now?' She stretched out as if it were she who was tired. Then, as an after-thought, she brought her face very close to mine and giggled. '*Il est très beau, ton père, n'est-ce pas?* He's very good-looking, isn't he? Your daddy.'

Her bright, flushed face was full of warmth and amusement, and I was filled with love for her.

'Oh yes,' I replied eagerly. 'He says he's the most handsome man in the office!'

And for some reason I didn't entirely understand, the two of us fell about laughing.

*

The best thing about Daddy and Mama going out, apart from the fun with Céline and the late bedtime, was the anticipation of what they would bring when they came back home. It was Daddy of course who thought of me, Daddy who hid in his pockets the mint and orange chocolates from the end of their meal.

That night, I was still awake when I heard them return, and I opened my eyes expectantly when Daddy crept in to kiss me. He started to make a great play of rummaging around, searching in the pockets of his sharply creased trousers, pulling out the square of silk in his jacket like a magician, in case the chocolates were hidden there. I squealed with delight when they were found.

The next day, I savoured them as slowly as I could, nibbling them in tiny bites and sucking them to make them last. They were the flavour of Mama and Daddy's glamorous nights out, when they were an ordinary, happy, harmonious pair.

REETA CHAKRABARTI

July 1st 1976

Who do they think they are, these girls who make all eyes at F? At first this was funny, not now so much. My peacock F, strutting about, flashing his feathers. He does not chase them but oh how he loves to let himself be chased. So much he likes the attention. I knew this man loves himself, but before I was sure of him, Bela Bela Belle he would murmur, his gaze full of love and longing. But now where is his mind, where is his desire? Is he true or is he not?

Men are weak, Bela, said Ma. He is weak perhaps. I still have a hold. But how to be always and forever beautiful Belle? Now I am also Ma, am I less to him? But he adores M, and also me for being her ma.

I also adore M. He tries to make her Daddy's girl, but even as she slowly grows towards him, to me she still comes for love and safety. The harbour of Mama. My baby girl.

What more does he want? Men will stray, Bela, said Ma.

Not that girl. Please not that one or any of them.

Please, F, don't want them.

CHAPTER 3

The classroom incident happened when I was 9 years old, and it exploded out of the blue with bewildering violence, shattering the only part of my life which I had relied on to be peaceful. It was the same year that Mama lost the baby, and while this latter event was to prove more consequential by far, it was the classroom moment that was seared on my memory – perhaps because childhood humiliation never fades.

Until that point, school had been a refuge from the constant arguments at home, as well as a place where I invariably shone. At breaktime, Katie and I acted out plays I had written, together in our corner of the field, away from real life and far from the louder children. We always avoided Tabitha, with her sharp tongue and scary self-confidence.

But the arrival of the twins in our class changed everything. We had never had twins in our school before, and the whole class flocked to Fi and Anne, fascinated that two people could look exactly the same. All of us were awestruck by their flaxen hair and ability to turn perfect somersaults. We were gripped by a fierce, unspoken competition to become Fi and Anne's best friend.

It slowly dawned on me that, in my case, this was not to be. Fi and Anne fell repeatedly quiet in my presence, as if deliberately so – stopping conversations when I walked in, whispering to each other under their breath.

One day I ventured to mention this to Katie.

'It's a bit different with Fi and Anne here. I really like them, of course,' I added hurriedly, not wanting to be out of step with everyone else. 'But it's different.'

Katie looked at me gravely. 'Yes,' she said, appearing to weigh her words. She looked away for a while, not wanting to meet my eye, and then in a rush, the words tumbled out of her. 'You know, Mivvi, it's really odd, but they said they don't like you. They said some mean stuff about you. It's so silly – I don't know why.'

She looked at me guiltily, as though she instantly wanted to take back her words. In an attempt to hide both her distress and mine, I gave a high giggle, although I could feel my cheeks starting to burn.

I was determined to bury any sign of alarm, determined not to cry. Why on earth would they dislike me? I hadn't done anything to them. I was bewildered and pretended to shrug it off, but an awareness of the revelation persisted, like a troublesome fly. Other incidents followed where I was treated differently.

We had started playing kiss-chase during the break, with the boys chasing the girls, and giving us a peck on the cheek if we were caught. I was a fast sprinter and could easily escape, only slowing down now and then to give the boys a chance. But one boy, sweet-natured Kevin who wore dirty glasses, had a different way of kissing me; he took my hand not my cheek, and gallantly pressed his lips against it. As he did so, he smiled through the fog of his specs, and I was both puzzled and touched. I wouldn't have minded if all the girls had their hands kissed so gently, but being singled out for such treatment was strange.

But the following week came the explanation. We went out to the playground at lunchtime under a leaden sky, and when the threatening heavens opened, we dashed back into the building, shrieking and sodden. Some of us went to the main hall, others to our classrooms.

As I approached the classroom door, I could see dimly through the misty glass pane that some children were already inside. I saw the flash of Kevin's broken glasses, and then the two blonde heads of Fi and Anne. In that instant, they spotted me too and abruptly slammed the door shut, pressing themselves hard against it so that I couldn't get in.

My heart started to race, but I smiled weakly, trying to hide my confusion.

Then I heard a chanting start up:

'Mivvi! Superstar! How many boys have you kissed so far? 24? Maybe more? Ten on the bed and the rest on the floor!'

And then they started to yell:

'*Paki! Paki! Blackie, Mivvi, Paki!*'

I felt my face go crimson, as humiliation and confusion coursed through me. Why were they calling me names? And why that? I had never thought of myself as dark-skinned – that was Mama, and anyway, so what? I was gripped by a tumult of fear and outrage, but I felt frozen, unable to react. Fi and Anne's faces leered at me through the glass, and even Kevin – sweet, treacherous Kevin! – was at their side, looking both gleeful and ashamed.

I might never have moved if it hadn't been for a sudden rough hand on my arm, grabbing me hard, and pulling me away.

'Those morons!' hissed Tabitha. 'Come on, let's get out of here.' She turned to the door and yelled, 'You can just get lost, you bloody cretins!' then shoved me down the corridor, away from my tormentors.

From that point onwards, I found myself protected by my new and intimidating friend. Everyone respected Tabitha, and Fi and

Anne kept a safe distance from us, only risking a furtive wrinkling of the nose in my direction if I was alone. Kevin was abashed by his momentary meanness and kept shooting me apologetic looks. Tabitha told me to ignore him entirely.

I had spent years fearing Tabitha, and being her friend was complicated. She could be warm and generous, defending me if anyone was mean, and sharing her sandwiches when Mama forgot to pack my lunch for a school trip. But if I did something awkward or clumsy, her kindness was displaced by a malicious pleasure that made me self-conscious and clumsier still. One day, I upset an inkpot all over my desk, and Tabitha cried with spiteful laughter. There were no cosy games of make-believe such as those I enjoyed with Katie. This was a friendship in which I had to shape up.

I tried to tell Mama and Daddy about being locked out of the classroom, but it was difficult to speak the words, and I stumbled through them haltingly. I knew that Daddy would be pained and that Mama would not understand, and I was right.

Daddy looked numb with anger, and it was all I could do to stop him from marching to the school there and then to confront the headmistress.

'No, Daddy, no,' I pleaded, 'it's alright now, really. They've stopped, they stay away from me now.'

Mama, though, seemed unsurprised. Instead, she looked thoughtful and almost amused. 'You should tell them they are whitey,' she said, 'or milky pudding.'

'Belle, Belle,' murmured Daddy.

I felt the lameness of Mama's advice. Daddy was white, so where was the sense in that? Besides, trying to insult them would only make things worse.

The alarming discovery that I was *different* made me determined to try to blend in more, and so I tried to limit Mama's appearances at school. She spoke loudly in public on the assumption that no one would understand her, and her voice, its accent still rich with home, drew mortifying attention. Sometimes she turned up in a sari, and I would go into agonies of embarrassment. I tried to persuade Daddy to come for consultations and concerts, for summer fêtes and Christmas bazaars, and gradually I edged Mama out of the picture. Mama made no complaint; she didn't like going out anyway, and so it was bright, sociable Daddy who became the parent I would publicly display.

After the hateful incident, I spent time scrutinising myself in the mirror, something I had never done before. A sturdy, brown-haired girl stared back at me. Her skin was the colour of sand – not the golden sand of Mombasa, but a dark yellow, sallow like a wet beach. Funny how I had never really noticed this before. Her palms were pale like everyone else's, but when she smiled, her gums were dark, almost purple, not pink like Katie's.

I practised smiling with my mouth shut, and then with my hand in front of my mouth; and in this moment of critical self-assessment I realised that my nails were bitten to the quick. I would chew them and the skin around them during Daddy and Mama's night-time rows, and the flesh was starting to discolour.

I put my hands hurriedly behind my back and peered at myself once more, confused by my own reflection. Maybe I had got darker? There were creams and things for that, weren't there? I was sure that Mama had mentioned them, but I had no idea of how to get hold of any. I saw a slight double chin suggest itself in the mirror and quickly held my head up high. That was something else that Fi had hissed at me in the corridor – '*Oi, tubby!*' – but then Tabitha had appeared, and Fi had glided innocently away.

I decided to embark on a concerted regime of change. Every day I washed my face three times, before school and after, and then once before bed, scrubbing as hard as my skin could bear. I was determined to be Daddy's daughter, not Mama's. I secretly took whatever cream I could find in the house, mostly from Mama's jar of scented night cream, and rubbed it vigorously into my reddening cheeks.

Day after day I peered at myself anxiously; I could see no difference, but perhaps these things took time? While Mama was rocking herself in her bedroom, and Daddy was out at work, I ran up and down the stairs, up and down, over and over, taking care not to trip on the snag in the carpet, wearing myself out. The words *Oi, tubby* repeated themselves in my head.

One day, when Céline came over to babysit, she caught me at it.

'What are you doing?' she asked, perplexed.

I blushed with embarrassment and felt lost for an answer.

'It's exercise,' I replied finally. It was the truth after all.

Céline looked sympathetic. 'Oh, Mivvi, it is a funny way to exercise. You could go swimming or something instead? But maybe your daddy has no time to take you?'

There was obviously no question of it being Mama. I shook my head.

Céline brought her face close up to mine. 'I think you look well just as you are,' she said gently, running her finger down my pudgy arm.

I looked at her gleaming pale skin and her reed-slim limbs, and while I returned her warm smile as genuinely as I could, all I could think was how easy it must be to be Céline.

FINDING BELLE

May 20th 1973

Today she took her first steps, my baby bird, one fat foot in front of the other, slowly slowly, and then suddenly her legs went running away under her! She so astonished and delighted with herself! She's gleeful, said Meera, joyfully clapping her hands, me and she, the spectators of M's giddy flight. Then she sits down heavily on her bottom, all cushioned and padded so no pain, and she and me and Meera laugh and laugh! Such sweet and simple pleasure. Do it again for Daddy, I say, let me take a picture, and my little M struggles up with Meera's help and does it again.

Sweet baby, and dear Meera also. I wish she could stay longer. It is better when she is here — I am not so alone. F has to work so hard.

In the afternoon, baby had her sleep and we both lay down with her too. The weather is hot and heavy — more like Mombasa summer than English May — so we two ladies were drowsy like the baby. We had siesta like at home. Meera hummed a lullaby for M, and I gave Meera shushuri, stroking her arm to make her sleepy too. When I give it to F, he says it tickles and he does not like. But Meera likes and she falls asleep.

F says Meera likes ladies not men, but this is just bad talk, just malice. What does it matter what she likes? To me she is my friend, and I am more whole when she is here.

CHAPTER 4

One day, my routine of self-improvement was interrupted by some startling news from Daddy.

'Sweet Pea, have you noticed something about Mama? She's growing big, isn't she?'

'Is she? Yes, maybe. Is it because she eats too much?'

'No!' Daddy laughed. 'Darling, she's going to have another baby. You're going to be a big sister!'

I stared at him. Another baby! I remembered wanting a little brother or a sister, but that had been ages ago, and in truth it had been to compete with Katie. The impending existence of a real baby was something else entirely. I did my best to look happy.

'We've wanted one for ages,' said Daddy, as he adjusted his tie. 'And, you know, maybe it will be good for Mama.'

'Will it be a brother or a sister, Daddy?'

'Well, I think your mama wants a little boy, but I really don't mind.'

I remembered the story of my grandparents' disappointment at my own arrival. 'Well,' I said, 'I don't mind either.'

The news explained a lot. Mama's face was puffy and swollen, and although I was far too big to sit on her lap these days, the space there had noticeably shrunk. She felt sick much of the time and spent hours of the day lying in her bed rather than rocking herself on it. She no longer sang, or even cooked very much. It was bewildering to think that Mama was getting bigger but also somehow disappearing.

Mama never came to pick me up from school anymore, so when Daddy was busy, sometimes Céline came to meet me. She worked in a boutique these days instead of for Tabitha's family, but she wanted the extra money, what she called the *argent de poche*. I always brightened at the sight of her at the school gate, all bangles and jangles and brightly coloured scarves.

Mama bristled when Céline was around. Maybe she just didn't like visitors, although she made an exception for Daddy's friends John and Bianca, who sometimes came to dinner. Mama didn't really have friends, but sometimes she mentioned someone called Meera, whom I couldn't remember.

But Céline had such a bright and sunny nature that she never seemed to notice Mama's sourness. If she stayed till the evening to make my dinner, she would drink lots of Daddy's gin, and I once saw her put her hand briefly on his knee. But Mama was there, so that was alright, although maybe she didn't see.

The same evening, once Céline was gone, I listened to their conversation in the kitchen, pretending to be engrossed in a game with Adèle.

'She's always telling this thing and that thing about sex,' whispered Mama.

'Oh, she's just young and carefree,' said Daddy. 'It's quite funny really.'

'But so many stories, of picking up this one, and wearing a thin little dress, and picking up that one! Who is she, does she think? And such crude talk, of doing this thing with them, and that thing with them! Why does she tell us? Such promise-coo-ity!'

I heard Daddy laugh lightly. 'Oh, I don't know, Belle, that's just her. She's just showing off, I guess. She's harmless.'

Mama snorted, and I played on.

*

Just when we needed her most, Céline announced that she was off to France for two weeks to see her family. Daddy was very put out; he was worried that the baby might arrive early. So, when Tabitha's mother stopped him at the school gate and volunteered to have me when the time came, he accepted with relief.

I had the usual lurch of excitement and nerves at the prospect of more time with Tabitha. I was so lucky to be her chosen friend, but it was so difficult to relax with her. Tabitha, with her quick wit and acid tongue, was clever and capable too; she had a treehouse in her garden, built with her own hands. Mama called Tabitha a tomboy. Whatever she was, Tabitha sneered at dolls and imaginative games, and I knew never ever to mention Adèle in front of her.

As always, my anxieties were outweighed by the sheer fascination of Tabitha, with her boldness and confidence as well as her underlying loyalty to me, even if she sometimes acted superior.

So, with a deep breath, I resolved to put my regime of self-improvement on hold, and to force my more adventurous self to the fore.

Tabitha's large house had a crooked staircase, and a cellar and an attic, and built-in wardrobes perfect for hide and seek. The floors were strewn with colourful rugs, and unlike at home, there were bookshelves everywhere, even in the kitchen. Tabitha's mother urged me to read and to borrow whatever I wanted, and in moments when Tabitha tired of my company, I curled up happily with these new treasures.

Her mother insisted that I call her Bree, and she asked me many questions about school and the books I liked reading. She was so unexpectedly kind that she made me feel shy. Strangely, there was no sign of Tabitha's father.

We sat down each evening to huge meals of stews and casseroles, and we all ate together, unlike the haphazard mealtimes at home. Bree drank a little wine with every evening meal, there was muesli for breakfast instead of cornflakes, and she baked her own bread, so dark and dense that it was almost black.

Tabitha took charge of me, as I had known she would, and for the first few days we enjoyed the novelty of being together. But her loftiness towards me eventually and inevitably emerged.

'Have you really never heard of Parmesan?' she asked, as we lounged in her bedroom after a spaghetti dinner.

I looked humble. It was the first time I had had spaghetti, but I wasn't going to tell Tabitha that.

'We have Cheddar,' I said, 'I quite like it.'

Tabitha smiled pityingly. 'Bree has always insisted on Parmesan, ever since we went to Italy.'

This was something new for me, calling a parent by their first name. I had never been to Italy either, but I smiled brightly nonetheless.

'Italy must have been amazing. I'd love to go.'

'Oh, we always have holidays abroad, Bree can't bear to stay here.'

'What about your dad?' I asked. 'Does he like to go abroad as well?'

'Yeah,' she replied nonchalantly. 'But Samuel and I go skiing with him. They're divorced.'

'Oh,' I said. I didn't know of anyone else's parents who were divorced. It added to Tabitha's mystique.

Their sleek Siamese cat Athena leapt onto the bed and settled next to Tabitha. Together they regarded me coolly.

'Bree makes lovely food,' I said. 'That bread is so good!'

'Yes,' drawled Tabitha, as if it were obvious. 'Well, you had some on our school trip. Remember, ages ago?'

'Oh, yes,' I replied fervently, 'it was so nice of you!'

Tabitha gave a small yawn. 'Bree often does that – packs me extra. Just in case someone else is going without.'

I was silenced. I hadn't known I had been a recipient of charity.

But Tabitha didn't notice. 'When did you say your baby brother or sister is due?'

'Oh, quite soon I think.'

'Bree had Samuel at home,' Tabitha went on. 'We heard her cursing and screaming, but it didn't go on too long, and then there was a baby. Bree says she just breathed him out.'

I hung on to my bright smile. 'I hope Mama – I mean Belle – will breathe it out too.'

*

The next morning, Daddy rang Bree to say that Mama was going into hospital. I tried to look excited.

'Your mother will be taken up with the new baby when it's born, Mivvi, but you mustn't worry, she loves you every bit as much as she always did.' Bree was frying us eggs for breakfast. She wore a *Ban the Bomb* apron over her cheesecloth shirt. Samuel was chewing toast with his mouth open deliberately to annoy Tabitha.

I grinned at Bree as if reassured. I was aware that she had no knowledge of what Mama was like.

She went on. 'Do you know, my dear, I noticed your skin is a little dry, on your arms and legs, so I've popped a small pot of moisturiser by your bed. Do take it home if you want to.'

I glanced down in surprise at my bare knees and saw a greyish dullness on my skin. Neither Daddy nor Mama had ever mentioned this, but more cream was welcome news, for knees and for face.

I looked at Bree gratefully, while Tabitha kicked Samuel under the table. 'Thank you, Bree, I will.'

'Don't do that, Tabitha and stop yelling, Samuel. Better manners with a guest here, please. Mivvi, you might want to pop some on your hands too – it will soften the skin on your fingers.'

I quickly sat on my hands, ashamed she had spotted my bad nails.

'I was a terrible one for chewing my nails,' Bree went on, 'whenever I was anxious.'

I was running out of replies, so I just thanked her again.

'It's a pleasure,' she said, 'it's a pleasure to look after you, Mivvi.'

*

My day at school was unremarkable, but that night, I was woken by Bree. She was sitting on the edge of my bed, a look of extreme tenderness on her face.

'My dear Mivvi, I hope I didn't startle you. I've just had a phone call from your dad. I'm so sorry, my dear – there's some very sad news. Your mum went into hospital as you know, but something went wrong – very badly wrong. She lost the baby.'

I felt her warm gaze on my face as my eyes turned wet, although inside, I felt nothing at all. For a brief second, I couldn't understand how Mama might have misplaced such an important thing. Then Bree took my hand and stroked my hair, and I willed myself to react with shock or sorrow, but all I could think was that I would not now be a big sister like Tabitha.

'Was it a boy or a girl?' I managed eventually as I reached automatically for Adèle, before remembering she wasn't there.

'A girl,' said Bree softly. 'A little girl.' She hesitated, and then added, 'She's with the angels now.'

I knew that Bree wouldn't believe in angels, but I did my best to look comforted by the idea.

'Thank you, Bree,' I stuttered, and as I submitted to her embrace, I felt a fraud for not being able to feel.

*

Mama stayed in hospital for several days, and I remained with Bree and Tabitha until she was allowed out. Daddy rang me twice, sounding tense and tearful. When it was time for me to go home, Bree packed my bag carefully, cramming in my new moisturiser and several books from their collection, before driving me back.

Daddy was waiting for me outside the house, and I rushed into his arms and held him tightly.

'Fairfax,' I said, and in the intensity of the moment, my abandonment of the word *Daddy* passed unnoticed. 'It's so sad.'

He looked distraught. He was unshaven, and his hair was out of place. 'Your mother's lying down upstairs. I'm sure she'd love to see you.'

I wasn't so sure, but I crept up dutifully. Mama was lying prostrate in a half-darkened room. Her eyes were open, but she didn't seem to take me in. I held her hand and stroked her arm gently, just as Bree had stroked me.

'Are you alright, Mama?' I asked softly. 'Belle, are you okay?'

She gave me a half-smile but seemed unable to speak. Her face, still puffy, looked soft, and her eyes were unfocused. Her long dark hair spread over the white pillow, and I felt that she was far away and vulnerable.

That was the night I dreamt of the silent rowers and of Mama vanishing into the distance. Overcome with panic, I ran trembling from my bed into her room. She opened her eyes momentarily, before shutting them sleepily and drifting once again out of reach. It must have been early, because my father wasn't there.

I stifled my sobs and got into bed next to her, wrapping her heavy arm around my trembling body. Her breath was warm on the back of my neck, and I drew comfort from its regular rhythm. Still, I kept her arm tightly around me, desperate to keep her close.

I had an ominous sense from my dream that I had to take my own comfort where I could, and that Mama's capacity to protect me was slowly ebbing away.

REETA CHAKRABARTI

April 6th 1972

Such tiredness and exhaustion but I am floating on oceans of joy. My baby sleeps so sweetly next to me. My first born. Her hair is soft brown like sugar. It has some of F's gold. Her fingers and tiny small toes like pomegranate seeds that I could suck. At noise she jumps even in sleep, her hands shooting up to grab — what? A branch or something for safety? My little monkey. And then she settles again.

I thought I carried a boy, and I know Ma will mind that I did not. I thought I too would mind but no. She is mine and now I am Ma. F shows his goodness and happiness at our girl — his face glows like the sun when he sees her, just like it used to.

He is a modern man, no judgement, no disappointment. Mivvi mivvi mivvi he calls her, like the ice-cream in the commercial, silly man. He will be a good father, I know it, and I will try and be a good ma.

Soon I can go home, surely. One nurse is nice, but the other is not, and speaks to me roughly. She tried to give me beef for dinner, after I had told her no. I think she did this on purpose. Some people do not know how to behave.

Home soon, with my precious, my newborn, my baby girl.

CHAPTER 5

After she lost the baby, Belle spent day after day in bed, and although Fairfax said she would rally soon, the house felt grey and mournful, as if the curtains were permanently drawn and family life, such as it was, was suspended. When Belle did manage to get up, she would drift aimlessly from room to room, barely registering who or what was there, and even though I had got used to doing without her, this phase felt new. At first, Fairfax made sure to come home early, but his usual work routine soon took over, and then Belle had to cope alone.

I tried to bury myself in reading and then re-reading all of Bree's books, and I moped quietly, not really because of the baby's death but because it was expected of me. Céline came sometimes and always behaved with quiet sympathy, and I tried to copy her.

But to our surprise, Belle hadn't yet lost all initiative. One day when I got back from school, Fairfax announced that Meera was coming to stay, just for a night.

'What, her old friend from before?' I asked. I had seen photographs of Meera in the album, all maxi skirts and shining eyes. Belle had told me that Meera loved children, and I hoped she would like me.

'Yes,' said Fairfax shortly. 'Your mother appears to have asked her to come.'

He didn't look very pleased.

The next day, Belle stirred herself in preparation for Meera's arrival, and before Fairfax was home from work, there she was at the door, throwing her arms around Belle, who stood overwhelmed in her friend's bear-like embrace.

'Belle! My dear, dearest Belle!'

Meera was the most beautiful person I had ever seen. She looked like my idea of a flamenco dancer, with thick black hair and skirts that swished and swayed as she walked. She was all movement and light, with a smile of such brilliance it made Mama's own face shine with pleasure. I think I fell immediately in love with her.

'Let me look at you,' said Meera, hugging Belle again. 'It's been so long! Yes,' she went on, 'it really has been a while, eh?'

I watched wonderingly as Mama opened up in front of Meera like a parched flower given water.

'So long,' she said. 'And now you really are Dr Meera, working in a hospital and all.'

Meera shrugged. 'It was a hard slog, but I got there.'

'You are very tenacious,' said Belle, and I was astonished to hear her use such a long word. Who knew she could talk this way?

'Well, you have this gorgeous creature to raise,' said Meera, gesturing at me, and I felt suddenly shy and grateful to be noticed.

My eyes widened as she leaned over and rummaged in her soft, tasselled bag, then fished out a package which she put in my hands.

'Your mother told me you're always writing. *Scribbling*, she said, but I'm sure it's proper writing. Go on – open it!'

My smile was as wide as my face as I pulled open the paper. I didn't realise that Belle knew I liked writing. There, under the wrapping, was a thick leather notebook with creamy-coloured pages and a proper ink pen. I was too overcome to do more than mumble my thanks, but Meera leaned in close, proffering her cheek, and I gave her a truly delighted kiss.

Then she leaned across and took Belle's hand in hers.

'But, Belle, tell me, how are you? It's such an awful thing to have happened. I'm so glad you called me.'

Belle looked weary. 'I am okay,' she said. 'I have to manage. Perhaps I am a little bit alone. Well, well, what can I do?'

This was the Belle I more readily recognised.

'Have you had to handle it alone? Fairfax is out a lot, huh?'

Belle nodded.

'It must be so difficult,' Meera said, looking at her with concern. 'I'm so sorry I haven't been in touch. I feel I've neglected you. You've … not made friends here?'

Belle shook her head. Her large, expressive face, soft in Meera's presence, was full of pain, and I noticed for the first time the dark circles under her eyes.

'I wish I lived closer,' Meera went on, 'we could see each other more often.'

Belle nodded wistfully.

Meera brought her face closer to hers, speaking almost in a whisper. 'And, Belle, how are you more generally? Those times that you told me about, the voices. Does that … does that still happen?'

Belle shrugged, as if to say *maybe,* and shifted her gaze to the floor. Meera searched her face and, seeing her evasion, looked beyond her at the kitchen. I saw it through Meera's eyes: a shabby room in an unloved house, chipped plates in the sink, stained cups on the shelf, the bin overflowing, the floor grimy.

We all sat in silence for a few moments, and then Fairfax walked in.

'Ah, Dr Sen, how are we?'

'Not so bad, Fairfax. And your good self?' There was an edge to their tones. 'Working hard?'

'Always,' said Fairfax, pouring himself a drink without offering Meera one. 'Someone has to. Anyway, cheers!'

*

Meera took my mother out to do some shopping, and after that, Belle roused herself to make a sumptuous meal of mutton curry and pilaf rice, one of her old favourites. After dinner, we sat listening to Meera's tales of hospital life, the sad stories of the ill children she had to look after, and the funny ones about her colleagues. She persuaded Belle to sing for us, and my mother's sweet voice, not powerful but in perfect tune, soared mournfully with songs learned from her own mother. When I was younger, I disliked how self-absorbed she was when she sang. Now I felt sad that it happened so rarely. Meera applauded loudly, while Fairfax sat reading the paper.

Afterwards Belle, still humming to herself, started to wash up, and I saw Meera beckoning to Fairfax to follow her out of the kitchen. When I heard them speaking to each other in hushed tones outside, I tiptoed to the door to listen.

'I'm so sorry for you both, Fairfax, but really, she seems lost.'

'She's fine – she'll rally.'

'I think she's very lonely.'

'Well, she won't go out.'

'It's unhealthy to be so isolated.'

'I agree, but I can't force her out, can I?'

'Couldn't she do with some … help? You know, more generally?'

My father's tone changed. 'Can I suggest you leave it?'

'But still, Fairfax, I'm worried about her. She doesn't look well.'
'Leave it – it's fine.'
'I don't think it is.'
'I can manage it, okay?'
'Has she seen anyone?' Meera asked, ignoring him. 'I mean, it's not just the baby, is it?'
'Am I not making myself clear, Meera? You look after yourself, and I'll look after my own.'

I heard Meera give a heavy sigh. 'Alright, alright, but please think about it. I'm serious. And one more thing – please get her some help around the house. She can't manage. Not right now. Even if it's just for a while. Please do that. You've got the little one to think about too.'

I edged in closer to listen, but foolishly forgot about Adèle dangling from my wrist, and she hit the wall with a thud.

Fairfax cleared his throat loudly. 'Mivvi,' he called, 'that's bedtime for you!'

To my alarm, he came swiftly around the corner, but luckily his look of irritation dissolved into the sweetest of his golden smiles.

'My little Sweet Pea, how you do creep around sometimes! Come on, up to bed, and I'll tell you a story.'

'I'm too old for stories!' I said, trying hard to salvage some dignity from the situation.

'Whatever you say. Up to bed.'

*

The next morning, we all had breakfast together, a rare event which I assumed was for Meera's benefit. It was the second day in a row that Belle had managed to be up and dressed before I left for school.

'Belle,' said Fairfax, 'your friend here thinks we need some help around the house. It's not up to her standards.'

'You know I didn't say that, Fairfax,' said Meera calmly.

Usually, Belle looked guilty if Fairfax criticised her, but now she replied steadily. Perhaps she was emboldened by Meera's presence. 'Well, I know it is different here, but I am used to help. To maids and to servants.'

Fairfax snorted. 'How many years have you been here now? Maids and servants indeed!'

But Belle would not be diverted. 'Tabitha's mother used to have Céline, did she not, to do all her dirty work? It would help me to have someone.'

'Well,' he said, 'I don't know about dirty work.' But he sounded more thoughtful. 'But it has got me thinking. Someone to help out might be a good idea.'

'Oh!' She hadn't expected him to relent. 'Not Céline though,' she added, in an odd voice.

'No, no, she's not free anyway – she works in that fashion shop now. But John mentioned a girl a few weeks ago. A Jade Evans. Someone he knows through church. She's looking for some casual work before going to college, just for a few months. Done some filing at the office apparently, although I've never seen her. He says she is a good girl, hard-working.'

I saw Mama and Meera both looking hopeful.

'I think I can scrape the money together,' Fairfax went on, 'and it's probably the right thing to do, at my stage and all that. Anyway, let's see if I can fix something up. There you go – I thought that might please you!'

His words were for Belle, but he was looking towards Meera, who sat smiling quietly into her tea.

FINDING BELLE

Fairfax was going to drop Meera at the station after he dropped me at school, and as we piled into the car, Belle stood in the doorway to wave us goodbye. Her housecoat flapped loosely around her hunched self, and as we drove away, I saw the momentary light in her eyes starting to dim.

CHAPTER 6

There was nothing about Jade Evans that suggested catastrophe. I looked at her flat shoes and her grey knee-length skirt, her neatly bobbed brown hair, and her small, grey eyes. The three of us lined up in the hallway as if for an inspection, and she stood in front of us, slight and pale, looking in need of a square meal. When she clasped her hands together, I saw that her nails were rough and bitten.

Belle towered over Jade like a large-eyed giantess and was clearly unsure how to behave. All the servants she had known had been from Mombasa, and here was Jade, a new breed entirely.

'Where are you from?' she asked, in an effort to put Jade at her ease, although it was Belle who appeared unsettled.

'From Yorkshire,' replied Jade primly. She had a flat voice to go with her pale face, and she spoke with a finality that closed off further questions.

There was a pause, and then Fairfax jumped in. 'Well, Jade,' he said, 'I expect John has told you what we're after – a little light housework, some shopping, the washing, some cleaning. My wife will see to the cooking and to looking after our daughter, but some help with these other chores would be most welcome.'

He turned his glorious smile on the newcomer, which did seem to ruffle her composure.

'Yes, of course, sir,' she murmured, showing the first flicker of animation. 'That's grand.'

'Very good,' he said. He was starting to lose interest. 'Oh, and by the way, do call me Fairfax. You may call my wife Belle, and this here is Mivvi. We don't stand on ceremony here.'

Jade murmured her assent again, but I saw Mama's face turn dark. Evidently this was not how it was done back home.

*

Jade Evans was every inch as conscientious as John had said, and our sad home started to revive under her care. Belle was always suspicious of strangers and stayed out of her way, but I was curious. I couldn't work her out. She would appear noiselessly, as if she wanted to remain invisible, but there was also something controlled and watchful about her.

I could not warm to her exactly, but my life was uneventful, and so I took to spying on her from a distance.

I slipped upstairs one day with Adèle in tow to study Jade through the door of my parents' bedroom. She was dusting the chests of drawers and polishing the framed photographs, one of the few embellishments in our bare home. She paused to look at an image of my parents on the beach in Mombasa, then another of their wedding day, and then my favourite, the two of them gazing tenderly at me, their newborn daughter. She lingered over these pictures, the housework forgotten.

Satisfied with this glimpse of the strange woman, I tried to steal past the door, but then Jade turned around to pick up one of Belle's saris from the floor – and I was spotted.

'Hello,' she said, with a hesitant smile. 'I'm just tidying up your mam's mess.'

She folded the sari, running her hand across the stiff brocade border. 'I've seen these in Leicester,' she said, her flat vowels stranger to me than Belle's voice. 'But you don't see them around here, not really.'

I felt defensive. 'She wears trousers too,' I said stoutly.

'Where's she from?' asked Jade.

'Mombasa,' I replied.

Jade frowned. 'Isn't that in Africa? I thought she was Indian.'

I had never considered this and thought it a silly question. Belle was surely both.

Jade put the sari in a drawer and then glanced at Adèle dangling from my hand.

'You play with dolls still, Mivvi?' she asked, in an amused tone. 'How old are you?'

'I'm nearly ten.' I looked down at Adèle, who was a companion as much as a doll, and I felt judged. 'How old are you?'

For the first time, Jade's pinched features relaxed into a laugh.

'I'm twenty! And I had no dolls when I was nearly ten. Well, that's just how it was.'

She turned away, and I sidled off quickly.

Jade made me feel uncomfortable. She certainly had none of the fun and allure of Céline.

*

Jade mostly came while I was at school, so often weeks would go by without my seeing her. She became for me a shadow person, felt only in the newly swept floors and the freshly clean sheets.

But she was there on the day when, out of the blue and to my dismay, Belle announced her intention to pick me up from school.

'Why does she want to come? I don't want her to. I can manage by myself!' I was mortified; apart from the occasional lift from Fairfax, I had now started walking home alone.

'It'll get her out of the house,' Fairfax had replied shortly, 'instead of her sitting around moping all day.' Then, perhaps realising he sounded too harsh, he added, 'Sweet Pea, it's been hard on her and hard on me too. But I'm worried that she never gets out. For some reason, she's decided she wants to do this, so let her. It's just this once. It won't hurt.'

So, when school finished, there was Belle, waiting at the school gate, some way off as I had trained her to do. Mercifully she was wearing a blouse and some slacks, not a sari, and despite my annoyance, I felt a pang of hopefulness at seeing that she had roused herself.

Still, I wasn't taking any chances. I rushed her off from the vicinity of school and then, once we were safely out of the sight of anyone I knew, I slackened the pace, and we ambled on together. We passed by Walton Park, where Belle used to take me when I was small, where I would feed the ducks and chase the geese. We got to the road at the bottom of the hill leading to our house.

Then, at the little picket fence of a detached house on the corner of the road, Belle suddenly stopped.

She reared herself up, vigorously and theatrically, and spat three times with venom at the garden.

My mouth fell open.

'*Saitan!*' she hissed, '*Badmaash!*'

'Belle!' I cried.

She appeared not to hear me. Her dark eyes were inflamed and her nostrils flared, ready for another attack.

'Belle!' I hissed again, horrified now. 'What are you doing? Mama, come on, come on – let's go!'

Belle seemed to snap out of wherever she was. She shook herself and muttered, 'Nothing, nothing,' then grabbed my hand to march on.

I was aghast. 'W-what were you doing?' I stuttered. 'Who are they, in that house? What have they done?'

Belle shook her head vigorously. 'They told me, they *know*,' she whispered.

'Who? Who told you what?' There was no one else in sight; the street was deserted.

'They did. They said there are bad people in there. Wicked people. Come on, let's go.'

She gripped my hand tightly and pulled me down the road. I felt blank with confusion and embarrassment, and I darted a look left and right in case anyone had seen – but the road was still empty. I shook myself roughly away and walked home as fast as my legs would move, leaving my mother trailing behind me.

My heart fell as I saw Jade at the front porch, emptying the bins.

'Oh, hello, Mivvi,' she said with mild surprise. 'I thought your mam was coming for you today?'

I was too full of anguish for speech, so I pushed past her and barricaded myself in the front room with the television on at maximum volume. A dim memory came back to me of another time when Belle had spoken to an imaginary voice, and the thought forced a bitter taste into my mouth. What a way of behaving, spitting and cursing like that – what on earth made her do it? What if somebody had seen her?

I wanted to gag, and I shuddered as I tried to push all the ugly thoughts away, burying them as deep as I could.

Behind the blaring sound of the television, I realised there was a knocking on the door, and then Jade appeared, armed with the vacuum cleaner. She looked at me with apology.

'Mivvi, I've got to do the front room. Sorry, I'm later than usual. I've got another job in the mornings now – I'm saving to go to college.'

I gazed at her uncomprehendingly. In that moment, there could be no reality other than my own.

'You alright?' Jade asked tentatively.

I couldn't bear her concern. I nodded brusquely before getting up to leave. Upstairs, the door to Belle's bedroom was ajar and I saw my mother sitting quietly, folded in on herself once again.

I slunk sulkily into my own room and pulled out Meera's notebook. I was in the middle of writing a play for me and Katie, based on the menace in the Pinkish Jungle, and in a rush of anger, I decided the anti-heroine would be modelled on Belle, and perhaps also on Jade.

I lost myself in the writing and was well into the second scene when there was another knock on the door.

'Hello again,' said Jade, in her high, flat voice. 'Last thing, I've got to strip your bed – the sheets need changing. You alright with that?'

I nodded and shut my notebook quickly, although there was nothing incriminating in there yet.

'What are you doing?' Jade asked me. 'Is it homework?'

'I'm writing,' I squeaked, instantly annoyed at myself for sounding guilty. 'A play.'

'A play?' Jade was amused. 'Who's going to watch that then?'

I shrugged. 'Maybe Fairfax, maybe Belle.'

Jade smiled in a way I found most patronising. 'Funny how you call them by their first names,' she said. 'I'd have said dad and mam myself. I see, a play. I never see the point of plays and stuff. I've not been to see one, ever.'

She began pulling the sheets off the bed. 'Your mam's very quiet, isn't she? Does she go to plays? Does she go out at all? I mean, not just the shopping and fetching you from school?'

I had no intention of confiding in Jade and felt a sudden prick of loyalty to my mother.

'Yes, she does,' I said as decidedly as I could. 'And she's perfectly happy!'

'Well, that's good,' said Jade, with another slight smile. 'I just wondered, you know, whether being in a family, you might be … looked after a bit more, you know…' She tailed off as I gave her my stoniest look. 'Well, she went out today, didn't she?' she went on, not unkindly. 'It must be hard sometimes though, for your dad.'

It was the longest conversation we had ever had. As Jade turned to leave, we both caught sight of Belle through the open door. She had slipped back into her dreamy self, sitting blank-faced and absent in the room across the landing, rocking herself gently to the rhythm of some silent tune.

Jade looked down at me, but I resolutely refused to meet her eye. I would share nothing with this stiff stranger, with her unwelcome prying and her awkward sympathy.

The last thing I needed was a witness to my family's inexplicable woes.

*

The change in Belle was becoming impossible to ignore. Her late-night rows with Fairfax had long ceased to be thrilling, and the arguments now spilled over into the following days, so that when I left for school, I had no idea which mother I would come home to: the docile version or the simmering one.

On the nice mother days, there would be tea waiting for me, a plate of sandwiches and fruit, or at least some bread and butter. But on the nasty mother days, there was nothing to eat, just a cursory hello from a brooding Belle. I could smell the anger coming off her, pungent like hot smoke. I tried to stay out of her way, writing my plays, burying myself in more books from Tabitha, clinging to Adèle. I wished I could spend more time at friends' houses, but I could never invite them back. Besides, Katie and I were drifting apart. I think she was frightened of Tabitha.

One clear, sunny afternoon, Fairfax came to pick me up from school, his appearance invariably a bright moment in my day. He had just got the car washed and waxed, and looked gratified as people turned to admire it gleaming in the sun. He let me sit in the passenger seat as we drove off, a small smile playing on his face.

I was tired and gazed absent-mindedly out of the window, then glanced round at him, at his hands gripping the wheel. On his left hand were three long, fresh scratches, as if from a bramble, or a cat.

'Fairfax, what's that?' I asked.

He didn't answer.

'What is it, Daddy?'

He bit his lip then and hesitated. 'Oh, nothing.'

'How did it happen?' I persisted.

He hesitated again, then said, 'It was your mother, Mivvi – she did it to me.' His mouth was contorted with hurt, or perhaps it was with shame.

I felt dumbstruck. It was inconceivable to me that Belle might hurt him. Fairfax was surely impregnable.

I stroked his injured hand gently, but he kept his eyes on the road.

'I don't know why,' he went on, talking to himself more than me. 'I don't know what's the matter.'

As we drove on in silence, I felt a spreading pain in my tummy and the rise again of the bitter taste in my mouth. It was as if my thoughts and feelings were all scrambled up together, and I tried to let the rhythm of the car dull my mind.

*

That weekend, it rained unremittingly in miserable grey sheets. Fairfax was working from home upstairs, and the day hung listlessly about me. For once, I was tired of reading, and so I began an invented game, dashing around the sitting room with Adèle.

'Sshh,' said my mother, from where she sat on the sofa. She was downstairs for a change, but I wasn't used to her presence and paid no attention.

'Sshh,' she whispered several times – and yet again, I played on.

If I had looked, perhaps I might have caught her changing expression, but as I leapt in the air to evade an unseen enemy, I was astonished to find myself suddenly caught mid-flight. I fell heavily to the ground and felt a stinging slap across my cheek, and then a burning sensation as Belle grabbed me by the ear and started twisting it.

'Shut up!' she yelled. 'I told you to shut up!'

I put my hands up to try to defend myself, but Belle was strong, and I felt my head propelled backwards and forwards as she twisted my ear with rage. My face felt on fire, and the hot pain seared through me.

Belle's voice boomed with fury. 'I have kept telling you!' she shouted. 'You stupid girl, I have kept telling you!'

Then suddenly there was a dull thud as my head hit the wall. I was stunned and went limp, but Belle, in a passion now and out of control, did it again. I felt the hard, cold wall once more against my skull.

Belle's voice was a screech and the room a blur, and I was too dazed to cry. It was only when Fairfax ran in and pulled my mother off me that I was able to start whimpering.

'Jesus Christ, woman – what the hell is wrong with you?' he hissed at Belle, cradling me in his arms as I mewled with shock.

His words brought Belle back to herself, and she slumped, the passion draining from her, her face ghostly and spent.

Minutes seemed to pass, and then she crouched down next to us, and took me in her arms. Her face was wet, and the two of us cried silently together, the assailant and the victim, locked in Belle's terrible predicament, while Fairfax, granite-faced, looked on.

*

That evening, after I had gone to bed, he came up to talk to me. We had all been subdued for the rest of the day, as if in mourning once again for the lost baby, but when I heard him coming up the stairs, I felt my spirits gently lift.

He perched on the edge of my bed, his face indistinct in the dark. 'You're a good girl, Mivvi,' he said softly.

My sore heart eased at his words. As long as I had his approval, nothing could be that bad.

'It won't happen again. I've talked to your mother, and she understands. She lost control, just this once. But, Sweet Pea,' and here he moved to stroke my cheek briefly, 'this is between us, alright? No one else needs to know about this, do you understand? Not just today, but all of it – everything that's happened. We'll just work it out together.'

I nodded. I couldn't imagine telling anyone about Belle – not Katie, certainly not Tabitha. Thank goodness I had said nothing to Jade.

'You do understand?' His tone was pressing. 'Don't say anything to anyone at school or anywhere else.'

'Yes, Fairfax, I understand.'

He let out a deep sigh. 'It's very important that it doesn't get out,' he said. 'There's something about your mother that's ... underdeveloped. She's ... unable to control her feelings sometimes. But you understand. You're a big girl now, Mivvi.'

I nodded again, comforted by my bond with him and flattered by his trust in me. It was my duty to help him; he was relying on me to be mature, and I couldn't let him down.

Fairfax touched me gently on the cheek again, then slipped away.

*

It was the only time that I would remember being the direct target of Belle's condition. For weeks after that, I kept my distance from her. I went to school, wrote my plays, spent time with Tabitha, avoided Jade. I became adept at pretending that everything was alright.

As the incident receded, Belle went on whispering and muttering to persons unknown, and my fear was replaced by a mounting fury. Where was the woman who was meant to mother me? Where was the care, the attention that I craved?

'I hate her, I hate her!' I cried to Adèle. 'Why can't I have a proper mother?'

But I was 10 years old, and Fairfax was counting on me to cope, to closely guard our shared shame. So I covered up my boiling feelings, even from myself, slamming a lid firmly on the turbulence bubbling away deep inside.

FINDING BELLE

March 30th 1971

So much time alone, and then suddenly two visitors, Meera and Maz! Good thing they were not together; that would have been too much difficulty. Maz comes in wonderment at this country. The milk is so creamy, he says, and drinks up two pints! The bread is so fresh, he says, so he eats up half the packet!

F is not pleased. I see his blue eyes becoming icy. He does not like to have Maz here; he fears he will not return home. Maz looks dog-like at F, longing to be asked to stay, wounded when it is clear he will not be welcome. He is angry too at Baba, in a bubbling volcano way, because Baba would not leave his home — he would not leave Mombasa, and now Maz says it is becoming too late. I do not understand these things, but Maz and Ma are both boiling at Baba. I am relieved not to be there.

But there is no big happiness here either. I do not tell of these things, but maybe Baba senses them. Maz says Baba is worried about me. Why should he be worried, I ask. But I know he is. Baba's letters say, are you okay my baby, my Bela, are you settling into the new home? He asks this even though now it is two and a half years I am here, a long time. He asks, does he treat you well?

To this, I know not the answer. Yes and no. Yes, because F sometimes remains under my spell, like a small boy with a basket of fruits — Belle Belle, he whispers, Belle Belle. But for so many hours he is not here, off with his work — making ends meet, he says. I think ends have been met for a long time. But he is not satisfied. He becomes mocking at me because I failed at the Montessori test. It's just me, the breadwinner, is it, he says, half affection, half scorn. He thinks Baba should have given us more money at the start. Poor Baba, who tried his best.

So the answer for Baba about his baby Bela is not clear, and I write fudged up letters to hide the truth. Then he sends Maz, who says come home for a while, Bela, Baba misses you, even as he himself longs to stay here! I feel sorry for him. He cannot stay all alone — he is only 17.

But how can I go back? F does not want it, and I do not want to submit to Ma's questioning. When will F send money, she will ask, when will he help Maz? On and on she goes in her letters, wanting more, wanting help, accusing F of not doing enough. In the rubbish they go — I read them and throw them away. What does she expect me to do? If F won't help, he won't help. I have asked him gently, but he gets annoyed. I cannot make him annoyed; he is my only comfort here.

No, Meera is my comfort also. Such fun she brings with her, such lightness in her person. She goes to night school, she says, for her first science exams, and then to medical school to become a doctor. F is not very warm to Meera. Who knows why. She teases him, and maybe he doesn't like it.

I tell her about the Montessori, and she is kind, she says, Belle, what does it matter, you work if you want to but you do not have to. She is not mocking. Then she says slyly, what about another path, Belle, what about a baby?

We giggle and laugh when she says this. Yes, I tell her, shyly, we have until now not been lucky, but I feel it will happen. Of this, I am sure. A baby! A little life inside, growing like a treasure.

Yes, that surely is the way ahead.

CHAPTER 7

What did Jade really know of Belle's deterioration? I lived in a state of anxiety over what she might witness, and while Jade remained impassive, I was sure she must have gleaned more than she revealed. At least – and of this I was certain – she never saw the worst of Belle's descents. Fairfax made sure of it: gently shutting the door on my simmering mother or putting Jade off until another day.

But Jade must have been aware of Belle, or at least of her absence – a broiling creature in a closed-off room. Maybe Jade was just indifferent to our plight. I didn't care. I just wanted her gone. She had been with us for nearly a year but was, thankfully, leaving soon to go to college.

On Jade's final day, Belle was in a docile mood. She followed Fairfax downstairs to the kitchen, looking worn-out but gentle, and gave me a weak smile as she came in.

'Mivvi,' she said, in a voice soft with exhaustion. 'My brother is arriving today. From Mombasa.'

'Uncle Maz?' I asked. I had seen pictures, but I had never met him.

'Yes,' said Fairfax briskly. 'He's coming for a week, he says. Well, we can manage that, I suppose.'

My mother turned to Jade, who was at the sink, doing the

washing-up. 'Jade, you will please make the bed nicely?' Her name sounded strange in Belle's mouth. 'And also towels.'

Jade nodded, wiped her hands and went to find the linen.

'Why is he coming?' I asked. We never had family visitors. Fairfax's father had died when I was small, and his mother before that. He had spoken of cousins in Canada, but they remained strangers to me. Belle's family had never come.

'Who knows? He's always talking about moving to this country. What on earth he'd do here though, I don't know.' Fairfax sniffed. 'Nor how he'd support himself.'

Belle looked downcast. 'He will not bother us,' she said quietly. 'Perhaps it will be nice to see him.'

I looked across at her. 'When I was small, you said little brothers were painful.'

'Well, well,' she replied, 'sometimes he was. But he is my brother after all.'

'Always after something.' Fairfax's voice sounded sour. 'Not at all what was suggested at your end.'

Belle shrugged. 'What can we do? Our fathers talked like that – both pretending to riches. Yours also. My father at least provided us with something.'

I felt the stirrings of another memory, this time of a row over money.

Fairfax's expression hardened. 'Anyway, it's him turning up *now* that I'm wondering about. I don't think it's out of family feeling. In fact,' he said, with a laugh, 'I don't think there's much of that at all.'

Belle looked impassive. 'He is my brother. He is as he is. What can we do?'

*

When I got back from school, Maz was installed in the front room, slurping at a cup of tea, a plate of cake set in front of him. Across from him, Fairfax was looking pained, and there was a faint smile on Belle's lips. It looked like she was having a good day. She had tied her hair up neatly into a bun, and had dusted her face with powder.

'Ah, Mivvi! My ice-cream niece! Let me have a good look at you!'

Maz unwound his wiry frame from the sofa, and we both took each other in.

He was smaller and slimmer than Belle, with a face like the grandmother in the old photographs, sharp and alert like a garden bird. His hair looked wet with coconut oil, and I could smell it, along with the burnt scent of his deep brown skin, as he bent down to graze my cheek with his lips. Fairfax was also appraising him, looking critically at his imitation brand jeans and his bright orange polo top. Maz had left his sandals by the front door, and his toenails were uncut. Fairfax adjusted his tie.

'Well,' said Maz, whistling softly, 'what have we here? A wheaten girl, a wheaten beauty! That's a fair child you've produced, Bela.'

I smiled at him uncertainly. It was the first time anyone had ever called me fair.

Belle shrugged and glanced at Fairfax, as if to say it was his doing.

'How old are you now, Mivvi?' Maz asked. In his mouth, my name sounded different, the vowels longer and more emphatic.

'I'll be eleven soon,' I replied politely.

Maz let out another low whistle. 'Eleven! Eleven whole years since I've seen you all! Longer, even.'

He settled back into the sofa, and it was Belle who responded. 'Well, well, it is a long way,' she said. 'It is not possible to travel so far all of the time.'

Maz chewed on his slice of cake and replied with his mouth full. 'Oh, it's not the distance, Bela, it's not the miles.' He was smiling, but there was something else in his tone.

'Well, it is also the government,' she said vaguely. 'They make it difficult to come, I suppose. I don't understand it all really.' Even if she didn't, it was odd to see Belle taking the lead in the conversation.

'Ah, but if you have family help, these things become easier,' said Maz. His tone was light and heavy at the same time.

Fairfax cleared his throat. 'As Belle says, there are laws and rules – it really isn't that simple. Anyway, here you are now, for a week's holiday, and that's … well, that's fine.' He frowned. 'You can look around, see the sights.'

'Find a job?' asked Maz, grinning.

Fairfax looked irritated, but I found my uncle strangely compelling.

'You can't do that, as you well know,' Fairfax replied shortly.

Belle poured her brother some more tea – a rare act of domestic care, small though it was. I couldn't remember the last time she'd poured me a drink.

Maz took another slurp and let out an exaggerated sigh of pleasure. Some of the hot liquid spilled into his saucer, and he lifted it high into the air and poured the contents into his open mouth.

I resisted a sudden urge to giggle. I was starting to wonder if Maz was deliberately trying to annoy Fairfax.

Jade, who was working later than usual as it was her last day, put her head around the door. 'That's me done, I'll be off now,' she said to no one in particular.

Maz eyed her with interest. 'Very good, Bela, a servant and all,' he murmured, so that Jade couldn't hear.

Belle made no reaction, but I felt his condescension towards Jade and for a moment pitied her.

'Well done, Jade – thank you for everything,' said Fairfax too loudly, and he jumped up from his seat. 'Well, that's it, I suppose,' he said, extending his hand. 'You've got this week's money, I hope? Good luck with the course! Who knows, perhaps we'll see you again in the office?'

The shadow of a smile appeared on her pale face as she mumbled that she hoped so too. She gave a sidelong nod to Belle and Maz, glanced once towards me, and then turned to leave our employment for good.

The conversation turned to other things.

'So, man,' said Maz, after a delicate belch, 'how come you're still in Milton Keynes? I'd have thought a hot shot lawyer like you was headed for the big time.' He narrowed his eyes slyly. 'Not managed London yet, eh?'

Fairfax tried to look cool. 'I didn't see the need. This is a new town. I wanted to be somewhere up and coming, part of a bold new project.'

'Also, it is less expensive,' added Belle. I could tell she wanted to support my father in front of Maz, but Fairfax didn't want her help.

'No, no, money is not an issue,' he muttered.

'Ah,' said Maz lightly. 'Well, I will reacquaint myself with your new town then. Expensive or cheap, whatever it is.'

Fairfax had had enough. 'Well, Maz, I'll leave you to catch up with Belle. I've invited John and Bianca for dinner tonight. You'll remember John – you met him at the wedding. I've just got some papers to clear from the study; it doubles up as the spare room where you'll be sleeping. I'm sure you'll be very comfortable there.'

Maz inclined his head graciously.

I remembered that I had left Adèle in the study, so I got up to follow Fairfax out. As I glanced back at Maz, he gave me a large and knowing wink.

*

I had hoped that Fairfax might say something interesting to me about Maz once we were out of earshot, but he was soon preoccupied and barely noticed me as he took a stack of papers out of the study and into his bedroom. I wandered in to fetch Adèle, not wanting Maz to see that I was still playing with a doll at my age.

As I scooped her up, my eyes caught sight of a small pile of dog-eared magazines in the corner of a low chest of drawers which were usually shut. I looked curiously at the top photo – and gasped. A half-naked woman pouted back at me, her bare breasts thrust out, her bikini pants covering little.

I glanced furtively at the door, but there was no sign of Fairfax, so I picked up the first magazine and opened it. It had a long story told in photographs, like a cartoon but with real people, titled, *He had to make love to every woman he met, or see the world die!* The man with this heavy responsibility was in his underpants in all the pictures, and all the women were in their bras.

I gave a contemptuous snort. I didn't really know what making love was, although Tabitha had tried to tell me once, but the story was clearly preposterous!

Then I picked up another magazine, this one more fascinatingly repellent, with page upon page of naked women lying on their backs, legs splayed, holding themselves wide open, with smiles a bit like Adèle's fixed on their faces.

I dropped the magazine in disgust. Why on earth had my father got these?

As if I had conjured him up, Fairfax appeared at the door.

'Mivvi, Mivvi,' he cried, his face twisted with alarm. He scooped up the magazines, and threw them into a high cupboard, somewhere I couldn't reach.

'Those are work magazines,' he said hurriedly. 'Just forget about them. Off you go, love, off you go.'

I blushed scarlet and rushed into my room with Adèle, choking back nervous giggles as I shut the door.

Then I threw myself onto the bed and lay gulping, convulsed with horrified laughter. It was a glimpse of a private Fairfax whom I had no desire to know.

*

'Helloo helloo!' yelled John, who could never speak quietly. He took up most of the hallway, but Bianca edged past him and enveloped me in an exuberant hug. John planted a loud kiss on Belle's cheek and pumped Maz's hand enthusiastically.

'Good to see you, Maz, after all these years – how are you, old boy?' he cried, although Maz was probably not 30.

Maz had changed into a stiff, shiny suit for the evening, with trousers that were too short for him. He wore socks but no shoes, and the other adults towered over him. His coconut hair was slicked back into a quiff.

He smiled shyly. 'I'm good, man, I'm good. Nice to see you and to meet your lady wife,' he said, nodding to Bianca, who gave him a generous smile.

She was wearing a purple mini-dress, and as Maz glanced down at the hem, she threw her hands in the air and exclaimed, 'I'm a Sixties child!'

He looked away, embarrassed, but John squeezed her arm, and she air-blew him a kiss. They had always doted on each other. 'Very good people,' Fairfax called them, slightly acidly, perhaps because they were both very devout Christians.

Belle had been even-tempered all day, and she had risen to the occasion by cooking a lavish *desi* meal, a glistening mix of Kenyan and Indian foods: hot curries, spicy chutneys, and rice sparkling with fruit. She had swathed herself in red silk, and applied careful make-up, and a *bindi* to her forehead. She looked like her old self in the photographs, looser and heavier, but still glamorous. I watched her with cautious relief.

It was Fairfax who was tense. He poured out large whiskies for himself and John and a smaller one for Maz, who frowned at his glass. Bianca had a whisky, too, but not Belle. Fairfax didn't like her to drink. He had told me once that it might 'alter the delicate balance of her chemistry.' She had lemonade like me.

'So, Maz, what are you up to?' asked John, his voice resounding with goodwill. 'How's life treating you?'

Bianca turned her green eyes on the newcomer. The whisky must have gone to her head quickly, as she laid a manicured hand on Fairfax's forearm to steady herself as she listened.

'Oh well, you know, I'm managing okay,' said Maz, with a weak smile. 'The opportunities are not so great at home, but things are opening up now, so let's see.'

'A coffee business, isn't it?' John asked. 'That you have with your father, I mean.'

'Yar, that's right,' said Maz, rolling his words. 'We are thinking of expanding if possible, maybe garments, some trade with here, maybe some with Pakistan.'

'Is that where your family's from?' asked Bianca, looking confused. 'I thought it was India?'

'It is India,' said Belle. I looked at her in surprise; she was usually content just to sit and listen. 'Our baba – that is, our father – his family is from Gujarat, and he went to Mombasa first with his parents when he was 14. Our ma is from India only – she went from Bengal state to marry him.'

'The first mixed marriage in the family,' said Maz, with a glint in his eye.

John shot a warm smile at Belle and Fairfax, but she gazed at her empty plate, and he studied the carpet.

'It was not so easy for Ma when she arrived in Mombasa,' continued Maz. 'Her mother-in-law, my father's mother, persecuted her.'

'Oh, surely not!' exclaimed Bianca. 'How awful!'

'It happens all the time,' said Maz, in a matter-of-fact tone. 'It is generational. Should I ever bring home a lady wife, my mother will also persecute her, for sure.'

'He is exaggerating,' murmured Belle quietly, without conviction.

I looked between them; Belle had often told me about Mombasa when I was little, but this was not a story I knew.

'Anyway,' Maz was now in full flow, 'poor *Thakurma* met a sad end.' He put his index finger to his temple and turned quick circles in the air. 'Lost her mind. Late life loss. Complete lunacy!'

Fairfax scraped back his chair sharply. 'Time for pudding!' he said abruptly. 'Come on!'

He started to clear the table and pulled Belle and Maz up to help. They went into the kitchen, and I found myself alone with John and Bianca. The curls of Bianca's piled-up red hair were starting to escape, and she was missing an earring.

'Mivvi,' she said, in an on-stage whisper. 'Love, how are you doing? How is your mum?' Her finely plucked eyebrows knitted together with concern.

'Oh, she's alright,' I said vaguely. 'The same, you know.'

'It's difficult for your dad, isn't it?' said John, on the other side. 'And for you too sometimes, I'm sure.'

I looked at them, faking dumbness. If there were anyone in the world I might confide in, it would be John and Bianca – or perhaps Meera, even though I had only seen her once. But Fairfax would never forgive me if I said anything, and what would I do then?

'You know,' John went on, 'you can always come to us if you need anything.'

'Any help, that is,' said Bianca, wrapping her arm around me. Her curls tickled my cheek. 'Although God is looking out for you, love – you know that.'

'Your old dad,' John said, 'bless him, super chap, and he worships you. But very keen on appearances…'

He tailed off as a large bowl of creamy rice with sultanas and cardamom was brought in with fanfare. Fairfax opened another bottle of wine.

'Have things calmed down over there?' John asked Maz, once everyone was served. 'You know, all that anti-Asian feeling?'

Maz shrugged. 'It doesn't just disappear. But we learn to live with it – we who are left behind.'

I saw Fairfax looking at him levelly.

'But you could come here surely?' asked Bianca innocently.

'Darling, you know the government doesn't make it that easy for people, not anymore,' murmured John.

'Too true,' said Maz. 'But my father wouldn't leave for Britain when we could – he said he loved Africa and would rather return to India if he had to. So now this is my situation. Unwanted in Mombasa and also in Milton Keynes!'

'Oh!' exclaimed Bianca, but Fairfax's face was dark.

'Come on, Maz,' he said, 'stop all this. It's not so easy; money is tight.'

'I don't need your money,' replied Maz lightly. 'I need your help. Anyway,' he went on, 'I hear you're planning to send ice-cream Mivvi to private school? That's what Bela tells me.'

This was the first I had heard of it. I looked up at my father in surprise.

'I am,' Fairfax said. 'She's a clever girl, and I'm sure she can get in.'

Bianca looked at me admiringly. 'Those exams are meant to be so difficult.'

I sat there, feeling flattered but bemused. Private school? All the talk in class this year had been about everyone going to Compton, the local school. I looked to Fairfax for an explanation, then quickly looked away. My discovery earlier that afternoon was still in my head.

'Good to hear you've got the money for that,' said Maz snidely.

It was getting too much for John. 'Now, what I want to know,' he bellowed to Fairfax, 'is how you've found our Jade? She's finished with you now, isn't she? I've promised her some secretarial work if she passes her college tests, which she's bound to do with flying colours!'

'She seems a pleasant young woman,' said Fairfax. 'Hard-working. I have tried to encourage her.'

'She needs a bit of boosting, that's what she needs,' Bianca declared. 'She had a hard start in life, but she's doing alright now. I think there's a fella on the scene too – Roy, I think he's called.'

'Well, I think if it all works out, she'll be a good asset to the firm,' John went on. 'Maybe she'll work for you again, Fairfax!'

I stole a quick look at Belle to see what she thought of this talk of Jade.

She looked impassive for a moment, but then opened her mouth to speak. 'She is a very silent girl,' she said reflectively. 'Silent and creeping.'

John roared with laughter. 'You have such a way with words, my dear Belle!' he exclaimed, and Belle's face broke into a mischievous grin.

How lovely she can look sometimes, I thought wistfully, *and how sharp she can be.*

When Maz got up to go to the bathroom, we all heard him hawking into the toilet bowl. Fairfax rolled his eyes, but John just smiled.

'It's fine, old boy – you just relax now.'

Bianca helped herself to another glass of wine when Maz returned, and she put her hand lightly over Belle's. Her costume jewellery shone garishly in the lamplight, but her smile was genuine.

'Are you looking after yourself now?' she asked, giving Belle's hand a squeeze.

'Surely the question is, are you letting this old rogue look after you?' yelled John, to a prompt hushing from his wife. He tried again. 'Make sure he gets you out and about,' he said, sounding furtive. 'He mustn't hide you away.'

Belle's smile was strained now. 'I am okay,' she said. 'I am managing.'

Fairfax busied himself with topping up the glasses.

'Of course you are,' said Bianca encouragingly. 'But it's best not to be too alone?'

'I'm here,' said Maz, with a big yawn. 'I can be company.'

'You're here for a week,' Fairfax snapped. 'It's very late. Mivvi, go on – off to bed now.'

I traipsed upstairs and lay in bed for a while, listening to the murmur of adult voices and replaying the conversation I had just heard.

That night, I dreamt of myself in a boater hat and a pleated skirt, armed with a large lacrosse stick and ready to clamber onto the school bus, which was empty apart from the driver, who was Fairfax. In the way of dreams, he appeared again in the school grounds, this time sporting a pair of antlers. Maz had also grown horns, and the two of them were sparring intently, too engrossed in their fight to notice me.

I woke up briefly when the front door slammed, then slipped back into a deep and blameless sleep.

CHAPTER 8

'Arr-rre, my head!' moaned Maz loudly at breakfast. 'What did you feed us, brother? I thought it was finest Scotch, not baddest hooch!'

Fairfax looked almost amused. 'Can't take your drink, eh?' he smirked. He was fresh and sleek in a crisp white shirt, as if dressed for the office. I wondered if this smart weekend look was for Maz's benefit.

Belle looked subdued. Her animation of the previous night had used up her small stock of energy.

I sat quietly at the end of the table, thinking over the previous day: the magazines in the cupboard, the conversation at dinner, the mention of private school.

'So,' Fairfax went on, taking a large gulp of tea, 'are you going to take a look around the town today, see the sights?'

'That I am,' said Maz. 'You fancy showing me around?'

'Sorry,' said Fairfax quickly, 'can't do that, old boy.' He had borrowed the phrase from John. 'I'm drowning in work. And Belle needs to rest.'

'What about Mivvi here? Let me take her with me. We can get to know each other!'

'Ah, no, that won't be possible. She's got lots of work to do too.'

'But it's Saturday!' Maz protested.

'She needs to start studying for those exams,' Fairfax replied firmly.

I looked up from my breakfast. 'What school is it, Fairfax?'

'It's in Buckingham, Sweet Pea – there's a school bus from here. It's a good school, for bright girls. You have a very good chance of getting in.'

I tried to look modest, but I could feel my heart leap at his praise. 'Will Tabitha try too, do you think?' I asked. 'And Katie?'

Fairfax shrugged and looked non-committal. 'Not sure. I don't think Katie's got it in her.'

Maz and I both looked at him askance.

'What?' said Fairfax. 'I'm only saying how I see things. Not everyone can be good at everything. Anyway, Mivvi's got to get preparing.'

I nodded, frowning. It felt disloyal not to defend Katie, but it was true that she never did that well in school tests.

Maz drained his coffee. 'You got it all worked out there, man. Okay, I'll take myself off then. Cheerio, or whatever it is you British say.'

*

Maz's week passed quickly. He stayed out late on Saturday night, and then took himself off to Birmingham on Sunday to see import-export people and 'meet some others who look like us'. Once the weekend was over, I saw even less of him. I was at school during the day, and he was out in the evening – 'meeting someone he's picked up,' Fairfax commented grimly.

Suddenly it was his last night. I was intrigued by him, but Belle was deteriorating again, and I was thankful that he was leaving. Everything in our house was on borrowed time.

I got back from school later than usual that day and was surprised to see Fairfax and Maz coming out of the study together, as if they had been discussing something. The door to my parents' bedroom was closed. Belle didn't come down that evening at all, and dinner was a Fairfax special, frozen pizza and ice-cream.

'How are your parents?' Fairfax asked Maz indifferently.

'Getting on, you know, but getting by. Your own father died, I heard?'

Fairfax nodded. 'A while ago. When Mivvi was very small.'

'I was sorry to hear it. He and Baba used to be good friends, before they fell out.' I wondered what Maz meant, but he didn't elaborate. 'Of course,' he went on, 'they made the introduction – that is how you came to meet and marry our dear sweet Bela!'

Fairfax shot Maz an acid look. 'And took her off your hands!'

Maz just shrugged. 'Well, you have a good life here, with servants and all.'

'What, do you mean Jade?' exclaimed Fairfax. 'She doesn't work here anymore, and anyway, she was hardly a servant! That's not how we view people here, Maz.'

'Still, you could share some of that success with family, you know?' Maz's bravado melted into a plea.

Fairfax drained his drink. 'Never mind about all that, just think about what we discussed.'

Everything was so tense between them, and I was longing for the evening to be over. It was a relief when Maz went out after dinner.

I made an excuse to go up to my room, but before I left, I turned to Fairfax while he was rinsing the plates.

'Fairfax, what is it with Uncle Maz? You don't like him, do you?'

Fairfax started to whistle tunelessly. 'I wouldn't say I don't like him, Sweet Pea. I just don't want more responsibility.'

'Why does he mean that?'

'Well, if he stayed, it would be me picking up the tab. His father set up that business, not him. Maz hasn't got it in him. Anyway, the father's business has gone wrong too now.'

'Why did the business go wrong?' I asked.

'I don't know,' he replied shortly. 'Anyway, my point is, Maz is just … a useless so and so.'

I was taken aback, but he didn't notice.

'Besides, that family,' he was talking to himself now, 'and their trap…'

As I moved to leave, his attention returned to me.

'Anyway, not to worry, Mivvi. It will all work out in the end.'

*

I found it hard to get to sleep that night. I heard Maz return late, and promptly retire to his room. Then I caught sounds of Belle's sharp voice, complaining about something to Fairfax, and I shivered under the sheets, praying that my mother would not humiliate us with a guest in the house. Perhaps Fairfax said the same to her, because the noise softened, and I slipped into a deep sleep.

I was woken later by sounds coming from my parents' bedroom. The streetlight shone through my thin curtain, and I got up and crept down the corridor to peer into their room.

Belle was lying prostrate on her back on the bed, wearing no clothes on top, her bare breasts hung low, her long hair streamed out over her shoulders and the pillow. Her eyes were red, her face was wild, and she was pounding Fairfax with her strong muscled legs, landing thumps with her feet against his chest, throwing her head from side to side in a frenzy of wordless groaning.

I could barely understand what I was seeing. Then, in that shocking moment, Fairfax, who was submitting to the assault, saw me in the doorway.

'Come see what your mother is doing,' he gasped, red-faced and solemn. 'Come in, Mivvi, and see.'

Aghast, I rushed in to defend my father and to quell the madness. Acting on pure instinct, I smashed my hand down on Belle's arm with all the force I could muster.

'Stop it! Stop it! Don't do that to him, stop it!' I shrieked, overcome by my own passion.

When I looked up, I saw a shadow at the open door, the silhouette of Uncle Maz, caught there fleetingly, watching the scene.

My slap must have brought Belle out of her delirium. The kicking stopped, and the moaning slowly subsided.

I could never remember what happened next. Did Fairfax take me back to my bed? What happened to the shadow at the door? It was all a blur.

*

In the morning, the wild mood had dissipated, and Belle had that meek and humble air that followed a torrid night – as if the spirits had left her.

As Maz prepared to leave, he made no mention of the scene he had witnessed, but his face was grave. There was a hushed conversation between my father and uncle in the hallway which I couldn't make out, but when Maz stepped out to the waiting taxi and mumbled a parting word to Fairfax, I heard my father's reply clearly: 'And you think about what I said. I'll be in touch.'

With a brief wave to me, Maz was gone.

That afternoon after school, I asked my chastened mother to show me some old cine film they had of me as a toddler, playing with Belle and Fairfax in a park. There were friends in the background; it was a happy group outing of the sort we never had now, at a time that I was too young to remember. But I did have an almost bodily recognition of my parents as they once were, light and lively and smiling, full of the optimism of the young.

The images jumped around soundlessly. Were they in love then, my parents? Watching it, I could connect the silent film version of Fairfax to the present-day father I knew and adored. But Belle remained as unknowable as her flickering, projected image. The lithe and lovely woman on the screen bore no resemblance to the defeated Belle who sat next to me now, battered by her own imagination.

PART 2 – 1986

CHAPTER 1

'I've brought you the files on the Baldwin case,' Jade said, as she placed the documents carefully on Fairfax's desk. 'There are also these papers to sign here, and I've just set up a meeting for tomorrow lunchtime with Mrs Goodwin.'

'Jade, what more could I want from you?'

Jade raised an arch eyebrow. 'I suppose that means coffee?' she asked primly.

'How well you know me.' Fairfax smiled. 'This time it's on me.'

'What, not just an instant? A posh coffee from the café?'

Fairfax had many qualities, but Jade knew that generosity was not one of them. He was clearly in a good mood. She took the proffered change.

'I think Mivvi greatly enjoyed her visit here yesterday,' Fairfax went on.

'Mmm.'

'Who knows – maybe she'll follow me into the law? She'd be a great lawyer. A barrister perhaps. I could have been one, you know,' he added casually.

'How old is she now? 13?'

'Yes, 14 soon. Doing very well at school. She's at the oldest one in Buckingham, you know. Private, of course.'

'Mmm, yes, I know,' Jade replied. Fairfax took every opportunity to say so. 'Alright,' she said, as she stepped towards the door, 'I won't be long.'

Seeing Mivvi again had stirred up mixed emotions in Jade. She had known the girl was coming, but it had still been strange to see her. Mivvi herself had seemed oddly surprised when they met, but surely Fairfax must have told her Jade was working here. It had been nearly two years now, after all.

Mivvi had changed. Back when Jade was working in the house, Mivvi had had an innocence with her fancy doll and her funny plays. It had made her endearing, despite her tendency to snoop. Jade had felt sorry for the girl, living in that oppressive house, coping with its tensions, fending for herself. But now, Mivvi was closed and wary, with none of that lightness of childhood. Maybe it was just puberty – she was certainly bursting out of her clothes.

Jade unconsciously ran a hand over her own flat stomach, and smoothed down her hair in the lobby mirror, pleased at her new style with its layers and highlights. Her recently bought pumps were killing her, but it was worth it for the extra three inches she gained, and she tripped delicately towards the revolving doors, trying to look casual through the pain.

She was still thinking about Mivvi as she stepped out into the fresh air. The girl might be an adolescent now, but she still seemed very clingy and needy around her father. There again, her mother had been very peculiar, perhaps that was why. Jade had never fully known what was wrong with Belle, but she had watched the empty woman with her haunted face passing long hours doing nothing, and she knew the worst was being kept from her. Sometimes, Fairfax would shut the door on his wife, and Jade would hear her pacing the room or speaking to no one in her throaty language, sounding cornered and angry. It was unnerving. But Jade hadn't wanted to know more, and her relief at finishing the job and leaving that claustrophobic house was only tempered by a faint, barely conscious regret that she would no longer see Fairfax.

She had marvelled then at how a man as vital as Fairfax could be with someone as unsettling as Belle. The first time she had met him in the house, with his staring wife and watchful daughter, she was too nervous to take him in properly, only registering briefly his matinee idol looks. But in the months that followed, as she worked in his home, his presence enveloped her, even when he wasn't there. She tidied his papers and ironed his shirts and studied the photographs of him as an impossibly handsome young man. He was much older than she was, of course, and her growing crush had just been a light fantasy of hers, something to dwell on during a lonely evening or a boring one with Roy.

As Jade paid for the coffee – Fairfax had not given her enough money – she thought over how her life had changed since those days. She was secure now, with a proper job and a proper salary, not just mopping up after someone else.

But Fairfax occupied her mind insistently, like a drumbeat she couldn't ignore. She had always considered herself a prosaic person, not given to romantic notions, but increasingly she couldn't get him out of her head.

At the beginning, as she settled in at the office, she had sat working quietly at her desk, watching him flashing his brilliant smile, exuding his easy charm. He had remembered her, of course, but casually and in passing as just another acquaintance, another of John's foundlings.

But diligent though Jade was, this gleaming man kept intruding on her thoughts, and she started to feel her bearings slip. She felt like Barbra Streisand in a film she had once seen, mesmerised by the beauty of Robert Redford, glowing and golden-haired in the sunlight. She hoped her confusion didn't show. He was beautiful as a woman is beautiful. Or like Robert Redford, bedazzling on a huge cinema screen.

'Thank you for the coffee,' said Fairfax when she arrived back at his office. 'Although I had hoped you'd bring me some double cream with it.'

Jade went to the office fridge and brought out a carton on which she scrawled *double cream*.

He smiled at her. 'Very good, Jade – you treat me very well.'

He hitched up his trousers so that they wouldn't crease as he settled into the big swivel chair next to her desk, ready for a break.

'I really do think Mivvi enjoyed being shown around,' Fairfax said.

'Uh-huh?'

'She's very bright, you know. And I am serious about her going to the Bar – if she puts her mind to it. She spends too much time mooning over those novels of hers, but hopefully she'll grow out of it.'

Jade nodded. 'I hate novels. Waste of time.'

'Yes, I agree. Much rather watch a film.'

'Hmm, yes, me too.'

It was warm in the room, and Fairfax rolled up his shirtsleeves. Jade's gaze kept returning to his arms, with their glint of golden down and warmth of burnished skin.

'I've finished the Summers case now, by the way. You'll sort out the final bill, won't you?'

'Of course.'

Fairfax smiled. 'Nice woman. I think she was very pleased with me. From Yorkshire, you know?'

Jade was distracted by the sight of more of him than usual on display. 'Oh yes?'

'That's where you're from, isn't it?'

'Yes, originally.'

'You don't sound very Yorkshire? Not now anyway.'

Jade shrugged innocently. She had worked hard at softening her accent.

Fairfax sat forward in his seat. 'And what brought you to Buckinghamshire?' he asked.

'There was nothing much to keep me in Yorkshire really.' She forced herself to concentrate. 'I was keen to get away and get a good job. London was too expensive, so I came here.'

'You see your family much?'

Jade hesitated. She usually headed this question off, but she wanted him to know.

'Sorry, am I prying?' asked Fairfax.

'No, no, not at all.' She took a deep breath. 'I don't have any family, actually. I grew up in care, with foster families for a while, but mainly in a children's home.'

Fairfax was looking at her with surprise and concern, and she felt her cheeks grow warm.

'It's alright, really,' she went on, 'I'm fine about it. I don't talk about it much, because people ask questions or feel awkward, but it was fine.' She spoke lightly, but it made her feel dizzy to be confiding such personal details to Fairfax. They had never had a conversation like this before.

'It must have been hard at times, though?' he asked.

'Yes, well, sure – yes, it was. The foster parents were … variable. It was quite … loveless at times. But the children's home was alright. I mean, the manager was strict, and the food was inedible, but actually, the kids got on reasonably well, and some of the staff were kind. I made a friend there, Helen Booth. She was older than me, and good at coping with it all. I really looked up to her.'

Jade fell silent for a moment. She caught sight of her animated reflection in the window, and hoped she hadn't said too much. Somehow, she didn't think Fairfax was interested in complexity.

'How did she cope then, this Helen?' asked Fairfax.

'Well, she was quite … churchy.'

Fairfax pulled a face.

'No, I didn't think that would be your thing,' Jade said, 'but it helped her. I don't know – I'm not that much into it either, but church people have been nice to me, especially John and Bianca. That's how I met John. His sister fostered me for a while.' Jade paused, aware she had been speaking in a rush. She wasn't used to saying these words; she usually kept her past entirely to herself.

'What happened to Helen?' Fairfax asked the question absent-mindedly. His attention was wandering.

'I'm not sure,' she answered, 'a couple took her on while I stayed at the home. I was pleased for her. Her health was never great, and I thought it would do her good, being somewhere permanent. I remember her praying that I would be fostered too. I don't know what happened to her after that.'

There was a pause, and Jade wondered if he had stopped listening.

'Ah well,' Fairfax said. 'Come on then, let's get back to work.'

Jade nodded. She had pressed things too far. Her struggle to survive was what made her special, but she worried that it also made her dull.

'Yes, sir, yes, boss,' she said in a sprightly tone. 'Enough church talk. I'll keep that for John and Bianca.'

'Ha yes. They do *goodness* – I really don't.'

It was clear to Jade that he liked to keep things light and uncomplicated. Funny, given the dark shadows in his own life. But she had struck the wrong note, and she resolved in future to return to matters of less consequence. She didn't want to risk him losing interest again.

*

Over the next coffee, which she bought, Jade told him about secretarial college.

'It was money very well spent. But the college itself – well, it was full of clones.'

Fairfax laughed. 'Clones of whom?'

'Of each other! Honestly, Fairfax, to a woman, they were all thin and blonde, with names like Laetitia. It was like a finishing school for the home counties. But,' she said slyly, 'maybe that's your type.'

Fairfax raised an eyebrow. 'I was raised in the Midlands,' he said, as if that were an answer.

'Anyway, none of them had ever met a Jade before. I suppose they didn't mean any harm – they just weren't very self-aware. And they never seemed to eat.'

'Never?' Fairfax smiled. 'They were a bunch of blonde clone corpses, in that case.'

'I used to eat all the peanuts when we went out for a drink – not that I went very often, but I ate them all just to hear them squeal. "Six calories a peanut," they'd scream, and I'd reply, "Calories is for fat people, and I ain't fat."'

Fairfax started to laugh, and Jade wondered where her garrulousness came from. She never told these stories, not even to Roy. But Fairfax seemed to invite her chatter, and she was desperate to amuse and entertain him. It probably took his mind off other things.

They were interrupted when John came in to call Fairfax to a meeting.

'So, when's she coming again?' he bellowed. 'Your little Sweet Pea?'

'Sometime soon, I hope, although she doesn't like being Sweet Pea anymore. And you don't have to shout.'

'Sorry,' whispered John. And then, lowering his voice further, 'How are things?'

'Fine,' said Fairfax quietly. He glanced over at Jade, who busied herself with some papers.

'Are we still on for dinner at the weekend then? Me and Bianca?'

'Yes, I think so. Yes, should be fine.'

'It's an okay time?'

'Yes. Come.'

'No one else around? She's so fond of Meera – has she seen her recently?'

Fairfax pulled a face.

'Oh, come on, she's nice!' exclaimed John.

'Well, she's got a job in Scotland, so she's not around.' Fairfax shrugged. 'You're right, she's fine. She's good for Belle.'

'I think more company generally would be good for Belle,' said John. Then he muttered something quietly, and Jade did her best to look focused on the papers. She couldn't hear what he was saying, but Fairfax was nodding.

'Yes, alright, I'll think about it,' he said. 'Yes – perhaps that's not a bad idea.'

*

That was how Jade came to be invited to dinner at Fairfax's house. The invitation was for Roy too; she knew she would not have been invited alone, but Fairfax had met Roy once at the office, and he must have been judged safe.

Jade was beside herself with anticipation. Fairfax's dinner parties were rare and selective, she knew, and visitors were tightly controlled. But she was nervous at seeing Belle again; she had no sense of how she would react to her presence at the table. Distracted and vague she might be, but Jade knew full well that she thought herself considerably superior to the former home help. *Well, she can look down on me all she wants*, she thought defiantly. *I don't care. I'm making something of myself. And her husband wants me there.*

She desperately hoped Roy wouldn't let her down. The two of them had limped along together for over three years, he always keener than her. At first, she had been flattered by his attentions, but over time she had come to find him irritating and dull. The contrast between him and Fairfax was stark: Roy short, thin, prematurely balding; Fairfax a modern Adonis, whatever that was.

Still, at least Roy never tried to go too far. If his goodnight kisses sometimes lingered too long for comfort, he never resisted her gentle pressure out of the front door. She knew he thought she was saving herself, and that suited her well. It meant she could cloak her lack of experience behind a point of principle, and besides, she didn't want to give herself to just anyone.

That Sunday, she went to church with John and Bianca, who was resplendent in a scarlet faux Chanel suit, its gold buttons glinting in the setting sun. Jade felt she needed sunglasses to look at her.

After the service, the conversation turned to Fairfax and Belle. 'They got married in Kenya,' John said. 'Did you know? It was a whirlwind romance, and I must say he was absolutely besotted with her. They married within weeks of knowing each other. I was in India at the time and flew out to be Fairfax's best man.'

'She's Kenyan then, is she?' asked Jade, curiously.

'Yes, but her family is from India, so I suppose she's both,' said Bianca. 'Their daughter's smashing, isn't she? So grown-up for her age.'

'Belle was dazzling when they married. Just stunning,' said John, giving his wife's arm a squeeze as if to reassure her that she was, too.

'Yes, you can see she was, I suppose.' Jade kept her tone casual. 'But she's changed, hasn't she?'

A look passed between them.

'She's not quite what she was, it's true. Belle has had … issues, you might say,' John said carefully. 'We're both very fond of the old girl, of course, and we'd do anything for her.'

'There might have been trouble adjusting, you know, coming here and everything,' said Bianca softly. 'Still,' she continued, 'we all have our crosses to bear, don't we?'

If that was a cue for Jade to ask more about Bianca's own life, she didn't take it. She was fond of the older woman, but her mind was on Fairfax.

The conversation moved on, and she half-listened to the couple's dinner plans, images of a hot Mombasa sea playing in her mind.

Bianca's voice intruded on her thoughts. 'I hear Fairfax has invited you to dinner next weekend, too.'

'Yes,' said Jade brightly. 'It's very kind of him. To be honest, I'm a bit worried about what to wear.'

John started to chuckle, but Jade was serious. Bianca never lost an opportunity to dress up, and Jade suspected that even faded Belle would make an effort. She had spent mornings after the couple's occasional dinner parties picking saris off the floor and rearranging heavy gold earrings and chokers back in their cases, although not before once or twice furtively trying them on.

'Just whatever you're comfortable in,' said Bianca kindly. 'Roy's coming, isn't he?'

'Mmm,' said Jade.

His evident delight at the invitation had irritated her. She felt the same way, but at least she had the dignity not to show it.

REETA CHAKRABARTI

January 15th 1970

What is wrong with these people? I speak to the shop girls and they do not hear me. They look straight through me. Why, am I invisible? F says these things are in my head, and I am not strong enough with them. I am strong alright! I think they are badmaashi. They do it deliberately. F says everything is multi-culti in UK now, but not in this place. In the big cities maybe, but not here.

But also he wants me to be different. He wants me to work. I did not expect this, but okay, I try to find a little work. I did the secretary course, so boring, but no one gave me a job. F said go in slacks and blouse to interview, not in sari, so I did that, but still no job.

So then I try this Montessori course, but it is difficult. Small children I like, but the course is so hard. F says I do not try enough. Maybe. At home, I did not have to try, and still I did well. Here there is no one to help, only F, and he is so busy. He is building himself up to be a big man. He has little time to be with me. And then he is always do this do that, no time to be still. He says to me, don't just sit there brooding! But I am happy to sit, and also the world outside is cold.

Sometimes I would like to be like him, always busy. His eyes dance. His hair shines. My F. With him, I am okay, but this country is not friendly. Only John and Bianca are sincere people, and also Meera, but she is far away. I wonder about writing to Ma, but what will she say? Only that this was my choice, and it is true, but it was her choice also. Ma wanted me to marry well.

FINDING BELLE

And so I have, so I have.
I will not sink.
I hope F will help me if I do.

CHAPTER 2

On the evening of the dinner, Jade decided to stick to what she knew worked, and put on a pale blue pussy-bow dress. The nerves, she convinced herself, were less to do with Fairfax, and more to do with the fact she rarely went out.

She and Roy arrived at the house promptly, and Jade's heart sank as she saw Bianca looking spectacular in a clashing combination of red and purple velvet, and Belle wrapped in a scarlet silk sheath with a slash of matching lipstick. She had miscalculated entirely.

Belle ignored her as she glided towards John and Bianca, the scarlet sari shimmering on her ample body, her face heavily made up, her abundant black hair snaking down her back. But if her face and clothes were dramatic and compelling, Jade felt sure her mind was elsewhere.

What is he doing with her? Jade wondered again, as she watched Fairfax raise a glass to Bianca. *What can they have in common?*

Jade had never been abroad, and was confused that this woman who looked Indian came from Africa. *No wonder she's all mixed up. I bet she's never done a day's work in her life – sitting around in this house, drifting and moping. Talking to herself, or whatever it is she does.*

She felt a strong rush of sympathy for Fairfax as she watched him pouring more wine. What had he done to deserve this marriage? However stunning Belle had once been, surely, he must want more?

She could see Mivvi across the room, watching television with the sound down. She had a notion that the girl was spying on them from the side-lines, and she had a childish urge to pull a face at her.

Before long, Roy went over to talk to Mivvi with a benign look on his weak face. He was a teacher, and fond of children – something else he and Jade did not have in common.

'Your name's like the ice-cream,' she heard him say.

Mivvi smiled at the unoriginal comment.

'It's lovely,' he went on. 'I used to like the strawberry ones.'

She smiled again, and their conversation turned to his job as a French teacher. Jade switched her attention elsewhere.

Belle was bringing in platters of food, which she laid on the side for a buffet, while Bianca was throwing her head back in ostentatious laughter at something Fairfax had said.

She grasped Belle's hand as she set down the food. 'Look at this, love! What a fantastic lot of nosh! And you look gorgeous!'

Belle's ghostly face broke into a huge smile, and Jade shuddered at the effect of beauty and vacancy combined. She wished she could find something to say. She felt gauche and tongue-tied; her office banter was of no use here. She was far out of the inner circle, and Belle was making sure she knew her place.

'Well done, old girl, this looks marvellous!' said John loudly.

The food did smell delicious, rich and aromatic, nothing like the gluey Indian take-aways Jade sometimes shared with Roy. The chicken biryani was much spicier than she was used to, but although it brought tears to her eyes, she was astonished that the indolent Belle could cook up such a feast. As everyone praised her, Belle glowed with animation and something approaching normality.

'You might enjoy French novels, when you're older,' she heard Roy saying to Mivvi as they came up to get food. How boring he was! What on earth had she been doing with him for three long years?

The wine was going to Jade's head, and she settled into her chair more unsteadily than she would have wished. She and Bianca were seated on either side of Fairfax, with the men on either side of Belle. Mivvi ate in front of the television, but Jade knew she was following every word they said.

Roy gazed up at Belle as she served him some mango chutney, his small face so flushed with pleasure that he resembled a cherry tomato. Fairfax continued to top up his guests' glasses. Bianca was getting increasingly merry. Her cheap jewellery glistened crudely in the electric light, and her cheeks, already red with rouge, flushed further with her heightened colour. She rested her hand on Fairfax's arm, and Jade felt the stirrings of jealousy.

'Mivvi's doing very well at school,' said Fairfax, apropos of nothing.

Everyone looked approvingly at Mivvi – apart from Jade, and perhaps Belle.

'I was also good at school,' said Belle. Jade looked at her in surprise; Belle rarely said anything about herself.

'I bet you were!' Bianca's voice was warm. 'And you're so talented, with your singing and all.'

'Were you good at school, Jade?' asked Belle pointedly.

'I moved … around a lot.' Jade took a breath, trying to suppress her nerves. 'I didn't have much time to settle anywhere really.'

'Jade was fostered,' Roy said to Belle. 'So, she went between different families and different schools.'

'I see,' Belle responded, as if this came as no surprise.

All the other adults knew of Jade's past, but still they eyed her with compassion. She saw Mivvi at her place in front of the television surreptitiously licking her plate.

'It's alright, really. I managed,' Jade said steadily. Now that she had spoken once, it felt easier. 'And I made up for things later – I got my qualifications. And here I am, in a good job.'

'And we all say well done to that,' cried John, banging the table in agreement.

Belle used this moment to clear away the plates, and Fairfax brought in the pudding.

'What are you doing with your days now, Belle?' boomed John.

'Oh, this and that, John, you know. I am a mother, after all,' said Belle vaguely.

Mivvi glanced around and pulled a face at this, and Jade caught Roy giving her an encouraging smile.

'Do you ever missh home, Belle?' Bianca was starting to slur. Her breasts teetered dangerously over the *kulfi* in her bowl.

'This *is* home, Bianca,' replied Belle, but her answer seemed mechanical.

'No, you know what I mean,' Bianca went on regardless. 'Your old home, the sun, your mum and dad, that cheeky brother of yours—'

Fairfax scraped his chair back and cleared this throat loudly. 'Belle is fine here,' he said tersely, 'brother or no brother.'

Through her own fog of alcohol, Jade remembered sensing his aversion to his brother-in-law – and how disparaging he had been of her the one time they had met.

'Now,' Fairfax announced with a change of tone, 'brandy anyone?'

Try as Jade might to focus, the room was starting to fade and blur, and the faces of the guests seemed to melt like waxworks in the heat and then congeal in front of her. Soon, the room began to spin, and the characters bobbed and drifted gently around her as if riding on a fairground carousel.

Bianca's painted face loomed in and out, her make-up running, her red curls awry as John's bellowing laugh crashed like cymbals in her head. The carousel turned, and Mivvi, large and suspicious, fixed her with gimlet eyes, and Roy's chinless face leered obsequiously. The room spun again, and there was Belle, pale and deathly, a scarlet kitchen assassin with a breadknife in hand.

But just as Jade might have swooned, a cognac bottle swam into view, and behind it was the gleam of Fairfax's sapphire eyes, the glow of his blond hair, and the dazzle of Venus on a moonless night that was his smile.

And it was in that moment, as the ghouls and phantoms danced their ghostly caper around her, that Jade's last defences were breached and shattered – and she knew she had to have him.

CHAPTER 3

Within two months, she had ended things with Roy. He wept, the poor man, and pleaded with her to reconsider, but she was immovable. They had nothing in common, and their relationship had run its course. He departed finally with a theatrical slam of her front door.

The next day at the office, she was pale and hollow-eyed, not from distress but from too much cheap wine. She knew it was unwise to drink so much before a working day, but she had needed the fortification.

Despite several strong coffees and large glasses of water, she still felt fragile when Fairfax called her into his office.

'You okay?' he asked. 'You look pale.'

'Yep, fine. Thanks.'

He looked at her intently, and then handed her a file. 'A new client, a Mrs Simpson. Not married to a former king though.'

He smiled, but Jade didn't know what he meant. She nodded dully.

'Jade, are you really alright? What is it?'

'Oh, nothing.' She chewed at a fingernail. 'Well, if you really want to know … Roy and I had a bit of a scene last night. It's over between us. Just as well, really.'

Fairfax looked solicitous. 'Why, what happened? A row?'

'Sort of, yes.'

'Sort of? What do you mean?'

Jade hesitated. What could she tell him? That she had been bored? That she was in love with him?

'What happened, Jade? You don't look yourself at all.'

His sympathy was overwhelming, and she felt a faintness at his proximity. He put his hand on her arm, and she took in his cologne as he patted her gently. On the back of his hand were three light scars. Strange that she had never noticed them before.

'Jade, he didn't hurt you, did he?'

She looked at him in alarm.

'He didn't, did he?'

His closeness made her mute. She gazed up at him, her eyes swimming with emotion.

'Oh my God, he did – he hurt you! I don't believe it. He seemed like such a nice man...' Fairfax tailed off, and then burst out again. 'The bastard! The bloody bastard!'

She was robbed of speech, but her face spoke volumes.

'Jade, this is terrible – you should report him! To the police, I mean.'

Fairfax's usual jaunty expression was now full of tender feeling. His face made her heart and stomach dissolve.

'No, no, Fairfax, I can't do that...'

'But Jade—'

There was a knock at the door. It was John, wanting Fairfax for a meeting. Jade turned away, so that John wouldn't see her expression.

'We'll talk later,' said Fairfax as he left. 'I want to know more.'

Jade's heart was thumping as the door closed behind him, and she grasped the back of his chair for support, letting out an involuntary whimper. The feel of him so close had thrilled and terrified her.

But what was she to do about his sudden conviction that Roy had hurt her? She felt dizzy with confusion and tried to still her racing heart by taking slow, deep breaths. *Really, it's not my fault.* Fairfax had jumped to his own conclusions. She herself had uttered no lie. *And he looked at me with such sweet care and concern.*

Roy was gone from her life; she owed him nothing. What did it matter if Fairfax had told himself a story? It was of no consequence; it hurt no one.

And besides, no one else will ever know.

When he came back from the meeting, Fairfax looked thoughtful. He asked Jade to step once more into his office, where they could talk alone.

'I'm rather shaken by what I've learned, Jade,' he said, closing the door.

'Look, don't worry about me,' she replied, managing to speak steadily now. 'It's finished – I've split up with him. It's not been right for ages.'

'Clearly not.'

'Fairfax.' Jade smiled wanly at him. 'I've looked after myself all my life – I'm sure I can manage this time, too. I'm an adult. I know what I'm doing.'

Fairfax looked at her hard, gazing straight into her eyes. Then he looked away and, as if summoning up some deep reserve of energy, he said, 'Fancy a drink tonight? I mean, let me take you out for a drink this evening, after work. To prove to you that not all men are brutes.'

Jade made a show of considering her options. 'Hmm, yes, I think I can do that. Yes, alright, that would be nice.'

*

They went that first time to a pub outside of town, where no one would know them, although all they were doing was having a drink. He put the radio on as he drove along the country lanes, and she was glad they could sit in silence. She found herself sliding down in the passenger seat until they got out of town, just in case.

At the pub, Jade opted for half a shandy and Fairfax for a whisky and soda. She was nervous, afraid that her office sophistication might desert her, but Fairfax was able to talk for them both.

As she listened, she noticed the shadows around his eyes, the slight thinning of his flaxen hair. What a hard life he had, and how little he deserved it. She glanced down again at his left hand, at the three faint scars.

Fairfax was either oblivious to her scrutiny, or blithely used to it; he carried on recounting all the interesting things he had seen and done in his life.

'I met John at law college, you know.'

'Mmm, I think he mentioned.'

'We hit it off instantly – outgoing types, both of us. He's from around here, and I sort of followed him. I thought about the Bar but decided against.'

'Yes.'

'I've still got ambitions though,' he said, draining his drink and looking wistfully at the glass. He was driving.

'Of course you have,' she murmured, then feeling she should say more, she added, 'You're so talented.'

He smiled at her appreciation. 'John's a very good lawyer too. A bit cautious perhaps – could afford to take more risks. Mrs Simpson was very pleased with me, called me very can-do!'

'Can you do another drink?' she asked hurriedly, then winced at her weak pun. She was desperate not to appear dull, but it was harder work than in the office. She feared her mascara had smudged.

'Why not?' he said heartily. 'One for the road? Your round.'

*

They met at the same pub the following week, and he told her more about his time in India and Africa, seeing the world before settling down to his career. He never mentioned Belle.

The week after, they met twice at a different place. Walking into a smoky room, the jukebox loud with the droning of The Smiths, they found the quietest corner they could. Fairfax said with a dark smile, 'I have to save you from loneliness, now that you've dumped your abuser!' They had to dip their heads close together to hear each other. She never mentioned Roy.

Over the following month, the drinks became essential to their weekly routine. Each time they sought out new out-of-the-way places, although all they were doing was having a drink. Sometimes he would go home first after work, and they would meet later at a prearranged place, which was never as exciting as she had to take the bus. She scrupulously avoided asking what he said at home about his evening outings.

He told her one day that theirs was a *'romantic friendship'*, and Jade revelled in his use of the word *romantic*.

Then, at the following meeting, drinks turned into coffee at Jade's flat, and she found herself in his arms.

It was the start of a magical time for Jade. 'Fairfax and I are lovers,' she whispered to herself, incredulous at her good fortune and the fulfilment of her impossible dream. She used the word in the old-fashioned sense, the *lovers* of a formal courtship, of two people in love, because Jade had not yet given herself to any man, and the idea of doing so immediately to Fairfax filled her with dread.

She could not however tell him this.

'What do you mean?' he said the first time, astonished at her restraint. His lips were tracing a whorl around her ear, and she could feel his breath hot against her.

'Fairfax, it's difficult. I need you to understand. It's … it's … you are married, after all!' She blurted out the first thought to come into her head.

He pulled back and looked at her warily.

'No, no, I don't mean to push you away,' she said hurriedly. 'It's just – well, let's wait a while, shall we?'

'What is this, some … churchy thing?' His tone was lighter as his lips began seeking out her own.

She nodded beneath the weight of his mouth. 'Yes, some churchy thing. Just exactly that.'

She knew she must appear quaint to him, but she needed to buy herself some time. Perhaps her fear would disappear. Perhaps he would grow to respect her scruples.

She worried that her timidity might diminish his interest in her – but then again, it might heighten it.

Her own inner life was transformed. Each morning, she would greet the day with a new excitement. *In just an hour's time, I'm going to see him.* Her pulse would race as he walked into the office. *Control yourself, girl, look demure, look professional.*

Sometimes, he would wink at her when he thought no one else was looking, and she would do her best not to blush or laugh. She lived in a state of hyperconsciousness of Fairfax, watching him constantly, feeling his presence even if he were out of sight. *When he is here and our hands brush, it feels like a delicious electric shock.* She became a changed character, her suspicion of romance abandoned. *I've spent so long alone, so much time having to be self-sufficient.* Now, Fairfax had swept in, and she became totally, hopelessly dependent.

They took every precaution not to be noticed. No one suspected them. Jade's low profile helped; she had never been the subject of any discussion.

Weekends alone were long and tedious, but even then, Fairfax was sometimes able to slip away and see her for a few hours. Jade supposed he made up a story for Mivvi rather than for Belle, who would be unlikely to ask any questions. But the two of them never discussed such mundane details, preferring to use their limited time to bask in the thrill of each other.

REETA CHAKRABARTI

September 1ˢᵗ 1969

You are my lover, F tells me. Silly, I say, brushing his hair from his eyes, I am your wife. You are my lover and my wife and my romance and my life. The love of my life. These silly things he says to me. I like to hear them. But is he true to his words? I think sometimes he is in love with the idea of love. I am an old romantic, he says. What's wrong with that, he says. Nothing nothing, I reply as he runs his hand up and down my spine, up and down. Nothing wrong with it, F, so long as you are true. So long as it is always me. So long as you love me for what I am, and not what you think I am. Or what you want me to be.

Why is there this small little worm in the apple of our love? My fears, my mistrust.

Perhaps it is only in my head.

CHAPTER 4

The year I turned 15, it seemed to me that my father was behaving differently, although I couldn't put my finger on how or why. His moustache was certainly new; he preened himself with it, wearing it first long and droopy, and then clipping it as if he were in the army. He began staying out late at work all the time, and even when he came home, he often went back to attend to some urgent matter.

I imagined he had a lot of responsibility now, and maybe Jade wasn't much help. I had been astonished to see her at the office that time, and again at the dinner party. She was so different from the wan, drab woman I remembered, now groomed and sleek. Even her voice sounded different, the flat vowels softened and made southern.

When Fairfax left the house for his pressing evening issues, he always looked his impeccable best, in a crisp white shirt and buffed shoes, his shaven cheeks glowing with the aftershave he had slapped on. I sometimes felt tearful as he kissed me goodbye. Without him, the house felt empty and purposeless, and I was stuck at home with Belle, with nowhere to go. I knew he had to work, but I did wonder, somewhere off-stage in my head, why he was quite so dressed up. Then again, that was Fairfax.

Our family life followed a bleak pattern these days, dictated by the cycles of Belle's mind. She was frequently beyond reality, consumed by the voices raging in her head. She whispered back to them furiously, cursing them in the slippery syllables of the language we could not understand, her speech explosive and accusatory. In the moments when she spoke in English, she sounded agonised and fearful: *'Get away from me!'* she rasped. *'Get out! Leave me alone!'*

I did everything I could to block out the sound, playing loud music or watching television at full volume, straining every muscle not to listen, not even to hear. But sometimes it all got too much, and in a fit of rage, I would rush in to surprise Belle, to shock her out of her madness. On those occasions, she would pull away from the window and away from her demons, looking guilty and fearful, like a cornered animal.

She oscillated between child mother and mad mother, all meek and lost, or all bulk and intensity. Fairfax was the only functioning adult in the house, and I assumed a role much older than my years, supporting my father, doing the shopping, taking over the housework. I had to be responsible for the home and for myself.

On the rare occasions I asked Belle for help, I swiftly regretted it. Once, when I was studying hard for my mocks and Belle was simmering, I unthinkingly asked her for some food. She emerged from wherever her mind had wandered to put some eggs on to boil. A full hour later, an acrid smell filled the house, as the boiling eggs ran out of water and rattled angrily in the dry pan. My heart was bursting with despair. I felt foolish for seeking care from a mother who was incapable of giving it; and yet a profound need to be nurtured and loved ate away at me.

With Fairfax out so often, I went back to preparing my own simple meals, which I ate alone in my bedroom, trying all the while to lose myself in a book, and to ignore the sounds of pacing and whispering, and of the deep loneliness of my adolescent soul.

When he was at home, Fairfax stayed in his study, trying like me to block out Belle's state. But whenever I knocked on the door for some company and conversation, Belle was always the dominant subject.

'I see your mother has been at it again,' he said one evening. 'I wish she'd pull herself together.'

I nodded. I knew he counted on me at these times, and I was determined to be grown-up about our situation.

'She doesn't go out when she's like this, I hope?' Fairfax sounded bitter.

'No, of course not. She doesn't like to go out anyway.'

'Good. At least she has the presence of mind not to show herself.'

I nodded again.

'You don't … talk about her, do you?' It was a question that obsessed him.

'No!' I cried. 'You know I don't – I promised!'

'That's good,' said Fairfax. 'This has to be just in the family.'

He gave a heavy sigh. I looked at him, taking in his tired eyes and the slightest of paunches suggesting itself around his midriff. He loosened his cravat – another of his new affectations – and I saw a strange mark on his neck, almost like a bite.

'I've no idea why she's like this,' he went on. 'I've said it before, I know, but I just don't think there's anything really *wrong* with her. Sometimes, she's perfectly normal.' Which was true. 'She's just kind of helpless and immature. It's like she … can't handle adult life.'

I had heard this so often that I had never once dreamt of questioning his judgement. But this time, I felt a slight pinprick of doubt. Could it really be true that there was nothing wrong with her? 'Fairfax,' I said tentatively. 'What about John and Bianca – do they think there's nothing wrong with Belle? And Meera?'

I saw his face cloud over. 'I don't know,' he said shortly. 'We don't talk about these things.'

'But they do … know about her. Don't they?'

He assented silently, and I knew it was deeply painful to him to acknowledge that our secret went any further than the two of us.

Then he said, 'Maybe she would have been better off somewhere else?'

'Where would she have gone?' I asked wonderingly.

He shrugged. 'It's true, I don't know.'

I dared one further question. 'And what about Uncle Maz? Did you ever talk to him about Belle?'

Fairfax's face hardened. 'Even if I did, it would have done no good – no good at all! He's a useless little shit!'

I recoiled, and Fairfax put his hand on my arm in apology. 'Sorry, love – that was too rough. But he's no use.' He put his hands to his temples and rubbed them in exhaustion and pain. 'Look, Mivvi, I've got some work to finish, so I might nip back to the office. I do wonder sometimes if your mother even cares for us. Who knows what on earth goes on in her head?'

I heard the pain in his voice, and for all my brief moments of doubt, my heart went out to him. He did suffer so.

*

But the following night, I heard unusual noises in the corridor, and got up to find Belle laying out blankets and a duvet on the floor outside my parents' bedroom.

'Belle, what are you doing?' I asked sleepily.

'Oh,' said Belle, trying to make light of it, 'your daddy has put me out of the bedroom, so I will sleep here.'

It was a winter's night, and I shivered in the corridor, with its floor of bare boards and lack of heating. Belle had been simmering all day – perhaps that was why Fairfax had shut her out. But this time, the demons had not taken hold of her, and she looked pitiful and resigned to her exile.

I felt miserable for her. 'Go and sleep in the study, Belle.'

'I cannot. He has put me out of that too – it is locked. It is okay, I will sleep here.'

I cast around for some solution. 'Come on,' I said. 'You can have my bed and I'll sleep here. I don't mind.'

But on this occasion, Belle wouldn't have it, and after I had helped her to lay the moth-eaten blanket over the thin duvet, she ushered me off to my room.

She looked wretched, bedding down on the floor, and I felt that familiar tug of love and anguish that only my mother could induce.

In the morning, I caught Belle folding away the bedding, and felt momentarily sickened at my father's heartlessness.

*

I was not without friends at school, but I was well-practised in keeping them far from the house. Unlike at primary school, no one had any inkling of who my mother was, and I went to great lengths to keep it that way. I was by now a seasoned storyteller about my ideal home life, and adept at inviting myself to other people's houses without ever having anyone back myself. There had never been any easy socialising at my home.

But it was impossible to put up barriers high enough for Tabitha. She rang up out of the blue one day, saying that Bree had business nearby, and that they would drop by to say hello.

Our friendship had cooled after we parted ways to go to different schools aged 11, and it had taken Tabitha a long time to forgive me for going to private school, which she had denounced as *'excloo-sive'* – that was apparently Bree's word for it. I had been stricken that I might be doing something that Bree disapproved of, although I didn't see quite why *I* was to blame for Fairfax's decision. Katie and I had drifted apart, but Tabitha had softened, and I still saw her from time to time.

Now I braced myself for my difficult friend, with her keen nose for my weaknesses, to turn up right on my doorstep. I was suffering agonies of worry about how Belle would behave, but putting Tabitha off had never been my forte.

The doorbell rang, and a lean creature in skintight jeans and thick black eyeliner was leaning against the doorframe, looking bored. I squinted at her – I hadn't seen Tabitha for a few months, and she was almost unrecognisable. As we embraced, I caught the stale smell of smoke on her breath.

'Sorry, darling,' she drawled, as I winced involuntarily. 'Bree disapproves too, but you know what she's like. Too liberal to tell me off! She's dying to see you, by the way.'

She made her way in.

'I can't stop for long actually. She's made an appointment to see the Aga man – something's wrong with it – so I thought I'd tag along and pester her for a new pair of jeans. How are you?'

She came further in without waiting for a reply. At least she didn't seem to take in the poverty of our surroundings.

'I'm good!' I said brightly, my heart sinking as I heard Belle's heavy tread coming down the stairs.

'Ooh, hello, Tabitha,' said Belle, a flush of recognition spreading across her slow face. She was dishevelled, her blouse was missing a button, but otherwise she looked presentable. 'How are you? It is a long time I haven't seen you.'

Tabitha smiled at her. She was so confident in herself that nothing ruffled her.

I did my best to match Tabitha's poise. 'She's just passing by, Belle.'

Belle stood uncertainly in the hallway, her stock of small talk already depleted. Before she needed to say anything more, a battered old Renault 4 pulled up outside, and Bree stepped out.

'Tabitha, we have to go – I'm so sorry, I've mistimed things. I'm seeing this man in fifteen minutes. Mivvi, my dear, Mivvi, how are you? Goodness you're growing so fast – let me take a look at you. But you're beautiful, darling, so womanly! Belle, are you there too? It's been so long! Good to see you too. Your lovely daughter, you must be so proud!'

Belle gave her a tired smile. Her blouse gaped now where the button was missing. She nodded gently; it was all she was capable of, but I preferred her silence to speech that was off-key.

As Tabitha stepped out of the house, Bree turned to her. 'Tab, why don't we have Mivvi round next weekend? You're invited to a party, aren't you? Why don't you take Mivvi? You can come and stay, darling.'

'If she doesn't mind being down with the *proles*,' said Tabitha, and she smiled as I gave her a light kick.

'Watch it, you. Umm, alright, yes, Bree, thank you, that would be lovely,' I said. A change might be good for me, even if it was only one weekend.

'It's a deal,' said Bree, and blew me a kiss as the two of them headed off.

*

Later that evening, Tabitha rang. 'Hey, Miv, great you're coming next weekend. Bring some good clothes, won't you?'

'Sure,' I said, uncertain that I had any.

'By the way, Bree said something that you might want to know.'

I felt a lurch in the pit of my stomach. The afternoon had passed off without incident; I thought we had got away with it. 'Oh yes?'

'It's about your mum. Bree thinks she's severely depressed.' Tabitha delivered this dart with matter-of-fact brutality.

I swallowed hard.

'She might be wrong, of course,' she went on, 'but I thought I'd let you know.'

'Did she ask you to tell me?'

'Oh no.'

'You know,' I said falteringly, 'she's alright, in fact – you know, she's always been a bit quiet.'

'Fine.' Once Tabitha had made her point, she was nothing if not peremptory. 'Great, well, see you Friday!'

I stood by the phone, feeling sick at our near exposure and at Tabitha's callousness. I considered calling off the weekend visit, but that would be an admission of guilt.

Instead, I went to find Fairfax, who had locked himself in his study. I perched on the edge of the spare bed, as he lounged moodily, and took a deep breath.

'Fairfax, Tabitha's mum saw Belle briefly today, and … well, Tabitha says she thinks that Belle is depressed. Severely depressed, she said. Is that possible? Do you think she is?'

Fairfax considered this, although in the gloom, it was hard to see his face.

'I'm not sure. Bree hardly knows your mother, and it's none of her business. She should keep out of it.'

I shouldn't have mentioned it. Fairfax always had his own explanation, and I found it near impossible to counter him.

'Your mother was always a little strange,' Fairfax continued. 'I remember things her own family said about her – no initiative or get up and go. Perhaps there was funniness in the family, I don't know. Anyway, whatever it is, she doesn't know how to look after you or me, or herself. And she doesn't seem to care.' He paused. 'I wonder sometimes if she even loves me.'

My heart felt torn. 'I love you though,' I said softly.

Fairfax gave my arm a gentle squeeze. 'Love you too.'

It meant everything to me to be able to talk to Fairfax like this. Belle was our shared dilemma, and these conversations reconnected me to him. If his assurances about her left me less satisfied than they used to, I had no sense that there was anything else he might have done for her.

All I knew was that Belle was incapable and that my father loved me very much.

Poor Fairfax, I thought. I might not have had much of a mother, but my father was the best.

*

As I packed my bag for Tabitha's, I was tempted to take the sky-blue maxi dress that hung in Belle's wardrobe, a present from Meera which was now too small for her. But Tabitha's cool friends would surely sneer, so I grabbed some jeans and a sparkly top and tried them on in front of the mirror.

The girl reflected back at me filled them more than I would have liked, but in other ways, I was happier with what I saw. She no longer had wet-sand skin, perhaps because at my *excloo-sive* school, no one had ever said anything nasty, although none of the words for mixed race really described the girl in the mirror: neither olive, nor coffee nor chestnut, and certainly not sun-kissed. As I looked at my image, I saw for the first time the outlines of Belle in my face; they were her eyes, her cheekbones. I felt ungainly and heavy in my top and jeans. But Bree had called me *womanly*, and Maz, all those years ago, had said I was *wheaten*! I started to laugh at the memory, and the glow of my happy reflection caught me unawares and gave me confidence. *You can do this, Mivvi*, I said to myself in the mirror, *you can*.

Bree enveloped me in a warm hug when I arrived, and I took in the baked bread smell of her hair.

'It's so lovely to have you, Mivvi. You look wonderful!'

'Well,' I said quietly, seeing that Tabitha wasn't listening, 'I'm all dressed up. I'm trying!'

'You look marvellous, dear,' came the reply, and I basked in her approval.

There was no rest that weekend. We went ice-skating, which Tabitha of course did with grace and boldness, skimming across the rink in her state-of-the-art skates, while I shuffled cautiously near the edge.

That night, we stayed up late, and Tabitha recounted the tales of her love life, the two boyfriends she had already been through, and a third whom she was targeting. She had a small bottle hidden in one of her drawers – 'Vodka, so Bree can't smell it.' I'd had the occasional sip of gin from Fairfax, and as I cautiously took small swigs from the bottle, I found I preferred his drink to hers.

The following evening was the party, which I steeled myself for. I led such a circumscribed life that I feared I had lost the ability to be natural with people I didn't know. Luckily, Tabitha detected none of this, and I threw myself into the ritual of getting ready, to achieve that look of having barely prepared. Bree breezed in and out of the bedroom, offering advice.

The bass was thudding when we arrived, and the house crammed with people. There was a table full of soft drinks provided by the parents, but bottles of beer and white rum had been smuggled in, and plenty of the guests had the flushed look of teenagers having their first real drink. The host thrust glasses of rum and coke into our hands. Tabitha adjusted her tiny skirt and looked around disdainfully.

'The interesting crowd are all outside,' she said, and I saw them through the window, with their assortment of piercings and dyed hair, puffing away with studied intensity. The orange tips of their cigarettes lit up the dark, like a dance of glow-worms. Tabitha muttered something about being desperate for a fag, and signalled that she would soon be back.

Free of Tabitha's presence, I looked around curiously. I wasn't overawed exactly, but I did want to talk to someone who wasn't trying to look cool. I caught the eye of a boy whose expression said he was searching for the same. He had curly black hair and skin the colour of Belle's. His wire-framed glasses perched precariously on his nose, and he had an air of being thrown together.

'You're Tabitha's friend, aren't you?' he said, coming over. 'She said you were staying for the weekend.'

'Yes, hi, that's right.'

'I see she's abandoned you already.'

'Already? Why? Was it inevitable?'

The boy smiled. 'No, but Tabitha likes being where it's at.'

I smiled in recognition of this description of my friend. 'And where is that then?'

'Well, not where I am, but that's okay,' said the boy. 'My name's Ashish, by the way, and you, I know, are Mivvi.'

'How funny!' I blurted out. 'I would have been called Ashish if I'd been a boy! That's what my mother told me.'

Ashish looked at me curiously. 'We must be from the same neck of the global woods then.'

'Sort of. My father's from here, so it's just my mother's side, and even then, that was actually her parents. My mother was brought up in Mombasa.'

He was interested and clearly expected me to go on, but I suddenly came to a halt. Although I was happier in my skin these days, I had spent so many years hiding this part of myself – the Indian and the African part – that I didn't know what else to say. Besides, I never talked about Belle.

'Well, my parents came here before I was born,' he went on, 'but we've been back there a lot – to the family home, I mean, in Calcutta. Every other summer holiday, in fact.' He nodded as much to himself as to me. 'It's good, if a bit mental.'

I looked at him encouragingly.

'The poverty hits you, of course, but there's a great energy to the place.' Warming to his theme, he went on. 'They're all communists – I mean, just in that state.' I looked quizzical and he grinned. 'My parents aren't very political, but my uncles over there really are. They're quite sniffy about Blighty.'

'What about you?' I asked. 'Are you political?'

'Not really, but I enjoy listening to my uncles pontificating. We did make a concession to them and called our cat Mao.'

I burst out laughing. 'That's brilliant!'

'We thought so too,' said Ashish modestly.

I wanted to ask him more, but the music was thumping. I smiled at him awkwardly.

'Do you want to dance?' he asked.

I hesitated. Ashish was nice, but he looked clever and earnest, and would surely be a terrible dancer.

'You think I'll be a terrible dancer, don't you?' he said. 'Come on, I'll surprise you.'

Outmanoeuvred, I followed him.

*

The next day, I woke with a dull pain in my head. My first hangover. I got up gingerly, took a gulp of water, and then started to pack my few things. The long weekend was over.

I fished out of my jeans pocket the piece of paper Ashish had given me, with his phone number and address, and carefully put it in my purse. I could feel a small smile playing on my lips.

I had spent the whole evening with him. He had proved to be a great dancer but had sent himself up with such happy abandon that I too forgot my usual self-consciousness. I found he shared my love of reading, and we had argued tipsily over our favourite novels; and then when we were completely drunk, we had argued some more.

Despite my delicate state, I felt a warm glow of pleasure at the thought of him. I couldn't remember the last time I had enjoyed myself so much. Even Tabitha's drawling verdict that the party had been boring could do nothing to dampen my buoyant mood. Tabitha was not used to this serenity in me, and when it was time for me to catch the bus home, she suddenly found herself busy with another engagement.

Instead, Bree walked down with me, and brought Samuel who skipped along behind us, acting out some action fantasy in his head. I silently willed Bree not to mention Belle.

'It's been so nice having you,' she said, as we got to the stop. 'It's like old times. Tabitha's very fond of you, you know. And you're good for her – you keep her grounded.'

I was surprised. I thought Tabitha regarded me as her duller friend. Samuel was making *kerpow* noises behind us.

Then Bree continued. 'Umm, I just wonder before you set off … how's your mother?'

'She's alright,' I said nervously. 'She's, you know, much the same. But fine.'

'Mivvi, I know this is perhaps interfering, but she's very isolated. It's not good for her.'

I nodded.

'I did mention it to your father ages ago, but it didn't go down well. You were small then, so I didn't say anything to you. I really didn't mean to offend him.'

I could feel my face turning scarlet. 'I think he's very proud,' I managed.

'What about the wider family?' she persisted gently. 'Is there any help there?'

I shook my head. 'No, they're all abroad.'

I could feel the tension rising in me, along with that spreading ache in my stomach that would sometimes afflict me. I looked up and with relief saw the bus rounding the corner.

Bree nodded. 'Yes, of course. Well, it must be difficult. Stay in touch, dear, and let me know if I can do anything to help.'

And at that, I kissed her gratefully and bolted for the bus.

When I got home, the dull truth of our situation struck me with a force all the greater for my having been away. Belle eyed me moodily, and Fairfax was nowhere to be seen. The impossibility of anything ever changing overwhelmed me at that moment, and I trailed wearily up to my bedroom to shut my family out.

FINDING BELLE

*

I had contorted myself over the years to adjust to Belle's cycles, and now the lack of action over time had created its own reality. I had seen that life outside could be different, but this was the only family life I had ever known. So I went on carving out spaces for myself, staying in my room as much as I could, slipping into the kitchen late at night for food when my mother was in bed.

Fairfax also had his own routine. Sometimes he was there in the evenings, sometimes not. There was the occasional oasis in the desert of my parents' marriage, when Belle's troubles seemed to dissipate, and the two of them were able for a while to live together in relative tranquillity. I marvelled when this happened, sometimes daring to hope that our situation was not irretrievable.

But if these periods of optimism were short-lived, I had other reasons not to despair. I was of an age now to feel separate from my parents, and to want to prepare for my own life instead of being trapped by theirs. I would escape, eventually. I still adored my father, but I depended on him less, and asked little of him, or about him. With Belle, I just kept out of her way.

REETA CHAKRABARTI

July 12th 1969

Today I put on the mustard blouse F bought me for our anniversary, with the golden jhumka earrings from Ma for our wedding. Getting ready for dinner with his work people. They look like bells, or bunches of golden grapes, he says. I put them on, and he stands behind, putting his hands on my waist, then his arms around.

We look in the mirror, he and me, his hair as golden as the jhumka, his eyes like summer sky. He put his hand up on my breast. We don't have to go out, he said, voice thick with love. We can stay here, he said, stroking my breast, let them eat our dinner for us.

I love him like this, lazy and funny, only he and me, no one else around, no talking or dashing about, just quiet and stroking.

You are in a swoon he tells me, and I say, what is swoon, but he only laughs and so do I. My Mombasa marvel, he calls me, my Belle of the ball.

I look in the mirror with his lips on my neck, and feel I am really marvel. Ma was right, I married well, but she cannot know these moments, private moments, not money, not work, not Mr Big, not the cold people outside, just F and me in a swoon.

Then John rings on the phone, and it is broken. But you can only break something that is really there.

CHAPTER 5

Like all lovers, Jade thought her taste of paradise with Fairfax would last forever. But as their first anniversary came and went, and then their second anniversary began to loom, the taste began to curdle.

It was not the relationship itself that troubled her, but the fact of her remaining at the periphery of his life when she should have been at its centre. She did love him so, and he felt the same way, she was sure. He did such sweet things for her, bringing chocolates and flowers, and daft things too, like growing a moustache. She found his vanity touching, he was like a little boy trying to please, so she refrained from telling him that she didn't like facial hair. They spent their time together quietly, content in each other's company, and she would urge him on as he talked of his ambitions at work.

But living in the magic of the moment was becoming less and less satisfactory, and Jade found herself increasingly longing to replace the woman who was his wife. The thought, which would have been so audacious a year or two previously, preyed constantly on her mind, driven by the intensity of their relationship.

There remained, too, the issue of her 'churchy thing' as he called her *pudeur*, which increasingly felt like a complication of her own making. Close as they were, she still couldn't confess her inexperience, and although she trusted him enough to go the whole way, she was unsure that doing so would bind him closer to her.

Given the choices she had created for herself, continued modesty might better further her cause than submission.

*

She made her first speech of entreaty to him one Sunday morning, after he had driven over to see her. She had tidied the flat, and bought in fresh flowers, knowing these were comforts he did not have at home.

'Fairfax, I need to say something,' she said carefully. 'We've been together a long time now. I think it's time that you considered your position and followed your heart. Your true heart.'

Fairfax raised his eyebrows and silently stirred more milk into his coffee.

She had to tread carefully. Fairfax hated confrontation.

She sat down close to him, adjusting her new, short skirt casually so that her slender legs could be seen. He put his hand on her thigh.

'Fairfax, darling,' she said, nuzzling his neck. She felt his hand move further up her leg. 'I love you,' she murmured, and she heard the sweet words repeated back to her.

His breathing became heavier, and she too felt desire, mixed with alarm. She decided to go on.

'My love, I want you so much too, you know that. But I can't. I can't until … you know what.'

Fairfax groaned, in frustration and weariness.

'You know what I'm saying,' she continued. 'Couldn't you possibly start to consider it now – consider leaving? Mivvi is almost grown-up, after all. You could come and be with me. We could be so happy together!' This last she said too violently, so she softened her voice, in the way she knew he liked. 'I've been alone for so long, Fairfax, and it's been so hard. I don't want to be alone anymore.'

Fairfax smiled weakly. He looked powerless. 'I don't know – it's very difficult,' he said, at last. 'Look, perhaps it's time to think again, about us, about what we are doing.'

'What do you mean?' she cried. 'No, Fairfax, what are you saying? How could we do without each other? Please don't talk like that. I've been so lonely.'

'Jade,' he sighed, 'my love, I know it's hard. Perhaps – I don't know, perhaps you should look for someone else? Someone who can love you as you deserve.'

This was going all the wrong way. 'Look,' she said, and she put her face up very close to his, so he could see nothing else. She wanted to steady him. 'You just have to take the decisive step. It will be fine. It will be for the best for everyone.'

Fairfax looked uneasy. 'I don't know, I just don't know,' he muttered. 'It's not that simple.'

'Everyone will just adjust,' she said, as confidently as possible. 'It's what happens. It will all work out fine.'

*

That time, she left it there. But the next time they met, she tried again.

'My darling, no,' she whispered, when his hands roved under her blouse, and then between her legs.

'Why not, come on.' His voice was thick, and she sensed her power over him. 'Please, Jade. I love you.'

'You know why. My love, only when we are really together.'

'Please,' he breathed, 'please. I want you, I need you.'

It was the moment. 'Fairfax, come and be with me. Come on. It's time – it's time to make the move.'

He fell away, sighing. 'Do we have to do this all the time?'

'No,' she said, 'no, of course not. But I'm thinking of us. I'm thinking of you, of what's best for you.'

'But I do care for Belle,' said Fairfax, almost indistinctly.

'That's because you are a good man,' said Jade, pulling him close again. 'But you're not happy together, are you?'

He didn't reply.

'You know, if you care for her, maybe the best thing you could do for her is to leave. She's not happy either, is she? It would be for her, too – you would be doing it for her.'

Fairfax looked at her uncomprehendingly. 'What are you saying?' he muttered. 'Look, perhaps we should just … stop. I mean, it's not like we've been up to all that much, anyway.'

'No, no, you don't mean that. You can't mean that.' Jade's heart was pounding, and her words came in a rush. 'Let's leave it now, but think about it, just think about it. Please.'

'How would they manage?' he mumbled. 'Without me? I can't.'

'But, my love, you want me, don't you?' She pressed herself closer to him. 'You know you do.'

He took a deep breath and pulled himself away. 'No, not now. I can't.'

The conversation had run away from her; she had again gone too far, too fast. But it was all she could do not to shout at him, *You're tied to a lunatic, to a mad and crazy woman! You've got me – you must want to escape.*

*

This was their cycle of entreaties and retreat, of Jade pleading and Fairfax backing off, of him threatening to end things with her and her hurriedly insisting what they had was enough for her.

He would say, '*Find someone else!*' She would weep, '*I can't do without you!*' Sometimes, she changed tack and tried to sound worldly and mature: '*I'm an adult – I know what I'm doing!*' Then would come another round of pleas for him to leave, and more ducking and weaving from Fairfax. It became a pattern, a repetitive, never-ending, exhausting pattern.

She felt drained at living this lie, pretending they were nothing but colleagues at the office, existing only on the scraps of his life that he gave her.

Even though she saw him every day, Jade started to write letters to him, to stop their meetings from always descending into recrimination. She slipped them into his hand at work or placed them carefully on top of a pile of documents only he would see. She even sent two to his house, concealed in anonymous, typed envelopes which looked official, but she stopped when he turned up at the office looking like thunder.

Writing was a sign of her desperation. She was not comfortable with the written word, but she reached for the language of love she read in magazines, baring her soul to him, telling him that she knew she was plain and ordinary, but that her love for him was true. On the subject of leaving Belle and his daughter, she wrote obliquely *these things are always a little bit messy*, and was proud to have found the right adjective.

This was a dark period for Jade. Her previously solid sense of self deserted her, and she knew she was at Fairfax's mercy. Again and again, she considered abandoning her resolve and giving in to him, but she feared deep down this might weaken her position. But if she held out, would he tire of her anyway?

She lived in a state of depression at their quagmire, and for the first time in her life, she turned away from her own image in the mirror. She had never been beautiful, but she had never cared before – she had been confident of her cool expression and intelligent face.

Now, a bitter and fraught woman gazed back at her. What to do, how to persuade him?

CHAPTER 6

My attempts to distance myself from my parents' plight came crashing down one weekend at a dinner party at our house, the first for many months. Meera was going to be there; she had recently quit her job in Glasgow for a new one in Luton and was a part of our lives again. Fairfax told me that John and Bianca were coming too, as was Jade.

'What happened to Roy?' I asked him. I didn't want to sound too interested in Jade, but I had liked Roy the one time we had met. 'I haven't seen him in ages. Is he uninvited?'

'Oh,' said Fairfax airily, 'they split up, him and Jade. Ages ago. Must be maybe two or three years ago now.'

'Really?' I frowned at him. 'I don't remember you mentioning it. Why?'

'Hmm, don't know the details, but he behaved badly. He was quite brutal to her, I think.'

I looked at Fairfax in amazement. Cherub-faced Roy? Brutal? He looked like he wouldn't harm a fly.

'Surely he can't have been? He always looked so gentle.'

Fairfax shrugged. 'Can't judge a book by its cover, you know.'

This irritated me, coming from Fairfax, who so prized appearances.

I looked at him closely, and realised that he had got rid of his moustache.

I waved at his face. 'Why'd you shave it off?'

'Ladies don't seem to appreciate moustaches,' he said enigmatically.

'I ain't no lady,' I said, managing a smile.

*

I had planned to go out for a burger with Ash on the evening of the dinner party, but he rang to cancel because of some family event. We were now firm friends, and I spent more time than I'd like to admit wondering if we were more.

Our first meeting after the party with Tabitha, ostensibly to swap books, might have been awkward, and I was worried that we would find our chemistry had just been party-induced. But we ended up talking for hours about books and school and people, and I found I could be myself with him, without any pressure to divulge anything.

Since then, we had spent nearly every weekend together, chatting or reading in each other's company, in cafés or at his house. I liked the mess of his curly black hair, which looked like Bianca's after she'd had a drink, and the carelessness of his worn clothes, and his precarious glasses. I told him nothing of the situation at home, but he was the first friend to whom confiding about my life did not feel impossible, should that time ever come.

But now, I had to reconcile myself to a night in. Meera swept in early, like the blast of spring air she always was, and sat talking to Belle in the kitchen as she prepared the meal. There was a splendour about Belle, and not for the first time, I wondered how my mother could still pull this off. She could spend weeks wandering around the house in a state of disarray, a big shambling ruin of a woman. But tonight, she had returned to a version of the majesty she once possessed, dressed in a violet-coloured gown that glowed like a jewel, with her hair tied up.

Most importantly, she seemed calm and present, as if some of her former power had been given back to her. As she listened to Meera talking about her move to Luton, Belle looked both animated and gracious, and I felt a pang for the woman she might have been.

But Meera wanted a private word with me and steered me into the front room before Fairfax got home.

'Mivvi, my sweet, I know it's awkward, but I've got to say, I am very worried about your mother.' She spoke quietly and intently, her soft brown eyes scanning my face.

'She's okay, you know – she's just the same.'

'I have been worried for a long time, Mivvi.'

I shrugged.

Meera hesitated, and then asked, 'Does she still hear voices?'

'How did you know?' I asked, startled.

'Mivvi, my dear, I am her friend. I know.'

I looked at her in alarm, feeling cornered. Fairfax would be furious if I told Meera anything.

'I'm not sure,' I ventured. 'Yes, probably. But it's just what she's like.'

Meera shook her head gently. 'You know it's an illness. It has a name.'

I stared at Meera as she told me what it was. It was a word I had heard before but had never understood. It sounded harsh, discordant, fractured.

'And what's more,' she went on, 'it's often treatable. And treatment is what your mother needs.'

At that moment, we heard Fairfax's key in the front door, and we looked at each other in complicit silence.

'Fairfax,' called Meera, 'I'm here with Mivvi – who I hear is soon turning 16! I can't believe it!'

'Dr Sen,' said Fairfax, in the dry tone he reserved for her. He gave her a peck on the cheek. 'Sweet sixteen she will indeed be.'

'Will you have a party, Mivvi?' she asked.

'Oh no, I don't think so. But perhaps I'll go out with friends.'

'Come on, Meera, I'm gasping,' said Fairfax, disappearing into the kitchen. 'Let me get you a drink.'

Meera nodded at me and followed him through.

I turned her words around in my head. A real medical condition. The possibility of treatment. But Fairfax had always been so adamant it was nothing clinical. I felt suddenly heavy, weighed down with the competing pressures in my life. It was so hard for me to talk to him about Belle – he became distant if I challenged him, and it made me feel anxious and insecure. I strongly doubted I had the courage to broach the subject again.

By the time John and Bianca arrived, Fairfax had already downed three large glasses of gin. As they all greeted each other, he uncorked the first of several bottles of wine.

I sipped my own small gin cautiously and wondered why I hadn't noticed before how much Fairfax drank these days. I liked drinking, in as much as I was allowed to, but watching my father, I felt wary of excess. Bianca, too, looked more bloated and blowsy than last time. I wondered again about her familiarity with Fairfax, but he barely reacted, and John never seemed to mind. Bianca flashed me a warm smile, reminding me how very much I liked her.

Jade was the last to arrive, and time had changed her again. She was more expensively dressed than before, her prim and demure self abandoned for a conspicuously assertive style. She had her hair up in a chic chignon and wore an Audrey Hepburn-style cocktail dress. But she had lost none of her awkward formality, shaking my hand woodenly and directing a forced professional smile at Belle.

My mother looked through her at first, and then asked sharply, 'Where is Roy?' to which Jade shrugged meekly. I wondered if it still pained Belle to have her former home help at the table.

I considered disappearing upstairs away from the dinner, but I had had enough of studying and any company was better than GCSE revision. I sat myself in front of the television, separate from the party, and started channel-hopping with the sound down.

The gin gave me a lift, and I watched the flickering screen in a distracted way, letting the noise of conversation wash over me. As I reached for the control, it fell and spun towards the table. I bent down to retrieve it – and stopped, as my eye caught sight of something that I couldn't immediately process.

One of Jade's stockinged feet was resting on Fairfax's ankle.

No, it was rubbing his ankle, moving up and down his calf inside his trouser leg.

I felt my face go scarlet. I looked up at Fairfax, who was impassively listening to an animated Bianca. What on earth was going on?

Fairfax? Fairfax and *Jade*? And here, in front of Belle – fondling each other under the table, betraying my mother in her own house!

I was hit by a wave of nausea, and slumped back on the sofa, turning away to hide my shock. That mean and leaden woman was sleeping with my father – that woman devoid of any single charm was carrying on with Fairfax.

I was filled with a surge of hatred such as I had never known before. Oh, I had hated Belle at times, hated her inadequacy and her madness, but that was nothing compared to what I felt now for Jade. What an obscenity! How long had this been going on for?

And Fairfax, my father. How could he do this to Belle? How could he do this to me?

*

I spent a sleepless night rearranging the recent past in light of what I now knew. My father's disappearances in the evenings, all dressed up – his absurd moustache – his ridiculous cravat! It all made sense now. I tossed and turned under the sheets, my head aching, feverish and eaten up with fury and pain.

Fairfax's life with Belle was hard – I knew that – but there could be nothing that justified this. Whatever Belle was, however hopeless she might be, she was my mother, and she had been *betrayed*. What did that wretched Jade woman want? Was she trying to take my father away? Was my family in jeopardy?

My head pounded and ached as I assaulted the image of Jade with words. *Cow! Bitch!* The scene replayed itself over and over in my head, Fairfax showing no emotion as Jade caressed him under the table, the woman's small eyes shining at him as she nodded her agreement to everything he said. Was that how she got him, by telling him how wonderful he was? Was that all he needed, a sly stroking of his boundless vanity? Did they do this all the time, had they been playing footsie at all of these dinners? Just how often had they insulted Belle, and humiliated her in this way?

I fell into a fitful sleep when it was nearly dawn and woke mid-morning with my head thick and heavy. For a moment, I thought I had drunk too much again, and then reality hit, and I slumped back on the pillow.

Now I just wanted to cry. My dear daddy, my darling Fairfax.

Perhaps it hadn't been his fault. Women always chased him, and he was so vain. Maybe this one had trapped him, and he couldn't shake free. Perhaps that was why he was impassive as Jade rubbed his ankle beneath the table. He never seemed to give an inch to Bianca, though she flirted with him shamelessly.

As I lay there, the morning sun streaming through the crack in my curtains, I started to formulate a plan. I had to find out how long this had been going on and discover some means of cutting it off. I had to save Fairfax for the family. I didn't know how, but if I could stop this madness of his and bring him back to us, perhaps I could talk to him properly about Belle. If Meera was right – and Meera must be right; she was a doctor – then perhaps we could get her treatment, and then surely our lives would improve.

First, I needed to know whether this was a passing fling – I shuddered at the word – or something more. Where might there be evidence? Presumably they saw each other every day at work and arranged their trysts there. But the office was small and public, and it would be hard for them to speak privately. Where else might there be messages between them?

Over the next few days, I reverted to my tactics of years ago, at the height of Belle and Fairfax's quarrels: creeping down the corridor and listening at doors. I knew my behaviour was ridiculous, but I was carried away by my need to save the family. On the rare evenings when Fairfax was at home, in his study with the door shut, I tiptoed up and waited mouse-like outside, straining to listen to his phone calls. Just as long ago, his low tones were barely audible, but I knew him well enough to make out the murmurings of affection. One time, his voice rose in contradiction of Jade, with a breathy, 'No, you're beautiful, you are!'

I felt bilious as I pictured Jade's wan, colourless face.

I had another idea, and one day when he was out, I went to rifle furtively through his papers in the study, confident I would never be interrupted by Belle. By now I was an unashamed snooper. As I looked through reams of legal files and papers, I found among them a photocopy detailing some money sent to Maz. It was a large sum – ten and a half thousand pounds. The document almost detained me, but I had to work fast – my mission was elsewhere – so I stuffed it back into the pile. I looked through old newspapers, postcards from friends, and unexpectedly, a couple of very old love letters from Belle. I started trying to read Belle's flowery, curly handwriting, but quickly put the letters back; it didn't feel right intruding on my parents' past intimacy.

I sat down and grunted with annoyance. Surely Fairfax must have something from the miserable Jade. If so, where on earth was it?

A sudden memory came back to me, and I balanced tentatively on a chair to reach up to the corner of the very highest cupboard, steeling myself in case I came across a pile of pornography. As I groped around, the first thing I pulled out was indeed two old copies of *Playboy*, which I gingerly replaced, but then, as I blindly felt around again – bingo!

I pulled out a few creased letters, which were hidden right at the back. The top two were written on scented pink notepaper, in plain white envelopes, with our home address typed on the front. The third letter looked different, but I hurriedly grabbed all three and scurried back to my bedroom, locking the door behind me just in case Belle broke the habit of a lifetime and walked in.

Jade's letters made for lurid reading. She wrote with a mixture of piety and panting, like the bodice-ripper paperbacks Ash and I sent up for fun.

We could be so happy together, she breathed. *You deserve so much better than her. You owe it to yourself to be happy.*

Then, later in the same letter: *If you would entrust yourself to me, I know that together we would grow...*

Despite myself, I started to laugh. What an absurd, florid style she had. Who did this woman think she was!

Then I opened the second letter and my laughter subsided.

If you care for her, you should leave her. You should set her free. It would be a measure of your love. I've had such a hard time, with Roy too as you know, and you helped me. You've helped me to feel better about myself. I would lose my bearings without you.

As I read, I experienced what Jade would have described as inner turmoil. I felt grubby looking at private letters to my father, but I was torn apart by his dirty betrayal. And what about the tale told in these letters? It was, after all, only Jade's version of their miserable story. Was it really possible that Roy had been brutal to her? I had not known him well, but he had seemed gentle and kind, incapable of harm, and I doubted her story was true. Perhaps she had invented it to make Fairfax feel sorry for her.

But what did Fairfax really want? He surely wouldn't leave us for that woman?

And how would we manage if he did?

The last letter was in different handwriting. It had been scrunched up but preserved at the bottom of the pile. It was dated simply *August 19th – Mombasa*, and as I read it, I realised with a start that it was from my grandfather.

Your words cause me great pain, he wrote, *and I would do as you request, but her mother will not allow it. You must do your duty, and I will speak to our son. They both expected more, but he must behave correctly. I am sorry it has come to this, but I beg you to look after our girl. We will never be a burden to you, of that I can assure you.*

I read and reread the short note, my heart beating fast. There were no clues as to what my grandfather meant. What was Fairfax's request, and why would Belle's mother not allow it? Why the statement that Maz must behave correctly?

I let out a sigh of frustration. How little I knew about my wider family and what had gone on in the shadows. There was no full date, so no clue as to whether this exchange had happened recently or years ago.

I placed my grandfather's letter carefully underneath the other two and then, after checking that the coast was clear, hurried into the study to replace them all in the top cupboard.

Back in my room, I sat down on the edge of the bed, breathing hard, as I contemplated the disaster the adults around me had made. It was obvious from the pink scented notes that Jade was doing everything she could to get Fairfax to leave us. What should I do? Was it time to confront Fairfax? Should I have a showdown with Jade?

Or – and this was dynamite – should I tell Belle?

FINDING BELLE

June 3rd 1969

I cannot tell why Maz has come. Naturally Baba has sent him, but does he have concern in his heart for me or concern only for himself? Bela Bela, Baba is worried, he says, Baba thinks you are too much alone. Maybe Maz also is worried, but when he arrives he behaves not so well. He wants help from F but competes with him also. Silly boy, he is only 15 years old — how can he compete? F is always worried about money, and I see now he is not a naturally generous man, but Maz does himself no favours.

I am fond of him still, though. He expected more from his new Sahib brother, but he gets pushed back and denied. F should be kinder to him, but he says money doesn't grow on trees, Belle! There is no magic tree, Belle! He is mean-faced when he mocks. Poor Maz only trying to make his own way, but not so lucky as F.

Ma expected more also. Only Baba just cares for me.

Dearest Baba. I miss him and send him my letters of reassurance — I am fine, do not worry for your Bela, all is good and happy in this place. This kingdom of opportunity.

CHAPTER 7

My sixteenth birthday was completely overshadowed by the tawdry secret I had stumbled upon.

On the day itself, Fairfax, oblivious to my stiffness, presented me with an ornate necklace. He had left the price tag on – presumably, it was meant to impress. He was planning to take me out for burgers with Tabitha and Ash, whom I had mentioned casually as a friend; but when he ruefully called that afternoon to say he had to work late, I was glad. *Get lost then,* I thought, *buzz off to your wizened little mistress, see if I care!*

The depth of my anger astonished me, but it was liberating too, and I enjoyed the occasion without him. The three of us drank cider, smuggled out of Tabitha's house, and I unwrapped my presents, which were exactly what I would have expected from each of them: *A Guide to Green Travel* from Tabitha, and from Ash, a specially bound anthology of two of the Brontës' works.

*

But there was soon another cause for Fairfax to celebrate – one which had him centre-stage. His law firm was announced the winner of a coveted Legal Society prize, and he personally was singled out for a Special Commendation. I watched as his delight at recognition battled with pique that it had taken so long. But he quickly swung into celebratory mode, hiring a dinner suit and buying a new silk tie and handkerchief for the ceremony.

Belle and I watched him set off for the dinner with John with all the solemnity of a war hero. Among the audience were journalists from the *MK Times*, who printed a story and a small front-page photograph of him looking handsome and grave at his own achievement.

He returned home ebullient, brandishing his small, Perspex trophy and grabbing me by the waist to swing me round the kitchen.

It was the old, buoyant Fairfax come to life again and I laughed, despite myself. My heart had hardened against him, but his delight in himself triggered an old impulse of affection.

'We need to celebrate properly, Mivvi! Not everyone could come to the awards — there's all the rest of the staff, and friends too. We're going to do drinks at the office, and I'm in charge of catering. I can get lots of cheap fizz and canapés. Help me with it, will you?'

'Umm, alright,' I replied. Spying on him didn't exclude giving him a hand.

'And you'll come to the party itself, of course, won't you?' he asked quickly.

'Let's see,' I said. 'I might be busy. I've got lots of exam revision.'

I had no intention of going to the party; the prospect of being in the same room as Jade was unbearable.

'But you can still come? Why don't you invite Tabitha?' said Fairfax, with a generous sweep of the arm. 'And Bree too? I'm sure they'd both like to be there!'

I stared at him. He had never wanted anything to do with Bree before.

'Isn't this just a work do?' I asked, more balefully than I had intended.

'Nah,' said Fairfax expansively. 'We can stretch to more. What about that boy – what's his name again, the one you're keen on? Hashish?'

'Ashish, Dad,' I said guardedly, 'and he's just a friend.'

He gave me an old-fashioned look. 'It'll be a big event,' he said, flicking back his hair.

'I'll ask them,' I lied.

But there remained the question of my mother. Belle had been simmering in the last few days.

'What about Belle?' I asked slowly. 'I suppose she won't want to come.'

'Good lord, no!' Fairfax exclaimed, his eyes popping. 'She hates parties anyway. No, no, she'll be much better off here.'

I nodded, and although I understood him, my heart felt heavy.

Fairfax looked intent. 'What a life this has been, Mivvi – I had no idea what was in store…' He tailed off as I looked at him sharply.

'Well, it's our life, and that's just how it is,' I said, and as he nodded wearily, I steeled myself for my next question. 'Perhaps we should try and get some advice on her, some help?'

The words sounded lame, as was always the case when I broached this subject.

Fairfax looked sceptical. 'I don't know. I don't like getting other people involved.'

His reaction robbed me once more of conviction, and I let it go.

'Who else will be going to the drinks then?' I asked, trying to sound casual. 'John and Bianca, I suppose? And that Jade woman?'

Fairfax gave me a keen look. 'All of them and more,' he said. 'Jade's alright, you know. She's not been happy – she had a hard time with Roy. It's taken her a while to find her feet again.'

The mention of feet brought to mind an unwelcome image.

'Well, I'm sure she'll find someone else,' I said, fighting the urge to snap at him.

Fairfax shrugged. 'Maybe,' he said.

*

He went on doling out invitations liberally. The editor of the *MK Times* agreed to come, and so did Céline. I hadn't seen her for years, but Fairfax said he had bumped into her and asked, and she had said yes, enthusiastically. I began to wonder if his office was big enough to contain what was rapidly becoming half the town.

Days before the party, I was startled out of my homework by a loud cry. I ran into the corridor, and saw, through the open door to my parents' room, that Belle was standing by the open window, her voice a high-pitched scream as she tried to fend off whoever or whatever was assaulting her mind. Her loud shrieks split the air with rage, as she launched a full-throated attack against her imaginary demons.

I went back to my room, and as I winced and cringed at my desk, I could make out words from next door: *'Get away! Get out! I have the power, get out!'*

At other times it was just noise, the shrill unrelenting sound of acute mental pain.

I was alone in the house with her, and I clamped my hands over my ears to try to muffle her sharp cries. I could feel tears rolling down my cheeks, and although I should have felt for my mother, I was wracked instead by my own deep isolation. I put my head under the pillow, but I could not shut out the wild sounds.

I knew she would return to herself in a day, maybe two, clawing her way back from this peak of insanity, but in that moment of extreme distress for both of us, it was no comfort.

As I sobbed, it began to dawn on me that Meera's diagnosis – *schizophrenia* – was the one I now knew to be true. Fairfax's vague references to *inadequacies* no longer made sense to me. It was an illness that consumed my mother – one that could be treated.

Belle's cries mixed with my own growing clarity that something had to be done, and that it was Meera who would help.

I was thankful our nearest neighbours were away; at least there was no one else to hear Belle's torment. There was only me, and I was used to it.

*

Fairfax came home so late that night, if he came home at all, that I didn't see him. The following morning, Belle's fit seemed to have played itself out, and she was quiet in her room.

Fairfax came downstairs, bleary-eyed and unshaven, saying he had slept in the bed in his study. I felt a strong physical aversion to him – a feeling normally reserved for Belle.

'Your mother has been in one of her states again.'

'It was yesterday,' I said quietly. 'I think she's calmed down now.'

'Do you think that's it? For the moment?'

'Yes, probably. Hard to tell. I haven't seen her.'

'I have to mention this party to her.'

He only thinks of himself, I thought. But last night, I had made a plan.

At that moment, Belle came into the kitchen. She looked exhausted and crumpled. I felt relief to see she was apparently over the worst, mingled with despair that she had succumbed again.

Fairfax stiffly wished her good morning, but relaxed as she looked at him humbly and asked if he would like a cup of tea.

Seizing his moment, he said to her casually, 'Belle, we're having some drinks at work on Saturday, to celebrate my award. Mivvi might pop by. But you won't like it, so no need to worry.'

Belle nodded.

It was time for me to speak.

'Meera will come and keep you company,' I chipped in quickly. 'In fact, I rang her and left a message.'

'You did?' asked Fairfax, puzzled. 'How do you even know her number?'

'It is on the fridge door,' said Belle. 'Stuck with a magnet.'

Fairfax looked blank; he had clearly never noticed this. 'Why did you just invite her like that?' he asked me.

'It'll be nice for Belle,' I said innocently. 'You'll be at the party, and she can have her friend.'

And I will stay behind and talk to her about getting Belle treatment – I added silently.

Fairfax shrugged. 'Okay. But you might be at the party, too, right? I'd like you to come, Mivvi.'

'I know,' I said. 'I'll see.'

CHAPTER 8

It was three days before the party, and I was continuing to resist Fairfax's pressure to attend. I was battling with some trigonometry revision after school when the phone rang.

'Mivvi! Little honey Mivvi! It's Maz, your old uncle.'

'Oh, hello, Uncle,' I said. 'How are you?'

'I'm good, doll, I'm good. Say, I'm here for a few days, and was going to drop round, see how my sis is doing, and all of you, you know. It's been a while, eh? How's Saturday afternoon?'

'Well, I should probably check with Fairfax? It'll be nice to see you, but he's got a do on Saturday evening, you know, a sort of party – he's won an award. He'll be quite busy…'

'Oh, a party! Great, I love parties!' he purred. 'Count me in. I've got some business with your daddy anyway.'

'Well, maybe I should just ask him first?' I insisted. 'Do you want to give me your number?'

But he had already hung up.

*

I braced myself for Fairfax's anger, but when I told him he seemed more annoyed at the timing of Maz's visit than at the fact of it. Belle sat with us, listening as I recounted the conversation.

'So, he says he's got some business with me, does he?' said Fairfax, gazing out of the window.

'Yes. Does he?'

Fairfax shrugged. 'I don't want it to be on Saturday though,' he said. 'We're going to be so busy! Did he really not leave a number?'

'He rang off too quickly.'

'Hmm. His company is doing quite well now, I hear. Just does as he pleases though,' muttered Fairfax.

'Does he have his own business now then?' I asked.

Fairfax nodded tersely.

'What is it, Fairfax?' I ventured. 'Why don't you like Uncle Maz?'

'Nothing, nothing,' he said, but then muttered, 'Bloody cheek just turning up when he wants to…'

Belle unexpectedly cut in. 'He must come,' she said. 'He is my brother.'

Fairfax stared. 'Really? I mean, he'll come, but why? He's got a wife now, hasn't he? Why does he have to show up this weekend of all weekends? Anyway, you've never shown much fondness for him.'

I winced. Why did he always put her down?

Belle looked Fairfax straight in the eye. 'He is my brother and he will come,' she said calmly.

Fairfax frowned. 'You don't even like him.'

'No,' she replied. 'Perhaps I do not very much like him. But he is my brother. And he will come. You will go to your party, okay. So, he will come.'

Fairfax glared at her, and then walked out of the room. I realised I had been holding my breath.

Belle appeared to gather herself. 'He is my brother,' she said, to no one in particular. 'He will come.'

*

That Saturday, I did help Fairfax with the shopping, loading crates of fizzy wine and boxes of canapés into the car. He was in a state of high excitement, marred only by his disappointment that I was still refusing to be part of it. For a moment, I did feel mean and churlish, but then I remembered Jade and her sour face.

Fairfax remained cheerful and unsuspecting, and little by little during the course of the morning, I found myself softening, succumbing to his own generous view of himself, his perennial invitation to others to bathe in his own glory. It was, I could recognise now, a display of his essentially selfish nature, but I gave in, just a little. It was simpler to feign the old patterns of our relationship.

'Give us a hand here with this crate, sweetheart,' he panted, and the two of us somehow got it into the boot of the car. He was sweating but exhilarated. 'Well done!' he cried. 'We're a great team, Sweet Pea, you and me.'

I raised an eyebrow at the old nickname, but without resentment.

I got through the chores, knowing that at least I wouldn't have to endure the party itself. Once he had gone, I would be able to talk to Meera.

*

Maz appeared at our house mid-afternoon. He was stockier than he used to be, with a small pot belly that hung over his belt. His still-abundant hair was flecked with grey, but no amount of coconut oil could tame it, and its bounce made him look still youthful. He was sporting an unfashionably wide rainbow-coloured tie.

'Party gear, eh, Uncle?' I said, trying to lighten the atmosphere that always developed around him.

Maz grinned at me wickedly. 'Am I early, babe? Never mind. You wouldn't fetch me a little Scotch, would you?'

Just at that moment, Fairfax came down. He ran a hand over his own thinning scalp and muttered a curt hello. Maz looked embarrassed about the whisky.

Then Belle came in, neater and tidier than usual, and they greeted each other.

'How are you, Maz?' she asked, with a pale smile. 'And congratulations,' she added, gesturing to the wedding band on his left hand.

'Ah,' Maz said lightly. 'Ma was starting to worry it would never happen. I'm okay, Bela, I'm doing well. You're looking not too bad yourself. Is that what I should tell Baba?' He looked at her keenly.

'Yes, tell him I am not too bad,' she said mechanically.

Fairfax cleared his throat. 'Yes, we wondered when we'd see you. Better late than never I suppose.'

At this, Maz tipped an imaginary hat. 'I had to wait until better times,' he said, smacking his lips at the whisky.

'And these are better times, you say?' asked Fairfax softly.

'Yaar, well, as you know, I've struck out by myself now. I'm doing textiles, import-export to India. It's going very well.'

Fairfax had poured himself a drink too and raised his glass with an ironic smile. 'Well,' he said, 'I suggest we go up to the study and have a chat, and then you can be on your way.'

'But I want to come to your party, Fairfax,' said Maz teasingly. 'I can come back, we can do business tomorrow. What?' he asked, as Fairfax darkened. 'Don't you want your *bhai* there?'

Fairfax eyed him suspiciously, but before he could respond, Maz turned his attention to Belle.

'Bela, where is your party gear? You gonna have to do better than that.'

'I don't know about parties,' she replied in a tired voice. 'I will stay here.'

Maz whistled through his teeth. 'You can't do that, Sis! It's a celebration!'

At that moment, the phone rang, and Fairfax went to answer it. While he was gone, Maz topped up his drink.

'That was Meera,' Fairfax said briskly when he returned. 'She can't come. Some emergency at the hospital.'

Belle's face fell in dismay, and I turned away to hide my own disappointment.

'Oh-ho,' Belle said. 'Oh-ho, no Meera. I will have no friend tonight.'

At this, Maz's face was almost tender. 'You've got me, Sis. I'll be your friend.'

She looked so crestfallen that he started to laugh, but kindly.

'C'mon,' he said. 'Come to the party! Come with me – I'll look after you! You still scrub up well, girl. Besides,' he went on, 'have you met hubby's worky friends? Don't you want to see what he gets up to with them?'

I held my breath. He couldn't possibly know; it was just his insinuating manner. He could never resist goading Fairfax.

I could feel my father stiff and breathing heavily next to me.

Belle eyed her brother steadily. Then she smiled. 'I hear you, Maz. Alright, I will come.'

'That's better,' he whooped. 'Time to party! I hope there's dancing, Fairfax? Wine, women and dancing!'

Fairfax looked as if he was straining every muscle to control himself. 'I think we've got some business to discuss first, haven't we, Maz? Do you want to step into my study?'

'You don't want business today, brother,' said Maz lightly, 'it's a party day. Today I'm here to check up on Sis. Mivvi, are you coming tonight, doll?'

'I've got revision,' I said, knowing how weak the excuse sounded. The whole reason for my staying behind had disappeared, but the prospect of seeing Jade filled me with dread.

Maz snorted. 'Revision! What sort of teenager are you? There's a party and you want revision! Come! Come with us!'

Fairfax looked at me pleadingly, the two men making common cause for the first time. 'Go on, Mivvi, it would be so good if you came.'

His eyes strayed over towards Belle, and I understood that he wanted me to keep an eye on her.

'Alright,' I said, with a weak smile. 'Revision can wait. I might see if Ash can come too?'

'Ash, Bash and Smash! Bring them all!' cried Maz, as if he were the host. 'Great stuff! This is going to be some party!'

*

'What do you mean you're busy?' I looked at Ash with sinking disbelief.

'Does it matter that much? My mum says I need to be home. We've got this uncle visiting. From India.'

'I've got an uncle visiting too, from Africa. He's always the unwelcome guest. Still, can you really not come with me?' I felt jittery with nerves. Who would be my ally at the party if Ash wasn't there? I knew it wasn't his fault, but I felt he had somehow failed me.

'You think I've failed you,' he said, perplexed.

'How do you always know what I'm thinking?' I exclaimed.

'Ah, you see, I was right.'

'Sorry, unfair, I know.' I sighed and put a hand on his arm, then withdrew it quickly. I didn't want to show too much emotional need.

'Why are you so against going to this party?' His glasses looked precarious, and he pushed them up. 'It's great your dad's won an award. You could just show up for a little bit.'

I nodded gloomily. How could I ever tell him about the wretched Jade, it would be so disloyal to Fairfax! Not that Fairfax deserved my loyalty.

'It's all very strange with Maz,' I mused. 'He's the uncle, Belle's brother. He's a funny character for sure, but Fairfax seems to hate him. I can't work out why.'

Ash looked sympathetic. 'My family all hate each other.'

'Do they?' I asked, surprised. I had thought it was only mine that was dysfunctional.

'Well, I don't think it's specific, no old grudges or anything – they just get a lot of satisfaction in putting each other down.' His eyes glinted. 'Behind each other's backs, of course. It's all a big competition.'

'I don't think this is the same,' I said. 'This dislike seems very specific. I just don't know where it comes from.'

'You know, you probably should go to the party,' he replied tentatively. 'I know there are these weird tensions, but he is your dad, and he has won this prize, or whatever it is. He probably just wants you there.'

I felt a streak of irritation at how simplistic Ash was, before remembering that he knew nothing.

Then he redeemed himself. 'Look, do you want me to get out of my family do?'

'Oh yes!' I cried. 'Oh Ash, yes, would you?'

He nodded. 'I mean, your dad wouldn't mind if I came, would he?'

'Oh no, he'd love it – I mean, he's inviting everyone,' I said glumly.

'Perhaps we can just put in a brief appearance, and then escape?'

'You really don't want to go, do you? It won't be that bad.'

I shrugged and tried to look resigned. It would undoubtedly be better with Ash there, but I had a foreboding about this party which was starting to exceed my hatred of Jade. A dark shadow seemed to cling to its every aspect, besmirching it like a black and noxious fog.

*

I waited for Ash at the corner of the street. Although the evening was cool, I felt a dampness on my brow, and tried to still my quickening breath. The road was quiet, apart from the strains of music and raucous laughter coming from the party. I kept looking anxiously from left to right, willing Ash not to be much later, and preparing to hide if Jade suddenly appeared.

Then I spotted an unlikely figure wearing a large blazer with gold buttons. He was walking towards me, one side of his round glasses stuck together with tape, his black curls unruly in the wind.

'Ash!' I gasped, as I ran up to greet him. 'What on earth are you wearing?'

'It's my father's,' he said sheepishly. 'My mother insisted I wear a jacket. It's a formal celebration, see.'

I kissed him demurely on the cheek, and we started to laugh. His ability to withstand looking ridiculous was one of the best things about him. He thrust a bunch of flowers into my hand, and a copy of *1984*. 'The book is for you, and the flowers for your mother,' he said.

With a start, I realised I had been so anxious about Jade that I had forgotten to worry about Belle.

We went in together, and I did a quick scan of the room. The first person I saw was the one I most wanted to avoid: Jade had been cornered by Maz, and was standing there awkwardly, twisting a paper napkin between her fingers, half-listening to him, her eyes following Fairfax around the room.

I didn't know if she had seen me, but I shot her a glacial look nonetheless, and then searched for Belle, who was safely ensconced between John and Bianca. Belle's eyes sharpened when she saw Ash by my side, and then narrowed further when she spotted Jade with Maz.

'Where is Roy?' I could hear her shrill voice asking Bianca, who then whispered a reply.

I looked around the room through the throng of people, and waved to Céline, who was clad in a dress so short even Tabitha wouldn't have worn it. Fairfax was at the far end of the room, talking animatedly to the newspaper editor, who had bottle-blonde hair and purple nails.

I took a deep breath, put on my best, sociable face, and moved in brightly to introduce Ash to those in the crowd whom I knew.

*

Jade was brittle with tension and wilting with the effort of trying to appear composed. She desperately wished herself anywhere but here.

She had been startled to see Belle walk in after Fairfax had insisted she wasn't coming, and now any faint possibility that she might relax had vanished. There was a time when Jade felt a thrill at being with Fairfax in Belle's presence, as she had done at the dinner parties, but now she felt spent and drained by their constant arguments about the future, arguments which she never won.

He had been standing right before her as she walked in, and as he raised an eyebrow to indicate Belle, he already looked unsteady on his feet. She would have gone to find refuge with John and Bianca, but they were taken by Belle, so she had slunk into a corner, determined to leave early – when to her horror she was joined by Belle's brother.

It took her a half-second to remember who he was. Suave, with greased-back hair, built more slightly than his sister, same nose, darker skin. He edged in to talk to her, standing too close, and Jade drew on all her strength to appear casual, neutral. Her skin prickled, and beads of sweat made her hair stick to her skin.

Out of the corner of her eye, she watched Fairfax working the room, pumping men by the hand, embracing women exuberantly. The hero of the night.

Maz was so close she could smell his aftershave. He looked wolfish, and she had a brief image of herself as Little Red Riding Hood.

'So, I remember you at the house,' he said. 'Many moons ago. You were just leaving – you'd finished work.'

'Yes,' she replied nervously. 'But I work here now, with Fairfax. And others of course,' she added hurriedly.

'You work with him, do you?' The man knew nothing, yet his words curdled with meaning.

'Yes, that's right. I suppose some would say I work for him, but it's not that sort of place.'

'Not that sort of place? What sort of place is it then?' he grinned. 'Democratic, is it? You British, you love your democracy.'

Jade attempted a smile. She felt sick with nerves.

'C'mon, I'm just teasing you,' said Maz. 'Here, have some more fizz.'

'No, thank you.' Jade shook her head. 'I'm not a big drinker.'

'Oh, come on, it won't hurt,' he insisted, topping her up.

She sipped it cautiously.

'So, you must know my big sis quite well?'

It was like walking through broken glass.

'Not very well,' she ventured. 'Of course, I saw her when I worked for them, and I've been to a few dinners at theirs. But I usually sit next to Fairfax – I mean, at the other end of the table,' she said weakly.

'The other end of the table, eh?'

Why did he keep repeating what she said?

'It's a pity you don't know her better. She's quite a character. My father worries about her, but then, Bela has married very well.'

His eyes didn't leave her face as he spoke.

Jade looked for a way out. She tried to catch John's eye, but he didn't see her.

'Would you like me to get some canapés?' she squeaked.

Maz laughed. 'No, thank you, I'm not hungry. But perhaps you are? You look like you need fattening up. Go on, why don't you grab yourself some of those nice little canapés?'

As Jade fled, she bumped into a young woman wearing long scarves and a very short dress.

'*Oh, la!*' the woman exclaimed, her French accent strong. 'I am so sorry. But you are in such a hurry!'

'Umm, yes, I mean, no,' gabbled Jade, her self-possession gone. 'I'm sorry as well, I was just after a canapé.'

The woman gave a light and silvery laugh, but it was not unkind.

'Parties make me hungry too!' She smiled slyly. 'Although not always for food.'

'I see,' said Jade stiffly. 'Well, each to their own, I suppose.'

The woman turned her smile up a notch, and with a wave of her fingers, she moved on.

Jade scooped up a salmon tart in case the wolfish brother was still watching and then scurried away across the room. Once she had recovered her composure, she risked a brief glance back and saw him now focused on the French woman. She was having a better time than Jade had had, throwing her head back to laugh loudly while he flirted with her.

Jade heard her say something to him in French, which made her think of Roy. Belle's brother moved in to top up the woman's glass, and as he did so, he touched her bare thigh with his hand, leaving it there too long for it to be incidental. The woman's eyes widened, but she did not move out of reach.

Jade might have looked away at this point if it hadn't been for Fairfax suddenly striding towards them. He seemed to address a sharp word to the brother, and then took the woman's elbow to guide her away.

Jade stared after them, frowning. What had just happened – who was that woman? Was it possible that Fairfax had other secrets too?

She began to cross the room towards him, shaking with confusion and rising anger.

*

I was trying to make small talk, but I was distracted by all the currents of tension running through the room. Even with Ash beside me, it was impossible to relax.

Belle looked alert and watchful. She had stayed close to John and Bianca but she, like me, appeared to be observing the scene. How much of it, I wondered nervously, could she read?

'Hey, doll, your boyfriend needs some new glasses.'

I hadn't noticed Maz suddenly at my side. Ash had gone to get drinks, and I saw the tape around his spectacles starting to unfurl.

'He's not my boyfriend,' I said, smiling. I didn't mind Maz's teasing.

'Maybe he should be,' he said suggestively, and I gave him a gentle poke in the ribs. 'Lots going on here tonight,' he went on, as if somehow he knew.

Ash wandered back, handing me a drink before holding out his hand to Maz. 'Hello, I'm Ash.'

'We're friends,' I said pointedly.

'Sure you are,' said Maz. 'Good to meet you, Ash. I'm her uncle Maz. So, are you a bookworm like my niece?'

'I guess that's what you would call me, yes.'

'Good, good. Your mama was a great reader, Mivvi, when she was a gal.'

'Really?' I said in surprise. It was always hard to tell whether Maz was joking or not, but I couldn't ever recall seeing Belle pick up a book.

'Oh yes,' drawled Maz, 'lots of books. All those funny poets, Keats and Yeets.'

'Yeats,' mumbled Ash.

Maz blinked at him. 'Pardon?'

'Mates,' I said quickly. 'Keats and Yeets were mates.'

Maz looked at Ash intently. 'You laughing at me, young man?'

'Certainly not,' said Ash hurriedly. 'I'm just a terrible pedant.'

'Mates like us,' I said loudly, desperate to stop Ash taking on Maz. 'C'mon, Uncle, tell me how things are.'

Maz was still looking levelly at Ash but brought his attention back to me. 'Things are good, Mivvi, they're going well. Got my own business, starting to do some exporting, to India you know.'

'And is that what Fairfax wants to talk to you about?'

Maz pursed his lips. 'No, not really. That's something else.'

At that moment, Belle turned towards us, and Maz winked at her. She looked at him steadily and her eyes narrowed. She was wearing a magenta gown, with heavy gold bell-like earrings, and bangles at her wrists. I marvelled at her splendour, wondering if these were her wedding jewels. Belle had made her face up heavily, the effect almost mask-like. Perhaps that was what made her so inscrutable.

I turned back to talk to Ash, so how events unfolded and why Belle did what she did, I could never subsequently say, but suddenly out of the corner of my eye, I could see Belle drawing herself up to her full height.

I turned quickly and saw her eyes darting about wildly. My heart started to thump. *Belle, Belle,* I whispered to myself, *no, please, please don't.*

'Belle!' I cried out, but it was too late. In that instant, my knowledge was also Belle's knowledge.

My mother had swept over to Jade and was spitting viciously in her face.

'Get out,' she hissed, 'get out of this place! You slut, you whore, you harlot!'

Now she was screaming. 'You filthy, filthy woman! You have come to my house and have sat at my table and eaten my food and think you can take him! He's my husband! He's mine! Get out! Get out!'

Jade stood, ashen-faced, Belle's saliva trickling down her cheek.

Fairfax stumbled towards Jade, crashing into a table of canapés on his way. John grabbed a napkin and started wiping Jade's face. Céline and the newswoman stared. Maz gawped. Ash stayed still as a stone.

'You bastard,' Belle hissed at Fairfax. 'You bloody bastard. You want to put horns on me, do you? Again! You *badmaash*! How dare you?'

I watched everything happening in slow motion. Fairfax's milk-white face loomed in horror at his shrieking wife and his shrinking mistress. The room had turned deathly quiet. I wanted to dissolve into nothingness and disappear. It was all out – Fairfax's betrayal, my parents' terrible marriage.

Fairfax seemed in the moment to slump, his big strong body folding in on itself at this sudden, violent exposure. Tears were running down Jade's cheeks. Belle was snorting like a bull, ready to charge again.

Bianca took over. 'Come on, love,' she said to Jade, reaching for her hand. 'We're taking you home.'

She gestured to John, who couldn't leave quickly enough. The other guests gazed at the ground or at the ceiling. Only Maz recovered his cool, and a malicious smile flitted across his sly features.

'You old dog, Fairfax,' he said under his breath. 'Well, you've got it coming to you now.'

Fairfax shot him a murderous look, his face now purple with fury and humiliation. Belle was bristling and agitated, and without thinking I went over to take her by the arm, pausing only to nod to a sorrowful-looking Ash before leading Belle out.

Fairfax followed us automatically, our family fleeing the scene of our mortification together.

*

We drove home in deafening silence. Belle sat ramrod straight in the passenger seat, while Fairfax kept his eyes fixedly on the road, stone-cold sober despite his drinking. I slunk down in the back seat, wishing myself anywhere but with them.

When we arrived, I hastily turned to head for my room.

'Stay,' rasped Belle. 'Let us hear together the story of your father's dirty work.'

'Belle, please, this is for us,' said Fairfax wearily. 'It's not for her ears.'

She gave him a withering look. 'You didn't think of that before, did you, when you started with that woman? Where was our daughter, where was I, when you started to fuck—'

Fairfax cut her off. 'Stop it, shut up,' he said curtly, 'Mivvi, go.'

I fled, but only to lie on my bed helplessly, listening to them fighting and counting the leaden hours as they passed. Belle was shrill with rage, but there were tears too and wailing, and a guttural crying I had never heard before. I couldn't hear Fairfax. Maybe he was crying too. Through the yelling, I thought I could hear the phone ringing repeatedly, but no one answered it.

I must have slept fitfully at some stage, but suddenly Fairfax was there at my door. It was the middle of the night. He sat down heavily on the edge of the bed, his eyes bloodshot, his face haggard.

'Mivvi, I'm sorry.' He was rasping. 'I can never explain to you – I can never make you understand. But it's been so difficult! You know that. It's been so hard.'

I was tense with distress and exhaustion, but I put my hand on his arm. 'Fairfax, I know, I know.'

It had been wretched, but he could have found another way of dealing with our misery.

'I've been so unhappy,' he went on. 'That's why it happened. It was just a sort of … distraction. She too was trying to break free … from, you know, Roy and all that. It was just escape, a temporary escape.'

My whole being shuddered at his self-pity, but I clung to the word *temporary*.

'I know what you must think of me. But I felt trapped by everything that happened. And now I have no option.'

I looked at him sharply. 'What do you mean, Fairfax? What are you going to do?' I felt a rising panic. 'Fairfax, don't leave us! Daddy, don't go – please don't go.'

Fairfax hugged me tightly. I could feel tears streaming down his face.

But he did not reply.

He left then and I fell into an exhausted sleep. When I woke, he was gone. Gone from my room, gone from the house and, I knew for sure, gone from our family.

*

After making their escape, John, Bianca and Jade drove wordlessly away. Shattered as she was, Jade cringed to think what a shock it must have been to the couple who had been her friends and mentors.

She slumped in the seat behind them, shivering and trembling as the images of Belle's assault replayed themselves in her head, like scenes from a nightmare: the monstrous woman, nostrils flared, eyes blazing, bearing down on her from across the room, Mivvi's taut face screaming at her to stop, and then the stream of spitting and hissing and screaming.

Jade thought she would never get the feel of the woman's saliva off her skin. Her powers of movement had deserted her and she had watched herself as if from outside her own body, paralysed before the violent abuse.

At last, the journey was over, and she thanked John and Bianca briefly, then rushed upstairs. Exhausted, she fell on her bed. Never before had she known such humiliation; her whole being burned with it. But the fever that coursed through her came also from knowing that her future with Fairfax hung in the balance, that he was deciding right at this moment between her and Belle.

What could she do? For the first time ever, she rang him at home; it had always been him who called her, but now she rang repeatedly, every minute – but he would not pick up. She briefly considered going to his house to beg him to come away with her, but she knew that would be folly.

In a frenzy, she grabbed his letters to her and wondered if she should send them to Belle, as irrefutable proof of his love for her.

He's mine, she thought, *he's mine*.

Her head pounded with conflicting urges – to act, to grab what was rightfully hers, or to attempt the long wait. Surely, he wouldn't abandon her? Surely, he would come?

It was nearly dawn when she heard his key in the lock.

He walked in, dragging a suitcase after him, looking distraught and destroyed, and Jade hugged him noiselessly, feeling his face wet with tears. She stroked his hair and murmured his name, with love and relief. The refrain ran over and over in her head: *He's walked out on her, he's left her. We are together.*

'I knew you were coming,' she said to him, 'I knew you would – I could hear you calling my name, it was you, calling me – Jade! Jade!'

She went on caressing him softly. *We are one*, she thought to herself. *I have won.*

*

I wandered dazed around the house, feeling everywhere the absence of Fairfax. Not everything had gone, but it was enough. Several suits, and the grey trousers he wore at home. His aftershave, and his badger shaving brush. His diary and a photograph of me that he kept in the study. It was daytime, and Fairfax might well just have been at work, but a heaviness hung in the air, a feeling of finality.

I went downstairs and started tidying up automatically, washing the plates in the sink, sweeping the kitchen floor. The house was still and silent; the only noise and movement were mine.

Finally, in the late afternoon, I went up to the bedroom which used to be my parents' and which was now Belle's. My mother was sitting motionless in an armchair by the window, gazing blankly at the scene outside. She acknowledged me wordlessly and shifted her dull eyes back to the window. I sat down next to her.

In another life with a different mother, I might have embraced her. As it was, we sat separately and in silence, united in grief, although I could never know what was going on in Belle's mind.

The summer air was heavy, and the evening windless and oppressive. We listened to the starlings screaming, and watched the sun begin its slow bleed across the sky. The light seeped away, and the scene thickened into an inky black. We stared on dumbly, looking but not seeing, as night fell on the house that Fairfax had fled.

But then Belle broke the silence. 'I kicked him out, you know.'

I started. 'What did you say?'

'I kicked him out. He didn't flee – I told him to buzz off. To get lost and to buzz off! Hard luck to him!' She seemed to cackle. 'Hard luck! The shabby man.'

I stared at her. 'But, Belle, how could you? How will we manage?'

Belle went on with her mirthless laughter. 'Oh, we'll manage alright. We'll make sure he helps us manage. Your Mr Blue-Eyes father. The traitor! He thinks he's so clever. He thinks he's such a big man! But he's a low-down, shabby little traitor. Him and that Céline too you know. Same thing. *Badmaash.*'

I felt a heaviness descend on me. Céline, too? Well, yes, maybe on some level I had always known. Could it be true that Belle had kicked him out? After all my hopes of keeping the family together, could it have been Belle who had blown it apart?

In despair, I tried to coax more out of her, but she now turned her face away and sat still and monumental as a statue. Defeated, I slumped back, allowing the silence and the obscurity to envelop us both once more.

CHAPTER 9

In the weeks that followed the party, nothing felt real. Every day I expected to hear Fairfax's key in the lock, and each evening I had to confront again the brutal fact of his departure. The heart of the family had been ripped out. Belle barely spoke, and the two of us existed together, enduring rather than living, unable to express our fears of what might become of us.

I made hurried trips to the corner shop to buy us milk, bread, cheese, and left drinks and sandwiches for her in the kitchen. Sometimes they disappeared, sometimes not. I tried to get the truth from her, whether she had really thrown Fairfax out, or whether he had left us of his own accord. But whenever I asked, Belle's face would become hard and agitated, and I quickly abandoned my attempts, afraid that I would trigger another of her attacks.

I had no idea of Fairfax's intentions, but I did receive one hastily written note through the letterbox, promising to send me money every month to keep the household going. It gave me shivers to imagine him furtively delivering the letter to the house that had so recently been his home. But it meant our survival was not in question. Only the shape of it, and how we would cope without him in the months and years that stretched ahead.

I withdrew from the world. I called in sick at school and unplugged the phone. I received messages through the letter box from Tabitha, telling me that she knew what I was going through. I put them in the bin. Once there was a letter from Meera, which I put to one side. There was a scrawled note from Maz , saying he was returning to Mombasa early as his mother was ill. *Look after yourself*, he wrote, *and also my sis. I know you will.* I put this in the bin too.

I opened the door once to Bianca, who seemed even more distressed than me. I hugged the weeping woman but sent her quickly away, unable to endure her sympathy, nor her fury at Fairfax.

I had no room in my life for anyone else's emotional needs.

*

The one person I did see was Ash, who faithfully knocked on the door every day for nearly a week until I finally let him in. We sat together at the bottom of the stairs, and he took my hand in his and stayed silent until I spoke.

'So, I suppose we're the laughing stock of the town?'

'I don't think that's anyone's reaction. There's concern about you.'

'Huh, I don't need anyone's concern,' I said bitterly. 'I can look after myself. I have done for years.'

'Is he sending you money?'

'Yes, he is,' I replied, more quietly.

'Have you seen him?'

'Not yet.'

'And your mother?' he ventured.

I shrugged. 'I don't know. She's hardly spoken. She's just kind of existing.'

'It must have been such a shock.'

'Yes, it must have been. I don't really know how she suddenly knew, but she did.'

'I meant it must have been a shock for you.'

I looked at the floor miserably. 'I knew.'

'What?' he said in amazement, and I nodded.

'I found out a while ago. I didn't know what to do. I was trying to think of some way to get them to split up.' I gave a hollow laugh. 'It sounds so daft, doesn't it? What did I think I could do? And then Belle blew it all apart anyway.'

I realised that my eyes were wet, and I wiped them surreptitiously with my free hand. I didn't want to cry in front of him.

'Mivvi,' he said eventually. 'I had heard before that your mother has been…' He hesitated and then stuttered, 'Un-unhappy.'

I stared at him. 'What do you mean? What have people said? Who's been talking about us?'

'No, no,' he groaned. 'No one has. Not in a nasty way anyway.'

'Is this all because of the other night?' I hissed at him. 'Because she acted so wildly? You said no one was talking about us!'

'I said no one was laughing at you. And no, not just the other night. One or two people, like Tabitha's mother, have said things before – that your mother might be depressed or something. And I have wondered. You never mention her. You talk about your dad all the time, but you never mention her.'

I felt suddenly breathless, as if my throat were constricted. Even now, even to Ash, it was so difficult to break the habit of a lifetime of concealment.

'We don't have to talk about it if you don't want to,' he said nervously.

I forced myself to breathe deeply and slowly.

'I'm sorry, I shouldn't have said anything.' He sounded wretched. 'Forget it, please just forget it.'

I exhaled and managed to squeeze his hand to signal a truce. I couldn't look at him, but I could feel his relief.

'I will talk to you,' I said. 'I will tell you. But not right now. It feels like too much.'

He nodded and awkwardly put an arm around me. This was a greater intimacy than we had known so far. We sat in silence and eventually I relaxed into him, and although his arm must have begun to ache and stiffen, I knew he had no intention of letting me go.

*

From then on, we saw each other almost every day. We sat in my bedroom listening to music or reading, separate but together. Sometimes if I needed to get out of town, somewhere anonymous, we took a bus to the Abbey, the nearby stately home with huge, peaceful gardens where no one else our age would go.

At home, Belle remained an ephemeral presence somewhere upstairs in the house, but occasionally there drifted down strains of her gentle singing, and sometimes even gurgled laughter. She was inactive as ever, but her mood was lighter, although she never left her room when Ash was there.

I had spent so long avoiding bringing friends to the house, but Ash was different; he seemed entirely without judgement, and I gradually found my anxiety thawing.

I told him about my strange childhood, haltingly at first and then more freely. I was 16, but I felt old beyond my years, and the very act of narrating parts of the past made me appreciate more fully how peculiar it had been.

'Did your father not want to help her?' Ash asked.

'Well, he didn't want anyone else to know. And I think he was in denial – he seemed barely to accept that there was anything wrong.' I felt keenly the weakness of my defence of him. 'And I guess I just believed him. Do you know, on some level, I still do? I think he persuaded himself it was all self-inflicted, and he kind of persuaded me too.'

Ash nodded.

'We don't have much of a relationship, me and her,' I went on. 'I don't really know her. It's been impossible to.'

'Maybe it's not too late?' he asked.

I sighed. 'Who knows? It feels like it is.'

'And what about getting her some help?'

'Medical help?'

Ash nodded.

I bowed my head. 'Meera, our friend who's a doctor, said that to me a while ago.' I made to chew a fingernail, and then promptly sat on my hands. 'I was going to talk to her on the night of the party, but she couldn't come. Maybe I should have acted earlier. I feel like I'm partly to blame.'

'Don't be silly,' he said roundly. 'You're not.'

'I will do it. I don't know if Belle will cooperate, but I'll ask for Meera's help.'

Ash nodded encouragingly. 'Yes, yes of course. Good. And how is it back at school?'

'It's alright actually.' I turned to him with a wan smile. 'I'd have stayed off if it hadn't been for the exams, and I was dreading it. I thought I'd get all these mocking looks and snide glances. But no, nothing. Just people noticing that I'd been off.'

Ash smiled back. 'I told you not to worry.'

'I know, and you were right.'

'And you've still not heard from your dad?'

I shook my head brusquely.

'Nope. A note about sending us money, but nothing more. I wonder how he's dealing with it all, being exposed like that.'

'It won't be easy.'

'That's for sure,' I declared and felt a sudden spark of anger. 'He'll be going through agonies of shame – I know he will. Ha! Serves him right. He's got exactly what he deserves!'

*

In the first flush of their new life together, Jade treated Fairfax as though he were an invalid. He called in sick at work, and then asked for further compassionate leave. He did look as if he were ailing; his face was pale and haggard, his shoulders hunched and his movements slow. Jade was solicitous, tenderly wrapping a blanket around his shoulders as he slumped on the sofa and coaxing him to eat even though his appetite was quite gone. She was shrewd enough to avoid any hint of triumph, and felt confident now to give herself to him completely – and this he accepted gratefully and greedily, with emotion which verged on the tearful.

She had hoped he would greet his newfound freedom with relish, but she was prepared to bide her time. She had waited so long – what were a few weeks or even months more? Besides, like her, he was probably still recovering from the shock of Belle's deranged behaviour. It was a monstrous injustice: the party should have been the crowning moment of his professional success, not the stage for a mad woman's ravings.

The two of them lay low for many weeks, continuing to live quietly and discreetly. Fairfax scanned the local paper every day in something approaching panic, but – as Jade suspected – the minor philandering of a local solicitor wasn't worthy of even a news-in-brief.

Secretly, she exulted that she had her prize at last, and she comforted herself with her conviction that he would come around soon. *He's just adjusting to a new reality,* she thought. *That's it. He couldn't stand it anymore and he walked out. He chose me. A family breaks up, and a new one forms, and eventually everyone just adapts, don't they?*

For so long she had felt as though she had lost her bearings, and now she spent every night under the same roof with the man she had longed for. There was deep pleasure and satisfaction in their new physical relationship, and she was confident it was a precursor to a formal union. She yearned for marriage; it surprised her how suddenly she had moved from simple possession of Fairfax to needing to be his wife. But her whole life had been lonely, and other people's stability, the resilience of their families, had always mocked her with their solidity and complacency. Not Fairfax's, though. She had seen through the fragility of his marriage, whatever façade he had tried to maintain.

Jade smiled at herself in the mirror. She had qualities that Belle would never have: resilience and determination and perseverance. She could cope with a morose Fairfax for a little while longer, confident that in time he would see he had made exactly the right decision.

FINDING BELLE

England
January 31st 1969

How to go on writing here. This flat land, these grey skies. Air full of water, always heavy and wet, not proper rain, just a moist film. These people live inside a cloud. But always they talk of it, so cheerful about their damp watery weather, congratulating themselves. How will I manage? I cannot understand them. They cannot understand me, although really, I think they can — this is just a pretence to make me small.

Such a small, lowdown place, all concrete and cars. F is full of excitement. Little boy, showing off his Belle to people. But it seems to me that no one wants to see. Meera did come to see, all the way from her home, just like Baba asked her to. She is so warm, and so real, not like the other fakery types. I like her — we can speak of home and our parents' home with no barrier. Also seeing John here is nice, although I cover my ears, and his Bianca, funny woman, overdressed, like an overripe mango. But nice also. Maybe she and F were something before me, she with her hugging and her kissing. But it is okay. Now he has eyes only for me.

My queen, says F, my Belle of the ball. But where are the balls? Only dinner here and dinner there, chit chat, work, money, everyone always wanting to be better than the other. I speak and they speak but our words slide over each other — it is not really talking. So, then I become quiet. F gets angry. Why don't you speak more, he says, but it is easier to be quiet.

His friends are polite, though. Not like the badmaash shop girls. So offhand and to a married woman like me! F doesn't understand. I must make him see. He works so hard, always it is work and the office.

Maybe I will adjust. I write to Ma and Baba telling them I am so happy. They mustn't know. And with F, I am happy. But this country is dull and without colour, without warmth, without welcome.

PART 3 – 1990

CHAPTER 1

'Belle!' I called. 'Are you ready?'

I could hear her stirring.

'We're going to the doctor, remember?'

Belle appeared at the top of the stairs, looking confused. She had trouble remembering things – a side-effect of the medication, although years of illness had also clouded her memory.

'Are we?' she asked worriedly.

'Yes, Belle, you know, we're going to the hospital for your check-up. To see Professor Brooke.'

'Oh-ho,' said Belle. 'Oh-ho. I had forgotten.'

She looked abashed. But in the past an unexpected outing might have agitated her; now she simply smiled sheepishly. The wildness that used to wrack her had faded away, and she was docile, co-operative. She was sleepier and slower with the tranquillising effect of the pills, but that was a small price to pay for the banishing of her demons.

'You do not have school?' Belle ventured. 'You have finished?'

'You know I have. Last week. Finished my A Levels, remember? Out in the big wide world now. It's the prize you get when you turn 18.' I couldn't tell how much Belle was taking in, but she smiled benignly. 'Well, you'd better get ready.'

But she still looked uncertain.

'There's nothing to worry about, Belle – the prof just wants to make sure you're doing alright. And you are.'

I went up and gave her a gentle pat on the arm. These days, I made an effort to be as cheerful as I could be around my mother, but physical affection towards her had never come naturally.

The meeting with Professor Brooke was more significant than I had let on. The end of my school days meant it was time to confront decisions about what I was going to do next. My friends were full of excitement at the prospect of flying the nest, but my own home had ceased to be a nest long ago, and while I did have hopes of flying away too, leaving a vulnerable mother was fraught with worries.

But it was a measure of how much Belle had improved that I was able to consider leaving at all.

As I waited for her to get ready, I thought of how much she had changed in the two years since I had plucked up the courage to ring the doctor. With Ash's encouragement and Meera's help, I had secured an appointment with the psychiatrist. But confronting Belle had not been easy.

'Belle, Mama,' I had said. 'I want you to come with me to the doctor.'

Belle had fixed me with her huge brown eyes. 'Why, are you ill?' she had asked gently. Her concern was touching.

'No, I'm not. It's you I want to take. You know why. The way you behave, you know sometimes – you're not well at all…' I had tailed off as Belle drew herself up.

'What is wrong with me?' she had said huffily. 'I am okay.'

But I had stayed determined.

'Yes, you are now, but sometimes you're not okay. Please, come with me, Belle. I'm doing this for you.'

Belle had stared at me suspiciously.

'This is not that Mr Blue Eyes, is it? Eh? Does he want to give me pills, eh? To harm me?'

'No!' I had groaned. 'This is nothing to do with him!'

'Is it that filthy maid servant he has gone to? Is it her?'

'Belle, stop this!'

Despite my own deep hostility towards Jade, I was aghast at her words.

'It's nothing to do with them!' I'd cried. 'In fact, it's precisely because he's gone that I want to take you! It's for your own good. Please!'

My words had had the right effect. The fire had slowly left Belle's eyes, and she had nodded. It was barely perceptible, but it was assent.

*

Now, we once again walked together into the hospital grounds, with me moderating my long stride to Belle's slow shuffle. The hospital was right next to Fairfax's office; the first time we came, I had had to rush Belle past the window in case they caught sight of each other. This time, I took pains to use a different route.

Professor Brooke's consulting room was painted in shades of cream and lavender, and there was a profusion of orchids on the mantelpiece above the fireplace.

'Good to see you again, Belle. How would you say you are?' the professor asked, looking at her over the top of her rectangular glasses.

'I'm alright really,' said Belle in a small, high voice.

'Are you? That is most encouraging. And those voices that you used to hear, have they gone?'

Belle smiled. 'Oh yes.'

'Quite gone?'

'Oh yes,' she repeated, beaming like a prize pupil.

'And you feel better now? More settled?'

Belle nodded.

'Do you remember, Belle, what it was like to hear those voices?'

'A little bit.'

The professor nodded encouragingly. 'Go on, tell me.'

'They were just bad people, you know, saying ugly things. Evil things. I told them I had a power to make them go. But they didn't go.' Belle squirmed as she spoke.

'It made you feel afraid, didn't it? And it's good we've made them go away?'

How childlike she looks, I thought, as Belle silently agreed. She was hunched up in her chair, watching passively as the professor made notes. There was less of Belle now. The pills had calmed her mind but reduced her person.

After the consultation, Belle waited outside so that I could have a private word with the professor.

'She's doing well,' said Professor Brooke. 'She seems calm and unruffled. And the voices have left her.'

'She's so much better than before,' I agreed. 'But … not normal exactly.'

'Mivvi,' she said gently, 'we always knew Stelazine would not be a miracle cure. You must remember it has helped her. You know that.'

'I do know.' I sighed. 'It's just the loss of time I regret. It's like so many years have gone, and so much of her personality has been lost. Professor, I wonder if I can ask you something? Do you think that Belle, my mother, can live independently? If I were to go away? We have friends who could keep an eye on her.'

There was a short pause as the professor considered my question.

'I think so,' she replied. 'You've been out at school during the day, haven't you? And you go out in the evenings sometimes, I'm sure. She manages, then? And are you certain she'll take her medication without you there? Yes? Then I think, if there are people you can rely on who are nearby, she'll be fine.' She lowered her glasses so that she could look me straight in the eye. 'You've got to get on with your own life too, you know.'

I felt a lump in my throat at her attention and concern. 'If she had been helped earlier,' I asked quietly, 'might she have recovered properly?'

'It's impossible to say, Mivvi, I'm afraid. But do you even know who a proper Belle would have been?'

I shook my head sadly. 'No, you're right. No point dwelling on hypotheticals.'

'She's no longer a danger to others, nor to herself. She's got back some of her life. Now you have to get back some of yours.'

The conversation was stirring up feelings of neglect and loss in me which were usually kept firmly tamped down. I managed a wan smile at the older woman.

'Do you have plans?' the professor asked. 'Where are you going to go?'

'Well, university. I've got a place. To do French. I used to know a French girl once. And a French teacher too. I never see them anymore, but…'

'They instilled a love,' said the professor. She smiled, then turned suddenly brisk. 'I'm going to have to see you out now, Mivvi, but good luck. And any problems – you know where I am.'

*

Back home, Belle lowered herself slowly into her armchair. Any small exertion exhausted her. She sat sunken in the seat, and her left foot shook involuntarily, another side-effect of the Stelazine. I did my best not to notice.

'Belle, I'm out this evening.'

'Okay.' But then her eyes narrowed, and her breathing quickened. 'To see the *badmaash* and his low-down filth?'

'No,' I said quickly. 'I'm seeing Ash.'

'Okay.' She seemed to relax. 'He is a good boy.'

I had tried hard to keep my relationship with Ash away from Belle, but despite her illness, she had proved a quick detective. However, I was struggling to break it to her that I was planning to leave home.

'Belle, the professor is very pleased with you. She thinks you're quite capable, that you can manage by yourself for a bit, if I go away.'

'Where will you go?'

'To university. In Bristol. To do French. I will be away for a few weeks at a time, but back here in the holidays. There will be a year for me in France eventually, but you'll have got used to it by then. I can teach, or study there.'

Belle looked dubious.

'It won't be that bad,' I went on as sunnily as I could. 'I could have gone for a while this summer, you know, to look after children with a family there, like…' I bit my lip before I said the name Céline. 'Anyway, I turned that down.'

Belle received this in silence. Her small face looked uncomprehending.

'I won't be very far away, Belle. And remember that Meera's coming – she's spending a few months at the hospital where the professor is. She'll be here for you.'

At this, a small light came into Belle's eyes. 'Ah, Meera, that is good, that is good,' she murmured softly. 'I will be happy to see her.'

'Meera's doing well,' I said. 'She's got a promotion to work here, although I think she really wants to go to London. She's a child specialist – you remember. She wants to be a consultant.' I could see Belle's attention drifting, so I brought the focus back to her. 'And Bianca will look out for you too when I go, and John, of course.'

'They take me out for drives.'

'I know.'

'The top of their car comes off, and the wind goes through my hair!'

'John drives too fast.' I smiled. 'And it's called a convertible. Their one extravagance.'

'He speaks too loud also,' said Belle.

She was starting to subside. It was time to end the conversation.

I had planted the idea of leaving, and for the moment that was enough.

*

Ash had just learned to drive, and he came to pick me up in his parents' car so that we could drive out to the Abbey and take a brief walk around the gardens. They had gone on being a place of solace for me. It was to be a brief walk, because I was due to see Fairfax later – another fact I had kept from Belle.

It was a bright summer evening, and the roses bloomed in clouds of snow white and salmon pink. A parakeet squeaked indignantly above us, and I laughed, forgetting for a moment my heavy load.

'How did it go?' he asked.

We passed another couple, who were holding hands; I was glad that Ash knew me well enough never to hold mine.

'The appointment was good – the prof was pleased.'

'And uni?'

'I've put the idea in her head. She was reassured by the fact Meera's coming.'

'That's great, Mivvi – well done.'

I rested my head momentarily on his shoulder, acknowledging his praise, then caught sight on the other path of a young woman in a sun dress who was tugging at the lead of a recalcitrant dog. It made me smile.

'I'll miss you when you go,' Ash said.

'You're off too!' I replied.

'That won't stop me from missing you.'

'Well, maybe I'll miss you too.'

'Ooh, so grudging,' he teased. He was used to my reticent ways.

'We'll see each other in the holidays,' I said in a matter-of-fact way.

We were able to make light of our coming separation; the prospect of university felt only like a slight interruption.

He squeezed my hand and asked, 'What time are you meeting your dad?'

'Soon.' I sighed. 'I'm sorry, I'd love to spend longer, but I did say I'd go round tonight. I just wanted to see you after the prof, you know. Thank you, Ash.'

I spoke simply, but my heart was full of gratitude towards him. He was the only person who came close to knowing everything I had been through.

The sun was low in the sky, and the woman with the dog was

silhouetted ahead of us as we got to the gate. Her expensive perfume drowned out the scent of the roses.

'Mivvi! Ah, Mivvi, you don't recognise me!'

Céline's hair was cropped now and her skirt covered her thighs, but her soft voice was instantly recognisable. I blushed at the sight of her.

'Céline, hello, gosh, it's you! It's been a while – I thought you'd left?'

'I have,' she replied. 'I went home a year ago, but I am back for a few weeks for work. I am in fashion now, you know – and I came by to see Tabitha and Bree. This is their new dog, but he does not like me very much! It is so nice to bump into you like this!'

She spoke lightly, without embarrassment or reserve. *She doesn't know that I know*, I thought, *she can't do*. I only hoped my own heightened colour didn't betray me.

'How is your mother? Things were difficult, no?' Céline asked.

'Yes,' I replied evenly. 'They were, but now she's alright.'

'That's good, that's good,' murmured Céline, shooting a smile at Ash. But I was reluctant to introduce them; my feelings about Céline were too complicated.

'And your father? He is with Jade now, I hear?'

I nodded.

'Is he well?'

I stared at Céline, suddenly lost for an answer.

'I've been so rude,' said Ash, jumping in. 'I should have introduced myself. I'm Ash.'

They shook hands with mock formality, and I felt once again the absolute necessity of Ash.

'He's fine, Céline,' I said eventually. 'Yes, they are together, and

I see him every so often.' And then, not knowing why, I added, 'In fact, I'm going there now.'

Céline's smile brightened. 'Ah! How nice! Please say hello from me. In fact,' and she groped in her handbag for a card, 'it would be very nice to see him again, perhaps quickly before I go. You will contact me if it is possible? I leave in two weeks.'

I took the card with her phone number and nodded blankly. 'Let's see. Sometimes he's busy.'

'Of course, of course he is busy!' Céline's tinkling laugh sounded like sleigh bells in the summer heat.

I could not dislike her, try as I might.

'And you, Mivvi? Still writing plays? Remember how you used to?'

'Oh, no,' I replied dismissively. 'All that's over now.'

'You do some writing now and then,' said Ash, 'about things that happen.'

'Like a diary?' asked Céline. The dog was straining at the leash.

'No, no. Bits and pieces. Nothing special.'

'Whatever you do will be special,' said Céline warmly. 'You were always a very clever girl, Mivvi. Ah well – this dog does not want me to talk more! Perhaps you will ring me if you can? It was lovely to see you again, and to meet you, Ash. *Au revoir!* Come on then, Ares.'

And with a light goodbye flutter of her fingers, Céline was pulled by Ares out of the gate.

CHAPTER 2

I perched on the edge of the frayed armchair, as Jade hovered over a tray she had set on the coffee table.

'Shall I be mother?' she asked, with her usual infelicity. 'Do you take sugar, Mivvi? I always forget! Never? And milk? I've put it in a milk jug – I do think it tastes better that way. Fairfax, darling, do go and get some biscuits, would you, there's a pet.'

I felt queasy at her pretensions. Why did she insist on speaking in this ridiculous way – was it her idea of being a host?

As Fairfax left to find biscuits, I looked around to avoid having to make eye contact. The room was furnished in Fairfax style, full of second-hand furniture and fittings, but with feminine touches from the mistress of the house, chintz fabrics and artificial flowers. The mistress was fussing over the tray, equally unwilling to make conversation now that Fairfax was out of the room. The passage of time had failed to make relations easier.

We heard Fairfax's footsteps in the hall.

'It's a year since we moved in!' Jade said to him brightly. 'Isn't that something?'

Fairfax's smile couldn't disguise his unease. He and I usually met on neutral ground, but he seemed to need to subject me to these occasional, excruciating meetings. *He's trying to normalise things*, Ash said once, but none of us ever managed to act normally.

At least Fairfax looked better these days. The first time we met after that shattering evening, it was at a café on the edge of town, and I had barely recognised him, unshaven and suddenly jowly, his fine blond hair uncut and unkempt, an unfamiliar whiff of tobacco on his breath.

Now, he was groomed again and smart, although his golden hair had thinned some more, and he had a resigned and chastened air about him. He was wearing a suit, even though he was at home.

'You don't miss your old flat?' he said to Jade fondly, and she shook her head with vehemence.

'No way!' she declared. 'I've always loved the idea of a maisonette!'

When Belle first heard what they had bought, she had mocked what she thought was their affectation. 'He moves in with a maid, and they live in a mansion-ette!' she had cackled, and I had rolled my eyes. I couldn't bring myself to join in my mother's snobberies, but now, as I suffocated slowly in my surroundings, Belle was very present in my thoughts.

Fairfax kept darting nervous glances at each of us. There was a fixed smile on Jade's strained face, and every so often she laid claim to him, stroking his cheek or his arm. Once, she ran her fingers over his hair, and I saw Fairfax flinch. I had a sudden urge to laugh.

'You know, Mivvi, that Jade is going to train to be a teacher?' Fairfax said.

'I'm leaving the firm,' said Jade, patting Fairfax's knee.

'Oh,' I replied, stifling a yawn.

'I think I'm outgrowing it,' Jade tinkled, 'and it's time for a new challenge!'

Fairfax nodded. 'It's a great idea. A bigger salary too.'

There was a long pause.

'So, school's over then, Sweet Pea – I mean, Mivvi?'

I nodded.

'Still thinking of plans?' he asked weakly.

The question of Belle hovered in the air.

I nodded again.

'Tell you what,' he said, springing up energetically. 'It's a lovely summer evening. Why don't I walk you home? Well, part of the way anyway,' he added, as Jade's face tightened.

Jade got up to see us out, and she moved in close to Fairfax, resting the top of her head briefly under his chin, as if to highlight her vulnerability. I shot her a vicious smile and slipped out of the door with my father.

'What are your plans then?' he asked again, as we took the shorter route through Walton Park, disturbing a flock of Canada geese, which took flight and then settled on the other side of the lake. 'Is it definitely French?'

'Yes, it is.'

'I thought you might do law. I had hoped so.'

I sighed. 'I know. It's just not for me.'

'And you are really going to go off? I thought you might stay nearby.'

'Bristol's better. The course is better.'

He nodded, and then asked weakly, 'So, you think she'll be alright then?'

'Yes, I think so. I took her to see the doctor again – you know, the one who got her on the pills. She thinks she'll manage. And there are people to look out for her.'

This was our way: talking of Belle without saying her name. But she was ever present in our dealings with each other – her health, her well-being, the very fact of her always hovered between us. In the years since he had left, Fairfax had gone on quietly supporting us, and the satisfying thought crossed my mind that Jade must be displeased by this.

Tough, I said to myself, *we're still his responsibility.*

But Fairfax had never once mentioned my crucial achievement of getting Belle treatment. It was as if it were nothing to do with him.

We walked at a leisurely pace, Fairfax apparently in no hurry to get home. We found ourselves by the lake, and watched a solitary swan gliding majestically over the surface, ignoring the eider which disrupted the peace with its mocking cry. But Fairfax was about to shatter the tranquillity too.

'So, Mivvi,' he said, taking a deep breath, 'I've got something I want to talk to you about. Jade is keen, has been keen for a while, that we get married.'

'How can you – you're already married?'

He gulped. 'I would need a divorce, Mivvi.'

'She won't agree.'

'But we're separated, Mivvi, and it's permanent. In a few years' time, I can get a divorce myself. She would just be delaying the inevitable. There's no point.'

'Well, I don't think she'll agree,' I said. I still had no idea whether he had been thrown out or whether he had fled, but whichever it was, Belle would refuse point blank to help him now.

'You couldn't raise it with her,' he asked tentatively, 'could you?'

'Me?! What are you talking about, Fairfax? No!' I was startled by his audacity. 'Certainly not – I'm not going to do your dirty work for you.'

Fairfax looked abashed.

'Besides,' I said more softly, 'she's reached a level of stability over the last few months. That sort of talk might tip her over the edge.'

Fairfax nodded sadly. His big, bronzed face – craggy now in

mid-life – was despondent, but he let the matter drop. *I wonder what sort of row Jade will give him when he tells her that I wouldn't do it*, I thought spitefully. *I bet she put him up to it!*

I shoved my hands obdurately into the pockets of my jeans and felt the sharp edges of Céline's card. *So, Jade wants to be Mrs Fairfax does she? Ha, let her wait!*

*

When I returned home, the present Mrs Fairfax came to the door, looking wary.

'You were a long time,' she said uncertainly.

'Yes, well, I had some things to do.'

'Did you go to see that man and his concubine?' asked Belle, suddenly acid.

How on earth did she know?

'I am not so stupid, you know.'

'I did see them,' I said slowly, thinking a half-truth would be best. 'They were out for a walk, and we bumped into them.'

'What is he, all lovey-dovey then?'

'He's okay.' I did my best to sound neutral. 'Don't know how he stands her though,' I added.

Belle brightened, and I took some comfort from her pleasure. *We've got to get our happiness where we can*, I thought, *Fairfax certainly has.*

But still, I did wonder about his true state of mind. Was this life he had made with Jade really what he had wanted?

REETA CHAKRABARTI

Mombasa
September 30th 1968

It is done. I am married. I felt such deep love as we exchanged our vows. F looked as if he were drowning in his happiness, and I too was wanting to drown.

Ma wept through the ceremony and the reception, mainly for show. She kept wailing, my baby girl is going away! So ridiculous, such a hypocrite — really, she is so triumphant that I have got him. Baba was also wet-eyed, and he took too many drinks at the reception. John arrived on time to be best man. He loves F so much, and I think he is a good man, although he talks very loudly.

Ma told every guest that her Bela is going to Bilayti. Always so embarrassing! When the time comes, I will not miss her. All the time before the wedding, she was giving me lectures — don't be moody! Stir yourself! Why is she always so critical, who can tell? Maz also, but then he is just irritating with his teasing. I will not miss him either, or maybe only a very little bit.

I am happy alone — maybe they laugh at this, but now I will be happy with F. One small piece of advice I waited for from Ma — what will happen on the wedding night — but of course it did not come. I know what happens, but I wanted to see if she would tell me.

When I went with F to the marriage bed, covered in jasmine flowers, F was so gentle — it was not pleasure, but it was not pain. In the mirror, the next day I looked, and I could see no change, but now I am a fully married woman. Now I know something new.

In Ma's country, the married ladies wear the red sindoor in the parting of their hair, to show they are no more maidens. Perhaps I will also do this. Marked by F.

He leaves in a week with John, to prepare he says for my coming — then he will return for me. It is okay, I will miss him, but I can wait. More I want to get away from Ma and her hot tongue. But she and Baba look upset all the time that soon I will go. Baba at least is genuine. He said to F, 'Now it's you who must take care of her,' and F replied so sweetly, 'Oh I will! I will!' My heart melted. He seems a little worried about money, but Baba has given us a handsome sum, to get us started, he said.

F's fair skin is toasted in the sun, and his fair hair is white gold. He gorges in the day on mangoes and passion fruit, and in the night-time on me. I have the fairest husband — there was so much female jealousy at the wedding! Will we have a child? Maybe a boy with his father's smile and brown eyes like mine. A blend of us both, a brown-skinned honey-haired child.

CHAPTER 3

Although it was at the law firm that Jade had found her one and only true love, she was impatient to leave. She was bored, and work had become redundant as a meeting place now that she finally lived with Fairfax. But his barely disguised delight whenever they talked of her planned departure surprised and irked her; it was a tiny spot of discontent marring her otherwise perfect bliss.

'It's such a fantastic idea,' he said warmly, as they discussed her plans again. 'You'll be such a great teacher! When will you leave? Soon?'

Jade looked at him quizzically. She was learning to interpret his enthusiasms, and this one increasingly seemed excessive. 'Well, the deadline to apply is next week. I can't count on being accepted, but there's no reason why I shouldn't be. You seem very pleased?'

'Of course, I'm pleased! Why wouldn't I be?' Fairfax ran a hand over his immaculate hair. 'I want you to do well. You'll thrive in a different place.'

Jade gave him a cooler look than usual. 'It's not that you want me out of there, is it?'

'No, no,' he said, too quickly. 'Why would you think that? No, no, no!'

She was not wholly convinced. Since the torrid night of the party, they had both had to endure furtive glances from malicious colleagues, but unlike Fairfax, she had ignored them and held her head up high. Besides, the public disclosure of their love had ultimately enabled what months – years, even – of tears and pleading with him on her part had not; it had brought them together, and it aggravated her that time had not blunted his sense of shame.

Still, she knew his aversion to confronting problems directly, so she adopted a softer approach, sitting down close to him, swinging her legs over his, half sitting in his lap.

'I know it's all been very difficult,' she said, trying to nuzzle his neck.

He squirmed. 'Sorry!' he laughed. 'It tickles!'

'But it has been difficult for you, darling, I know that.'

He made no reply, and she could feel him tensing, just slightly.

'It's not been that bad, has it?' she ventured.

'I don't know,' he murmured eventually. 'I don't like to think about it.'

'I know it's hard,' she said, stroking his hand. 'But that night finally brought us out into the open. Not the way either of us wanted, I know, but here we are.'

He was silent again, doing nothing to dispel her suspicion that he would feel less mortified in the office once she had vacated it.

'Will you miss me?' she asked.

'I'll see you every night,' he said softly, on safer ground now.

'What about John? Has he thawed a bit?'

Fairfax sighed. She knew he hated talking about it. 'No, not really. He's still very cold with me. And Bianca is starchy and correct if I ever see her.'

Jade sniffed. Fairfax's oldest friends, who had once been her friends too, had sided with Belle. So much for loyalty.

'Anyway, once I qualify, we'll have more money,' she said, 'and that's something to look forward to.'

'We'll have less while you train,' said Fairfax, before adding hurriedly, 'but you must go ahead, of course.'

We have so little because you insist on paying for that woman and her daughter, muttered a voice inside Jade's head. She tried to ignore it.

'Fairfax, couldn't we go away for a while? A short holiday somewhere quiet? It would be so lovely.'

Fairfax looked doubtful. 'We've just bought this place. And we're about to lose your income too, for a while. Things are tight, as you know. I … lost some money a while ago, and…'

'What do you mean?' she asked.

'Oh nothing, it was a few years back. But we haven't got any spare right now.'

Jade felt another spot of discontent float to the surface and couldn't help herself. 'Of course, you're very generous to your daughter and your ex.'

'What does that mean?' he replied stiffly. 'I've got to support them. Mivvi is still in education, and Belle is pretty helpless.'

'But she *is* your ex,' Jade said pointedly, and then hurried on, 'I mean, of course you have to provide for Mivvi – I do appreciate that. But you are very generous to them.'

Then came another thought she could not stifle: *And you're not known for your generosity.*

They sat quietly for a few moments, in mutual knowledge of what would come next.

'Fairfax, you know I want us to get married.'

He sighed. 'We've talked about this before. She'll never agree to a divorce.'

'But you've left! You're not going back. I know she's unreasonable, but surely even she must see that?'

Fairfax looked weary. 'I can't force her, Jade, can I? If she won't, she won't. Once the five years are up, and we've been separated all that time, I can divorce her. But until then, I'm powerless. Anyway, what's the problem? We are together, aren't we? You've got me.'

And you've got me, thought Jade, *in every single way, in ways which mean we should be married.*

'Did you ask Mivvi to talk to Belle?'

'I did, and I got exactly the reaction I'd feared,' said Fairfax flatly. 'I should never have asked her. We should leave Mivvi out of this.'

Jade would have been delighted to leave Mivvi out of their lives completely. Her visits to them were torture, the air humming with their mutual dislike. Fairfax knew it and felt it, but they were all apparently hostage to these brittle occasions. Mivvi would perch on the edge of the armchair, ready to make her escape, darting critical looks around their new home.

Jade usually took revenge by claiming Fairfax as her own, moving in close when they rose to say goodbye, slotting herself under his chin so that she stood between them. She knew she was being immature and spiteful, but she had to signal her ownership and show who was in charge.

*

But she soon found that Mivvi knew how to stir the pot too.

Ten days after their last tense encounter, she arrived at the maisonette with an uninvited guest – a stranger who, Jade realised with a start, was the beaky woman from the fateful party. What she had seen between this woman and Fairfax had been forgotten in the aftermath of Belle's attack. But here at the door stood Mivvi with the very same person, draped in silky scarves and smiling shyly.

Mivvi played the dumb innocent. 'Look who I bumped into!

Céline's over for work, Fairfax, and she said she simply had to see you!'

Fairfax looked dumbstruck as they walked into the hall.

'We won't stay long,' said Mivvi brightly. 'Céline just wanted to say hi.'

Jade stared at them both with an animosity she couldn't hide as the newcomer settled herself in the best armchair and fixed Fairfax with a lighthouse smile. She had long, lanky legs, and she reeked of perfume.

'Good afternoon, Jade,' she said, with French formality. 'We bumped into each other once. And here we are again! I am Céline.'

She smiled up again at Fairfax, whose usual poise had deserted him. He cleared his throat several times and then asked Jade if she would make some tea.

'What, no whisky?' asked Céline with a light laugh, before turning to Jade. 'I'm not being serious – tea would be nice.'

Jade returned her look with icy courtesy and went into the kitchen. Moments later, she heard Fairfax and Mivvi whispering to each other in the hallway.

'Why have you brought that woman here?' he asked in a strangulated tone.

Mivvi sounded defensive. 'I'm sorry – she insisted, and I couldn't just put her off. But it's okay, isn't it? I thought you always liked her?'

You wicked cow, thought Jade, pouring boiling water over the teabags. She slammed some biscuits onto a plate.

'It's complicated, Mivvi,' he muttered, 'it's complicated.'

'Well, I gathered Belle didn't like her, but doesn't Jade either?' Mivvi's voice was a model of daughterly incomprehension.

Jade kicked open the kitchen door murderously and took through the tea.

*

'Who was she to you then?' Jade snapped, when Mivvi and Céline had left after a seemingly endless half hour. 'You never properly explained – tell me now!'

Fairfax busied himself with clearing away the tea. 'She's just someone we used to know – she did some childcare for us when Mivvi was small.'

'Why did she just show up like that? She seemed uncommonly pleased to see you.' Jade couldn't quite believe she was using this tone with Fairfax, but it spilled out of her uncontrollably.

'Are you being sarcastic?' he said tersely. 'If so, it doesn't suit you.'

'She just sat there, making eyes at you,' shot back Jade. She could feel herself becoming tearful. 'Who *was* she?'

'Jade, will you stop this? She's someone who used to help us out ages ago. Apart from that night at the party, I haven't seen her in years. She clearly just stopped by to see Mivvi, or bumped into her or whatever it was, and then tagged along here. That's all.'

'But she seemed so focused on you.' Jade tried to keep her voice steady. 'Was there something between you two?'

'Look,' he groaned, 'I haven't seen her in ages. Please stop.'

'What was going on that night at the party? Why have you never told me?'

Fairfax looked sullen.

'Was there something between you, Fairfax?' This time, Jade's voice was hard and sharp.

'Why are you making such a scene? What the hell does it matter? Alright, yes, if you really want to know, we fooled around a bit. But it was nothing – just a few casual encounters, that's all. And it was way before you, way before, so why does it matter?'

'But were you married to Belle?' asked Jade tightly.

'Well, if she was helping with childcare, it doesn't take a genius to work out that yes, I was,' muttered Fairfax. 'Look, I'm not proud of it, but it happened. I was under a lot of stress, and it was an escape. I shouldn't have, but it didn't mean anything. It was a brief infatuation, a few afternoons – that's all.'

Jade stared at him. 'Does Mivvi know?'

'God help me, I hope not! Please, Jade, let's just move on. Shall we? Can we? In fact, I need some air – I'm going out. See you later.' Fairfax grabbed his jacket, and swung out of the front door, slamming it as he left.

Jade stood looking at the shut door. She could feel her illusions falling away, as if a silken band covering her eyes were drifting slowly to the floor. She had assumed that only she had the power to rescue Fairfax from his unhappy marriage, that their relationship was unique and special, that it had to be her. She wondered dully if his casual infidelity to Belle meant that he might do the same to her.

Her settled sense of their joint selves had had solid foundations until now. Here it crumbled, like rock suddenly friable.

CHAPTER 4

'Here she is!' called Bianca from the front door, as she ushered in a windswept Belle. Meera brought up the rear, her hair tangled and tumbled. Belle's cheeks were flushed with fresh air and excitement, and Bianca's long earrings were caught up with her curls.

'Was that fun?' I asked Belle indulgently.

'Oh yes,' she replied. 'The wind was in my hair! But also, Bianca drives more carefully. It is good.'

'I know,' said Bianca, rolling her eyes, 'John's not half a demon on the road! Only when it's safe though.'

'His one weakness,' I said, with a grateful smile. Belle's weekly spin in the car with Bianca or John did her the power of good. She had just enough energy to chat for a short time, and then she could sink into the passenger seat and gaze out at the scenery without having to speak.

Even with Meera here, she stood passively between us, giving over the reins of the conversation.

'Why don't you go and sit down, Belle?' said Meera. 'You look tired. Mivvi will see us out.'

Belle turned away submissively.

'How did you both find her?' I asked, after she had gone.

Meera nodded thoughtfully. 'She is very docile now. Quiet and calm. Sometimes even reflective. She mentions Mombasa sometimes, and she told me today that she was born in India.'

'Was she?' I asked, surprised. 'But I thought my grandparents got married in Mombasa?'

'They did, but they went back to Calcutta when your grandmother was pregnant so that she could have her baby there,' said Bianca. 'That was the tradition apparently.'

'I never knew,' I said, smiling. 'Whenever I spoke about her when I was small, I used to say she was from Africa and India, and it turns out that I was right!'

Bianca put her arm around me. 'You getting ready to leave?'

'Yes,' I said, 'pretty much.'

'Got your place all lined up? Bristol, isn't it? Clever girl!'

'I have, and I'm not particularly, but thank you.'

'And Ash, where's he going? Is it Edinburgh?'

I nodded and then asked tentatively, 'And you are really fine to keep an eye on Belle, the two of you and John?'

'Of course! Don't be silly, love. As if you have to ask! You know we are,' said Bianca. 'We'll be a holy little trinity – don't you worry about her.'

'I know, I know. Thank you.' I felt a lump in my throat. 'It's just that her life is so limited.'

'But she's calm,' said Meera. 'She's calm and she's quiet, and that is a good enough life. A good enough life for Belle.'

The two women headed towards the front door, but Meera turned back to me.

'Oh, by the way, I almost forgot! Your uncle Maz is here and was wondering if he might be able to see you?'

'Really?' I asked. 'Why doesn't he just ring? He's got our number.'

'Yes, it's odd, isn't it? I think he was worried he might get Fairfax on the line, which is strange given that he doesn't live here anymore! Anyway, he did seem a bit nervous.'

'How did he get your number anyway?'

'He said it was the old Asian tom-tom,' laughed Meera, and I rolled my eyes. 'Yes, well, you know what he's like. He'll have got it from family in India – my uncle and aunty used to know your grandparents when they were kids. It's a small world, in some ways. I don't know why he doesn't ring you directly. Anyway, shall I let him know that he can turn up?'

I smiled. 'He doesn't usually ask for permission. But yes, he can. Thanks for the warning.'

*

After Meera and Bianca left, I went to find my mother in the front room. She was huddled in an armchair, looking absent-mindedly at her hands. Her body was still, apart from the tremor in her foot; that was part of her now, just as the voices had been part of her before. I had never broached the topic of Belle's illness with her, but something about my conversation with our two friends emboldened me.

'They think you're doing well,' I said.

Belle smiled but said nothing.

'Belle. Mum, can I ask you something?' I tried to speak with delicacy. 'Do you feel better? The voices have gone, haven't they? You told the professor they have.'

Belle's eyes widened, but she nodded.

'What was it like? Can you tell me?'

Belle fidgeted in her seat. 'It was no good. It was angry voices. I tried to keep them away. They made me afraid.'

'I see. Yes, I can imagine you were afraid. But you know, you used to make me afraid.' I said this as gently as I could. 'The way you behaved. I know it wasn't your fault, though.'

Belle sat looking defenceless in her chair, like a chastised child.

'Well, well,' she said, as if these things just happened. 'Well, well.'

We sat in silence for a few moments, and then I said, 'I'm only sorry we didn't get help for you sooner.'

At this, Belle sat up. 'Who is we? Your father?'

'Well, yes.'

'That man, he does what he wants,' she observed. The tremor in her left foot grew more pronounced.

'I know. But he did look after me when you were sick.' I took care to use the past tense.

'He looked after you as he chose.' Belle's eyes gleamed. 'He does his own pleasure, not for anyone else. Mr Big Look at Me. Always free of duty.'

'It was difficult for him,' I said. 'It was difficult for all of us.'

'Not so difficult for Mr Big Man. He only cares for the big stage, not for the home.'

I changed the subject, feeling foolish for imagining I might have a reckoning with Belle. There was too much bitterness, and she remained too unstable.

Any proper evaluation of the past would have to come from me, and from me alone.

*

It was in this frame of mind that I started to wonder when Maz would appear. In the two years since the party, he had rung me twice – two hurried phone calls which I suspected were made at my grandfather's behest. Maz had given me news for Belle of her mother, who was sickly; and he had been solicitous in his way, each time trying to offer me money. It had made me smile that Maz who was always after something should suddenly be so set on giving help – help which I refused as we had plenty from Fairfax. But if anyone could tell me more about Belle, it was him.

I was unsure exactly what I wanted to ask him, but the knowledge that he was around made my need to see him grow. Meera gave me the number he had left, and I rang several times, leaving messages on an anonymous answerphone.

I had all but given up on him when one afternoon, in that long hot summer of 1990, the doorbell rang, and there he was on the front step, leaning lazily against the wall.

'Hey, doll,' he drawled. 'Can I come in?'

He had filled out since I had last seen him and glowed with a new air of prosperity. I took in his slim-cut suit and slip-on Italian shoes, which he wore without socks. His cream linen shirt was fashionably crumpled, and he had applied enough aftershave to rival Fairfax.

I led the newly stylish Maz into the front room and at his request poured him a large whisky from a bottle that Fairfax had left behind.

Belle was upstairs, but I delayed fetching her. I wanted some time alone with him.

He sighed with theatrical pleasure at the drink, and slouched on the sofa with exaggerated ease, his legs wide open, his arm thrown expansively over the back of the sofa, as if entirely at home.

'So, your daddy gone, eh?'

'Yes,' I replied calmly. 'You know he has. It's been two years.'

He drummed the chair with his hand. 'Oh well, that's true, it has.'

'Meera said you wanted to see me,' I said, feeling there was no point in wasting time.

He nodded, frowning slightly. 'You managing?' he asked, looking at me more closely.

'Yes, we're alright. He provides for us, so yes, we're managing.'

'You okay for money?'

'Yes, like I said, we're fine. Fairfax has gone on paying for us.'

Maz nodded slowly. His face, so often clownish, looked set and serious. 'I'm doing better now, you know,' he went on. 'I had a tough few years, relying on the old man – your grandfather, working in his business. But then I struck out on my own, and it's all come good.'

'I see,' I said, wondering why he was telling me all this.

'And I thought the chances would be here in the UK, but they're not! They're in India!' Maz's face shone with pride at his own success. 'Lots of exports you know, textiles, coffee. They're opening up, and so are we!'

'I'm happy for you, Uncle,' I said simply.

'Hey, no Uncle please, that makes me feel old! Call me Maz! You call your old ma Belle, so call me Maz.'

'Maz it is,' I said, smiling.

'So, Mivvi, I will ask one more time, let me help you out, give you some of my success.'

'No, Maz, really there's no need.' I was amused at his persistence, but it stirred a memory of something else: that receipt I had found among Fairfax's papers, noting a large sum transferred to Maz.

'Maz, I know this is an odd question, but did Fairfax ever give you any money?'

Maz looked blank. 'Not that I recall, doll. Not for me.' He picked out an eyelash that had fallen into his glass.

I let the matter drop – I could hardly reveal that I'd been snooping. It was just another of the many things I didn't understand.

Maz took another long sip of his whisky. 'What about your ma? How's her health?'

'She's alright.'

FINDING BELLE

A scene from years previously flashed into my mind: Belle on the bed beating Fairfax with her legs, Maz's fleeting shadow at the door.

'Her health is better. She's more stable.'

'Is that because he's buggered off? Sorry, doll,' he added, as I shifted uncomfortably. 'I know he's your pa and all. But she's quieter without him, eh?'

'She just seems to have reached an equilibrium, I guess. She's doing well.'

'Good, good,' he murmured. But he did look culpable. *As well he might*, I thought. He had never done anything to help Belle.

'I wanted to talk to you, Maz.'

'I know, doll, I got your messages. I wanted to talk to you, and you wanted to talk to me. So how can I help?'

'I've been wondering about Belle. You know, how she was before she got ill. Who she was.'

Maz let out a short laugh. 'Hey, these are big questions! Who she was, I cannot say. But how she was ... well, you know, she was alright, she was like you and me. Quiet always, I guess. A little turned in on herself. But she was alright.'

'Did you get on with her?'

'No!' He laughed again. 'But I was her kid brother. What do you expect?'

'She told me once that you were painful,' I said with a wry smile. 'A long time ago.'

'And you know what, she was probably right!' He drained the whisky and smacked his lips with pleasure.

'What happened to her, Maz?'

'I don't know, doll. She came here, and it all went wrong. Why, I don't know.'

'Was there ever any sign that she might be ... you know, unstable?'

These were direct questions, but I felt that I could be straightforward with him.

'No,' he said, shaking his head. 'I would not say so.'

'And there was no one else in the family who was ill in the same way?'

He shook his head again. 'My grandma, yes, but that was only in her old age.'

'Did you worry about her? Belle, I mean.'

'Our daddy did. Worried a lot.'

'And your mother?'

'No, well, Bela and our mother, they never – how to put it – they never saw eye to eye.'

'Why not?' I asked.

Maz scratched his head and took a while to reply. 'Your grandma has always been quite critical, critical of all people, but most of all of Bela. Bela could do no right. I think your grandma didn't like having a girl. I don't know – I'm no Dr Freud. But Bela grew to be beautiful, and then your grandma hoped for a good marriage for her. A rich marriage.'

'To a rich man?'

'Aye, yes, indeed. And that's what she thought Fairfax was. My daddy knew your Fairfax's daddy and the introduction came that way. Fairfax Senior gave the impression that he was richly endowed. But then they fell out, Fairfax and his daddy.'

I listened intently. I had never heard about this estrangement before, although I vaguely knew that Fairfax held some resentment against his father.

'What happened?' I asked. 'Why did they fall out?'

Maz shrugged. 'Of that, I am not entirely sure,' he said slowly. 'But I do know of your grandma. She thought our lives would be enriched too by this marriage. Rich son-in-law, richer parents-in-law. We all thought that. But it didn't turn out that way.'

'That's not Fairfax's fault, though.' I had spent so long being angry at my father that it felt strange to defend him.

Maz looked non-committal. 'He didn't bring the money my ma had expected. Then she hoped he would make his own money and help. That didn't happen either. Ah, well.'

It was all mystifying. I sipped my tea and turned the conversation back to my mother. 'Have you worried about Belle, Maz?'

Maz looked me straight in the eye. 'I have,' he said steadily. 'I have, and I am pleased that you have helped her. So, I have wanted to help you.' He shifted about in his chair.

So he knew about Belle's treatment; Meera must have told him.

'We don't need that,' I said. 'But thank you.'

We were silent for a moment, and I thought again how much he had changed. Even the music of his voice was different, his accent softer. And he spoke much more fluently than Belle.

'You speak differently from my mother,' I said abruptly. 'Sorry, random remark – but you do.'

Maz grinned in his old wolfish way.

'Your ma can also speak like me. Or she used to. Maybe she's sat there too much in her head. It does funny things to you, doesn't it?'

As he spoke, Belle came down the stairs. She must have heard us. When she walked into the room, I was struck by their resemblance to each other now. Belle stood in the doorway uncertainly, and stiffly received the hug which Maz enveloped her in. I could see she was pleased to see him, but spontaneous affection was beyond her.

'So, brother, you are here after a long time,' she said, smiling at him wanly.

'I've been keeping tabs on you, Bela, don't you worry. I know you are in good hands, now.'

'And how are you here?'

'You know, I travel a lot, and I thought I'd stop by. I made some connections in Birmingham, and I came to look them up. Came to look you up too.'

Belle eyed him curiously. 'You have not been so much interested in me, Maz,' she said after a pause.

'I did my best, Bela, under the circumstances.' He spoke softly, but I saw that he wouldn't meet her eye.

'You are happy at my misfortune?' she asked, without reproach.

'No!' he cried. 'No, Bela, no! Whatever I thought of that man, no! We have worried about you.'

'Baba has worried about me,' said Belle sadly.

'We all have.' Maz spoke with gentle sincerity, but I had a nagging suspicion that he was keeping something back.

Still, I found it touching to see them, brother and sister, one prospering, the other surviving, both still able to reach each other after many intervening years.

'How is Baba?' asked Belle, looking forlorn. Maybe she was able to have family feeling after all.

'He's alright,' said Maz. 'Still fit and strong, goes for his morning walk every day, does his yoga. The business is not going so well. Sometimes he talks about going back to India.'

'Why would he do that?' I asked.

'He says he would be happier among his own. He loves Mombasa, but things changed some years back, just before you were born. Indians were suddenly not so welcome. Perhaps we were sometimes to blame too,' he added reflectively.

'And Ma?' asked Belle.

'She is not so good. You know she had a stroke last year. It was a small one, but it has affected her.'

'Oh,' said Belle. A spasm of pain crossed her face, and I wondered if it was her mother's illness or the dark memories of the past that caused it.

'Do you miss Mombasa, Bela?' asked Maz gently.

'Sometimes,' she said, looking wistful. 'But I do not miss Ma much.'

Maz chuckled. 'India is better – there's a lot happening there. You should come.'

Belle smiled pleasantly. We all knew that her travelling days were over.

I left them to talk for a while, contented to see my mother relax and reminisce, and grateful to Maz for making the time. If Belle could maintain this level of stability, I felt I really could leave for university without concern.

After an hour, I heard Maz stirring and went back downstairs.

'Mivvi, I am off. Well, Bela, it has been good to see you. You're looking alright. Your daughter's a good girl. I'll tell Baba I found you well.'

'Okay,' said Belle. He hugged her again, and this time, she softened into his embrace. 'Okay, Maz, okay, go well.'

As I went to see Maz out, I had a sudden impulsive thought. 'Maz, should I come to Mombasa? Should I come and see my grandparents?'

He looked at me levelly. 'No-oo,' he replied, exhaling softly. 'Mivvi, doll, you're a sweetheart, but it's complicated. Besides, your grandma is not in the best of health. I'll tell them though. I'll tell them what a sweetie pie you are.'

He grazed my cheek with his lips, and that was the last I saw of him.

CHAPTER 5

At last, the day came for me to leave for Bristol. Ash had left a few days beforehand, and I had wished him an overly emotional goodbye, struggling to fight back tears. We had agreed not to visit each other during termtime, but I was sceptical about whether our resolve would hold. In an attempt to keep things light, we teased each other with threats of going off with someone else, but the thought of gawky, geeky Ash with another girl was so impossible it made me smile. He really was mine.

I busied myself with my final packing. Tabitha, who was off to Oxford, had offered to help me, but I had already had to endure her condescension about Bristol, so I gently refused. Fairfax had bought me my train ticket and given me extra money for taxis at each end. Despite everything, I found the gesture touching, because I knew he thought taxis an unnecessary expense.

I had said goodbye to him the previous day, and we had hugged each other with genuine feeling.

Now, I got together my suitcase and a small backpack, trying to minimise what I would have to carry. Belle was drifting around the house, disconnected from my activity.

As I padlocked the case, I heard the taxi draw up outside.

'Belle, I'm off,' I called, as my mother came down the stairs.

'Where are you going?' she asked vaguely.

FINDING BELLE

'You know, I'm off to university. To Bristol. I told you.'

Belle looked blank. 'Oh, okay, well, goodbye then.'

That was it. No affection, no concern. *Well, what did you expect?* I thought bitterly, feeling foolish for harbouring the hope that I might get a normal, loving reaction. I felt my chest tighten with the suppressed pain that I always carried around, usually so tamped down, but now taking me over. *Belle. Mama.*

I stepped into the car, willing the habitual numbness to return.

*

To my surprise, though, as I settled into university life, I began to receive occasional letters from Belle, written in her distinctive spidery hand. Despite their bad grammar, they were unexpectedly fluent, and at times almost conversational. She had nothing much to say, but contact was clearly important to her, and she was able to write with an elegance that belied her speech. Her weekly routine was unchanged – Meera, John, Bianca, the car rides – but at least it was stable.

Fairfax would phone me occasionally, but he never sent a handwritten letter, and I marvelled at my mother's well-hidden talent.

During term, I managed to shrug off some of the burdens of home. Ash and I quickly broke our resolution and visited each other, able now to be together on a more adult basis, without having to contend with parents and family. Fairfax came to see me once in my first year, his face bursting with pride at my undergraduate self, my rejection of Law all but forgotten. He seemed to have recovered some of his natural flair.

When I returned home in the vacations, I found Belle calm and unchanged. Ash and I had by now abandoned any pretence that we were not committed to each other, and I felt that for the first time in my life, a balance had been achieved, despite its competing tensions.

In my third year at university, I went abroad to study in Nice. The glamorous city held out the promise of good times, but the other students felt much younger than me, and I found myself more alone and detached than in Bristol, almost by choice.

I buried my loneliness in my work and in books, ploughing slowly through piles of new novels, borrowing liberally from the university library, and working my way through the nineteenth and twentieth centuries on park benches and in gardens, or propped up under a parasol on the beach. Novels, I concluded, were invariably about unhappy families, and the infinite ways in which human beings torment each other.

My reading gave me more language to describe my own unhappy situation: Fairfax was solipsistic and a narcissist, and Jade opportunistic and unscrupulous, words that I could hiss in my head. Meera was altruistic, and John and Bianca benevolent.

But Belle – what was Belle?

Before I left, Ash had given me one of the region's most famous novels, *Tender is the Night*, which I devoured in two sittings on the beach. I thought at length about its portrayal of the mentally ill Nicole, based on Fitzgerald's real-life wife Zelda, and wondered whether here I had finally found words to describe Belle.

Nicole suffers a deep trauma in her childhood and goes through periods of insanity which are hushed up by her husband, Dick Diver – but Nicole slowly recovers, and then it is Dick who deteriorates – so, I thought, no ultimate parallel there.

I spent time re-reading the two novels that Ash had given me for my sixteenth birthday, and I lingered over one of them for days, asking myself again whether here I had found Belle.

FINDING BELLE

I started to write down thoughts and memories in the notebook I still had from Meera, prompted by my reading to record random stories from my past.

*

Then, one afternoon when I was sitting in my room, deep in another book, Meera rang.

'Mivvi, my dear, I'm so glad I've caught you! Now, I don't want you to be too alarmed, but it's your mother. She's alright, but there was an accident, and I felt I had to let you know.'

I almost dropped the phone. 'Jesus, what happened – is she okay?'

'Yes, she is – it could have been much worse. She was cooking, and you know how unmindful she is – we think she left one of the gas hobs on. The sleeve of her dress caught fire! Thank goodness John had just arrived – he grabbed a blanket and threw it around her. Her arm has sustained some burns, but she's alright. She's out of hospital now, and resting at home. John and Bianca are with her. So please don't worry too much. She's on the mend now.'

I felt faint at the news, it was just the sort of accident I had feared.

'I'll come home,' I said immediately.

'You don't need to – she's alright, you know. And we can look after her.'

'I know, and thank you so much, but I need to see her. Tell her I'm coming. I hope Fairfax hasn't been in touch?'

'No, he hasn't, and I wouldn't tell her if he had,' said Meera. 'You know how she can react to any mention of him.'

*

Within hours, I was on a plane, and late that night, I walked back into my home. Bianca was there in the front room, her hands clutched together as if in prayer.

'Mivvi, love!' she cried, and the two of us embraced. 'You needn't have come, but it's lovely to see you.'

'Where is she?' I asked. 'In her bedroom?'

Bianca nodded, and I went upstairs.

Belle's room was gloomy. A bedside lamp was on, but it did little to light up the obscurity. Belle was lying in bed, one arm in a bandage, her head lolling to one side, a dull glaze in her eyes. My heart sank.

'Belle, Mum, it's me.'

Belle fixed her eyes on me, as if struggling to concentrate. I wondered if she had been sedated.

'Mivvi,' said Belle, in the disembodied voice she put on when she couldn't focus. 'Mivvi, I was on fire.'

'I know, Mum – it must have been horrible. Are you alright?'

Belle giggled softly. 'Oh yes, I'm alright. I'm always alright. Little Bela, she'll always be alright.'

I wondered if Belle had remembered to take her pills. Her eyes had a feverish quality, as if they might start to dart around, a sure sign that one of her old fits was imminent.

'Mum, I think you need to take one of your pills – you know, not for the burns, but the other ones.' I rummaged in the bedside drawer and found them. 'Have you had one? You need two a day, remember?'

'I don't know,' said Belle. 'I don't think so. I had this accident.'

I poured her some water, and she obediently swallowed her pill, then settled back against her pillow, smiling weakly. I felt for her uninjured hand and held it lightly.

There was a knock at the door. Bianca put her head round, looking worried.

'Mivvi,' she whispered, 'Fairfax is here! He wants to see her. But I don't think it's a good idea at all!'

I gasped. 'Bianca, no! No, he can't come in!'

'No, no, I thought not.' She made as if to scurry off, still murmuring *no*.

But he was already behind her at the door, anxiously running a hand through his hair, his face riven with concern.

'Belle, Belle, it's me. I had to come. I know what you think of me, but are you alright?'

He got no further.

Belle began to gasp, her eyes bulging, her nostrils flaring. I shrank back as my mother began to scream.

'You! You! You *saitan*! How dare you show your face here! Who do you think you are – you'd betray me with that woman, would you? Get out, get out!'

Bianca grabbed Fairfax and shoved him out of the door and down the stairs. I could hear her scolding him – 'I told you, such a stupid idea, all wrong' – and the low rumble of his voice in reply.

Belle slumped back against her pillow, exhausted by her passion.

I stared at the empty space where Fairfax had been, incredulous that he could be so obtuse. Just because he had moved on with his life, he had the presumption to assume that Belle had too! As if she had anything to move on to! Fairfax, who nursed such deep grudges, but expected sad, mad Belle, to somehow forgive him.

Unless I had got it all wrong. Was it possible that he still harboured feelings for her?

I looked in stunned silence at Belle, whose face was stony and pitiless, her eyes also fixed on the space Fairfax had just vacated. Any semblance of madness had evaporated, and in its place was a look of profound and unalloyed hatred.

REETA CHAKRABARTI

Mombasa
September 15th 1968

Getting married is an exhausting business. There is so much to be done: choosing the most sumptuous sari, deciding the guest list, the menu, the invitations, and all this before the actual ceremony! Thank goodness it is a small wedding. F says now that his father will not come — there will be no one from his side. His mother has passed away, and he only has cousins who live far. But he says his friend John is in India and may come to be his best man. I hope so. The servants are making such a fuss about getting the house ready for the reception, I am almost looking forward to no longer having to deal with them.

F and I went to the photographer's studio to have some portraits taken, and we will have more after we are married; it is a nice idea of Ma's. I put my hair up to show off the earrings she gave me, and I could feel Fairfax desperate to kiss my neck. We posed well together, I could tell. The photographer was most admiring. Fairfax is only slightly taller than me, but he looks strong and capable in the pictures, and barely able to hide his delight at our upcoming union.

I try to withhold myself a little. Where will my power lie over the years if I give it all away immediately?

CHAPTER 6

Jade strode confidently through the school gates, with the glad feeling that each new morning had brought her since the start of term. She felt the wind lifting her freshly bobbed hair, and adjusted the stiff new leather bag to sit comfortably over her shoulder. It was a present from Fairfax to celebrate her new job, and felt like a pleasing sign of her newfound success. She had spent so many years preparing and planning for this, and here she was in exactly the right work, teaching exactly the right subject. Maths was so logical; there was always a correct answer.

She was an assertive teacher with an easy talent for crowd control, and she had already won the grudging respect of even the most recalcitrant pupils.

'Morning, miss.'

'Morning, Jake. But do up your tie.'

It was pay day, her first since starting as a teacher just a few weeks ago, and it added to her buoyant mood. She had never had so much money before, and it had come at just the right time, what with Fairfax cutting down his working hours. 'To give younger colleagues a chance,' he had declared magnanimously, and Jade had acknowledged this with a quiet smile. She never embarrassed him with reminders of the past, and if he wanted to spend less time in the office, she wouldn't dream of asking why.

Her only worry had been that this was the school where Roy had worked, and she had feared running into him – but to her relief it emerged that he was long gone. As a forward-facing person, she didn't like to dwell on the past.

But now, as she stepped into the staff room, the past loomed up before her in the shape of a petite woman with feathery, chestnut-coloured hair. She walked towards Jade with her arms outstretched, and a beaming smile.

'Helen!' gasped Jade in amazement. 'My goodness, Helen! What are you doing here?'

Helen held her in a warm embrace, and when she finally pulled away, Jade saw tears in her bright eyes. Helen, so sickly in her youth, looked blooming with health and radiant at finding her old friend.

'I suspected it was you,' Helen said, her voice husky with happiness. 'I'm a teaching assistant, and when the headteacher said your name, I had a funny intuition! But I told her not to say anything. I've been wondering when we'd run into each other – I wanted it to be a surprise.'

'Well, it really is,' replied Jade with wonder. Now that it was sinking in – her only real friend from childhood right in front of her – she felt a slight prickling of unease. She had remade herself so successfully. She didn't want anything from the past to get in the way. But she had always admired Helen. What was there to feel nervous about?

They agreed to meet the following day after school in the café at Walton Park, and after an hour of catching up and reminiscing, Helen took Jade's hand in hers.

'We had some tough times, eh? But we've come through it all, and now look at you, a proper teacher. And married?'

'Not married,' said Jade, with a sniff. 'Not yet anyway. But hopefully soon. And you?'

'No, not me,' said Helen, with a modest shrug. 'No one on the scene. But I'm happy enough. I'm only part-time at the school – it gives me time for other things. I play in a band, and I work some afternoons in the gift shop at the Abbey. It's a charity, and they need volunteers. It keeps me out of trouble!' She flashed a brave smile, and Jade felt the slightest hint of satisfaction at knowing herself more secure than her old friend.

'You were always resilient, Helen,' she said warmly, trying to compensate. 'And determined to be cheerful, however hard it was.'

The two of them fell silent for a moment, remembering.

'I used to look up to you so much,' Jade confessed. She felt bashful at her admission, but confident enough to make it.

'Get away!' said Helen, laughing, but she looked pleased. 'Well, the home was okay wasn't it, better than the foster families, where I knew I didn't belong. At the home, none of us belonged, and so we all did!'

'Yes, too true.' Jade nodded. 'And you were everyone's big sister! That's how I saw you anyway. Tell me,' she went on 'did you ever try to contact your birth parents? I knew you wanted to.'

Helen made a face. 'My mother, yes, but it was a big mistake. She didn't want to know. My father, I've no idea about. It hurt at the time, but I'm over it now. It's fine. What about you?'

'No,' said Jade, decidedly. 'I never wanted to, and I never will. I'm not interested.'

Helen smiled. 'Always living in the present, Jade.'

'Yes, maybe,' Jade replied with a shrug. 'It's served me well enough.'

'Sounds like you've got someone else helping you now though,' said Helen slyly. 'What's he like? I've heard he's very handsome?'

Jade felt a jolt of surprise. She had brought Fairfax into the staffroom once or twice, and there had been a small flutter of interest among her colleagues. But she hadn't realised they had been the subject of discussion.

'Ah, there's been talk of him then, has there?'

Helen nodded. 'Yes! You know how people are.'

'Well, he's...' Jade tailed off, wondering how to summarise Fairfax. 'He's ... well, he's wonderful.'

Helen burst out laughing. 'That was very unfair, asking you to sum up your partner!' She squeezed Jade's arm affectionately. 'I'm happy for you, Jade. Not everyone finds true love. You're a lucky woman.'

Jade nodded. She felt, on balance, that she was.

'I mean it, Jade – you really have been very lucky!'

Jade looked at Helen's beaming face and saw only the purest goodwill shining from her clear green eyes. Her friend was evidently delighted at her great good fortune. But disconcertingly, Jade couldn't make an unequivocal reply, and she battled to quell the spot of discontent threatening to surface.

'There's a stepchild, I hear? Your beau told the head there was,' Helen went on. 'Well, I know you're not married, but he's got a daughter?'

Now Jade did feel a stab of annoyance. Being talked about was one thing, but being linked in the public imagination with Mivvi was another matter entirely.

'Oh, we don't see much of her,' she said airily. 'They're not very close.'

'A pity,' said Helen, in her affable way. 'Otherwise you'd have had a ready-made family.'

Jade moved quickly to close off this line of enquiry. 'I'm not into children. In the classroom is fine, but I've never thought of myself as the family type.'

'Well, you never know,' replied Helen. 'You just never know.'

REETA CHAKRABARTI

Mombasa
August 25th 1968

I am to be married. What strange and sweet words to write. Our romance has been short and intense, a whirlwind courtship. The future that F has drawn for me so confidently, I will now share with him. I cannot say I know this man well. But I feel I see in him an open heart and a good nature. He is ambitious, and maybe I am part of his desire for success. But also, he does desire me for myself — that I can see in his every look and touch. Soon I will know him as I've known no other man. I wonder at it, but I don't fear it.

His proposal was old-fashioned, so touching! He spoke to Baba before asking me, and yes, he went down on one knee. I am not easily moved, but the sight of this beautiful man gazing up at me imploringly touched me to the core.

Baba is becoming morose at the idea that I will be far away in F's country, and even Ma is sounding gruff, her way of expressing emotion. But I don't fear this either. Ma says that over there, there will be no one to help, I will have to do all the cooking and cleaning and washing. So, Ma, I said to her, shall I say no to him because I can't take a servant? She was quiet then. Baba, I think, has been explaining to F that our finances are not as strong as they were a few years ago, but F is too besotted to pay much attention. I think Baba exaggerated his success to F Senior when they were in correspondence. Well, that is what men do.

F is full of ideas and plans. We will go and live in a new town, he says, far away from his own father, who will not be at the wedding. Something

FINDING BELLE

has happened but I do not know what. I asked Baba and he told me not to worry. Just be happy, Bela, he said, and I am. I do not want to pry.

F is a qualified lawyer, and intends to join an up and coming practice. This is the way he talks, up and coming, on the go, seizing opportunities, grabbing life. His jewel-like eyes glow and I am carried along by him. Ma has told me I will have to shape up — no more sitting around daydreaming, Bela, she says, as if I too will always have to be rushing around. I won't. I don't think he expects it of me. I will be at home for him, being his wife. He will take care of me. He is a dependable man. I can see that.

And he needs me. I can see that too.

CHAPTER 7

Jade had given up trying to persuade Fairfax to get a divorce. Her repeated pleas got her nowhere, and she feared that her reproaches were reminiscent of their early days together. But just as she became resigned to waiting until the final hour, the unexpected news came that Belle had suddenly relented.

'What do you mean she said yes?' she asked Fairfax, her heart leaping in wonderment.

He shrugged. 'Well, she has – I don't know why. But I thought you'd be pleased?' He looked rueful as he said this.

Jade flung her arms around his neck, her face shining. 'Ah, of course I am. It's wonderful! It really is! I'm just, I suppose, surprised. I thought she was just going to string us along until the bitter end!'

Fairfax looked uneasy. He never joined in her outbursts against Belle, rare though they were.

'Has it got something to do with that accident?' she asked. He had mentioned that Belle had suffered some kitchen mishap.

Fairfax shrugged again. 'Maybe. I don't know why it would.'

'You didn't go and see her, did you?' she asked, struck by a sudden jealous fear.

'Me? No! Oh no, no, certainly not!'

He was so emphatic that she was reassured. She laid her head on his shoulder. 'So,' she said softly, 'aren't you going to ask me to marry you?'

This time he didn't miss a beat. 'Jade Evans,' he whispered in her ear, 'will you marry me?'

'Yes!' she cried. 'Oh yes, yes! Yes, I will! Fairfax, yes!'

*

The time was long past for a white wedding, so she rushed to book them a registry office ceremony as soon as Fairfax's divorce came through. She wanted to formalise their relationship quickly before there could be any impediment, fearing that she might somehow be denied at the eleventh hour. Her delight at learning she would finally get her longed-for prize was marred only by anger that Belle had kept her in suspense for so long.

When the day came, she stood solemnly next to Fairfax before the registrar, feeling herself a picture in cream lace, with a braid of pink flowers in her hair which Helen had carefully fashioned for her. Fairfax wore a beige linen suit with a pink tie that matched the flowers. He looked handsome as sin, Helen told him laughingly, as she dusted a fleck off his lapel.

Jade felt giddy and light-headed, and the registrar's words momentarily faded as she remembered a voice from the past: Maz, at the fateful party, telling her in his insinuating way that his sister had married well. Why this memory reared up now, she couldn't say.

But then Fairfax turned to her with the ring and she was brought out of her reverie and back to this moment, the culmination of all her desires. They kissed chastely but tenderly, and then it was done.

I have married him, she thought with both joy and disbelief, *I really have married him.*

The reception was small, just Helen and a few colleagues from school. The invitation was for adults only; Jade hadn't wanted any whining children spoiling their big day.

Helen sidled up to her over the champagne. 'It's just friends from school then?' she asked. 'No one from his side?'

'No, he thought about it,' Jade said casually, 'but his parents have passed away, and he only has cousins in Canada. He really wanted to make it my day.'

John and Bianca had been invited, but they had sent their excuses, which Fairfax had accepted without demur. Jade was unconcerned; the couple belonged to a previous era. There would be new friends for them now, should they want them.

'And why is his daughter not here?' asked Helen. She had drunk her champagne too fast, and her flushed cheeks made her look like a fresh apple.

'On holiday with the boyfriend,' said Jade shortly, trying not to show her relief. Mivvi still had a year to go at university but had almost dropped out after her mother's kitchen drama. Fairfax and the doctor Meera had persuaded her not to, but at least she was far away now.

'I see,' said Helen sympathetically. 'Well, hopefully Fairfax doesn't mind too much.'

Fairfax is also relieved, thought Jade, satisfied that they had this in common.

'Oh no,' she said airily. 'He just wants her to lead her life.'

Helen hiccupped happily, and the two of them burst out laughing. How had life delivered this, Jade wondered as she hugged her friend: the man of her dreams now officially her husband, and the best friend she had ever had returned to her?

Her happiness was complete, and in that moment, it felt as if nothing could spoil it.

FINDING BELLE

*

Of course, there were some small dissatisfactions in Jade's married life, chief among them that Fairfax continued to send Mivvi money for herself and Belle, even though they were now divorced; and although Jade resented this deeply, she knew she could not stop it.

In most other respects, she was content. Fairfax had so much more time for her now that he worked part-time. *One has to move on*, he had said, *one can't stay stuck in the same place*. The crushed look that he had worn for months at their beginning had all but vanished, and if his previously healthy self-esteem remained dented by those distant past events, it was not entirely extinguished.

Jade was worldly enough to take his vanities and small self-deceptions in her stride, particularly as Fairfax was so supportive while she poured her energies into her new career. He cooked up big meals in the evening while she was engrossed in lesson plans and marking, experimenting with new dishes – *Lasagne tonight darling!* Or *today it's coq au vin!* – and always washing up when she came home late after consultations.

He never complained, instead throwing his energies into a new environment. 'I need to get away from that stale old law firm,' he declared one day. He then volunteered to help run the gift shop at the Abbey, where Helen worked occasionally too.

She would be a good influence on him, Jade thought with satisfaction: steady, sensible and utterly reliable.

REETA CHAKRABARTI

Mombasa
August 8th 1968

F has already stayed two weeks longer than he meant to. He cannot tear himself away, and I am so glad — I would be desolate if he left. We are courting, I suppose, if sly looks and laughs, and walks round the garden, and strolls on the beach count as a courtship. It is all done, of course, under the careful watchfulness of Ma. We are easy in each other's company, and he is confiding in me more and more about his hopes for his future. Whatever he does, he wants success, he says. F is a performer, a blue-eyed showman. Now the show is solely for me, and I am happy to applaud him, perhaps even to adore him.

He has told me about some of his life in England. It is, he says, a land of opportunity. He has had some bad news from his father; there has been some fighting between them. He told me this, but then did not want to say more. Let us think only of happy things, he said.

He seems to know a lot, but sometimes he is ignorant. When we were walking on the beach yesterday — happily Ma stayed in the car with the driver — F said I would know much about British ways, as I had grown up here, and we had belonged to Britain for centuries. No, I said, you are wrong, Fairfax — the British were here only for a few decades; the Arabs preceded you, and before them were the Portuguese! He looked abashed not to have known this, and to save him, I gently took his face and turned it towards the Fort, telling him this imposing edifice was built by the Portuguese, and what a fine example of European skill it was. He smiled then.

FINDING BELLE

It was late in the evening, the sun was starting to set, and the sky was shot through with deep pinks and oranges. I knew that Ma would be fretting, but before we left, F gave his camera to one of the local boys to take a photograph of us.

We look like a picture postcard of paradise, F said, and he rested his arm gently around my shoulders. I never want to forget this, he said.

CHAPTER 8

When I returned home from my summer travels with Ash, I was taken aback by how much Belle had changed. I had only been away for three months – three glorious care-free months before my final year – but Belle's face looked distinctly grey and sunken.

I pulled my case into the hall, glancing back to make sure Ash was waiting at a distance as instructed. Belle knew about him, of course, but I hadn't directly told her who I was travelling with, and with her usual lack of curiosity, she hadn't asked. I didn't feel like launching into an immediate explanation.

Belle struggled to her feet, breathing heavily with the effort, and I winced at her pasty, shabby figure; I had forgotten how much she wore her illness on her body, but I felt a touch of shame and tried to overcome my old childhood instincts.

'Mivvi,' sang Belle, in a weak, high voice, 'you have come home.'
'Belle.'

I gave her a perfunctory kiss on the cheek, unable to soften into a maternal embrace.

'You've been alright? You've managed well? The others told me that you have.'

Belle shuffled away from the door to make way for me. 'I have been alright. They looked after me, John and Bianca.' And she smiled. 'Also Meera. She has gone to London now, but she comes often. She is coming next week.'

'That's nice,' I said, pulling my backpack into the hall. The door was still open. 'Did she ring you?'

'No, I asked her to come.'

This was unusual for Belle. I saw her looking out into the street, her eyes sharpening as she watched the curly-haired figure loitering on the pavement.

'I had a good time away,' I said, trying to divert her.

But it was too late.

'Does your friend want to come in?' Belle asked pointedly.

'Hmm, I'm not sure,' I said weakly.

But Ash realised he had been seen and came up, smiling. 'Hello, Belle, good to see you.'

'Hello, Ashish. Do you want to come in? I can make you a cup of tea if you like.' It was another unexpected turn; Belle was rarely hospitable to my friends.

'So kind of you, Belle, but I'd better be off to my folks. Otherwise they might imagine evil eventualities.'

Belle would not have understood this, but she giggled lightly as if she did.

'You go in, Belle, I'll see him off,' I said.

'Okay.' But Belle did not move.

'Go on, Belle,' I said, giving her a gentle nudge.

Belle's eyes shone, and she chuckled. 'Okay, okay, Ma is going. Off I go. Off I go,' we heard her saying to herself as she ambled into the front room.

'I'm so sorry,' I whispered, rolling my eyes at Ash.

'Don't be.' He spoke back softly. 'She gets to you more than me, naturally. Well, I'd better go. What are we going to do – no more living in each other's pockets?' He kissed my neck gently.

'You not sick of me by now? Three whole months together?'

'I might just have to get back into that pocket,' he murmured. His curls were tickling my face, making me giggle.

'Go on,' I said. 'I'll see you tomorrow.'

'And the next day, and the next.'

I kissed him on the tip of his nose and pushed him gently out of the front door.

*

After unpacking, I went to find my mother. Belle was in her usual place in the armchair by the window in her bedroom. Despite her reduced appearance, she had a small gleam in her eyes.

'This boy, you like him,' she said, looking up at me.

I eyed her warily. She could seem so out of things, but then there were these sudden flashes of sharpness.

'Yes, I do like him. He likes me too, mind you.'

She ignored my wry tone. 'I see. Okay. But I want to tell you. Do not only marry for love.'

'What!' I exclaimed. 'Who's talking about marriage?'

'I know, you modern girls. But you understand, it is not enough. Make sure he is a good boy.'

I was at a complete loss for words. I had never had an intimate conversation with Belle before.

'That man has got married,' she went on, 'to his hussy woman.'

'I know, I know, but we don't have to talk about them,' I said hurriedly. 'Anyway, Ash is good. And it's not like that, like what you are suggesting. We're just, you know, seeing what happens.'

'Not too much seeing. Be careful.'

'Belle, stop it,' I said hotly. 'You don't know anything about him. He's a good person, a kind one. Honest and straightforward.'

Belle nodded in acceptance. She seemed to drift off for a few moments, and then suddenly spoke. 'When I was your age, I could only do kishy-cuddly with a boy.'

'What!' I cried again, with a snort.

'Yes,' said Belle, with a mischievous smile. 'My mother said, "*Only kishy-cuddly is okay. But don't do anything else, you understand,*"' and here she mimicked her mother's shrill voice. '"*Don't do anything else!*"'

A gulp of laughter escaped me as Belle began a throaty and wicked chuckle. '"*Don't do anything else!*"' she said repeatedly, and we started to laugh infectiously and then uncontrollably – and soon we were clutching each other, stripped of inhibitions, choking with merriment, and together.

*

I told Ash what had happened the next day.

'It was so funny! She was suddenly so knowing!'

He smiled his dolphin-smile, sweet and enigmatic. 'Maybe she has the right idea?'

'What do you mean?'

He looked at me questioningly over the top of his glasses. 'You know, about getting married.'

I was astounded. 'You can't be serious!'

'Why not?'

'Well,' I spluttered, 'well, we're only 21!'

'True,' he conceded. 'But ... do you want to be with anyone else?'

I frowned and shook my head.

'Are you likely to marry someone else?'

I couldn't believe that he was in earnest. 'Is this a joke?'

'Nope.'

'Don't you think it's a bit … early?'

'Dunno,' he said, shaking his head. 'Should I go down on bended knee?'

'God, no!' I cried, cuffing him gently over the head. 'Goodness, you're full of surprises, Ashish.' I bit my lip, looking at him. 'Let me think about it.'

'Very romantic,' he said, but he was still smiling.

'What made you think of it?' I asked, resting my head against his shoulder. My initial astonishment was starting to fade.

'Dunno,' he said again. 'Your conversation with your mother maybe. Also, perhaps your father getting married.'

I shuddered. 'Ugh, thank goodness we were away.'

'You made sure we were away.'

'Thank goodness.'

'Anyway,' he went on, putting his arm around me, 'I wondered if him and Jade might set you thinking.'

'*You've* set me thinking. Anyway, we've still got a whole year apart.'

'I know. Long engagement.'

He twinkled at me, and even though I wasn't going to give him an answer, I began to wonder if his idea was so fantastical after all.

We sat for a few moments in companionable silence, which he broke with a question. 'So, term in two weeks, eh?'

I nodded. 'Last two weeks of freedom. I might try and see Tabitha before I go. She keeps pretending she hates Oxford, but it's such a façade. It's painful.'

'She's got to keep up the rebel's pretence?'

I wrinkled my nose and laughed. 'I am fond of her though,' I said.

'So am I.'

'Anyway, you've trumped her now!'

Ash had got a place in London to do a doctorate in English literature.

'But you think you'll just commute?'

He nodded. 'Yes – like I said. It'll be cheaper. I'll come and see you in Bristol as often as I can. And then when you're finished, let's see. Maybe we'll stay here, maybe we won't.'

'Hmm.' I sighed. 'Not sure we could afford London, not yet.'

'Maybe not.'

'If we stay here, I'd want to be nearer Belle than Fairfax, though,' I added.

'I think you mean nearer Belle than Jade,' he replied.

'Ash, you know me far too well.'

He took my hand and started encircling my ring finger mischievously. I withdrew it gently but pulled him close. His talk of marriage was so unexpected, but it touched me deeply. It was true, I thought. Who else did I want to spend the rest of my life with anyway?

CHAPTER 9

When Meera came the following week, it was clear that she too was concerned at the change in my mother, although she didn't seem surprised.

Belle had been in a state of feverish anticipation of Meera's visit, as if she were planning something – but her excitement couldn't conceal her essential fragility. She had asked Meera to bring some henna with her – I wasn't sure why – and Meera brandished it triumphantly before hugging us both. She was sleek and groomed now, no longer the Seventies flower child she had once been, but to me there would always be an air of flamenco about her.

'She seems suddenly very frail,' I said to her, once Belle was out of earshot.

'Yes, I know, she does. But it's been happening gradually,' said Meera gently. She pushed back a strand of glossy black hair from her face. 'She's had so many years of ill health. It takes its toll.'

'Is there something wrong?' I asked anxiously. 'I mean, apart from the obvious. Something else?'

'Well, while you were away, she did have chest pains. I know,' Meera held her hand up as I started to remonstrate, 'I would have called you if I'd been really worried. But I got her checked out, and they just said to keep an eye on her.'

'Has she got a weakness? A weak heart?'

'Yes,' said Meera. 'She's on some additional medication, and you know her, even though she's absent-minded, she has always taken her pills. Bianca knows about it, and I was always going to tell you. Belle has led a stressful life. Being ill in the way she has puts other demands on the body. But don't worry, Mivvi – we will all look after her.'

I nodded, reassured by Meera as always, and after a while I left them both together.

Much later, as dusk was falling, I heard their voices and Belle's soft chuckle, and I went upstairs in search of them.

Belle was sitting at her dressing table, peering at herself in the mirror, while Meera perched on an armchair. Wrapped around Belle's head was the *pallu*, the loose end of a glimmering red silk sari she had swathed herself in, a rich brocaded fabric that shimmered like a snakeskin. Heavy gold bells hung at her ears. She had made up her face as she used to do many years before, with powder too white for her, and lipstick too stark.

But I saw only my mother taking care of herself. All that was missing was the vermilion streak in her parting, which would have shown that she was married.

'Belle! Goodness, what are you doing?' I gasped. 'You're so dressed up!'

Belle smiled at me in the mirror. 'It is my wedding clothes. Am I beautiful?'

'Yes,' I said softly, although Belle's face was cracked and lined. 'You are. But why?'

'I just wanted to,' replied Belle in a dreamy tone. 'Just one more time.'

I turned questioningly to Meera, who shrugged and smiled. 'That's what she said to me too. And why not?'

I looked at my mother in bewilderment. It was so at odds with her loathing of Fairfax. Her hands and feet were adorned with swirls and whorls of the henna that Meera had brought – it had clearly all been planned. I would have to get the whole story from Meera later on.

But it was late, and Meera started to yawn. 'Sorry, I'm such a bore, I've just come off nights. I'm going to have to go to bed.'

'You're staying though, aren't you?' I asked.

Meera nodded. 'Yes, too late to go back now. I'll wake up early and creep out. No need to get up for me, Belle. You should get some sleep too.'

Belle roused herself from her reflections and nodded in the same dreamy way. It was as if she were drifting off already.

*

The next morning, I went downstairs and put away the dishes, made myself some breakfast and watered the plants on the kitchen sill. Meera had departed noiselessly, leaving an empty coffee cup and a handwritten note of thanks and kisses. I rang Ash and arranged to see a film with him that evening, then glanced at the university reading list for the final year. I wondered why Belle hadn't come down, but I didn't want to disturb her.

By early afternoon, there was still no sign of her. I called up the stairs. 'Belle, it's time to get up!'

Hearing no answer, I went up and knocked tentatively at her door.

'Belle? Mum? It's after lunchtime you know. It's time to get up.'

The silence continued.

'Belle? You okay?'

I eased open the door with a sudden feeling of dread. Belle was lying motionless on the bed, her grey hair still swathed in the red silk, the mask of powder and rouge still heavy on her face. The gold bell earrings were splayed on the pillow, and her face wore a look of ineffable peace.

I started to whimper, and a sob escaped me as I dropped to my knees by the bed – and then I began to howl like an animal. I took my mother's hennaed hand and pressed my own wet face against her fingers, feeling her for a last time.

There was no need for control; there was no need to keep it all held in, as I had done for so many years.

This was the end. This was my mother's end.

*

When I was able to get myself to the phone, I contacted Meera, who raced back. Her appearance prompted a fresh wave of weeping in me, and we held each other tightly as I wailed, and Meera cried silently. Only hours before, we had been marvelling at Belle in her bridal clothes, and now she was gone.

'It's almost as if she knew,' I wept.

'It feels like that,' said Meera quietly. 'It can't have been, but it feels like that.'

She released me gently, and we turned to look at Belle.

'Was it a sign of love?' I whispered. 'But it doesn't make any sense. She was enraged by Fairfax. She hated him.'

'You can only hate people you once loved,' said Meera. 'But I don't think it was about him. She was reliving her youth – her happiness and her hope. She didn't say so, but I think it was that.' She turned to the door. 'You spend some time with her, Mivvi. I'd better get everything started, everything that needs to be done.'

I sat with my mother and let the reality of her death sink in. All the different women that Belle had been came into my mind. Wild and tempestuous. Possessed by fury and rage and voices. But sometimes placid and accepting. An elegant letter-writer and sometime singer. A mother with a warm and comforting lap. A teller of funny stories.

She could have died in a kitchen fire, but from her face, from her final resting face, it seemed that her passing away had been quiet. A peaceful death for an unpeaceful person.

It was an early autumn day, and as I mourned next to Belle, the light started to fade in the room just as it had all those years ago, when the two of us had sat together bleakly, bereft at Fairfax's desertion.

Now it was my mother who was gone, and whatever troubles I had faced through the years, whatever the grief and neglect I had suffered, I could feel almost physically the severing of a vital link, and I sat stunned and overwhelmed by the loss I would have to endure.

CHAPTER 10

Jade was thrown into confusion by Belle's fatal heart attack. Her life with Fairfax had finally become settled, and she was flustered by this ultimate act of disruption from her great rival. The more she considered the news, the more she was stricken with annoyance that there would inevitably be fuss and drama.

To her great irritation, Fairfax was distraught. She heard him sobbing in the bathroom, and although she called out to try to comfort him, he wouldn't let her in. Jade had been feeling off-colour herself for a few weeks, which added to her difficulty in striking the right note.

It was impossible to remember Belle with any sympathy, but she did her best to appear kindly, and to give Fairfax the space he needed to process whatever it was that was going on in his head.

'The funeral's on Saturday,' he said to her, a few days after the news.

She nodded soberly and patted his knee. 'I suppose I shouldn't come?' she asked, with a note of self-sacrifice.

She felt torn between her antipathy towards Belle and a fresh anxiety at being excluded from Fairfax's past.

'Oh no,' he replied, shaking his head vehemently.

Jade suppressed a frown.

'Mivvi's been in touch with her university, to tell them what's happened,' he went on. 'They've been very sympathetic.'

Jade tried to look sympathetic too. 'It'll be hard, the funeral,' she said, moving closer to him on the sofa. 'Will you be alright? Without me, I mean?'

He nodded. 'You wouldn't want to be there. I'll have Mivvi. And John and Bianca are coming – it might be nice for me to see them.'

'I see.'

'And then there'll be other friends of Mivvi's, and that boy she's keen on. Dr Sen, too, I suppose.'

None of this was reassuring. Jade bit her bottom lip. 'You know, Fairfax,' she said in a rush, 'I think I really ought to come after all.'

He turned his big, sad face towards her. 'Really? Why? Won't it be ... you know ... painful?'

She ran her fingers lightly over his chest. 'I think I'd like to be there to support you.'

He looked doubtful, and his expression decided her.

'Yes, my love, I'll come. Even if it's painful, I don't want you to have to go through it all alone.'

And she took his lovely blond head and buried it in her shoulder, sparing him the conflict of emotions playing on her face.

*

In the run-up to the funeral, Jade felt taut with nerves. She bought herself a suitable outfit for the occasion – a black fitted dress, black high heels, and a little pillar box hat with a veil. Funeral-chic, she thought, as she looked at herself in the mirror.

On the day itself, she felt jittery and sick, but the clothes lent her a stylish mystery. Fairfax, though, emerged in a crumpled suit, his tie askew. She straightened it hurriedly. His face was white and drawn.

At the crematorium, he and his daughter hugged each other with a particular intensity. Jade squeezed Mivvi's arm, and murmured, 'I'm so sorry, Mivvi,' squirming all the while at her own insincerity. John and Bianca both looked wretched, and Meera's face was swollen with crying. Jade had braced herself for Maz, but he was nowhere to be seen.

There were more guests than Jade had expected, more even than Fairfax had listed, and she was taken aback at the numbers. She was introduced to a willowy girl called Tabitha and her mother, who seemed exceptionally upset.

Before the service began, everyone came up to offer their condolences, and Fairfax, whose face was set in an expression of profound grief, became more emotional with each well-wisher's speech. Jade felt uncomfortable and then increasingly affronted as Fairfax unaccountably assumed the role of the bereaved husband.

If this is an act, she thought angrily, *he's got to snap out of it now!*

But the queue of guests waiting to speak to Fairfax never seemed to end. Soon the service was underway, and there had been no private moment for her to remind him of who he really was.

As the service ended, Jade saw Fairfax turn and embrace a weeping Bianca – and in a flash, she saw in them what she had seen with Céline years previously.

A rage rose within her. If Fairfax had a past with Bianca, why had he never told her? Surely this wasn't happening again!

Jade hid her face and her feelings behind her veil, and got through the rest of the funeral somehow, waiting with agitation until she could speak to Fairfax alone.

*

I found the smell of the lilies on the coffin overpowering. Too sweet, too intense, and utterly cloying. It mingled with the burning incense, which was Meera's idea. I tried to breathe through my mouth and to concentrate on the celebrant's eulogy.

'Belle was loved by all who knew her. She had troubles in her life, but her abiding legacy is one of love.'

But I felt empty and disconnected from the funeral, and my thoughts kept wandering. There was comfort in the pressure of Ash's knee against mine, but although he knew about Belle, he had never really known her. I looked across the aisle at Meera, who was sobbing uncontrollably, and I felt a strong surge of love for my mother's only friend. I stole a glance at Fairfax, on my other side, looking white as a ghost, and then at Jade, dressed up like a mourner from a magazine, inexplicably wearing a veil.

'Born in India, her early years were innocent and carefree, brought up as she was in the sunny climes of Mombasa in Kenya.'

Who had related this garbage? Was this from Fairfax? None of the words came anywhere near to describing Belle, nor relating with any truthfulness the life she had really had. I wondered if my own contributions sounded insipid in the celebrant's mouth. But he seemed a gentle, well-meaning person. Perhaps it was simply that Belle was impossible to narrate.

The one person who might have come close to knowing the real Belle was Maz, but he had been unable to come. 'Visa issues,' he had told Meera on the phone, although that had never been a problem before.

He had sent a card of condolence, including words from Belle's father, words of sorrow and despair that his child should have died before him. His wife, Belle and Maz's mother, had died the previous year. What a terrible double loss for the old man.

The congregation stood up as the celebrant's speech came to an end, and I tearfully hugged those I loved in turn: Ash, Fairfax, Meera, John and Bianca.

As we gathered to watch the coffin disappear into the flames, I saw a tear-stained Bianca put her arm around Fairfax. Despite my grief, there was something in the gesture that made me suddenly understand. Fairfax and Bianca. Perhaps it was not such a surprise after all.

I could feel Jade bristling next to me, but as the coffin slid out of view, I lost all sense of my surroundings and surrendered myself to weeping for Belle.

*

Back home, Fairfax sank into an armchair with a deep sigh.

'So,' Jade began, trying not to let her voice falter, 'what was all that about then?'

'What do you mean?' Fairfax asked wearily. 'What are you talking about?'

'You know what I'm talking about.'

'It was a funeral, wasn't it? Nothing more.'

'Stop being all innocent.' She heard her control slip. 'What was that with you and Bianca? What did it mean?'

He sighed again. 'It didn't mean anything, Jade. We're old friends – or we used to be, anyway. She froze me out after everything that happened, but today – well, I guess it just didn't matter anymore. We go back a long way. Nothing more.'

'Nothing more?' Jade repeated tightly. 'You seemed to hold her very close for *nothing more*. I always noticed she used to paw at you, but I thought it was just her? Why did you let her? Why didn't John ever say anything?'

Fairfax's face hardened. 'Jesus Christ, Jade, what are you going on about? We've been at a funeral, for God's sake. Besides, this is all history. No, it's prehistory.'

'What does *that* mean?'

Fairfax looked exhausted. Jade studied him as she hadn't in a long time. His face was puffier than it used to be, his hair thinner, his bright eyes dimmer.

'Look, I knew Bianca years ago, through John. This was before they were together – before I was with Belle too. He was working for a charity through the church, helping people who'd fallen on hard times make a new start. Bianca was one of them.'

'And that's how you helped her?' she snapped. 'By sleeping with her?'

'What's with the moralising? I wasn't helping her – John was! We just had a few nights together, alright?' His face was red, and he hissed at her. 'It was never going to be anything more! John knows, and it's okay, because it was before them. She drinks too much – she always has done – and she gets very friendly, but it doesn't mean anything. She's alright, Bianca – she's a good sort.'

'She wasn't drunk today though, was she?' Jade retorted.

'No, of course not! But, although you may not be able to get your tiny mind around this, she was actually very fond of Belle. She and John looked after her when I left, as you well know.'

Jade stared at him. Fairfax was rarely sarcastic.

'Why are you talking to me like that? What the hell is going on here, Fairfax? You hated Belle! She made you miserable!' She paused, then went on more softly, 'Look, I know it's been a hard day. But don't forget, you had to get away from her. You had to be free of her.'

Fairfax looked away from Jade and stared out of the window.

At first, she thought he was composing a reply, but the silence dragged on.

'So, are you going to respond?' she asked uncertainly.

'Jade, Jade, what is all this?' He too spoke more softly now. 'We've just come back from a funeral, from Belle's funeral. She was my wife, you know.'

'And I'm your wife now!'

'Yes, of course.'

'So, what was happening back there? Why did you act as if you were still married to her? At the funeral, it was like she was still your wife!'

Fairfax started. 'No, no, she wasn't. I lost her as my wife a long time ago – well before I met you.'

'And you were happy to leave her – you were happy and relieved to finally be with me!'

There was another long silence from Fairfax. Jade's heart started to thump wildly.

'Fairfax,' she said, her voice trembling, 'you were, weren't you? You were?'

Fairfax seemed to sag. His words when they came were strangled, as if he were forcing them out. 'I didn't know how to cope with her. I just didn't know what to do. She was so beautiful when we married. I loved her so much and wanted her so much. But she changed when she came here – I don't know why. She seemed to slowly collapse. I thought if she had something to occupy her, something more than Mivvi, things might get better. But they didn't. Nothing helped, nothing made her content. I couldn't bear people to know, and I didn't know what to do. I thought people might start to talk about us.' His voice cracked. 'I couldn't stand it.'

Jade's heart softened as she listened to him. 'Fairfax, it's all over now.'

But it was as if he didn't hear her. She had a panicked feeling that she was losing a piece of him.

'Fairfax,' she said quickly, 'listen, it was all so traumatic, but it's over now. And that night, when she found out about us, it was for the best. I know it was awful, but it was for the best. It was meant to be.'

Fairfax stared at her. Again, he said nothing.

'Fairfax, love,' Jade said weakly, 'you don't regret it, do you – you don't regret it? No!' she cried suddenly. 'Don't answer that! I don't want you to.'

Fairfax was holding his head in his hands. He shook his head slowly as she spoke.

He doesn't regret it, she thought fiercely, *he doesn't*, he doesn't! But in the back of her mind, the suspicions were there. That he hadn't left of his own accord, that he had been thrown out. Or perhaps he had left only because the truth had been so violently exposed, because if he didn't then stand by his passion for her, what on earth had it all been for?

Jade felt a rush of nausea and she fled to the bathroom, where she heaved into the toilet bowl, her stomach churning violently.

CHAPTER 11

I was drained after the funeral; I simply wanted to curl up in my bed and block out the world. But some things still had to be done.

I summoned up the energy to contact Bristol, where the staff readily agreed to my missing the first few weeks of term and were so sympathetic that I started to cry all over again on the phone. But I had put to the back of my mind the issue of what to do with the house. It belonged in reality to Fairfax, and he would surely want it to be sold – yet I couldn't contemplate having to leave, let alone the idea of having to live with him and Jade.

For the moment, I was not alone. Ash moved in for a while, John and Bianca came regularly to see me, and Meera came up from London when she could. Tabitha dropped by too, bringing love and cakes from Bree.

Although the house was busy, Belle's absence coursed through it, and I marvelled at how my passive mother could have left such an active mark. I spent long periods sitting in her bedroom, looking through the folded garments and silks, absorbing the last of the scent of her creams and perfumes.

In one drawer, I found some old photographs, separate from the family albums – pictures of Belle and Maz as children with their parents, my grandparents, a soft-faced grandfather and a sharp-featured grandmother. I scanned these new images carefully for any signs of myself in them.

Under the photographs was an old, scuffed book which I realised with surprise was a diary from the Sixties, half-filled with Belle's distinctive flowery hand. It resembled the notebook Meera had given to me years ago, which I still treasured.

The pages of Belle's book were yellow, the paper fragile and easily torn; the entries seemed to stop abruptly a few years after I was born.

I tried to start reading it, but I felt myself welling up and couldn't continue, so I put it away in the drawer for another time.

*

I didn't see Fairfax until a fortnight after the funeral. We needed to give each other space to grieve in our own way. That Fairfax did mourn Belle, I had no doubt. His grief at the funeral had been raw and genuine. But when he arrived at the house – a house he had been forbidden to enter while Belle was still alive – I couldn't read him. He appeared diffident and sheepish, unlike his usual jaunty self.

'Mivvi, how are you?' He embraced me tenderly. 'It's been such a shock.'

'I'm alright. Adjusting to it, I guess. She was such a presence. Strange really. I never properly knew her, and yet she was a force in her own right.' My words felt strained.

Fairfax nodded. 'You never had much of a relationship with her, did you?' he continued, matching me for awkwardness.

'Well, it was difficult to have one, wasn't it?'

He nodded again. 'She loved you, you know.'

'I don't really think she knew me,' I said, with a sigh. 'How could she? Anyway,' I went on, knowing it would be easier to focus on practical matters, 'what do you want to do? With the house, I mean? It's yours, after all. Do you want to sell it?'

I must have asked this question wistfully, because Fairfax took my hand.

'We won't rush into any decisions, Mivvi. Eventually, I suppose we will sell it, yes. We could do with some more money, and I can then provide you with a nest egg, for when you settle somewhere yourself. But we can take some time.'

I was grateful for his tact. Sometimes, Fairfax knew exactly how to behave. But a feeling persisted that he was keeping something from me.

We sat quietly for a few moments. An early autumn English sun lit up the side of Fairfax's face, and his thinning blond hair shone momentarily with its old lustre.

'Not everything was bad, you know,' Fairfax said, after a while. 'We had some good times. And did you know, Mivvi,' he added, as if it had just occurred to him, 'you were nearly a big sister? Do you remember?'

'Vaguely. Belle lost a baby, didn't she? Why do you bring that up now?'

'Just … memories, you know.'

I turned to look at him. Grief took people in different ways, but I couldn't work out what he was trying to say. His face was shining, as if he were beseeching me.

'Fairfax, what is it?'

'Mivvi,' he whispered to me, 'you *are* going to be a big sister! We're going to have a baby. I'm going to be a dad again!'

I stared at him.

'Don't look like that!' he cried, more joyfully now. 'I know, I know, it seems ridiculous at my age – I mean, I'm going to be 50! It wasn't exactly intended – it was never part of Jade's plans. But now it's happened, I'm more excited than she is! There's life in me yet, Mivvi! Come on, be happy for me.'

He said this pleadingly, his big, handsome face appealing for my generosity. I felt a tumult of conflicting emotions, but I knew I couldn't possibly deny him the blessing he needed.

'Fairfax,' I said, embracing him tightly, 'a daddy again!' I was suddenly tearful at the thought, whether in sorrow or in joy, I couldn't tell. 'I have to say,' I managed, 'I'm completely astonished!'

He laughed with relief and hugged me back. 'I know! No one was more astonished than me! Mivvi, my love, my Sweet Pea, thank you.'

I watched him through the window as he left. He ran his hand through his hair in his achingly familiar way, and as he put his key in the ignition, he checked his look quickly in the rear-view mirror.

How well I know him, I thought, *and how much he can still surprise me.*

Nothing in the world was predictable, and now a new arrival might mean a new life for all of us.

*

A week later, I drove with Ash to the grounds of the Abbey. Belle's ashes were in a small urn, hidden in a bag. *I'm carrying my mother*, I thought, *instead of her carrying me.*

The two of us walked quietly, almost reverently, to the lake. We waited until a group of people had moved on, and then we slipped deftly under the barrier that cordoned off the water. There, between a beech tree and a willow, I carefully scattered my mother's ashes, turning the urn so that they hit the water in rounds and swirls.

Ash held me by the waist, to share the moment, and to stop me from falling in. I emptied the urn slowly, and chanted softly, 'Goodbye, my mother, goodbye, Belle, goodbye.'

The ashes settled briefly, then started to float away towards the ducks and the reeds on the far side, and I didn't at first think about the past and my life with Belle. Instead, I found myself imagining the future – perhaps even my own motherhood. Yet, somewhere, a thought was starting to take hold – that to throw off the heavy weight of my beginnings, I would have at some stage to confront them properly. I didn't yet know how.

As I stood there with Ash's arms wrapped tightly around me, I was filled with a sense that despite my goodbyes, this was not my final farewell to Belle; that I was still to persevere in my search for my elusive mother - in the hope that one day I might succeed in finding her.

PART 4 – 2000

CHAPTER 1

Ruby was rummaging in the large cardboard box I kept in the spare room of my flat, looking for old clothes and toys to play with. She emerged wrapped in an old silk scarf and clutching Adèle.

'Goodness, Ruby,' I laughed, 'I'd forgotten about that old doll! She's looking the worse for wear!'

Ruby tied the scarf around her slender neck more tightly. 'Where is this from?' she asked.

'It was my mother's,' I said. 'She loved silks and bright colours.'

'Your mummy's dead now?' asked Ruby. She enjoyed asking questions to which she knew the answers.

'Oh yes, she died before you were born,' I said gently, although Ruby looked unconcerned.

She fixed me with her large grey eyes, her smile disconcertingly like our father's. 'When is Daddy coming?' she asked.

'He'll be here soon. Come on, let's get that doll cleaned up – she's got years of dirt on her.'

We were scrubbing Adèle's face with a wet cloth when Fairfax arrived.

'How are my two gorgeous daughters?' he cried, as Ruby ran into his arms. I watched him scoop her up just as he used to do years ago with me. How I had loved him back then, with the same trust and simplicity that Ruby showed now.

'Had a nice time?' he asked, nuzzling my little sister, who wriggled in his embrace.

'Uh-huh,' she said, waving Adèle around in the air. 'Look what we found!'

'Oh, I remember that old thing,' laughed Fairfax. He looked easy and relaxed in his polo shirt and chinos, his usual Abbey outfit.

'Was it busy?' I asked. 'In the shop?'

'Nice and steady,' he replied, looking at the doll. 'She hasn't worn well, has she? You used to take her everywhere, Mivvi. I am amazed you still have her.'

'There's a load of stuff I'm amazed I still have – old things of mine and Belle's. I'll sort through it all one day.'

'It's my birthday next week,' whispered Ruby, confidentially.

'I know,' I whispered back. 'And I even know how old you're going to be.'

'Six!' she cried triumphantly, and Fairfax hugged her as if it were indeed a victory. *He's so good with her*, I thought. Small children always brought out the best in him.

Ruby pirouetted over to me and put her arms around my expanding waist.

'Helloo!' she called, her face pressed against my tummy. 'Helloo, baby! It's Aunty here!'

I laughed and squirmed. 'You're tickling me!' I said, ruffling Ruby's hair fondly. 'I'm sure baby has heard you.'

Fairfax's face was tinged with concern. 'You still feeling better?' he asked.

'Hmm, yes, thankfully.'

'Your mother was the same – very bad morning sickness at the beginning.'

'Your mother, not my mother,' sang Ruby lightly.

'Yes, Fairfax, you said,' I replied. 'But my sickness went on all day. Anyway, it's disappeared now, thank goodness. I've got my second scan next week.'

Fairfax beamed. 'So exciting! But you don't want to know the sex?'

I shook my head. 'I wouldn't mind, but Ash wants a surprise, so no. He can't come to this scan, though – there's a lecture he can't get out of.'

'I've a little hunch that it will be a boy,' said Fairfax, with a twinkle.

Ruby and I looked at each other with amusement.

'Silly, Daddy, you don't know!' cried Ruby, cuffing him over the head.

'She's right, you don't!' I smiled at him indulgently. The prospect of the baby had brought us closer together, and time had softened my antagonism towards him. But I was careful to preserve a little distance from him, just in case.

Fairfax tapped the side of his nose knowingly.

'Just a little intuition of mine. Are you thinking of names?'

'Yes,' I said vaguely, 'but we haven't decided.'

'If he's a boy,' Fairfax went on, 'I might call him Harry.'

'Why?' I exclaimed, laughing but indignant now too. 'You'll call him by the name we give him!'

Fairfax had the decency to look abashed. 'Well, yes, of course. It's just ... you would have been Harry if you'd been a boy.'

'But I thought I was going to be Ashish?' I asked in surprise, while Ruby chanted Ash's name to Adèle.

'Ah, that was your mother's choice of name for you. I would have gone for Harry.'

'I see.'

He hesitated, his brow furrowed. 'You're not still thinking of moving away, are you?' This subject was a new preoccupation of his. 'Now that the baby's coming?'

His pressure on us to stay close was one of the reasons I remained wary of him. Fairfax seemed to think he had claims on me, despite everything he had done.

'Well, we are thinking of moving at some stage, yes. You know we want more space. It's great having this little flat, but it's small. And the commute is exhausting for Ash. It'll be even more so with a baby.'

Fairfax looked untroubled by Ash's journey. 'But what about your job?'

I tried to look – and stay – even-tempered. 'I'll go back to it for a while after maternity leave, but I'll find something else in London when we move. Perhaps in publishing. The OU has been great, but I don't want to be there forever.'

'But I'll miss you,' said Ruby wistfully. She was sitting on the floor cradling Adèle and started wiping imaginary tears from the doll's eyes with the cloth.

I smiled down at her. 'Oh, Ruby, we're not going yet, and when we do, it won't be far. We'll come back lots, and you can come and visit too.'

Ruby was mollified, but Fairfax still looked grave.

I changed the subject. 'By the way, Meera's been in touch. She sent one of her out-of-the-blue cards. Anyway, she's leaving Oz, and coming back for good!'

I spoke lightly, mindful of his attitude towards Meera.

'I thought she was in New Zealand?' he asked.

'Australia. But she's got the travel bug out of her system, she says. She's going to India first to see family, and then coming home. Did I tell you she has a child now? Bianca told me.'

Fairfax looked surprised. 'Really? I didn't think she was that way inclined? How strange!'

I didn't understand his expression, but I just pressed on. 'I suppose she must have had it very late, but good for her. It's just lovely, isn't it?'

'A lovely baby! A lovely lovely baby!' sang Ruby.

Fairfax's face twitched as he glanced down at Ruby.

'Well, funny, I suppose I thought she was just a career girl,' he said, looking confused. 'Never mind, we can talk about it later.'

'Ash is keen to take our little one to India, as soon as we can travel,' I said, thinking I would start to prepare this particular ground now. 'He wants to show the baby off to his uncles and aunties.'

Fairfax looked uninterested. 'Ah well, after the baby's born, you might decide you want to stay here after all,' he said.

We won't, I thought, but I kept my own counsel.

*

Once they had left, I folded away Belle's silk scarf, and tidied up the contents of the box which Ruby had half-tipped out. Our flat was far too small for clutter. Ash and I had been very happy here in our first marital home, bought with the nest egg that Fairfax had promised and duly delivered after the sale of the old house. But the flat had filled up quickly, mostly with books and more books, and the lack of space combined with the prospect of the baby made it feel almost oppressive at times.

I hung on to Adèle to clean her up properly. Under the dirt, the alabaster was cracked in places, giving her a late middle-aged look. She wasn't even that old.

I waved her at Ash when he came home.

'Oh, it's Doria Gray,' he said, and yelped as I slapped him playfully.

'She helped me through some hard times, this doll.'

'Are they better now?' he asked, with a nudge.

'Oh yes!' I said. 'Infinitely.'

I watched him ease off his shoes, and then pour himself a small glass of white wine. He looked tired but he never complained, however difficult the day had been. He waved the bottle at me questioningly, out of habit; he knew I hadn't had a drink for months.

'How was work?' I asked, leaning across to him and rubbing his temples gently.

He smiled and shut his eyes. 'Fine. The students are keen and clever.'

'I bet you're a generous professor.'

'Not yet a professor.'

'You know what I mean.'

'How was Fairfax? And Ruby?'

'Ruby sweet as always. Fairfax excited about the baby and … you know, irritating.'

Ash raised an eyebrow. 'What was it this time? Us moving? Did you mention India?'

'He didn't seem interested in India, but he goes on and on about us moving house. I mean really, after the way he's behaved!'

'Yes, it's funny he's so possessive,' mused Ash. 'Given what happened, as you say. Well, we've hung on here for so long. Too long!'

'I know,' I sighed.

Ash had wanted to leave for years, but we had stayed on after Belle's death, and then I had got my Open University job, and we delayed moving again. But now I was as restless as he was.

'He knows the commute does me in,' said Ash. He didn't hold it against Fairfax; he just wanted to spend less time on a train.

'Well, he's always been selfish,' I replied. 'Belle used to say Fairfax did exactly as he pleased, regardless of anyone else.'

Ash took a sip of wine and looked across at me. 'You miss her, don't you?'

'Do I?' I said sadly. 'I'm not sure. I worry sometimes that I'm cold, frozen in relation to her.'

'No,' he replied, his voice gentle. 'You had to say goodbye to her a long time before she died. That's just coping. But I have been wondering, is there any family of hers in India, anyone we could visit?'

'I don't think so,' I said. 'I think Maz is often there, but I've no idea where. We could track him down, I suppose.'

'You're never sure of him, are you?' Ash asked.

I considered the question before replying. 'I quite like him actually. But the bad blood between him and Fairfax always stood in the way. There was some strange thing about money too – but I can't ask either of them, so I'll probably never know.'

'Your grandfather might know?'

'The grandfather I've never met.' I sighed. 'I did wonder once about going to Mombasa, but Maz seemed to think it would be a bad idea. I didn't pursue it. Oh well, never mind.'

We sat quietly for a few moments, but the idea of Fairfax was still gnawing away at me.

'I think Belle was right,' I said eventually. 'Fairfax does just think of himself. It's funny – he brings her up more in conversation now. He says, "your mother this, and your mother that." Ruby's little ears always prick up.'

'Maybe he just feels it's safe to now? Especially if you're seeing him without Jade.'

'That's true,' I admitted.

Ash moved a pile of books from the kitchen table. 'And you barely see Jade these days.'

'Also true. But when I do see her, I tolerate her more. I have to, because of Ruby.'

'Don't tell me you're warming to her,' said Ash cheekily.

I pulled a face. 'I think that's impossible. But I haven't always behaved well either.'

I was thinking of my humility when I finally understood what it meant to grow up in care, and how I had worried that my scorn for Jade's awkwardness was essentially snobbery. I regretted too my ambush of Fairfax and Jade with Céline all those years ago, a childish and spiteful response on my part to a chaotic time in my life.

But warming to Jade was out of the question.

Ash patted my gently swelling belly. 'How have you felt today?'

'I've felt good! I think I can feel it, you know, moving around. It feels like bubbles popping – at first I thought it was wind! But it's the baby. I know it is!'

Ash kissed me lightly and then opened the fridge for dinner.

Somehow, the prospect of our baby kept throwing my past into even sharper relief. I often thought of Fairfax's fiction that Belle was responsible for her own illness. He might have believed it, but it was a fiction nonetheless, and one in which he had recruited me against my own mother. I felt a helpless anger at my younger self for having been his willing foot-soldier.

'He does drive me mad,' I mused out loud.

'Your old dad? Your mad old dad?'

'Yes! Sorry. Just thinking. Brooding. Well, I'm allowed to, I guess!'

I smiled at Ash sheepishly. This stirring up of old memories and feelings was doing me no good. I got up to help him with dinner, trying to focus my mind on the present.

*

A week later, I put the phone down after calling an ecstatic Ash, and flashed an unrestrained look of joy at the hospital receptionist. Everything was developing exactly as it should, the doctor had said, no cause for concern whatsoever. As I gazed at the scan, I had marvelled at how fully formed the foetus was – a baby in miniature and entirely, recognisably human, perhaps even with Ash's nose!

I hugged myself with something approaching glee as I walked out of the hospital, buoyant with the promise of what was to come. The day was bright and mild, and I decided to drive out to the Abbey and treat myself to lunch there. Fairfax's office was opposite the hospital, and I considered dropping in to tell him the news but decided instead to savour the moment alone. I didn't want to share my joy with anyone until I saw Ash later.

The Abbey gardens were in full bloom with the first warmth of spring, the borders ablaze with salmon pink azaleas and thick purple bushes of rhododendrons. I walked through them, feeling giddy with happiness and unashamed of the smile on my face. I would head to the lake, where we had scattered Belle's ashes, and eat my sandwiches there. The ducks could have the crusts.

As I walked past the gift shop, I saw the back of an unmistakable blond head. *Ah*, I thought, *he's here today, not at the firm.* I had been amused and perplexed when I had first heard of Fairfax's plan to work in the Abbey shop; he had never shown any interest in culture or charity before. But it kept him busy, I supposed – a later life hobby for a man now not far off sixty.

He was standing at the counter, taking off his badge in preparation for someone else to take over. His blond hair was framed by an arc of William Morris wallpaper behind him, as if he had grown a floral halo. I had a strong instinct to slip behind a tree to avoid having to see him, but I checked myself quickly. *What are you doing, don't be silly*, I thought, *it's just Fairfax*. He turned around, and just as I moved to wave to him, he gestured towards a woman across the other side of the shop.

I stepped back and took in someone with chestnut hair and a kindly face. *It's that Helen who knows Jade*, I realised. *Of course, she comes here too.* I watched the two of them through the glass, as they smiled at each other and turned towards the conservatory café.

Then, just as I was about to slope away quietly, I caught sight of Fairfax raising his hand to give Helen a fleeting stroke on her cheek.

I now did swiftly slip behind a tree, suffused with a small burst of evil glee. The old rascal! Was he really up to his former tricks again, cheating this time on Jade? And with one of her supposed friends!

I knew I shouldn't crow, but I couldn't help feeling a rush of malicious pleasure. I caught a small boy staring at me and flashed him a beaming smile. *What goes around comes around*, I thought, *at least where Fairfax is concerned!*

*

I had plenty to tell Ash that evening, but when he heard about Fairfax, he frowned.

'Well?' I prompted him. 'It's funny, isn't it? Although also terrible,' I added. I could tell I was enjoying the discovery too much for his liking.

'Well, but it's depressing though, isn't it?' he said eventually. 'I know we don't adore Jade, but do you really want another upheaval for him? And what about Ruby?'

I felt my face fall at the reprimand. How could I have forgotten Ruby?

'If this is serious, Jade won't let go lightly,' Ash went on. 'In fact, she'll hang on for all she's worth. Who knows quite what your father sees in her, but they've been together for a long time now, and a split would be awful for Ruby. Jade's quite casual in her mothering, but she is still her mother. And you certainly don't need that stress in your life right now.'

I nodded, chastened. 'You think I'm being malicious, don't you?'

'No,' he said, his baby owl eyes shining. 'But I thought you were coming round to Jade, just a little bit?'

'I was, I am, I know,' I said, wishing that Ash weren't quite so decent.

'Anyway, he just touched her cheek. Perhaps there's no more to it than that.'

I laughed. 'You innocent, you!'

But I did wonder if Ash was right. *I've no way of finding out though*, I thought half wistfully. *My snooping days are over.*

I chewed over the episode for several weeks. It was base of me, I knew, but it was also light relief, as I lingered over the fickle Fairfax and the jilted Jade. *No*, Ash said, *she's not jilted, he hasn't left her. But alliteration is such fun*, I countered with a grin. I felt like a child laughing at the adult world, a luxury I had never had in my actual childhood. But my levity stemmed from an absence of real shock at his behaviour; I knew well by now that Fairfax was not a man of principle. The thought of jeopardy to Ruby was sobering, but I suspected deep down that he was not serious about Helen, just as I thought now that he had not wanted to leave Belle. It was simply that he was unable to be faithful. I had no intention of confronting him, confident that in a short time I would be moving away with Ash, creating our own family, cementing our own future, and leaving Fairfax's chaos behind.

CHAPTER 2

The baby was born in late October, a skinny, dark-haired boy with an annoyed expression and an old man's furled-up face. I had expected to find him beautiful and was surprised at how comical he looked.

'Our millennium baby,' I whispered to Ash.

'We're not going to call him Harry, are we?' he whispered in return.

I smiled. 'No.'

I felt dazed and serene, and filled with a huge surge of protectiveness towards this tiny scrap of human being. It was a feeling I would later recognise as love.

'He's a perfect baby with enormous hands and feet!' the midwife said. 'It means he'll be tall!'

Like his grandparents, I thought contentedly.

We called him Robin Arjun, a name for each of his countries.

*

Ash took leave from work, and the three of us settled down in the nest of our new family. Our first visitor at home, who had already been to see us in the hospital, was inevitably Fairfax. Now, as before, he stood speechless with happiness, gazing at the marvel that was

Robin and swallowing hard to contain himself. I had seen this side of him when Ruby was born, but it touched me all the more with my own child.

'I'm so proud, Mivvi, so proud,' he said, barely getting the words out.

Grandparents are meant to be besotted, I thought, as Fairfax tenderly cradled the baby.

'You're very practised,' I said, smiling at him.

'An expert with the babies, that's me,' he whispered and fell silent to watch his grandson's sleeping face.

Later that day, as I watched him leave, I wondered if this would be healing for us. Through the window, I saw him walk more slowly than before to the shiny car parked next to our battered one, and then duck down to catch his reflection in one of the wing mirrors. *Same old Fairfax,* I thought, *grandfather or not.*

I often wondered about Belle, and how she might have felt about becoming a grandmother. She had not loved children as Fairfax did, but my first memories of her were of warmth and refuge; early on, I knew, Belle had been well enough to be loving. I did feel wistful that my mother was not here to share the joy of Robin, even though she might have struggled to participate.

How strange it was, after so much time, to experience still the competing emotions that Belle could trigger in me.

*

The next afternoon, I was sitting quietly with Robin asleep in my arms. Ash was out getting provisions. I was in a dreamy state, from too much contentment and too little sleep. The doorbell rang, and I found Fairfax and Ruby standing on the doorstep.

'Oh, hello,' I said, with some surprise, 'I wasn't expecting you?'

'I've just picked Ruby up from school, and we were passing, so we thought we'd drop in,' he said brightly. 'Is that alright? I'm not disturbing you, am I?'

'Oh no, no, of course not,' I answered, and then, fearing I was being too formal, I gave his arm a squeeze. 'Come on in, you can make some tea.'

In the end, it was me who made the tea, as Fairfax had to have his cuddle with Robin. Ruby sat next to him, looking speculative.

'You're an aunty now,' I said softly to her, and she nodded solemnly. 'Don't wake him,' I warned.

'Oh, we won't,' whispered Fairfax. 'I'm very good with babies, as you know.'

When I came back, Ruby was holding Robin, looking tentatively down at him.

'Remember to support his head,' said Fairfax.

'I am,' she said indignantly.

'Shhh,' he said, 'keep your voice down. Isn't he lovely?'

They sat and gazed at him for a while, a miracle of new life.

'I've been telling everyone about him, at work and at the Abbey,' said Fairfax, relieving Ruby of the baby. 'You know, I think he's got my eyes.'

I squinted at Robin. 'Maybe? I think he looks more like Ash.'

'Well, yes,' he conceded, 'he does look like Ashish. At the moment anyway. Babies change. But I do think he's got my eyes.'

I glanced at Ruby, who raised her own eyes to the heavens, and we exchanged a secret smile. I enjoyed sharing these moments of scepticism about our father and his certainties.

But after a while, the lack of sleep started to catch up with me, and I found myself yawning.

'I think I'm going to have to have a nap,' I said apologetically. 'I was up for most of the night.'

'Yes of course,' said Fairfax, gingerly handing Robin back to me. 'We'll pop back in tomorrow, shall we?'

I had a moment's hesitation, and then I remembered. 'Ah no, we've got Tabitha coming with her boyfriend. Did I tell you she's expecting too? Due in the New Year. I'll see you soon anyway – maybe next week? I'll give you a ring.'

Ash was halfway through the door before I'd finished speaking.

'Fairfax, Ruby, helloo!' He spoke softly, careful not to wake the baby. 'I'd forgotten about Tabitha. When's she coming?'

'Tomorrow, just after lunch,' I said, handing him the sleeping baby.

'Time to prepare,' he said archly.

'Why, don't you like Tabitha?' Fairfax was looking on in interest. He had always been suspicious of Bree.

'No, no, I do like her, Fairfax. But one needs to be prepared – for the Tabitha onslaught.' Ash grinned. 'Anyway, see you both soon.'

*

'You didn't tell me that Marco was coming, too.' It was the next day, and Ash was dabbing a milk stain off his irretrievably stained shirt.

'I did tell you – you've just forgotten.'

'I screened it out.'

'You're not a fan.'

Ash gave up on the stain. 'He's so self-righteous.'

'He doesn't get your jokes.'

'Too right-on for jokes. He'll also prance around with his wretched camera.'

'Well, it is his profession. And he is Tabitha's chosen one. Anyway,' I said soothingly, 'get it out of your system before they arrive.'

At that moment, the doorbell rang.

'Look at you!' I said, when I answered the door, giving Tabitha a hug. 'Blooming or what! Pregnancy suits you – but then most stages of life suit you.'

Tabitha patted her bump. She was looking sleek as a cat, and it astonished me that she could be so trim while six months pregnant. The sight of her was an unwelcome reminder of my own rounder, post-partum self.

'Where's Robin? Asleep?' Tabitha whispered theatrically. 'Sorry, I shouldn't have rung the bell.'

Marco came in from locking up their bike.

'We've bought a tandem,' he said, glowing with perspiration. 'We can attach a trailer to it when Baby comes.'

He was taut and lean, and gleaming with health. Ash pulled his fraying jumper tighter around his thin body.

'Like a stretch limo on two wheels,' said Ash.

Marco showed no sign of understanding him. 'We've got to think of what we're doing to the planet,' he went on, 'and the sort of world we're bringing Baby into.'

'You drive, don't you, Mivvi?' asked Tabitha, taking one of the oat and linseed cookies she had baked herself.

'Yes, we bought a used car with some of the proceeds from Belle's old house,' I said, unable to keep a note of apology out of my voice. 'Fairfax was aghast. Second-hand, and it's not silver!'

'I had wondered about getting driving lessons,' said Tabitha absent-mindedly. 'But I don't agree with cars, ideologically.'

I didn't dare meet Ash's eye.

'We'll all get electric cars eventually,' said Ash, 'but manpower is good. What about a rickshaw? That would keep Marco fit, pulling you along.'

Marco never listened when Ash spoke.

'Hey, it's a gorgeous day,' he interrupted. 'Once the baby's awake, how about going to get a beer – not for you, Tab – and some food?'

'I can't think of anything I'd like less,' said Ash.

Happily, only I seemed to hear him.

But Robin was fast asleep, and the impossibility of waking a sleeping baby kept us all indoors, talking quietly. Just as we at last heard him cry, the doorbell rang again. Ash went to fetch Robin, and I headed to the front door.

Fairfax's ruddy face loomed down at me from the doorway, and Ruby's luminous one gazed up.

'Mivvi, love,' he said apologetically. 'We were just passing by again – I wasn't at work today and did the school pick-up, and we just thought we'd pop by and see how the little prince is doing. I assume Tabitha's gone?'

I was disconcerted to find him here after I had told him I wasn't free.

'No, they're still here actually. I'm so sorry, Fairfax – I know you've come all this way but…'

Fairfax looked abashed, but he was quickly in the flat, pulling Ruby in with him. I bent down and planted a kiss on her curly head.

'Ah, I thought they were coming after lunch, and it would be safe now. You know, Mivvi, I could murder a coffee.'

I stood there wearily, wondering if my gathering irritation was at all reasonable.

Then Ash came towards us with a wailing Robin, and Fairfax's face brightened.

'Ah, that's a healthy cry!' he said approvingly.

'He needs a feed.' I took Robin from Ash, wondering how our tiny flat was going to accommodate all these people.

'You go ahead and feed him,' Ash said to me. 'Once you're done, we can go for a walk.'

I gave a small sigh of relief. Ash always had everything worked out.

*

We stepped out into the crisp November day. The sky was bright and the chill gave the trees a brittle appearance. We walked fast to keep off the cold, and I was glad of the warmth of Robin's little body strapped in a sling against my chest. I walked with Fairfax, while Tabitha and Marco led the way with Ash. Ruby trailed behind us, kicking stones in a desultory way.

'I'm going to have it at home, of course,' I could hear Tabitha telling Ash. 'Bree had us at home, both me and Samuel, so it's got to be done!'

Fairfax glanced at me and rolled his eyes, and I permitted him the shadow of a smile. He ran his hand over Robin's soft and ruddy cheek.

'Ow!' he cried suddenly, as one of Ruby's stones hit him square on the ankle. 'Ruby, what did you do that for!'

She smiled guiltily. 'Sorr-ee!' she sang, but then went on scuffing up the gravel.

'She's been a bit moody recently,' Fairfax told me quietly. 'I'm not sure what's got into her. She's usually so sunny-tempered.'

'Ouch!' I cried as a large piece of gravel hit me on the back of the leg. Robin gave a whimper.

'Aw, come on, Ruby, give over!'

She looked sheepish and skulked past us towards the others.

'Hey, Ruby,' said Ash. 'There are lots of conkers here. Why don't you gather some? You can take them into school.'

Tabitha and Marco looked at her indulgently. It was beyond them to imagine having a child as old as she was. 'You can ride in our trailer, when we get it,' said Tabitha, smiling.

'That would be nice, wouldn't it, Ruby?' I said brightly. 'Although I suppose you might be a little bit big for it.'

At that, she pulled a face.

'Let's go and get a juice and some cake, and we can warm up,' said Ash, holding his hand out to Ruby. 'Some people are still small enough to need regular feeding and watering.'

We huddled into a small café, where Marco was disgruntled to find that they didn't sell beer. Ruby munched happily on a muffin, and Ash got the waitress to heat up some water so that he could feed Robin.

'A bottle?' asked Tabitha, looking askance.

'Mmm, it means Ash can feed him too,' I said. 'Very useful for the middle of the night!'

A look passed between Tabitha and Marco, which I studiously ignored.

'Wobin want some muffin?' said Ruby in an exaggerated baby voice. She made to push some cake into Robin's tiny mouth.

'No, no, Ruby! He's far too small!' I cried, pushing her hand away gently.

'Here, Ruby, you have this juice – it's only for big girls.' Ash placed himself firmly between me and Ruby, then took Robin and carefully positioned his head away from his eager young aunt before beginning to feed him.

Ruby seemed to forget about the baby and sat humming to herself, wrapped up in her thoughts, while Marco and Tabitha seemed wrapped up in each other.

Fairfax was sitting at the end of the table, close to me, looking round at the feeding Robin.

'You must feel so well set up now,' he said to me. 'Lovely baby, nice husband, cosy little flat.'

'Well, yes,' I said cautiously, hoping he wasn't about to start up again about our moving.

'It's so good you don't have stairs,' he went on.

'What's wrong with stairs?'

'Well, Robin, of course,' he said. 'You might trip and drop him.'

'I'm not a child, Fairfax!' I replied, with a laugh. 'I think I can work that one out for myself!'

Fairfax stiffened. 'Well, one learns these things. The grandparents know a little bit more than the parents, you know. I'm only trying to help.'

'Did you ever trip and drop me?' I asked, perplexed. 'Or did Belle?'

'No, I don't think so,' he mumbled, 'but it's a good reason for staying put.'

Robin burped loudly, and the tension was broken.

'Hey, Rubes,' said Marco, fishing in his rucksack. 'Why don't you take him for a moment, and I can get a photo? I'm doing some black and white ones for an album.'

'He's very good,' purred Tabitha. 'He's got a full centre spread in *Living and Lawns* next month. Only turned professional last year!'

Ash carefully put Robin in Ruby's arms, where he lay awkwardly as Marco fussed over his camera.

'Remember to hold his head now,' I said, feeling a little anxious.

Ruby was busy pulling faces at the lens, and Ash's arms appeared repeatedly in shot as he hovered protectively over Robin.

'That's gorgeous!' cried Marco. 'Just fab, keep smiling, Rubes, keep it coming! Ash, not too close!'

But Robin suddenly looked as if he might slip straight out of Ruby's grasp, and Ash quickly closed his arms around the two of them. The baby, startled by the abrupt movement, threw back his head and started to howl.

'Oh dear, that's done it,' said Fairfax cheerfully, as Robin's querulous cries filled the little café.

'It's what you've got to look forward to!' Fairfax winked knowingly at Tabitha and Marco, who suddenly looked at their watches and jumped up, declaring they had to be at an antenatal class.

Robin's shrieks grew more acute, and Ruby clapped her hands over her ears and started singing loudly to drown him out. I glared at her, irritated and exhausted, and took the screaming Robin from Ash. But I couldn't pacify him, and Fairfax made not a single attempt to quieten Ruby.

'Bedlam,' said Ash levelly. 'Come on, Mivvi – let's go.'

*

Late the next morning, the doorbell rang again unexpectedly. I got up wearily, expecting Fairfax, wondering if I was ready for a confrontation. But there on the doorstep was a beaming Meera Sen, holding the hand of a little boy with a shy smile. She thrust a huge bunch of flowers towards me.

'Meera!' I gasped. 'Oh my goodness, what a wonderful surprise! Bianca told me you were back. It's been so long. And look who you've brought with you!'

We hugged like the old friends and allies we were, and her small son joined in the embrace, grabbing us tightly behind our knees. When we finally stepped back, I saw that Meera's abundant hair was now shot through with grey, and she had shadows under her bright brown eyes.

But she was still Meera, lively and vital, and when she swept in, it was like a rolling back of the years.

'He's called Kiron,' she announced, pulling the boy into her lap as they settled onto the sofa. 'We dithered over whether to give him a European name or an Indian one, but my partner Ally insisted it should be Indian. She carried him, so I thought it only right to give way.'

I gazed at Meera as everything fell into place. And her partner had carried the child – she must be the younger of the two. Although, now that I looked at Meera properly, it was clear she was younger than Belle had been, although I had always viewed her as of my parents' generation.

'He's so lovely!' I said warmly. He really was, with his liquorice eyes and shiny dark hair.

'I have chocolate cake,' I whispered to him conspiratorially, as if Meera might object, and as Kiron looked to his mother for permission, he wrinkled his nose with pleasure.

'Where is he then, your little Robin?' Meera asked, after I had brought in the cake and some tea. She fished in her bag for some toy cars for Kiron to play with, and a soft toy for Robin. 'I've bought him a teddy. I was wondering what he'd like, but of course he's too young to like anything at all!'

Right on cue, Robin let out a yelp from his cot, and I fetched him to feed while we talked. Kiron settled on the floor, engrossed in his car game.

'So, you're back for good?' I asked her.

'Yes. Six years away was plenty. It was great, but … time to come home.'

'And where will you live? You're not coming here, are you?'

'Noo, I've got a job in east London, and we've just put down an offer on a small house there. Ally's a doctor too, although we don't work in the same hospital.'

'Wonderful! We're hoping to move to London soon too,' I said. Robin's arrival had put the project on hold, but hearing Meera's news gave me a fresh longing to leave.

'You must come and see us when we are all set up,' she urged.

'Oh, I'd love that!'

We sat in silence for a few moments, listening to Kiron's *vrooms* and Robin's soft gurgles, and then Meera spoke.

'Mivvi, there's something I wanted to say to you…' She hesitated, as if she needed to prepare her words. 'While I was away, I was thinking a lot about the past, about your mother, and … well, sometimes I worry I didn't help as much as I could have done. When you were a child, I used to try to look out for you. It was a delicate business, being both family friend and a doctor – I had to be careful to observe boundaries. But I knew your mother long before her illness kicked in. I was anxious about her, and it worried me that your father seemed very … out of his depth.' Meera spoke these last words slowly; she had clearly given them thought.

'My father spends a lot of time putting himself first,' I said, more aggressively than I had intended.

Meera raised her eyebrows and smiled in sympathy. 'It must have been hard for you. It was not a healthy situation, and you were stuck in the middle of it.'

'But you tried to talk to Fairfax about it, didn't you?' I asked. 'About getting Belle help?'

'Yes, several times, but he always batted me away.' Meera sighed. 'I knew more than I should have done, or that's what your father thought anyway. He didn't want to confront what was happening, and he convinced himself that you and he could go on living an ordinary life despite it. Anyway, I just … I wanted to say that I'm sorry. I feel I should have done more.'

'What more could you have done? If he wouldn't let you?'

Meera shrugged, a sad smile on her lips.

'The trouble was,' I went on, 'I think Fairfax just buried his head in the sand and wouldn't acknowledge what was going on. He never even tried to get a diagnosis.' I spoke hotly, the words tumbling out of me. I spoke about this so rarely, and only ever to Ash.

Meera remained quiet, her eyes fixed on the carpet. This silence was so unlike her that I began to feel uncomfortable.

'Meera, what is it?' I asked tentatively. 'Have I said something wrong?'

Meera shook her head slowly.

'What is it then?'

'I don't know what he has or hasn't told you, but … what you just said isn't entirely correct.'

'He's said nothing to me,' I said, frowning. 'We've never properly talked about what happened.'

Meera looked grave. 'Mivvi, I don't want to make things difficult between you and your father.'

'Oh, they've been difficult enough over the years, I can tell you. What happened?'

'Well,' she said carefully, 'he did know what was wrong. He asked me to come and see her many years ago, when you were maybe,

I don't know, 9 or 10 years old. Your mother was very isolated. She was lonely, depressed. Clinically depressed. It started after she lost the baby. Anyway, she was beginning to hear voices. I told him that she needed to see a specialist, that the symptoms pointed to schizophrenia. She needed help. But he … went into denial.'

There was a long pause as Meera's words sank in.

'You told him,' I said flatly. 'He knew. All that time, he knew perfectly well what was wrong.'

Meera sighed. 'Yes,' she said gently. 'Of course he knew. But he couldn't act on it. He wouldn't accept it. But you did it, Mivvi. You got Belle the help she needed.'

My heart started to thump. So, he *had* known. It had not been wilful ignorance on his part. He had known for years and done nothing. And he had duped me for so long, until I was finally old enough to take action for myself.

I felt light-headed, and Meera fetched me a glass of water. I drank it back, then she took my hand in hers.

'Are you alright?' Meera asked. 'It's a shock, isn't it?'

I looked down at Robin, still asleep in my arms, and across at Kiron, who was playing on, oblivious. I hardly knew what to say. 'Yes and no,' I said at last. 'On some level, I've always known. Or suspected.'

'Don't judge him too harshly,' Meera said softly.

I turned to her in astonishment. 'How can you say that?'

'People can find themselves in situations they never imagined,' she said. 'Some people just don't know how to handle it.'

'But he failed her! Miserably!'

'He didn't do well by Belle. But he always loved you, Mivvi, whatever else he did or didn't do.'

Kiron came up to his mother and started rolling his cars along her arm and over the top of her head. She didn't flinch and it made me smile, despite everything. I wondered if I would ever be as patient a mother as she was.

His play broke the tension in the room, and we talked about other things until Robin started to stir.

'Well, I'd better be off, I suppose,' said Meera, pulling Kiron towards her and reaching for his jacket. 'Are you alright, Mivvi? In all these years, at least since you've been an adult, I've never known whether to tell you or not.'

'I'd rather know the truth,' I replied. 'Yes, I'm okay. I'll need time to process this, but … I'm alright.'

'We'll see each other soon?' she asked, as we embraced and I got another knee hug from Kiron.

'Oh, yes,' I said, hugging her tighter, 'we most certainly will.'

*

'I feel like a fool,' I said to Ash that evening as I related Meera's visit. 'I can't believe I accepted his story for so long.'

'You mustn't blame yourself. You were very small when he was telling you these things about Belle. You trusted him. This is his wrong, not yours.'

'But I should have been gentler towards her, kinder.'

'You weren't given the chance to be. Besides, it must have been very difficult to be around her all that time, given the way she was.'

I leaned my head against his shoulder, and he put his arm around me, pulling me close. Robin let out a snuffle, and we both tensed. We were getting very little sleep, and we counted on these early evenings for some peace. To our relief, he settled down again.

'It's strange to think I knew so little about Meera when I was growing up,' I went on, 'I just saw her as my mother's friend, I suppose. She was so good with Belle. Do you know, when she first turned up, I was quite annoyed when I went to the door – I was expecting it to be Fairfax again.'

'He just can't keep away from the action, can he?' Ash said.

'Is that it? Do you think that's what this is about?'

'Maybe,' he replied. 'I mean, who knows? But we suspect things aren't great with Jade, if he *is* carrying on with that Helen woman. And he does like to be at the centre of things.'

'Only if things are going well,' I said. 'He's nowhere to be seen if they're not.'

Ash nodded slowly. 'You know, if you really are starting to feel that way, maybe we should start our house hunting again in earnest.'

'Oh yes,' I said fervently. 'You betcha.'

Ash reached for some essays to mark, and I picked up my novel. I usually enjoyed the quiet and calm of the evening, but I couldn't concentrate. However much I tried to push it away, the conversation with Meera kept disrupting my thoughts. How could Fairfax knowingly have left Belle to drown in her illness? What a dereliction of duty, all to bolster and protect himself. Just as Belle had always said of him, he was selfish to the core.

Not for the first time, I wondered bitterly whether his conscience ever troubled him. Or did he tell himself the same lies and evasions that he had shamelessly related to me?

CHAPTER 3

Fairfax eased himself out of his armchair, stifling the groan that habitually came with any movement upwards. He caught sight of a jowly stranger in the mirror and promptly turned away. Actually, he thought he looked very good for his age. No one would imagine he was in his sixth decade. His old suits didn't quite fit him, but the tailor had let out the waistbands and waistcoats, and if he buttoned up his jacket, he looked nearly the same as three decades ago. He did his exercises every morning and took the stairs instead of the lift. He had even cut back on the gin and whisky.

He looked at the photograph of his 30-year-old self on the mantelpiece, glancing casually at the camera, suave in his velvet jacket. He didn't look all that different now. Age just required a little more attention to detail – a touch more dye on the sideburns and eyebrows, a little cosmetic treatment from the dentist. But he was still essentially the same man.

But much in the world around him was changing. His gaze fell on the photograph of Mivvi, not far off thirty now herself, grinning back at him in that unselfconscious way that she had. Fairfax did wish she would dress up more; she was a fine-looking girl, and a little make-up would really enhance her. But she always looked irritated if he so much as hinted in that direction.

She had cut her hair too, which suited her face, but sometimes it really was too short. She didn't want to look like a man, did she? Or maybe she did. It was becoming impossible to decipher his older daughter.

Ashish was only just present in the margins of the photo, a portion of his face caught startled behind his glasses. Bad framing, thought Fairfax, although it fitted his son-in-law's nebulous personality. Well, he supposed they seemed happy enough.

Fairfax looked more closely at Mivvi's face, softer here than in real life, a synthesis of him and Belle. Perhaps it was her judgemental attitude towards him that made her look harsher in the flesh. She had become impatient and sharp lately, correcting him all the time, disagreeing with his views on principle. She thought him too dim or oblivious to notice, but he noticed alright.

Quite what he had done to deserve this, he had no idea. He was the same steady, loving father he had always been, but she seemed determined to keep him at arm's length. Of course they had had difficulties in the past, and there had been that extremely rocky period – the end of his first marriage, the beginning of his life with Jade. But he didn't dwell on these things. He could understand Mivvi's resentments about Jade, but he had expected time to lessen the militancy of her dislike.

And now, just as the family was growing and renewing with Robin's arrival, Mivvi had decided to become prickly and aggressive. It was most vexing. She behaved as if he were bothering her when he turned up to see his own grandson, and her heavy hints about moving house were verging on the cruel. Just when she had made him a grandfather.

Fairfax frowned at himself in the mirror, forgetting for a moment its unflattering reflection. He had done everything for

Mivvi. She had been his little Sweet Pea, brown-eyed, chubby and restless. She had so many strange notions back then, calling him Fairfax instead of Daddy, and creeping around the house with that funny doll of hers. Over time, she had taken against her mother; that had been inevitable, with the way that Belle behaved. But the two of them – he and Mivvi – had been so close. And he had done so much for her – turning up conscientiously at her school events, charming her teachers, taking care of her single-handedly.

Fairfax sighed to himself. Ingratitude – that was what it was. It characterised a whole generation; younger people had little idea of the sacrifices their parents made for them. Well, their fathers anyway.

But his other daughter was also unexpectedly giving him cause for concern. Little Ruby beamed back at him from another photograph, looking happy and secure in Mivvi's arms. She must have been around 4 years old then. Fairfax loved this picture of them, and Jade had permitted it to be placed just next to their own wedding photo. But Ruby, now nearly 7, had started behaving oddly too, as if she were sulking about something. He wondered if she needed more of her mother's attention. Jade was out at school all day, and worked late into the evening, leaving Fairfax to supervise bath time and bed. He didn't mind, but perhaps there was something else going on, some upset for Ruby in class. Jade had tried to talk to her about it, but without success.

Well, what could he do? He was never very good at this sort of situation. She would surely open up to her mother, if she needed to.

*

The next evening, Fairfax was reading to Ruby, while Jade sat at the kitchen table, books, papers and marking spread out before her.

'Daddy,' Ruby asked, her voice clear as a bell, 'why are me and Mivvi sisters?'

Jade went on working, but Fairfax knew she was listening.

'You know, Ruby, I'm your dad and also her dad.'

'Yes, but Mum isn't her mum.'

'No, but you know this. Mivvi's mother is dead. I used to be married to her, but now I'm married to your lovely mum.'

Jade pulled a face at the word lovely.

'So, we're not *really* sisters,' said Ruby.

'Well, you are. I suppose, strictly speaking, you're half-sisters,' said Fairfax. 'And Mivvi's very fond of you, as you know. That's sisterly.'

At this, Ruby was silent. 'Anyway, I don't want to be an aunty,' she said, kicking the edge of her seat.

Fairfax chuckled lightly. 'Oh love, does it sound too grown-up? You don't have to be Aunty – you can just be Ruby. Though I rather like being Grandpa.'

'I don't really like it,' she muttered. Then, in an undertone, 'Anyway, I know that Mivvi's mum was a crazy.'

Fairfax stiffened. He shot a hard look at Jade, who went on with her work.

'Now, Ruby,' he said, with as much mildness as he could muster, 'that's not a good word. And we mustn't speak ill of the dead.'

The room went very quiet.

'Well, never mind,' he went on lamely, 'but don't do it again,' at which Ruby gave the chair another kick and sloped off to her room.

Fairfax turned to look at Jade. 'What's wrong with the girl?' He spoke quietly, in case Ruby was loitering outside and listening. 'And where did she get *that* from?'

'I'm not responsible, if that's what you mean, Fairfax,' said Jade, peering over her glasses. She had taken to wearing them lately, and they gave her a professorial air.

'Well, who would she have got it from then? I have never talked to her about Mivvi's mother.'

Jade sighed. 'Look, Fairfax, I didn't use that word with her, if that's what you mean. But Ruby has been asking a lot of questions recently, ever since Mivvi's son was born.'

'What would that have to do with anything?'

'I don't know. Perhaps she's trying to work out how she fits in. But she seems unsettled, and I don't think she's happy at school. She won't tell me what it is. I did go and talk to her teacher, but he doesn't know. He seemed to think it had something to do with home.'

Fairfax felt another burst of surprise. He hadn't realised that Jade had been making enquiries without informing him. 'I don't like her using words like that to describe Mivvi's mother though,' he said. 'Whatever she was like.'

'I don't know where she got it from, Fairfax.'

There was a long interval, and then Jade spoke. 'Fairfax, I've been thinking – doing a bit of research, in fact. There's that school, Bletchley Manor, about twenty miles away. It takes weekday boarders – do you know the one I mean? It was in the paper the other day. It sounds wonderful. I think it could do Ruby a lot of good.'

Fairfax stared at her. 'What do you mean? Send Ruby away?'

'No,' said Jade, in a comforting tone. 'I mean, not in any permanent sense. We'd see her every weekend, and of course during the holidays. The results there are great, and it seems like a well-run place. I really think she could thrive there.'

Fairfax gawped at her. He'd had no inkling of this.

'But I would miss her so,' Fairfax said, whispering in his alarm. 'She's not even 7 years old.'

'They take them from seven,' said Jade briskly. 'Honestly, Fairfax, I think it might be the best thing for her. She's an only child, and I think she's quite lonely, in a way. I'm so busy, and you, my love, are busy too at the office, and doing your other bits and pieces, like the Abbey.'

He looked blank. 'If she's unhappy, won't sending her away make her feel worse?'

Jade considered this. 'Not if it's presented as an opportunity, which it very much is. You know, Fairfax, I want Ruby to do well. *Really* well. Look what I've done with myself – Ruby could do even better.' She was warming to her theme now. 'I spent all my time in a children's home – I mean, I know it was different. But it made me what I am, self-sufficient and independent. And for Ruby, it would be great, she would be with all these clever kids!'

'Yes, but you didn't have any choice, Jade,' said Fairfax, feeling disconsolate. 'Ruby does.'

'Well, I just think we should think about it – there's no need to decide now.'

Then he made his false step. 'I don't know, Jade. It would cost, of course. The fees are very high there.'

Jade's face hardened immediately. 'Really? That would be a concern, would it? You spent all that money on Mivvi's education, didn't you? I seem to remember lots of talk about her at the big school in Buckingham. I'm sure you would want the same for Ruby as you did for Mivvi.' She sighed, packing up her papers. 'Think about it, Fairfax. Sleep on it.'

*

The next day, as Fairfax left the office in the afternoon, he saw Bianca walking along the street towards him, side by side with Meera Sen and the doctor's little boy.

He was surprised to see them together, but it seemed that they had kept up a friendship after the doctor had moved away.

Meera wished him a cheery hello, while giving him one of those penetrating looks of hers. He always felt uneasy in her presence. She knew too much, that woman – always poking her nose into business that wasn't hers. There was something else too, that had troubled him throughout the years; when he caught her dark eyes resting on his face, it wasn't admiring, as with most women. He had always had his suspicions about her, and Mivvi had confirmed them only a few weeks ago when she told him that Meera's partner was a woman.

'Ah, a lesbian, well, that's quite alright,' he had replied in a worldly tone, 'I don't mind about these things at all.'

Mivvi had glared at him sourly, as she always did, given the slightest chance.

Now, he made an effort to make small talk with Bianca and Meera, chatting about Robin and Meera's little boy. Then came one of those disconcerting moments that always happened with Meera.

'Well, Fairfax,' she said abruptly, 'I wasn't sure if you'd be interested, but given that I've run into you like this, I've had some news of your father-in-law. Ex-father-in-law of course. His wife died a while ago, as you probably know, and he's packed up and gone back to India.'

'Oh,' replied Fairfax.

'Maz is travelling a lot, and the old man felt he had nothing to keep him in Kenya any longer. My aunt told me all this – you know I was in India recently. Anyway, I just thought I'd mention it.'

Fairfax hadn't thought about Belle's father in years. 'Where's the old man gone? He's from … western India, isn't he?'

Meera nodded. 'Yes, but he's gone to live with his sister. She married a Bengali too, so he's joined her in Calcutta, well it's called Kolkata now – it's where my family is from. And Ash's family too, in fact.'

Fairfax narrowed his eyes. 'I see,' he responded, and then said casually, 'You know, Meera, no need to mention this to Mivvi. It's all in the past.'

She fixed him with that cool gaze of hers. 'I've already told her. It would have been strange not to, wouldn't it?'

'Of course,' he said airily, 'well, that's quite alright.'

Bianca smiled at him benignly, her green eyes full of soft enquiry. 'Why shouldn't Mivvi know, Fairfax?'

'No reason at all,' he said emphatically. 'It's quite alright.'

He was bubbling with irritation and moved to close the subject down. Still, he heard himself asking, 'Did you hear anything else? About the old man, I mean.'

'Not much. I suppose he's gone to end his days there. He's sad at the loss of his wife and daughter, and sad at the life that Belle had … That sadness we all feel in relation to Belle.'

That was the trouble with this woman, Fairfax thought angrily as he strolled on down the street. Stirring things up for no reason. He had no intention of talking about the past anymore, and certainly not with Meera.

There were so many pitfalls to avoid, he thought wearily. Meera's meddling, Mivvi's scepticism, Jade's sensitivities. All he wanted was a peaceful life.

*

He got home to a quiet house. Ruby was with a friend after school, and Jade wasn't yet back from work. Fairfax absent-mindedly poured himself a very small whisky, just to enjoy the late afternoon sun.

There had been no more talk about Ruby going to boarding school, but Fairfax knew the subject was far from closed. When Jade set her mind to something, she would invariably have it.

She had not turned out to be quite what he had expected. The Jade he had first known had been so quiet, so unassertive, that he had barely noticed her. Then gradually he'd become intrigued by her strange mix of knowingness and fragility, that cool and flirtatious tongue concealed in a meek and demure demeanour. But she was steely, too – he knew that now. The way she had gone on at him all those years, weeping and sobbing at him to leave Belle, wearing him down, determined to have him – he felt now as though it had all been a strategy. Women always wanted so much – they were always trying to change men. Why couldn't they just leave things be?

Still, there had been a couple of exceptions to this rule. One had been Céline – it had probably been unwise, given his situation and the age gap. But it had been such fun, and without a hint of complication on her side!

The sun cast a warm ray of light across his armchair, and a smile of pleasure played on his face as his thoughts turned from Céline to Bianca – not Bianca as she was now, but the young and carefree one, who adored life and friendships and lovers. They had that in common, a greediness for life, all those years ago, before he'd met Belle, and before Bianca got together with John. Fairfax and Bianca were never going to be a couple, but for a few brief days together, it had been wild.

He remembered them streaming down Park Lane at high speed on his moped. 'Hold on tight now,' he'd shouted to her, feeling her pressed up behind him.

'Gawd!' she'd screeched, as he stepped up the speed and then went as fast as he dared.

He remembered feeling her scarf blow into his face and swerving sharply at the swirl of lava lamp colours, making her scream again.

'You're gonna get us killed, Fairfax, you bloody maniac!'

Fairfax smiled wryly. Ah, the craziness of youth.

He had agreed to look after Bianca for a couple of days, once John's charity had got her off the streets, and he had perhaps taken his task too much to heart. She was certainly looked after in every way.

Fairfax grinned to himself. What did it matter? They had done no harm – they were adults, and they knew it was just a bit of fun. Delicious Bianca.

She had been very starchy towards him for a while, but both she and John had softened after Belle's death, and if their friendship wasn't the same as before, at least they no longer gave him the cold shoulder. They had proved to be such a solid couple, she so loyal to him, he so tolerant of her excesses, and unembarrassed by her past.

In this respect, John was broader-minded than him, Fairfax had to admit. He had set his sights on someone considerably higher than Bianca. But then again, John and Bianca had endured, unlike him and Belle.

Fairfax dismissed the thought quickly. He couldn't have known how Belle was going to turn out. So how could he be blamed?

He poured himself another small peg of whisky, and shut his eyes, letting the sun play on his face. The one person he could rely on for simplicity was Helen. There, at least was an occasional escape from the flatness of his life.

He let out a deep sigh. It was hard to admit that his world had shrunk, but ever since that terrible night with Belle and Jade, nothing had been the same. He had delayed going back to work for as long as he could, but compassionate leave only lasted a few weeks, and then when he did go back, everyone had looked at him differently. There was never a single direct comment, but he had caught the smirks and the stifled asides alright. It had been most vexing! Who the hell were they to point the finger? He hadn't done anything that bad. Why should he be judged on a little infidelity?

He had considered moving to a different firm in another town, but Mivvi had still been young, and leaving her would have been a terrible wrench. Besides, he had needed to stay close to keep an eye on what was happening with Belle. Then there was Jade, busy with her new career. These forces had conspired to keep him where he was, so he had dealt with the blow to his dignity by detaching himself from work and trying to find interest in life's other pleasures, his children and grandchild, and, as it turned out, Helen.

The friendship with Helen had come upon him unawares; he had never planned to get involved with anyone else. Not that it was really an involvement. One major upheaval had been enough. He was with Jade now, whatever their shortcomings together. And yet, there was no point being in each other's pockets the whole time. One needed one's little escapes.

He would never have dreamt of any liaison with a good friend of Jade – but then Helen had stopped working at the school, and the two women had drifted apart. Either that, or Helen had become too busy to see Jade; he couldn't remember precisely. But, with him cutting down his hours at the firm, and Jade spending so much time in school, working in the Abbey gift shop took on a new significance.

There he would often see Helen and go for coffee with her or a drink. Happily, neither she nor anyone else at the Abbey had any inkling of his history with Belle. This fresh environment restored his confidence with people, and in himself. Helen was petite like Jade, but with a softer face that exuded goodness.

Fairfax had thought her a spiritual soul, until one day he had caught her looking at him playfully. He had felt a rush of his old self.

That's it! he thought. *That's what she does – she gives me back the old me!*

Nothing serious had happened between them – or if it had, it had only been on occasional afternoons when he had got carried away. He certainly didn't intend anything more with her. It was a *romance* in the old-fashioned sense, he thought, *a romantic friendship*. And that was how it would stay.

The whisky finished, Fairfax got up, smiling in a contented way.

You have to know how to enjoy life, he thought to himself, *and I do. There's no point regretting things. You have to adapt and be flexible, know when to advance and when to retreat.*

He did a little fencing move in front of the mirror and winced at the pain in his back. He thought of all the women in his life, of Belle and Mivvi, of Bianca, Céline and Helen, and of Jade and Ruby.

He thought of his old friend John, his earnest son-in-law Ashish, and his little prince Robin.

I'm a respectable man, he thought to himself, *and I've done well for myself. I've come a long way.*

He ran a hand through his thinning hair, settling it in a sweep across his head. When he heard Jade's key in the lock, he went to greet her, ready for whatever next life had in store.

CHAPTER 4

I settled Robin in his cot for his afternoon nap, wanting him rested and in a good temper before Fairfax and Ruby arrived. Mercifully, my father's impromptu appearances had tailed off over the weeks and months, and this particular visit was prepared for and planned.

Although Fairfax had mentioned nothing, I suspected that his absence was connected to Ruby. On the last few visits, she had been diffident and withdrawn, not wanting to talk or to hold Robin, even though he was so winning now, smiling and cooing and curious about everything. Perhaps I hadn't been as attentive to her as I should have been, but the tiredness of the first months had been all-consuming.

Whatever it was that was affecting her, I had decided not to make anything of it. It must be difficult for her, being suddenly displaced as the baby of the family. She was sure to adjust and come around to Robin soon enough.

The intervening weeks had also given me time to recover from my conversation with Meera. I kept veering between wanting to confront Fairfax with his cowardly dishonesty and wanting to run far away from him and his mess. Ultimately, I did neither, in the knowledge that I would get away soon enough when we moved house. In the meantime, I was glad he had stayed away.

Robin was still asleep when they arrived, and I ushered them quietly into the front room. Fairfax was pleased to see me after the long interval, and eager to hold the baby once he was awake. Ruby looked less sulky than before, and greeted me with a shy smile and a brief hug.

'I've got chocolate cake, Ruby, and I've dug out Adèle for you – she's in Robin's room. I'll go and get her.'

A faint smile of amusement flitted across her face. 'Thank you, but I'm not so into dolls anymore.'

'Goodness, you're much more mature than I was at your age!' I said, with a laugh. 'I went on playing with Adèle until I was, ooh let me see, almost a teenager.'

Fairfax smiled. 'Older even than that, if I remember rightly.'

'I was a very slow developer. Not like the precocious youth of today!'

We sat and chatted, and despite Meera's revelations, I found it easy enough to talk normally to Fairfax. Ruby's presence precluded any mention of anything serious, so we talked casually of smaller things. I knew that such occasions would become rarer once we moved, but if I could manage to maintain this level of detached friendliness, I could cope with him visiting us once in a while.

To amuse him, I recounted the story of Tabitha's latest visit. She had come with her baby daughter, whom she had named Hera. Marco had got a three-month job on a foreign photo shoot, so the tandem and newly bought trailer were gathering dust in the outhouse while he was away. Hera woke screaming at all hours of the night, so in desperation, Tabitha had given her a bottle to help her settle, and now she was a convert.

'"Really, Mivvi,"' and here I put on my most supercilious Tabitha voice, '"all that breast is best is just brainwashing, right?"'

I felt a touch disloyal for mimicking my friend, but it didn't stop me from telling the tale; and besides, Fairfax was lapping it up.

'It's always like that when they come, utter mayhem. Bottle or no bottle, Hera wails all the time. If ever I mention them, Ash says, "Hera, ye Gods!"'

The allusion was lost on Fairfax, but he laughed uproariously anyway. He loved gossip, as long as it was about other people. Ruby smiled at our merriment, and seemed content to sit and listen to us talk.

Fairfax had told me that Jade had in mind a new school for her, and although I was perplexed at the idea of Ruby being sent away, I did wonder if it might help her relax. Perhaps she just wasn't happy where she was. But I didn't want to raise the issue while she was in the room.

Presently Ruby started looking bored, and said grudgingly, 'Perhaps I will go and get Adèle anyway, just for something to do.'

I hesitated. 'She's in Robin's room, though. Are you sure you can go in quietly? It would be better not to disturb him for another half hour or so.'

'I'll creep in,' whispered Ruby.

'Right you are,' I whispered back. 'Nice and quiet now.'

'She seems well, Fairfax,' I said, once Ruby was out of the room. 'Sunnier than recently.'

Fairfax looked thoughtful. 'She's alright. Still a bit troubled at times, but it comes and goes. Jade is very set on this idea of sending her away, and strangely Ruby seems to be quite excited by it too.'

I looked at him sympathetically. 'It's just you who's not keen.'

'I'd just miss her so,' he said sadly. 'But let's see, it's still to be decided.'

There was a sudden yell from down the corridor. Robin was awake.

'What a pity,' I said, jumping up ruefully. 'I was hoping he'd stay down for longer. I guess I shouldn't have let her go in. Oh well, never mind.'

Robin's cries were getting louder and more plaintive.

'Coming, coming!' I called, as I went towards his room. 'There we are, it's alright,' I said soothingly, lifting him out of his cot. 'Here I am, it's all alright.'

But he was shaking in my arms, gulping in air between his sobs. This was not how he usually cried.

'There we are, petal, it's alright.'

But Robin kept crying.

Fairfax appeared at the door, making cooing noises. 'He's making a racket, isn't he?' he said admiringly. 'Fine pair of lungs. More noise than usual, I must say.'

'Where's Ruby gone?' I asked. There was no sign of her.

Fairfax shrugged. 'Must have found the doll and scarpered because she woke Robin.'

I cuddled my son to try to quieten him. 'Maybe he's wet – I'll change him.'

I unbuttoned the top of his overalls, and slipped them down over his little body, but Robin cried even more loudly.

There, on his left arm, was a bright red weal, a spreading bruise standing ugly against his pure brown baby skin. It was as if he'd been squeezed or pinched, and with ferocity.

Fairfax took a sharp intake of breath. 'Oh, Mivvi, oh my goodness, little Robin, poor little thing!'

I looked at the injury, appalled, and forced myself to think straight. I had to protect Robin, but I could not allow this to turn into a big family drama.

I changed him quickly, fetched some cream for the bruise, and then held him close so that his little cheek was pressed against mine. His strangulated sobs slowly started to die down.

'Let's go and find Ruby,' I said to a sorrowful-looking Fairfax.

Ruby was under the kitchen table with Adèle, any pretence of being too grown-up for toys gone. She studiedly ignored us as we came into the room.

'Ruby,' I said firmly but gently. I didn't want to frighten her. 'Ruby, come on out. We have to have a little talk.'

Fairfax stood next to me, looking wretched.

'I'm playing,' hissed Ruby.

'You need to stop playing and come and tell us what happened.'

When she failed to answer, I handed Robin to Fairfax, and crouched down by the table.

'Ruby, listen to me,' I said slowly. 'No one is angry at you, and no one is going to tell you off, do you understand? But what happened just now must never happen again. Robin is very small. He can't defend himself. You don't have to like him very much, but you must promise me not to hurt him again. Ever.'

Ruby's face was tight as a fist. She twitched her nose angrily and started pulling at Adèle's hair.

'You do hear me, don't you?'

She still made no reply.

I stood up and reached for Robin. 'Fairfax, I think you should take her home. Let everything calm down, and then we can talk again.'

'Yes, yes, of course,' he said hurriedly. 'Come on, Ruby, leave that doll now, and let's go home to your mum.'

'She's not at home, she's at work,' Ruby muttered.

'She'll be back soon. Come on.'

They walked out to the car, Fairfax clutching his little daughter's hand, an expression of bewilderment and dismay etched on his face. Ruby's lips were pursed, and she stared doggedly ahead. As I watched them go, I thought for the first time that the girl looked just like Jade.

Robin was quiet now, and I mechanically stroked his hair. Family troubles could erupt from any source, I thought, even the most innocent.

Outside, the silver car pulled away, and they were gone.

*

Jade was home earlier than usual, and Ruby ran soundlessly into her arms, burying her face against her mother's body. It was unusual, Ruby rarely appealed to her so directly.

Fairfax stood beside them helplessly. He was unable to decide whether silence was better than explanation, and whether they would unite against him if he told what had happened. He opted for silence, until Ruby stopped sobbing.

Once the girl was calmer, Jade sent her upstairs so that they could talk.

'It's just a bit of sibling rivalry,' said Jade coolly, once Fairfax had finished telling her. 'Not that I'm condoning it – of course not. But Ruby is young and isn't always in control of herself.'

'But to hurt him like that!' Fairfax burst out, as if he himself had borne the injury. He ran his hand through his hair. 'I don't know, Jade – it's very disturbing. I mean, Robin isn't her sibling, is he? It's not as if he's our son.'

'I didn't mean rivalry with Robin – I meant with Mivvi.'

Fairfax was astonished.

'Fairfax, you're such an innocent sometimes,' said Jade, looking almost amused. 'You dote on Mivvi, perhaps too much, I don't know. And you're besotted with Robin. That's a grandparent's prerogative, I suppose – I don't know about these things. But Ruby, I imagine, watches it all and takes it all in. It affects her. I think she feels side-lined.'

'But I adore Ruby too!' said Fairfax plaintively.

'Of course you do, we all do,' said Jade. 'It will blow over. Ruby's got a fright, and she won't do it again. I'll send Mivvi a card telling her Ruby is sorry. Don't worry too much.'

Fairfax wondered how Jade could be so practical and so unemotional.

'Perhaps this episode does show us something,' Jade went on, after a pause. 'A change of environment would really do Ruby good. It would stop her from brooding on family matters. She's keen on Bletchley Manor, you know – I've talked to her about it. I really think you should reconsider.'

Fairfax, who didn't think he had much say in the matter, nodded slowly. 'Maybe you're right,' he said quietly. 'But, if she were to go away now, mightn't it look as if we were punishing her? She must never hurt Robin again, that's for sure, but she might take against us for inflicting too harsh a punishment.'

'Nonsense,' said Jade briskly. 'She'll be only too pleased to be sent off. You underestimate her independence. She's like her mum.' And here Jade put her face very close to Fairfax's. 'A free spirit.'

'An indomitable will,' murmured Fairfax, lightly kissing her lips, despite himself.

'So, it's a deal,' she murmured back. 'Sealed with a kiss.'

CHAPTER 5

'They've sent her away, you know,' I said.

'Who? Who've sent who away?'

'Whom.'

'What?'

'Who've sent whom away.'

Ash narrowed his eyes at me. 'You're worse than I am. I assume you're talking about Ruby?'

'Yes,' I said soberly, despite his teasing. 'I hope she didn't think it was because of what happened here. Fairfax assured me the two weren't connected, but I don't know if Ruby knows that.'

'But she was alright the last time you saw her, wasn't she?'

'Yes, she was. But she did look very chastened.'

'Well, she'll have known you were watching her closely with Robin.'

'Like a hawk! But I was gentle with her. I did think Jade's card was a bit cold though.'

Ash looked at me wryly.

'What? What have I said?' I cried. 'It *was* cold!'

Ash put his arm around me. 'It was – you're right.'

'Anyway,' I went on, 'I feel quite sorry for Fairfax now, whatever he's done. He looks bereft without Ruby. I don't know what he does with his time. Mopes around probably.'

'Helps out even more at the Abbey shop?' asked Ash cheekily.

'Well, he *has* started turning up here all the time again,' I said, ignoring him. 'My heart sinks every time, but I am trying to be patient. I do feel for him – in this instance anyway.'

'Have you told him about India?'

'No, not yet. When I mentioned it a while ago, he didn't seem interested. I'll talk to him about it tomorrow.'

Ash nodded. 'And have you decided about Belle's father? Are you going to tell him that we might see him?'

'I don't know,' I said slowly. 'Fairfax knows he's in Calcutta now – Kolkata in fact, I must remember to call it that. Meera told him – but he's never once raised it with me. So I feel reluctant to raise it with him.' I hesitated and then went on, 'I've never told you this, but … I found a letter from Belle's father to Fairfax once.'

'Found?'

'Well.' I could feel the embarrassment rising. 'It was when I was snooping on Fairfax, trying to find out about him and Jade. I couldn't understand it, it was something about a request that Belle's parents couldn't fulfil. It sounded really intense. Anyway, it's all just made me wary of saying anything.'

'He'll twig though won't he, surely? Even if you don't say anything?'

I shrugged. 'He might. There again, he's a great one for going into denial. If something's inconvenient, he just spirits it away – whoosh!'

Robin clapped delightedly at the sound and started to repeat it as he propelled himself around the kitchen in his walker.

'Anyway,' I said, above his cries, 'why shouldn't I go and see my grandfather? I don't need Fairfax's permission, do I?'

'No, of course not,' Ash said, with a smile. 'You must do exactly what feels right.'

*

The next day, I went for a drive with Fairfax out towards Bletchley, so that he could show me Ruby's new school from afar. Robin sat silently in his car seat, wide-eyed at the sight of sheep.

'There it is,' said Fairfax, pulling over to point out a large, Victorian red-brick building at the top of the hill, with wide lawns and an imposing iron gate. 'Looks very distinguished, doesn't it? And posh!'

I did what was required and looked admiring. 'And she really has settled in alright?' I asked.

'Oh, yes. I have to admit that Jade's decision was well-judged. Ruby's much sunnier now when she comes home for the weekend.'

He looked nonplussed that Ruby could so easily do without him. I patted his arm.

'Come on, the decision's been taken,' I said, 'and it sounds like it's for the best. Ruby seems happier to me too. I get letters from her from school, like a pen pal!'

Fairfax shot me a grateful look. 'It feels like all of that has blown over, then?' he asked, glancing back at Robin.

I nodded. 'Yes, I think so.'

'Good. Anyway,' said Fairfax, starting up the car again, 'I've got much more time on my hands without Ruby, so I can be around to help you more! With Robin, I mean.'

I bit my lip and tried to compose myself. 'Actually, Fairfax, I've been meaning to tell you, we're setting off on our trip soon. To India – you remember I mentioned it? Ash is very keen to take Robin for his first birthday. It's amazing to think it's only three weeks away! Anyway, we leave in a fortnight.'

Fairfax gripped the wheel silently. 'I see,' he said eventually.

'And is that really a good idea, Mivvi? India is a hard country to travel in.'

'We've just got to get there,' I said, in a reassuring tone. 'Then we'll be looked after by his family. His parents are there at the moment too. We're not really travelling around.'

'But, you know, diseases and bugs and things,' he replied vaguely. 'Tummy bugs, dysentery, even Delhi belly – that could be dangerous for a baby.'

'We'll be careful,' I said, keeping my eyes fixed on the road. 'To be honest, I'm more worried about the flight and keeping him quiet.'

Robin gurgled and whooped, and I blew him a kiss.

Fairfax looked thoughtful. 'Do you want some help?' he suddenly asked, flashing me an uncertain smile. 'I mean, shall I come with you?'

'*What?*' I was used to his impetuous ways, but this was extreme.

'Oh, you know, to give you a hand. And I like an adventure!'

'Well, no, I...' I trailed off, torn between irritation and confusion. 'I don't think it would be appropriate, would it? I'm meeting Ash's wider family for the first time – it would be strange to turn up with you!'

The tips of his ears flushed, and he looked wounded. I didn't know what to say. Surely he couldn't have been serious?

The subject of Belle's father loomed unspoken between us.

'Alright, well it was just a suggestion,' he said huffily. 'Best be getting back now – I've got lots to do.'

We drove back to Milton Keynes in a silence punctuated only by Robin's exclamations at the wonderful outside world around him.

*

'How was the drive?' asked Ash that evening.

We had finally got Robin down. His sweet temper had vanished as soon as we got home, and I had spent hours trying to get him to sleep. I felt thoroughly frazzled.

Now, Ash was chopping some olives to put in the spaghetti sauce, while I slumped on the sofa, exhausted. At least our open-plan flat meant he could cook and I could sprawl.

'It was alright,' I said, 'until Fairfax offered to come to India with us.'

Ash looked round at me, astonished.

'Don't worry, I put him off! Such a mad idea, but he looked quite resentful when I said no.'

'And no mention of your grandfather?' he asked. He was dipping the spaghetti into the boiling water, watching the ends curl.

'No, mercifully.'

'Well, well,' he said thoughtfully. 'What a strange creature Fairfax is. I don't think he's very self-aware, is he?'

I was exhausted and Ash's reasonableness grated. 'Why are you defending him?' I snapped.

'I'm not!' Ash exclaimed, surprised. 'I just think he's very unreflecting. Now, I was going to ask, have you been in touch with the OU about when you're going back?'

I scowled at him. 'Are you trying to head me off here, Ash? Changing the subject? It's not very subtle, is it?'

'No!' he cried. He looked guiltily towards Robin's room, but there was no sound. 'No,' he said more softly. 'I'm not, it's just … well, he gets you into such a state sometimes.'

'And am I wrong to get into a state? Isn't it the only way to react to his presumption?'

Ash sighed heavily. 'Look, Mivvi, why are you taking it out on me? It's not my fault. I'm sorry he's like this, but it's not my fault.'

I felt the rebuke. 'I'm sorry, okay, you're right.'

But Ash was nettled now, standing back from the hob, dinner forgotten.

'You know, sometimes I wonder if you don't spend more time thinking about your wretched father than you do about me.'

I stared at him in astonishment. Nothing could be further from the truth. 'I do not! Really, Ash, I do not.'

'Well, it feels that way sometimes,' he muttered, looking immediately embarrassed by his petulance.

I put my arms around him. 'I only go on about him because he causes me so much trouble,' I said ruefully. 'You don't cause me trouble. You are in no way the problem.'

He nodded. 'Alright. Truce. And sorry. And as well as sorry, I actually came home with some good news. I've got the tickets. We're all set. My uncle will send his driver to meet us at the airport. It's all sorted. We really are going.'

I kissed him and then rested my head against his shoulder, so that he wouldn't see how emotional I felt. This journey to his parents' country and to the country of Belle's birth felt momentous to me, and I was filled with excitement and nerves at the prospect of meeting my grandfather.

When we returned home, I would hand in my notice, and then we would move to London. It would cause Fairfax pain but at least I wouldn't have to contend with his behaviour for much longer. His sense of entitlement with Robin infuriated me. His lack of responsibility towards Belle enraged me. But in all this time, I had found it impossible to stand up to him.

There was something else that gnawed away at me, too. Now that I was a mother, I couldn't possibly imagine allowing Robin to experience what I had gone through. Why had Fairfax allowed it all to happen? Why had he not protected me more?

I felt a radical shift away from him, like a satellite turning away from a star, rejecting the false path on which I had been set.

CHAPTER 6

The cacophony hit me with physical force.

'*Ayjay, ayjay, aashhun* please!'

'*Dao, dao, aye khane esho!*'

The air resounded with the voices of porters and drivers calling to each other and to the stream of travellers being disgorged from the airport, but in a language so clear and precise it suggested that despite the apparent bedlam, everything was in fact running smoothly.

I stood beneath the big neon sign of *Netaji Subhas Chandra Bose International Airport* with Robin strapped in behind me, the two of us gawping with amazement at the lean, wiry men navigating laden trolleys twice their size. The yellow taxis, fat as bumblebees, snaked around the concourse sounding their horns even when stationary and adding to the raucous symphony.

Ash was scanning the road looking for his uncle's car, flanked by two porters who had grabbed our bags as soon as we emerged, and who now stood supportively next to us. Ash's shirt sleeves were rolled up and he looked surprisingly at home.

It was dusk, and as insects darted through the gloom, I could taste the air, hot and smoky, with a flavour of sweetness that wasn't cigarettes or woodsmoke.

'Cow dung,' said Ash, reading my thoughts. 'People who can't afford fuel dry it and burn it instead.'

I smiled at him wonderingly as Robin clapped his hands and started to whoop behind me.

'Ded! Ded!' he cried at the sight of a porter balancing a huge suitcase on his head, perfectly upright despite its weight. Without missing a step, the man turned his eyes towards Robin and flashed him a brilliant smile.

'Here he is,' said Ash. *'Ayje, aashchay,'* he added to the porters, who were suddenly joined by many others, and as Ash greeted the driver, they all started manoeuvring our bags into the car.

I stood a little helplessly to one side, feeling large and ungainly next to these active, sinewy men, their movements almost balletic and choreographed. A loud horn blared right next to us and made us jump.

'Come on, Mivvi, let's go,' said Ash, after handing out rupee notes to the porters. 'Hold on tight to Robin – I'm not sure if the seat belts work.'

We drove as smoothly as the potholes would allow, our driver expertly dodging slower cars, hand-pulled rickshaws and, in one heart-stopping moment, an emaciated cow standing sadly in the middle of the road. I watched agog as another driver, impatient at a junction, mounted the grass verge to get around the traffic and narrowly missed a bicycle. A moped carrying an entire family weaved carefully past us, a tiny child sandwiched between its father and the handlebars, the mother and another child holding on tight behind them.

'Mental, isn't it?' said Ash happily.

I nodded back in silent agreement. There was simply no other word for it.

We arrived at a large gated complex in a more peaceful neighbourhood and were ushered into a front porch, its windows framed with intense pink and purple bougainvillea. A young man came out to help us with the bags, swiftly followed by Ash's parents and another elderly couple, the man bespectacled, the woman wrapped in a cotton sari. We hugged Ash's mother and father, Indrani and Rohit, and then Ash deftly dipped to the ground to touch his uncle and aunt's feet and then his forehead in a sign of respect.

'*Mama, mami, ayjay amar bow Mivvi ar amader chhele Robin,*' Ash said, gently pushing me forward with Robin in my arms.

I felt suddenly flustered and could feel myself flushing, conscious of my lack of knowledge about this culture and language which were, after all, partly mine. But then Robin reached out to his great-aunt's shoulder to touch the border of her yellow sari, and cooed with such unequivocal pleasure that everyone began to laugh, and I felt blessed with my sunny child and my sudden acquisition of a place in this land.

'*Namaskar,*' I said, bringing my palms together in salutation as Ash had taught me to do. 'It's so wonderful to finally be here.'

*

Our first two weeks passed in a whirl of family visits and sight-seeing. One of my first struggles was to follow how every relative had a name for their position in relation to me. 'This uncle is our *Jethamasya*,' explained Ash patiently. 'It means he's my father's elder brother. His son calls my father *Kaku*, meaning he is his father's younger brother.'

He laughed at me as I went cross-eyed with concentration.

'But,' he added, 'you can get away with Uncle and Aunty. Always! With anyone older.'

I gave myself over to eating five meals a day, as every visit to a new uncle and aunty included copious hospitality, and I obligingly munched my way through *mishtis* and *samosas,* and large clay pots of rich, sweetened *lal dahi.*

We visited family in old colonial Kolkata houses, their outsides grimy and unremarkable, their interiors gracious, high-ceilinged and cool; and then other relatives in modern, compact apartments, whole families crowded into spaces smaller than we had in Milton Keynes. It was autumn but still hot and humid in the city, and I was grateful for the ever-present ceiling fans, and for the abundant lemon water or *nimbu pani* that I was offered. If the streets smelt of pollution and bad drains and sometimes – miserably – of excrement, the homes smelt of spices and mustard oil and rich, heady incense. I felt my senses alive in a way I had never felt at home, perhaps because it was all so unfamiliar and new, but also because it was a country that thrust itself on me and into me, whether I liked it or not.

Robin was feted in each and every household and started to respond to Bengali words, bringing cries of admiration and approval. I was keenly appraised by the women of the family, and pronounced *'very fair'*, which brought back a sudden recollection of Maz. I made one long-distance phone call to Fairfax, but the crackly line made it difficult to speak, and I felt disconnected from him in more ways than one.

Ash was determined to show me the city in all its aspects, and I was hungry to take it all in, marvelling at the colonial vestiges that were the Victoria Memorial and St Paul's Cathedral, so incongruous in the shimmering Kolkata heat, as if monuments had been plucked wholesale out of London and unceremoniously deposited thousands of miles away.

FINDING BELLE

At home, I listened for many hours to Ash's uncle Manoj, who was no longer a communist, but was spending his retirement in charity work and in bemoaning the deep inequities of their society; and when I watched the street dwellers in their pavement homes, and the barefoot children sent out to beg, I felt a new appreciation for my own material comforts, which I had always taken entirely for granted.

Uncle Manoj insisted we visit the museum of the celebrated anti-British freedom fighter, whose name I recognised as the one emblazoned across the airport; and I felt a strange exhilaration at the acts of resistance it memorialised, despite my confusion at his wartime alliances with Japan and Germany.

I went respectfully to the home of Tagore, Kolkata's revered man of letters, and for the first time in my life, I attended worship at a temple, sweet with the incense I was growing to adore, and replete with icons and carvings too sensuous for religion.

We went for long strolls on the Maidan, where hundreds of boys were engrossed in games of cricket, each one a budding Test match star, and where young girls stopped us repeatedly to coo over Robin. Everywhere we went, we were objects of interest, not least at the city zoo, where we attracted more attention than the animals. I got used to people murmuring *memsahib* when I passed by, and I thought ruefully of how hard I had tried as a child to be the very person I was now being cast as.

*

Indrani and Rohit threw a small family party for Robin's first birthday. I carefully dressed him in a cream-coloured *kurta* and he was proclaimed a mini Rajah by the company as he clapped his hands at the single candle in his cake. Indrani and Ash's aunt dressed me in a blue sari, pinning it strategically in case it unravelled, and put a smear of red *sindoor* in my parting. I submitted to being their doll, despite feeling unequal to this new identity.

While the guests were passing round tea and samosas, Ash nodded his head slightly towards a very elderly couple who were sitting apart in a corner, listening to one of his uncles animatedly relating a tale.

'They are Meera's uncle and aunt,' he said quietly. 'They know your grandfather.'

'Oh!' I said. Belle's father had been preying on my mind. We had one week left in the city, and a meeting had still to be arranged.

'Who is he to me?' I asked him. 'My maternal grandfather?'

'Your *Dadu*,' Ash said. 'An easy one to remember. Shall we go and talk to them?'

We left Robin with Indrani and went over to the old couple.

'We have been waiting to speak to you,' said Meera's aunt, nodding at me gently as we sat down.

'We are not so mobile, so we sat until you came to us,' said her husband.

'He is waiting to see you, you know,' continued his wife. 'He knows you are here.'

'Who does?' I asked automatically, and instantly felt foolish. 'Does he?' I corrected myself.

Suddenly, Belle's father felt very close.

The old lady chuckled. 'This is a small community, you know. And not so much happens in our lives. We knew you were coming. We told him.'

'I should … make an appointment to see him,' I said earnestly, hoping they didn't think I was reluctant.

The couple started to laugh.

'No, no, no appointment needed,' said Meera's uncle. 'That is not the way here. You are his *nati*, his grandchild. You just turn up.'

'Really?' I asked, looking to Ash for confirmation.

'You do not need to ask your husband this question,' said the old lady, who was starting to gather her things. 'When you go back to *Bilayti*, give our love to our dearest Meera. She is a very good girl. But first, go and see your grandfather. He must see his *nati* and her son, while you are both here. He is an old man – well, we all are old. And so he must see you now.'

*

Two days later, Ash, Robin and I were ringing the bell at the large, double-sided wooden door of one of the imposing old houses of south Kolkata. The doors swung open slowly, but we could see no one there, just a long flight of unlit stairs that led up into a gloom.

At the top stood a young girl – 'the maid,' whispered Ash – who had let us in by pulling a long rope attached to the door handle, and we walked up not into gloom but the gentle light of an open verandah shaded by trees and rattan awnings that were half-lowered, sheltering us from the strong afternoon sun. The young girl gestured shyly for us to sit and brought us glasses of sharp *nimboo pani* while we waited.

Robin was drowsy in Ash's arms, and I was glad of the excuse to be silent, unable to put any of my thoughts into words on the cusp of this long-awaited meeting. Ash squeezed my hand. The taste of the lemons helped to cleanse my anxious mind, and I focused instead on the incessant traffic down below, the impatient horns and the shouting of traders. Periodically, a large crow landed on the balustrade and eyed us sceptically.

The curtain separating the verandah from the main house moved, and out stepped an elderly man. He was tall and spare, with a head of thin white hair, and a body so slender that he should have stooped, but he held himself up straight and erect. His face was thin and chiselled, with skin that looked like parchment, as though it might crease if it were touched. His eyes were small and alive and rested expressionlessly on my face, and then on the half-sleeping Robin.

'So you have come,' he said softly, after what felt like an age. 'You have finally come. My great-grandson and my granddaughter. My *nati*. And you look just like your mother, just like my Bela.'

He held out his arms to me, and I went to him, feeling the tears swimming in my eyes, my heart and throat full of emotion. I took in the hot smell of his skin and felt the wetness of his own eyes as he bent to kiss my forehead.

'Let me look at you again,' he said eventually, moving back. 'You look very fine. Maz was right. Come, sit and let us talk.'

Ash and I settled into a long wicker sofa lined with cushions, and my grandfather, after tenderly stroking the slumbering Robin's head, sat opposite us. He rested his hands on his knees with his fingers curled and his palms upright.

'This is usually my hour of meditation,' he said. 'I will not meditate, but the body has its own habits.'

'We are disturbing you?' asked Ash carefully.

The old man shook his head, smiling, and gestured to the young girl to bring us tea and sweets.

We drank and ate in relative silence. There was so much that I wanted to know but I was unsure where to start.

Eventually Ash spoke. 'Can I leave this little fellow on a bed somewhere?' Robin was now fast asleep. 'I thought I might take a walk and let you both catch up.'

I smiled at him gratefully. We had agreed that the old man might speak more frankly if I was alone.

After Ash and Robin had left, I turned to him.

'Grandfather, *Dadu*, I should have come to see you earlier, either here or in Mombasa. I don't know what was stopping me. I'm sorry it's taken so long.'

The old man inclined his head.

'You are here now – that is what matters. And you must have come with questions. I too have questions.'

I nodded, inviting him to go first.

'Did she suffer much? Bela? Was there much suffering?'

I felt a lump in my throat. But I had a duty to respond as truthfully as I could, so I took a deep breath. 'She did suffer, yes. She was lonely and isolated. And misunderstood. I didn't understand her either, not for many years, and I feel a lot of guilt about that.'

'You were a child,' he said. 'Children cannot understand unless things are explained to them. I do not think your father explained.'

'No, he didn't,' I said sadly.

The old man looked away, and for a moment I wondered if he had lost the thread of the conversation. But when he turned his face towards me again it was twisted with regret. 'I considered coming to see her – several times, I considered it. But travel to your country was not made easy for us. My late wife was also not in good health. And then, we were unsure of the welcome we would receive.'

'From Fairfax? I mean, from my father?'

The old man inclined his head.

'Why?' I asked softly. 'Why did relations become so difficult between you?'

He gave a thin smile. 'That is very hard to relate. It is complicated. Parts of it will also be difficult for you to hear. But you are an adult now. And you have sought me out. So I will try to tell you.'

He paused to gather himself, and I did not dare move for fear I might disrupt his thoughts.

'There were great expectations on both sides before your parents married,' he said eventually. 'I knew your father's father, a very successful trader – or he was when I first knew him. He made a lot of money and was ambitious, for himself and for his son, although I think their relations were not good. In my early days in Kenya, I too enjoyed success and relative wealth, although not as much as he.

'This was how things stood before Fairfax came to court Bela. His visit was known of by his father – perhaps Fairfax was trying to earn his approval. I don't know. But in the months leading to your father's visit, I suffered a heavy financial loss when a deal went wrong. When Fairfax arrived, his father came to know about my new difficulties, and told his son to walk away.

'But Fairfax was already smitten with Bela and ignored him, and he and his father quarrelled. I think their relationship was never repaired. It became the end of our friendship too. But it meant your father brought little money with him when he asked for Bela's hand in marriage.'

The old man paused and sighed. 'Ah, what to do! Such good times and such bad times! We had been hit so badly by my financial loss, and we had hoped that Fairfax might save us. But I was not going to deny Bela her happiness. I scraped together some money somehow, a large sum in those days, to give to them as a wedding present, to celebrate their union, and also in the hope that he might understand our generosity and might repay it later on in other ways, when he was successful – by helping us, you know, as family helps family.'

'But he never did,' I said weakly.

The old man inclined his head.

'Generosity was never his strong point,' I said with sadness.

'I understood that he felt precarious,' said my grandfather. 'He was estranged from his father – he had to make his own way. And at the outset, I did not doubt his feelings for Bela. His love for her was clear. But I asked him to look after her. I told him, *you have to look after her now.* This he was not able to do.'

'He was ashamed,' I whispered, 'of her illness.'

He nodded. The memories were flooding back. 'She would write to me in the first few years, letters in which she tried to hide her misery. I sensed what was going on, but she would not admit it. Also, your grandmother would not allow for Bela to be unhappy – she was very determined for her marriage to be a success. I did not know what to do. So I sent Maz sometimes to see how Bela was, but perhaps that was a mistake also.'

'Why?' I asked.

'The boy was fond of his sister, but he was jealous of her life also. For him, the West represented opportunity. It was a chance that she had, and he did not. I am afraid your father made it very clear he would not help him.'

'Out of pure meanness?'

He shook his head. 'Not only that. Resentment also. Bela was sinking, and I think somewhere within himself, your father blamed us. He thought there was mental instability in the family. There was not. My own mother became ill in this way, but this was to do with old age, nothing else. But Fairfax thought we had tricked him and came to resent us.'

'How do you know?'

'Letters. Not many of them, but there were letters, bitter letters between us.'

'What did he ask you to do, *Dadu*? Many years ago, I found a letter,' I stumbled, not knowing how to explain to him. ' Let's just say, I came across a letter from you, saying that you couldn't do as he asked. Or rather that your wife, my grandmother, wouldn't allow it. What was it?'

I spoke tentatively, but the old man looked as if he had been expecting my question.

'This will be difficult for you to hear,' he said slowly. 'After your mother lost her second child, she became very ill. You were still young, perhaps 9 years old – your father was struggling. Maz came to see you all after the baby died and said Bela was very sick. Your father made him a proposition.'

My heart began to beat wildly. 'What did he say?'

'He offered him money to take Bela away,' said my grandfather flatly. 'Ten and a half thousand pounds to take her back to Mombasa with him. Five thousand pounds was the money I gave them on their marriage. Your father doubled it and provided the airfare. Ten and a half thousand pounds to give away your mother.'

I stared at him in shock. 'No,' I gasped. 'It can't be true.'

He turned his face to look at me directly, his eyes full of pain, and I knew he had spoken the truth.

'But what was his plan?' I asked. 'Did he intend she just stay in Mombasa for a while, or … did he want to send her away permanently?'

'This was unclear,' he said. 'I think even your father did not know in his own mind exactly what he wanted. But he did want her away.'

I was open-mouthed with shock and anger, but even then,

the questions tumbled out of me. 'But he knew that Belle was ill, didn't he?'

'Yes, he knew. But he was too weak to help her. He was mortified that she should let him down. You live in a small town; he was worried people would come to find out.'

'Yes,' I said faintly. 'He was always worried about appearances.'

'And then,' he went on darkly, 'he dishonoured her.'

I gulped. The idea of discussing Fairfax's betrayal of Belle with my grandfather was unconscionable. My face must have been so full of alarm that the old man held up his hand.

'*Bas*,' he said. 'Enough. He is your father, and he used to be my son. That is enough. But I have to finish the story.'

'There's more?' I wasn't sure how much more I could stand.

'Yes, but the wrong which remains to be told is now on my side of the family. It is a wrong that I will put right. We owe you, Mivvi. We owe you the money.'

I blinked, not comprehending. 'What do you mean?'

A spasm contorted his face. 'You have to forgive us. Let me continue the story from our side.' He sighed, as if to steel himself, then went on speaking. 'Maz took your father's money and brought it back to us, with the request to take Bela back. I would have done so without the money, but my late wife was adamant that Bela could not return. I suffered much anguish over this, but she would not give way. It would bring shame on us to have her back – this is what my wife kept saying. So, I wrote to your father telling him we could not do as he asked, and I begged him to look after Bela.'

'That's the letter I saw,' I said. 'And the money?'

'Maz was charged with returning it to your father. At first, he said he would give it back if your father got Bela some help. But your father refused. He was furious – he called it blackmail. So, then Maz delayed and delayed returning it, even though I kept insisting that he must. But my own business was doing badly, and Maz was trying to set up by himself. He needed help that I could not give him.'

I stared at my grandfather, as the pieces slotted into place. 'So he used Fairfax's money?'

The old man nodded. 'Yes. To his shame and to my shame, he kept the money. There was one time when he was going to give it back, when he came to see you. You were 16 years old, I think. But on that night, Bela found out about the other woman, and your father's indecent conduct with her, and he left the home. My son seemed to think this absolved him of his duty to return the sum.'

'I see,' I said wonderingly. 'But you know, *Dadu*, there was a time when Maz was repeatedly offering me money! Was he trying to return it then?'

'He was. Your father's money helped make him a wealthy man!' He permitted himself a small smile. 'Maz is a selfish boy, but he is not a wholly bad person. He has felt guilt, and has wanted to return it to you. But you kept refusing! Now you must take it.'

I looked at him silently. How little I had understood over the years – how blind I had been. Fairfax had tried to sell Belle back to her family, and Maz had kept the money. It was a torrid, lurid story, and it was hard to think straight.

'What has happened to Maz?' I asked distractedly. 'I haven't seen him for years.'

'Oh, he is busy enjoying the high life,' sighed the old man. 'He is mostly in Mumbai. Calcutta, or Kolkata as we call it now, is too sleepy for him. I get an occasional message from him, though. He will turn up sometime. He may turn up in Milton Keynes too – you never know.'

We heard Robin give a yelp and then a cry from inside the house, and I looked ruefully at my grandfather.

'He's given us a long time to talk,' he said. 'Perhaps he knew it was important.'

I went inside to fetch Robin. His face looked squashed from sleep, and his black curls were woolly and unruly like Ash's. When I brought him back to the verandah, he managed a shy smile at his great-grandfather.

'Bela never saw him, did she?' he asked, with an expression of deep regret.

'No, no, she didn't.'

'But this is her achievement. A daughter like you and a strong and healthy grandson. What more could she have wanted?'

I managed to smile, knowing the question needed no response.

Just as I was wondering when Ash would return, the doorbell rang and the young girl emerged from the shadows of the verandah to pull the long rope. I started; I had thought we were alone.

'Do not worry,' said the old man, seeing my surprise. 'She knows no English. She just wanted to sit and watch you. She thinks you are from a Bollywood film!'

We both laughed and the tension eased for a moment, although the familiar sight of Ash made me suddenly aware how exhausted I was. Robin greeted his father with a joyous cry and as Ash took him in his arms, he looked hesitantly at me, his face full of concern.

I knew it was frowned on in India for couples, even married ones, to show physical affection in public, but I longed to feel his arms around me, to feel the certainty and solidity that Ash represented. Instead, he sat down close at my side so that I could feel the pressure of his body and the warmth of his skin.

'Aapna der kothha hoichchhe?' Ash asked my grandfather.

The old man shook his head, smiling. 'You forget Ashish, that I am not Bengali! That was my late wife. I have come here because my sister also married a Bengali. Her husband is also deceased, so we live together. Two old people. I like it here – it suits me. But I know only a few words of the language.'

'Of course – sorry. I did know that,' said Ash. 'I just wondered if you'd had a good conversation?'

'We did, yes.'

Ash looked between us, and he must have seen the tiredness in both our faces.

'Well, perhaps we should leave you now then,' he said gently.

'Wait a little while,' said the old man. 'You have come so far, and it may be some time before we meet again. You would surely like to see some pictures of your mother?'

'Yes,' I said gladly, despite my exhaustion. It did seem too soon to leave.

We spent another hour looking at photographs of a young Belle and a younger Maz, and I felt a strong pang for what life might have held for my mother in a different place, with a different husband.

Then Robin started getting restive, and Ash suggested again that we go.

'Yes, that time has probably come,' said the old man, suddenly formal. 'But tell me one thing first,' he added, turning to me, 'why do you not use your name?'

'But I do!' I said with surprise.

'That is not your real name,' he said, shaking his head gently. 'This name – Mivvi – is what your father called you. It is not the name your mother gave you.'

'The name I used when I married you,' said Ash, his face softening.

'Malini,' I said carefully, as if handing the two men a precious gift. 'My name is Malini.'

The old man bowed his head, accepting the gift.

'Malini and Ashish, I do not know much Bengali. But here, when people leave, we say to them *esho*. This means come back. So, as we part, I say to you both *abar esho*.'

'*Aajbo*,' said Ash. '*Nishchooi aajbo*. We will most certainly come.'

We descended into the hurly burly of Kolkata at rush hour, the perpetual noise and intense activity, the city alive and anonymous and indifferent to my distress.

I had come to India in search of answers, but as the revelations of yet more lies rang in my ears, I found the truth almost too much to bear.

I held on tightly but discreetly to Ash's hand in the car as we were driven home, Robin's innocent chatter a welcome distraction from my dark thoughts. All I could think was when we got home to England, I would have to put as much distance as I could between the three of us and Fairfax, such was my mounting disgust at the father I used to adore.

CHAPTER 7

Home was grey and flat when we got back, and I was surrounded by possessions I now knew I didn't need. I longed to move away and to get on with the next phase of our lives.

We had said regretful farewells to Ash's family, and although his parents were soon due back in Milton Keynes, a piece of my heart remained in Kolkata. I wrote a long letter to my grandfather, which I drafted and redrafted several times, and although I did eventually send it, the words could not do justice to all the emotion of our meeting, and what I wrote felt trite and stilted. He sent a short note back to me, urging us to come again, and telling me that Maz was making preparations for the money to be sent to me.

The jetlag lingered, and I found myself waking repeatedly before dawn. With Robin still asleep, I would head into the kitchen with a notebook – no longer Meera's, that had long been filled with my scribblings – and write down impressions and memories of our India trip, trying to keep it all alive on the page.

To my relief, Fairfax was away with his family in Yorkshire when we got back. He rang me on my return.

'Mivvi, we're away for half-term. I'm so sorry to miss you but we're back next week for Ruby's school. And Jade's, of course. I'll see you then?'

'Oh, that's okay,' I replied, as airily as I could. 'No rush.'

'Jade suddenly wanted to come back up here. We went to some place called Haworth. Bloody boring. Poured with rain!'

I made sympathetic noises.

'Anyway, did it go alright? Robin didn't get a bug? And you got to meet Ashish's family?'

No mention of Belle's father.

'Yes,' I said, as casually as possible, 'all good and no bugs.'

'Excellent. I'll ring you when we are back. I'm so glad we don't live up here!'

I knew I would need all my resources not to confront him the moment he returned. Even now, in full knowledge of the truth, I wondered if my courage wouldn't desert me at the last minute. I felt trapped in my small town and trapped in the past. All I could hope, with near desperation, was that I might be able to flee soon.

Days after our return, the estate agent in London rang. There was a small, terraced house on the market, two bedrooms, a patch of garden, no chain and affordable.

'The bathroom is avocado,' said the estate agent on the phone. 'A bit retro, I know. But the house is in good nick.'

We took the train down to see it the next day. The bathroom was the only weakness. In all other ways, the house was perfect: big rooms, high ceilings and flooded with light. There was even a dining room, an unheard-of luxury, with French windows opening onto the garden. I had visions of Robin as a toddler, running in and out on a warm summer's day.

'I think you've moved in,' said the estate agent. 'Mentally, I mean.'

'Oh yes,' I sighed happily. 'It's lovely! And we are so ready to be here.'

*

After months of stasis, everything moved fast. Our offer on the house was accepted, and we put our own flat up for sale and immediately found a buyer. I handed in my notice at the OU and began scanning the papers and the websites for jobs in London.

I saw Fairfax again with Robin, and such was my preoccupation with our plans and the move that I managed to control any outburst. I felt entirely detached from him. But I failed to mention that we were soon to leave Milton Keynes.

Still, a miserable fury would overtake me whenever I thought of him, so I threw myself into packing. The flat filled up with boxes, and the news came through from the estate agent that we were to sign for the new house in a fortnight.

We were elated, and I braced myself to speak to Fairfax, swearing to Ash that I would talk to him only about the move. The rest was too raw and would be kept for another time.

'Fairfax,' I said, when he next came by, 'I've got some news. You know how we've been talking for a long time about moving house? Well, it's now finally going to happen. We've found a place in London, just on the outskirts.'

He looked puzzled. 'But you didn't tell me. Is this soon?'

I spoke quickly. 'Well, yes, it is, but it all happened quite fast. We've been looking for a while, and then all of a sudden, we just stumbled across the right house. It's a lovely place, perfect for us, two bedrooms and even a little dining room. And a sweet garden, which is small, but fine, you know, and it really isn't very far away – you can come and visit sometimes…' I tailed off.

Fairfax was swallowing hard. 'Why do you want to go?' he asked, forlornly. 'Aren't we all quite happy here?'

'Yes, we're fine, but ... we need to move. You know that.'

'But I'll miss you,' he said.

'I know, Fairfax, but we'll stay in touch.'

'And I won't see Robin.'

'Of course you will – you'll come and visit. And we'll come and see you. It's just London. It's not far.'

'Ruby is gone and you'll be gone. And I won't see Robin grow up.' His voice turned hoarse. 'You'll cut me off from him.'

'No, don't be silly, Fairfax! There's no question of that. But Ash can't go on commuting. And we just need more space than we've got now. This flat is too small, you know that.'

'You can have more space nearby, can't you? I can help you if you need it – financially, I mean.'

'No,' I replied softly, 'thank you, that's really good of you, but we need to be nearer Ash's work. And I'll have more opportunities there too.'

Fairfax sat brooding, and I felt myself growing impatient. I was bottling up so many things, and I just needed to get this over and done with.

'What is this, Mivvi?' he said, turning towards me, frowning. 'It feels as if you want to get away from me. Is this some sort of punishment? I think sometimes you're angry with me, but I don't know why.'

'No, no, Fairfax, it isn't. I'm not.'

'I've always tried to behave well in my life, you know. I know things went awry back then, but they're alright now, aren't they? And I've always tried to do the right thing by you. I've always done the right thing.'

I looked at him, biting my lip. He really believed what he was saying.

I paused before replying. 'I'm not sure it's possible to always do the right thing, but never mind. I don't think anyone can really say that about themselves.'

'What do you mean by that?' Fairfax said gruffly. He was more aggressive than I had anticipated. 'Things have been difficult, but I've managed – I've come through. I have no regrets about what I've done.'

'Fairfax,' I said weakly. I had utterly failed to keep it light.

'I thought I was helping you with Robin,' Fairfax went on, in a wounded tone.

'You have helped.'

Fairfax turned his pale blue eyes on me. 'Mivvi, he is my grandson, you know.'

I gazed back at him with mounting irritation. Why was he so aggravating?

'And the grandparents often know a bit more than the parents,' he went on, insensible to the effect he was having on me.

I could contain myself no longer. 'Yes, you've said that before,' I replied drily. 'In which case, I could certainly have done with some grandparents around when I was small.'

Fairfax's face tightened. 'What's that meant to mean?'

'You know what it means. Why do you always have to pretend?'

'What do you mean, *pretend*? What are you talking about, Mivvi?'

I took a deep breath. There was no going back now. 'The pretence about how it was back then. That it was all fine in our house. It's as if all that matters is what other people thought. Or how you felt. How hard it was for you. You never give a moment's thought to how hard it was for me, do you?'

Fairfax looked astonished. 'I did everything I could for you. It wasn't my fault your mother was ill.'

'You say that so readily now, don't you, that Belle was *ill*. But why did you spend so many years saying there was nothing wrong with her? Why did you never get her any medical help? Why did she have to wait for me to help her?'

Fairfax looked at me warily. 'It's all very well for you to say these things, to sit here in judgement,' he replied, his voice shaky. 'You've no real idea what it was like. The rages, the madness.'

For a second, I wavered. This subject had forever been taboo. 'I do know what it was like, Fairfax, I do. I was there, remember? But she wasn't in control of herself. She needed help.'

He paused before replying. 'You say that so easily, Mivvi, but when you live with someone for years, the changes happen slowly. They come upon you gradually – you don't see them at first. And then you find yourself living with them, and somehow coping. Anyway,' he said, petulantly, 'I'm not a doctor, am I? How was I really to know?'

'I'm not a doctor either,' I said sadly, 'but I knew. I knew that screaming at demons was not normal. You should have done something.'

'That's just the arrogance of the young, always thinking they know better,' said Fairfax roughly.

'If you'd helped her, she might have had a chance. We might have had a chance as a family.'

Fairfax fell silent, his expression clouded. We could hear Robin stirring in his cot and didn't speak until he had quietened again.

'I did love your mother, you know,' Fairfax said softly, 'I really did love her. But then it all went so wrong. She grew distant and strange, and then eventually behaved in … that way. I felt I'd been … duped. By her family. They never said anything to me.'

'Perhaps there wasn't anything to say, not back then?'

He shook his head. 'I'm not sure. I think maybe there was. I don't know – I didn't pay much attention to it at the time. Clearly, I should have done.' He spoke bitterly. 'What was I to do?'

'You should have helped her. Meera told you to help her, didn't she? She told you Belle was ill. You did know.'

Fairfax's face stiffened, but I was beyond caring.

'You tried to get rid of Belle instead, didn't you?'

He turned and stared at me. 'What do you mean by that?'

'What about the ten and a half thousand pounds?'

Fairfax started. 'What?'

'The money you gave to Maz to take Belle off your hands.' The words, hard and cold, tumbled out of me like stones.

Fairfax looked suddenly haunted. 'You saw him,' he said weakly. 'You went to see the old man.'

'What happened, Fairfax? Were you trying to get rid of Belle? Were you?'

He put his head in his hands and stayed like that for what seemed like hours. When he eventually spoke, his face was ashen and ghostly. 'I couldn't cope, Mivvi,' he whispered. 'I couldn't cope with the moods and the rages, the paranoia and the imaginings. And there was no one I could tell.'

'You could have got her medical help.'

'And had the whole town knowing my business? Have everyone know that I'd failed? I couldn't! I couldn't!'

'And were you going to abandon her permanently?' I felt sharp as steel, as cold as a diamond.

'I don't know. I don't think so. Just for a while. To think. To give me some space and time to think. And to get some peace.'

'And then? Maz reneged on the deal, didn't he, and kept your money?'

'They wouldn't have her back,' he said bitterly. 'Or at least her mother wouldn't. Maz kept promising to return the money, but he never did.'

'Not until you got her help.'

'What?'

'He would only return the money once you got Belle help. That's what he said, didn't he?'

'I don't know,' muttered Fairfax, 'I can't remember.'

'Really?' I said sarcastically, marvelling at his selective memory.

'Really!' he repeated emphatically. 'He was just … he was just a grasping little chancer.'

'And you, Fairfax, what were you?'

'What do you mean?' He looked livid. 'Don't talk to me in that tone of voice!'

'Were you trying to get rid of Belle so that you could be with Jade?'

'No!' He was outraged. 'No!' he shouted. 'No!'

'Weren't you? Why else try to get her off the scene? It would have been very convenient, wouldn't it? Otherwise, why not just go on muddling through, as you did for so long? You just wanted her out of the way, didn't you, for your grubby little affair!'

I had gone beyond every boundary I had ever set myself, and I didn't dare stop to think about what I was saying.

Fairfax glared at me with undisguised fury. 'You know, Mivvi, you're a clever girl and all that, but not everything has a neat little explanation.'

'You're just trying to avoid telling the truth.'

'No!' He was yelling at me now, all scruples about the sleeping baby forgotten. 'That's not how it was! Life isn't like those story books of yours, you know, not everything ties up nicely with a little beginning, middle and end. Not everything has a reason! Life isn't like that – real life is about managing, just managing with whatever the hell is thrown at you! I was desperately trying to cope with your mother, and then Jade ... That just sort of happened. You've got a bloody nerve, trying to parcel it all up like this! It was all just a mess – just one big bloody mess!'

He gasped and grabbed a cup of cold tea, swallowing it all in one gulp. He too had never ventured onto territory like this before. Perhaps he had never allowed himself even to think about it.

We sat in stunned silence at what we had unleashed. I thought that we were finished, but then he spoke again.

'Anyway, I stayed with Belle, didn't I?' he said defensively. 'I stuck it out for a long time.'

I stared at him in astonishment. 'What are you saying? You didn't stay with her – you left her! You abandoned us.'

Fairfax shook his head forcefully. 'No, well, yes, but that was not meant to happen. It was just sort of forced on me, wasn't it? I know I shouldn't have been doing what I was doing, but I wasn't going to leave you. I just didn't expect your mother to find out. And to make such a scene about it! I had no option.'

I could scarcely believe what I was hearing. 'So, what, you left out of *embarrassment*?'

'No, not exactly, but ... with everything out in the open, what else could I do? I had no choice. And I didn't abandon you – I kept providing for you, for both of you. You know I did.'

It always came back to money with him. I saw myself small and concentrated, like a missile. 'Belle said she threw you out.'

Fairfax looked ahead stonily.

'That's right, isn't it? She threw you out.'

'I've nothing more to say.'

'Admit it, Fairfax – why pretend? She got rid of you, didn't she? She's the one who dumped you. She's the one who kicked you out – not the other way around!'

'I've nothing more to say,' he said, his face purple with fury. 'You'll get nothing more from me. Nothing!'

We were shouting at each other again. 'So, what's going on now, Fairfax? What are you doing with that Helen woman? Is this your way of staying with Jade?'

Now it was Fairfax's turn to stare. 'Well, Mivvi, have you been snooping on me or what?'

'Why don't you just answer me?' I bellowed.

'I'm under no obligation to answer to you!' he cried. 'But it's … well it's just a friendship with Helen.'

'A *friendship* – that's not what it looked like!'

'It is – it's a romantic sort of friendship, that's all! We get on well. We're very close.' Fairfax was now looking cornered. 'Things can be less than smooth at times between me and Jade. Life just isn't that simple, you know. Anyway, what's it to you? You've never liked Jade! You've never made the slightest attempt with her. What the hell do you care?'

I looked at him through a dull fog. No, I didn't care about Jade, and I didn't care about Helen either. But I did care about Fairfax. I had cared for him a great deal. But, over and over again, he had revealed himself as half the man I had thought he was. Fairfax, my failed father. My deeply disappointing dad.

He stormed out without looking at me or even seeing Robin, slamming the front door as he went.

Alone, I slumped onto the sofa with exhaustion, flayed by the viciousness of our exchange. I had breached every taboo, and what had I gained by it? With the catharsis of truth came the fear that I had lost the only parent I had left.

Robin started to wail, and I fetched him to feed, weeping as I did so bitter tears onto his soft and innocent little head.

CHAPTER 8

As a rule, Fairfax never talked to Jade about Mivvi, but that evening, he couldn't contain his feelings. He could never repeat the very private accusations the girl had hurled at him about his past dilemmas, but her cruel words and judgements were too much to bear alone.

He gave an emotional description to Jade of his daughter's shocking ingratitude for all the numerous sacrifices he had made to look after her. Although this was unfamiliar territory for them, Jade turned out to be consoling and wise.

'You've been under her thumb emotionally for years, Fairfax,' she said gently, 'and you've let her get away with a lot. It's understandable – she is your daughter. But you've done so much for her, and now maybe it's time to be firmer. Don't let yourself be hurt by her.'

Fairfax had never thought of his relationship with Mivvi in these terms before. He looked at Jade in wonder at her powers of perception.

'Yes, Jade, I think you might be right,' he murmured. 'I think I'm going to stay away from her for a while – for a long time in fact. She's hurt me profoundly with her insults today.'

Jade nodded with sympathy.

'You know, Jade, I've not talked about this before, but I know it's been hard for you with Mivvi – I do know that. There's no reason why the two of you should get on, apart from me of course – but you've always done your best, I know that.'

Jade gave a modest little smile.

'Mivvi has been hard work for you,' he said. 'Unyielding.'

She gave him a warm squeeze of the hand, and then in that way of hers, brought her face up close to his.

'It's so wonderful to hear you speak of all this,' she said softly. 'You know what you're doing, Fairfax? You're liberating yourself from the power she has over you. You're setting yourself free.' She stroked his hand gently.

'You know they're moving house, she and Ashish? She was always threatening to, and now they really are.'

Jade's eyes shone with compassion. 'Let her go.'

'But what about Robin? He's my grandson, you know.'

'He'll always be your grandson, Fairfax, wherever he is. He'll always be attached to you. But it's good that they're moving, and that Mivvi will be further away. You've got me. You've got Ruby. You don't need anyone else. Just let go.'

Fairfax gazed at her shining face. In that moment, all thoughts of Helen evaporated, and he was struck anew by his love for Jade.

'Oh, I will,' he said, with deep emotion. 'Yes, I really will!'

CHAPTER 9

It was more than a year before I spoke to Fairfax again, and it was up to me to make the first move, knowing full well that the wound to his pride after our blistering words would be insurmountable and that he would be incapable of getting in touch with me.

For many months, I had no desire to see him. I rushed off with Ash and Robin to our new London home as soon as we could. The pangs of regret I felt as we left Milton Keynes were not for him but for my childhood self, and for Belle too. The day before we left, I drove to the lake at the Abbey to say goodbye to her.

As promised, I had received the sum of ten and a half thousand pounds, delivered by money transfer from Maz, and a postcard on which he had scrawled *'Returned to owner, hope you're good. M.'* I considered getting in touch with Fairfax, whose money it rightfully was, but I suspected that would add insult to injury, and so I decided to view it instead as an early inheritance. I used half of the amount to furnish our new home, and set aside the rest for our next trip to Kolkata.

We started afresh in our cosy new house, where I copied Bree's style as I remembered it from many years previously, furnishing the rooms with pinewood and bookcases and old Persian rugs. I think that somewhere deep down I wanted to recreate the homeliness and security of Tabitha's childhood, such a contrast to the mayhem of my own.

We paid visits to east London to see Meera and Ally, and Meera soon became a firm friend not just a mentor, and Kiron a big brother to Robin.

I thought long and hard about Fairfax's furious defence of himself, wondering if it was really true that he had acted not through calculation or design but out of simple panic and helplessness. I did not know if I believed him; but I did acknowledge his accusation that I sought pattern and motive where perhaps there was only chaos.

I could never absolve him, but over time I softened, and when I eventually resolved to contact him, I wrote him an old-fashioned letter – not an email or a text – in the way that Belle used to write to me.

Hello Fairfax, it's a long time since we have spoken. How are you? I think of you.

I enclosed two photographs of Robin to remind him, if he needed it, that he was a grandfather.

I had no idea if I would get a reply, but three weeks later a stiff and formal letter arrived in the post.

Dear Mivvi, thank you for your correspondence. I am fine. Robin is looking well.

It led to us staying in touch, haltingly at first and then more regularly – and finally Fairfax came to visit us, without Ruby or Jade.

At the beginning, he was tense and tight, carrying the injury to his dignity on his sleeve. But over time, hints of his old cheerfulness re-emerged, triggered by his love for Robin.

'Fefa,' said Robin, his attempt at Fairfax. My son was sitting in his grandfather's lap, ruffling his hair, the only person in the entire world who was allowed to mess with his coiffure. Fairfax looked as if he might melt.

'Fefa,' Robin said again, grabbing his tiepin and trying to extract it from his tie. 'Typin,' he said knowingly, to peals of laughter from my father.

'What other two-year old knows the word "tiepin", Mivvi?' he exclaimed. 'I know he's my grandson, but really he is extraordinary!'

I knew that we would never refer to our brutal fight, just as I knew that something had permanently ruptured between us. But contact, however constrained, was better than war, and it meant that I could maintain my links with my little sister, too. Fairfax began visiting more often with Ruby, and sometimes even with Jade – and then in his unique way, he soon behaved as if nothing had ever been wrong.

I feared the return of the old, controlling Fairfax, but it was mitigated by the miles I had put between us. Ruby, now 8 years old, had forgotten all her old animosity towards Robin, and the two of them were becoming close friends. Seeing them together made both me and Ash think how much we had missed as only children, and we started talking about trying for a second baby.

After each visit was over, Ash breathed a sigh of relief. He did not dislike Fairfax; in many ways, he was fond of him. But there was too much history for him ever to relax fully.

In the months following our move, Ash and I took our time unpacking the numerous boxes of books, sorting through them meticulously for the shelves around the house. In the final box was the old, faded leather diary which I had found after Belle's death, hidden away in a drawer along with photographs of Mombasa. I had not forgotten it, but I had been waiting until I was ready.

The diary had been carelessly kept and many of the pages were stuck together and tore as I gently tried to prise them apart. I cursed at my clumsiness, which left some of the entries illegible. The ink was faint and the handwriting, with its loops and curls, hard to read. But I knew this was a task I had to carry out. Slowly and painstakingly, I started to decipher the first entry.

As I read, I realised the voice of the writer was not a Belle I had ever known – not the placid, passive mother of my infancy, nor the troubled mother of later years, but a different character: knowing, playful, daring and full of hope.

FINDING BELLE

Mombasa
July 15th 1968

So, he has come, the fair stranger, bringing with him a letter of introduction from his father. The man has hungry eyes of a startling blue. I watch him watching me.

Ma is full of excitement — she says he is mine if I want him. He has very good prospects, she keeps saying, and he's so handsome! He is very handsome, and he knows it too; he smiles as if sharing the pleasure of his own beauty. But I can play at that game too. I return his smiles shyly and modestly, but I know how to shine, in my own way. Ma has put out my most flattering robes and saris, in magenta and emerald, all flowing and translucent. I glide around, looking innocent and exotic, and poor Mr Fairfax appears hypnotised.

When he arrived, he was all eagerness and heart. He pretends to be experienced, but is not able to disguise his wonderment at life outside his little island. Baba met him off the boat from Bombay, and F told us stories of his journey here over dinner. He quaintly came by ship instead of by plane to prolong the adventure, he said. His eyes shine like pale sapphires when he speaks, and if I am next to him at dinner, our hands brush when we pass glasses and plates of food. He told us about the characters on board the big ship — an old sea captain called Spider Jones who drank three glasses of gin every day before lunch, a Punjabi officer, who'd fought against the Japanese, and also a playwright of the London musical theatre, who wore silk cravats, and looked as wolfish towards the young men as the young women.

F loves to tell stories. He is exaggerating these people and their peculiarities I'm sure, but his timing is impeccable, and they make for a good tale. Baba and Ma were falling about themselves laughing. Too much so, I thought. We want to make him feel welcome, and I am more interested in him — much more interested — than in any of the others, but still, we should maintain some mystery.

I felt triumph as Ma took in his admiring expression at me, she who called me an ugly duckling not so many years ago. I am swan enough now, and she looks full of gratitude. She expects little of me, I know that, but I will show her.

I can see him from my window, standing in the shade of the mango tree, talking earnestly with Baba and Maz. It's the tree that Maz fell out of when he was small, trying to climb too high to pick a mango just out of reach. What a concussion he suffered! Baba and Ma were worried he'd done himself permanent damage.

But there he is, boasting to Mr Fairfax about our business, all that boring import and export stuff, even though he is only 14 years old! He does not tell of Baba's money problems, and for this I am glad. Who knows what F would think of that.

Right now, F is looking at the mangoes as if they are magical, poor man. The best they have at home is the apple tree. I see him glancing up at my window now and then, but I don't think he can see me.

I can have him if I want to.

And I think I do.

CHAPTER 10

It took me several evenings to decode the few short entries, setting to work after Robin was asleep. My progress was slow but I persevered, copying out the extracts as I went along, marvelling at the stories I had never known, understanding anew the stories I had heard before, and enjoying the fluency and energy of Belle's writing.

There were big gaps in the diary, but as I read through to the final years of the book, my mother's voice became almost familiar to me, like the ghost of the faraway past. It was Belle as I knew her when I was 6 or 7 years old, just graspable at the edge of my memory, my mother by now struggling and alienated in what for her was a cold and unwelcoming country. Her writing changed too, the language more disjointed, a reflection of what was happening to her mind.

As I came to the end, I sat lost in my thoughts, unaware my face was wet with tears – and this was how Ash found me when he wandered upstairs.

'Goodness, what's the matter? Are you alright? Is it your father?'

'No, it's … my mother,' I said, smiling wanly as he passed me a tissue.

'Ah, the diary. Have you finished it? It must be very churning.'

I nodded. 'Yes, that's the word. Fragments of a person whom I knew but didn't know. Couldn't know, really.'

'Has it revealed anything?'

'Nothing of substance. More about the woman she was, before I was born and before my memories of her, and then from years ago when I just about remember. There's a lot about her love for me, things she could never express later on. It all stops a few years after my birth.'

He bent down and kissed my forehead. 'I don't want you getting upset about your family again.'

'Oh no, this isn't the same. It's … the pathos of it, I suppose. The what might have been – you know, if she'd been happy. Perhaps none of it would have happened.'

'All these things you can never prove,' he said gently.

'I know,' I replied with a sigh. 'But it's not about proof. I'm just imagining. Imagining how it might have been different. Trying to make sense of it all.'

Ash left to make dinner, and I remained where I was, gazing absent-mindedly at the diary, my head crowded with thoughts about the past. I had spent so long fighting with the contradictions of Fairfax that I had neglected any proper consideration of Belle, blaming the parent I had loved and pitying the parent I had not. But this glimpse of my mother as healthy and loving gave me a new understanding of what Belle had been, and with it, a new sense of myself too.

I started to rummage in the desk drawers and fished out my own old notebooks, including the one from Meera, with all the fragments of memories over the years – writing I had done at home, in Nice, in India.

Was it possible that I might recount the story in all its mess and its muddle, and put Belle at its centre? I would need to find the right vehicle for the story, and use creativity where I did not have evidence. The character I would call Fairfax had been the towering figure of my childhood, but maybe Belle could be restored to her rightful position, even if she were always to remain to a large extent unknowable.

If I managed honestly to set down the past, in all its contradictions and complexity, I might at last come to terms with what had happened and who I was.

So I – Mivvi and Malini, too – pulled out the keyboard and switched on the computer.

I closed my eyes briefly to gather myself, and then opened them and began to write.

The words started to flow:

After Mama lost the baby and then lost her self, I had a vivid and terrifying dream…

Acknowledgements

I would like to thank my agent **Mary Greenham** and my literary agent **Kerr MacRae** for their unstinting support and encouragement in finding a good home for this novel. I'm very grateful to **Martha Ashby** at HarperFiction for taking me on, and for inspiring some of the key moments in *Finding Belle*; and also to **Lynne Drew** at HarperFiction who believed in the project, and who stood by me in moments of self-doubt. My thanks too to **Katie Lumsden** who went through the text with a careful eye, and made helpful and clever suggestions. My biggest thanks go to book doctor extraordinaire **Sally Orson-Jones** for her wisdom, insight, honesty and for making me laugh at my mistakes; and to **Paul Hamilton**, who patiently read every word of every draft, and who provided considered, thoughtful criticism throughout.

GLOBAL MARKET BI

Investing in China: The Emerging Venture Capital Industry

Jonsson Yinya Li

With editorial contributions from Adamas

GMB

Publisher's Note
Every possible effort has been made to ensure the information contained in this book is accurate at the time of going to press. However due to the fast changing nature of Chinese law in this area the legal advice given should be treated with care. The publishers cannot accept responsibility for any errors or omissions, however caused.

No responsibility for loss or damage occasioned to any person acting or refraining from action, as a result of material in this publication, can be accepted by the editor, the publisher or any of the contributors.

This first edition published in Great Britain and in the USA in 2005 by GMB Publishing Limited.

Apart from any fair dealing for the purposes of research or private study, or criticism or review, as permitted under the Copyright, Designs and Patents Act, 1988, this publication may only be reproduced, stored or transmitted, in any form, or by any means, with the prior permission in writing of the publisher, or in the case of reprographic reproduction in accordance with the terms of licences issued by the Copyright Licensing Agency. Enquiries concerning reproduction outside those terms should be sent to the publishers at the undermentioned addresse:

GMB Publishing Ltd
120 Pentonville Road
London N1 9JN
UK
www.globalmarketbriefings.com

Distributed by Kogan Page Ltd
120 Pentonville Road
London N1 9JN
UK

22883 Quicksilver Drive
Sterling VA 20166–2012
USA

© GMB Publishing and Contributors 2005

ISBN 1-905050-13-5

British Library Cataloguing-in-Publication Data

A CIP record for this book is available from the British Library

Typeset by Digital Publishing Solutions
Printed in the United Kingdom at the University Press, Cambridge

Contents

Foreword Shi Jianxin, Minister Counsellor, Embassy of the People's Republic of China in the UK	vii
Preface Martin Bloom, UK Chairman, China-UK Venture Capital Joint Working Group	ix
About the Author	xi
Endorsement Prof. David Crowther, Professor of Corporate Social Responsibility, London Metropolitan University	xiii
Introduction Jonsson Yinya Li and Prof. Mannie Manhong Liu	xv
Acknowledgments	xix

Chapter 1. Why Invest in the Chinese Market?

China's venture capital system	1
VC activity	2
Case study: Five factors affecting stock markets in 2004–2005	20
Stages in the investment	21
Establishing perfect legal circumstances	23
New provisions and new rules on foreign VC investment	26
Investment system reform	30
VC's acclaim for an SME Board	31
Milestones of Mainland China's venture capital industry	33

Chapter 2. Criteria for Successful Investments in China

The criteria for investors	53
The functions of the management team in a venture capital project	54
Overseas or local Chinese students	56

The operation of the founders of Harbour	58
Biotech R&D commercialization	70

Chapter 3. Creative Products and Markets in China

Internet and e-commerce market development	81
QQ: The number one Chinese instant messenger	93
3721: The power of Chinese characters on the internet	106
Case study 1: B2B in China	113
Case study 2: Small electric appliances doing well	116
Case study 3: EVD: The next big home-viewing revolution	118
Case study 4: An e-tailer with a lot riding on bicycles	120

Chapter 4. Due Diligence and Investment Monitoring

Penshibao's fraudulent accounting	123
Areas for venture capitalists to consider when developing a due diligence model	131

Chapter 5. IPO Exits and the Stock Exchange in Mainland China

IPO: The main exit route for capital investment	139
Stock exchanges in Mainland China	142
Case study 1: The Chinese SME Board – no glory, but a dream come true	147
Case study 2: Chinese internet firms line up for IPO	163
Kingdee and UFSoft: Different IPO exit choices for Chinese domestic SMEs	170
Case study 3: Pioneer in the digital age – Wang Wenjing elected as '2003 China digital figure'	174

Chapter 6. Successful Venture Capital-Backed SMEs in China

IPO success on NASDAQ for Ctrip.com, the Chinese SME travel portal	179
VC investment for a start-up enterprise	187
The software manufacturing market in China	193
Telecommunications in China	200

Chapter 7. Best Practices in Products and Services for M&A Operations in China

Mergers and acquisitions in Mainland China	209
AsiaInfo: From venture-backed company to an M&A player	224

Chapter 8. Insight into the Potential and Traditional Sectors

The financial miracle of online gaming	245
Online games are all the rage in China	253
Soaring revenues win industry respect	254
The first media venture capital experience	259
VC investment in traditional industries	270
Legendary Mengniu: An exercise in capital restructure	273

Appendices

Appendix A.	Regulations on Administration of Foreign Invested Venture Capital Investment Enterprises	293
Appendix B.	Interim Provisions on the Acquisition of Domestic Enterprises by Foreign Investors	311
Appendix C.	Chinese Overseas Students	325
Appendix D.	President Calls on Students Abroad to Contribute More to Nation	329
Appendix E.	Term Sheet Sample	331
Appendix F.	The Winners of 2003's Best Companies Survey in China	341

Bibliography   *345*

中文序言　　Chinese Foreword

這是一本為數不多的全面論述中國風險投資的英文書。它不僅綜述了中國風險投資事業，并涵蓋了中國的創業、中小企業、知識產權和購并市場等各方面的法律和經濟現狀。隨著中國經濟的驚人的增長，中國風險投資事業也不斷發展壯大。中國市場已經成為國際風險投資的新的聚積地。目前大量國際風險資本的進入，使得全面介紹中國風險投資市場的英文資料成為當務之急。本書的出版恰逢時宜，可作為國際資本進入中國市場的有效指南和得力工具。

劉曼紅（Mannie Manhong Liu）2005年6月于美國波士頓
中國人民大學教授、博士生導師、風險投資研究所所長、北京市政府金融顧問、維新中國有限公司董事長
中國科技金融促進會風險投資委員會名譽副主任、美國波士頓中國金融研究中心主任

中文序言和介紹　　Chinese Foreword and Introduction

《Investing in China: The Emerging Venture Capital Industry》（《投資中國——蓬勃興起的風險投資業》）一書是作者李引亞（俊辰）在風險投資（也被稱為"創業投資"）、非公開權益資本、資本市場、人力資源管理、公司財務管理、行政管理等方面研究和實踐的成果。李先生曾就中國風險投資業的發展接受英國廣播公司（BBC）等知名媒體的采訪，其他報道其人其事的中文媒體（部分）有：新華社（中國）、《人民日報》（中國）、《大公報》（中國香港）、《文匯報》（中國香港）、香港中國通訊社（中國香港）、（香港）無綫衛星臺TVB（歐洲）、新浪網（中國香港、中國）、國際日報（北美）、《新歐僑報》（英國）、《新中原報》（泰國）、《星進日報》（泰國）、《新民商報》（阿聯酋）、《大衆日報》（中國）、《神州學人》（中國）等（英文媒體略）。

李先生是旅英多年的年輕學者和實踐者，是英國研究中國投資業以及傳媒、金融、信息技術（IT）和商務管理等方面的專家。其人其著被譽為"最年輕的全球華人經濟作家，最令人期待的投資領域專著"。李先生現在擔任歐金中國發展有限公司董事長、歐洲中國金融商務研究所常務副所長、英國科教文絲綢之路協會主席、EU Chinese Journal報社總編輯兼市場總監、中國人民大學風險投資研究所高級研究員，并持有微軟認證專家（MCP）、微軟認證系統工程師（MCSE）和微軟認證數據庫管理員（MCDBA）等證書。

風險投資已被公認爲企業技術創新和經濟發展的"發動機"和關鍵環節。中國政府充分認識到了風險投資的重要性，并致力于推動風險投資事業的發展。包括《中國國民經濟和社會發展第十個五年（2001–2005）計劃》等重大政策文件在內，中國政府都指出了風險投資的重要性：「完善風險投資機制，建立創業板股票市場，鼓勵發展多種所有制的創新型中小企業」。《Investing in China: The Emerging Venture Capital Industry》（《投資中國——蓬勃興起的風險投資業》）是第一本以英文語言寫作，集中介紹中國風險投資業、高科技行業和傳統行業、以及典型案例的書，總共分為八章，包括為什麼投資中國、成功投資的標準、創新產品、盡職調查和投資監控機制、首次公開發行和證券市場、成功的風險企業、兼并和收購、潛質行業和傳統行業及附錄中的法律法規和調查報告。

該書由歐洲國際商務、經濟和投資類權威出版社GMB Publishing在英國和美國兩地同時出版發行，并由英國著名經濟學家、資深編輯顧問、資深專欄作家喬納森·魯偉德（Jonathan Reuvid）先生進行全書的審定。Global Market Briefings從1992年就開始專注于國際商務、金融、投資等類型書籍和刊物的出版，并贏得歐洲、美洲、亞洲等國家和地區權威政府部門以及世界500強中諸多企業的關注和支持，其執行董事彼得·查德威克（Peter Chadwick）是英國著名的傳媒出版專業人士。除了英美兩地外，《Investing in China: The Emerging Venture Capital Industry》（《投資中國——蓬勃興起的風險投資業》）一書由引領世界經濟出版、歐洲最大的、經濟商務類權威出版社Kogan Page發行至加拿大、澳大利亞、新西蘭、南非以及歐洲、美洲和亞洲等的其它國家和地區。

該書首版的英文序言由中華人民共和國駐大不列顛及北愛爾蘭聯合王國大使館經濟商務處施建新公使銜參贊、英國財政大臣高登·布朗（Gordon Brown）領導的英中風險投資聯合工作小組英方主席馬丁·布魯（Martin D. H. Bloom）、中國投資界的權威學者和實務人士劉曼紅（Mannie Liu）教授和聞名歐、美、亞等洲的公司社會責任資深專家大衛·克勞斯（David Crowther）教授等分別撰寫。

作者李引亞（俊辰）先生特希望借此機會感謝尊敬的父母、師長、親人以及施建新公參、劉曼紅（Mannie Liu）教授、大衛·克勞斯（David Crowther）教授、馬丁·布魯（Martin Bloom）、喬納森·魯偉德（Jonathan Reuvid）、理查德·莫爾（Richard Morel）博士、彼得·查德威克（Peter Chadwick）、何家金、于興國、夏榮梁（Julian Ha）和王瑛等。

作者李引亞（俊辰）先生目前正在募集風險投資基金，基金擬投資領域為：傳媒出版、信息技術、咨詢、中國改制國有企業和中小企業等。作者聯系方式為：jonsson.li@gmail.com。

李孝諄（Hau Shun Li）2005年6月于中國香港
香港中國通訊社副總編輯

"志在風中飛常伴，馭于雲內情時飛。"
（注：考慮到海外普遍使用繁體中文，本屆中文簡介故採用繁體字。不便之處，敬請見諒。）

Foreword

The UK is an important trade partner of China; its trade volume with China totalled some US$19.7 billion in 2004, the third largest of European countries. The UK is also the biggest European investor in China, and the two countries are highly complementary in fields such as oil, pharmaceuticals, banking, insurance and transportation. Many UK companies have set up their representative offices or business operations in different areas and diverse industries in China, while more and more Chinese companies (be they state-owned or not) are also successfully establishing their businesses in the UK. Sino–British economic and business cooperation is developing at an even faster rate; China welcomes foreign investors.

China has achieved extraordinary economic success over the past 25 years with an average annual GDP growth of over 9 per cent. According to the latest figures from the National Bureau of Statistics of China, China's GDP growth rate in 2004 was 9.5 per cent. However, the dramatic development has been gained at the expense of huge capital input, tremendous consumption of resources, relatively low economic efficiency, inferior productivity and environmental pollution. This kind of economic growth model, characterized as high input and low output, is not sustainable. The way for China to achieve sustainable economic development in the next two decades should be based on innovation. Technology development, management upgrading and system improvement will generate resources and vitality for the new economic growth model, with venture capital being the real engine to power that growth. The development of an innovative economy and the experiences of the UK, US and Israel clearly indicate that venture capital has become strategically important to China's economic growth. However, it has encountered a variety of obstacles that have confined the growth of this promising industry like a roaring lion in a cage.

This book is rather timely, useful and important for the foreign investor to discover more about venture capital in China. It will serve as a platform for overseas professional investors, companies seeking trade and investment opportunities in China and business students to develop a clear understanding of China's current investment situation.

As the Economic and Commercial Counsellor's Office of the Embassy of the PRC in the UK, it is our great honour and undoubted duty to work as a bridge in the development of our bilateral relationship. We sincerely hope that through this book and our office, companies in the UK and elsewhere that are interested in starting business with China can find useful information and effective assistance.

Shi Jianxin
Minister Counsellor
Economic and Commercial Counsellor's Office
Embassy of the People's Republic of China in the UK
formerly Minister, Commercial Counsellor's Office,
Embassy of the People's Republic of China,
United States of America

Preface

Industrialization is a seemingly inevitable but slightly mysterious process that each of today's major economies have passed through at some stage – almost a rite of passage. Beforehand, its timing and extent are hidden from view, although seemingly predictable with hindsight. Each country has emerged from its cocoon in a slightly different way, with implications for later developments.

Its is now time for the world's most populous country to proceed along this path, a path it is constructing as it goes, changing the blueprint and rewriting the rules as it learns from the experience of those who have gone before. Its impact will be extensive and perception of this has been slow to impinge on those not directly involved. Yet in the past year, the by-products of this have been constantly in the western news as Chinese technology companies begin to extend their international spread.

The pace of this industrialization will grow even more intense as time proceeds. There will be ebbs and flows, but the direction seems irreversible. At one level, it will change relationships between nations. At the other, it will change relationships between companies as different parts of the supply chain of a range of industries fragment and reconsolidate. The best of the Chinese companies have already leveraged their strong domestic position into international positions of strength through their own growth or through audacious deals in taking over major international competitors. Others will undoubtedly follow.

What makes this different from those that preceeded on the path to industrial development is the role that venture capital is coming to play in this process. Jonsson Yinya Li considers the role of venture capital against this wider backdrop, providing fascinating case studies of venture-backed companies that will be among the leading global players of the 21st century – sooner rather than later. He unravels the internal dynamics that are driving this process.

Jonsson Yinya Li's book is the first comprehensive work documenting this process and identifying the opportunities and dangers that lie ahead. Many of the companies involved with these momentous developments are venture backed. A challenge for Chinese businesses will be to develop international marketing and branding skills. In addition, some sectors, such as biotech, face larger challenges and are behind electronics and telecoms in their pace of development. The viability of the Chinese venture capital scene augurs well for these companies to acquire or organically grow the skills needed to become world players. In fact, the venture groups backing these companies may even be the channel through which these skills are obtained and acquisitions made.

Jonsson Yinya Li sets out the ways in which this process has been adapted from western models to become a uniquely Chinese approach dating from the mid-1990s. The Chinese government saw the need to do more than just direct public funds into high technology industries and instituted a range of policy initiatives to promote the growth of venture capital and of the firms that engage in it. This has led to a proliferation of home-grown venture capital firms. Some invested in technology companies created by scientists and entrepreneurs returning from education and work overseas, many with experience of working for foreign global corporations. Increasingly, domestic Chinese talent is coming to the fore as the elite Chinese universities create the technologists and entrepreneurs of the future, often moulded by experience working in foreign and local firms.

There are many issues facing the fledgling venture industry in China. These include strong competition from foreign venture firms. Companies also have to contend with the peculiarities of the Chinese legal system. Due diligence, in particular, is fraught, and there are cases of individual investments of major venture firms failing at this first stage. Lessons are provided to identify problems. Nevertheless, this remains a hidden danger for the unwary.

Yet despite this, progress is being made. Some domestic venture firms are attracting foreign investors, while others are partnering with foreign firms in order to upgrade their skills and follow best practice. The future is always uncertain. Yet the first steps in the growth of Chinese venture capital have now taken place. They are now documented in this fascinating account.

Martin DH Bloom[1]
UK Chairman
China-UK Venture Capital Joint Working Group
© Martin DH Bloom, 2005

---

[1] Martin Bloom is the author of an account of the industrialization of Korea: Bloom MDH (2002) *Technological Change in the Korean Electronics Industry* Paris: OECD Development Centre.

About the Author

Jonsson Yinya Li, BSc, MA, also named Junchen Li, is Director, GBVC China Ltd; Chief Editor and Chief Economics Commentator, *EU Chinese Journal*; Marketing Executive, *EU Chinese Journal* (UK) Ltd; and Senior Research Fellow, Venture Capital Research Institute (VCRI) of Renmin University of China.

Mr Li received a master's degree in International Finance from London Metropolitan University and held the position of President of the Chinese Students and Scholars Association (CSSA) of London Metropolitan University and Ministers of the Strategic Ministry and Liaison Ministry of CSSA of the UK. He was invited to speak as one of the only eight representatives at the United Kingdom First Annual Academic Conference of the Chinese Students and Scholars, which was held at the University of Nottingham by the UK's CSSA, Oxford University, Cambridge University, Imperial College, University College London and others.

Jonsson Yinya Li is a Microsoft Certified Professional (MCP), Microsoft Certified Systems Engineer (MCSE) and Microsoft Certified Database Administrator (MCDBA). In his capacity as senior research fellow of the VCRI of Renmin University, he played a leading part in a keynote research project, Venture Capital and High-Tech Industry, which was operated by the Ministry of Education PRC. In employment terms, he has worked as a European chief representative of VCChina Ltd, assistant general manager at Fuzhou Cangsong Economy Development Ltd, co-director of the advertisement office and the computer office, personal assistant and assistant to the chief editor at *Yang-En Gazette*, assistant to the project manager at China Venture Capital Institute (Hong Kong) and assistant to the chief editor of Fujian *Legal News*. Having gained practical work and applied business and investment experience in China and the UK, Mr Li has a solid understanding of the political, business and cultural characteristics of China and Europe, particularly the UK.

He has written published articles, both in Chinese and English, for several popular newspapers and magazines in the fields of business, finance, management, culture and the law.

Jonsson Yinya Li is currently raising funds for investment among media, IT, manufacturing and consultancy companies in England and potential SMEs in China, and to construct mergers and acquisitions for the state-owned enterprises in Mainland China.

Figure AA.1 Author with Bo Xilai, the Minister of the Ministry of Commerce of China

Endorsement

China is presently the fastest growing economy in the world and will probably continue to be so for a considerable period of time. This, of course, makes it an important economy from the perspective of any potential investor. It is also a unique market in the way in which its stock market and financial markets are developing, and in the way in which issues such as governance are evolving. These developments will, naturally, continue and the Chinese markets and their regulation will be able to learn from mistakes made by some of the rapidly developed post-Soviet economies.

The growth rate of the economy is currently running at 8 per cent per annum and fuelling this level of growth is dependent on the provision of adequate finance for investment. It would not be an exaggeration to state that one of the important sources of this finance is venture capital. This means that understanding this market and, more importantly, understanding the role of venture capital in the development of the Chinese economy, is crucial for anyone involved in – or contemplating becoming involved in – either this market or this industry. The rate of change in the venture capital sector is phenomenal and this work will not only introduce potential investors to the context and rules of the sector, but will also acquaint the reader with the latest happenings at the time of publication. Apart from explaining the rules of operation of this section of the economy, this book also incorporates such distinctive features as an explanation of the ways in which mergers and acquisitions could be used to realize a successful return on the capital invested. The last chapter looks at the opportunities afforded by the very new online gaming business within China and the problems which need to be considered and overcome.

This makes this an important and timely book in which the nature of the Chinese market and the role of venture capital are thoroughly explained in a very readable manner. The main points outlined in each chapter are backed up with practical and up-to-date examples, articles and case studies, which outline the main issues surrounding the Chinese venture capital sector. And all of these are explained by a person who not only understands the venture capital market but also the Chinese economy and the way in which it is developing. For anyone interested in this topic – and particularly for anyone contemplating involvement in the sector – this book is essential reading.

Professor David Crowther,
Professor of Corporate Social Responsibility,
London Metropolitan University, UK[1]

---

[1] Professor Crowther also holds the following positions: Visiting Professor, St Petersburg State Polytechnic University; Honorary Council Member, Ansted University, Malaysia; Fellow of North American Academy of Arts & Sciences; Honorary Doctor of Applied Science, External Research Professor, Université Francophone Internationale, Belgium; Académico de Mérito, Muy Ilustre Academia Mundial de Ciencias Tecnología Educación y Humanidades, Spain; Certificate of Registration as International Expert in Social Education, Association Internationale pour l'Ecole de Promotion Collective, Togo; Affiliate, Corporate Citizenship Research Unit, Deakin University; Faculty member, New York College of Advanced Studies, USA; Treasurer/Membership Secretary, Board Member, Standing Conference on Organizational Symbolism (SCOS).

Introduction

This book is largely the product of work that the author has conducted over the years in the venture capital sector of Mainland China. Despite a large body of literature that exists on venture capital projects in most parts of the world, there is a lacuna of publications that place and discuss this interesting and diverse topic within the context of Mainland China. Until recently 'westernized' businesses have largely been reluctant to invest in Chinese enterprises. This is due, in part, to the economic isolation of the old planned economy of the communist government in China, and also due to a lack of understanding of the intricacies of the Chinese venture sector.

However, in light of recent events, namely the entrance of China into the World Trade Organization (WTO) and the increasing openness of the Chinese economy in the last decade, the author felt that it is time to bridge the gap and publish a work that would introduce potential venture capitalists to the opportunities and risks involved in investing in Mainland China. Many of the mainstream economic journals such as *The Economist* praise the advances made in the Chinese economy; furthermore, current foreign interest is justified by the size and potential of the Chinese markets.

Nevertheless, to increase your chances of a successful investment in China, it would be necessary to understand the context and business culture of the Mainland, which is distinct from that of Hong Kong and many of the neighbouring Asian countries and regions. In writing this book, the author's goal was to provide well organized, comprehensive and up-to-date coverage of the topics that take advantage of his many years of research in this area.

At present, the amount of small and medium-sized enterprises (SMEs) that are backed by venture capitalists is increasing at a rate of unprecedented growth, and has also fuelled in no small part the staggering 9 per cent GDP of this economic powerhouse. Under the rapidly developing economic environment in emerging China, the author hopes this book can lead more foreign investors to better know the venture capital industry, especially in respect of the

IT industry, which has the most potential power for development in China.

With about a quarter of the world's population and one of the world's fastest growing economies, China's attractive market has seen a rapid inflow of foreign capital, mostly in the form of international joint ventures. Venture capital now represents another important source of capital inflow. In the next few years, as a result of WTO entry, China will open its markets, eg in telecoms, insurance, banking, automobiles, gradually. More and more funds have been invested in China as foreign direct investment, including foreign venture capital investment, in the last few years. Based on the experience and results of developing venture capital in the US and in European countries, the drive for venture capital investment in China is sure to be the right choice.

In its five-year (2001–2005) plan, the Chinese government has already placed emphasis on basic research as a driver of the economy and on innovation as a means of capturing the benefits of venture capital investment. Obviously, venture capitalists can help Chinese investees to create a better organization, and foster a more cooperative, as well as more competitive, business. China's venture capital industry has undergone a consolidation stage since 2002 as a result of a slowing global economy and receding international venture capital investments. It must be recognized that the development of China's venture capital industry will be a lengthy process that will gradually mature on the back of the country's continued reforms and openness, as well as the development of its science and technology.

The year 2004 was one of extraordinary recovery for venture capital in Mainland China and Asia. In terms of exit activities, fund raising, new markets and new paradigms, a healthy rise could be seen. In the Asia Pacific region, venture capital has not only weathered the crises of 2001–2003, but has also strengthened its value-added role in assisting companies to create value through enhanced business strategies and management, financial engineering, good governance and communication. Many SMEs supported by venture capital have achieved excellent returns – as evidenced by the steady stream of exits throughout 2004. The rate of change in the venture capital sector is phenomenal and this book will not only introduce potential investors to the context and rules of the sector, but will also keep the reader up to date with the latest happenings at the time of publication.

This publication has been divided into eight chapters. The first outlines the benefits of venture capital investing in the Mainland

Chinese market, while also providing up-to-date information on the new and existing rules for venture capital investment. The author lists the new provisions and new rules on foreign venture capital investment as a separate part in Appendix A and Appendix B to make readers familiar with the current legal environment of the Chinese venture capital sector and know how to carry out investment more effectively in Mainland China.

The second chapter goes on to detail the criteria that would ensure successful venture capital investment in Mainland China, as well as outlining the potential risks and pitfalls to look out for. The 3721 technology is the leading online real name search engine service provider, and seller of internationalized domain names in the Chinese alphabet. The current acquisition by Yahoo-HK attracted many venture capitalists' attention.

The third chapter outlines some of the creative products and markets in the Chinese IT sector, while the fourth hammers home the importance of careful due diligence and investment monitoring within China. This was evidenced in the case of the Penshibao launch.

The main reason for making investments is to realize returns, preferably sizable returns. Chapter Five considers how to establish successful IPO strategies to ensure that the exit mechanism of your investment will be successful; Chapter Six illustrates the importance of these strategies by highlighting some of the success stories of venture backed SMEs in China. The story of Ctrip (an online travel service company) covers the last case of a successful Chinese SME to list on NASDAQ. Its shares rallied and jumped more than 108 per cent when the stock reached a high of US$37.35 over the IPO price of US$18 on its first day of NASDAQ trading, which was the largest first-day rise of a company in New York in the previous three years. Ctrip's success on NASDAQ is given the accolade of being the most successful and best example of exiting in the Chinese venture capital industry for 2003. The experience of GTT – an electronic ceramics R&D corporation – covers the creation and development phase, explaining how venture capital allowed the high-tech firm to grow and the internal organization operated in terms of 'producing, learning, and research'.

The last two chapters relate to very new and dynamic issues within the Chinese venture capital sector. Chapter Seven looks at the ways in which mergers and acquisitions (M&As) can be used to realize a successful return on capital invested. M&A is one of the most important financing methods for venture backed SMEs. For foreign investors wanting to enter China by M&A, they need to define their China business strategies and to choose proper business models that will better enable them to exploit the opportunities. AsiaInfo is a successful story in the field of M&A. This is the most detailed case in this chapter and covers the history of the company from its formation to the present situation.

The last chapter looks at the opportunities afforded by the very new online gaming business within China and the problems that need to be considered and overcome. Shanda, the leading online game operator in China, is something of a legend with regard to making profit and blazing the way for the Chinese online game industry, with the assistance of Softbank Asia Infrastructure Fund. Chapter 8 also analyzes venture capital investment in the traditional sectors, such as the media and dairy industries.

As this book goes to press, The China Internet Network Information Center (CNNIC) has just released its 16th China Internet Survey Report. According to the report, by the end of June 2005 China had 103 million internet users, up 18.4 per cent year on year. The number increased by 9 million from January. Broadband users increased 23.8 per cent year on year to 53 million. The number of computers in China connected to the internet reached 45.6 million, up 25.6 per cent year on year. This rapid increase in internet use will provide an enormous boost to China's e-commerce markets (B2B, B2C, C2C, online gaming, email, instant messenger, online payment, online purchasing, online advertising, domain registration, etc).

The main points outlined in each chapter are backed up by use of practical and up-to-date examples, articles and case studies, which outline the main issues surrounding the Chinese venture captial sector today. There are also extensive appendices at the back of the book that provide complete and up-to-date rules and regulations for foreign investors, provisions for foreign firms acquiring domestic enterprises in China, as well as current business surveys.

Jonsson Yinya Li
and Professor Mannie Manhong Liu
April 2005*

---

* Professor Mannie Manhong Liu has a doctoral degree of economy from Cornell University. She served as a research fellow of Harvard University from 1993 to 1997 and is currently a professor and PhD student mentor of Renmin University of China. She is also Financial Advisor to Beijing Municipal Government, Director of Boston China Finance Research Center in the USA, Director of Private Equity and Venture Capital Research Institute of Renmin University of China, Honorary Vice Director of VC Association of China.

Acknowledgements

There is a long list of people to thank for their helpful criticism of earlier texts and for assistance in preparing this book. I would also like to thank the sponsors of this book, the international law firm, Adamas, for their contribution and all those at Global Market Briefings who worked on the book, including the managing director, Peter Chadwick, the senior editorial consultant, Jonathan Reuvid, editorial project manager, Cecilia Thom and copy editor, Helen Cartwright.

I also need to thank Dr Richard Morel, a British civil servant, who used his spare time to help me to modify the organization of the book. Without his hard work and sincere help, this book wouldn't have been published. I also very much appreciate the input of Mr Jeffrey Sheng, a consultant in the field of private equity, who gave me advice on the structure and provided some information on cases.

Thanks also to my many friends in the field of media in Hong Kong, Beijing, Shanghai, Chongqing, Shenzhen, Wuhan and Fuzhou, and to express my appreciation to those in business, especially the private equity and venture capital field, whose insightful comments and suggestions were invaluable to me during the revision process:

- Mr Peter Chadwick, Managing Director of Global Market Briefings (GMB Publishing Ltd);
- Dr Chang Whui Min, Attorney at Law, Adamas, Shanghai;
- Professor Chen Gongmeng, Director of China Venture Capital Research Institute Ltd (Hong Kong), Director of China Accounting and Finance Research Centre of Hong Kong Polytechnic University;
- Professor David Crowther, Professor of Corporate Social Responsibility of London Metropolitan University, Honorary Council Member of Malaysia Ansted University, Honorary Dr of Applied Science of Université Francophone Internationale of Belgium, Affiliate

of Corporate Citizenship Research Unit, Deakin University of Australia;

- Ms Ashley Yanping Guan, Graphic Designer of *EU Chinese Journal;*
- Mr Julian Ha, Director of Evolution Securities China Ltd;
- Mr He Guojie, Chairman of Guangdong Technology Venture Capital Group, Chairman of Guangdong Venture Capital Association;
- Mr He Jiajin, Director of MoneyTT International Ltd, Director of Futsing Finance Ltd;
- Dr Heng Ko Lei, President of Chinese Professionals Association (UK), First Deputy President of The Promotion of China Re-Unification Society in UK, UK Promoter for Beijing 2008 Olympics Bid;
- Professor Josh Lerner, Jacob H Schiff Professor of Investment Banking, Harvard Business School, Arthur Rock Center for Entrepreneurship;
- Mr Hau Shun Li, Deputy Chief Editor, Hong Kong China News Agency;
- Dr James Jianliang Li, Assistant to Director of Beijing Radio, Vice President of Simul Cast Co., Ltd.;
- Professor Mannie Manhong Liu, Director of VC Research Institute of Renmin University of China, Director of Boston China Finance Research Center, USA, Financial Advisor to Beijing Municipal Government, Honorary Vice Director of VC Association of China;
- Mr Liu Jie, Executive Vice-Secretary General of Guangdong Venture Capital Association;
- Mr Martin Bloom, UK Chairman of China-UK Venture Capital Joint Working Group, Partner of Cambridge Accelerator Partners;
- Dr Meng Tianshan, Financial Advisor of China Development Bank;
- Dr Richard Morel, British Library;
- Mr Richard Pascoe, Director of China Policy Institute of Nottingham University;
- Mr Jonathan Reuvid, economist, corporate strategy consultant, Senior Editor of Global Market Briefings and Senior Consultant Editor of Kogan Page;
- Mr Jeffrey Sheng, Director of Co-win Venture Resources;

- Mr Shi Jianxin, Minister Counsellor of Economic and Commercial Counsellor's Office of the Embassy of the People's Republic of China in the UK;

- Mr Wang Baoqing, Minister Counsellor of Science and Technology Counsellor's Office of the Embassy of the People's Republic of China in the UK.

As I promised confidentiality and anonymity to all content informants, I will not list them here; although I cannot thank them by name, their generosity and openness were remarkable.

I would also like to thank my father Hongjiang Li and my mother for the moral and financial support that they have given me throughout.

Jonsson Yinya Li
jonsson.li@gmail.com
May 2005

1

Why Invest in the Chinese Market?

China's venture capital system

China's present venture capital (VC) system still relies heavily on funding from the government and its state-owned enterprises (SOEs). Therefore, it needs to be transformed into a privately driven investment sector. Historically, the motivating force behind the development of the VC industry has been the need of private equity capital to create a venture. To venture capitalists, funds are being invested for profit, while to the entrepreneurs, the support most needed from venture capitalists is long-term equity funding and management input. The scope of this book extends from the provision of 'seed' money by 'angel' investors through mezzanine finance, up to long-term funding and flotation.

While many factors may hinder China's establishment of an effective VC system, there has been a misunderstanding as to how the Chinese define and understand 'venture capital'. In English, the word 'venture' is defined as taking risk in a commercial context in order to create a new business; in Chinese, however, the word 'venture' in venture capital is often translated as just 'risk'. Therefore, in China, the term 'venture capital' is often understood as simply 'risk capital', which could include any equity investment or unsecured debt in a more established business. Consequently, the more precise meaning of 'venture', ie taking risk to create a new business, is often lost in the translation. Given the contentious translation of 'venture capital' it is generally wiser to accept that the Chinese definition of VC in Mainland China is 'risk capital' in the western sense.

As high-tech industries currently induce high risks, VC is often being mistakenly thought of as capital invested in high-tech products or industries. Under the influence of China's past planned economy, most people understand neither the function nor the process of using VC to foster entrepreneurship and the building of private ventures. Many erroneously believe that the government can foster the development of VC investment simply by directing public funds towards investment in high-tech industries. As such, growth of the VC industry has not been driven to date by market forces, but by economic planning.

VC is also known as private equity investment in China, as the recipients of most VC investments are companies that are not listed on the stock exchanges. Most investments take the form of equity and the financial instruments used are shares or loans convertible into shares at a predetermined price in the future. Invested enterprises can be high risk companies, small companies specializing in the new and high technologies at early stages of development, or those companies that have just established a market.

VC is a new phenomenon and has only become prominent in China since the mid-1990s. Traditionally, the four Chinese state-owned banks provided loans for technical updating and loans for capital construction to SOEs. Both types of loan resulted in an increased production capacity; however, one of the failures of this system was that these loans were not accessible to small and non-state owned enterprises. Therefore, in order to make good this shortcoming and to foster the development of small and medium-sized enterprises (SMEs) – especially those associated in the fields of science and technology, resources, export and community services – the government began to carry out the following policies and measures in the late 1990s:[1]

- establishing government controlled VC funds at national, provincial and local levels to give direct financial support to SMEs;
- provision that government guarantees and interest payment subsidies would be made available for SMEs;
- providing incentives to encourage portfolio investment in SMEs;
- increasing proportions of state bank loans to SMEs, and the allocation of funding priorities to SMEs at city banks and cooperative financial institutions;
- permitting qualified SMEs to raise funds in the bond market;
- permitting second board listing of high-tech SMEs in the near future.

VC activity

In 1999, 92 technology-oriented VC funding groups in China managed RMB4.3 billion (US$518 million), to which the Ministry of Science and

---

[1] Riquelme H, and Lilai X. *Venture Capital, Venture Capitalists' Decision Criteria, and Implications for China*, Graduate School of Management, La Trobe University, Melbourne, Vic 3083 Australia. A presented paper at the International Conference on the Chinese Economy: Achieving Growth with Equity, 4–6 July 2001, Beijing.

Technology added RMB3 billion (US$361 million) in the form of an innovation fund for high-tech SMEs.[2] The total (RMB7.4 billion) did not include the foreign fund. The number of registered VC funds was estimated to have reached 100 in the first quarter of 2000; about 28 per cent of the total VC investment went into 'seed stage' projects, 54 per cent went into start-ups, and 18 per cent into expansion projects. It was also revealed that 89 per cent of VC investment projects were involved with the New and High Technology Industry Development Zone.[3]

This outcome is largely the responsibility of provincial and municipal governments, who have been taking a very active investment role. A typical example of this was an injection of RMB100 million (US$12 million) from the Liaoning provincial government, to support small high-tech projects brought into the province by overseas Chinese scholars during Innovation Week in June 2001.[4] To foster innovation, some special committees are drafting significant laws and regulations, and a clear, concerted innovation policy is likely to be endorsed in the forthcoming National People's Congress, which will be held in Beijing in 2006. This will certainly exert a very positive impact on VC investment in China.

The Chinese government promulgated the new Regulations on the Administration of Foreign-invested Venture Investment Enterprises (RFIVCIE) in January 2003. These new RFIVCIE were put forward jointly by the Ministry of Foreign Trade and Economic Cooperation, Ministry of Science and Technology, State Administration for Industry and Commerce, State Administration of Taxation and State Administration of Foreign Exchange.

It is important to note, however, that a market does not suddenly become viable for all forms of VC investment. The environment evolves, becoming more supportive to certain types of investment than others. Investors can look to Europe where, although the issues of transparency, intellectual property (IP), and legal protection and liquidity have been addressed, there is not yet a significant, entrepreneurial VC market by US standards. To be sure, there are pockets in the UK, southern Germany, southern France and Scandinavia, but nothing to compare with the US. This is a major reason why European investors interested in VC tend to go to the US. On the other hand, there are substantial VC funds coming from the US, such as the

---

[2] Yu Yongda, *Chinese Venture Capital Development Current Situation and Prediction*, Hermes Corporation, 8 January 2001.
[3] Ibid.
[4] *The Notification on Second Innovation and Creation Week of Overseas Chinese Scholars (2001, Shenyang and Dalian, Liaoning Province)*, Silicon Valley Chinese Overseas Business Association, April 2001.

'incubators', as well as additional funds in Paris and Australia. Since 2001, the successful experiences of Far Eastern countries and Israel have been attracting more investors, including China, to those countries.

China excites investors for numerous reasons, such as its strong entrepreneurial culture, solid record of technological innovation and engineering excellence, as well as its large domestic market. All of these elements are required for a successful technology-based VC community, but the situation for private equity will be different. Currently, some of the elements required to support an environment for a viable and sustainable technology-based VC investment environment – at least for very early-stage companies – are only beginning to emerge in China. Issues of law, transparency, IP and liquidity are matters of tremendous concern to early-stage venture investors. As they are addressed, and as investors build experience and confidence in working on a trans-Pacific basis, the level of investment will increase. Ultimately, investment decisions are based on 'perceived' risk and reward, all viewed through the lens of an investor's 'comfort zone'. However, this process is not unique to China; in the past, the same process has occurred in varying degrees in Singapore, Israel and India.

Today, most investors are very excited about the opportunities in China but, as with most things, changes will not occur overnight. The question for an investor who is bullish about future opportunities should be: 'what can I do today to build up my understanding of risk and reward in venture capital?'. Five years ago, almost no-one in the US venture community would have dreamed of investing in a company engaged in development work in China. Today, the climate of opinion has changed and there are notable examples of success. Hence, the level of investors' comfort has grown in line with levels of experience and success. This process will continue until investors move into the next phase of technological VC investment in China and make direct investments in Chinese companies. Again, some of this activity is happening today but, typically, within the context of larger start-ups and investors with direct VC experience in China who have a physical presence within the country.

During the first half of 2004, VC investment maintained the warm recovery trend of 2003: more than 80 enterprises attracted VC, which accounted for about US$438 million.[5] Nevertheless, in relation to the demand for VC backing, Chinese VC development is still in its infancy compared with that of western countries, especially in technological and commercial applications. The extent of this underdevelopment is apparent when reviewing small-scale financing, low to average investments, low investment funds and the few cases involved – these are clearly highlighted in Tables 1.1–1.5.

---

[5] *The 2004 Third Quarter of China Venture Capital Investigation Report*, Zero2IPO Ltd.

Why Invest in the Chinese Market?

Table 1.1 The venture capital development and trend in China from 1996 to 2001

		1996	1997	1998	1999	2000	2001
Newly subscribed VC investment	Total amount (RMB100 million)	5.9	40.1	27.9	102.3	166.8	32.2
	Percentage increase over previous year	20	111	37	98	81	9
New VC investment firms set up	Total number	4	15	21	40	102	45
	Percentage increase over previous year	–	275	40	90	155	-167
Total amount of investment (RMB100 million)		n/a	n/a	n/a	n/a	n/a	15.08

Note: In 2003, there was US$992 million of VC investment and 173 cases in Mainland China, compared with US$420 million in 2002 and US$520 million in 2001. The capital invested increased by 137% in 2003 over 2002.

Percentage of each venture stage during the investment						
Seed	17.1	7.8	14.2	12.9	12.6	17.8
Start-up	80.8	13.1	66.9	41.3	28.3	21.4
Growth	2.1	79.1	14.1	38.0	26.4	22.0
Expansion	–	–	4.8	2.6	27.9	23.5
Mature	–	–	–	5.2	4.9	15.4

Exit	Number of exit cases	Exit channels				
	38	Initial public offering	Merger and acquisition	Management buy-out/management buy-in	Sales	Liquidation
		2	7	6	16	7

Source: *China Venture Capital Journal* (2002) and *China 2003 VC Annual Report*, Zero2IPO.

Table 1.2 Venture capital firms' investment in 2002

VC firms	Number (sample)	Number (known capital)	Management capital (RMB 1 Million)	Available capital investment to mainland (RMB 1 million)	Average available capital investment to mainland (RMB 1 million)	Exit number	Actual investment and percentage (RMB 1 million)	VC-backed companies (number and percentage by VC firms involved)	Average capital investment per case (RMB 1 million)
Mainland domestic	269	149	4,177	4,109	28	42/22	194.8/46.5%	168/74.3%	1.2
Foreign	38	36	101,795	5,967	166	16/12	208.6/49.8%	58/25.7%	4.9
Joint venture	18	15	540	420	28	n/a	14.6/3.5%	n/a	n/a
New firms	34	34	6,400	1,300	n/a	n/a	n/a	n/a	n/a
Total (excluding new firms)	325	200	106,512	10,495	52	58	418	226	n/a

Source: China 2002 VC Annual Report, Zero2IPO Ltd

Table 1.3 The most influential VC investment in Mainland China in 2002

Participating VC firms	Venture-backed enterprises	Investment amount (US$1 million)
Warburg Pincus, DragonTech	Harbour Network	42
Warburg Pincus	Zhejiang University ZDSoft.net	15
Government of Singapore Investment Corp (GIC), Intel Capital, Softbank China Venture Capital (SBCVC)	Linkage Technology (Nanjing)	14
Walden International, Legend Capital	Precom, Inc (Silicon Valley)	9.5
Legend Capital, Investor Growth Capital (Asia)	NSFocus Information Technology (Beijing)	2.98

Source: *2002 China VC Annual Report*, Zero2IPO

Table 1.4 Venture capital firms' investment in 2003

VC firms	Actual investment and percentage (RMB1 million)	Investee number and average by VC firms involved
Mainland domestic	159/16%	More than 100
Foreign	780/78.6%	63
Joint venture	53/5.4%	
Total	992	n/a

Source: *2003 China VC Annual Report*, Zero2IPO

Table 1.5 Stages of investment in 2003

VC firms	Sample number				180	
Newly subscribed VC management funds	Total amount (RMB100 million)				3702	
	Number of VC firms				76	
New VC investment	Total amount (RMB100 million)				3715	
Percentage of each stage during the investment	Seed	Start-up	Growth	Expansion	Mature	Preparation for IPO
	59	138	101	43		70

Points to note
1. VC investment distributed unevenly and focused on Beijing, Shanghai, Shenzhen and other developed regions.
2. The hotspots centralized in e-information, biomedicine, electrical instruments, internet and telecom.
3. VC firms are mostly owned by governments.
4. The stages of VC investment are concentrated on the periods of growth and expansion.
5. The main business is project investment. Earnings are derived from the projects' dividends.
6. Share deals accounted for 82 per cent of exit mechanisms. IPO exits accounted for less than 20 per cent.
7. The multivariant trend was apparent in project management and monitoring modes.
8. The governance environment should be improved.

Source: *2003 China VC Year Book*, CVCRI and *China 2003 VC Annual Report*, Zero2IPO

Some policy recommendations for the development of China's VC industry have been suggested. They are as follows:

- *to amend the Company and the Partnership Acts to provide a more flexible and effective operating environment for the VC industry.* Partnerships are the usual form of organization used in countries with mature VC industries. The structures available in China are much more rigid, making it more difficult for investors and fund managers to divide profits and risk. Currently, China has no law on regulations regarding limited partnerships. Some provisions in the Partnership Act even hinder the development of limited partnerships.

- *to accelerate the enactment of an Investment Fund Act as well as a Venture Capital Investment Management Act.* Their aims should be to broaden the sources of capital available for the VC industry. VC companies in China currently face major restrictions on their funding sources; therefore, China should learn from and apply overseas experience, by introducing the investment funds to provide a structure for VC organizations.

- *to establish a multilevel securities market system to improve the exit mechanism for VC investment.* Exit mechanisms are key to the VC market and small capital markets; over-the-counter markets, such as those of Japan, can play an important role in the smooth exit of venture capital.

- *to promote the use of stock options as a form of management incentive for new ventures.* China should speed up the enactment of the Stock Option Management Regulations to regulate the issuance of stock options. At the same time, the Ministry of Finance should publish related policies on accounting and taxation treatments for stock options.

The sharp rise in activity

It could be stated that the VC industry in Mainland China is developing with the global proliferation of the internet. After surviving 2000–2001's 'low tide' and the adjustment of 2002–2004, the VC industry in China is finally gathering strength. The US$40 million from Softbank Asia Infrastructure Fund (SAIF) to Shanda and the successful initial public offering (IPO) of Ctrip.com International Ltd (Ctrip) not only burnished *de novo* expectations for the internet industry, but also brought a glimmer of hope to the outlook for the Chinese VC industry in 2005 and the following years. As a result of a lot of favourable information and driving factors, the Chinese VC industry is starting to warm up.

The US, Japan and Europe are in a phase of economic recovery, while China, India, Russia and other developing countries are experiencing a phase of high-speed economic growth. In the capital market, the National Association of Securities Dealers Automatic Quotation (NASDAQ) topped 2000 for first time in two years on 9 December 2003.[6] This was followed by a significant rise in VC investment in the Asia and Pacific region at a time when VC investment in the US and Europe was declining. Against this encouraging backdrop, the total amount of VC investment in Mainland China climbed sharply to around US$990 million, which is more than the total for 2001 and 2002 combined.[7] This is 2.37 times more than for 2001 and 137 per cent more than in 2002. There were more than ten instances in which companies attracted in excess of US$10 million; this indicates the

---

[6] Krantz M, 'Nasdaq tops 2000 for first time in 2 years', *USA Today*, 29 December 2003.
[7] *China 2003 VC Annual Report*, Zero2IPO Ltd.

Chinese economy's capability for growth, as well as the attraction of international capital to the Chinese market.

However, 2003 was not a rewarding year for most of the domestic Chinese VC firms, which only received approximately US$160 million on investments in some 100 cases, accounting for 16 per cent of the total amount.[8] Their first task was to survive and then to demonstrate their ability. In order to survive, domestic Chinese VC firms avoided direct competition with their foreign counterparts that hold abundant capital and placed emphasis on biomedicine, new materials and traditional industry. Chinese VC firms showed their ability in numerous ways: they thought up 'brilliant' ideas for financing models, project management and exit channels in order to accumulate practised experience from the 'real' competition in the Chinese VC industry. The venture backed SMEs that were preparing for IPOs acquired US$310 million, about 32 per cent of the total amount. The US$780 million invested by the foreign VC firms into 61 companies accounted for more than 80 per cent of the total amount of investment.[9] It is clear that, at present, it is the foreign firms that dominate the VC industry in China; the successful achievements tend to be from foreign VC firms because they provide nearly all the big investments.

The main influence driving the increase in the Chinese VC industry is the global transfer of VC investment, which can be seen clearly in the fields and sectors that have attracted it. In 2003,[10] information and communication technology (ICT) sectors still gained the largest portion of investment. Only integrated circuit (IC) manufacturing acquired huge internal investment – at more than US$400 million, it accounted for 40 per cent of the total amount. The telecom industry also received some US$200 million in investment. Through research, it becomes clear that the main reasons for this are that most of the internet enterprises in which investment has been made have matured and need further capital investment.

Due to its favourable geographic location, Beijing, the capital of China, has obtained the majority of investment and projects. From the capital distribution by location in the Yangtze River Region, however, the Shanghai core has acquired more capital, totalling US$500 million, against Beijing's US$180 million.[11] Investment in the Guangdong (Canton) River Triangle Region reached around US$75 million, while the Middle and Western Region took US$50 million and North East Region US$10 million. The software and telecom enterprises based in

---

[8] Liu C and Li J 'Ten PRC ministries push Chinese domestic VC firms', *21st Century Economy Report*, 23 October 2004.
[9] *China 2003 VC Annual Report*, Zero2IPO Ltd.
[10] 2003 Statistics of Ministry of Information Industry PRC.
[11] *China VC 2003 Review and 2004 Expectation*, Venture Capital Research Institute of National Research Centre for Science and Technology for Development, 19 March 2004.

Beijing and Shanghai respectively, attracted the majority of the available investment.

Transition from 2004 and the flourishing forward trend in 2005

The *2004 China Venture Capital Development Research Report* shows that China's VC industry continued 2003's 'warmer' trend because of better Chinese macroscopical economy and establishment of the SME Board. The VC investment was more vibrant and presented four new points.[12]

Magnification trend for VC management scale
The results of analyzing 111 samples of VC management organizations show that there is RMB43,899.5 million invested, which is a growth of 34.93 per cent over 2003's RMB11,365 million.

Table 1.6 The percentage comparison between 2003 and 2004 by different scale VC management organizations

RMB million	2004	2003
0–50	15%	23%
100–200	Drop 1% in 2004 comparing with 2003	
200–500	28%	21%
More than 500	Increase 4% in 2004 comparing with 2003	

Source: 2004 China Venture Capital Development Research Report, CVCRI

Middle-South and East China became the new places for VC investment
The analysis of 140 questionnaires indicated that the level of VC funds invested was RMB5.245 billion, which was 41.7 per cent more than 2003's RMB3.7 billion. Absolute VC investment in 2003 rose to RMB3,791 million in 2003 with a growth of RMB762 million over 2002. There were 526 investment projects in 2004, an increase of 201 cases over 2003. Undoubtedly, Beijing, Shanghai and Shenzhen are still the hotspots for VC. However, Middle-South China and East China became the newly favoured places for venture capitalists. Some

---

[12] *2004 China Venture Capital Development Research Report*, China Venture Capital Research Institute (Hong Kong), 2005 China Venture Capital Forum, Shenzhen, 9 April 2005.

RMB480 million (26.5 per cent), RMB440 million (24.3 per cent) and RMB100 million (0.6 per cent) of total investment by 108 VC companies surveyed was invested respectively in the Middle-South China, East China and North-East China areas. There were 108 VC management firms providing the information for accumulated investment projects for eight areas in China. The total statistical number of the invested projects was 1606, including 565 (35.2 per cent) in East China, 292 (18.2 per cent) in Shenzhen, 187 (11.6 per cent) in West China, 151 (9.4 per cent) in Beijing, and 153, 126, 115, 17 investment items in Middle-South China, North China, Shanghai and North-East China respectively. Table 1.7 lists the clear distribution. Mergers and acquisitions (M&A) became the most frequently used exit channel (Table 1.8). The primary business for VC companies is project investment (Table 1.9) with the main earning coming from project dividends and exit income (Table 1.10).

Table 1.7 Accumulated projects for eight areas in 2004 (sample: 108 VC companies)

	Total	East China	Shenzhen	West China	Middle-South China	Beijing	North China	Shanghai	North-east China
Number	1606	565	292	187	153	151	126	115	17
Percentage	100	35.2	18.2	11.6	9.5	9.4	7.8	7.2	1.1

Source: 2004 China Venture Capital Development Research Report, CVCRI

Table 1.8 Exit channels in Mainland China in the last three years (sample: 36)

	Merger and acquisition	Initial public offering	Management buy-out	Other	Total
Projected numbers	49	4	14	56	123
Percentage	40	3	11	46	100

Source: 2004 China Venture Capital Development Research Report, CVCRI

Table 1.9 VC companies' primary business (sample: 100)

Project investment	Investment and financing service	Management consulting	Investment banking	Securities investment	Real estate	Other
89	34	30	19	13	9	5

Source: 2004 China Venture Capital Development Research Report, CVCRI

Table 1.10 Sources of income (sample: 96)

Source of Income*	Dividends from invested project	Exit project	Management consulting	Finance adviser	Securities investment	Other
97	67	52	26	21	18	12
Percentage comparing with the samples	70	54	27	22	19	13

* The selection statistics allow for choice of more than one option. For example, the sample company can choose the 'dividends from invested project' and 'exit project' together.

Source: 2004 China Venture Capital Development Research Report, CVCRI

VC investment focused on the exploration and expansion stage
According to the analysis of the stages of 198 new VC investment projects, Chinese domestic VC companies still focus on VC-backed enterprises in the exploration or expansion stages, but there is an increase in seed capital investment.

Table 1.11 VC investment for different stages in 2004 (sample: 198)

	Start-up/seed	Exploration	Expansion	Maturity
Number (%)	47	72	56	14
	(24)	(36)	(28)	(7)
Capital Distribution (%)	16	35	30	19

Source: 2004 China Venture Capital Development Research Report, CVCRI

It can be said that VC investment is still strongly focused on the stage of exploration and expansion, which received roughly 65 per cent of the total capital investment (Table 1.11). Under conditions of fiercer competition in the middle and final stages, and because the estimated value of VC projects was driven up, Chinese domestic VC companies are transferring their attention to enterprises in the seed/start-up stage. The situation illusrates the enduring attraction of ventures for VC management organizations, boosted by the improving environment for VC investment in China.

In 2004, Doll Capital Management (DCM) reviewed five Chinese domestics in the middle and later stages (MLS) but discarded them because of their high estimated value. DCM then transferred its investment strategy into start-up enterprises. In the fourth quarter of 2004, Carlyle Group invested US$27 million in two start-up enterprises.[13] All of this could be a signal for growing VC early stage (ES) investment in 2005 although MLS investment will be dominant. The ES investment can not only bring a more generous return, but also incurs less competition than MLS. In 2004, many funds were set up for ES enterprises, such as the Gobi Partners' Gobi fund, JAFCO Investment's JATF2, and Tsinghua Venture's Chinese Environment Protection Fund 2004, which augur a flourishing future for VC development in ES funding following an increase in the number of start-up enterprises.

New overseas VC management organization became the net 'gold diggers'
Foreign VC organizations always play an important role in the Chinese VC industry, with the early pioneer investors, such as IDG, Walden International and SoftBank, achieving success. The new foreign VC entrants include Venture TDF, US Goldman Sachs, UK 3i, British CDC Capital, Chengwei Ventures, Carlyle Investment, Pacific Venture Partners and MCM China. More than 55 per cent of investment has come from the foreign VC companies, which promoted not only the overseas IPOs for Shanda, Mengniu, Tencent and Lining, but also invested most of the domestic sectors' leading enterprises, eg Alibaba, FocusMedia (China), Versa Technology, Topsec, Datang Microelectronics Technology (DMT), UnionPay, Asia Netcom and Mobi Development.

Semiconductor Manufacturing International Corporation's (SMIC) list made Silicon Valley's mainstream VC companies, such as NEA and DCM, well known to Chinese enterprises. As one of the most valued

---

[13] 'Ten Trend for Chinese VC in 2005', *Shanghai Securities News*, 24 February 2005.
[14] UUMe.com was founded in 2003 by James Liu and Fred Rao, Silicon Valley veterans who both graduated from the renowned Stanford Business School. UUMe.com pioneers the online social networking service in China. This online community enables people to facilitate real world dating, friendships, job-seeking and other transactions that are better conducted within a trusted network.

VC companies in the US, NEA has invested US$150 million since its first year in China. Other Silicon Valley VC companies include the investor of UUMe[14] (Accel Partners) and BCD's investors (Granite Global Ventures, Redpoint Ventures and Venrock Associates). In fact, besides maintaining investment in the US' life science field, VC companies in Silicon Valley have shifted some of their centre of gravity into China and India. Foreign VC companies, especially those from Silicon Valley, will undoubtedly give an important original impetus to the whole Chinese VC industry. The famous European 3i Venture, which invested in Dalian HiSoft and CSMC Technologies, will soon open its Shanghai office.

Among foreign corporate VC companies, Agilent Technologies invested the IPFIII fund of AcerVC in 2004 through limited partnerships (LPs). To date, LPs in Mainland China include not only corporate ventures, such as Cisco Systems, IBM, Motorola, Agilent Technologies, NTT DoCoM, and Alcatel, but also financial institutions, eg International Finance Corporation (IFC) and Asian Development Bank (ADB). However, because of the long time in preparing to grasp the investment opportunity, LP investment won't be the primary mode for foreign capital and foreign direct investment (FDI) in 2005 and subsequent years. Those planning actual investment action for foreign corporate VC include Nokia Venture, Time Warner Investment, SVB, Unilever Technology Venture, Shanghai Bell and Alcatel. In line with the gradual prosperity of Chinese venture capital, VC funds from the Middle East are expected to become leading players in China in 2005 and the years immediately following.

For the new foreign VC investors, there will be two opposing patterns: on one hand they will associate with other domestic VC organizations to invest in some large-scale MLS enterprises, such as SMIC; on the other hand it will be better for them to invest in some ES enterprises, such as the investment in Up Technology in 2003 and advanced micro-fabrication equipment (AMEC) in 2004, which related to business with multinational companies or in corporations backed by other VC organizations. Furthermore, more attention should be paid to offshore hedge funds that take part in the later and pre-IPO stages.

According to the most recent data available from the National Bureau of Statistics of China, China's GDP growth rate in 2004 was 9.5 per cent. This astonishing development has been gained, however, at the expense of huge capital input, a tremendous consumption of resources, relatively low economic efficiency, inferior productivity and environmental pollution. An economic growth model such as this – which is characterized as high input and low output – is not sustainable. The way for China to achieve sustainable economic development in the next two decades should be based on innovation. Technology development, management upgrading and systems improvement will generate resources and vitality for the new economic growth model, with venture capital being the real engine to power the growth.

Firstly, the investment sum will continuously rise. In the following years, the Chinese VC industry will generate new opportunities:

- US mainstream VCs are accelerating their entry into the Chinese market;
- the new technology is maturing and bringing new and broader investment opportunities, such as third generation (3G) and digital television (DTV).

From 2003 and 2004's statistics, it was the huge VC investment projects that dominated the total investment sum; for example, US$300 million VC was invested into SMIC in the third quarter of 2003, and US$82 million into Alibaba and US$72 million into DMT in the first quarter of 2004. These multimillion dollar investment cases held a major share of the full year's capital investment, distorting the composition of the investment sum. According to the statistics of Shanghai Securities News, there are 32 projects out of 253 (12.6 per cent) that attracted more than US$10 million each, but which accounted for 65.8 per cent of the total investment sum of US$1.269 billion. Under these circumstances, the primary factor in 2005's investment increase will be the incidence of similar cases as in 2003 and 2004.

For foreign VC investors, financial system reform, which is the favoured policy for VC and consummation of the legal system are still the focus of attention. There is no denying that a high level of risk in the Chinese VC system virtually increases the opportunity cost for VC. Generally, 2005's domestic VC is continuing to rise in China; with the interest of foreign VC, such foreign investment will be greatly enhanced in 2005 compared with 2004.

Secondly, there will be a greater focus on high-tech and non-IT investment. The hotspot for 2004's investment was centred on the field of IC fables and wireless value-added service. Including 87.1 per cent IC fables, US$420 million was invested in 40 cases in the IC sector, accounting for a third of all VC investment in 2004. Besides IC fables and innovative wireless value-added services, 3G, digital TV and applications based on broadband will bring forward more investment opportunities. However, non-IT sectors and traditional industries, including manufacturing, services, media, consumables, environmental protection, new materials, energy projects and education will also attract attention. Successful cases to date involve FocusMedia, Target Media, Mengniu Dairy and Ningxiahong Chinese Wolfberry Industry Group (NXH).

Thirdly, more overseas IPOs will be supported by VC. With the opening up of NASDAQ in the third quarter of 2003, overseas capital markets have opened their doors to China. Up to 22 December 2004, with the assistance of VC companies, 21 VC-backed enterprises, including Ctrip, SMIC, Shanda, Finance Street, 51job.com and eLong, realized overseas IPOs and raised US$4.67 billion. In 2005, IPO plans for NXH, FocusMedia, Baidu.com and Spreadtrum Communications will attract the attention of investors. The IPO market will be centralized on NASDAQ and Hong Kong Stock Exchange Mainboard. As a result of the China Aviation Oil (Singapore) matter, Chinese enterprises will take a passive attitude towards the Stock Exchange of Singapore in 2005 and for some years following. At the same time, however, more IPOs bring deeper conformity to the same sector. Shanda and AsiaInfo's M&A are the best example. Forthcoming IPOs will be clustered in the field of internet service, IC fables and traditional industry.

Domestic and foreign VC firms

Even after WTO entry, China still maintains greater control over certain industries, including banking, financial services and insurance, than other member states. It seems that China has finally opened the door to foreign VC investment.

At the start of 2004, Zero2IPO Corporation short-listed companies for the '2003 China Domestic Top 20 VC Investment Firms', as well as the '2003 China Foreign Top 20 VC Investment Firms'. Many may ask why it did not just select the 20 strongest VC investment firms in China; perhaps the answer is that there wouldn't be any domestic Chinese VC investment firms in a listing of the 'Strongest 20 VC Investment Firms in the China Market'. To focus on the strongest ranking would totally ignore the development history of the Chinese VC industry; furthermore, it would be statistically biased and not represent the true state of affairs, thus making any forecasts spurious.

Chinese domestic VC firms are in a state of relative atrophy. The Zero2IPO research reports show that the ratio of domestic to foreign VC firms' investment remains at around 1:3, which means that the gap will widen in 2005. Up to the end of 2004, there were no more than ten active domestic VC firms, including CDH, Shanghai NewMargin, Legend Capital, Guangdong Technology Venture Capital Group (GDTVCG), Sandong High-Tech Investment Corporation (CDHTIC), Shenzhen Capital Group Company Ltd (SZCG) and Canton Venture Capital Company Ltd (C-VCC). Although some of the domestic firms can compete with foreign VCs, most of them still lag far behind. Whether or not domestic VC firms can escape from their 'rat trap' depends on two important factors, namely the time it takes to push for a real full-scale VC Board, and the putting into effect of the related rules and regulations. It can be said with confidence that the situation of foreign VC firms leading China's VC industry won't be changed in 2005 or the following three years.

NewMargin Corp appears in the ranking list three times. Although the management fund for NewMargin is not huge, the company is keeping active in the field of China VC and has made outstanding achievements among the domestic VC investment firms since its foundation. Two students from Stanford University conducted a Chinese VC investment market investigation[15] for 2003 and reached the conclusion that there were three contributory factors for a successful investment in the Chinese VC industry. These are: local practice, international experience and high interposition of management. Coincidently, the researchers of MIT drew amazingly similar results through a project that focused on NewMargin as a case study. NewMargin's success was a result of the above three factors. The partners included two Chinese and two Americans, who cherish the opportunities of participating in corporate management and try their best to improve the strength of the venture-backed SMEs in which they have invested. According to information available up to February 2004, all of NewMargin's projects made money and none had failed.[16] Three VC-backed enterprises were listed in 2003 and five VC-backed enterprises carried out IPOs on Hong Kong's stock exchange in 2004.

In China, the VC industry is taking its initial steps, while everyone is looking for a successful VC investment model. From 1999, the Chinese VC industry developed steadily from 'strength to strength' in all its fields.[17] Enterprises that became involved during this period not only made themselves more mature, but also learned more about venture-backed enterprises and the ruling time dimension in VC development.

Comparing foreign VC management firms against local VC management firms it becomes clear that local VC firms have not been affluent in the financing sector. However, there are at least three advantages of cooperation with local VC management firms. First, it is easy for them to communicate with a project and to understand better the project's value because local VC firms share the same culture and similar concepts. Second, they can understand rare investment opportunities through an intimate knowledge of the local market. Finally, they can use Chinese, not English, expertise to their advantage.

Venture funds are mostly sourced from foreign capital; why is this? The reason is that China doesn't have a suitable political, social funds

---

[15] *The Change of Venture Capital,* Shenzhen Vene Capital Association, 9 February 2004.
[16] Guo W 'NewMargin broke the silence' *Economics Observer* 19 March 2004.
[17] Cheng Siwei, 2003. 'The Strategic Consideration for Developing Chinese Venture Capital', Issue 10, *People's Tribune.*

and economic environment for VC. Thus, there is a reluctance to hand over funds to be managed by Chinese VC management firms. All the social funds are constrained under the current Chinese VC situation. Society would like to invest in real estate, steel, cement and other traditional sectors that belong to the category of visible profit industries. The 'fresh' industries in which VC is invested are finding it difficult to be accepted, so the domestic fund for VC is currently fed on illusions. There should be at least a five- or six-year period of evolution before the scale of VC investment is formulated.

Some researchers contend that domestic VC firms are now transferring their investments to traditional industries, especially in the medium and later stages of their development. These two points have brought about suspicion of the appropriate VC investment standard for start-up enterprises; in actual fact, the VC firms' investment standard has not departed from rapid growth enterprises. Irrespective of an organization's stage of development, the industry or terms, and as long as Chinese enterprises have the ability to expand rapidly, VC investor firms would be as attracted to them as they are to enterprises in the US. The difference is that traditional industries in the US are declining sharply, while in China similar traditional industries have the space and opportunity to rapidly expand.

One unique opportunity in China at present is the retreat of government capital and the advance of that from the private sector. If the events of the past two years are anything to go by, 2005 will be a climax year for new start-up enterprises, which will compel foreign VC firms to pay more attention to China.

The economy of China is expanding rapidly; in 2003 GDP growth rate was measured at 9.3 per cent[18] and a similar growth of 9.5 per cent was recorded for 2004. These figures are certainly gestating more high-growth companies. The rapid growth of the Chinese economy also means that there are more investment opportunities. VC is well placed at the right time in the Chinese market environment. VC firms drive the opportunities for wealth and spur the increasing economic trends without hindering the economy's health. Trials, practice and development in the next three to five years will make the role of Chinese domestic VC firms clearer.

---

[18] *2003 Annual Statistics (Emendation),* National Bureau of Statistics of PRC, 14 October 2004.

Case study: Five factors affecting stock markets in 2004–2005[19]

The performance of China's stock market may be affected by government policies on five aspects, market observers noted in January 2004. Policy on the management of state-owned assets is deemed as a major factor contributing to the stock market.

The performance of the stock market in 2003 showed a big impact resulting from the measures implemented for the management of property rights in listed companies and, in large companies, from asset reorganization among enterprises. With the increasing depth of reform on the state-owned assets management and supervision system in 2004, relevant policies were expected to affect the operation of the stock market to some extent.

The setting up of a 'second board' market in Shenzhen in May 2004 is viewed as a key factor that will give impetus to the development of the stock market. The Chinese authorities have decided to promote venture investment and build a second board market, which will encourage efforts to establish a multilayer capital market system, improve the structure of the capital market and enrich capital market products.

The policy on IPOs and the reform of both the IPO verification commission system and the guarantee system promoted by the national securities watchdog is having a significant influence on the issue of new stocks. The new policy will also help to guarantee the qualifications of listed companies at the root.

Assets management by securities firms will open a new channel for more funds to flow into the stock market and will be conducive to increasing institutional investors' economic capacity. The draft amendment to the securities law was submitted for examination and approval to the nation's top law-making body in April 2004. The original law, which was put into effect in 1999, contains some rules that are no longer compatible to the development of the stock market – a revised law will boost the its development.

---

[19] Quote from Xinhua News Agency, 27 January 2004.

Stages in the investment[20]

From the western point of view, there are five stages in the development of venture-backed companies, which can be defined as:

1. seed;
2. start-up;
3. other early stages (exploration);
4. expansion;
5. maturity (exit).

Such terms are used by the majority of VC firms to define the 'stages' of a company's development and are determined by the purpose for which the financing is required. This can be complex, thus it is necessary to explain these stages in the investment process.

Seed

> *To allow a business concept to be developed, perhaps involving the production of a business plan, prototypes and additional research, prior to bringing a product to market and commencing large-scale manufacturing.*[21]

Only a few seed financings are undertaken each year by VC firms in China; the same can be said of the UK. Many seed financings are small and require too much hands-on support from VC firms to make them economically viable as investments. There are, however, some specialist VC firms that are worth approaching, subject to the investment companies meeting their other investment preferences. Business angel capital should also be considered, as a business angel on a company's board may be more attractive to VC firms when later-stage funds are required. AsiaInfo's success could not have been achieved without the support from a business angel to raise the funds.[22]

---

[20] The stages described are taken from BVCA and PricewaterhouseCoopers (1998) *A Guide to Venture Capital* London: PricewaterhouseCoopers and BVCA.
[21] BVCA and PricewaterhouseCoopers (1998) *A Guide to Venture Capital* London: PricewaterhouseCoopers and BVCA.
[22] AsiaInfo, *The Place to Use Your Ability,* AsiaInfo, 1996.

Start-up

To develop the company's products and fund their initial marketing. Companies may be in the process of being set up or may have been trading for a short time, but not have sold their product commercially.[23]

Although many start-ups are typically 'smaller' companies, there are an increasing number of multimillion pound funds available for start-ups in the UK. The information from the British Venture Capital Association (BVCA) shows that around half of its members will consider high-quality and larger start-up propositions. However, there are those who specialize in this stage, subject to their meeting the firm's other investment preferences. Around 10 per cent of financings each year are related to start-ups. Currently, many Chinese would like to start up their own 'tech' companies but are unable to do so due to a shortage of funds. Bearing the strength of the pound sterling in mind, this may be a good opportunity for businessmen from the UK to invest in China.

Other early stages (exploration)

To initiate commercial manufacturing and sales in companies that have completed the product development stage, but may not yet be generating profits.[24]

This stage has been attracting an increasing amount of VC over the past few years, accounting for some 10 per cent of the number of financings each year in the UK and about 20 per cent of those in China.

Expansion

To grow and expand an established company. For example, to finance increased production capacity, product development and marketing, and to provide additional working capital. Also known as 'development' or 'growth' capital.[25]

More UK companies at this stage of development receive VC than any other, generally accounting for around 50 per cent of financings each year.

---

[23] BVCA and PricewaterhouseCoopers (1998) *A Guide to Venture Capital* London: PricewaterhouseCoopers and BVCA.
[24] ibid.
[25] ibid.

Maturity (exit)

In BVCA's opinion, there are nine alternative routes in this period. They are: MBO management buy-out (MBO), management buy-in (MBI), buy-in management buy-out (BIMBO), institutional buy-out (IBO), secondary purchase, replacement equity, rescue/turnaround, refinancing bank debt and bridge financing.

Chen Siwei, Vice Chairman of the Standing Committee of the National People's Congress of China – often referred to as 'the father of the Mainland China's VC industry' because of his contribution to it – suggested that ventures go typically through four stages of development, including start-up, exploration, expansion and maturity. The responsibility of venture capitalists is to nurture their ventures into maturity before profiting through the exit mechanisms. Therefore, the growing capital needs of a venture during the exploratory and expansionary stages should be provided by venture capitalists instead of being raised from the public through a premature IPO. Listing entrepreneurial ventures before their maturity is essentially shifting to the public risks that should, in reality, be borne out by venture capitalists, and is a move that can have serious consequences. Of the four development stages of an enterprise, the exploratory and expansionary stages are most the crucial to the success of the enterprise and should as such be the focus of venture capitalists.

Establishing perfect legal circumstances

A favourable legal environment is a prerequisite for the creation of wealth. Borrowing from the successful experience of the US in fostering the growth of its VC industry through legislation, China may be able to overcome some of the obstacles that currently hinder the development of its VC industry. However, to do so China must first perfect its legal system in order to accelerate the development of VC investment.

Since 1974, the US Congress has passed and modified a series of laws that have promoted the development of VC investment. It revised the Limited Partnership Act in 1974 while cutting the capital gains tax from 49.5 per cent to 28 per cent with the aim of encouraging private equity investment. The rate was again reduced to 20 per cent in 1981.[26] Congress also revised the Employee Retirement Income Security Act (ERISA) Prudentman rule in 1979, allowing pension funds to engage in VC investment as long as they did not jeopardize the safety

---

[26] Kelly DePonte (2004) *The Evolution of Private Equity Secondary Activity in the United States: Liquidity for an Illiquid Asset*, Probitas Partners.

of the overall portfolio.[27] In 1980, this rule passed the Small Business Investment Act, which redefined VC companies as 'venture development companies', thereby exempting them from registration with the Securities and Exchange Commission (SEC), quarterly reporting requirements and other restrictions. In the same year, it changed the rules on the ERISA safe harbour, which exempted VC companies from being guarantors to pension funds. This reduced the risks for venture capitalists in accepting investment from pension funds.

The above changes in legislation have had a great impact on the development of the VC industry in the US. The most important change has been in the ERISA Prudentman legislation, which used to prohibit pension funds from investing in VC. With its removal, pension funds began to pour into the VC industry. Congress further passed legislation in 1992 and 1993 to encourage banks to increase their lending to smaller ventures while offering credit guarantees in case of default.[28] Various laws were also passed in the 1990s to strengthen protection on intellectual property rights.

It can be seen from the US experience that the government can create a favourable environment for the VC industry through proper legislation that removes the legal obstacles to its development. The US legal system has been dynamic enough to keep up with the changing economy and, in doing so, has offered potentially valuable lessons for China's future endeavours.

To improve the operating environment for its VC industry, China should remove all the legal restrictions that currently impede its development. Borrowing on the experience of some foreign countries as well as local governments, the following steps are perhaps the wisest ones to take:

1. *Enact Law of PRC on Venture Capital*. This should provide a legal framework within which the VC industry can operate. This law should clearly define and classify the roles of the VC company, its trust banks as well as the venture-backed firms. The law should also spell out the rules for investment, capital structure, company finance, taxation and the exit mechanism.

2. *Enact Law of PRC on Limited Partnership*. The current Company Law in China does not allow for the establishment of a limited partnership, which is a major form of VC investment vehicle in foreign countries. To encourage the use of limited partnerships as

---

[27] Josh Lerner (2002) 'Boom and bust in the venture capital industry and the impact on innovation,' *Economic Review* Atlanta, October.
[28] Kelly DePonte (2004) *The Evolution of Private Equity Secondary Activity in the United States: Liquidity for an Illiquid Asset*, Probitas Partners.

a vehicle for venture capital investments, the government should establish a 'Law of PRC on Limited Partnership'.

3. *Revise laws relating to the VC investment industry.* The government should:

- revise the Company Act by clearing the restrictions on the establishment of limited partnerships and changing registered capital requirements;
- revise the Banking, Insurance and Securities Acts to allow these financial institutions to invest in VC;
- revise the tax laws to provide more incentives for new start-up high-tech ventures. This may include a lower tax rate for capital gains, lengthening the tax holidays from the current two to three years, allowing the use of accelerated depreciation methods, and providing special incentives for the management of high-tech ventures;
- strengthen laws that protect intellectual property rights.

VC firms have many different features when compared with common-product and service enterprises, but China's Company Law only suits product enterprises, while the Partnership Law only suits service enterprises; thus it is essential that special regulations relating to VC firms are drafted. Considering that the Company Law has provided the legal basis for drawing special regulations with the article 'the State Council can make special stipulation', it is also practicable to introduce *the special regulation for venture capital firms*.

By investigating the legal problems in the process of VC investment, the special regulations for venture capital firms should outline nine legal schemes to promote innovation for China's VC firms:

- permitting VC firms to invest all of their assets into venture business;
- permitting VC firms to invest in special stocks such as convertible preferable stock in order to effectively protect the investors' benefits;
- introducing a main sponsor so that the main sponsor can raise funds through private-placement offerings;
- permitting VC firms to register capital by its shareholders' commitments, in order to avoid leaving capital unused;
- permitting VC firms to entrust their capital to professional investment consultant companies in order to develop the venture capitalist's team;

- permitting VC firms to acquire performance-related compensation in order to establish the incentive mechanism;
- permitting VC firms to pre-draw management fees in order to establish a cost-constraint mechanism;
- stipulating that a VC firm must be dismissed after 12 years in order to establish an effective risk-constraint mechanism;
- constricting the proportion of debt of VC firms in order to establish an effective debt-constraint mechanism.

New provisions and new rules on foreign VC investment

The Chinese government announced new provisions on foreign VC investment in 2001. On 28 August 2001, Interim Regulations on the Establishment of Foreign-invested Venture Investment Enterprises (IREFVIE) were promulgated in China by the Ministry of Foreign Trade and Economic Cooperation (now the Ministry of Commerce), the Ministry of Science and Technology and the State Administration for Industry and Commerce. The Regulation was brought into force on 1 September 2001.

The provisions and items stipulated were widely regarded as both bold and favourable because they removed virtually all the regulatory barriers that previously prevented overseas VC firms from fully participating in China's burgeoning VC industry. Foreign venture capitalists can now choose from the following investment modes to participate in:

1. wholly-owned subsidiary or offices in China;
2. joint ventures with a qualified local investment firm;
3. cooperative agreement with a local qualified investment firm.

For the first time, foreign VC firms can operate completely independently and on an equal footing as domestic companies in China.

To be able to operate as a legal entity in China's VC industry, either independently or collaboratively, a primary foreign VC firm should meet the following criteria outlined in the IREFVIE:

- VC investment is the firm's primary business;
- the firm's cumulative capital under management over the past three years is at least US$100 million;

- the firm's cumulative capital on venture business that has been invested in the past three years is not less than US$50 million;
- the firm has capable professionals who have acquired more than three years' experience in the VC industry;
- the firm must invest at least US$20 million in a newly created subsidiary or joint venture;
- in a joint venture, only while the total shares owned by foreign VC firms are more than 25 per cent do the venture-backed enterprises have the right to get the preferential treatment as the foreign-invested enterprises.

In the event that a group of foreign VC firms decide to establish a VC firm in China, either by themselves or with local firms, only the primary VC firm needs to meet the above criteria. In other words, VC firms can still operate in China as a secondary foreign VC firm without meeting these requirements.

However, as more foreign investors became involved in VC, improved laws and regulations were needed. Hence, on 30 January 2003, the Chinese government promulgated the new Regulations on the Administration of Foreign-invested Venture Investment Enterprises (RFIVCIE). These new RFIVCIE (Appendix A) were put forward jointly by the Ministry of Foreign Trade and Economic Cooperation, Ministry of Science and Technology, State Administration for Industry and Commerce, State Administration of Taxation and State Administration of Foreign Exchange.

'The Regulations', which became effective on 1 March 2003 and the IREFVIE promulgated in 2001 were repealed on the same day. The law introduced concepts and mechanisms from the international private equity fund community to develop and supplement China's existing foreign investment law system, and to enable overseas private equity fund promoters, managers and investors to establish VC investment-oriented limited partnership funds with Chinese characteristics in China for the first time.

The promulgation of the RFIVCIE satisfied policy objectives and met the needs of industrial and market development. The introduction of more overseas capital has long been one of the main policy objectives of the Chinese government, and was the major policy consideration in promulgating the RFIVCIE. China's flourishing high-tech industries need huge amounts of capital investment, management support and experience in capital operation, which was an industrial development consideration behind the promulgation of the law. China's need to cultivate its own private equity investment industry was the market consideration behind the formulation of the law, which will enable overseas fund investors and managers to more effectively use domestic RMB funds and enjoy simplified examination and approval procedures for investments.

However, because private equity funds and related concepts have not been formally introduced and there is a structural deficiency in China's existing foreign investment laws, even foreign investors of non-corporate VC enterprises will inevitably face problems during the implementation of the RFIVCIE. These problems include the legal effect of the agreed upon limited liability, taxation treatment, the investment time horizon, the scope of business, capital withdrawal and termination of liquidation procedures. Some of these problems will be resolved with the constant development and improvement of China's laws, and some will be avoided after investors make the necessary structural adjustments. It should also be noted that although the RFIVCIE offers some convenience to overseas investors, they should also learn about, and comply with, related restrictions under other laws – such as the regulation for the merger and acquisition of resident enterprises by foreign capital, and the use of foreign capital to restructure SOEs – when applying to set up VC investment enterprises and engage in domestic VC investment activities.

According to the new Regulations, foreign-invested venture capital investment enterprises (FIVCIEs) are foreign-invested enterprises established in China by foreign investors alone or with companies, enterprises or other economic organizations registered under Chinese law whose business activities are venture investment. FIVCIEs can be either in the form of non-legal persons or in the form of corporations. Investors in a FIVCIE with non-legal personal status are jointly and severely liable for the debts incurred by the FIVCIE. The investors in a FIVCIE with non-legal personal status must also provide, in the FIVCIE contract, that the obligatory investor will bear joint and several liabilities for the debts of the FIVCIE, and that other investors will bear liability to the extent of the capital contributions subscribed by them.

The agreed amount of contribution and the limit of management capital has been reduced under the existing Regulations. The minimum contribution of non-legal personal FIVCIEs is US$10 million; for corporation FIVCIEs, the minimum is US$5 million. Each investor, with the exception of the obligatory investors, should invest no less than US$1 million into an FIVCIE. The time limit for capital contribution was extended from three to five years, and the regulations defined the term 'venture capital investment management enterprise (VCIME)'. VCIMEs' registered capital or total investment must be not less than RMB1 million or the equivalent in foreign exchange. VCIMEs can be in the form of a corporation or in the form of a partnership, and can be entrusted to manage more than one FIVCIE.

A FIVCIE must have at least one obligatory investor; this obligatory investor can be either foreign or Chinese. The obligatory investor must have managed a total of no less than US$100 million for three years before it applies to establish a FIVCIE in China, and US$50 million out of that US$100 million must have been used as venture investment. If the obligatory investor is a Chinese company, it must be a company that has managed a total of no less than RMB100 million (US$12 million) for three years before it applies to establish FIVCIEs, and at least RMB50 million out of the RMB100 million must have been used as VC investment.

A FIVCIE can engage in the following business:

- purchasing equity with all its own funds, including establishing new enterprises, investing into established enterprises, purchasing shares from established enterprises and other methods permitted by law;
- providing venture investment consulting services;
- providing management consulting services to the enterprises in which it has invested;
- other business approved by the authority.

A FIVCIE must select an appropriate exit mechanism when selling or using other methods to dispose of its shares of enterprises in which it has invested. The exit mechanism includes:

- assigning all or parts of the equity it holds in the enterprises invested by it to another investors;
- entering into an equity buyback agreement under which the enterprises in which it has invested buys back the equity held in it;
- when the enterprise in which it has invested satisfies the conditions for listing, it may apply to list its shares on a domestic or overseas stock market. In this event, the FIVCIE can lawfully transfer the shares it holds through the open market.

FIVCIEs can be managed by themselves or by another FIVCIE or VCIME. The VCIME can be domestic or Chinese, foreign-invested or wholly foreign. The implementation of the new RFIVCIE is bound to help China to usher in more complex institutional investors and many experienced international private equity fund managers, thus greatly improving the country's existing level and quality of foreign capital and promoting the development its VC industry.

Investment system reform

On 25 July 2004 the State Council's Decision on Reform of Investment System was promulgated.[29] In Chinese Premier, Wen Jiabao's words, 'pushing the investment system reform forward is of great significance for a perfect market economic system and more effective macrocontrol'.[30] The core of the reform is to give full corporate control to the market in terms of resources allocation by relieving enterprises of intervention from the government. This means that enterprises should play the leading role in investment activities, make investment decisions at their own discretion and shoulder risks of losses, while banks should extend loans on their own account.

The government, on the other hand, expects to perform its well defined duties, which involve formulating development plans and industrial policies and guiding the social investment with legal and economic levers. The government should make more scientific investment decisions in a more democratic way through an optimized decision-making process for government investment projects. A strict system will hold decision makers responsible for their loss-making investments. Beyond all doubts, such reform will play a positive role in adjusting the structure, deepening the whole reform and switching the model of economic growth.

The local governments and departments were asked to push the reform forward actively and steadily and focus on the following points:[31]

- *The investment management system.* Decisions of investment should be made by investors, ie businesses, and the parties benefiting from the investment should take risks. Businesses will never have to go through any approving process for non-government sponsored projects. Instead, they will be subject to a confirmation system or a registration system. Large enterprises will be free to make investment decisions and companies will have more channels to fund their projects. The government encourages social capital funds to step into industries and fields as long as laws and regulations do not deny their entering into these areas. Financial institutions should improve their fixed assets loans system and sharpen their ability of loans check-ups to ward off financial risks.

---

[29] Lin Jian, Lu Xiaoping and Lei Linghao, 'China to further reform on investment system', *People's Daily* and *Shanghai Securities News*, 23 July 2004.
[30] Wen J *Deepening the Reform and Improving the System* Xinhua News Agency, 27 February 2005.
[31] WEN Zhao, 'The shoulder heavy responsibilities for the reform of investment system', *The Economic Observer*, 18 August 2004.

- *Targeting the government investment mechanism.* The purpose is to make government-funded projects more productive. Government investments are mainly channelled to social and economic fields that concern national security and for which the market doesn't work well. Decisions should be made scientifically and democratically. Responsibilities for a project should be defined well and the approval process should be streamlined. The capital should be put under proper control and the structural form should be optimized. The operation system for non-profit government investment projects should be in place as early as possible. Local governments should attract social capital into utilities and infrastructure projects.

- *Strengthening and improving the macrocontrol of investment to achieve a balanced aggregate and better structure.* Legal, economic and administrative measures should be combined with economic tools including market access, prices, interest rates and taxation to leverage the investment of the whole society. The government should navigate the social investment through planning, policies, information disclosure and market access control.

- *The supervision of investment to secure an orderly market investment and structure.* Corporate investment, government investment and investment intermediaries will be put under the watch of a comprehensive supervision system. Various investors should act within the legal framework, which is expected to be in place as early as possible and administered carefully.

Deepening the reform of the investment system serves the same aim as strengthening and improving macrocontrol, that is to say, promoting the stable and fast development of the Chinese national economy.

VC's acclaim for an SME Board

The main reason for making an investment is, of course, to realize a return, and the bigger the better. VC investment is no exception. Exit is the final stage of VC, achieved either through an IPO of the shares in a primary stock market or through an arranged sale to a financial or strategic buyer of the company. Western venture capitalists focus on exit through IPO. The successful timing of a venture-backed IPO provides significant benefits to venture capitalists, because taking companies public when equity values are high minimizes the dilution of the venture investors' ownership stakes.

After 14 years' stock exchange market development in Mainland China, on 27 May 2004, the SME Board opened on the Shenzhen Stock Exchange (SZSE). On 17 May 2004, with the approval of the State

Council, the China Securities Regulatory Commission (CSRC) had authorized the SZSE, one of the country's two exchanges, to establish an SME Board under the Main Board and endorsed the implementation plan. The SME Board debut brought glad tidings to all venture capitalists and VC investment companies, and resulted in the execution of the long-shelved listing plan for the establishment of a SME Board in Shenzhen. As the first region to develop VC investment in Mainland China, Shenzhen leads the country in the number of investment institutions and the amount of capital for research and development (R&D) and development of venture-backed SMEs and high-tech enterprises. Until November 2003, Shenzhen had registered 197 VC investment companies,[32] which together combined to realize a third of the investment nationwide. Although the SME Board is not a real Chinese Second Board or VC Board, most venture capitalists still applauded warmly, since it gives VC companies the first ray of hope for an exit mechanism. Establishing a NASDAQ-style Second Board in Mainland China is still a dream for investment bankers in the years ahead. VC companies suffered a tough period over the past five years after the Chinese government decided, in 2000, to delay the creation of a Second Board.

After the worldwide low tide in VC, lots of high-tech projects have completed their seed, start-up and exploration stages to become profitable in their expansion stages in the last three years. Since the VC Board was not in place, the investors had lost a major channel to exit through IPO after cashing in on their projects and the development of both the venture capitalists and venture-backed SMEs had therefore stagnated. The development of the VC industry is preconditioned upon the flourishing of start-up SMEs in the high-tech sectors. Chinese official statistics indicated there are more than 1500 SMEs eligible for listing on the SME Board[33] – more than any overseas market in terms of flotation resources. The revitalization of listing shares in SZSE has aroused Shenzhen's ambition to become a regional financial centre.

---

[32] *Shenzhen, The Most Active Region of Chinese National Venture Capital Investment*, Xinhua News Agency, 10 March 2004.
[33] Deng Nan, (Vice Minister of Ministry of Science and Technology) 2004. 'Breakthrough the bottleneck of high new industry for SMEs', *Chinese Economic Weekly*. Issue 22.

Milestones of Mainland China's venture capital industry

Date	Organization/institution	Milestone
1984	State Science and Technology Commission (SSTC)	Science Technology Promotion R&D Centre of the SSTC (renamed as PRC Ministry of Science and Technology (MOST) on 10 March 1998) organized research concerning the New Technology Resolution Revolution in Mainland China and brought forward the suggestion of building a VC system to promote the high-tech development.
January 1985	Central Committee of the Communist Party of China (CCCPC), State Council (SC)	*The Decision on Science Technology System Reform* was issued by CCCPC and the SC, proposing that 'VC can be set up to support the rapid changing and risky high-tech development'. The concept and practice of VC was first introduced into Mainland China's sci-tech policy system.
1986	SC, Ministry of Finance (MOF), China New Technology Venture Capital Company Ltd (CNTVCC)	With the approval of the SC, in order to support the implementation of the Torch Project and SSTC, MOF co-funded CNTVCC (the first shareholding company engaged in VC investment in Mainland China). SSTC and MOF held 40% and 23% of the shares respectively. CNTVCC provided services such as investment, loan, rental, financial guarantee and consultation etc. (The company has now closed.)
1988	SSTC	The Torch Fund was set up by the SSTC and listed in Singapore. With a fund of US$100 million, it is used for the development of China's new technology enterprises. The Torch Fund is a typical VC fund.
1989	SC, Ministry of Foreign Trade and Economic Cooperation (MOFTEC), Hong Kong China Merchants Group	With the approval of the SC and MOFTEC, (renamed as PRC Ministry of Commerce, Ministry of Foreign Trade and Economic Cooperation (MOFCOM) on 10 March 2003), CMHK, SSTC and

Date	Organization/institution	Milestone
	(CMHK), SSTC, Commission of Science, Technology and Industry for National Defence (COSTIND	COSTIND set up a joint venture, China Ke Zhao Hi-tech Co Ltd – the second VC company and first Sino–foreign VC investment company in Mainland China. It is mainly responsible for commercial transformation and industrialization of national high-tech achievements. The projects funded are mainly the projects for sci-tech promotion, such as Torch Project (35.7%), 863 Project (11.6%), Project of Promoting National Sci-tech Achievements (6.3%), Sparkle Project (10.4%), Project of Transformation from Military to Civil Use (1.5%). The industries of investment are mainly high-tech: bio-engineering and medical, new material, mechanical electronics and information etc.
1991	SC	SC issued the Temporary *Stipulations for China's High-tech Industry Development Zones*, which proposed that 'VC funds can be established in development zones for the establishment of high-risk high-tech industry. VC investment companies can be set up in the mature high-tech development zones under possible conditions'. The regulation demonstrates that VC had begun to draw the attention of the government.
1991	SC	The *State Council Notice with Regard to Approve National High-tech Industry Development Zones and Other Policies Regulation* (1991 National No 12) pointed out the support of building VC funds on high-tech zones.
1991	SSTC, MOF, Industrial and Commercial Bank of China (ICBC)	SSTC, MOF and ICBC co-set up the National Science and Technology Venture Capital Development Centre (NSTVCDC).
1992	Shanxi Sci-tech Fund Development Corp (SSFDC), Guangdong Sci-tech VC Investment Corp	The first sci-tech VC fund was established in Shenyang. Multiple methods investment, such as credit guarantee, subsidy interest, discount

Date	Organization/institution	Milestone
	(GSVCIC), Shanghai Science and Technology Investment Corp (SSTIC), Zhejiang Sci-tech VC Investment Corp (ZSVCIC)	interest and shareholding, were used to provide VC for enterprises. Such VC companies (or funds) were set up in Chongqing, Taiyuan, Jiansu, Zhejiang, Guangdong and Shanghai (eg SSFDC, GSVCIC, SSTIC and ZSVCIC).
1992	IDG, Beijing Science and Technology Commission (BSTC), Shanghai STC, Guangdong STC	PTV-China (renamed as IDGVC in 1993), the subsidiary of US International Data Group (IDG), entered China in 1992 and cooperated with BSTC, Shanghai STC and Guangdong STC to establish three VC investment companies that invest Sci-tech sectors professionally.
May 1995	CCCPC	CCCPC and the SC issued the *Decision on Speeding Up the Progress of Sci-tech*, with an emphasis 'to develop sci-tech VC industry and establish the mechanism of sci-tech VC'. The document further clarified the strategy of developing with science and education in Mainland China
1996	SC	The SC issued the *Decision on Deepening the Sci-tech System Reform During the Ninth Five-year Project Period*, focusing on the exploration and development of high sci-tech VC systems and the commercialization of sci-tech production.
June 1996	SC, State Economic and Trade Commission (SETC)	SC approved the SETC (renamed MOFCOM on 10 March 2003) to implement 'technological VC projects', focusing on the fact that 'enterprises should play an important role in VC project and commercializing the new technologies'.
1996	National People's Congress (NPC)	NPC issued *PR China Law on Promoting Sci-tech Achievements to be Commercially Transformed*, stipulating that the state treasury fund for science-tech transformation be used in the guiding fund, discount loan, subsidiary fund and VC. Article 24, in the third part, stipulates that national government encourages setting up the

Date	Organization/institution	Milestone
		sci-tech transformation fund and VC fund. The fund source could be provided by national, regional, corporate, state-owned organizations. The fund should be used to support the commercial transformation of high-risk, high-devotion, high output and accelerate the industrialization of science-tech results. This is the first time to put the concept of VC into the law clause.
1996	SSTC	SSTC undertook full preparation for detailed research of the VC system. It sent visiting scholars to study the US Small Enterprise Investment Act, protection of intellectual property and VC. SSTC also carried out the investigation and analysis for the exploration of domestic VC development from 1984 to 1996.
November 1996	SSTC, People's Bank of China (PBC), Bank of China (BOC), Industrial and Commerical Bank of China (ICBC), China Construction Bank (CCB), Agriculture Bank of China (ABC)	SSTC held the Province and City Science-tech Finance Promotion Colloquium in Changsha, the capital of Hunan Province, with many senior representatives from SSTC, PBC, BOC, ICBC, CCB, ABC, and provincial and city science and technology commissions (STCs) present. All the participants would like the SSTC to strengthen the R&D of the VC system.
1996		By the end of 1996, there were more than 20 VC investment organizations in China, which were founded by the local STC and Finance Department.
1997	SSTC, Tsinghua University	Deng Nan, the vice-president of SSTC, was confirmed to be the head of VC R&D Project. Collaborating with experts of Tsinghua University, SSCT brought forward four requirements: 1) clearly explain the VC system; 2) explain the relation between the VC and capital market; 3) create a blueprint of the VC mechanism; 4) suggest the policy regulation and law with both innovation and feasability.

Date	Organization/institution	Milestone
1997	Shenzhen VC R&D Guidance Team (SVCRDGT)	SVCRDGT was set up.
March 1997	Shanghai Pudong Venture Capital Company Ltd (SPVCC)	SPVCC was established with its first-period capital of RMB10 million.
June 1997	SSTC	SSTC and experts carried out investigations and surveys in Shenzen.
October 1997	Wuhan Security Investment Fund (WSIF), Shenzhen Nanshan Venture Capital Investment Fund (SNVCIF)	Mainland China's fund industry formally broke the ice with WSIF and SNVCIF.
November 1997		After the *Interim Regulations on Security Investment Fund Management* was promulgated, the Security Investment Fund developed rapidly. The overall scale of open-end and closed-end funds was expanding to a great extent and quickly.
1997	Venture Capital Consulting Company (VCCC)	VCCC was set up in Shenzhen, dealing with strategic investment banking business in the high-tech industry.
1998	State Planning Commission (SPC)	The Macro-Economic Academia of the SPC set up a task group to conduct a feasibility study on the establishment of a VC fund in Mainland China's mechanical industry.
January 1998	Premier Li Peng	Premier Li Peng presided over the fourth meeting of National Sci-tech Leaders Team. The meeting decided on a general blueprint of VC mechanism for high-tech enterprises and started the experimental units.
February 1998	SSTC, Vice-Premier Zhu Rongji, SPC, PBC, China Securities Regulatory Commission (CSRC), Financial Study Centre of China Academy Social Science (FSCCASS), International Finance	SSTC asked Vice-Premier Zhu Rongji (who held the position of Premier from 17 March 1998 to March 2003) for instructions that SSTC would like SPC (renamed as State Development Planning Commission (SDPC) on 2003), PBC, CSRC to take part in the R&D of VC together. Then the Ministry Coordination Team (MCT) came into

Date	Organization/institution	Milestone
	Research Institute of Bank of China (IFREBOC)	existence, led by the SSTC and aided by SPC, MOF, PBC and CSRC. The two research teams led by FSCCASS and IFREBOC started up formally.
March 1998	CPPCC, China National Democratic Construction Association (CNDCA), SSTC, SETC, MOF, PBC, CSRC	During the Ninth National Committee of CPPCC, CNDCA Centre Committee brought forward the *Proposal of Using of Reference from Western Countries and Speed up the Mainland China's Venture Capital Industry*, which was well known as the 'No.1 Proposal'. Then the Proposal Committee of CPPCC held the Proposal Consultative Meeting and invited SSTC, SETC, MOF, PBC, CSRC. Venture capital drew the attention of Chinese top leaders and became a popular topic in the economic field.
May 1998	Ministry of Science and Technology (MOST), Beijing Council of Trade Promotion (BJCTP)	In Beijing Municipality MOST and BJCTP organized 'Beijing High Sci-tech Industry Week', aiming at international exchanges for high-tech industry. Financial scholars explored and exchanged ideas on 'the development of high sci-tech and venture capital' and drew great attention from the theorists and entrepreneurs of the industry.
July 1998	Hangzhou Meeting	There were more than 15 VC investment organizations from Zhejiang, Shanxi, Guangdong and Liaoning in Hangzhou, the capital of Zhejiang Province, to hold a communication meeting in the field of VC investment.
September 1998	MOST, Hong Kong Stock Exchange (HKSE), Hong Kong Growth Enterprise Market (HKGEM)	Deputy Minister of MOST met with Andrew Sheng, Chairman of HKSE and Peng Ruchuan, Director of China and International Development of HKSE to discuss the VC system and Mainland China's high-tech enterprises' flotation in HKGEM.
October 1998	MOST, CSRC	MOST put forward a new suggestion for CSRC solving the high-tech enterprises' IPO in A-share market IPO quotas and formulating a policy for

Date	Organization/institution	Milestone
		encouraging the overseas IPO of high-tech enterprises.
October 1998	FSCCASS	The VC Research Experts Team (part of FSCCASS) reported their results to MCT and MOST.
October 1998	Renmin University of China	The Venture Capital Development Research Centre of Renmin University of China was set up and became the first formal VC research organization among the universities in Mainland China.
26 October 1998	MOST, IDG	MOST declared in Beijing that it would introduce US$1 billion from IDG, an American information service enterprise, in order to set up a high-tech development fund.
27 October 1998	Beijing High-tech Venture Capital Company Ltd (BHVCC)	BHVCC was established with registered capital of RMB310 million. Its aim was to support the high-tech industry of Beijing.
28 October 1998	Beijing Sci-tech Venture Capital Company Ltd (BSVCC)	The first company with the name of 'venture capital' was registered as BSVCC with a registered capital of RMB500 million. The business scope covers the investment of high-efficient agriculture, bio-medicine, software systems etc. It also operates a registered guarantee fund, which means it provides loan guarantees when registered capital of a newly established company is not sufficient for a bank to make the loan.
October 1998	Mannie Liu	Professor Mannie Manhong Liu's book, *Venture Capital: Innovation and Finance* (first edition), was published and served as an important influence in the industry's insiders.
November 1998	Vice-Premier Wen Jiabao, Li Renjun, Deng Nan, Li Lanqing	Li Renjun, Member of Standing Committee of National Committee of the CPPCC and former Vice-Director of SPC, wrote a letter to Vice-Premier Wen Jiabao about the promotion of venture capital in China. Later, Wen suggested officially to forward Li's letter to

Date	Organization/institution	Milestone
		Deng Nan, deputy minister of MOST, because Deng was currently organizing a team on the VC research. Vice-Premier Li Lanqing also made comments.
December 1998	MOST; Education, Science, Culture and Health Committee of NPC (NPCESCHC); Financial and Economic Committee of NPC (NPCESCHC)	MOST reported the VC research work for NPCESCHC and NPCFEC.
December 1998	MOST	MOST officially sent the *Report on Establishment of China Sci-Tech Venture Capital Mechanism* to the SC.
January 1999	Vice-Premier Wen Jiabao, MOST, CSRC	Vice-Premier Wen Jiabao made an official comment requiring CSRC to execute the suggestion in the report by MOST.
March 1999	Premier Zhu Rongji, CSRC, MOST, Li Lanqing, Zhu Lilan, SC	Premier Zhu Rongji made an official comment on the MOST report and the CSRC suggestion. This needed confirmation for the sci-tech venture capitalists to support the SMEs and required MOST to do further research and hand in a new scheme and report for the SC. Vice-Premier Li Lanqing required Zhu Lilan, the Minister of MOST, to do further research with other ministries and then co-sign to wait for the examination and approval of the SC.
March 1999	NPCFEC	The Draft Lead Team and Advisors Team of NPCFEC's *PRC Law on Fund Investing in Securities* were set up. Drafting out the *PRC Law Fund Investing in Securities* initiated in due form.
March 1999	MOST	After inviting the heads of SPC, SETC, MOF, PBC, State Administraion of Taxation (SAT) and CSRC, Zhu Lilan, the minister of MOST, followed the instructions of the SC and chaired the meeting on VC research.

Why Invest in the Chinese Market? 41

Date	Organization/institution	Milestone
23 March 1999	MOST, Ministry of Education (MOE), Ministry of Personnel (MOP), MOF, PBC, SAT, State Administration For Industry and Commerce (SAIC)	Seven ministries including MOST, MOE, MOP, MOF, PBC, SAT and SAIC issued *Several Stipulations on the Promotion of the Transformation of Sci-tech Achievements*, highlighting 12 measures and policies.
April 1999	SPC, SC	SPC sent *Interim Rules on Industrial Investment Fund Management (Draft)* to the Legislative Affairs Office of the SC.
21 May 1999	SC	SC issued the *Temporary Stipulations on the Tech Venture Capital Fund of SMEs of Sci-tech Type*, submitted by MOST and MOF. The SC decided to build up SME Technical VC Fund with RMB3 billion and to have it administered by the SME VC Fund Administration Centre. SMEs of sci-tech type would also be given discount loan and assistance without interest (limited to RMB1 million) and capital (with 20% registered capital as its limitation).
June 1999	MOST, SPC, SETC, MOF, PBC, SAT, CSRC	Seven ministries (MOST, SPC, SETC, MOF, PBC, SAT and CSRC) united to report the *Instruction for Establishing China Sci-tech Venture Capital Mechanism*. Li Lanqing and Wen Jiabao, the SC leaders, scheduled the establishment of the sci-tech VC system, and promoted cognition and practice for society.
14 June 1999	Shanghai	Shanghai Municipality issued *Some Stipulations on the Transformation of High-tech Achievements*. In this document, the Shanghai Municipality funded RMB600 million to the financing of high-tech VC. One month after the issuance of the Stipulations, Shanghai Council Science-tech identified 125 projects as major industrialization projects. The 125 projects are involved in the industries of information, new material, environment protection and bio-medicine etc. With a fund of

Date	Organization/institution	Milestone
		RMB1.86 billion, they attempted to introduce VC to solve the problem of the shortage of funds for these ventures.
16 June 1999	SETC	SETC issued the *Guiding Opinions on the Establishment of Pilot Schemes of SME Credit Guarantee* to promote the investment guarantee agencies on all levels to support the financing and the VC of sci-tech SMEs.
20 June 1999	SC	The SC compiled *Speeding Up the Construction of Zhongguancun High-tech Park*, submitted by the Beijing Municipality and MOST. According to the planning, Zhongguancun will be built up into a top sci-tech park on an international level within 10 years.
July 1999	Xu Kai	Xu Kai wrote the comment on instruction by seven ministries, which mentioned that for the five aspects of sci-tech VC mechanism, seven ministries held common views and principals. As a result functionality departments can make the regulations themselves in advance.
July 1999	New Margin, China Science Academia (CSA)	Shanghai NewMargin Venture Company Ltd (NewMargin) was founded in Shanghai by SPC, SEPC, CSA, Shanghai Alliance Investment Company and China Foundation of Science and Technology for Development. Shanghai Alliance Investment Company is an investment vehicle of Shanghai Municipal Government; the China Foundation of Science and Technology for Development was set-up by the State Development Planning Commission, State Economic and Trade Commission, and the Chinese Academy of Science. Since its founding in 1999, NewMargin has been one of the most active venture capital firms in China. It currently manages committed capital of over US$100 million, focusing investment in

Date	Organization/institution	Milestone
		high-growth companies in China, in particular companies in the IT, healthcare/life science, and new material and environmental protection industries.
20 August 1999	CCCPC	CCCPC and the SC produced the *Decision on Strengthening Tech Innovation, Developing the High-tech, and Realizing Industrialization*, planning for the promotion of progress and the development of high-tech industries in the new situation, fostering the capital market that benefits the high-tech industries, and establishing the VC mechanism step by step.
22 August 1999	SC	The SC convened the National Technological Innovation Conference.
26 August 1999	Shenzhen Venture Capital Company Ltd (SZVC)	SZVC (renamed Shenzhen Capital Group Company Ltd (SCGC) in October 2002) has always stayed at the forefront of China's venture capital industry since its inception, with RMB 700 million as its first registered capital. Of the RMB700 million, RMB500 million was funded by Shenzhen Investment Administration Company, entrusted by Shenzhen Municipality. So it could be said that SZVC was initially a government-backed VC firm incorporated with a total paid-up capital of RMB1.6 billion. Until 2004, there were 13 wholly-owned subsidiaries, stake controlling companies, joint venture investment companies and venture management companies, which altogether combine a total investment capital exceeding RMB 3 billion. In October 2000 the Board of Directors and the meeting of the shareholders decided to increase the first registered capital of RMB700 million to RMB1.6 billion. By October 2000 the company had negotiated 1000 projects, assessed 79 projects and invested in 38 projects with RMB360 million.

Date	Organization/institution	Milestone
August 1999	Shanghai, Shanghai Venture Capital Company Ltd (SVCC), Shanghai Sci-tech Venture Capital Committee (SCVCC)	Approved by Shanghai Municipality, SVCC was locally funded with RMB600 million in 1999. As the government solely supported company, it was an individual legislative body transformed from Shanghai Sci-tech Venture Capital Centre. As a professional institution, it would be operated in accordance with international VC practice under the guidance of SCVCC. Market-oriented, it would draw various funds from home and abroad and form a varied system of financing and investment in order to promote the development of the transformation of high-tech achievements.
October 1999	Shenzhen High Tech Trade Fair (SZHTTF)	The first session of SZHTTF was inaugurated in Shenzhen. In the forum, Deng Nan spoke the topic of Providing Financial Support System for the Development of Mainland China's High-tech Industry.
October 1999	Beijing Venture Capital Association (VCAB)	VCAB held the preparation meeting, which was formally set up in March 2000 with the approval of the Beijing Civil Affairs Bureau.
December 1999	NPCFEC	NPCFEC convened the International Proseminar on Draft the Investment Fund Law.
30 December 1999	SC	With the SC leaders' approval, the General Office of the State Council transmitted and issued National No 105 Document, *Some Opinions on the Establishment of Venture Capital Mechanism*, which was brought forward by MOST, SPC, SETC, MOF, PBC, SAT and CSRC.
2000		With 10 years of development, 100 venture capital companies had been built up with capital of RMB8 billion. Among these companies, 90% were wholly or partly funded by the government.

Date	Organization/institution	Milestone
February 2000	SVCC	SVCC set up funds with Shanghai JiaoTong University, Fudan University and Shanghai Zhangjiang High-tech Park. The funds were equally shared and the operation entrusted to a professional VC investment management company.
July 2000	CSRC, SC, MOST	According to the CSRC's *Regulation of Share Issue for Venture Backed Enterprises (Draft)*, the Legislative Affairs Office of the SC solicited the opinions on the share arrangement and the complete draft from MOST and other relative ministries.
October 2000	SZSE	According the nine rules of the VC Board, SZSE solicited the opinions on whether the rules were suitable for the VC Board or not from society.
October 2000	Shenzhen Venture Capital Association (SZVCA), Shanghai Venture Capital Association (SHVCA)	SZVCA and SHVCA were set up.
11 October 2000	Shenzhen	The first regulation on VC came into being in Mainland China. It was the *Temporary Stipulation of Shenzhen Venture Capital of High-tech Industry*, which was formally published by Shenzhen government's No. 96 document. It was an audacious exploration of Shenzhen with regard to establishing VC.
December 2000	NPCFEC	NPCFEC convened the second International Proseminar on drafting the Investment Fund Law.
1 January 2000		*The Regulation of Zhongguangcun High-tech Park* was enforced. The Regulation is the first Regulation dealing with high-tech areas that imported the content of VC. In its first clause of the third part, Promotion and Assurance, it stipulates the four rules for VC investment corporations: 1) developing the VC business; 2) the

Date	Organization/institution	Milestone
		organizational structure and form; 3) the registered capital; and 4) exit ways.
14 February 2001	Kingdee, IDG, HKGEM	Kingdee Software, venture-backed by IDG, was listed in the HKGEM and became the first of Mainland China's independent software companies to appear in the international capital market.
2 March 2001	Beijing	Beijing Municipality issued *Limited Partnership Management Measures (No. 69)*, which aimed at setting and accelerating the standards for the development the VC investment companies in the form of limited partnership.
8 May 2001	AsiaInfo	AsiaInfo, 'the Engineer of China' and largest internet software provider, acquired a strategic equity stake in Intrinsic Technology. Under the terms of the agreement, AsiaInfo and its partner, Fidelity Ventures, invested US$8.2 million into Intrinsic Technology in order to acquire a significant minority stake of the company. The structure of the agreement allows AsiaInfo to see whether the technology becomes as profitable as projected, and then to use its option to invest additional capital and increase ownership by up to 51%, thus consolidating Intrinsic's revenues with its own over the subsequent two years.
14 August 2001	TianLu (Beijing) Venture Capital Investment Centre (TLVCIC)	With RMB500 million, the first limited partnership VC corporation in China, TLVCIC was established in Beijing. The RMB500 million capital was from Xinjiang Tianye Company Ltd, Xinjiang Shihezi Development Area Economy Development Co Ltd, SinoTrust (Beijing) Management Consulting Ltd, which contributed the amount of RMB40 million, RMB9.5 million and RMB0.5 million respectively. The SinoTrust's Chair of the director of the

Date	Organization/institution	Milestone
		board and president, Zhao Min, is appointed to be the Limited Partnership Affair Administrant. The foundation of TLVCIC is the first Mainland China limited partnership VC corporation after *The Regulation of Zhongguangcun High-tech Park and Limited Partnership Management Measures* were issued by Beijing Municipality.
1 September 2001	MOFTEC, MOST, SAIC	IREFVIE were implemented in China by MOFTEC, MOST and SAIC.
2001	SVCCL, H&Q Asia PAcific	The VC fund in Mainland China accessed US$84 billion. US$518 million was invested in 216 venture-backed enterprises. SVCCL, now SCGC, was the most active domestic VC firm and invested in a total of 36 companies. The biggest investment was from H&Q Asia Pacific, which invested US$70 million in a semiconductor project in Shanghai. The main focus was IT, service, medical treatment, telecommunication and environment protection. There are in total 133 domestic VC investment companies distributing around 22 provinces and municipalities. Guangdong, Beijing, Shanghai, Shandong are the best regions for VC development. Investment by foreign VC firms comes mainly from the US, Singapore, Hong Kong, Japan, Taiwan and Europe.
2002		2002 was the 'lawmaking' year. China's NPC paid more attention to WTO-related legislation for helping Chinese laws meet world standards and enhance the transparency of China's legal framework. There were more than 2300 acts to be amended in the fields of goods, services, intellectual property rights protection; more than 830 acts to be abolished; and more than 6000 items by governmental examination and approval of administration to be repealed. Some regulations about VC

Date	Organization/institution	Milestone
		system development were issued in Beijing, Tianjin and Hefei.
1 January 2002		*The Regulation on Foreign-invested Telecom Management* was enacted.
March 2002	Hong Kong Polytechnic University (HKPU), China Venture Capital Company Ltd (CVCC), *Hong Kong China Venture Capital Journal (HKCVCJ)*	Originating with HKPU and CVCC, *HKCVCJ* commenced publication.
1 April 2002	SPC, SETC, MOFTEC	*Instruction Catalogue on Foreign Investment Industry* (revised edition) with its attachment was brought into force. These were promulgated by SPC, SETC and MOFTEC on 4 March 2002. The *Instruction Catalogue on Foreign Investment Industry* was approved by the SC on 29 December 1997 and promulgated by SPC, SETC and MOFTEC on 31 December 1997. Promulgation was abolished when the revised edition was issued.
12 April 2002	Alcatel Shanghai Bell, NewMargin	Alcatel Shanghai Bell and NewMargin founded the Telecom Technology Fund, the first-ever investment vehicle exclusively dedicated to China-originated telecoms technology with an initial investment of US$18 million.
19–20 April 2002		The first China Venture Capital Conference was held in Beijing.
June 2002	TianLu (Beijing) Venture Capital Investment Centre (TLVCIC), CSRC, SinoTrust	Within a year of being established, TLVCIC (the first limited partnership VC firm) was forced to be disbanded. According to the requirement of the CSRC and the Partner Company Law, Xinjiang Tianye Company Ltd withdrew the investment capital and parted with SinoTrust. TLVCIC's establishment was dependant on the *Limited Partnership Management Measures,* which were issued by Zhongguangchun Park of Beijing Municipality and does not have national power. In the eighth clause, PRC Partner Company Law regulates

Date	Organization/institution	Milestone
		that 'all the partners must assume unlimited liability with all the company's property'. In terms of CSRC's regulations, the listed company must not invest huge capital in the project and the company that demands the listed company is charged of unlimited liability with the property. As a listed company, Xinjiang Tianye's investment in TLVCIC exceeded the 50% of its net asset, so it broke the regulations of CSRC. According to TLVCIC's disbandment and the coming foreign VC funds, amending the Partner Company Law and Company Law was voiced by VC industry insiders.
June 2002	Warburg Pincus	Warburg Pincus announced the accomplishment of raising a Global VC fund valued at US$5.3 billion, which would be invested in US, European and Asian enterprises with another US$2.5 billion fund. In China, Warburg Pincus had invested US$300 million.
11 June 2002	Walden International	Walden International announced the appointment of Dr Jack Q Gao as General Partner and Managing Director of its China operations. Leveraging his 14 years of industry experience in the US and Asia, Dr Gao also contributed his strategic insight and technological expertise in identifying prospective investment opportunities in China's high-growth IT and software sectors. Walden International is a leading global VC firm, providing early-stage technology companies with the advantage of an unrivaled global network since 1987. The firm's international VC funds comprise approximately US$2 billion in committed capital. Walden International's global organized network of multicultural professionals spans the US, Hong Kong, China, Singapore, Japan, Taiwan, India, Malaysia and Philippines.

Date	Organization/institution	Milestone
19 June 2004	China Venture Capital Association (CVCA)	CVCA was incorporated in Hong Kong with a representative office in Beijing at the suggestion of Warburg Pincus. CVCA has 93 member firms, which collectively manage over US$100 billion in private equity funds. Examples of successful companies backed by CVCA member firms include AsiaInfo, UT Starcom, Sina.com, Sohu.com, Netease.com, Shanda, Eachnet, Mengniu and several other fast-growing businesses.
21 June 2002	Kan Zhidong, China Southern Securities (CSS)	Kan Zhidong, former General Manager of SZVC was appointed as the President of CSS. Kan left CSS at the end of 2002 because of the complex internal management.
29 June 2002	NPC	NPC passed the *PRC Promotional Law for Small and Medium-sized Businesses*.
1 December 2002	State Administration of Foreign Exchange (SAFE)	*The Provisional Administrative Measures on Foreign Exchange Issues on Securities Investment by Qualified Foreign Institutional Investors*, which was issued by SAFE on 28 November 2002, became effective. The Measures govern the foreign exchange procedures for qualified foreign institutional investors (QFIIs). QFIIs are required to entrust a single custodian to handle all formalities under the Measures. Under the Measures, QFIIs must apply to SAFE for an investment quota of not less than US$50 million or more than US$800 million. Investment quotas may be transferred in whole or in part to other QFIIs with SAFE approval.
17 December 2002	PBC	PBC issued Notice on *Issues Relating to Applications to Engage in Custodian Business of Domestic Securities Investment of Qualified Foreign Institutional Investors by Commercial Banks*, which became effective on the same day. The Notice clarifies

Date	Organization/institution	Milestone
		procedural matters in relation to applications by commercial banks to serve as custodians for QFIIs.
2003		VC investment focused on Beijing, Shanghai and Shenzhen. China formed the Beijing Zhongguangcun High-tech Park, Shanghai Zhangjiang Park, and Shenzhen New High-tech Area: the three highlights for VC. By the end of 2003, the governments of Beijing, Shanghai, Shenzhen, Tianjin and Zhejiang had pushed forward 91 regulations about the preferential policies and consultation documents of VC investment.
1 January 2003		The *Government Procurement Law* came into effect to help regulate overall government procurement. Article 10 states clearly that, 'government procurement should buy domestic goods, engineering projects and services.'
30 January 2003	MOFTEC, MOST, SAIC, SAT, SAFE	Scheduled to come into effect on 1 March 2003, RFIVCIE was promulgated by MOFTEC, MOST, SAIC, SAT and SAFE. IREFVIE, promulgated in 2001, were repealed on the same day.
21 February 2003	Standing Committee of the Third Shenzhen Municipal People's Congress (SZMPC)	The *Regulations of Shenzhen Special Economic Zone on Venture Capital* was adopted at the Twenty-second Meeting of SZMPC.
March 2003	China Venture Capital Research Institute (Hong Kong) Ltd (CVCRI)	CVCRI was established on the initiative of Professor Cheng Siwei, Vice Chairman of the Standing Committee of the NPC. The institute is a joint venture between Hong Kong Polytechnic University and China Venture Capital Company Ltd. Headquartered in Hong Kong Polytechnic University; it set up an operating institute in Shenzhen, which is registered as the Shenzhen Zhongtou Venture Capital Research Development Company Ltd on 28 May 2003.

Date	Organization/institution	Milestone
28 October 2003	NPC	The long-awaited *PRC Securities Investment Fund Law* was passed by China's standing Committee of NPC and would become effective on 1 June 2004. The passage of this law was the most comprehensive attempt by the Chinese government thus far to regulate the nascent investment fund business. Previously, the Chinese government had relied on a series of administrative regulations, most notably the *Provisional Measures on the Administration of Securities Investment Funds*, promulgated in November 1997, to regulate this vibrant business.
10 December 2003	Ctrip.com	Ctrip.com International Ltd was listed on NASDAQ, under the ticker symbol CTRP. Ctrip.com became the seventh Chinese internet-concept company listed on the US VC market after AsiaInfo, China.com Sina.com, Sohu.com, Netease.com and UTStar. Its shares rallied and jumped more than 108% when the stock reached a high of US$37.35 over the IPO price of US$18 on its first trading day before easing back later to close at US$33.94, with a gain of 88.56% on the IPO price.
July 16 2004	SC	The SC's *Decision on Reform of Investment System* was promulgated. In his directions on the implementation of the Decision, Chinese Premier, Wen Jiabao, stressed that pushing this reform forward was of great significance for a perfect socialist market economic system and more effective macrocontrol.

2

Criteria for Successful Investments in China

The criteria for investors

Three criteria

There is much empirical research on the selection criteria that western venture capitalists can apply when evaluating new venture proposals. The identification of useful selection criteria has been researched using different methodologies such as simple rating of criteria,[1] verbal protocols,[2] construct analysis[3] and quantitative compensatory models.[4] Most studies using these different methods have concluded that there are three main aspects of a successful investment (outlined in Figure 2.1). In order of importance they are:

1. the human resources, such as the management team;
2. the market; and
3. the competitive product.[5]

---

[1] MacMillan I, Zemann L, and Subbanarasimha P. (1987) 'Criteria distinguishing successful from unsuccessful ventures in the venture screening process' *Journal of Business Venturing* 2(2): 123–137.
[2] Fried VH, and Hisrich RD. (1994) 'Toward a model of venture capital investment decision making' *Financial Management* 23(3): 28–37.
[3] Riquelme H, and Lilai X. (2001) *Venture Capital, Venture Capitalists' Decision Criteria, and Implications for China*, Graduate School of Management, La Trobe University, Melbourne, Vic 3083 Australia, A presented paper at the International Conference on the Chinese Economy: Achieving Growth with Equity, 4–6 July 2001, Beijing.
[4] Muzyka D, Birley S, and Leleux B. (1996) 'Trade-offs in the investment decisions of European venture capitalists' *Journal of Business Venturing* 11(1): 273–287.
[5] Riquelme H, and Lilai X. *Venture Capital, Venture Capitalists' Decision Criteria, and Implications for China*, Graduate School of Management, La Trobe University, Melbourne, Vic 3083 Australia, A presented paper at the International Conference on the Chinese Economy: Achieving Growth with Equity, 4–6 July 2001, Beijing.

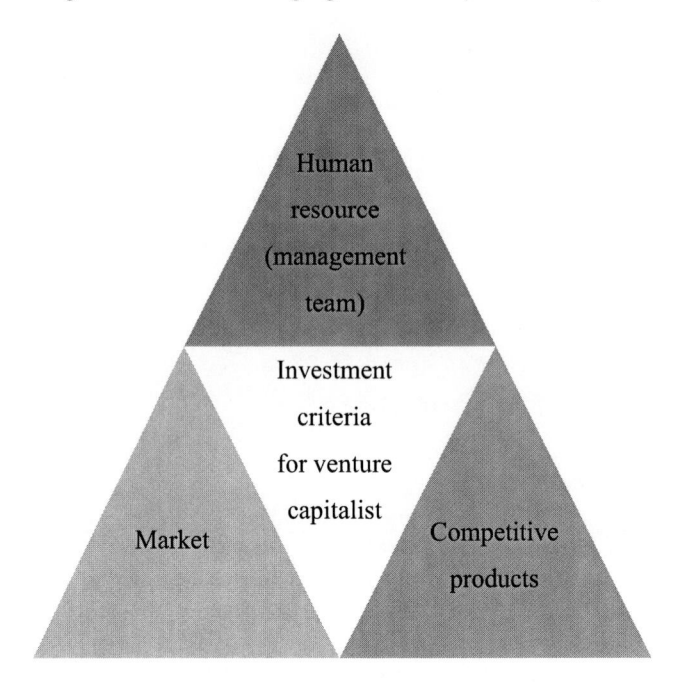

Figure 2.1 Investment criteria for venture capitalists

As they purport to discriminate between successful and unsuccessful businesses, these aspects should form the core of the venture capitalist's mental model when evaluating a business proposal. This chapter will focus on the human resources aspects for successful investment.

The functions of the management team in a venture capital project

Due to the current trends in law and economic development in China, it will be difficult to establish a 'reputable' culture for venture capitalists or investment partners within a short period of time. As a result, there has been deep investigation into the functions of management teams within venture capital (VC) projects – this has become necessary to enhance the chances for successful VC investments in China. To evaluate the effectiveness of the project management team, it is first necessary to evaluate the track records of the team members. Once this is done, a set of quantitative measures should then be used to test the effectiveness of the project team and to provide information, based upon which team members who have proved to be outstanding can be rewarded.

Due to the unique difficulties that arise from VC business, it is essential that VC companies establish project management teams of highly skilled individuals to manage their ventures. As these companies take direct equity stakes in the high-growth small and medium-sized enterprises (SMEs) in emerging industries, they must strive to prevent high risks occurring within the project management process. The underlying reason for this is that the management of VC operations differs from bank financing management. VC emphasizes shareholding operational management, not only because the average holding period for VC investment is long, but also because each process in the venture carries predictable and unpredictable management risks. As such, the importance of shareholding operational management after the investment outlay cannot be ignored.

It is absolutely essential to install a project management team in order to realize the investment goals. The person in charge of the project management team should have several years' practical experience in VC investments and possess managerial experience in a variety of entrepreneurial contexts. The skills and abilities of the team members should encompass different professions and management disciplines, the complementary aspects of which can be utilized by the project manager.

It is essential that the project management team evaluates the operating environment in conjunction with the companies' management to ensure that sound decisions are made, and that the project develops in accordance with corporate goals. The team should also investigate the viability of any proposals for the transfer of equity stakes, IPOs, mergers and acquisitions (M&As), spin-offs, repurchase or liquidation. Senior members of the project management team should participate in investment assessments and investigations of related VC projects. The aim of this will be to track the performance of VC projects and to take appropriate action on investments so that there is a return on the VC funds.

Before the safe withdrawal of funds invested in the venture, team members should be endowed with the powers to track the operations and management of it. An important yardstick for evaluating the effectiveness of the management team is whether it can complete allocated tasks within the stipulated time period. It is to be expected that when VC is introduced to a company it will be necessary to redefine its long- and short-term objectives as well as its operating strategies. If the VC company invests in a venture during the initial stages of development, it is likely that the venture will lack an established management system. Even SMEs in their growth stage need much substantial assistance to ensure there are significant improvements in their corporate management structures.

Overseas or local Chinese students

There is a special human resource policy in the Chinese economy. In the late 1970s, China's launching of the drive for reform and opening up triggered a kind of 'gold rush' for young Chinese people to study overseas.[6] Some critics once cried out against the so-called 'brain drain' and feared that China might lose her young, energetic talents forever. According to the statistics of the Ministry of Education, from 1978 to 2003, over 700,200 Chinese academics studied on foreign campuses, mostly in developed countries.[7] Of them, around 70,000 (approximately 10 per cent) were financed by the government, but the majority used their own financial resources to study overseas. Around 172,800 of overseas Chinese students had returned home by the end of 2003. Statistical analysis has revealed that around 77 per cent of the government-financed students have returned.[8]

Deng Xiaoping once said that he would like to see the number of Chinese students studying overseas rise and, in accordance with his wishes, the government has adopted more flexible policies since the 1990s to give greater freedom to these students. Over the past 25 years, a series of favourable policies has been issued by the government to help returning students in more various ways compared with any period in the past.[9]

Over 76 industrial and technological parks have been established across the country with the aim of helping returning students to start or develop their own businesses. So far, over 4,000 SMEs run by 15,000 such students have established ventures in these parks.[10] Playing a huge role in China's modernization, returned scholars make up the majority of the country's top scientists and engineers. At present they account for 81 per cent of the academics in the Chinese Academy of Sciences, 54 per cent of the members of the Chinese Academy of Engineering, and 72 per cent of the leading scientists in the country's numerous national research projects, particularly the '863 High-Tech Program', initiated in March 1986.[11]

Similarly in the US and Europe, many foreign VC firms see the educational background, professional experience and moral character of a company's founder as essential to its success. From 1998 to

---

[6] 70s Persons Golden Figure, Simmani Network, August 2003.
[7] 2003 Overseas Chinese Student Situation Press Conference, Ministry of Education, 16 February 2004.
[8] ibid.
[9] Yonghua HE, Liyu XIN, and Luo H *Deng Xiaoping is the Founder of Overseas Chinese and Overseas Chinese Students* China News Agency, 23 August 2004.
[10] Li N 'Encourage overseas student to come back China' *Beijing Review* 30 August 2004.
[11] *High-Tech Program* CAS Online: www.cas.cn

2000, foreign VC companies preferred to invest in tech-ventures established or managed by Chinese overseas students, such as AsiaInfo and Sohu.

Why did they prefer to invest in companies established by Chinese overseas students? The main reason is that many foreign VC firms were doing VC business for the first time in China, using the selection methods that they used in western countries to select their deals in China. Having studied in western countries, the returned overseas students were closer to the standards that they associated with success. Therefore, in comparison with local entrepreneurs, returned overseas students had an advantage in attracting foreign VC funds when that industry was just being established in China.

Secondly, most of the returned overseas students came from English-speaking nations, such as the US, UK, Canada and Australia, whose education systems have good reputations. Furthermore, they are more familiar with the cultural mores of western countries making the communication process easier. Many of the returned overseas students have acquired work experience in multinational corporations such as Cisco, Lucent, Intel and Microsoft, or investment banking firms like Morgan Stanley, Goldman Sachs, Barclays Capital, Lazards, Lloyds TSB and so on. Thus, they mastered the best technology and understand international business activities. Of course, when they set up or manage a company, their products and services should be unique. Nevertheless, the most important factor for their success is that they should operate and manage the company according to international standards and use the advanced management skills and ideas that they acquired while studying abroad.

However, more recently foreign VC firms have shifted their investments from returned overseas students to local successful entrepreneurs and foreign VC companies' senior managers in China's markets. Gradually, they noticed the weaknesses of returned overseas students when it came to exploring opportunities, business models and relations. After 2000, therefore, more and more local entrepreneurs were successfully raising funds from foreign VC firms that were becoming more aware of the advantages that local entrepreneurs offered. Usually educated at China's elite universities and coming from large private companies, these entrepreneurs tend to be more familiar with China's markets and have an advantage in exploring new markets. In general, however, overseas Chinese students still have more advantages on balance than locally educated entrepreneurs.

The operation of the founders of Harbour

Bright future for a telecommunications manufacturer

While regulatory and structural issues continue to hamper investment into China's telecommunications sector, VC firms are taking note of solid growth as a basis for investment opportunities. Price wars, unpredictable policy, limited legal and intellectual property (IP) protection, and constant technology shifts make China's telecommunications market treacherous terrain for start-ups. Although China produces a wealth of engineers, the struggle remains to find talented managers that can navigate Mainland China's minefield and turn technology products into businesses.

Financially, SMEs in Mainland China struggle to operate on a large scale due to the difficulty of raising capital. Domestic loans for small businesses are nearly non-existent, while the domestic VC industry is just taking off. In addition, the lack of exits and restrictions on foreign VC investment limits overseas funding channels. Domestic listings for SMEs are rare. Talk of a NASDAQ-style second board for new technology companies has largely faded into the background. The recently launched SME Board on the Shenzhen Stock Exchange (SZSE) cannot be called a real second board (as detailed in Chapters 1 and 5).

Domestic telecommunications firms such as Huawei Technology Co Ltd (Huawai) and Zhongxing Telecom Equipment Corp (ZTE) are another inhibitor of start-up success in Mainland China. Enjoying government backing and Mainland operating cost efficiencies, these major Chinese vendors have used aggressive sales forces and low-pricing strategies to attain the scale to compete on their home turf with global vendors such as Motorola and Nokia. Providing comparable products for as little as half the cost of those from foreign companies, these large domestic firms are still able to replicate the nascent technology emerging from small domestic start-ups and then leverage existing sales networks to get the products to market. Unlike major foreign vendors such as Nortel and Cisco, which make expensive acquisitions of small firms with innovative technology, Huawei and ZTE stifle acquisition exits by finding ways to do it on their own.

In a growing trend, however, Chinese entrepreneurs that have gained experience, contacts, and telecommunications market knowledge at companies such as Huawei are beginning to set up ventures of their own. Harbour Networks Limited (Harbour), founded by former Huawei employee, Li Yinan, is a prime example. In May 2002, Harbour completed a US$42 million second round of funding led by

Warburg Pincus.[12] During previous years, the company, which specializes in end-to-end broadband IP solutions, grew from 60 employees to over 650 and actively pursues both domestic and overseas products. When firms such as Harbour attain the scale to expand their business abroad, their low-cost base ensures international competitiveness. To some extent, Harbour's success is the personal success of the founder Li Yinan (Li), a successful choice from the management issues point of view.

Building up Harbour

Harbour was established in 2000 and is a Beijing-based telecommunications manufacturer, committed to developing, manufacturing, marketing and serving a full line of broadband IP network equipment and solutions for China's telecommunications carriers, service providers, enterprises and government offices. Harbour's main product is the next generation of broadband IP instruments. The company has always been dedicated to the field of 10GB IP telecom networks, large private networks, intelligent optical networks and next generation networks (NGN). It has also been making efforts to become recognized as a trustworthy total network solution provider for all of its customers.

Harbour Building was completed and put into use in May 2004. Located in Zhongguancun Software Park, Harbour Building covers 1 hectare and can accommodate 2500 people. Zhongguancun Software Park was elevated to a state-level software industry base in Beijing in 2000 by the State Planning Committee and Ministry of Information Industry (MII) because it is a key base in the Capital's '248' Major Enterprise Project and a leader among software parks in Beijing.[13]

Since its inception, Harbour has maintained a rapid and stable development for four successive years. In 2003 it had contract sales of RMB1 billion, up 122 per cent over the previous year.[14] Harbour currently has 1800 staff of which 1050 are employed in research and development of network products. To date, the network products of Harbour are applied on a large scale in the networks of China Telecom, China Netcom, China Mobile, China Unicom and China Railcom. They are also adopted by the government, education, finance and electrical power industries, as well as large and medium-sized enterprises. Therefore, it comes as no surprise that up to June 2004 Harbour had applied for 145 patents and 18 software copyrights.

---

[12] Yan S, 'Li Yinan wants to copy Huawei' *21st Century Economy Report* 14 January 2004.
[13] Harbour Online: www.harbournetworks.com
[14] Yao C, 'Harbour's experience on solving the problems of personnel and finance' *Sohu IT* Issue 171, 2004.

Harbour was founded by Li and several colleagues from Huawai. Before founding Harbour, Li was the former vice CEO of Huawei, which was founded in 1988. Now Huawei has become the biggest provider of telecommunications instruments and solutions in China. When Li joined Huawai and became Vice CEO in 1993, he was only 27 years old.

In October 2000, Li left Huawei and founded Harbour. Initially, Harbour positioned itself as a distributor of low-end internet instruments. Its business model was similar to that of RAD Data Communications in Israel, which relied on one or two big telecommunication instruments manufacturers and provided solutions and services for their customers. Due to Li's successful work experience and Harbour's professional services, the new company developed very fast. In 2001, Harbour's sales return reached RMB150 million.[15] However, being a distributor was only the first step for Li, who aimed to build a giant telecommunications firm. His goal was to be a middle telecom provider of broadband IP instruments. As a distributor, Harbour built tight relations with all its customers, while at the same time it began to invest in research and development (R&D) and to manufacture its own products. In June 2001, the company introduced its first set of products into the markets and by August, Warburg Pincus and Dragontech had invested US$19 million in Harbour as seed funds.[16]

As Li had established a solid reputation at Huawei when he left, Warburg Pincus kept an eye on him and his new business. Warburg Pincus had years of experience in doing VC business in China; it knew what kind of tech-ventures would become extinct. In selecting a candidate, the company usually focused on the industry prospects and background of the founder, as well as the market strategy, management and manufacturing elements.

Currently, Harbour has offices and technology support centres in 28 principal cities throughout China including the Hong Kong Special Administrative Republic (SAR) as shown in Figure 2.2. At the same time, Harbour has penetrated overseas markets such as North America, Japan and Southeast Asia, making every effort to become a trustworthy 10GB IP networking solution provider.[17]

Some will contend that Harbour should not have set up so many offices and tech-support centres with regard to the cost of building subsidiaries. Such a view is an economic one, but any manufacturer should see the customers' benefit as of primary importance if it wants to establish strong support, an essential in developing a long-term Chinese market that creates value for customers. Customers would

---

[15] Li N 'Li Yinan's Harbour' *China CEO & CIO* 19 March 2004.
[16] Chen Z 'Is Harbour a fairy tale?' *21st Century Economy Report*, 15 January 2004.
[17] Harbour Online: www.harbournetworks.com

Figure 2.2 Harbour's offices and technology support centres

like to have good partnerships with companies that have stability, long-term prospects and credibility.

The founder

Li Yinan passed his exams and entered the youth class of Huazhong University of Science and Technology when he was 15 years old. By June 1993, as he was able to solve difficult problems, Li had registered in Huawei and became an engineer within two days. He was quickly promoted to be Director of Engineering. Within two weeks, he was made Vice General Manager of the Central Research Department. Shortly after this, he was elevated to be General Engineer and was promoted head of the Central Research Department within two years. He finally took the seat of Huawei's Vice President when he was 27, led thousands of research personnel and developed dozens of technological products that have provided advanced services and huge economic profit. In 2000, when Li used his bonus of RMB10 million to set up Harbour, he had just turned 30.[18]

---

[18] Li N, 'Li Yinan's Harbour' *China CEO & CIO* 19 March 2004.

Acute and clever venture capitalists did not let Li out of their sight. Warburg Pincus knew that Li was a suitable person for them to invest in because Li had achieved great success in Huawei. Under his leadership, Huawei had been one of the biggest telecommunications instruments manufacturers with an annual sales volume of RMB25.5 billion.[19] Furthermore, he was familiar not only with technology but also the market.

It could be said that Li used Huawei, as Harbour was initially appointed as the network distributor of Huawei, in order to enter the data network facility market. The benefits were clear: on the one hand, Harbour could fish outside the rules of marketing and manage the social relationships, on the other hand, it accumulated abundant benefit from the lower threshold of being the network distributor. The Harbour top management team was drawn wholly from Huawei. Besides Li Yinan, Peng Song, the vice president of Harbour, was the former deputy president of Huawei's domestic market department. The administrative vice president, Lu Xin was the former general manager of the Technology Data Telecoms Department in Huawei.

The core Harbour teams of exploration and sale systems were wholly comprised of former personnel from Huawei. But Li, who was described as Huawei's chief technology officer, did not want Harbour to remain in the position of an agent. Due to the abundance of technology and R&D engineers, Harbour quickly produced its own products and pushed them onto the markets. The first transition opportunity for Harbour was the contract they won from Ningbo Netcom, a project valued at RMB30 million.

Market prospects

China will face another tide of investment for its backbone telecommunications industry. Warburg Pincus believes that both the local area network (LAN) and broadband markets will be changed by three factors:

- the IP broadband network is regarded as the next generation network because of its low price and high quality of data transferring;
- the merger and reconstruction of China's telecommunications carriers will give new instrument providers a larger market;
- the operators are shifting their investments from hardware to software. [20]

---

[19] ibid.
[20] Yan S., Li Yinan wants to copy Huawei, *21st Century Economy Report,* 14 January 2004.

As China's telecommunications market faces ever increasing competition, the rigid state-mandated spending plans in hardware and infrastructure are giving way to flexible, market-based investment, with the objective of attracting and retaining consumers. Reflecting this transformation, operator investment in developed markets will be strong in areas such as broadband office storage server (BOSS), broadband access (asymetric digital subscriber line (ADSL), LAN), virtual private networks (VPN), call centres and intelligent networks. Therefore, conditions are right for companies such as Harbour that rely on operator spending for the latest low-priced products and services.

Although Huawei and ZTE are the heavyweights in this field, the Chinese market is so large that one or two heavyweights alone could not satisfy the needs of this fast-growing market; it also needs some energetic medium-scale enterprises. Furthermore, while Huawei is aiming for the high-class market to compete with Cisco, Harbour is committed to becoming a multinational medium-sized enterprise in broadband IP network. So far, this policy has not only allowed Harbour to survive, but also to make profits.

Harbour Network's revenue is rising annually: RMB76 million in 2000, RMB147 million in 2001, RMB410 million in 2002. Harbour Networks recorded contracted revenues of RMB1.2 billion (US$145 million) in 2004, as compared with RMB1 billion (US$121 million) in 2003. Realized revenues were RMB900 million (US$109 million) in 2004. In December of 2004, the company recorded monthly sales revenues of RMB200 million (US$24 million) from domestic and overseas markets. The company generates most of its revenues from China.[21] At present, in the field of broadband IP networks, Harbour holds about 7–8 per cent of the market while Huawei holds 10–15 per cent.[22]

Harbour's technological edge was a very important element in attracting Warburg Pincus' investment. Li had been the Vice CEO in charge of R&D in Huawei, and most of Harbour's main members in R&D came from big telecommuications manufacturers such as Huawei, Motorola and Siemens. Harbour has its own in-house, full-line broadband IP network equipment and its products include ethernet switches, application specific integrated circuits (ASIC) for ethernet, high-capacity backbone intelligent multilayer switches and world-class broadband IP network solutions from backbone to access. Its products have been widely deployed on the backbone networks of carriers and enterprises.

---

[21] Interfax Information Services, Emerging Company Profile for Harbour Networks, http://www.interfax.com/4/72025/news.aspx, 24 June 2005.
[22] Harbour Online: www.harbournetworks.com

Internal management

Li recognized a development opportunity in relatively lower-value projects and low-grade products. While Huawei always competed with Cisco for the high-grade customers, Harbour's success could not leave out those at a lower level. In Huawei's internal creation plan, the company's sales package is for professional SMEs who are scattered over the market, but it continues to hold tightly to its good customers, such as the telecommunications carriers. This situation provided a good market-exploring opportunity for a new entrant.

At the very start, Harbour aimed at the business sectors with the most potential but whose potential markets were not fully explored. These included the customer sectors, such as education and the online civil service. In building channels, through subsections of industry, Harbour has spread out an in-depth strategic structure with many industrial agents. Harbour and the agents devote their time on products and share the profits together. Through a series of plans, Harbour has built a stable base in those industries that had been neglected in the governmental, educational, medical, financial, electric power and mining sectors.

The stock of available capacity for the telecommunications industry is currently decreasing while that of other industries in the information process will take up a larger proportion of the telecommunications facilities market. The proportion of Mainland China's network facility market purchased for the telecommunications industry declined from 40.5 per cent in 2001 to 30.1 per cent in 2002. That of the educational sector, however, increased from 11.3 per cent in 2001 to 12 per cent in 2002.[23] Ignoring the relationship between Huawei and Harbour, it could be said that the birth of Harbour was an inexorable result of the fragmented network facility in the domestic markets, and that this kind of situation reflects the market's trend towards deep sectoral development.

For new SMEs, it is important to be ready for the challenge of the markets. In its fifth year, Harbour is still recognized as a new company in the market and it relies on its customers' trust. But establishing trust cannot be achieved in a single day – Harbour must do so with its good services and effective product promotion. It is also important to build, train and coordinate the team. The members of the Harbour core team have considerable experience in the related industries. Such factors helped Harbour capture funds from international investment organizations and thereby acquire international operational experience.

---

[23] Statistics of Ministry of Information Industry, 2003.

Presently, China's domestic network market is highly competitive because there are new SMEs continuously emerging in this sector. Everyone can sense the speed of the changes in the network industry. The development of the traditional telecommunications industry depends on the accumulation of experience and technology with market strength. Most of the facility manufacturers are in large-scale enterprises, whose involvement extends from manufacturing their products to service provision. But the successful SMEs in the field of networks are smart action enterprises. Within such a fast-changing network environment, Harbour has developed by adjusting its policy to adapt to the continuing changes and competitive situation. The lesson to be learned from Harbour is the requirement to recommend new products and modify any policy according to the needs of the changing market.

From its foundation, Harbour was organized like other enterprises; that is, as a large-sized facility provider involved in all stages from R&D to construction, to distribution and, finally, after-sale services and organizational structure. R&D is destined to be a hard road and now many SMEs depend on original equipment manufacturers (OEMs) to enter the market quickly, but Harbour has always undertaken the hard-headed research itself. The network equipment manufacturers have been able to survive so long because they own the technology that they market.

Harbour's mergers and acquistions

On 29 December 2003, Harbour announced the official acquisition of Shenzhen Telen Technology.[24] The corporate name remained Harbour Networks Limited after acquisition and Harbour integrated competitive resources such as R&D teams, product technology, marketing and sales, customer service and manufacturing using the combined resources of both Harbour and Shenzhen Telen. This has greatly strengthened its leading position in data-com markets, and was a win-win strategic move for both parties involved. With the acquisition, Harbour inherited Telen Technology's multiservice transport platform (MSTP) world class technology as well as patents; it is now in a position to continue developing those technologies.

As a leading MSTP optical networking equipment provider, Telen Technology was established in 2002 and had an R&D team of 200 high-calibre engineers with an in-depth understanding of optical networking and rich industrial experiences. Based on their proprietary ASIC core chipsets, Telen Technology had applied for over 40 patents and launched OpCity Genius 2000/5000/8000/10000 serial products.

---

[24] 'The Merger between Harbour and Telen' *China Telecom World*, 5 January 2003.

Certified and permitted to enter public networks by the Ministry of Information Industry, Telen Technology's products range from Schlieren Thermal Mapper-1 (STM-1), STM-4, STM-16 to STM-64, providing a complete and stable new generation MSTP solution for metropolitan area network (MAN) transmission. Big carriers have begun to deploy OpCity serial products commercially. Based on the combined competitive advantages from Harbour and Telen Technology, the new Harbour can create more customer value and provide more end-to-end solutions, including MSTP optical networks, 10GB core routers and switches, ADSL/very-high-speed digital subscriber line (VDSL) broadband access systems, soft switch and NGN integrated access.[25]

It is worth noting that Huang Yaoxu, the founder and president of Telen, was also from Huawei. Huang was the head of the optical network business in Huawei; following the acquisition, he became the deputy general manager of Harbour.

Huawei's report for the third quarter of 2003 showed it to be ranked second in the global long distant wave market but the company is a long way ahead of its competitors. Before Harbour acquired Telen, Huawei did not count Telen as one of its competitors; since Harbour's acquisition, however, Huawei has been forced to reconsider this judgement.

Although the effects of acquiring Telen were not felt until the end of 2004, it aroused people's interests. Experts in the telecoms sector are sure this acquisition will enhance the strength of Harbour. Telen's optical network products will be an important element in Harbour's ambitious RMB2 billion sales goal.

The effects of Harbour's acquisition influence not only itself, but also have an impact on the optical networks market. Now, the optical networks market will open up not just for Huawei and Zhongxing, but for UTStarCom, Harbour and Photonic-bridges. The competition of optical networks in the next few years will be at its fiercest!

In fact, M&A has become an important tool for Harbour to accelerate its accumulation of technology and extend the range of its product line. At the China International Telecom Fair held at the end of 2002, Harbour exhibited two core routers named 'PowerHammer16008/16016', which support the technology of 10GB ethernet networks and provide the ten high-capability general purpose operating systems (GPOS) with high consistency. Behind the vast array of confusing technological terminology, it means that Harbour now owns the best high router products. Since then, the name of Harbour has started to appear on the lists of important rivals of many network manufacturers.

---

[25] Harbour Online: www.harbournetworks.com

Two products that have aroused competitors' attention are from Obade Ltd, which was acquired by Harbour in November 2002. Obade was created in the terms of a typical international start-up at the beginning of 2002. Its business strategy from foundation was for it to be acquired as an exit mechanism. The merger with Obade ensured that Harbour owned all the router products from the low-middle to high levels, while retaining its own brand of switch machines. In 2003, Harbour's growth rate was at 122 per cent and it broke through the sales barrier of more than RMB1 billion, largely as a result of the merger with Obade.[26]

With the support of its investors, Harbour had also completed other small acquisitions. The clear purchasing aim is to strengthen its technology and extend the range of its product line.

Exit strategy and VC firms' investment

In order to exit its investment, Warburg Pincus and Harbour registered a holding company in Hong Kong, which made the Harbour (Beijing) branch the subsidiary of the holding company. It is the aim of Warburg Pincus to ensure that Harbour is listed on the Hong Kong Mainboard Stock Market or NASDAQ. Li would not like to approach the capital market on the basis of Harbour's scale of operations. Listing has a lower capital cost than obtaining public funds support, which is really a very important task for most SMEs. Listing, however, is just the start for a successful SME, not the end.

In August 2001, Warburg Pincus invested US$16 million and Dragontech Venture invested US$3 million into Harbour, giving Harbour substantial funds of US$19 million.[27] This ensured it did not need to be a distributor and could devote its efforts to selling its own products. The Harbour workforce increased from 50 to 650.[28] In May 2002, within its first year of operation, Harbour had completed its second round of fund raising. Warburg Pincus and Dragontech Venture invested a further US$42 million into this tech-venture, of which US$37 million was from Warburg Pincus and US$5 million was from Dragontech Venture.[29]

Besides its direct investment, Warburg Pincus also acted as a guarantor for Harbour and helped Harbour to borrow US$350 million from China's banks;[30] at that time, Harbour had about RMB1 billion cash in hand. The company was able to raise the funds because it had achieved

---

[26] 'Harbour acquired Obade' *China Telecom World* 19 November 2002.
[27] Yan S, Li Yinan wants to copy Huawei, *21st Century Economy Report* 14 January 2004.
[28] Harbour Online: www.harbournetworks.com
[29] Huang JJT *China Focuses on Venture Capital and M&A: New Rules on Foreign VC Investments Open up Easier Access* Jones Day Ltd, August 2003.
[30] Yan S, 'Li Yinan wants to copy Huawei' *21st Century Economy Report* 14 January 2004.

RMB2.41 million profits in the second year from its establishment. Such profits stimulated the development activities of this new SME.

Many venture capitalists were interested in investing into Harbour, however Li finally chose Warburg Pincus. The most important reason for this was that future aspirations, management style and the operations model adopted by both Warburg Pincus and Harbour were the same. This would ensure harmony among shareholders and in business operations, with the long-term prospect of creating value for customers and then becoming a leading enterprise. In fact, there have been many SMEs in Mainland China experiencing shareholder conflict but, unlike others, Li appears to be fully satisfied with the cooperation of Warburg Pincus.

Warburg Pincus has increased Harbour's value by introducing international leaders with management experience and knowledge into Harbour. Combined with the Chinese local management experience and people, they have helped to create an excellent and dedicated enterprise.

Before acquiring Telen, Li signed contracts with a German investment company, Deutsche Investitions und Entwicklungsgesellschaft Mbh (DEG), and the Federation of Manufactured Home Owners of Florida Inc (FMO), who provided a 5-year loan of US$200 million. DEG has invested in more than 30 projects in Mainland China valued at more than €1700 million.[31] DEG believes that China's capital market will be opened in the future. The long-term loan to Harbour is a zero-interest mortgage but also it is the only secured loan. The loan will ensure that Harbour undertakes M&A using its own funds to enrich product lines rapidly so that it can fully expand its capacity to satisfy customer demand and explore new market areas.

In 2001 and 2002 Harbour's liability/asset ratio was at a low level and it was carrying only 30 per cent with which to support stable development. However, as a result of the lower liability/asset ratio, the company has been able to employ financial leverage at the high points of its business development. After taking on board the loan from DEG and FMO, the liability/asset ratio is now about 40 per cent.[32] However, Li still feels that the current ratio is low and that it should be around 50 per cent to be in line with the telecom facilities industry norm. In the future, Harbour will consider how to attract more corporate finance through short-term loans.

---

[31] Zhou Z, 'Harbour Network merges with Shenzhen's Jun Tian' *Pacific Epoch* 6 January 2004.
[32] Yan S, 'Li Yinan wants to copy Huawei' *21st Century Economy Report* 14 January 2004.

Success of the business model and native entrepreneurs

Harbour's success was due to a good business model combined with successful native entrepreneurs. The business model was robust: Harbour started as a distributor of low-end network instruments, depending on one or two big manufacturers and providing its customers with low-end instruments and services. Its business model was like that of RAD of Israel, which helped to build a solid customer network. When its own products had matured, Harbour stopped selling products from other companies and began to sell its own. In China, this business model proved both effective and successful.

After 2000, more and more foreign VC companiess paid attention to tech-ventures founded by successful entrepreneurs and management from China's private enterprises. Successful native entrepreneurs understood the intricacies of the Chinese market and, at the same time, had an abundance of management experience, making them the right persons for foreign VC firms. Harbour shows how the investment skills of Warburg Pincus also helped it to gain the essential bank loans to supplement its VC funding.

Li recognized the importance of technology and an operations model. From a technological perspective, Harbour realized that its customers would not easily accept them if they only provided the same technological capacity as some of the large-scale enterprises, because they would not feel that Harbour created value for money for them. The direction for Harbour to take was to add more value in technology and new ideas, and to create a new field of vision for business managers. Regarding its operations model, as a young SME, Harbour focused on the field in which its efforts are absorbed. Based on maintaining a high quality of service and decreasing operating costs, Harbour can feed back advantages to the customers so that they will appreciate the development of new technology and the predominance of favourable pricing.

In the past few years, the broadband IP network market was so 'hot' because of China's opportunity to build an information-based society, which passed through a development process to eliminate market competition when all manufacturers were busy building their broadband compatible networks. Through such an adjustment, many others in this sector have realized that they should not only provide a stable and credible network, but also offer broadband guarantees, billings, security and customer management services. Furthermore, it will be better to supply more value-added business to create a new broadband profit model so that the whole broadband industry can develop in a healthy and structured manner. Within the broadband industry supply chain, Harbour should provide a low-cost network building blueprint as a basic equipment provider to let the telecom carriers build a flexible telecom network. In a word, Harbour should find its own niche in the broadband industry supply chain.

Harbour has its own stable corporate financial management experience, holistic operational experience and a compelling management team. Its future is bright.

Biotech R&D commercialization

The road for commercialization

VC provides financial resources to support private firms in transforming basic knowledge into proprietary and commercial applications. The availability of VC funding for biotechnology is key to the existence of the industry in the US. In the fourth quarter of 2003, US venture capital in biotechnology reached to US$1.1 billion and exceeded investment in the software industry for two quarters.[33] However, so far VC has played a limited role in the commercialization of biotechnology R&D in China.

Virtually all R&D in Mainland China was funded and monitored by the state prior to economic reform, thereby creating an incentive structure for individuals and institutes to gain state grants to carry out scientific research without being able to exploit its final results commercially. Chinese R&D institutes have developed a bureaucratic management system under the centralized economy, and their operating procedures, lacking a market-driven culture, were mainly established to meet policy and/or reporting requirements.

In 1985, the Chinese government decided to extend its reform policy from the agricultural and industrial sectors to a national R&D management system by emphasizing applied R&D in order to drive economic growth through more cooperation between researchers, industrial firms and entrepreneurs.[34] A national leading programme, the 863 Plan, identified biotechnology as one of seven priority areas for development. However, few biotechnology projects have been implemented due to the substantial uncertainty in commercializing biotechnology R&D in comparison with the large number of projects in electronics, information technology (IT) and new materials. At last in the 1990s, the Chinese Academy of Science (CAS) established a Chinese biotechnology research institute (SEBC) to spearhead the transformation of biotechnology R&D results into marketable products

---

[33] Bioon Biotech Information Network Ltd, 30 July 2004.
[34] Hui P *Looking Back the 20 Years of Chinese Software Industry (1984-2004)*, Ministry of Science and Technology of PRC, 28 July 2004.

and technologies through academic–industrial alliances.[35] It was decided to locate SEBC in Shanghai, where the strongest research and industrial base in the field of Chinese biological engineering resides.

SEBC has undergone gradual changes in terms of its strategic objective, organization structure and project selection procedures in response to the rapidly evolving environment under economic reform. However, the limited success of its commercialization efforts show that market demand is not sufficient to bridge the gap between technological potential and commercial exploitation. Market-based financing is found to be of critical importance to commercialize R&D successfully in a transition economy because the severity of budgetary constraints underlies the difference between centralized and decentralized models of R&D management.

There are two lessons that can be drawn from the development of SEBC. First, an R&D management system in a transition economy serves as a link between the change in institutional environment and the implementation of organization strategy. An R&D management control system based on vaguely defined property rights is a formula for costly conflicts, operating inefficiencies and the squandering of resources. Despite the high expectations, advanced facilities and its preferential location, SEBC was unable to achieve a critical mass of technological entrepreneurship for commercial success because of the lack of an effective R&D management system.

Second, external financing, especially VC, is the key to an effective R&D management system. Internal financing allows soft budget control, which is accountable for the disappointing economic performance of R&D institutes under the centralized economy. In contrast, external financing provides a market-based monitoring mechanism to deter ethically hazardous and adverse selection problems associated with R&D investment decisions and project evaluation. Capital budgeting and project evaluation are two essential financial control tools without which no investment in large-scale, long-term biotechnology R&D commercialization projects is feasible.

The hard road of SEBC indicates the importance and absolute need for an R&D management system, especially in the transition period of the Chinese economy and against the background of the SEBC experience. Unclear IP rights meant that SEBC could not set up an effective financial control system, seriously restricting its ability to raise external funding for its commercial projects. The result was that neither the business nor its operation could achieve its plan. As for reducing the problems of choice for R&D investment decision making and project estimation, the importing of marketing expertise and finance, especially

---

[35] *High-tech Program* CAS Online: www.cas.ac.cn, 12 April 2003.

VC, which can provide a supervisory and monitoring mechanism, is very important to the success of a commercial R&D operation. The board of directors of SEBC decided to adopt two measures to improve the project's financial control system: SEBC will only take part in projects where it has the controlling rights and the investment return rate should not be less than 10 per cent.

Biotech opportunities in China

Biotech opportunities in China will flourish because labour costs are low and clinical trials are much easier to perform in a relatively homogeneous and large population. Investors can expect incentives or subsidies from the government as biotech is classified as high technology.

Chinese scientists are good at developing upstream high-end technology, but come undone when dealing with the downstream and commercial aspects of it. R&D budgets are extremely low by western standards. Scientists also have difficulties in industrializing new technology for various reasons. Many of the drugs have dozens of companies producing them or about to produce the same industrialized product. China has more than 1000 biotech enterprises and research institutes, which employ in excess of 10,000 R&D staff. The current general scale of the biopharmacy industry is around RMB8 billion, which includes RMB3 billion of blood production, RMB0.5 billion of diagnosis reagents, RMB1.5 billion of biogene drugs and RMB3 billion of biochemistry pharmaceuticals.[36] The research capability of Chinese scientists in the field of biotech is very strong. China has made great progress and strongly advanced the world's knowledge in the study of human gene groups and disease-related genes, the plant gene atlas, gene chips, dry cells and gene transplant animals. Another programme that is about to start is a gene-group testing project to study Chinese traditional medicine on a molecular level and to separate its active composition. Should this programme be successful, it will open up a new territory for drug development – this is a field at which VC firms should certainly look.

Among the biotech drugs for which China has its own proprietary technology, there are liver cell growth factors, human origin alkaline fibre cell growth factors, therapeutically mono clone antibodies, and human blood replacement, all of which have finished or almost finished clinical testing. These drugs are really innovative and have the potential to sell internationally. There are other investment opportunities in the start-ups of returned overseas Chinese scholars. These

---

[36] 'Chinese bio-tech industry is under the opportunity of investment' *EBiotrade Network* 9 January 2004.

people are entrepreneurs who have mastered world-class technology and should be able to exploit the competitive advantages of low R&D costs and a huge potential domestic market.

However, generally speaking, the technology level of the Chinese biotech industry is not competitive when compared with that of the US and Europe. Among the domestically manufactured biotech drugs on the market, very few are produced with proprietary technology, which has become a big problem for China following its WTO membership. R&D projects are usually conducted over a very long period of time and success rates are low; furthermore, IP protection remains an unsolved problem.

Despite the low technology level of most Chinese biotech companies, biotech stocks listed on the Chinese stock market have been climbing high in recent years, but this does not mean that the industry is booming in China. Rather, it is just another stock market bubble. Gene chips have also been hot property during the last two years in China, where several R&D companies were established to try to produce gene chips for medical diagnosis.

Shortages of early-stage research funds and VC support have been the bottleneck for the biotechnology industry. Despite the rapid development and huge potential of China's biotechnology sector, the industry is still in its infancy and, as a result, remains too weak to attract foreign VC. The 'Medicine in the 21st Century Tri-Conference' and 'Bio-Forum 2004', held in Shanghai by the World Biotechnology Forum, a New Jersey-based non-profit organization, did not give biotech professionals any good news. The New York Stock Exchange, NASDAQ and International Finance Cooperation were invited to the event. Lots of foreign-based VC firms are starting to pay close attention to the Chinese mainland's biotech industry, but this isn't cause for optimism because they are just looking for sectors in which they may invest in over the next five years. Compared with Singapore and Taiwan, the Chinese mainland still lacks human resources, good manufacturing process certificated plants, a fair environment and good IP protection for drug innovation. These are the major obstacles blocking foreign venture capitalists' efforts to pour their money into China's biotech sector. Statistics indicate that China has more than 50,000 life-science researchers and more than 300 public laboratories nationwide,[37] but the overall research level remains quite low. Although numerous overseas researchers and scientists have returned to the Chinese mainland in recent years, the nation still needs talented people to upgrade its overall level of drug innovation.

---

[37] *The Current Situation, Problems and Countermeasures of Bio-technology Industry In China*, Institute of Scientific & Technical Information of China, August 2004.

Since China's WTO accession in December 2001, the IP rights laws and some regulations have been amended to comply with the Trade-Related Aspects of Intellectual Property Rights (TRIPS). Implementation of the laws and regulations in Chinese regions outside of Beijing and Shanghai, however, has not been good. Compared with the overcautious attitude of foreign venture capitalists, domestic investors have been quite active in the biotech industry. Funding by state-owned firms has been a major force in the sector. Statistics indicate that the Chinese government plans to invest US$10 billion and create 1 million employment opportunities before 2010 to boost the development of the nation's biotechnology industry.[38] Various levels of local government, which regard the sector as their future economic pillar, will also contribute. China's pharmaceutical market will grow tremendously over the next 10 years, especially given the State's preferential policies that support biotechnology and the sector's huge potential. In some cities such as Shanghai, Beijing and Shenzhen, where most biotech resources and enterprises are located, biotech investments have paid off.

The third phase of clinical trials of H101 (gene engineering adenovirus injection), an anti-cancer medicine developed by Shanghai Sunway Biotech Co Ltd (Sunway), has just been concluded. H101 will be the first oncolytic drug in the world to be marketed commercially to stop the metastasis of cancer cells. Sunway has US$15.34 million in registered capital and is venture-backed by state-owned Shanghai Alliance Investment Ltd (Shanghai Alliance). Shanghai Alliance has invested some RMB100 million (US$12 million) in Sunway since 1997.[39]

Chengdu Venture Capital Co Ltd, in southwest China's Sichuan Province, is another example of success. The state-owned company, established in 2001, has invested in two 'seed' biotech projects. One project generated profits of 16 per cent in its first year.[40] Its government backing gives certain and strong support because biotech projects usually take R&D members more than a year to investigate carefully and take up, since there are great risks in investing in the biotech industry with its long life cycle. Many venture capitalists express great interest in developing biotech products but withdraw after they learn how long R&D takes to develop a new drug (an average of 8 years), the possible

---

[38] Sun Guohong, *China Could Not Lose Again in the Field of Biotechnology*, Tianjin Binhai New Area Government, 23 July 2004. (In this article, the author also mentioned that China has dropped behind India in the software industry to too great a degree. Ten years ago, India established the world's first biotech valley. The Indian government also set up the BioTech Ministry, as well as the Ministry of Science and Technology, which is unique in the world. Furthermore, India established the International Biotech Research Centre and gathered the best international scientists.)
[39] Suway Online: www.sunwaybio.com.cn
[40] Chengdu Venture Capital Association.

great risks and the huge investment needed. China's incomplete market system and unequal taxation policy, combined with the difficulties in withdrawing investments, have created obstacles for venture capitalists eager to invest in the nation's biotech industry.

Besides public funds, VC also plays an important role in the biotech field. A recent significant event in the biopharmaceutical sector was the first gene therapy approved in China. In October 2003, the Chinese State Food and Drug Administration (SFDA) issued a drug licence to Shenzhen SiBiono Gene Technologies Co Ltd (SiBiono) to commercially produce the world's first gene therapy drug, Gendicine™, for the treatment of head and neck squamous cell carcinoma.[41] Gendicine™ uses an adenoviral vector plus p53 tumour suppressant gene delivery system. Shenzhen Yuanzheng Investment Ltd (Yuanzheng) invested in SiBiono during its difficult period although there was only a 30 per cent probability of success. However, the result vindicated Yuanzheng's judgement. So far, more than RMB70 million of funds have been injected into SiBiono. VC has provided abundant funding for the company to build a solid foundation for its biotech industrialization.

Currently, foreign venture capitalists have decided to invest and are looking to extend further into the biofield of technology and the products of Chinese herb exploration, chemosynthesis, raw material medicine, non-prescription medicine, clinical research, etc. The venture capitalists should pay full attention to the risks of Chinese biotech industry investment. In general, a bio venture-backed project should expect a 12–16 year cycle and a cost of US$0.8–1.2 billion for its return.[42] However, the good environment, abundant resources, relatively lower cost and the special disease chart, are all the reasons why foreign venture capitalists focus on Chinese biotechnology.

VC-made genes to be in the vanguard

SiBiono is a pioneer in developing gene therapy in China. As the first professional company of this nature, SiBiono has achieved great success, which would not have been possible without VC investment. In October 2003, the Recombinant Human Ad-p35 Injection, trademarked as Gendicine™ and developed independently by SiBiono, successfully obtained the drug licence, production approval and good manufacturing practice (GMP) certificate from China's State Food & Drug Administration (SFDA).[43] SFDA approved the manufacture and use of

---

[41] SiBiono Online: www.sibiono.com, 15 September 2004.
[42] Mark Tang, President and Managing Director of World Technology Ventures, August 2004, reported by TEDA-WASTON International Forum On Biotechnology and Biomedicine.
[43] SiBiono Online: www.sibiono.com, 15 September 2004.

Gendicine™ after clinical trials found that it markedly improved the survival rate for patients with cancer of the head and neck. Gendicine™ is the first commercialized gene therapy product ever approved in the world. Doctors are now extending the treatment to patients with lung and stomach cancer. Undoubtedly, Gendicine™ is a milestone in the field of gene research and high-tech biotechnology and will have an impact on the whole world's medical and health system, making an important contribution to the course of improving human health.[44] Table 2.1 shows the milestones of SiBiono's development programme.

Table 2.1. The milestones of SiBiono's[45] Development Programme

Date	Matter
11 March 2004	Manufacturing facility for Recombinant Human Ad-p53 Injection (Gendicine™) is granted a GMP certificate by the State Food & Drug Administration.
20 January 2004	Recombinant Human Ad-p53 Injection (Gendicine™) is granted a production certificate by the State Food & Drug Administration.
16 October 2003	Recombinant Human Ad-p53 Injection (Gendicine™) is granted a new drug licence by the State Food & Drug Administration.
15 September 2003	Zeng Qinghong, member of the Political Bureau of the Central Committee of the Communist Party of China, Vice President, visits SiBiono GeneTech.
8, 9 July 2003	Dr W French Anderson, called 'father of gene therapy' visits SiBiono GeneTech, and takes the post of advisor to SiBiono GeneTech. A cooperation research development contract is signed between Dr Anderson and SiBiono GeneTech.
7 January 2003	Zhang Dejiang, member of the Political Bureau of the Central Committee of the Communist Party of China and Party Secretary of Guangdong Province, pays a visit to SiBiono GeneTech.
22 November 2002	SiBiono is granted the Pharmaceutical Manufacture Permission by the Guangdong Drug Administration.
November 2002	Recombinant Human Ad-p53 Injection is listed as a special science and technology project in the National Tenth Five-Year-Plan by the Ministry of Science & Technology.

---

[44] Tao S 'The first approved commercialized gene therapy product in the world' *People's Daily* 1 March 2004.
[45] Shenzhen SiBiono GeneTech Co Ltd website: www.sibiono.com, October 2004.

Date	Matter
November 2002	A labour union is set up in SiBiono GeneTech and will act on behalf of employees for their interests.
3 July 2002	Recombinant Human Ad-p53 Injection is granted a production technology patent (No. ZL 98 1 23346.5) by the State Intellectual Property Office.
December 2001	The Ministry of Science & Technology lists the Recombinant Human Ad-p53 Injection in the National Science & Technology Programme.
December 2000	A gene therapy manufacturing plant is built in Shengzhen High-Tech Park.
7 October 2000	The State Food & Drug Administration approves the Recombinant Human Ad-p53 Injection to take phase II clinical trials.
July 2000	The Ministry of Science & Technology lists Recombinant Human Ad-p53 Injection in an innovation fund for high-tech SMEs.
December 1999	Recombinant Human Ad-p53 Injection is listed as a key industrialization project by Shenzhen municipal government.
January 1999	The Ministry of Science & Technology lists Recombinant Human Ad-p53 Injection into biotech development projects in the 863 Plan.
28 December 1998	The State Food & Drug Administration approves Recombinant Human Ad-p53 Injection to take phase I clinical trials.
9 March 1998	Shenzhen SiBiono GeneTech Co Ltd is established.

Dr Peng Zhaohui is the founder, Chairman and CEO of SiBiono. He was educated in China, Japan and the US. Peng has devoted more than 10 years to the field of gene therapy; his achievement in the birth of Gendicine™ will not only enable China to take the lead in the international competition of commercialization of the gene therapy industry, but also indicates that the technology chain in Shenzhen has been extended to technology innovation.

The location for accomplishing Peng's dream is Shenzhen. As an overseas Chinese company, because of the choice of first fundraising and the funding environment, Peng laid down roots in Shenzhen. On Christmas Day 1997[46] Peng started his undertaking in Shenzhen.

---

[46] Li Bin, 'The first gene therapy medicine in the world,' *Shenzhen Economic Daily*, 23 October 2003.

The first capital for Peng's foundation was from the Science & Technology Bureau of Nanshan District of Shenzhen (STBND). Peng once said that he would never forget STBND's favour although the government department abandoned the investment following a change of policies.[47] At that time, STBND sent professionals and experts to Beijing for a feasibility demonstration with the help of academics and authority departments. There was some debate among industry insiders over such a mysterious field, but Shenzhen and STBND had the foresight to see its value and meaning. Before Peng carried out his formal procedures for leaving Japan, STBND had prepared all the facilities and some personnel, including a fund of RMB2.4 million, offices and personal assistants. On March 1998, SiBiono settled in Nanshan, Shen.

High-technology projects belong to a highly committed industry. In the early stage, there won't be any output, only contribution. At the toughest time Yuanzheng decided to invest in SiBiono. Peng told Yuanzheng frankly that investing in SiBiono was a long-term project and that perhaps there would be no return for 8 years. Furthermore, because of the high risk, there was only a 30 per cent likelihood of success. The results proved Yuanzheng's unique insight to have been right. Until the end of 2003, RMB600 million was injected into SiBiono through VC, which established a stable base for the development of SiBiono.[48]

In this period, many cities wanted Peng to take the project away from Shenzhen, but he remained there – the reason being that he considered the mechanism for developing high science and technology to be nearly perfect in Shenzhen. As a result of its sound formulation, the gene project would have also been successful in other cities, but Peng judged that it would be successful much quicker in Shenzhen.

There are two special features of the Shenzhen system:

- *Harmonization with the international trend in corporate property rights systems.* SiBiono can be said to be a pure knowledgeable company. The IP rights account for the major part of the equity. According to the modern US structure of legal person governance, SiBiono was set up by the CEO who assigned his IP rights to the company; the investors did not oppose these provisions.

- *The relatively mature mechanism for industrial growth.* Shenzhen High-sci and Technology Area is a figurehead of the Chinese life sciences industry. In the last 10 years, two neighbours, Shenzhen Kexing Biotech Co Ltd and Shenzhen Kangtai Biological Products

---

[47] ibid.
[48] ibid.

Co Ltd, were rated highly and became famous domestic brands in the gene project industry.

Bill Gates once predicted that the next person to amass his fortune will be in the field of gene exploration and development. Peng and SiBiono are currently defining the scope of this new industry. SiBiono decided to import international investors and multinational pharmaceutical companies to expand the production scale of Gendicine™ from 2003's 200,000 annual output to 1 million per year. Gendicine™ was estimated to have a US$100 million market in 2004.[49] For Peng, the next river to cross is developing to be the world's best in terms of sales achievement and profits.

---

[49] Rusconi S, *Towards First Commercialization of a Gene Medicine Product in China?* December 2003, original from: www.unifr.ch/nfp37/sibiono.html

3

Creative Products and Markets in China

Internet and e-commerce market development

Market growth and current trends

According to the China Internet Network Information Centre's (CNNIC's) 13th statistical survey on development of the internet in China (published in January 2004), there are 79.5 million internet users in total, of whom 39.6 per cent are female and 60.4 per cent male. Breaking this down into types of accessing methods, there are 26.60 million users of leased lines, 49.16 million dial-up users and 5.52 million ISDN users with a residual 17.40 million users accessing the internet via broadband connections. Figure 3.1 shows the users by different geographic regions.

China is now the second largest internet country user in the world – this huge user number is building a strong base for development of the Chinese internet industry. The flourishing internet market in China drives the development of related industries, which belong mainly to the SMS and online gaming sectors. As a result of the internet platform, an online game has its live earth and developing space; the online game operator, represented by Shanghai Shanda, and the telecom carriers realize the incremental profit.

The statistics detailed in Table 3.1 show that the number of websites accessed increased sharply between July 2002 and January 2004. The total bandwidth of leased international connections is 27,216MB

Table 3.1 Website usage from January 2001 to January 2004

	January 2001	July 2001	January 2002	July 2002	January 2004
Number of websites accessed	265,405	242,739	277,100	293,213	595,550

Source: 13th China Internet Development Situation Statistics Report, CNNIC, 2004

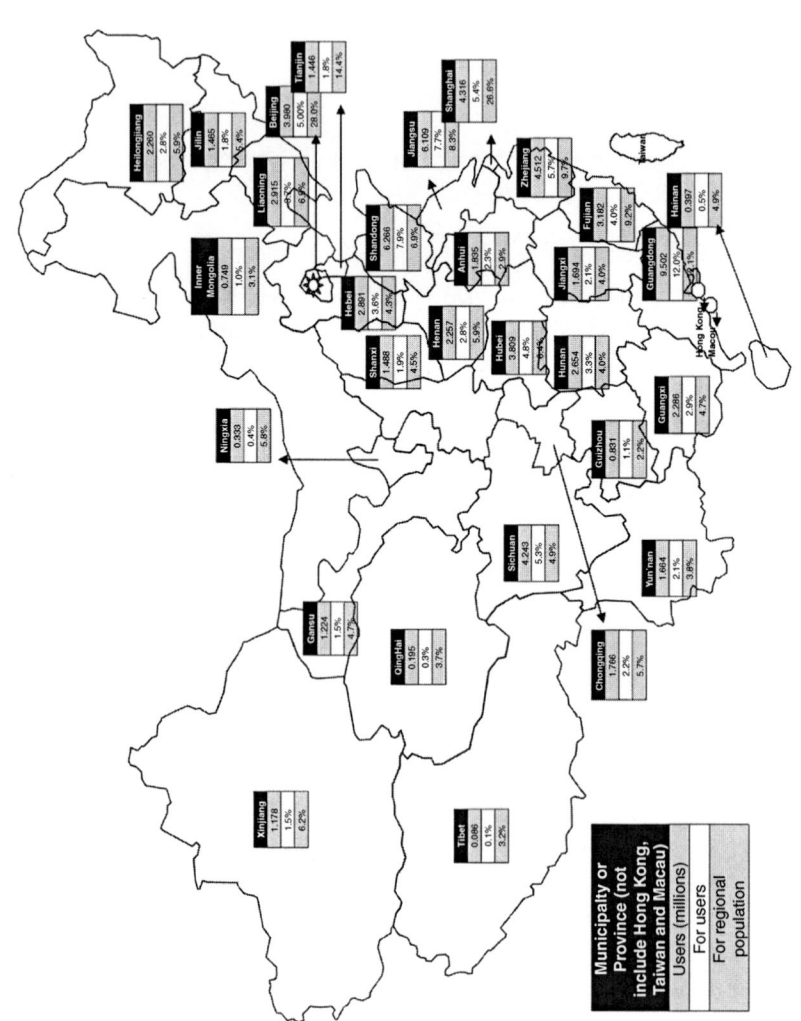

Figure 3.1 Internet users (millions) by geographic region in China

according to CNNIC's statistics. Countries directly connected to China's internet market include the US, Canada, Australia, the UK, Germany, France, Japan and South Korea.

Internet and e-commerce in the new century

2004 is the tenth anniversary of Chinese internet development.[1] Within these ten years, as a new industry, the internet market has come a long way and altered radically. It is a happy time for investors in the internet industry because most companies made profits in 2003. It could be said that the CEOs of internet-based small and medium-sized enterprises (SMEs) have found a clearer approach to attracting revenue, customers and broadband. Current Chinese internet users are good at e-commerce, which is evident given the development of online advertising, online gaming, online shopping, multimedia messaging service (MMS), internet banking and internet trade. Now, users will not just stop at their previous online services, such as checking the news and e-mail, but are very interested in new products marketed by internet-based SMEs.

The three largest Chinese websites have begun to make profits and their share prices are increasing. When NASDAQ's index was at the bottom, the three websites had already gained strength on the stock exchange. After Sohu, Sina and Netease attracted low share prices of US$0.52, US$1.02 and US$0.51 respectively in 2001, the share price unexpectedly increased ten times to 50 times its value![2] China-concept stocks started to come into their own. As a result of the good performance of online gaming, the net income of Netease increased by 50 per cent in 2004 compared with 2003, which reached RMB903.6 million. The net profit increased by 37 per cent (RMB441 million). Ding Lei was awarded fifth richest man in Mainland China in 2004.[3]

Developing clearer models for making profit has been the key to the successes of the three website firms. Each has its own unique features. Sina is good at news links, thus advertisements within the news page have become the main money-maker. Netease keeps ahead in the technological sectors; it makes higher profits more than Sohu and Sina because of a popular online game, *The Legend of West Journey 2.0*. Sohu positions itself as representative of technological fashion – its short message service (SMS) and *Classmates' Record* make the same

---

[1] *1994-2004: The Ten Years of China Internet* Sohu IT Online: http://it.sohu.com, 2 September 2004.
[2] Wang N, Liao X 'Chinese enterprises run to NASDAQ again' *21st Century Economy Report* 31 July 2003.
[3] 'New Fortune Press Conference: 500 Richest Men in Mainland China' *New Fortune Journal* 28 April 2005.

profits as online advertisement sectors. Of course, the three websites are also exploring new business opportunities: Sina has acquired an online game website and decided to build up its SMS community, Netease is now rivalling Sina in the field of news links for more online advertisement, while Sohu made a decision to expand further into the online games industry.

2003 opened with mergers and acquisitions (M&As) and initial public offerings (IPOs) at record levels for the internet-based SMEs, such as Ctrip, 3721, Sohu, EachNet and ELong. Sohu acquired China's biggest online game website, www.17173.com, and the most influencial real estate website, www.focus.cn. ELong secured US$15 million from the venture capitalists, www.tom.com, and was one of the first players to launch wireless interactive voice response (IVR) services through the acquisition of Wu Ji Network, the leading wireless IVR service provided in China. US venture capital firm Tiger Technology Fund has been one of the more ambitious investors, who injected RMB52 million into www.Joyo.com, the Chinese business-to-consumer (B2C) website, to become one of its top investors after domestic software vendor Kingsoft and computer giant Lenovo (formerly Legend).[4]

In 2003, EachNet, the leading online trading community in China, was acquired by eBay for US$180 million. In 2002, eBay acquired a 33 per cent interest in EachNet, for US$30 million in cash. Also included in the purchase price was an option for eBay to purchase the remaining 67 per cent of EachNet.[5] Founded in Shanghai in August 1999 by two US-educated Chinese entrepreneurs, Shao Yibo and Tan Haiyin, EachNet will further extend its e-commerce leadership in China and gain a foothold in one of the world's fastest growing internet markets. Today, EachNet has 3.5 million registered users who trade a wide variety of items from clothing and antiques to computers and real estate. China is the fourth largest e-commerce market in Asia and eleventh in the world, and its online commerce is expected to nearly double every year for the next four years. The relationship with EachNet is an important step forward in eBay's strategy to build a truly global marketplace. Over the next three to four years, China's e-commerce revenue is projected to be more than US$16 billion.[6] Together with EachNet, eBay will be well positioned to help develop this emerging market and benefit from its growth long term. Following the capital investment by eBay, the fomer EachNet website,

---

[4] Wang R 'The Tiger Fund would like to acquire the two internet bookshops, DangDang and Joyo' *21st Century Economy Report* 15 January 2004.
[5] Steiner I *eBay Completes EachNet Acquisition* AuctionBytes Online: www.auctionbytes.com 17 July 2003.
[6] Lee M 'Online auctioneer bids 2b yuan turnover for No 1' *The Standard* 7 September 2004.

www.eachnet.com, has disappeared and was integrated with the same platform as eBay to become www.ebay.com.cn.[7]

Real name, online game and search navigator services have prospered in the Chinese internet market. In 2003, the whole range of internet services, including connection, online SMS, advertisements, search navigators, registration of domain name and internet downloads made RMB18.97 billion and achieved a growth rate of more than 60 per cent.[8] The internet service industry has become the largest fractionized market in the Chinese IT sector.

Due to the high speed of changes in the market environment, distribution agents have a very important role to play. For instance, online real name service achieves great success as the internet service product most used by traditional models, expanding the number of agents. 3721's outstanding achievements in the field show that the traditional markets are head and shoulders above online sales within the current economic environment. Dependence on online sales price ranking, not only for the internet real name service but also other internet service products, such as the registration of search navigators, has led to slow development because of localized characteristics for product services and the absence of professional knowledge for the operation to terminate customers. Many tasks, including sale promotions and after-sales services for real (but not online) markets, need to be dealt with by independent agents who can exploit their advantage of knowing local markets needs to help expand the services. Online sales could not be detached from sales achievement, so the 'line-down' channel to market (the sale channel on the traditional market independent of the internet in Mainland China) will definitely be the main sales route for most network business distributors.

Currently, internet services are still in their early stages of development. However this market may expand, customers will only receive those applied technological services from businessmen who provide high quality services. In other words, to provide an effective rival service, SMEs should assure that they can deliver good services and can manage their employees, procedures and technology tightly to deliver effective market solutions. Eventually, the weaker SMEs will be forced out of the market. The winners will be those SMEs that have the ability to design carefully and continue the development of their business model, and that have an effective team to gain trust and credibility in the capital market.

---

[7] *EachNet Integrate Online Credit* eNet Online: www.enet.com.cn 28 June 2003.

[8] CCID Research *The Value Return of International Internet*, CCID Consulting, 29 March 2004.

In early 1999, China Telecom teamed up with the Information Centre of the National Committee of the Economy and Trade, to promote three internet access programmes, namely Government Online, Enterprises Online and Family Online. These three programmes have had a profound influence on the growth of digital multimedia businesses and the e-commerce sector. E-commerce applications by industry sectors are shown in Table 3.2, while Figures 3.2 to 3.6[9] reveal the main industries in China that are now investing in the information sector.

Table 3.2 E-commerce applications by industry sectors

Industry sector	Estimated investment fund for IT systems in 2004	Use
Domestic banks	RMB18 billion	Complete application, internet banking, interbank transfer system, internet security and hardware upgrade
Stock exchange	RMB9 million	Upgrading information system
Social welfare and insurance	From RMB96 billion (2003) to RMB152 billion	Five IT subsystems including retirement, unemployment, social medical/health insurance, industrial injury and birth control (operating independently but on the same platform)
Electric power	RMB5.9 billion (28% more than 2003)	Strategy support system, resource conformity, network security
Health	RMB3.5 billion (25% more than 2003)	Public health information system, clinic information system, medical and health insurance system, regional health information, doctor workstation, pathology image system, electronic medical case history, laboratory information system
Government	RMB40 billion (increase of 16% over 2003)	Online government affairs, public service system (including the emergency dictate system and online office system), town and mountain area's IT building, software, information security

---

[9] Source of Figures 3.2, 3.3, 3.4, 3.5, 3.6: CCW Research, November 2003.

Industry sector	Estimated investment fund for IT systems in 2004	Use
Transportation	RMB10 billion (increase of 19.8 % over 2003), RMB8.35 billion in 2003 (increase of 21% over 2002)	Railroad's transport management information system (TMIS), dictate management information system (DMIS) building, airline's global distribution system (GDS) application, transportation's electric data-exchange information (EDI) system, e-commerce, highway and regional network management, regional information transport system building and human resource and logistics management
Education	RMB22.68 billion in 2003 (increase of 19.8% over 2002); investment growth rate in 2004 was 8%	Campus computer network, education information service, multimedia education and online education
Large-sized manufacturers	RMB9.35 billion, accounting for 47.9% of the manufacturing industry total (RMB19.5 billion), an increase of 22.6% over 2003 (RMB7.63 billion, accounting for 46.2% of RMB16.5 billion for the whole manufacturing industry)	Enterprise IT system

Entering the World Trade Organization (WTO) should mean that China's telecommunications and finance markets will open up resulting in a greatly enhanced competitive market environment and lower costs of internet usage, which will bring about beneficial developments in e-commerce. On the other hand, some obstacles exist, which will hinder the wider acceptance of e-commerce. Such obstacles include internet security, internet infrastructure, credit record systems, e-commerce related regulations, coding standardization, payment through the internet, knowledge levels of executives on e-commerce, availability of technological talent and third-party material flow and distribution systems.

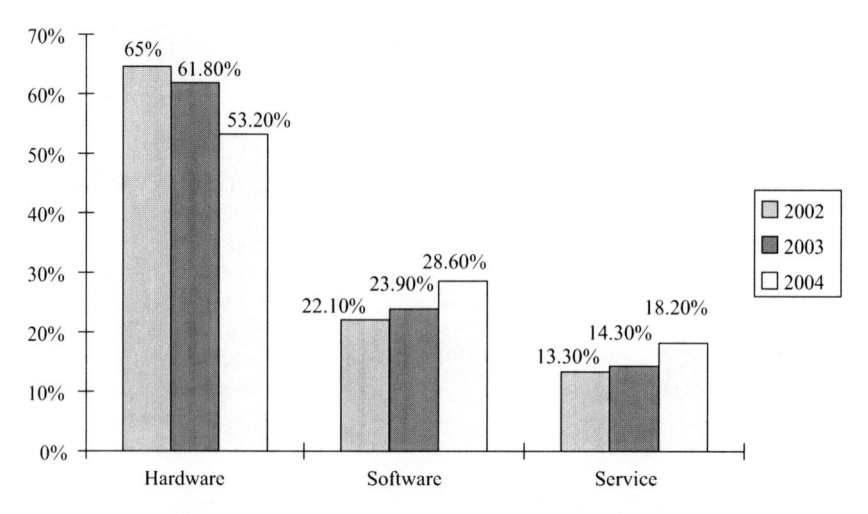

Figure 3.2 Banking industry investment structure (2002–2004)

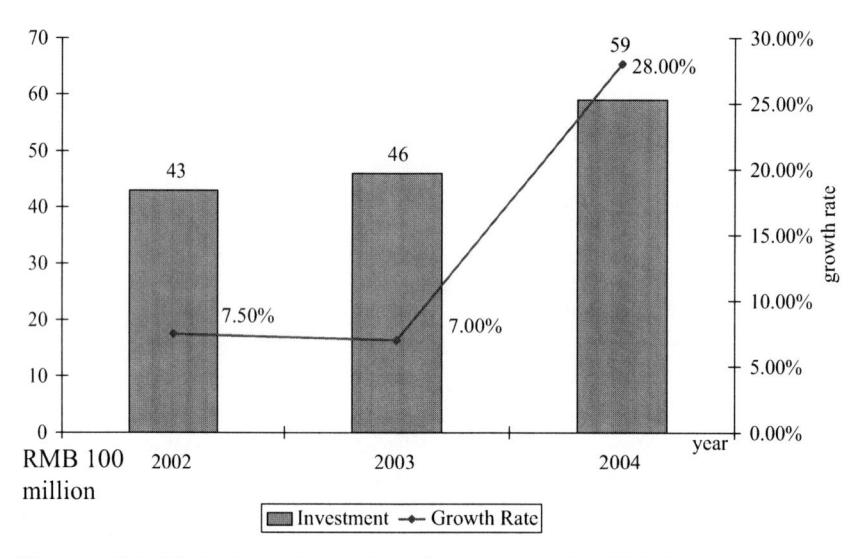

Figure 3.3 IT stock scale in electric power sector (2003)

VC backing for e-commerce

After three difficult years, the Chinese e-commerce market was rejuvenated in 2003. The speed of financing, which exceeded people's anticipation, could be described as a 'blow-out', with companies such as IDG (International Data Group), Tiger Fund and Softbank actively represented and all expecting to make huge profits in the next round of stimulating Chinese internet SMEs. In 2004 and 2005 competition

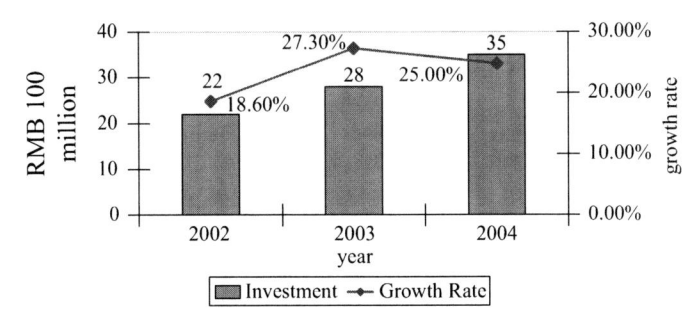

Figure 3.4 IT stock scale in health industry (2003)

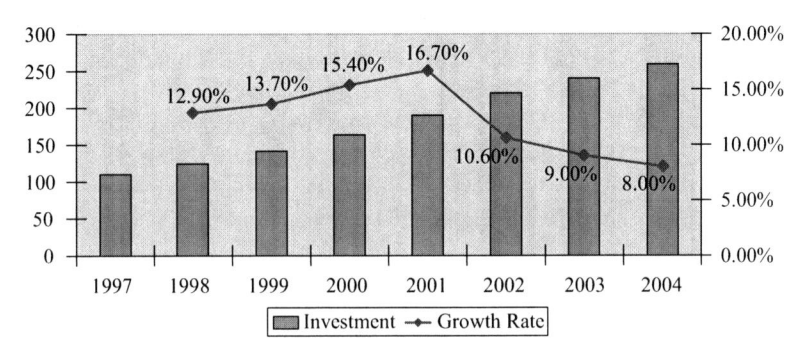

Figure 3.5 Education industry invests in information technology

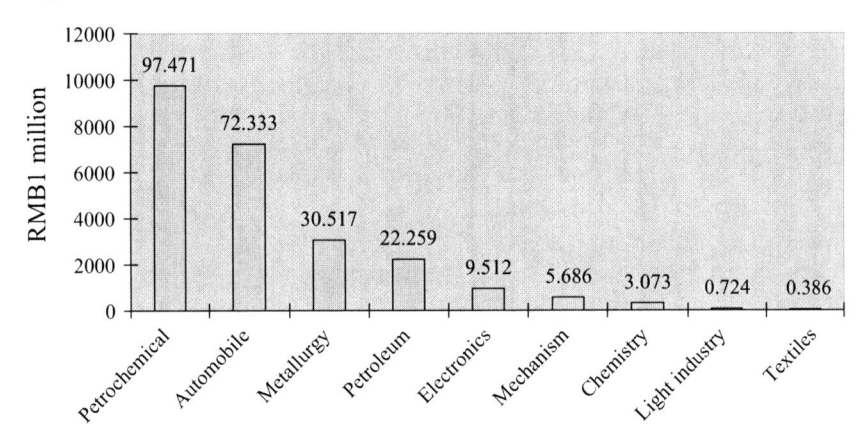

Figure 3.6 Investment forecast by manufacturing sector

in China's internet industry started to move from text messaging, advertising and online games to e-commerce.

Chinese-based Alibaba.com, a global trade sourcing website and the world's largest internet business-to-business site, received US$60 million funding from a Softbank-led syndicate of investors[10] and plays matchmaker to small and medium Chinese firms and overseas buyers. Until February 2004, Alibaba.com Corp, a home-grown competitor to eBay Inc and Yahoo! Inc, had raised US$82 million in VC, the largest amount ever accrued for a Chinese internet start-up firm.[11] The cash is helping it to improve its technology and to aggressively expand its internet auction site, Taobao.com, to compete with its two better-known US rivals within the highly competitive Chinese market. Alibaba, which is profitable, did not rule out future acquisitions or a stock-market listing. Ma Yun, the CEO and founder of Alibaba, anticipated the coming 'internet war' and felt that Taobao, which launched in May 2003 with an investment of US$12 million, would compete directly with Yahoo! and eBay, which Alibaba recognized as formidable opponents. Alibaba aimed to triple sales in 2004 to US$90 million from some US$30 million in 2003 and US$10 million in 2002.[12] Finally, the firm generated over US$12 million in free cashflow in 2003. Backers in Alibaba's latest round of financing are US-based firms Fidelity Investments, Granite Global Ventures and China's Venture TDF Technology Group as well as Japan's Softbank. Alibaba is sitting on a huge pile of cash, which could be put to good use in acquiring other businesses; moreover, a stock listing could also be in the offing. Its main objective at present is to run the business well. Listing on a stock exchange should be a natural process and not an undertaking for its own sake; thus, Alibaba will list at some point in the future.

Thanks to the funds from foreign venture capitalists, Chinese websites that are involved in e-commerce currently have money to spend. Dazzling professional internet concepts, such as online shopping, online action, B2C, C2C and B2B will become mainline products.

Why, when it failed four years ago, has e-commerce received venture capitalists' attention since 2003? The first reason is the profit announcements from many of the Chinese e-commerce websites. The latest statistics from CNNIC indicate that there are more than 270 million customers in the present e-commerce market compared with a mere 350,000 in 2000. CNNIC's internet survey shows that 40.7 per cent of internet users purchased from an online shop within the last year compared with only 8.79 per cent in 2000. This is not peculiar to the Chinese e-commerce websites receiving investment, but because of the impetus from the global internet industry revival. As an

---

[10] Wang H 'Alibaba raised US$82 million and aimed at B2C website' *China Business Post* 17 February 2004.
[11] ibid.
[12] Liu J *China's Alibaba Raises $82 Million in Venture Capital* Reuters, 19 February 2004.

example, Amazon's price-to-earnings (P/E) ratio once stood at more than 80:1 – three times higher than the P/E ratio of the S&P 500.

In addition, Chinese internet SMEs universally yielded a good return for advanced venture capitalists. For example, IDG – as a result of EachNet's acquisition by eBay and 3721's acquisition by Yahoo! – gained a rich return on its investment in the Chinese internet industry in 2003. Furthermore, QQ, one of IDG's investments, is making RMB0.5 billion profit annually. The listing information of some of the famous website SMEs, like DangDang – a Beijing-based retailer that sells more than 300,000 different Chinese books, CDs, DVDs and computer games online – stimulates the e-commerce concept.[13] The generous investment from overseas venture capitalists has spurred the venture-backed websites to spend money more audaciously. The total budget for Alibaba is US$49 million although it made profits of only RMB100 million.[14] The budget includes the US$12 million for its Taobao enterprise and US$37 million for the software research centre.[15] Alibaba's goal in 2004 was to make a profit of RMB10 million per day; in 2005, the company decided to make great efforts to reach RMB10 billion in revenue per day.[16]

Although VC is stimulating the market, the competition of Chinese domestic e-commerce SMEs has let people see its potential. Having obtained VC, Joyo began a price war with DangDang. The competition to distribute for only RMB1 pushes the war into increased intensity.

With such investment, the elimination game in the whole market has begun. Taobao lasted only six months before falling under the advertisement war and was forced out of the market by its opponent EachNet. EachNet signed an exclusive contract with DangDang and Tom.com, which prescribed that those firms could not put any advertisement or send any sales promotion to EachNet's competitors; doing so would be regarded as breach of contract. EachNet's competitors included Taobao, Yabuy, Ebid and Guaweb; Yahoo! Auction were, thus, effectively excluded.

Internet development in China

There are three problems for the Chinese domestic internet-based SMEs that need to be solved. Firstly, malignant competition exists in the same sector with similar profit-making models. The CEOs of

---

[13] DangDang Online: www.dangdang.com
[14] *Alibaba: The Biggest Private Equity Investment*, Thousand Dragon Online: www.qianlong.com 18 February 2004.
[15] *The Foundation of Internet Business* Alibaba Online: http://china.alibaba.com 30 Setpember 2004.
[16] *The War of E-Commerce* eNet Online: www.enet.com.cn 19 Feburary 2004.

NetEase and Shanda entered the list of rich men quietly depending on the online game. After that, it seems that everyone sobered up and focused on product exploration, cooperation and copyright. The sector has developed its own strong specialist competition and there is an active trend towards different forms of competition. This situation should arouse professionals' interest.

Secondly, new ideas for development should be explored and researched as soon as possible. Through collaborative analysis of the internet's development, it is not difficult to understand that there are other factors, besides good content, for a website that can generate profits, such as 'building network platforms' and 'springing internet users'. Business exploration of the internet is inseparable from network platforms. Dredging games, chat rooms, message boards and advertisement market sectors based on the internet are the new focus for attention and the application of effort by network platforms. At the same time, the expansion of new business happens to correspond to the demand of internet users. Therefore, during the business expansion phase, the CEOs of websites need to concentrate on the two points mentioned above to cultivate internet users' loyalty. The internet is not only a new industry; it is also a technology and application. As such, effective cooperation with traditional industry will be the best course of action for both to gain profits.

A third point to consider is the role of the internet in society's development process. The role of the internet *per se* is not a single one but a synthesis of numerous roles. As a new type of media, the internet provides people with abundant information and instant interaction. From a technological perspective it enhances work efficiency, while for the entertainment sector, it has opened up new types of entertainment, such as the online gaming, broadband film and television. The degree to which the internet has improved development depends on the role and life orientation endowed upon it by its users. It is certain that, in the future, the internet will become a daily necessity for users.

The development of the internet has been compared to a long-distance runner just starting its journey. After five, ten, and then 50 years' growth, the internet revolution will have profound impacts on various aspects of Chinese society and life. The change that the internet has instigated for Chinese users is obvious; browsing the internet for news, sending and receiving e-mail and searching for useful information is only the beginning of what internet technology applications can offer. Broadband for the family, the representative of new generation networks, is spreading through Chinese internet builders' hands, which will exhibit a clear blueprint for free time internet lifestyles for Chinese and foreign users alike.

It could be said that internet development in China must be unique because there is no other country that accounts for a quarter of the global population, but the development of the internet industry should not be independent of planning, layout and management.

QQ: The number one Chinese instant messenger

Tencent's creation

'Don't call me, QQ me!' a lively penguin said on a flash picture; this is a popular advertisement in the world of network. Now, there are many ramifications with the penguin symbol to be sold in notable places on some famous Chinese websites, such as Sina.com. This penguin is a record holder for the Chinese domestic internet industry with the largest number of registered users (320 million[17]), largest number of active users (92 million[18]), largest number of online users at the same time (7 million[19]) and the highest daily advertisement display (1 billion[20]). This is QQ, the main product of Tencent Technology Limited. Tencent, currently one of China's biggest instant messaging and mobile services companies, posted an operating profit of RMB322.2 million and revenue of RMB735 million in 2003 and has approximately 600 employees.[21]

QQ, the adherent of ICQ ('I Seek You') internet beep pager (BP) machine, is engaged in an international lawsuit with ICQ. Because of this connection, QQ, previously named OICQ, has accounted for more than 95 per cent of China's market and stands third in the world of ICQ products.[22] Also, in the near future, QQ symbols will be embedded into electronic machines, such as video compact discs (VCDs), DVD players, televisions and even the newest mobile phone produced by famous foreign manufacturers. Shenzhen, the current location of Tencent's headquarters, is well known as the rapidly developing commercial city that is located just across the border from Hong Kong, which many consider to be one of China's most important gateways to the outside world.

---

[17] *Tencent QQ Leads Chinese Instant Messengers* QQ Online: www.qq.com, 18 September 2004.
[18] *Sina Acquired LanmaUC* eNet Online: www.enet.com.cn, 17 May 2004.
[19] *Tencent QQ Leads Chinese Instant Messengers* QQ Online: www.tencent.com, 18 September 2004.
[20] *QQ Customer Online Ad Statistic* WideNet Online: www.zsonline.com, 31 August 2001.
[21] *Tencent's Flotation Would Make Ma Huateng As a Billionaire* World Executive Institute Ltd Online: www.icxo.com, 9 June 2004.
[22] Tencent Online: www.qq.com.

Tencent's dominant market share in the instant messaging industry in China and its comparatively cheap offer price made it much favoured among investors. It made a big splash on the Hong Kong market and its IPO, which was arranged by Goldman Sachs, was 158 times oversubscribed. When the stock started trading on 16 June 2004, the price jumped 12 per cent, and its volume of almost 440 million shares made it the second most-traded stock on the Hong Kong Stock Exchange. By 18 June, however, it had already given up most of its gains and sank below the threshold of HK$4, close to its listing price of HK$3.70.[23] Tencent raised about US$199 million.[24]

The first step

QQ is an instant messaging service product that allows users to write to each other on computers, mobile phones and pagers. The inventors of instant messaging service products are three young Israelis. They invented ICQ in 1996 and in 1998, AOL bought the product for US$287 million[25] when its registered users numbered 12 million or more. Today, there are over 100 million ICQ users worldwide. ICQ's main markets are in the US and Europe, but it is becoming the biggest instant messaging service system around the world.

Ma Huateng and his college friend, Zhang Zhidong, set up Tencent in 1998. At that time, Tencent was simply a newly established small company in Shenzhen that provided value-added software and systems integration services and strode forward aggressively. The owners were six youths who were full of enthusiasm to carve out a niche of their own. The rudiments of QQ were invented in 1999; after investment rejections by several companies, including Guangdong Telecom, QQ was offered as a free service on Tencent's own website. When the owners found that there were more than 100 users online simultaneously, they felt surprised and then pleased. Due to the increasing number of users, they had to contribute around half of the firm's running costs to pay for the RMB2000 of servers' service charges, without making any profit. Luckily, they did not give up at this tough time. At this time, there were many similar products, such as PICQ, TICQ, CICQ, GICQ, which are all followers of ICQ. Furthermore, Sina.com had its own Sina BP. Sohu, Netease and Yahoo! provided a similar service. There was no Chinese version of ICQ in 1999. Tencent never knew that it would

---

[23] Einhorn B, *Fear and Fascination in Cyber China* Online Asia, Business Week Online: www.businessweekasia.com, 21 June 2004.
[24] Tencent Online: www.qq.com
[25] Dulles VA *The AOL/ICQ Acquisition* http://diamond-back.com/icqlies3.html, 24 October 2004.

be so dependent on QQ in the prevalent competitive environment. Three years after its foundation, Tencent started to make profits.

Financing from venture capitalists

Ma Huateng, the president and CEO of Tencent, was refused loans by banks and domestic investors because regulations made it impossible for them to provide loans for businesses other than registered users. Providing loans for fixed capital was forbidden. Ma insisted that the value of Tencent would be in the future but not the present. Finally, IDG and Pacific Century CyberWorks Ltd (PCCW) each invested US$1.1 million but only in 1999 after Tencent had amended its business plan six times. The precondition was that the number of registered users should more than 4 million; however, in the first six months of 2000, Tencent's user base had exceeded 40 million.[26] The speed at which users increased could not be forecast even by those in the industry.

In June 2001, MIH, the subsidiary company of the South African media group Naspers Ltd, was involved in a buyout of 46.5 per cent of the share capital, which was equal to US$320 million that time.[27] Before the joint venture, the founders owned a 60 per cent stake, with 20 per cent each held by PCCW and IDG. Now Tencent is owned by the South African-based media group Naspers with a 46.5 per cent stake, while a further 46.5 per cent of the company is owned by its founders and a group of Chinese entrepreneurs. The remaining 7 per cent belongs to IDG.[28]

All the evidence shows that ICQ regrets that it lost out on the huge Chinese market. To remedy this loss it accused QQ of encroaching on its rights because the name of QQ at that time was OICQ. The name of OICQ had, however, been registered at the National Industry and Commercial Registering Bureau. This lawsuit will continue for at least the next five years, although Tencent changed the company name from OICQ to its nickname of QQ.[29] Changing names will not change the market share. As long as Tencent does not appear to be defeated by its problems, it will be difficult for competitors to lure users away from OICQ(QQ). QQ has become established as China's most popular

---

[26] Mu G *IM Software: The Seaman in the Internet Epoch* Space Online: www.yesky.com, 27 September 2004.
[27] Vanek M *Naspers to Offer Tencent* Moneyweb Online: www.moneyweb.co.za, 5 December 2003.
[28] Qiu W 'Ma Huateng's personal fortune accessed to RMB 900M because of Tencent's IPO' *21st Century Economy Report* 17 June 2004.
[29] Yu F *The Changing Face Enigma: The OICQ Changed to QQ* CCID Consulting, 9 September 2004.

service due to its powerful functionality, ease of use and security. Now, only Tencent is widely recognised as the professional instant messaging service provider in Mainland China.

QQ's personalized character lies behind its success. It provides a unique internet-based service where users can select a number of different ways to communicate, build relationships and browse the internet using a comprehensive and user-friendly software client. For example, Tencent designed the lively colourful head portrait (which is brown when it is offline); whenever the users change their machines, they will find information about QQ because Tencent has put the information in the server. Such detail shows the essence of QQ's quality: simple but carefully and meticulously designed. The current Yahoo! Messenger and MSN Messenger have both taken on board the merits of QQ.

New business model

It could be said that Tencent is technically a derivative, but there was no business model for QQ to copy from ICQ. AOL does not depend on ICQ to make profits, rather it is simply a free service for AOL's users. The difference for Tencent is that they need the money.

Advertising on QQ was the first money-making method adopted. Tencent was the first service provider in the world to advertise 'ICQ products' – a method that ICQ learned from QQ after several months. It was unimaginable for any websites to conceive of a display capacity of 100 million users per day and a 1 million click quantity daily.[30] Advertising companies do business with Tencent monthly, because they can afford the advertisement fee by display or click quantity due to such high usage. QQ's click and display quantity made it the biggest carrier of China's internet advertisements.

The second idea was to operate jointly with telecommunications carriers; Tencent was the first internet company to do this. BP carrier was the first collaborator with Tencent, but BP service is a unilateral one. How could communication among people be unilateral? Communication should surely be bidirectional.

Next, Tencent engaged in a project with China Mobile. Wireless and fixed-line value-added services provide instant messaging services between QQ and mobile phone or other terminal devices.[31] Mobile QQ is the first and most popular mobile instant messaging service and wireless data service in China. Mobile QQ allows the customer's PC-based instant messaging service to become integrated seamlessly with

---

[30] *QQ Customer Online Ad Statistic* WideNet Online: www.zsonline.com, 31 August 2001.
[31] QQ Online: www.tencent.com

his/her mobile phone, permitting the customer to stay in touch with PC or mobile-based contacts from just about anywhere. Tencent has maintained a leading position in scale and functional features such as Feichang QQ Nannv, 12586 online entertainment, QQ whisper, QQ gas station, application for QQ numbers via mobile phone or IVR, ringtones and picture downloads, DIY SMS, SMS subscription and news services. Mobile QQ is available on China Mobile and China Unicom's networks across all major provinces in China.

Tencent's mobile network coverage for its wireless data services is the most extensive in China. Tencent's current suite of mobile services offers some of the following functions[32]:

- sending instant messages between mobile phones and PCs seamlessly;
- receipt of messages sent to user's PC-based QQ client remotely on a mobile phone;
- checking the presence status of other QQ online contacts to verify if they are online and available for instant communication;
- profile information on other QQ subscribers and potential contacts delivered to user's mobile phone.

Tencent's third profit-making approach was to let agents conduct the brand's derivative business. Three years ago, Tencent licensed its penguin logo to a Guangzhou private dress company for an unusually high price. The agency right was contracted for a year. In addition to the agency licence fee, Tencent deducts a percentage from sales. People's high regard for the Tencent penguin is one of sentimental preference. Many people open QQ as they start work in the office or their study at home. Gradually, the penguin is endowed with human feelings. Soon, there will be a chain of new unified Tencent penguin shops and a cartoon that stars the QQ penguin may be shown on television in the near future, which will make huge profits for the brand owners.

At present, the profits from mobiles and other electronic products are tiny for both foreign and domestic manufacturers. Such manufacturers would like to cooperate with Tencent to exploit their added value. Tencent is also looking for a new field beyond the PC terminal because the QQ service is almost free, except to a few paying users. But now, it seems that a new series of popular services by QQ are emerging, such as QQ super boy and girl: these are special update QQ products for supporting more friends on the contact list of one account (200 as

---

[32] ibid.

opposed to 50. QQ mailer has found new terminals: for example, mobile telephones and television.

Unless extensive expansion has been planned, Tencent does not, at present, have any financial difficulties. Its management team insists that venture capitalists play by their rules; for example, they won't allow venture capitalists to take part in the day-to-day operation of the company.

Tencent has in-house regulations for cost control. Whatever the circumstances, the company won't pay for commercial advertisements. Every kind of cost application has to be pre-qualified by a 10 times projected return. Tencent do not provide land lines or distance calling services for staff because they require that all employees use QQ as their communication tool for contacting headquarters and corporate branches. However, maintaining a system that has more than 1.8 million people online at any one time requires money to support the telecom carriers' operations. Increasing business volume by 800,000 registered users per day requires that Tencent puts one double central processing unit (CPU) and 1GB RAM into its servers costing more than RMB70,000 per day. The huge cost of more than RMB1 million per month has put pressure on Tencent to introduce fee-paying membership.[33] Now, the registered fee for QQ is RMB2–20 per month payable via mobile, ChinaVnet, Xiaolingtong, the 168 services of China Telecom or by credit card.

Enterprise QQ with IBM

Enterprise Service is a real-time communication solution designed to enhance efficiency and reduce communication cost within an enterprise, as well as between enterprises and customers. Real Time eXpert (RTX) is the first core product launched; Tencent is in the early stages of commercializing this service.

Tencent launched RTX, the enterprise version of QQ, in October 2003 and then immediately unveiled a surprise partnership with IBM to crack the enterprise market. As a result, Tencent RTX will be sold to IBM corporate clients. Tencent's Enterprise messaging head, Shen Weibiao, and IBM software development president, Lin Hongyi, have indicated that Tencent and IBM plan to work together beyond Tencent RTX.[34]

However, many people regard QQ as merely an entertainment tool; consequently, it will be very difficult for Tencent to succeed in the

---

[33] Qiu W 'Ma Huateng's personal fortune accessed to RMB 900M because of Tencent's IPO' *21st Century Economy Report* 17 June 2004.
[34] QQ Online: www.tencent.com

serious enterprise level market. Nevertheless, the real aim of Tencent is obviously to provide virtual services through an enterprise version of QQ.

Tencent still exercises the power of denying free registration, which is a serious drawback for users. Unfortunately, if Tencent cannot let its product differ from those of competitors or maintain its own customer appeal and originality, then Windows/MSN Messenger is likely to take possession of the Chinese instant messaging market. Although users will incur a cost for a changeover, rivals like Microsoft know how to secure sales, while Tencent makes small mistakes in its business profit strategies. Thus, anything is possible. In such a rapidly changing market, Tencent could fall from grace without rhyme or reason, as its adversaries did before.

To date, Tencent has established a web portal to help it compete in a market that is home to some of the world's best performing stocks. Its aim is to become a mainstream internet portal that focuses on entertainment. It believes that its customer base and messaging services are already moving in that direction. Tencent's entertainment portal, www.qq.com, which features flashing cartoons, banner advertisements and its penguin logo is divided into sections including not only news, entertainment, fashion, sport, games, cars, jokes and chat rooms, but also services including QQ game portal, QQ dating, QQ show, QQ home, QQ alumni, QQ E-CARD, and massively multiplayer online game (MMOG) Sephiroth, to name but a few. QQ game portal consists of board games, card games, games of skill and QQ show chat rooms. These personalized value-added services combine entertainment in vogue with communication. Sephiroth, a 3D MMOG game that Tencent licensed from Imazic of Korea, is currently one of the most popular online games in China.

IPO on the Hong Kong Stock Exchange

Since 2003, Tencent has considered joining rivals with an IPO. One of the investors, South African media group Naspers Ltd, said on December 2003 that it was considering an IPO of its Tencent joint venture in 2004. Such news pushed its share price up more than 4 per cent. Naspers said it was 'investigating the feasibility' of a Tencent IPO.[35]

In 2003, there was speculation that an IPO of Tencent held sometime in 2004 could raise anywhere between US$100 million and US$200 million, with some analysts even predicting that it could raise up to US$2 billion! This would mean a significant return on investment

---

[35] *Tencent Considers Nasdaq IPO* Datamonitor Online: www.datamonitor.com, 10 December 2003.

for Nasper's stake, which it bought for US$34 million. The US$2 billion, half of that for Naspers, represents approximately 25 rand per Naspers' share. This potential was the factor behind a 4.3 per cent rise in Naspers in Johannesburg to a new year high of 42.75 rand, building on gains of 5 per cent after it announced its consideration of a Tencent IPO.[36]

By floating, Tencent joined the listings of a number of its local rivals. Tencent's dominant market share in the instant messaging industry in China and comparatively cheap offer price made it highly favoured among investors on 16 June 2004 when it finally floated in Hong Kong. Tencent sold its IPO shares, raising US$199 million, with the offer price P/E ratio at 14.8 times on forecast earnings for 2004 of at least RMB444 million (US$53.6 million) based on Tencent's announcement of 2004 half-year results. According to Tencent company sources, more than half of its revenues comes from providing games, news and other services to mobile phone users in China. Shares in Tencent closed at HK$4.15 on 16 June 2004 (US$0.532), hitting a high of HK$4.625 (US$0.593) earlier in the day[37] as the second most actively traded share on Hong Kong Stock Exchange's main board.

In fact, the good prospects of Tencent for investors were apparent at its issue. Tencent reported that its public offer was 158 times oversubscribed, with international placement significantly oversubscribed, suggesting that investors haven't lost their appetites for select Chinese IPOs. The overwhelming demand for the offering triggered a 'clawback' mechanism, which increased the number of shares in the Hong Kong public offer to about 50 per cent of the total. Table 3.3 shows Tencent's IPO information in detail.

Being in the same field of business operations as online service providers, Tencent's successful listing in Hong Kong provided a 'push' for those ISPs, such as KongZhong Corp (KongZhong) and China Asia United Telecom Network Corp (ChinaAUTNC). KongZhong applied for an IPO to the US Securities and Exchange Commission (SEC) on 4 June 2004 and hoped to raise more than US$100 million. Its initial prospectus, however, didn't include the number of shares to be placed, the number of shares on public offer or the scheduled share price. ChinaAUTNC became one of the multiple internet bar enterprises on March 2004, which is also interested in listing on NASDAQ.

Listing has not only increased sharply Ma Huateng's personal assets, but also provides an opportunity for cashback on the stock

---

[36] 'Tencent IPO bid to seek US$1.5 billion' *The Standard*, Global China Group, 4 April 2004.
[37] Feng D *Tencent's Management Team Won't Cash Out Within 2004* ChinaByte Online: www.chinabyte.com, 17 June 2004.

Table 3.3 Tencent's IPO information

Tencent Holdings Limited (Code 0700)			
Date of listing	16 June 2004	Market	Hong Kong Stock Exchange (Main Board)
IPO price	HK$2.77/3.70	Offer price	HK$3.7
Major shareholder(s)	MIH QQ (BVI) Limited		
No. of placing shares	420,160,500	No. of public offer shares	42,016,000
Nominal value	HK$ 0.0001	Weighted average P/E	0.000
Adjusted net asset value per share	n/a		
Global coordinator	Goldman Sachs (Asia) LLC		
Sponsor and lead manager	Goldman Sachs (Asia) LLC		
Co-lead manager	n/a Co-manager n/a Co-sponsors n/a		
Underwriters	Goldman Sachs (Asia) LLC, The Hongkong and Shanghai Banking Corporation Limited (HSBC)		
Legal advisors to the underwriters	Freshfields Bruckhaus Deringer, Haiwen & Partners, Shearman & Sterling LLP		
Receiving bankers	Bank of China (Hong Kong) Limited		
Lot size	1000	Market cap	HK$6218 million
Public offer/placing (%)	10.00	Annual dividend yield (%)	0.000
Diluted P/E	0.000	Adjusted net tangible asset value per share	HK$1.17

exchange. Ma, the President and CEO of Tencent, whose personal assets are valued at more than RMB700 million, can cash out for HK$180 million because his personally owned company, Advance Date Services Limited, holds 14.43 per cent of the shares in Tencent. Other top members of the senior management team also saw their stocks rise from Tencent's IPO. Tencent's prospectus and related information identifies 12 enriched individuals, including Ma. Tencent Holdings Limited shareholders consist of 12 natural persons and one artificial person, who together account for 50 per cent of the shares. Following Tencent's IPO, 12 natural person shareholders own at least HK$175 million worth of shares at book asset value, including the five main founder members, Ma Huateng, Zhang Zhidong, Zeng Liqing, Xu Chenye and Chen Yidan.

The listing of Tencent resulted in at least five people becoming billionaires and another seven, multimillionaires. Tencent's prospectus shows that Zhang Zhidong, the company's chief technology officer, is one of the two executive directors and responsible for special technology R&D. Zhang is the sole owner of Best Update Internal Limited, which holds a 6.43 per cent stake in Tencent and can cash out HK$80 million.[38] The other three main founders' shareholders' holdings are unknown because the prospectus doesn't identify shareholdings of less than 5 per cent. Zeng, Xu and Chen are all aged around 30 and hold the positions of Chief Operations Officer, Chief Information Officer and Chief Administration Officer respectively.

The threat from competitors to Tencent's main product

Currently, Tencent is surrounded by an ocean of hidden competitors. The strongest rivals are not AOL but MSN/Windows Messenger (MSN) and Windows Messenger. Windows/MSN Messenger is part of the Windows platform, such as 2000 and XP, and allows users to communicate instantly with co-workers, friends and family all around the world right from their computers. With Windows/MSN Messenger, users can communicate using text, voice and video, while their productivity is enhanced even more with the ability to share applications or a whiteboard. Windows/MSN Messenger gives users control over with whom to talk and when, by blocking specific users, to view the typing status of 'buddies', and to decide who to add to their contact list. Windows/MSN Messenger is the instant messaging client of choice for businesses in managed environments with connectivity to exchange instant messaging servers and session initiation protocol (SIP) based instant messaging servers, along with connectivity to the MSN service.

Instant messaging is only one of the functions of Windows/MSN Messenger. Microsoft wants not only the market that is occupied by QQ in China, but is also looking for an approach to change the current market situation of instant messengers worldwide. The Dot-Net strategy of Microsoft is to explore internet operating systems so that all of the international electronic information can be supported by Microsoft's operating systems. At present in China, in order to add a friend to your contact list, it is necessary to update a telephone number, QQ number and MSN user name, each being vital contact information. To stay in line with other IM providers, QQ is also striving to provide its customers with more and more services.

The Vnet Instant Messenger (VIM), a newly developed instant messenger software from China Telecom, was launched commercially at the start of 2004. In the plans of China Telecom, VIM will be not only a simple instant messenger, but also a value-added service

---

[38] Qiu W 'Ma Huateng's personal fortune accessed to RMB 900M because of Tencent's IPO' *21st Century Economy Report* 17 June 2004.

platform, which brings the fictitious internet operators together to provide such services as internet telephone, audio, video, e-mail and future 3G to build the functions of management and collaboration in a company internally. VIM forms an outstanding individual communication platform to compete with ambitious video service providers (VSPs). Thus, it seems highly likely that VIM will be a strong competitor for QQ.

Many Chinese value-added service providers are experimenting with virtual services such as Honglian95, Runxun and Zhongqi Networks, which already have licenses for commercial experimentation in this new sector. A telecommunications expert thinks that MSN and Tencent are very close now to VSPs. MSN and QQ have so many users that, when MSN and Tencent transform into VSPs, they will be much stronger than any of the other value-added service providers and, thus, more likely to become the strongest competitors for China Telecom.

The operators of VIM have claimed that individual exploration of instant messenger tools and systems is not different for telecommunications carriers. The potential threat from China Mobile and China Unicom is also worth heeding. With a binding personal mobile communication terminal and the appearance of basic platforms for wireless internet value-added service, China Mobile and China Unicom spread their own instant messenger system easily for the benefit of their existing huge number of customers. The commission from Mobile QQ is the most important source of profit for QQ and Tencent. Mobile carriers operating their self instant messenger will definitely affect Tencent's revenue. China Telecom can also enforce a restrictive policy, such as forbidding QQ to pass its ADSL.

Under the pressure from the telecom carriers, the management team of Tencent is carrying out preparations on two fronts. At the same time as looking for a win-win result with contact telecom carriers on Tencent's own initiative, the company is engaging in a public relations campaign aimed at the authorities to protect its benefits by a governmental policy of strongly restricting the action of telecom carriers.

On the other hand, the restriction of advertisements, cold calling, virus inrush, chargeable functions (such as QQ membership, making friends and increasing speeds for video chatting) and the inhibition of amusing entertainment images during usage of the working position function have been a secret worry for QQ and Tencent, causing them deep concern. With bigger differences in customers' income, culture and age levels, the requirement from customers for QQ has become more complex, forcing QQ to increase the number of its functions by giving more attention to the details in its interface. However, by following such a policy, the orientation of QQ becomes more opaque.

At the same time, it seems that QQ has thrown its efforts into the wrong area. Every kind of group feels that there are some special needs that could not be satisfied and that many unnecessary functions exist. The search for a better performing instant messenger service has been the reason why those customers who pay more attention to convenience and practicality are leaving QQ.

Until the end of 2003, the most frequently used instant messenger was QQ, which accounted for a 74.3 per cent market share. MSN took 11.23 per cent and NetEase Popo held 4 per cent.[39] However, no-one suspected the potential threats to QQ from MSN from the monopoly status of Microsoft's software and their great efforts to explore the Chinese market. Currently, Microsoft cannot enter the telecom value-added services business because the Chinese government is strictly auditing foreign investment in the telecommunications sector. Once the Chinese authorities unleash the restrictions on foreign manufacturers in this sector, MSN will have a heavy impact on QQ. There is no need for pessimism, however, because the present advantage of QQ is still clear. If it had a single pure application software, Microsoft could annihilate its adversary easily with free-binding, such as Internet Explorer and Realplayer. However, Microsoft is not ready to replace an instant messenger, such as QQ, because of the high cost, strong customer loyalty and the closed link with users. Furthermore, it seems that Microsoft does not have a plan to develop its internet and instant communication activities in Mainland China, which is not its core business.

NetEase announced that the registered users of Popo exceed 10 million per month. Although such a number does not increase its ranking in the market, it has threatened QQ's place. Depending on the resource advantage of portal websites and free texts for mobiles, and adding on the technological guarantee of the R&D team headed up by Ding Lei, the impact on the future instant communication market is apparent.

On the very day of the QQ's IPO, internet giant Yahoo! went live commercially with its new instant communication software, Yahoo! Messenger 6.0 (Chinese Version). As the leading updated version in the first non-English speaking countries and with a two-month lead over the other 20 counties, the emergence of Yahoo! Messenger 6.0 (Chinese Version) indicated Yahoo's emphasis on the Chinese market. Yahoo! Messenger 6.0 (Chinese Version) claimed it would not consider introducing charges within two to three years and would not show any advertisements in Yahoo's promised service. Otherwise, Yahoo! Messenger 6.0 (Chinese Version) bound itself to a self-writing messenger function for users to send SMS to mobiles free of charge, which is

---

[39] iResearch Associates *An Online Survey on China Instant Messenger Market*, iResearch Inc, 15 March 2004.

obviously aimed at QQ as the only service to adopt charging among instant messengers in Mainland China.

Tencent's next gold strike: value-added service and online games

In its stock market prospectus, Tencent predicted spending HK$818 million on its new business strategy – on aspects of instant messaging, entertainment and new internet operations – and putting HK$250 million to strengthen other current business expansion. Up to the first quarter of 2004, instant messenging and entertainment accounted for 96.1 per cent of Tencent's general revenue. According to Tencent's 2003 financial report, it is apparent that Tencent is not short of money; according to the company's sources, its profits were RMB107.3 million in the first quarter of 2004, a rise of 87 per cent compared with the same period of 2003. Based on such figures, Tencent would make a net profit of RMB444 million for the year. Even if it were not listed in Hong Kong, Tencent has the power to carry out M&A and business expansion activity. Why, therefore, did Tencent persist in its IPO and how will it use the HK$818 million?

M&A is inevitable for Tencent. Only through operating a series of M&A ventures after exhausting financing channels, can Tencent have the strength to compete with internet giants Microsoft and Yahoo! At present, the main profit of Tencent could be separated to three parts: internet value-added services (IVS, including QQ member service, community service, game and entertainment services etc), mobile and communication value-added services (MCVS) including mobile QQ, chatting, SMS ringtones etc) and internet advertising. As a result of a decrease in the MCVS profit proportion and an increase in the IVS profit proportion, exploration of new opportunities for IVS has become a necessary focus for action.

Deployment of the IPO funding will involve e-commerce and music value-added services. In the near future, following the IPO, Tencent will develop in two directions. First, it is uniting its own information resource as Yahoo! Messenger to form more modules in the QQ platform and combine the qq.com's website information into QQ, and will eventually become the biggest internet community nationally, classified geographically. While the internet community retains the large and regular users, Tencent will show itself as a player and pitch its goal as becoming the DangDang and Taobao in the field of e-commerce in order to channel e-trade through its website. Second, Tencent would like to follow Shanda's model with the aid of its QQ platform to expand its online game players. Tencent has built an R&D team of online games to include more than 100 people. In addition to its former small entertainment game, Tencent decided to go commercial with a large online game and would possibly use its substantial funds to acquire a suitable online game research institute.

Confronting the competition and unpredictable future change, Tencent is continuing to mine users' demand alongside the instant messenger. From August 2003 to August 2004, QQ game, Tencent's entertainment online game (EOG) platform, attracted more than 630,000 concurrent players.[40] With the highest number of concurrent users per day and average online users, the QQ game has overrun its rivals and has taken the lead in EOG. The current EOG market, however, cannot be equated with the former instant messenger market because QQ does not have any monopoly advantage in customers' channels. In addition to QQ, Tencent has recently released Tencent Messenger (TM) for young professionals and a multipage browser Tencent Traveler (TT). Furthermore, Tencent's EOGs do not have special merits. With QQ, the function of EOG will be increased. Tencent's objective is to become a game web portal.

Tencent's peak performance depends on QQ's startling and explosive increase. The products are still there, but markets are no longer the same. QQ and Tencent are experiencing a change in roles from the situation of outshining others several years ago to the current one of market fragmentation by rivals.

3721: The power of Chinese characters on the internet

3721's technology standard

Founded in 1998, Beijing-based 3721 Technology Co Ltd (3721/Beijing 3721) – China's leading e-mail and online real name search engine service provider, (with internationalized domain names in the Chinese alphabet) – has more than 450,000 corporate users every day.[41] Most portals, such as Sina and Sohu, apply such technology to their search engines. 3721's sales network has extended to more than 20 major cities in the country. While 3721.com's Chinese language service reaches 60 million web surfers,[42] such an achievement justifies 3721's claim that 90 per cent of Chinese internet users employ its services.[43]

The seven-year-old firm's flagship search service allows users to type and input Chinese characters directly into the browser address

---

[40] QQ Online: www.tencent.com
[41] Wang H 'Coming out the marketing misunderstanding' *CIW Weekly* 14 June 2004.
[42] '3721 seeks overseas listings' *China Business Weekly* 31 August 2003.
[43] 3721 Online: www.3721.com

line to find information, instead of typing in URLs and domain names in English. Thus, there is no need for users with poor English to remember web addresses for search sites such as Google, Baidu or the portal websites, such as Sina. China has become the world's second largest internet market in terms of users, with nearly 80 million people jumping online.[44] If this trend continues, SMEs must design features to capture a portion of this growing sector. 3721 makes nearly all of its money from charging 150,000 websites a basic fee of US$60 for inclusion on its search engine.[45] Sites can pay as much as US$600 for a premium placement, while 150,000 governmental, educational and non-profit websites are listed for free.[46] The service reached 90 per cent of China's internet users, or 68 million people at the end of June 2003.[47] By October 2003, 3721 had 4000 agents and 300,000 business customers.[48]

Another service allows users to set up an e-mail forwarding address composed of a few Chinese characters for use with their Roman-letter accounts. That service was introduced in August 2003. Such innovations in providing Sino-centric services on the internet have been key to 3721's success.

During this period of growth, 3721 has forged a technological alliance with 3721 Network Software Co (3721 NSC), which is incorporated in Hong Kong. 3721 NSC was acquired by Yahoo! at the end of 2003. The *China Daily* issue of 22 November 2003[49] carried the story as a major headline, reporting that 'US internet giant Yahoo! made another stride towards tapping the potential of the world's most populous market with the acquisition of a leading Chinese software development company, 3721'. The negotiations between Yahoo! and 3721 came about as the Internet Corporation for Assigned Names and Numbers, the net's supervising body, was deciding whether to add suffixes in non-Roman character sets to its domain name database. People can surf the web using different languages, but site addresses must currently end in a Roman-language suffix such as .com or .org.

In brief, 3721's business involves selling Chinese-language keywords for Roman-alphabet domain names to help local internet users find websites more easily and efficiently. The company sells software that people can install into a web browser to access the Chinese

---

[44] *13th China Internet Development Situation Statistics Report*, China Internet Network Information Centre (CNNIC), January 2004.
[45] *3721 Claimed that it will List Abroad and Raise for More than RMB300 Million*, Unifytruth, Sohu IT, 21 August 2003.
[46] '3721 seeks overseas listings' *China Business Weekly* 31 August 2003.
[47] 3721 Online: www.3721.com
[48] *3721 Expands its Business*, Beijing Yitianrising Technology Co Ltd, 7 November 2003.
[49] *Yahoo Acquires Leading 3721* People's Daily Online: www.people.com.cn

keyword service. This means that a Chinese company can maintain its brand when local web users either search for the name of the company or type in the company's web address. 3721 charges US$115 a year for 'specific' keywords, such as company and product names, and US$1,300 a year for 'generic' keywords, such as categories or broad industry names, for example, 'laptops' or 'restaurants'.[50] Web users can download browser software to accept Chinese language keyword inputs; Chinese language web portals should support 3721 keywords.

Selling search-related services has been a priority for Yahoo! Earlier in 2003 the company bought Inktomi's web search business for US$235 million[51] and then bought the private search company Overture Services for US$1.63 billion[52] – two deals aimed at generating more revenue from search activity.

Investment attracted from two venture capitalists

In April 2002, shortly after accepting VC investment from US-based IDG, 3721 aroused the interest of the investment company JAFCO Co Ltd, a leading global VC firm that was focusing on a balanced investment strategy in the IT sector. JAFCO invested almost US$10 million of registered capital into 3721.com, and will invest another US$100 million in the Chinese market in the near future.[53]

JAFCO Co Ltd, the parent company of JAFCO Asia, was established in 1973 and went public on the Japanese over-the-counter (OTC) market in 1987. It was listed on the Tokyo Stock Exchange in January 2003 and is currently the largest VC firm in Japan, with an aggregate of approximately US$3 billion under management worldwide. It operates seven branches in Japan with more than 100 investment professionals and its investment focus ranges from IT venture investments, non-technology VC investments and management buyouts to biotechnology investments. International venture capitalists have a lot of faith in this emerging Chinese industry.[54] JAFCO has confidence in 3721 and is confident of making a profit from the investment.

Zhou Hongyi, 3721's chairman and president, attributed the company's success in attracting the world's top two investment companies within two months at a time when most venture capitalists were withdrawing from the world market, to their universal and simplistic search capabilities. 3721 ensures that all Chinese companies can be

---

[50] 3721 Online: www.3721.com
[51] Baertlein L *Ask Jeeves Rekindles Web-search Merger Talk* Reuters, 29 May 2003.
[52] *Yahoo! Search Engine Analysis* SEO Logic Online: www.seologic.com
[53] *IDG Prospers in China Tech* The Deal.com The Deal LLC: www.thedeal.com, 3 December 2003.
[54] JAFCO Ventures Online: www.jafco.com

searched for on the internet simply by typing the key words of the company's name or brand in Chinese characters or Pinyin on the address bar of the explorer. It also promotes a strengthened software package designed to provide timely information services.

With the help of the software, Chinese internet surfers will be free from the frustration of searching fruitlessly for websites in English. Once the free software is downloaded by internet users from 3721's home page or its associate websites, users should find it easy to use Chinese or Pinyin to search for what they need.

Most companies spend a large amount of money building up their websites, but their contents are often unsatisfying. According to Zhou, the company's software package allows enterprises to get the most out of the internet, giving them widespread promotion of their brands as well as further promotion of their e-business. In Zhou's words when interviewed: '3721 has never positioned itself to be a broad and big internet service provider. Instead, 3721 devotes itself to carrying out technology research to further improve its services to enterprises'.[55]

There is a famous saying in the IT industry that echoes Zhou's remarks: 'top level enterprises define sector standards, those at the second level focus on brands and those at the bottom levels can just sell products'. This principle is gradually being recognized and accepted by Chinese IT companies, which have discovered the importance of standards and are pressing for them. Datang Telecom Group is one of the fastest growing IT companies in China due to its TD-CDMA[56] whose standard is recognized as one of the three international 3G telecoms technology standards, together with the European WCDMA[57] and the US CDMA2000.

---

[55] Shun Feng, Zhou Hongyi's Operation Strategy, URL: http://www.cinet.cn, 20 June 2005

[56] There has been an enormous amount of market hype recently around the proposed 802.16 standard, commonly known as WiMAX. Beyond the hype, however, another standard has quietly emerged as the leading standard in the global next-generation broadband wireless market. This standard is TD-CDMA, also known as UMTS TDD. TD-CDMA actually already delivers the vision that WiMAX proponents such as Intel are promising for the future. TD-CDMA performance has been proven by commercial networks that have been deployed over the last two years and the dozens of operators around the world that are already deploying TD-CDMA networks. Source: Neff DJ and Axcera *UMTS TDD versus WiMAX: Which Standard Will Rule Next-Generation Broadband Wireless?* http://axity3g.axcera.com/umts_vs_wimax.pdf

[57] WCDMA is short for wide-band CDMA (Code-Division Multiple Access), a 3G technology that increases data transmission rates in GSM systems by using the CDMA air interface instead of TDMA. WCDMA is based on CDMA and is the technology used in UMTS. WCDMA was adopted as a standard by the ITU under the name 'IMT-2000 direct spread'. Source: www.webopedia.com (The only online dictionary for computer and internet technology definitions), www.webopedia.com/TERM/W/WCDMA.html

3721's development in one of China's provinces provides an example. In 2002, with a booming economy in East China's Zhejiang Province, more and more local enterprises were seeking to establish online businesses. In July 2002, 3721 announced that it would open up a sales and technical branch in Zhejiang Province, indicating the company's intention to enter into the country's southern and eastern provinces. The move aimed to help more local enterprises join the tide of real name search engines, which would make it easier for native Chinese people to access their websites. As a result, 3721.com extended its sales network to more than 20 major cities in the country.

Yahoo!'s purchase of 3721

Yahoo! moved into the growing domain name business in Asian markets with its purchase of 3721 NSC. On 21 November 2003, Yahoo-HK and 3721 NSC announced that the two companies had signed a definitive agreement under which Yahoo-HK would purchase 3721 NSC.[58] Under the terms of the agreement, Yahoo-HK agreed to pay approximately US$120 million in cash over two years subject to certain conditions.[59] The cooperation will help Asian SMEs to reach an increasing number of consumers and will build a bridge into global markets, while at the same time supporting the continued growth of the Asian software industry. In other words, this deal could be said to signal Yahoo!'s first successful foray into the domain name registration market. It does sell domain names, but only through Yahoo! Domains Property, which is simply a facade for network solutions. Such moves have strengthened Yahoo!'s presence in the vast and rapidly-growing Chinese market as both a brand and as a search resource.

3721 NSC has become a wholly owned subsidiary of Yahoo-HK and there are no current plans to alter the management structure of either company. The transaction was subject to customary closing conditions but was completed in 2004 and gives Beijing 3721 access to Yahoo! technology, products and services.

The deal comes as talk was building in financial markets over whether several Chinese internet companies were planning to go public in the near future, including 3721 NSC, Baidu.com, Alibaba.com and Joyo.com. Company officials have said they would like to list the company on stock markets in Hong Kong or Singapore. However at present it is unclear whether 3721 and Yahoo! plan to move forward with a public offering. To be a public company helping to support 3721's

---

[58] Berniker M 'Yahoo's $120 million search finds new symbols' *ClickZ News* 21 November 2003.
[59] *Yahoo Buys Chinese Software Company* Xinhua News Agency, 24 November 2003.

growth, which is aligned to the growth of the Chinese internet industry, 3721 would prefer a listing in Singapore because the Hong Kong market is looking sluggish while the Singaporean government has been very open to China-based private firms. 3721 has the advantage that one of its backers, IDG, has had considerable experience in taking Chinese companies public in Singapore.

Post-acquisition, 3721 NSC specializes in the design of keyword search engines on the internet, while Beijing 3721 is responsible for sales. 3721 NSC is a software development company incorporated in Hong Kong and has a technological alliance with Beijing 3721 Technology, a provider of internet services in China, which operates the search engine 3721.com. 3721 NSC designs keyword search engines and bills itself as a seller of Chinese language keywords for Roman alphabet domain names. Its keywords are supported by Chinese language web portals and it has developed a range of leading and proprietary technologies that contribute to providing an enhanced user experience on the internet and help Chinese language users to move around the internet. 3721 NSC claims that 90 per cent of Chinese internet browsers use its real name service.[60] The Hong Kong-based software firm controls Beijing-based 3721, which has the same board structure as 3721 NSC; both are managed by Zhou and his wife. There is no doubt that Yahoo! and 3721 NSC will bring together innovative technologies that can improve the experience for both users and businesses in Asia.

Before the announcement made by Yahoo! and 3721, there was media speculation that 3721's price tag might be as high as US$120 million.[61] The media reports alluded to Zhou as being the source of many previous acquisition rumours. The top position at Yahoo! China has remained vacant since Cheng Hongshou left in April 2003 and Zhou was expected to assume the presidency of Yahoo! China when the transaction went through. The jewel in 3721's crown is its 300,000 strong enterprise customer base,[62] seen as a good fit for Yahoo!, which generates approximately 50 per cent of its US revenues from SMEs. In March 2004, as expected, Zhou Hongyi was appointed on a one-year contract as the new president of Yahoo! China.[63]

Yahoo!, which has been very aggressive in the search engine market with acquisitions of US-based firms in the past two years, has gained strong support to develop the SMEs market on the Chinese mainland.

---

[60] Berniker M 'Yahoo's $120 million search finds new symbols' *ClickZ News* 21 November 2003.
[61] *Yahoo Buys China Internet Firm 3721.com for 120 Million Dollars Cash* Agence France-Presse, 21 November 2003.
[62] *3721 Expands its Business* Beijing Yitianrising Technology Co Ltd, 7 November 2003.
[63] 3721 Online: www.3721.com

The US giant, which first came to China five years ago, has been developing slowly in the market. Its portal business only made US$1.64 million in its first seven months in China from online advertising, while China's biggest portal, Sina Corp, made US$20.35 million.[64] Yahoo! is, therefore, very anxious to develop the Chinese mainland market now and wants to seek a breakthrough with the 3721 NSC acquisition. However, whether Yahoo! can integrate successfully 3721 NSC's advantages of keyword and real name searches into its portal business is still an open question for the Chinese domestic internet sector. At the least, by striking the 3721 NSC deal, Yahoo! is now in the business of selling domain names in China and has established relationships in Hong Kong and Beijing. However competition is intensifying with a raft of companies, including leading internet portal Sohu.com, and search engines like Baidu and Google all trying to grab a share of the market.

Yahoo! will aim to use 3721 NSC's double-byte search technology. Unlike languages, such as English and those of other countries that use just one byte of information per word, this technology uses two bytes and so is useful for languages such as Chinese and Japanese. As a further result of this acquisition, Beijing 3721, as a noted pioneer in selling keywords in China, through its technological cooperation with 3721 NSC and its affiliates, will have access to a broad range of Yahoo! technology, products and services. Looking forward from the current situation, it can be forecast that China will have 154.4 million broadband internet users by 2007 compared with 84 million in 2004.[65] The online search market in China is growing rapidly and will be worth billions of dollars over the next few years. 3721 is the most utilized Chinese language internet directory in China. 3721 is, therefore, a comfortable fit with Yahoo!'s global strategy of beefing up its search engine business.

Included in the 3721 NSC technology portfolio is the ability to enable keyword search through the Internet Explorer browser address bar in addition to other search tool bars. In addition, 3721's double byte character technology enables non-English language based users to enter search terms in local languages. 3721 NSC's technology will complement Yahoo!'s already robust search services and enable Yahoo! to continue growing its global search strategy.

Now, the Chinese government has established new rules for registrar companies that manage internet addresses in China, such as having a minimum of RMB1 million (US$121,000) in start-up capital, at

---

[64] Berniker M 'Yahoo's $120 million search finds new symbols' *ClickZ News* 21 November 2003.
[65] Midler N *IDC Statistic* IDC, 14 October 2004.

least 15 employees and offering 24-hour customer service.[66] New Chinese internet regulations say that these firms 'must have strict and effective filtering mechanisms for cleaning bad and offensive domain names, which should be carried out once a day,' via China's Ministry of Information Industry's website, www.mii.gov.cn. In an official recognition of the rapid growth of internet usage in China, The China Internet Network Information Center, which maintains a national registry of names, said that it had at least 300,000 unique websites and adds around 10,000 new addresses every month.[67] At first, many people didn't understand the 3721.com's model; they thought it had to be proven in the US in order to be successful in China. People from the US, however, already speak English.

Case study 1: B2B in China

Alibaba.com's unique experience[68]

Business to business (B2B) is currently the buzz word of internet China. However, due to the insufficient infrastructure, high cost and mainly lack of technical know-how, formidable hurdles remain in bringing Chinese enterprises online. It is hard to arrive at a specific figure about the internet *status quo* of Chinese enterprises as different organizations deliver different statistics. Some references, however, may help to give the picture. According to CNNIC, the government-funded internet monitor in China, there were 22.5 million people with access to the internet by the year 2000. Quite a sizeable part of the so-called 'internet population' consists of students surfing for fun. Most people use the internet for e-mail and news. Business is so far an emerging concern for more mature net users.

There are approximately 15 million PCs in China; only about 10 million have internet applications. Less than one per thousand of Chinese enterprises has its own website. To make matters worse, only 70 per cent of the valid 'dot coms' are actually in operation. Against this rather gloomy general picture, B2B is making headway in sectors where outside competition is fierce and decision makers are more sensitive to new ideas and tools. Foreign

---

[66] *China Tightens its Rules on Internet Address Managers*, Reuters, Beijing, 22 November 2003.
[67] *13th China Internet Development Situation Statistics Report* China Internet Network Information Centre (CNNIC), January 2004.
[68] Jack Yun Ma, CEO and Founder of Alibaba.com, International Symposium on Government and E-Commerce Development, China, 27 November 2000.

trade, and especially exports, is one of these sectors. The Ministry of Foreign Trade and Economic Cooperation (now MOFCOM) was one of the first government departments to launch a website in 1998. The ministry moved all its administration functions online before the end of 2004 and set up online quota, data collection and foreign exchange management systems. Many exporting companies began to use the internet as a complementary source of generating business information. E-commerce has been identified both at the policy level and executive level as a 'must' in order to expand exports.

One typical example, which was reported by the *New York Times* in June 2004, is that of a 28-year-old Chinese trader who successfully sold some US$15,000 worth of sleeping bags and tents to Turkey through trade leads posted on Alibaba.com. This young man is assigned by his employer, a subsidiary of the powerful China Technology Import & Export Group, to evaluate the use of the internet in imports and exports. Although most of his colleagues in the company still do their business as usual, he surfs the world's major trade sites daily, looking for potential partners. This example illustrates the role of B2B sites in exports. So far, the internet remains a source of trade information rather than of trading itself. With online banking and other services at the embryo stage, the absence of relevant legislation and die-hard concerns about security, it is too early to urge enterprises to complete deals online. Information seems to be the only mature and widely acceptable product of B2B e-business in China.

Information is the most needed and pragmatic product. Over the years, with or without government preference and protection, import and export companies, mostly state-owned, have already established a set model of doing business from sourcing suppliers and buyers to finally shipping the goods, such as the maximum and minimum signatures and seals required on a contract. There are also a lot of interests, legal or otherwise, involved at each stage of a transaction, making it difficult to cut some service costs even though there is strong tendency to do so at policy levels. However, we believe that, following China's WTO entry, 'life and death' issues will iron out significant concessions. Another interesting phenomenon is that a dominant majority of Alibaba.com's members in China are between the ages of 22 and 35. To them the internet is a help and fashion, which 'my friends are all using'. To people younger than these, such as students in college and the coming generation of traders, the internet is an important part of their lives.

The internet cafe of China University of Foreign Trade and Economics, a university sponsored by MOFCOM and an important supplier of talent to state and export companies, is always full at night. It will not take too many years for e-business to become a popular tool in China's import and export companies. I have said repeatedly in China that in the e-time, the first batch of traders to be kicked out of the game will be those middle-aged people who have a lot of customers but who do not care about e-commerce. Many people would be disappointed that we have found through surveys among Alibaba's members that B2B transactions are not what the enterprises, especially SMEs, want at the current stage. 'You are a great site, but just don't tell me you are going to do transactions. I am very comfortable with my bank,' is a typical answer from most of our members. Why? The purpose of doing transactions online is to save cost and time. But for SMEs, the small volume of each transaction makes the cost saving insignificant. Also, time is not a concern for businesses in developing countries where labour is cheap. What these business people want is to sell their products to more markets. Therefore, again, information proves itself to be the paramount benefit of B2B e-commerce for SMEs.

Based on these findings, in the coming 20 months the online transaction will continue to be a mirage. Having learned this much about B2B in China, it is easy to understand why Alibaba.com is the Alibaba.com you see on your screens. The internet experience is like surfing. The tide now can only get you here. We have set out from nowhere and travelled a long way to this prestigious place. Alibaba.com was started in March 1999 when B2C was the hottest topic in the internet world, with only a rough idea and a small amount of pocket money. However it has been growing at an exceptional rate, thanks to its good product and good customer service. To date, Alibaba.com is a trade community of more than 530,000 registered members, who contribute over 2000 trade leads to its four sites every day. They now boast 1.5 million page views a day – quite an impressive achievement for a business site.

Alibaba.com's most cherished principle is the win-win-win (3W) principle, which generates members and high member satisfaction. The first win is the members' win; the second is the partners', which include such respected names such as Softbank, Goldman Sachs and Investor AB; and the third win is Alibaba itself. Only when members and investors benefit from its services can Alibaba.com be a successful company. Customer service is always a priority. Once a member visits the site, Alibaba.com will try its best to make him or her come again and again by providing valuable information, customized services and constantly developing new value-added services.

Value is what matters to many business people. There are a lot of people worrying about the Alibaba.com revenue model, especially after the NASDAQ went nose down. Actually, Alibaba.com predicted and prepared for the market crash beforehand. Its new revenue models will be different from the existing models, which themselves are far from mature. Revenue will come from several channels when Alibaba.com thinks that the market is ready. As the Chinese sage Deng Xiaoping once said in another context: 'no matter whether it is black or white, the cat that catches the mouse is good'. B2B in China should have its own characteristics that help Chinese users to catch the mouse, in this case, business opportunities. And the final winners are those who can combine their strengths in the traditional industries with a good mastery of e-commerce tools.

Case study 2: Small electric appliances doing well[69]

Small electrical appliances are outselling their larger counterparts in China's ever-expanding market. A survey conducted by the National Bureau of Statistics indicates that the potential market for small electrical appliances will be worth about RMB350 billion (US$42 billion) over the next decade. As demand is expected to increase by more than 30 per cent annually over the next ten years, analysts widely consider the next two or three years as a golden period for the development of China's small electrical appliances sector. It appears that small electrical appliances, which have traditionally sold well in China, are still popular. Consumer demand continues to increase as people's living standards continue to improve. As a result, several factories that formerly manufactured large electrical appliances have begun producing small electrical appliances instead.

Between January and November 2003, the production volumes of microwave ovens, electric cookers, grease pumps, water heaters, vacuum cleaners, dishwashers and electric heaters surpassed those of the previous year by 49.9 per cent, 44.5 per cent, 13.6 per cent, 33.9 per cent, 36 per cent, 150 per cent and 57 per cent respectively. Small electrical appliances, in contrast with large electrical appliances and despite having lower per-unit costs, have greater profit margins. Small electrical appliances sold in China generate gross profits in excess of 30 per cent; larger electrical appliances, less than 5 per cent. Foreign companies have rushed to get their small electrical appliances into China's market since 2001, when China joined

---

[69] Yan X *Small Electrical Appliances Doing Well* National Bureau of Statistics and *Business Weekly* 13 January 2004.

the WTO. Statistics indicate there are nearly 200 kinds of small electrical appliances in developed countries, and that each family owns between 30 and 40 of these household goods. In China, however, there are fewer than 100 types of small electrical appliances and each family owns just a few of these items. This indicates there is great potential for the market to grow. Small electrical appliances generally have a lifespan of about six years. That means most of the small electrical appliances will have to be replaced in the near future, which will result in a purchasing frenzy.

In terms of the market, what will be the situation in China this year? In large, provincial-level cities, people are mostly interested in strongly branded small electrical appliances. Due to their advanced technologies, international brands – such as Philips (The Netherlands), Panasonic (Japan) and Braun (Germany) – are dominant, even though they sometimes cost three times more than domestic brands. Fewer domestic brands that copy famous international products are entering the local market. Previously, more than 20 such items entered the market annually. That figure has fallen to seven. Also, due to the enormous market potential, many of China's manufacturers of large electrical appliances have begun making small electrical appliances.

Consumption of domestically made small electrical appliances has grown rapidly. As a result, production of water coolers, household dishwashers and household sterilizers have soared by more than 40 per cent annually in the past few years. Imported small electrical appliances, however, remain more popular. Philips, Panasonic and Braun have solidified their footholds in China due largely to their advanced technologies and their products' attractive appearance. There is tremendous need in western China for small electrical appliances and that need is growing. These markets are ready to be exploited.

Statistics indicate that nearly 37 per cent of the small electrical appliances in western China were purchased between five and eight years ago. They will soon need to be replaced. On the other hand, new products – such as water coolers, microwaves, DVD players and sterilizers – are desired by most families. Statistics also indicate that more than 25 per cent of Chinese families plan to purchase such products this year. As for traditional products – such as electric cookers, electric fans and electric irons – domestic products remain popular in western China. Consumers think highly of domestic brands Medi, Haier and Kelong. More than 69 per cent of consumers in western China know about the firms that produce water coolers, sterilizers or dishwashers. In China's coastal areas, that number falls to 43 per cent. Despite the great prospects, some negative issues warrant attention. These are highlighted below.

Lack of competition

In spite of the increasingly large volume of the market, few small electrical appliance factories have taken shape. The Bureau's survey indicates that there are fewer than 50 competitive enterprises.

Inferior technology

Instead of producing competitive products, some domestic enterprises have to fight each other, in terms of pricing, for market share. As a result, profit margins of China's small electrical appliance manufacturers have declined – to less than 10 per cent. However, well-known brands continue selling for significantly more money; for example, an electric razor made by a Chinese firm sells for about RMB30 (US$3.60), while a razor by Braun costs at least RMB200 (US$24).

Poor management strategy

In terms of functions, small electrical appliances can be classified as for:

- kitchen use, such as microwave ovens, electric cookers and family sterilizers;
- family use, such as the electric fan, vacuum cleaner and electric heater;
- personal use, such as the electric razor, electric iron and electric toothbrush.

Currently, China's appliance manufacturers are concentrating mainly on products to be used in both the kitchen and for family purposes.

Case study 3: EVD: the next big home-viewing revolution[70]

China, the world's largest manufacturer of digital versatile disc (DVD) players, has launched a new format to end its dependence on foreign technologies, but insiders question whether the so-called

---

[70] Jiang J 'EVD: Next big home-viewing revilution?' *China Business Weekly* 13 January 2004.

enhanced versatile disc (EVD) players will be financially viable and/or accepted globally.

Jiangsu Shinco Electronics Group, one of China's largest DVD player producers, promoted the first high-definition disk players in 2004. Some 100,000 EVD players have entered China's market. They are available in 18 cities, including the Hong Kong Special Administrative Region. The players cost up to RMB1998 (US$241), compared with an average RMB800 (US$96) for a DVD player. The image quality of an EVD player is reportedly five times better than that of a DVD player and the discs can store a greater amount of data. Eight other major manufacturers of DVD players, such as Shanghai-based SVA Electronics Group, will eventually unveil their own EVD players.

Liu Dan, sales manager of E-word Technology Co Ltd, said high patent fees for DVD prompted the company to switch to EVD technology. Chinese enterprises must pay the 6C patent licensing alliance – Hitachi, Matsushita, Toshiba, JVC, Mitsubishi and Time Warner – US$4.50 for each DVD player they produce. China produced more than 30 million DVD players last year, which accounted for about 70 per cent of the players in the world market. E-word Technology is creating the national standard for the production of EVD players, Liu told *China Business Weekly* in an interview. The first draft of this national standard has been submitted to the Ministry of Information Industry (MII) for approval. The company has applied to the 6C alliance for 20 EVD patents; seven have been approved. Since the end of 2001 when China entered the WTO, Chinese enterprises have expressed increasing interest in holding their own intellectual property (IP) rights.

Lopez-Claros Augusto, chief economist with the World Economic Forum, said that in 2002 China spent RMB60 billion (US$7.2 billion) in R&D of new technologies. China became the third largest country, after the US and Japan, in terms of its investment – at 2.5 per cent of its GDP – on R&D projects. Augusto said that the country's technological competitiveness will come to the fore within six years. While seeking to hold their own IP rights, producers are being driven by demand in the high-end market to develop and enhance EVD players, which are specially designed for high-definition television (HDTV). 'With improvements in people's living standards, the consumption of HDTV has increased dramatically,' said Chen Changfeng, manager of Shinco's advertising department.

Statistics from China Audio Industries Association (CAIA) indicate that the sales volume of HDTVs has captured 20–30 per cent of the overall television market. It has doubled in recent years. 'Consumers can only enjoy the high image quality of an HDTV with an EVD player,' Chen added. Higher prices (compared with DVD players) will not make it difficult to promote the EVD players: 'EVD players are aimed at high-income people or super fans of audiovisual products. They are able to pay three times the price of a DVD player,' Chen declared.

People questioned the viability of DVD players a few years ago when they first entered China's market. Now, DVD players are an important part of modern people's daily lives, an unnamed CAIA official told *China Business Weekly*. An estimated 1.8 million EVD players were manufactured in 2004; 3 million in 2005; and 9 million are estimated to be made in two years' time. Analysts doubt whether EVD players will be widely adopted in the rest of the world. The international market has adopted DVD players as the standard: 'Compared with Chinese consumers, who tend to follow trends, European consumers are more rational in terms of products' functions,' stated an industry observer. 'It is not an easy job to persuade them (consumers) to give up their DVD players and buy an EVD player, which has many of the same functions.' Also, it is too early to say if Hollywood studios, which drive the world's video software business, will release their films on EVD. Negotiations between MII officials and several large Hollywood film distributors to have about 100 movies released on EVD are going well, the SVA spokesman said. 'The first film on EVD will be available in Chinese shops by the year's end,' he said.

Case study 4: An e-tailer with a lot of riding on bicycles[71]

To make sure that the packages arrived safely, DangDang arranged for a fleet of delivery men to zip around China's biggest cities on bicycles, delivering their packages to the customers' offices or homes. Peggy Yu once thought that the key to e-commerce success in China was to emulate Amazon.com. A 38-year-old native of Sichuan Province with an MBA from New York University, Yu is the co-founder of Dangdang.com, a Beijing-based retailer that sells more than 300,000 different Chinese books, CDs, DVDs and computer games online. Yu launched DangDang in 2000 with her husband, Li Guoqing, at a time when e-commerce was in its infancy in China. ('The name, DangDang, is a play on the Chinese word for cash register,' Yu says.) She did her homework, studying the SEC

---

[71] Einhorn B, An e-tailer with a lot of riding on bicycles, *E Commerce Times* 14 March 2004.

filings of Amazon and other American dot-coms to learn the details of the business.

As a student of American e-commerce, Yu tried to get Chinese customers to point, click and buy. That wasn't easy in a country where credit cards aren't very popular and people don't have the tradition of ordering things from catalogues. Still, Yu was determined to give it her best shot: 'I really pushed very hard for online payment,' she recalls. 'I was giving away coupons as credits for people who paid with credit cards'. The problem wasn't just the shortage of credit cards – even those who had cards and wanted to use them online encountered difficulties.

Reality check

Yu says that she learned that the servers in different provinces and cities run on different schedules. So a bank in south-eastern Fujian province may shut down at 12 midnight, while one in Shanghai may run 24 hours. 'But neither the consumer nor DangDang know about that,' says Yu. Moreover, China's postal service was not reliable and there was no credible nationwide alternative like FedEx. The whole thing quickly became exasperating. 'It was pretty much a "mission impossible" situation,' says Yu. So Yu and Li, DangDang's co-presidents, shifted their strategy. As Yu puts it bluntly, 'we faced up to reality'. Instead of depending on customers to use credit cards, DangDang focused more on encouraging would-be buyers to pay via money orders or even old-fashioned cash-on-delivery (COD).

Relay race

To make sure the packages arrived safely, DangDang arranged for a fleet of delivery men to zip around China's biggest cities on bicycles. These 'bicycle boys,' as Yu calls them, distribute about 15 to 20 orders a day, delivering their packages to the customers' offices or homes. If the order is COD, they then collect the cash, give it to the courier company, which then transfers the money to DangDang. In some ways, this system is better for DangDang than if people paid via credit cards. 'It works out very well,' says Yu. 'First, DangDang doesn't have to pay the finance charge that retailers pay to banks for credit card payments'. Typically, retailers in China pay close to 3 or 4 per cent charges for credit card transactions. DangDang has to pay its courier companies a 5 per cent shipping charge, but Yu says that's not a problem since it's simply tacked onto the original price of the item. 'It's paid by the customer,' says Yu. 'COD really works. It gives us a method to provide service to customers and to get our revenue collected.'

Security money

How can she be sure her trusty bicycle boys won't run off with the money? For the courier companies to get business from DangDang, they have to make safety deposits equal to three days' worth of revenue, which can range from US$6000 to US$12,000. Says Yu: 'If they miss one single payment, then we can just cut them off'. That hasn't happened yet. The courier companies have a similar security system with the bicycle boys, mostly migrant workers from the countryside who have joined the millions of Chinese flocking to the prosperous big cities along the coast. The workers have to pay a deposit with the courier companies to secure their jobs. A lot is riding on the honesty of those delivery boys. Any day, the amount they carry can be more than their month's salary – about US$66. And, says Yu, it could be 'two or three times more for the efficient ones'.

The dark tower

Since they get paid according to how much they deliver, these bicycle boys need to work fast. According to Yu, few of them like to deliver to big office towers, where security guards might slow down their progress. One particular black spot is the Motorola building in Beijing. 'It's got 16 floors,' explains Yu, 'the wait there can be 40, 50 minutes'. In China, a land of 1.3 billion people, DangDang's delivery strategy makes sense. But the US is a different story. 'With the labour costs in China so low, I think it is possible,' says Yu. 'I don't think it's possible in a high labour cost country like the US'. The new tactics seem to be working. DangDang is one of the few online retailers to have survived the aftermath of the net crash in 2000. As Yu points out, while there were about 300 online booksellers back in 2000, there are only a handful left today.

Learning to walk

Yu won't comment on press reports that the privately-held company recently received an US$11 million infusion from a US venture capital fund, but will say that more than 2 million customers have purchased from DangDang, with an average order today of about US$10. Back in the early days, 'we were e-commerce babies,' she adds, but now, 'we are entering the toddler years'. For that, Yu owes thanks to all those bicycle boys racing around town.

4
Due Diligence and Investment Monitoring

'We look for innovative technology that can be a national leader and international pioneer. And it has to have very strong market potential,' said Chen Yuchen, who manages two biotech research and development projects for the Shanghai Municipal Fund. One of these projects is concerned with trying to produce a new breed of cotton – a softer, stronger fibre created by splicing together the hair genes from a rabbit and a lamb. This 'transgenic' cotton is expected to hit the world market. The other is also a genetic engineering product – one designed to make trees grow faster. This is something China desperately needs in order to reforest its landscape. 'These Chinese scientists come to us with just the idea,' stated Chen, '…most of them do not have the personality or the training to conduct negotiations and raise the necessary money to finance the project'.

Penshibao's fraudulent accounting

On 15 March 2000, JAFCO Venture (HK) proceeded against Wang Xianglin (Wang Xl), PSB-BVI and PSB-Beihai for defrauding JAFCO Venture for investment by illusive financial records. JAFCO Venture solicited the Guangxi Superior Court to judge that PSB-Beihai had to compensate JAFCO Venture US$6 million and the accrued interest.[1]

Restructure and financing: cooperation in the PSB and JAFCO Venture

Founded in the Bobai county of Guangxi Autonomous Region of the Zhuang Minority (Guangxi Province) by Chairman Wang Xl in 1985, the Guanxi Beihai Penshibao Co Ltd (Penshibao/PSB-Beihai) has been based in Beihai since 1995. The company has a registered capital of RMB70 million, and is now one of the leading hi-tech enterprises that

---
[1] Hu P 'Penshibao's Resturcture Tragedy' *China Youth Daily* 7 August 2001.

integrates production and services of various agrochemicals. It is also the biggest manufacturer of foliar fertilizers in China.

The flagship product of the company, PSB Foliar Fertilizer Series – which claims to be cost-effective, of high efficacy, environmentally friendly and to engage wide-spectrum applications – is known as 'China's Fertilizer King'. It, therefore, comes as no surprise to learn that the brand name of Penshibao or PSB is revered as the number one agricultural merchandise provider in China.[2] However, in 1998 the company became conscious that its development process was obstructing its family management. It still used the same methods from 1992 in its sales promotion strategy. Wang Xl encountered a bottleneck of administration, thus forcing him to innovate and reform.

Re-established in 2003 as an independent VC partnership, JAFCO Venture is a joint venture between Nomura Securities and JAFCO. Its first fund, JAFCO Technology Partners I, closed in July 2003 with capital to the value of US$100 million.[3] With a new investment team of highly experienced venture capitalists in place, the fund's charter aimed at investing early in expansion-stage technology companies. The company's goal is to invest in venture opportunities of firms with a true 'breakout' potential; in such cases JAFCO Ventures can meaningfully add value with capital, as well as the experience of seasoned VC investors and the deployment of their Asia business development teams.

For the sake of 'secondary start-up', Wang Xl had the interest of an overseas list for financing. In 1998 Penshibao entrusted Core Pacific-Yamaichi International HK Ltd (CPY-HK) to conduct a promotion service to encourage foreign entry into the Hong Kong Stock Exchange. Introduced by CPY-HK and its initial investigation listing, JAFCO Venture was interested in investing into PSB-Beihai because of PSB-Beihai's famous brands and its outstanding record. JAFCO Venture began to negotiate with Penshibao for cooperation and, in accordance with JAFCO Venture's investment requirement, Wang Xl registered Baoshi Development Co Ltd in the British Virgin Islands (PSB-BVI). At this point PSB-Beihai became a full capital subsidiary company under PSB-BVI. Finally, JAFCO Venture went along with the subscription of equity to make the investment and, after JAFCO Venture's due diligence, it decided to invest in PSB-BVI in July 1999.

In August 1999 PSB-Beihai signed an investment agreement with JAFCO Venture in Hong Kong. The NJI No.2 Investment Fund and NJI No.3 Investment Fund invested US$6 million and got 15.68 per cent of the issued RP shares of PSB-BVI. Both parties agreed upon

---

[2] Penshibao Online: www.psb.com.cn
[3] 'One to one interview with the president of Penshibao: how did Penshibao hand in the bad luck?' *China Economic Times* 2 July 2001.

a US$4.5 million loan for PSB-Beihai with an annual interest of 4 per cent.[4] US$1 million of this loan was awarded to Wang Xl for his hard effort and secular undivided profits for PSB-Beihai, while the remaining US$0.5 million was sent out as agency fees. Figures 4.1 and 4.2 clearly outline the process of this investment.

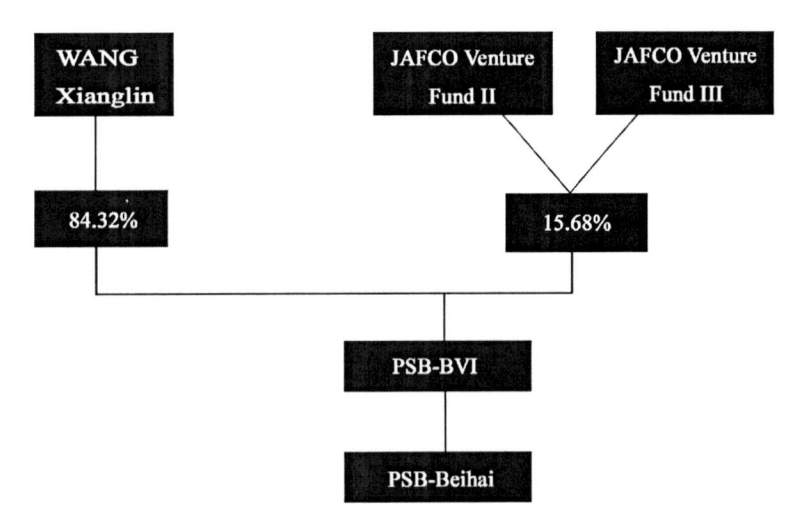

Figure 4.1 Percentage breakdown of investment

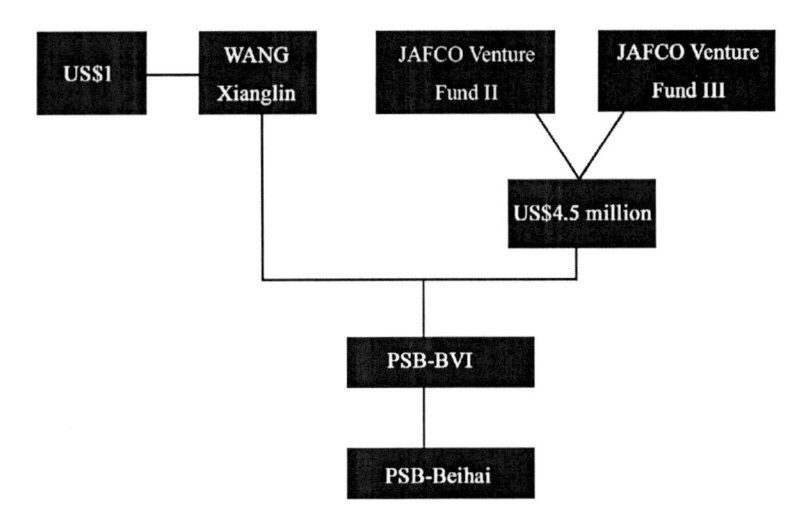

Figure 4.2 Monetary breakdown of investment

---

[4] ibid.

The exit mechanism of the investment fund was also agreed. If PSB-BVI succeeded in listing in Hong Kong before 1 January 2003, JAFCO Venture's 15.68 per cent RP share would change automatically into ordinary shares. However, if PSB-BVI failed to make it into the stock exchange then JAFCO would have the right to redeem the RP shares with an annual interest of 12 per cent.[5]

In order to protect its benefits within the company, JAFCO Venture made some protective terms in the shareholder and purchase agreements. These agreements stipulated that:

1. Directors of PSB-Beihai should be nominated by PSB-BVI.
2. The CFO should be recommended by JAFCO Venture.
3. The CEO of PSB-Beihai could be recommended by JAFCO Venture or Wang Xl. The hiring and firing of the CEO should be agreed by both parties.
4. Firing the Vice General Manager, CFO and Head of Marketing of PSB-Beihai should be approved by PSB-BVI.
5. JAFCO is entitled to appoint two directors to the board of PSB-Beihai.[6]

Bó Lè Associate Ltd (BLA) is an international executive search company that specializes in the Asian market with extensive experience in recruiting for a wide range of industries and well-established regional network, including 11 local offices in the Asia region. For PSB-Beihai's continued development, and at the request of the venture capitalists, Wang Xl decided through BLA to find a CEO and general manager with first-class experience in the building and management of world class corporate systems.[7] According to the agreement, in 1998 BLA recommended that Wang Weizun (Wang Wz) become the CEO of PSB-Beihai.

Wang Wz graduated with an MBA from Chinese Europe International Business School (CEIBS), the leading China-based international business school, and worked for China First Auto Works as a unified planner from July 1985 to November 1987. From there he moved to Changchun Auto Sheet-metal Works Factory as the Director from December 1987 to November 1990, and then to Maoming Kleit Co Ltd as General Manager from March 1993 to December 1994. At Maoming Kleit Co, he transformed the enterprise from being in deficit

---

[5] ibid.
[6] 'The water of Penshibao is too deep and too muddy' *Southern Weekend* 5 April 2001.
[7] 'One to one interview with the president of Penshibao: how did Penshibao hand in the bad luck?' *China Economic Times* 2 July 2001.

to being one of the best quality enterprises. After this he went to Shaoxin Yinghong Co Ltd as General Manager (January 1995–May 1997), Taitai Pharmaceutical Co Ltd as Deputy General Manager and Shenzhen Seashore Co Ltd as General Manager (June 1997–November 1999). At present he is employed as Director of Public Relations of CEIBS.[8]

At the same time as Wang Wz's designation, the CFO, Shui QiLing, was appointed by JAFCO Venture. Wang Wz recommended Duan Liming and another 11 professional managers to form the management team of PSB-Beihai.

Discovery of fraudulent accounting

Shortly after entering PSB-Beihai, Shui had doubts relating to the authenticity of the accounts. To ensure true corporate operation, Shui and Wang Wz conducted a thorough check into the financial situation of PSB-Beihai, and claimed that PSB-Beihai had forged financial documents and other financial records. All the financial data relating to PSB-Beihai's RMB63.54 million profit and RMB171 million sales[9] – which were the reasons behind the cooperative venture and equity exchange between JAFCO Venture and PSB-Beihai – were forged. The discovery of possible fraudulent accounting meant that JAFCO Venture, as the investor, had been fooled by Wang Xl. Soon, the management team reported the extent of the fraudulent accounting and displaced some financial documents to JAFCO Venture. From 26 January 2000, 13 members of the management team, including Wang Wz, Shui and Duan, left PSB-Beihai in quick succession. In their haste and in an effort to protect the evidence, they also took the laptops and mobile phones that had been provided by PSB-Beihai.[10]

On 14 March 2000, Shiu Nam Lui, the principal of the investment department of JAFCO Venture, brought accusations against PSB-Beihai via Guangxi's Superior Court. These accusations included compiling veracious accounting statements, lying to procure investment and infringing rights and interests. JAFCO Venture asked the court to pass judgement, compelling PSB-Beihai to compensate JAFCO Venture to the tune of US$6 million as well as the accrued interest.

The shareholder and purchase agreements outlined that if PSB listed in Hong Kong's Growth Enterprise Market (GEM) before

---

[8] *Wang Weizun's CV* Suzhou Industry Park Human Resource Development Ltd Online: www.siphrd.com
[9] Ning H, 'Penshibao's case shows new clues: former General Manager oppugned corporate fraudulent accounting' *The Economic Observer* 23 February 2004.
[10] 'One to one interview with the president of Penshibao: how did Penshibao hand in the bad luck?' *China Economic Times* 2 July 2001.

1 January 2003, then the RP shares held by JAFCO Venture would be changed into common shares before any IPO. If PSB failed to list before 1 January 2003, JAFCO should be entitled to put the shares to the company at a price of 112 per cent of the principal amount invested by JAFCO Venture. Only then would the company take up the securities. The sales revenue of 1998 was forged to be RMB171 million rather than the genuine figure of RMB39.05 million. Furthermore, the stated annual profits of 1998 were forged as RMB63.54 million from RMB1.23 million. The half-yearly sales revenue of 1999 was also forged as being RMB132.8 million rather than RMB26.32million. Finally, the reported profits from the same period were forged as RMB55.36 million from RMB6.41 million.

Wang Xl, the president of PSB-Beihai, denied these facts regarding the 'fraudulent accounting disturbance' and its effect upon JAFCO Venture's charge. He said to the media that he did not know the methodology behind PSB-Beihai's financial statement[11] because the capital evaluation report, compilation statement and the reports for JAFCO Venture were done by CPY-HK's Yi Lok, who was the project manager. PSB-Beihai was only responsible for providing related data on the orders of Shiu Nam Lui and Yi Lok. Wang Xl recalled that Yi Lok refused to provide PSB's original financial data to CPY-HK via Wang Xl because the number and amount had to be recognised and modified by Yi Lok.

In July 2000, Wang Xl reported the case to security authorities, Beihai City Polices, claiming that the CEO, Wang Wz, CFOs Shui and Duan and other managers stole and transferred PSB-Beihai's important financial credence, business licences and some related certificates, and laptops. They fabricated the existence of the Department of Direct Sale and took RMB131,000[12] from the treasurer in the name of that department's working capital fund. Wang Wz was arrested on the charge of business bribery in his Shenzhen home in November 2000, but no-one really believed that he broke the law.

Wang Wz was hailed the 'hero of exposing fraudulent accounting' by the media in China. After he was sent to jail, 397 MBA holders jointly supported Wang Wz and queried the actions of public security sector.[13] This matter also triggered a large-scale and long-term discussion about the credit problem of professional managers and entrepreneurs. Two people involved in this matter, Wang Wz and Wang Xl, were ranked in '2001's Top Ten Chinese World News Persons' by Hong

---

[11] Zhang J 'Former CFO, Shui Qiliang was sentenced to 7 years' *China Business Times* 27 February 2004.
[12] ibid.
[13] 'The water of Penshibao is too deep and too muddy' *Southern Weekend* 5 April 2001.

Kong Phoenix Satellite Television and Sina.com.[14] Wang Wz ranked second and, due to society's support, became the honoured guest of the famous TV programmes in Mainland China, *Dialogue* and *Face to Face*.

One year later, on 20 August 2001 the public trial of PSB-Beihai's accountancy fraud began before Guangxi Superior Court. JAFCO Venture's special representatives were enlisted from Japanese headquarters and Chinese legal-affair representatives from Beijing's Junhe Law Office. These groups, together with Wang Xl, had come to a compromise that involved signing a new agreement, which ensured that the old shareholders and purchase agreement was completed. JAFCO Venture gave up its shares in PSB-BVI. The investment by JAFCO Venture in 1999 was regarded as the 'bank loan' to PSB-BVI, but far less than US$6 million. PSB-Beihai had to pay US$1.35 million to JAFCO Venture. The remaining sum had to be paid within 8 years. High-class representatives indicated that JAFCO Venture attached importance to this negotiation.

On 15 July 2002, the People's Procuratorate of Haicheng District decided not to submit the case to the court on the grounds of insufficient evidence. At that time, the two other criminal suspects, Shui and Duan, were still wanted by police. In March and November 2003, they were arrested separately by the Beihai Public Security Bureau.[15] On 9 February 2004, the People's Court of Haicheng District tried the case of Shui openly. On the afternoon of 26 February 2004, the People's Procuratorate of Haicheng District and People's Court of Haicheng District announced that Shui, the former CFO of PSB-Beihai, had been found guilty of corporate bribery and post embezzlement and would be sentenced for 7 years.[16]

The overseas financing from co-win to co-fail

With the end of Shui's case, there is still speculation as to who is responsible and PSB's case resulted in too many unanswered questions. PSB-Beihai has several famous brands, covers large markets and owns numerous patents. JAFCO Venture holds enough VC funds and is one of the top four international investment companies. They complement each other so well that they should be a promising couple with whom to go into partnership. However, a lack of due diligence and investigation resulted in them finally facing the courts. This case

---

[14] Phoenix Satellite Television Online: www.phoenixtv.com
[15] Lu Y 'Wang Weizun: the next is me' BlogChina Online: www.blogchina.com, 8 March 2004.
[16] Zhang J 'Former CFO, Shui Qiliang was sentenced to 7 years' *China Business Times* 27 February 2004.

included the matter of Wang Wz as well as the previous affair between PSB-Beihai and JAFCO Venture.

The agreement between PSB-Beihai and JAFCO Venture is a typical example of VC investing agreements for future profit in Mainland China. The registration of company headquarters in the British Virgin Islands is a general instrument by which Chinese domestic SMEs and overseas venture capitalists cooperate in consideration of exiting an IPO of venture capital and foreign exchange.

PSB-Beihai should not have fabricated an immoral business record in order to gain investments and the opportunity of listing. After this incident in Mainland China, PSB-Beihai's method of fraudulent accounting was declared publicly to dissuade investors from investing in PSB-Beihai again. Although JAFCO Venture conducted due diligence on PSB-Beihai, they still suffered from this case. On the other hand, JAFCO did not employ auditors to audit financial records of PSB-Beihai. They made a decision based on the accounting reports of one of the top five accountancy firms in the world. However, no-one could ever guarantee that you won't face another Enron. It is important to employ auditors to audit companies when conducting investments in China.

The experience with PSB-Beihai became an unlikely way in which JAFCO Venture could enhance its reputation in the field of investment. At the same time, the traditional industry would find it increasingly difficult to get financing as a result of PSB-Beihai's case. Now, JAFCO Venture has decided to increase investment in the high-tech sectors by 100 per cent. This is not only a lesson for PSB-Beihai but also outlines important issues for those SMEs that tried to enter the stock exchange market too hastily over the last few years.

From a managerial perspective, professional managers should hand in such evidence to the legal department, but not to JAFCO Venture, one of the investors, which has important profits related with PSB-Beihai. On the other hand, professional managers holding positions such as CEO/CFO should be aware of legal procedures when working for private enterprises in China. According to the enterprise's strategic development, listing in the market is an artifice of combining outside resources but not the aim of development. As a private enterprise which used to suit family management, it was difficult for PSB-Beihai to understand how to transfer management within the confines of capital market logic. The right procedure must adjust the management pattern by regulating the range of business operations and the running scope. Generally, to employ professional managers, participating corporate administration currently only adapts to the mature stage of the venture for relatively large-scale enterprises and entrepreneurs. The start-up stage only is suitable for a model of family management; there needs to be a transition area between the start-up, growth and maturity stages. PSB-Beihai was in a transition phase but adopted for only a single step, making failure inevitable. At this stage, professional managers could be used as assistants or innovators but not as CEOs. Thus, management transfer must be progressed slowly, step by step. During the transition period, mastering and assigning power of control is very important.

Could the Guangxi Superior Court be in a position to accept and hear the case? PSB-Beihai thought not due to the purchase and shareholders' agreements provided, which should be governed and construed in accordance with the laws of Hong Kong. They also contended that all the involved parties should submit to non-exclusive jurisdiction of the Hong Kong courts in respect of this agreement. However PSB-Beihai's appeal was not accepted by Guangxi Superior Court, forcing the company to appeal to the Supreme Court of China. The High Court ruled that Guangxi Superior Court should hear the suit related to commercial cheating but could not judge the suit related to the dispute of shareholder agreement and purchase agreement.

Although Guangxi Superior Court was granted the right to hear the case, it was still very difficult for the court to judge. First, JAFCO Venture appealed to the court that PSB-Beihai pay back JAFCO Venture's US$6 million and the accrued interest. However, the problem was that the US$6 million was invested by JAFCO Venture into PSB-BVI and not PSB-Beihai. Thus, PSB-Beihai got the sum of US$4.5 million by means of a loan and has only an obligation to pay back the amount according to the loan agreement. Second, according to the purchase and shareholders' agreement, PSB-BVI would buy back the shares that JAFCO Venture held if the company failed to list in Hong Kong. The same agreement also provided that the transfer of any PSB-BVI shares must be agreed by all shareholders in PSB-BVI. Wang Xl was a major shareholder of PSB-BVI and would not agree. Third, the loan agreement failed to stipulate a payback date. For PSB-Beihai, there was not enough evidence to prove that the company forged financial records – but who knew when the key evidence would appear?

Areas for venture capitalists to consider when developing a due diligence model

Obtaining more information about a company

There are lots of tech-ventures in China, yet it is not easy for foreign venture capitalists to gain accurate information about them because the Chinese government agency in charge of corporate records maintenance tends to be inaccessible to the public. The government unit in China vested with the authority to register companies and maintain company records is the State Administration for Industry and Commerce (SAIC), which functions through its various provincial or local offices. The functions of SAIC mirror similar corporate registration and records maintenance functions of the Companies Registry in the Hong Kong SAR, or the Secretary of State's offices in the US. However, foreign VC firms also find it difficult to communicate with technological entrepreneurs about the business models, strategic plans, human resources and financial management, due to the different backgrounds and experiences between them. Furthermore, foreign VC companies tend to not have enough personnel to do this work, and so it is not easy for them to find a suitable deal.

Some foreign venture capitalists will look for deals by way of introduction from business colleagues. Others may find their deals by establishing strategic partner relations with local VC companies and science parks. Most of the best deals of Warburg Pincus were initiated by introductions through acquaintances or friends. It usually finds its deals through domestic friends such as lawyers, financial advisors, auditors, accountants or entrepreneurs. In this way it can acquire a better view of the company's financial situation and its fundraising needs before it makes an approach. IDG established close relationships with science parks and science departments from big cities, such as Beijing, Shenzhen, Shanghai, Guangzhou and Xi'an, making it easier to learn more about the target deals. Many companies may falsify financial statements, so be sure to check:

- the authenticity of the company's return;
- all sales contracts of the company;
- bank records of loans;
- research to ensure the company has a good record of paying taxes prior to investing (many companies in Mainland China have special ways of manipulating the taxation system in order to evade taxes).

Almost all domestic VC firms in China were founded after 1998. Although they have invested in more than 400 projects in China, they still have to wait for investment returns, so they lack the skills and knowledge necessary to conduct due diligence effectively. Furthermore, they did not know what to look out for and what investment criteria should be established. Most of them are tumbling now; some giant domestic firms, such as Shenzhen Capital Group Co Ltd (SCGC) and NewMargin Venture Capital, have established their way of doing due diligence by learning from existing investments and by establishing strategic partnerships with foreign venture capitalists. In some collaborative deals, these firms have undertaken some due diligence together with foreign VC firms and they have learned from these companies and finally developed their own methodology.

Agency problems and solutions

How to deal with agency problems between the venture capitalists and entrepreneurs in order to achieve a win-win situation is of special interest to academics and the VC communities in China. At a time when China's system of credit and trusts still leaves much to be desired, how can VC companies in China minimize their risks? For instance, traditional private enterprises or family firms in China suffer from serious problems regarding fraudulent accounting. The management of enterprises remains largely family dominated and people are unwilling to adopt international management and financing systems. As hi-tech enterprises face relatively high risks in R&D as well as marketing activities early on, it is easy for the strategic decisions of entrepreneurial ventures to deviate from the direction that results in a maximization of shareholders' value. At the same time, employees of the ventures may also take their companies' secrets to other companies. Survival of many entrepreneurial ventures and the growth of China's VC companies hinge on satisfactory solutions to these and a whole range of similar problems.

Many cases of VC investment in China reflect the agency problems between venture capitalists and entrepreneurs. Before signing the contract SMEs sometimes hide information, which mainly includes the feasibility of hidden projects, the abilities and credibility of the management team and the financial conditions of the company. After signing the contract, these SMEs may then hide the 'action', such as the entrepreneur's strategic decisions, capital usage, operational management and protection of intellectual property.

Some analysts propose five solutions to such problems that may exist between the venture capitalists and entrepreneurs:

1. Due diligence investigation is an effective way to solve the hidden information problem before signing a contract.

2. Finding out about voting rights, seats on the board of directors and repurchase rights should be a priority so as to check the powers of an entrepreneur for engaging in hidden activities after signing the contract.

3. The right of knowledge and other prohibitions stipulated in investment contracts as well as post-investment corporate governance are relatively good ways to prevent hidden actions by entrepreneurs with regard to fund usage and operational management.

4. Confidentiality and non-competitiveness clauses within the investment contract are the most effective measures to protect intellectual property.
5. Investment in stages, convertible debt, convertible preference shares, cashflow rights and contingency provisions can also play a role in restraining hidden information and hidden activities by the entrepreneur before and after signing a contract.

Although invested contracts are by no means perfect, foreign VC companies have figured out ways to deal with such problems. Some of these measures may be effective in China. Nonetheless, due to the current Chinese legal and regulatory limitations, many instruments designed to minimize risks, such as convertible securities, cannot be used. At the same time, public knowledge regarding the VC industry is still insufficient in China, as many entrepreneurs still do not understand the characteristics of VC. Therefore, the catalyst for the development of China's VC industry lies in the establishment of a solid legal mechanism as well as a basic understanding of the operating mechanisms for the VC industry by the general public, so that venture capitalists can legally and appropriately avoid risks and protect their own interests.

In the deal structures, in order to protect the interest of VC, there should be protective terms in the agreement, as highlighted in Table 4.1.

Table 4.1 Protective terms in agreement

	Protective terms in agreement	
Right	Agreement	Others
Dividend right	Terms of the share purchase agreement and rights agreement	Rights and preferences of Series A preferred
Conversion rights	Right of first refusal and co-sale agreement	Liquidation preference
Voting rights	Confidentiality and invention assignment agreement	Redemption
Rights of first offer		Automatic conversion
Information rights		Anti-dilution provisions
Registration/ offering rights		Protective provisions
		Change in control

What legal documents should foreign venture capitalists review as an important part of due diligence? Table 4.2 shows how to sign a legal contract in Mainland China.

Table 4.2 Forming a legal contract

	Main points	Secondary points
General	1. Company chart	
	2. Company details	Certificate of incorporation, memorandum of association and articles of association, or similar constitutional documents
		Minute books, share register and other corporate records, or alternatively advise when these can be viewed
		Details of any agreements or arrangements, including pre-emption, option or nominee agreements or arrangements, between shareholders
	Business activities: in respect of each company, briefly describe its main activities, the location of its principal place of business, any overseas offices and the regions in which it operates whether by way of joint venture, franchise or otherwise	
Shares	1. Share details	Particulars of share capital, showing total capital, authorized and issued (if appropriate), classes of shares and number of shares in each class
		List of all shareholders showing the number and type of shares held, whether the shares are fully or partly paid up and whether any shares were paid for in any way other than cash
		Copy of the up-to-date register of members
	2. Other interests: details of any interests that a company has in any other companies, partnerships, associations or other entities including copies of any shareholders' agreements or arrangements in respect of such interests including but not limited to joint ventures in the PRC	

	Main points	Secondary points
Financial position	Funding	Disclosing sources of funding from banks and other financial institutions, including the amount and extent of utilization of all facilities
		Disclosing debt or other securities issued by any company (with copies of the principal documentation)
		Disclosing all lieu, mortgages, debentures and other charges on any property (including but not limited to real property) of the company; with copies of all relevant documents
Compliance	Licences: a list and copies of all licences, permits, consents, approvals, authorizations, certificates, applications, registrations and declarations required to be issued, obtained or made in respect of the operations of each company in any jurisdiction in connection with its business	
Assets	Ownership: details of any assets	
Agreements	1. Hire purchase: any hire, hire purchase, leasing, credit sale, conditional sale or similar agreement and any factoring agreement	
	2. Agency: any agency, management, franchise or distributions agreement	
	3. Standard form: all standard-form contracts, other than employment contracts, and details and status of any franchise renewals or arrangements currently under negotiation in respect thereof	
	4. Major supplies: ie those accounting for more than 5% of goods of that nature supplied to the group. Also the value of purchases from such suppliers in the last financial year with copies of any material agreements or arrangements between any company and its suppliers	
	5. Acquisitions or disposals: all agreements relating to the acquisition or disposal of shares, business or a significant asset	
Employees	1. Employee details: list of all key employees of each company with brief details of the job they perform, their length of service and the terms of their employment as well as information about numbers of other employees in business area and location	
	2. Key employment contracts	
	3. Standard-of-contracts	

	Main points	**Secondary points**
Real property	1. Details: list of all real property owned, used or occupied, giving a full description of each property and the way in which it is used	
	2. Documents: in respect of each of the properties	If applicable, a copy of the title deeds or other such documents
		Copies of all licences granted to or by the company, evidence of the current and other related charges with copies of any relevant documents, eg correspondence relating to last renewal or rent increase
		List and evidence of third party rights, restrictions on use and transfer, and copies of most recent valuation
Insurance	List of policies: a list of insurance policies taken out by or for the benefit of each company, identifying classes of risks covered and amounts insured	
	Unusual terms: details of any unusual terms of restrictions in the insurance policies, or of any premiums that are in excess of fair market value, or of any circumstances which could make any policies invalid or unenforceable	
Intellectual property	1. Owned or used: details of any intellectual property rights, including patents and computer systems, a list of registrations and applications for registration and copies of any agreements relating to such intellectual property rights	
	2. Licensed: details of any intellectual property rights used by the company belonging to the third party, including the name of the third party and details of the arrangements relating to the use of such intellectual property rights	
Other matters	Competing interests: details of any direct or indirect interests, of any nature whatsoever that the directors or shareholders of the company, or their families, trusts or other companies controlled by them, may have in any businesses that may compete with any company	
	Copies or summaries of any other documents or matters, not within any of the above categories, which are significant in relation to a company, its business or prospective investor and that a prospective investor could reasonably expect to want to be aware of in assessing the value of the company	

5
IPO Exits and the Stock Exchange in Mainland China

IPO: The main exit route for capital investment

The absence of the most profitable exit mechanism in Mainland China

The main reason for making an investment is, of course, to realize a return: the bigger the better. 'Exit' is the final stage of VC, achieved either through an IPO of the shares in a primary stock market or through an arranged sale to a financial or strategic buyer of the company.

Most private equity investors in China also initially expected to exit through IPOs.[1] But because of policy limitations, exiting via the stock exchanges within China has proven problematic for SMEs. A comprehensive range of laws on securities markets, disclosure and accounting standards is not yet in place. The selection of which firms may list on the stock exchange in China remains principally a state decision. The central government's position is that venture-backed firms already have strong financial resources and therefore should not need the capital that a stock offering would provide. The funds that can be raised through a stock listing should be directed instead towards state-owned enterprises (SOEs) that are in desperate need of restructuring. So many enterprises do not consider the option of listing locally in China, but look towards either strategic buyers or a listing on a foreign exchange such as The National Association of Securities Dealers Automated Quotation System (NASDAQ), Stock Exchange of Singapore Dealing and Automated Quotation System (SESDAQ), Growth

---

[1] Liu Qian and Liu Jin, Chinese VC Anticipating For Spring, *Nanfang Daily*, 13 October 2003

Enterprise Market (GEM) of the Hong Kong Stock Exchange and Alternative Investment Market (AIM) of the London Stock Exchange.

A study based on interviews[2] showed that in Mainland China the only major exit strategies readily available are to locate a strategic buyer, have the firm itself buy back the stock or obtain a rare overseas listing. The latter two are usually difficult and subject to much regulation. Thus, strategic buyers represent the most likely exit mechanism, whereby a buyer – typically a western firm – would acquire a funded Chinese firm. One VC firm reported it was able to exit an investment in China by selling its interest in a paper plant to a major western firm. This firm supplied the local Chinese company with some inputs including machinery and certain raw materials such as chemically-related items. By investing in this Chinese company, the western firm was able to sell more inputs upstream, while also gaining entry into the Chinese market. However, finding such an ideal strategic partner to help exit an investment can be difficult, and laws regarding the transfer of assets can be particularly restrictive and hard to interpret. Also, such a strategic partner would typically want a majority stake in the venture. Thus, the VC firm will not only need to sell its portion of the stock, but probably convince the Chinese firm to sell part of its shareholding as well, and it is difficult for most Chinese business owners to accept becoming a minority shareholder in their venture. Moreover, when exiting via a sale to a strategic partner, the multiple paid on the firm's revenue stream will result in a return significantly lower than that traditionally associated with an IPO.[3]

International venture capitalists

In the west, most VC firms are organized as limited partnerships with a limited life. Thus, the aim is to exit their investments through the usual exit strategy of an IPO, before the VC partnership is finished. The venture capitalists may not exit completely. And in the case of a listing they may retain some quoted shares if further growth appears likely. A stock market listing has various advantages and disadvantages for the entrepreneur, outlined in Table 5.1.

In the discussion of VC investments generally, most attention has focused on exits through IPO. The successful timing of a venture-backed IPO provides significant benefits to venture capitalists in that taking companies public when equity values are high minimizes the dilution of the venture investor's ownership stake. Also, the venture

---

[2] Brutona, GD and Ahlstromb, D (2003) An institutional view of China's venture capital industry: Explaining the differences between China and the West, *Journal of Business Venturing*, **18**, pp 233-259
[3] ibid.

Table 5.1 Advantages and disadvantages of flotation

Advantages	Disadvantages
• Realization of some or all of the owner's capital	• Possible loss of control
• Finance available for expansion	• Unwelcome bids
• Marketable shares available for acquisitions	• Requirement to reveal all price sensitive information which may also be of interest to your competitors
• Enhanced status and public awareness	• Onerous disclosure requirements and continuing obligations, such as costs and management time
• Increased employee motivation via share incentive schemes	• Increased scrutiny from shareholders, press and media
	• Perceived emphasis on short-term profits and dividend performance
	• High costs of gaining quotation

Source: BVCA (1992, 1998)

capitalists' governance may be biased where they have incentives to offer bad advice to their investors in the matter of premature IPO timing. When thinking of going public, the entrepreneur will need to decide:[4]

1. Whether the business is suitable for flotation. The company must meet the commercial tests of the market, which include a demonstrated sound trading record, good financial control, good management, an effective board of directors, good prospects, no major uncertainties or risks in the foreseeable future.

2. Which market for flotation.

3. Whether to raise further finance as part of the flotation by issuing new shares, as opposed to selling a percentage of the shareholdings of existing owners.

4. How much control to surrender.

5. What method of flotation to use.

---

[4] BVCA (British Venture Capital Association) (1992) *A Guide to Venture Capital*, Price Waterhouse, London

Over the last two decades, venture capitalists have helped to create such well-known corporations as 3Com, Apple Computer, Cienna, Cisco Systems, Digital Equipment Corporation, Federal Express, Genentech, Hotmail, Intel, IVillage.com, Lotus, Microsoft, Oracle, Vitesse Semiconductor and Yahoo, amongst others. Clearly, attaining a high return depends on the investment exit route used, as shown in Table 5.2. For venture-backed firms, IPOs are traditionally the preferred exit route since the average return is 22.5 times for first-round, 10 times for second-round, and 3.7 times for the third-round investments.

Table 5.2 Distribution of venture capitalist exit routes and realized gains

Exit route	Percentage of firm	Average gain (multiples of original investment)
IPO	30	2.95
Acquisition	23	1.40
Company buyback	6	1.37
Secondary sale	9	1.41
Liquidation	6	-0.34
Write-off	26	-0.37

Source: Bygrave WD and Timmons J (1992) *Venture Capital at the Crossroads* Boston: Harvard Business School Press

Stock exchanges in Mainland China

In the last two decades of the 20th century, the Mainland's economy grew at an electrifying rate, averaging 9.7 per cent per annum.[5] Along with this, China's securities market experienced only a little over ten years' operation of the Shanghai Stock Exchange (SSE) and Shenzhen Stock Exchange (SZSE)[6] compared with western stock exchanges' operations of over 200 years.

---

[5] *Economy Analysis of Mainland China*, China Economic Analysis Working Papers No.2 August 2003, Cross-Strait Interflow Prospect Foundation

[6] Xie Zhichun (2003) The Lurch and Curing Measures for Chinese Securities Market, *Shanghai Securities News*, 23 September; Xiao Zhuoji (2000) The Challenge for Chinese Securities Market After the Entry of WTO, *China Enterprise News*, 9 October

The SZSE and SSE

The SSE was founded on 26 November 1990 and was in operation by 19 December that year. It is a non-profit-making membership institution directly governed by the China Securities Regulatory Commission (CSRC). The SSE based its development on the principles of 'legislation, supervision, self-regulation and standardization' to create a transparent, open, safe and efficient marketplace.[7] SSE endeavours to realize a variety of functions, such as providing a marketplace and facilities for securities trading, formulating business rules, accepting and arranging listings, organizing and monitoring securities trading, regulating members and listed companies, managing and disseminating market information. After 15 years' operation, SSE has become the pre-eminent stock market in Mainland China in terms of the number of listed companies, number of shares listed, total market value, tradable market value, securities turnover in value, stock turnover in value and the T-bond turnover in value.

By the end of 2002 it had over 35.6 million investors and 715 listed companies, with a total market capitalization reaching RMB2.5 trillion.[8] In 2002, capital raised from the SSE market surpassed RMB61.4 billion,[9] and a large number of companies from key industries, infrastructure and high-tech sectors have not only raised capital, but have also improved their operation mechanism as a result of listing on SSE. In the opening years of the new century, the SSE is faced with great opportunities and challenges to boost market construction and regulation. Combining cutting-edge hardware facilities with favourable policy conditions, Pudong has become an exemplary role model of Shanghai's economy. The SSE is fully committed to the goal of state-owned industrial enterprises reform and the development of Shanghai into an international financial centre.

The SZSE, established on 1 December 1990, is the other stock exchange of Mainland China. Located in the strikingly modern and dynamic coastal city of Shenzhen, the SZSE has been committed since its establishment to creating an open, fair and efficient market. The evolution of the SZSE mirrors that of China's securities market, by characterizing the entrepreneurial spirit of the city where it is located.[10]

Over the past 15 years, the SZSE has developed from a regional into a national market, with listed companies and members throughout the

---

[7] *SSE Online*, www.sse.com.cn
[8] Zhang Y (2004) *China's Stock Market after Entry of the WTO* 2005 China Economics Summit, 24 May 2004.
[9] ibid.
[10] SZSE Online, www.szse.cn

country. It enjoys an important share of the gross national market in terms of listed companies, market capitalization and trading turnover. The total funds that it has raised in the market since it opened have exceeded RMB250 billion;[11] thus it is playing and will continue to play an important role in the national economy.

In general, the achievements of China's stock exchanges can be summarized as follows:

- setting up of regulatory framework;

- establishment of nationwide automated trading system;

- phenomenal advances in market size;

- professional teams formed in securities industry.

Figure 5.1 shows the automated trading system of Chinas stock market.

According to SZSE research, the market statistics up to the end of March 2001 showed that there were 1209 listed companies and US$770 billion turnover of equities and mutual funds in 2000. Market capitalization was US$615 billion, accounting for 61.2 per cent of GDP.

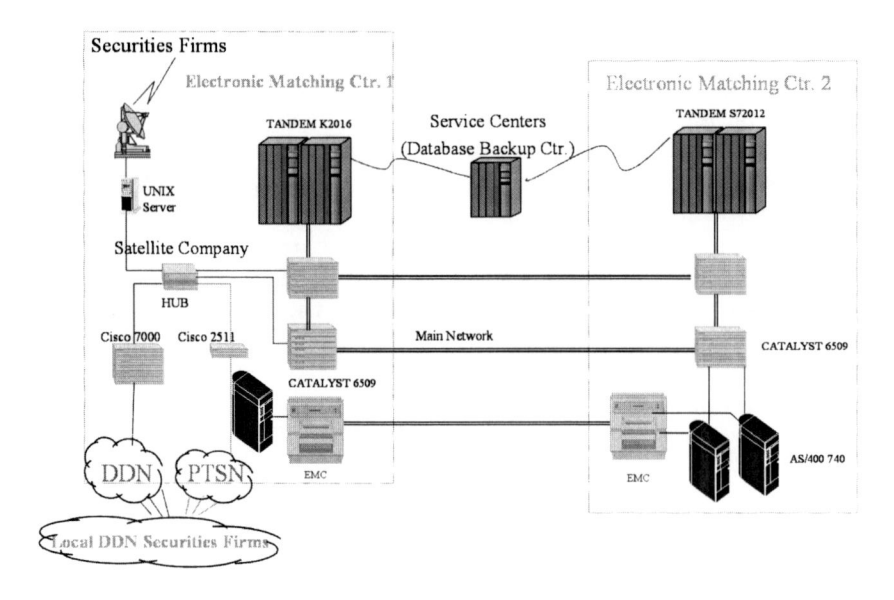

Figure 5.1 The automated trading system of China's stock market

---

[11] Zhang Y (2004) *China's Stock Market after Entry of the WTO* 2005 China Economics Summit, 24 May 2004.

There were 61.41 million investor's accounts, representing 4.7 per cent of total population and 13.5 per cent of the urban population. The statistics indicated that there were 101 securities firms, 14 fund management companies, 151 investment consultancy firms, and around 180,000 employees in the securities industry.[12] Over the past 15 years, China's stock market has facilitated the development of China's economic growth and market oriented reform. It has also greatly stimulated the transformation of social concepts and ways of life. It has laid a solid foundation for meeting the challenges brought about by China's entry into World Trade Organization (WTO). But problems still remain, such as:

1. imbalanced market structure;
2. segmented market;
3. small size of market;
4. market not fully open to the international community;
5. need for strengthened law enforcement.

The market size is very small compared with the US, as Table 5.3 demonstrates.

Table 5.3 China's stock market size compared with that of the US

	China's stock market size	Compared with US
Number of listed companies	1209	7.5%
Market value	US$580 billion	16% of NASDAQ 4.7% of NYSE as of end of March 2000
Capital raised in 2000	US$18.6 billion	14% of NASDAQ

Source: Shenzhen Stock Exchange (2002)

The above problems are common to all fledgling markets, but behind these problems lies huge opportunity. It is necessary to strive to achieve better results. Consequent to WTO entry, the China securities industry will:

- allow foreign securities institutions to trade in B-shares directly;

---

[12] Zhang Yujun (2004) *China's Stock Market after Entry of the WTO*, President & CEO of SZSE, 13 August.

- allow the establishment of Sino-foreign joint venture securities firms and fund management companies;
- encourage more Chinese enterprises to seek overseas listings;
- allow foreign enterprises to issue stocks in China;
- allow foreign capital to be invested in China's stock market;
- optimize laws and regulations as well as strengthen law enforcement;
- consolidate the financial intermediaries and let them play a more important role in the market;
- launch a new third market;
- promote self-regulation in the industry;
- train and attract more talented professionals;
- open up the market and promote innovation;
- emphasize standardized operations to enhance competitiveness.

With the improvement of supervision skills and market conditions, China's stock market will open more to outsiders. The gradual opening up of China's stock market will provide the US and other foreign institutions with excellent opportunities to invest in China, which will be an important channel for China to join the international market and finally become a well-developed market.

Over the past 14 years, China's two Main Boards have accumulated rich experience and laid a solid foundation for the future sound development of China's stock market. Looking forward, the China securities market will emerge in the international community as both established and powerful.

Investors are also more rational in picking stock and base their judgment more on the fundamentals of the listed firms. The power and energy sectors, which are expected to benefit from rising prices in coal, electricity etc, will be more favourable for fund managers in their portfolios. Stocks in the public utilities and banking sectors also expect solid growth. The Chinese economy will be one of the biggest driving forces for the stock market recovery in 2005.

China's economic growth in 2004 was 9.5 per cent and the momentum is expected to be maintained in 2005, which would generate improved corporate results in general. An improving global economic climate will also benefit the Chinese capital market, which is opening up at a growing pace, following the adoption of the qualified foreign institutional investors (QFII) system and the launch of a batch of Sino-foreign joint venture securities houses and fund management firms since 2003. A report issued by Morgan Stanley in 2004 said that international investors had favoured Chinese stocks in 2003 and would maintain their share in the next few years[13] as more large Chinese companies are expected to be listed overseas, including the China Construction Bank, one of the 'Big Four' state-owned banks. More overseas investment funds will be established to target Chinese equities. The large volume of new share issues expected will also affect the enthusiasm of investors that Chinese companies, especially the banks, still need to improve management and internal controls.

Four years after China's entry to the WTO, China's stock market has been gradually moving in the direction of deregulation, with the adoption of a series of market-driven rules. The CSRC will continue to improve the market mechanism in the bourses in the coming years and encourage product innovation. The commission has begun to reform the share issue system to improve the quality of listed companies. The sponsor system, which adds more responsibilities and liabilities to the underwriters on the quality of stocks, will reduce administrative interference in listings and increase public supervision during the process. On the other development, to ease the shortage of funds for SMEs and the pressures of expansion on the main board, China initially launched the long-awaited Second Board market in May 2004.

Case study 1: The Chinese SME Board – no glory, but a dream come true

Whatever the consequences may be, the foundation of the SME Board of Shenzhen Stock Exchange indicates that investors have taken a fresh approach to Shenzhen, the city of entrepreneurial spirit.

Since 12 October 2000, the date of Changsha Zoomlion Heavy Industry Science & Technology Development Co Ltd's (Zoomlion) listing, Shenzhen stopped listing the new corporate share for 1311 days.

Although the faces of the SZSE's staff appear calm, there is no doubt that they are very happy in their hearts at the launch of the SME Board. A member of staff admitted there would be no champagne or big party. But the atmosphere is quite different compared

---

[13] Han Yaling (2003) Does Chinese Stock Exchange Like Casino?, *People's Daily Overseas Edition*, 7 April

> with the breaking news. A distinguishing feature is the increased number of meetings. Heads of department have to attend at least three more meetings per day.
>
> Unbroken sunshine covers the Shenzhen city to its zenith. Shenzhen is now in the running and the happiness has begun. But no glory, just a dream come true.

Abandoning the innovation of a VC Board finally brought about the naissance of the SME. Although the SME Board is not the anticipated creative equity market for prominent players in some circles, the SZSE was reborn and finally resumed its listing for new shares.

There was a late celebration ceremony. On 27 May 2004, in Shenzhen Wuzhou Guest House, honoured guests and senior representatives from China Securities Regulatory Commission (CSRC), national ministries, Guangdong Provincial Government, and Shenzhen City Government toasted with champagne and due ceremony the full operation of the SME Board.[14] After six years' gestation, appeals, enthusiasm, hesitation, debate and reiteration, in some people's eyes there is still no VC Board. But the arrival of the SME Board may be on the curve of gradual progress towards a VC Board, or might only split differences of opinion among various interest groups. Time will provide the final answer.

Is there any meaning and rationale for an SME Board? A possible reason for reducing the cost for listing is that the creative speed of the Chinese domestic capital market system is slower than the actual potential. From the VC Board concept to a real-life SME Board, Mainland China's equity market has only moved forward half a step and made the SZSE wait for three years and six months. During this period, many domestic VC investment companies and venture-backed SMEs have met a different fate; the ardour and enthusiasm of many professional venture capitalists have been exhausted by the long delay.

On 17 May 2004, a day of historic significance for the SZSE, the CSRC gave an official, written reply to the SZSE that authorized it the SZSE to set up an SME Board under its Main Board. The SME Board mainly arranges share issues and IPOs for good potential growth companies with a turnover of under 50 million shares[15], and high-tech SMEs which have drafted applications to list on the Main Board. The SME Board should also confirm the suitable issue scale and type of business according to the market.

---

[14] Zeng Zijian, SME Board Started Its Trip, ZHU Lei, *Chengdu Business News*, 27 May 2004

[15] The Potential Power of SME Board, *Huaixin Investment & Homeway Online*, 31 May 2004

From the implementation documents, the main points of the SME Board can be summarized as follows. Two fixed points are:

1. the law, regulation, and rules are the same as for the Main Board;
2. IPO companies should conform to the listing qualifications and information disclosure required.

The four points of independence are:

1. separate operation;
2. separate supervision;
3. separate code;
4. separate index.

The operating rules of the SME Board are the same as for the main board stock exchange.

Simply speaking, the requirement for listing the SME Board is still very high, which is different from qualification for the other countries' Second Board compared with the main board stock exchange. Full marketability in the Chinese capital market is still under discussion. Ownership shares are still split between tradable and non-tradable shares. The appearance of such an SME Board has aroused differing opinions in all circles. Various problems that arose with the Main Board will possibly emerge again, because CSRC did not introduce any innovations for auditing the IPOs of the SME Board and still follows the existing measures of the Main Board. The administrative authority considers that this expedient will leave room for system innovation and make the SME Board a completely separate VC Board in due course, but under this policy and the burden of its history, such as split equity structure and the imperfect Main Board system, the SME Board will soon lose its halo.

Wang Shouren, secretary of the Shenzhen Venture Capital Association, points out that the reason why the administrative authority did not open the VC Board in one step is based on the situation of the present Mainland China economy. The step of first setting up the SME Board and then creating the conditions for transition to a lower requirements and full marketability VC Board tallies with the situation of Mainland China. Looking at past appearances to perceive the core meaning, it is clear that the SME Board is not simply a reproduction of the Main Board. Because the scale of SMEs is generally small and they experience higher risks in operation and marketing development, stock speculators will be more active, which will force the administrative authority to adopt a conservative strategy on SME listing standards and equity distribution. Under current Chinese stock market conditions, if the CSRC were to agree to reduce IPO qualifications for entry to the SME Board, there would be many enterprises based on a mixture of the genuine and the false and over-promoted companies which would infiltrate the SME Board and leave it in an awful mess. So the inauguration of the SME Board is a first step in constructing a VC Board and instilling the confidence to build a multilevel capital market in Mainland China.

There is no doubt that the SME Board has increased the enthusiasm of foreign venture capitalists because it has opened up the VC exit mechanism in Mainland China. At the Third Plenary Session of the Sixteenth Central Committee of the Communist Party of China (CCCPC), the CCCPC adopted the *Decision on Issues Regarding the Improvement of the Socialist Market Economic System*, which, for the first time, explicitly previewed the establishment of a multitiered capital market system to facilitate venture capital investment and the building of a VC Board market, and which mentioned that a single-tiered capital system would address further reform and the opportunity for development.

The multitiered capital market system is a synthesized concept. There are six action points to China's strategy to forge a multilayered capital market system, which are:

- widening the financing channels of securities dealers;
- actively and steadily solving the problem of equity separation in listed companies (negotiable shares held by the public and non-negotiable shares held by the state and legal persons);
- encouraging lawful funds to enter the stock market;
- improving experimentation in the qualified foreign institutional investor (QFII) system;
- improving taxation policies for the capital market; and
- actively and steadily developing the bond market.

According to this strategy, China will establish a multilayered capital market system, including a main board market and a Second Board market for venture capital, and markets for corporate bond and futures products. The strategy includes plans to regulate the operation and governance of listed companies in various ways, including an improved management system for share issuance. There are plans to boost the development of intermediate services for the development of capital markets and increase the supervision and regulation of the markets through an improved legal system and capital market credit rating system.

Honouring its WTO commitments on the securities sector, China will continue its efforts to open up its capital market to foreign investors and venture capitalists.

The UK and US models

In terms of the London Stock Exchange (LSE)'s multilayer capital market, the LSE enables companies from around the world to raise the capital they need to grow by listing securities on its markets, which includes the two primary markets of the main market. Secondly, the trading services of the LSE provide the trading platforms used by broking firms around the world to buy and sell securities and tap quickly into equity, bond and derivative markets. The LSE's derivatives business is a pioneering diversification beyond its core equity markets. EDX London is the LSE's international equity derivatives exchange. The UK-covered warrants market is one of the world's fastest growing investment markets. The LSE hosts five blue-chip issuers offering over 650 warrants and certificates on single stocks and indices in the UK and around the world.[16] Such a structure could be a good example for the Chinese government to develop its own multilayer capital market.

The US has formed a capital markets structure which is led by the New York Stock Exchange (NYSE) and supported by the NASDAQ and other regional markets. Such a multitier capital market system can not only help different natural enterprises to enter the market by many alternative financing channels, but also guarantees that listed companies and investors can engage in optional deals and investments consistent with maintaining and ensuring investors' profits.

NASDAQ is the largest US electronic stock market. With approximately 3,300 companies, it lists more companies and, on average, trades more shares per day than any other US market. It is the home to category-defining companies that are leaders across all areas of business including technology, retail, communications, financial services, transportation, media and biotechnology. NASDAQ is the primary market for trading NASDAQ-listed stocks. Approximately 54 per cent of NASDAQ-listed shares traded are reported on NASDAQ systems.[17] In addition, the US NASDAQ is not only a pure stock exchange market for SME or high-tech enterprises but is also a multitier stock market that includes four levels, NASDAQ National

---

[16] London Stock Exchange Online: www.londonstockexchange.com
[17] The NASDAQ Stock Exchange: www.nasdaq.com

Market, NASDAQ Small-Cap Market, Over the Counter Bulletin Board (OTCBB) market and Pink Sheets market.

Developing a multitier capital market in China

In order to build a multitier capital market in Mainland China, the system should be actively expanded with a VC Board, an OTC Market, an Agency Share Transfer Market, a Technology and Equity Exchange Market etc, while at the same time continuing to develop the Main Boards of the SSE and the SZSE. But it is also necessary to introduce innovation to the current legal system whilst establishing the multilevel capital market. Security Law and Company Law still have to be refined further, especially to accommodate the criteria of multielement markets, such as the OTC, equity exchange and agency share transfer.

All this would be accomplished in an action programme for building the multitier capital market in China. But how can the SME Board transform into a real Second Board – the VC Board – in a rapid and uncontroversial manner? Will the current Agency Share Transfer System act as the permanent recycle bin for the withdrawal of companies? How can a repeat of 1997's experience of losing control of the local OTC market be avoided during the period of positively developing the regional stock exchange market? How can the establishment of an OTC market be brought into the multitier capital market blueprint in a suitable manner? Basically, there are still many problems to be solved. The road should be walked step by step.

Cooperation between HKGEM and the VC Board of SZSE

Besides the NASDAQ, foreign VCs investing in China usually exit their venture-backed firms in China by making an IPO in a second favourite place, the Hong Kong GEM. At present, there are more than 60 Chinese companies listed on overseas exchanges. Among these, nine are listed on the HKE and the NYSE concurrently, three listed on the HKE and the LSE concurrently, and one listed on all three concurrently. There are about 100 red chip shares listed on the HKE, NYSE, NASDAQ and other overseas exchanges. The theme of the GEM is capital formation for growth companies from all industries and of all sizes having a focused line of business. The GEM's acceptable jurisdictions are Hong Kong, Bermuda, the Cayman Islands and Mainland China. There is no profit requirement for the GEM compared with the HK$50 million required for the Hong Kong Main Board. For the shares of companies with a market capitalization of less than HK$1 billion at the time of listing, a minimum public float of 20 per cent of the issued share capital is required subject to a minimum of HK$30million. For companies with a market capitalization of HK$1 billion or above at the time of listing, a minimum public float of 15 per cent or such higher percentage of the issued capital as will result in at least HK$200 million worth of shares being in public hands at the time of listing is required. There must be at least 100 public shareholders at the time of listing.[18]

The debate as to whether Mainland China currently needs to develop a Second Board, the VC Board, is highly controversial although the SME Board in the SZSE has been operating since May 2004. Opponents point to the poor performance of similar markets overseas, notably the NASDAQ, which hit new lows in 2004, although it seems to favour 'Chinese concept firms'. At the same time, lower standards for companies to be listed increase the risks for investors. Moreover, with many problems remaining unresolved on the Main Board, the creation of a VC Board will only lead to even more problems. On the other hand, those supporting the establishment of the VC Board have argued that the current poor market sentiment abroad is only the result of over-expansion in the IT industry. There continues to be a huge demand for a wholly healthy Second Board in China and high market risk can be controlled by tighter supervision. Currently, the running SME Board of SZSE could not be regarded as a whole and integrated Second Board.

Why does China still need a whole Second Board on the mainland when there is already a GEM in Hong Kong? Will the creation of a similar market in Shenzhen lead to vicious competition for market resources, thereby increasing the risk for both? What are the relationships between the Second Boards in Hong Kong and Shenzhen?

There are strengths and weaknesses in the market development of HKGEM and the VC Board of SZSE. It is important for them to complement each other and develop their strengths accordingly. The capital market shows that market efficiency hinges on effective competition by all participants and the premise for effective competition lies in the cooperation of competitive markets. Investors may demand geographical diversity and liquidity in their quest for capital appreciation and therefore specialization enables each regional market to play its specific role and the cooperation and development of Second Boards in Hong Kong and Shenzhen will satisfy this demand. If the opening of the Shenzhen VC Board provides a market base for capital flows, only cooperation with Hong Kong can guarantee the safe and smooth flow of such liquidity, reducing the risks caused by its inherent weaknesses.

The future VC Board of SZSE will not influence Hong Kong's GEM because the aim of a Second Board is to solve the problems of Mainland

---

[18] Growth Enterprise Market Online: www.hkgem.com

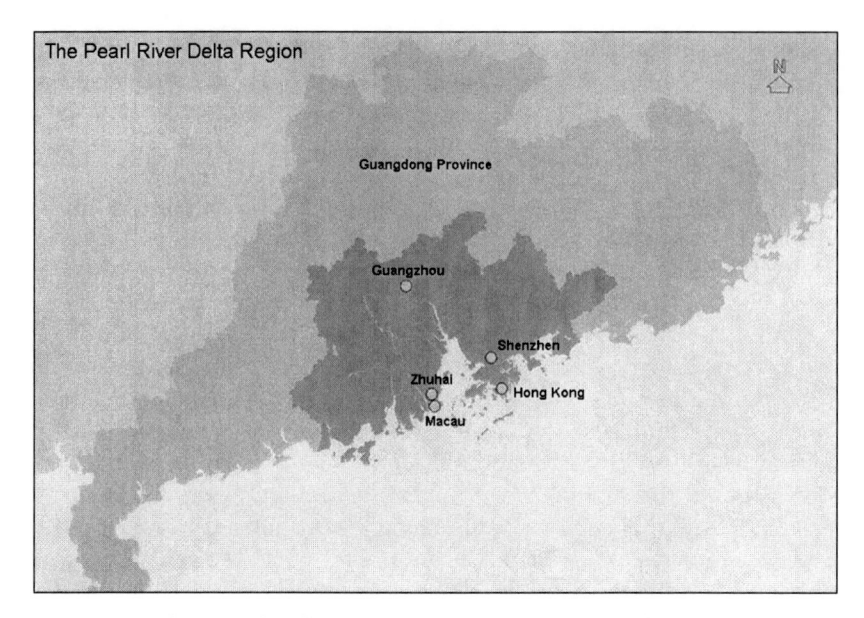

Figure 5.2 Geographic location of Hong Kong and Shenzhen

China's stock exchange and SME financing. From this listing viewpoint, there are so many SMEs interested in coming into the stock exchange that the Second Board of the SZSE is not able to identify clearly those SMEs which will list or intend to list on the GEM. Furthermore, according to market expectations, the threshold of the SZSE Second Board will not be much lower than the main board unless it sets different selection criteria for each market. The current decrease in the number of SMEs planning to list on the GEM is not because of the information offered by the SZSE Second Board but a reaction to the new rules and policies pushed by the GEM. From the point of market cashflow, unless there is some policy concession, the possibility of large outside funds entering the SZSE is small, even after the strong drive for a VC Board on the SZSE.

Figure 5.2 shows the geographic relation between Hong Kong and Shenzhen. Therefore, it will be best to follow capital market disciplines and establish the VC Board as soon as possible in order to benefit from its complementary relationship with the Hong Kong market. Such cooperation and competition between the Second Boards in Hong Kong and Shenzhen will foster growth in the high-tech enterprises within the two cities and boost economic growth.

The road ahead for SZSEs' VC Board

The plan to build Mainland China's Second Board originated in 1999 but has been delayed many times because of social and economic policies and circumstances.[19] In May 2004, China Securities Regulatory Commission (CSRC) and the State Council of China approved a project to found and test an incomplete Second Board, the SME Board. SMEs have the opportunity to list on the current SZSE, whilst the larger new share issues will be placed on the other Chinese stock exchange, the SSE. The securities authorities would like to develop the SZSE into a stock exchange similar to the US NASDAQ. China will soon reduce listing standards to allow smaller and new SMEs to grasp the opportunity of stock exchange financing, but the timetable is still under discussion. In fact, it would be best to build a high transparency Asian 'NASDAQ' in Hong Kong because of its high profile reputation in the Far East, but this is very difficult to achieve since all other Asian countries have their own strong *amour-propre* and like to be recognized by others.

International business and market competition accelerate the tempo for building a Second Board in China. The rivalry between capital markets is one of the key factors in national competitive power. At the crux of competitive capability for capital markets are the listing resources. Compared with foreign capital markets, there are many obvious advantages for Mainland China's domestic listing resources, which should devote much attention to encouraging SMEs to use IPO channels to solve their financing problems. Mainland China should take the opportunity to build a VC Board for its huge domestic market and also to accelerate its development. However, the SZSE VC Board must be the last and only one; one good Second Board should guarantee enough large transaction volumes. There are many regions in China and if every region wanted to possess of its own Second Board, the whole stock exchange would be damaged. Europe paid a high price for having numerous Second Boards. The Second Board in Germany has closed down, and another Second Board in Switzerland is breaking down. In Europe, the AIM exchange of London is the most mature; therefore no other Second Board is needed. According to London Stock Exchange AIM Statistics (April 2004), the average AIM company had a market capitalization value of GBP27.1 million and there were 809 companies quoted on AIM. AIM is becoming an increasingly attractive market for international companies, especially for Mainland China's

---

[19] Zhou Yi (2004), Cheng Siwei – the Promoter of VC Board Market, *Securities Times*, 2 April

SMEs, particularly since the closure of the German Neuer Markt and the winding down of EASDAQ.

If the VC Board of SZSE wants to captivate the attention of international VCs, transparency of market, definition of laws and rules need to improve drastically. The Second Board in any country should be established over eight to ten years. After that period, the continuing success of the Second Board will be trusted by international venture capitalists. In comparison with Europe, Asia still lags far behind in some aspects of its attraction for international VC investment. The gap will be narrowed in the years ahead because of the emerging Asian economy. In the next two to four years, China will rank amongst the top ten in acquiring international VC investment.

Before pushing for the VC Board, there are two important problems, which need to be solved. First, the equity structure should be normal. The situation of the 'big share' on the Main Board must be changed. The VC Board should not allow family members to hold most of the shares in a listed private enterprise, so that public investors can really exercise their shareholders' rights. Secondly, the same share should always have the same price to create a good impression of markets that operate openly, fairly, and correctly. On issuing shares, the same price for all shares must observed, instead of selling shares to the initiators of the flotation as a privileged clique for only the nominal value or lower than nominal value, and then driving up the share price to public investors. Such kinds of unfair share issues should not be allowed to reappear on the Second Board.

Accelerating construction of a VC Board could satisfy the strong demand for financing Chinese domestic SMEs. Furthermore, the VC Board should not only provide a financing channel for SMEs, but also play an exemplary role. Within the current mass of SMEs in Mainland China, there are only a few that have the opportunity to list on the SME Board. China's rudimentary Second Board, which opened in May 2004, included in the first listings eight SMEs, of which most operate high-tech businesses. But the beginning of the SME Board will start up a social business undertaking mechanism and will encourage SMEs to observe listing standards in the operation of their businesses and, at the same time, promote their sale.

Exit strategy is not only a high profile topic for China's VC industry; it is also an urgent problem that needs to be solved for its industries. Not only is exit being affected by investment strategies, it is also a major factor in deterring investment strategies. Analysis of traditional VC paths, in the absence of a Second Board and the imperfection of China's capital market, suggests that the focus of China's VC exit strategies may be transferred to M&As.

At present, investment should be guided by the market and exit opportunities. Current profit-oriented financial investments focus primarily on financial yardsticks at the time of investment. Considerations of strategic investment and industry chain investment can be added to the basis of financial investments. Strategic investment is primarily aimed at realizing the strategic value of the company, taking into consideration its technology and markets.

Furthermore, venture capitalists can develop their own exits using existing securities markets and can use their control of a listed company to acquire the investment projects of the VC companies. This will provide an exit for VCs. The implementation of such an exit strategy requires that the proportion of shares held by the venture capitalists cannot be too small and that the development of the investment project must be good. The execution of such a strategy also requires the use of a large number of connected transactions, the approval of which by regulatory authorities is highly uncertain.

Venture capitalists should also consider three aspects in relation to exit. They should free themselves from the constraints of thinking that venture capitalists can only invest in early stage projects. They should instead invest in projects that are in their growth and mature stages. Moreover, venture capitalists should change their present attitude of over-emphasizing investments but de-emphasizing services. They should use value-added services to foster the growth of the enterprise and to speed up their exit.

Table 5.4 Chronology of China's Stock Market (1990–2004)

Date	Event
1 December 1990	Shenzhen Stock Exchange (SZSE) began its test run.
19 December 1990	Shanghai Stock Exchange (SSE) was inaugurated and began formal operations, with 22 exchange members, 45,000 registered investors and 30 stocks listed. The SZSE also started trial operations the same month. It was formally launched the following July.
28 August 1991	The Securities Association of China, a national self-discipline organization in the securities industry, was launched in Beijing.
29 November 1991	Shanghai Vacuum Electron Devices Co Ltd issued the first B shares on the Mainland to be traded formally on the SSE. The company was listed in Shanghai in February 1992.
1992	China started issuing shares to foreign investors.
October 1992	State Council Securities Commission and China Securities Regulatory Commission (CSRC) were established

Date	Event
	successively. SSE and SZSE were transformed from regional to national stock exchange markets.
April 1993	The State Council issued the Provisional Regulations for Stock Issuance and Trading, the first to regulate stock trading and issuance in China. More securities-related rules were issued later in the year.
15 July 1993	Tsingtao Beer, the first H share, was listed on the Hong Kong Stock Exchange.
1 July 1994	The PRC Companies Law was enacted.
March 1995	Transaction volume and deal numbers on the SSE greatly exceed those of its counterpart, SZSE. Enterprises based in Shanghai, Jiangsu and Zhejiang, the Yangzi River Delta Area, displayed their superior economic strength.
May 1995	China Construction Bank, Morgan Stanley and other institutions launched the China International Capital Corporation, the first joint venture investment bank in China.
1996	Stimulated by Hong Kong's upcoming return to Chinese sovereignty in the following year, the SZSE increased input in its facilities and services. Since August, transactions volume of the exchange exceeds that of SSE. The annual growth of SZSE Composite Sub-Index ranked first worldwide, reaching 174.92 per cent in this year.
July 1996	Shanghai-based Shenyin Securities and Wanguo Securities merged. This was the first major merger in the Chinese securities industry, producing the country's biggest shareholding securities house, Shenyin & Wanguo Securities.
October 1996	CSRC issued a notice to clamp down on price-rigging behaviour in the securities markets. On 16 December, the *People's Daily* published an editorial on the front page, attacking speculative behaviour and price manipulation on the stock market and urging investors to become more rational. The market then staged a sharp correction.
24 March 1997	Beijing Datang Power Co Ltd was listed on the London Stock Exchange, becoming the first Chinese company to enter the European capital market.
21 May 1997	The authorities issued a circular to prohibit state-owned enterprises and listed companies from taking part in stock trading.
1998	CSRC forbad all Mainland Chinese enterprises from voluntarily choosing their IPO locations.
19 May 1999	The Shanghai composite index and Shenzhen sub-composite index rallied by 4.64 and 5.03 per cent respectively, starting a strong bullish run that lasted for two years.

Date	Event
1 July 1999	The PRC Securities Law came into effect.
October 1999	The State Council allowed insurance companies to purchase securities investment funds, enabling them to enter the stock market indirectly.
August 2000	*Proposed Draft of Listing Rules for the Second Board (VC Board)* was issued. SZSE was authorized to conduct relevant issue qualification examinations.
September 2000	SZSE stops new listings. In Mainland China, only SSE retains the IPO right for domestic enterprises.
October 2000	*Caijing* magazine published an article that disclosed price manipulation and other irregularities of fund management companies, triggering public debate and official investigations.
April 2001	The delisting system was introduced to the stock market. Shanghai Narcissus Electric Appliance Co Ltd became the first listed company in China to be delisted from the bourses.
1 June 2001	The hard-currency B share market was opened to domestic retail investors.
14 June 2001	The State Council unveiled rules aimed at reducing State holdings in companies to finance social security funds. It ruled that companies launching IPOs or additional share offerings should in the meantime sell State holdings equivalent to ten per cent of the offer value to public investors and that the money raised should be put into social security funds.
23 June 2002	The State holding selling plan was aborted.
1 December 2002	China formally introduced the qualified foreign institutional investors (QFII) scheme that allows foreign institutions to invest in A shares, bonds, funds and other approved instruments were previously limited to domestic investors.
2 February 2004	The State Council issued a document to boost the development of China's capital market, announcing a series of reform measures and urging all government departments to enhance their coordination.
17 May 2004	CSRC authorized the SZSE to establish a small and medium-sized enterprise board (SME Board) under the Main Board and endorsed the implementation project.
27 May 2004	SME Board debuted on SZSE.
25 June 2004	The first eight SMEs were listed on the SME Board in the Shenzhen Stock Exchange.

Table 5.5 Milestones in the establishment of the SME Board and the preparation of the VC Board Stock Exchange in Mainland China (1998–2004)

Time	Participants	Event
March 1998	Chinese People's Political Consultative Conference (CPPCC), China National Democratic Construction Association (CNDCA), Cheng Siwei (Chairman of CNDCA)	On behalf of CNDCA, Chairman Cheng brought forward the famous VC plan, *Expediting China's Venture Capital Industry*, commonly known as the No. 1 Proposal.
July 1998	SZSE	SZSE issued a study report on the Second Board, the first of its kind in Mainland China.
December 1998	State Council (SC), State Development Planning Commission (SDPC), China Securities Regulatory Commission (CSRC)	SDPC lodged the *Project of Researching Establishing the VC Board Stock Exchange* to SC. SC required the CSRC to feed-back research opinion.
March 1999	CSRC, Shanghai Stock Exchange (SSE), Shenzhen Stock Exchange (SZSE)	For the first time, CSRC confirmed plans to establish a High-tech Enterprise Board in SSE or SZSE.
17 April 2000	Zhou Xiaochuang (CSRC Chairman)	Zhou stated that his commission had made full preparations to launch a Second Board.
May 2000	SC, CSRC	After discussion of the request for instructions to establish the Second Board stock exchange from CSRC, SC received the CSRC's opinion in principle to name the Second Board the Venture Capital Board Stock Exchange (VC Board).
April 1999 – May 2000		More than 2000 venture backed enterprises applied for IPO listing on the VC Board of SZSE. Finally, 238 venture backed enterprises applied for VC

Time	Participants	Event
		Board listing, which included 79% of companies that set up in 1999.
June 2000	SZSE	The launch of the second transaction and clearing system in SZSE marked a great leap forward.
October 2000	SZSE	SZSE halted IPO issues on its Main Board.
End 2000 to 2001		A global crash hit technology-heavy stock markets worldwide signalled by a slumping NASDAQ index. All markets had to revise their rules to raise quality thresholds for listed enterprises and consolidate market foundations.
November 2001	Zhu Rongji (ninth Premier of the People's Republic of China State Council from March 1998 to March 2003)	Zhu Rongji declared in Brunei that the stock exchanges of Mainland China should learn from the experience of Hong Kong and other advanced countries first and then push for the VC Board after straightening out the Main Boards.
November 2001	Cheng Siwei (Vice Chairman of the Standing Committee of the National People's Congress of China)	In Hong Kong, Cheng Siwei announced that the Mainland China VC Board would not be set up in the near term.
14 October 2002	NPC	The Standing Committee of the NPC passed the *Law on Promotion of SMEs*, calling for measures to broaden direct financing channels for SMEs.
November 2002	CSRC, SZSE	In the report for CSRC, SZSE suggested developing the establishment of a VC Board step by step.

Time	Participants	Event
March 2003	Song Hai (Vice Governor of Guangdong and a deputy to the NPC), National People's Congress (NPC)	Song Hai submitted a motion to accelerate the building of a growth enterprise market, co-signed by a dozen Guangdong NPC deputies, to the First Session of the tenth NPC.
October 2003	Central Committee of the Communist Party of China (CCCPC)	At the Third Plenary Session of the Sixteenth CCCPC, CCCPC adopted the *Decision on Issues Regarding the Improvement of the Socialist Market Economic System*, which explicitly put forward that a multi-tiered capital market system would be established to facilitate venture capital investments and the building of a VC Board market.
February 2004	SC	SC promulgated a document, *Various Opinions of the State Council Concerning Promotion of the Reform and Opening and Stable Development of Capital Markets*, stating that measures would be taken to establish a multitiered stock market system, perfect the venture capital investment system, explore the financing channel for SMEs, and accelerate the building of VC Board market in a progressive manner.
May 2004	CSRC, SZSE	CSRC authorized the SZSE to set up the SME Board.
25 June 2004	SZSE	The first eight SMEs were listed on the SME board in the Shenzhen Stock Exchange.

> **Case study 2: Chinese internet firms line up for IPO**
>
> Let us consider the way that 'hot' London nightspots, such as bars, pubs and nightclubs succeed: nightlife organizers build board and extensive support for a new establishment, and then depend heavily on party promoters to invite only the 'right' people. Some places would rather stay empty than let in the 'undesirables'. The whole point of the velvet rope in front of such bars, pubs and clubs is to create impossibly long queues and to generate even more buzz and hype so as to create a scene of bustle and excitement. After all, what would happen if an A-list patron should encounter a 'ne'er-do-well' inside? The bars, pubs and nightclubs would lose their 'buzz', and the ever-fickle in-crowd would find new ways to expend their enthusiasm, time and money.
>
> The IPO market works in exactly the same way; the sponsors, promoters, brokers and bankers put together an A-list of the best companies, create a buzz and then introduce a velvet rope. Unlike nightspots, however, there are no bouncers to keep out the undesirables. Without a bouncer to keep an orderly flow of respectable companies into the market, the IPO market will quickly fill up with a lot of B, C or even D-list companies that would have had a hard time going public even during the internet mania of the late 1990s. Let's hope that investors continue to press for only the highest-quality new stock offerings and that the invisible hand of the market restrains many of the most speculative new candidates for IPO.

Investment enthusiasm for potential internet development

Many Mainland China internet companies are renewing their IPO fervour. Foreign investors are also investing in these companies, preparing to gain from future listings. The US VC firm, Tiger Technology Fund, has been one of the more ambitious investors. On 16 October 2003, Tiger injected RMB52 million (US$6.28 million) into Joyo,[20] the Chinese business-to-consumer (B2C) website, to become one of its top three investors with an interest of about 20 per cent, after the domestic software vendor Kingsoft and the computer giant Lenovo

---

[20] Wang Ruohan (2004) The Tiger Fund would like to acquire the two internet Bookshops, DangDang and Joyo, *21st Century Economy Report*, Beijing, 15 January

(formerly Legend), which control about 50 per cent and 20 per cent respectively.[21] With investments from partners like Tiger Technology, Kingsoft and Legend, Joyo.com will lay a stable foundation for future manoeuvres in capital markets at home and abroad. This VC investment will no doubt become a strong driving force in the takeoff of Joyo.com. According to an interview with Lin Shuixing, president of Joyo.com, the company had been making a profit since the second quarter of 2003 and would register an annualized 70 per cent growth in revenues for the full year, based on a 'conservative estimate'. In 2002, Joyo.com's revenues reached nearly RMB100 million (US$12.08 million) while the figure for the first nine months of 2003 had already exceeded RMB105 million (US$12.68 million).[22]

In 2003, Tiger Technology Fund and Blueridge Capital invested US$15 million in eLong.com.[23] Softbank Asia Infrastructure Fund (SAIF) invested in online games provider Shanda in March 2003, pouring in US$40 million for a stake of around 25 per cent, the largest single venture capital investment in a Chinese internet company at that date.[24]

China's internet market grew to almost 80 million internet users at the end of 2003.[25] The estimate for 2005 is 126 million.[26] It is not difficult for investors to see the huge potential in Mainland China. There are bright prospects for China's internet industry and the solid performances of China's top three portals listed on the NASDAQ are encouraging other firms to launch IPOs. Online advertising, one major area of business in the internet industry, stood at US$60 million in 2002; it increased by around 50 per cent in 2003 to US$90 million and is forecast to expand further to US$162 million by 2007.[27] At the same time, whilst most dotcoms were struggling to find practical business models after the internet bubble burst in 2000, many Chinese internet companies established their own models and have since begun to claim profitability.

Now, both internet users and enterprises are discovering the importance of the internet and are willing to pay for any services which they consider to be of use. While mobile messaging services continue to

---

[21] Joyo Bookshop Online, www.joyo.com
[22] ibid
[23] Chen Gang et al (2004) The Second IPO Tide of Chinese Internet Companies, *China Internet Weekly*, 15 March
[24] Shanda Online, www.shanda.com.cn
[25] 13th China Internet Development Situation Statistics Report, *China Internet Network Information Centre (CNNIC)*, January 2004
[26] ibid
[27] 2003 China Online Advertising Research Report, iResearch Inc, *China Internet Research Center*, 17 January 2004

help drag Sina, Netease and Sohu out of heavy losses, Timothy Chan, head of Shanda, has been ranked the tenth richest person in China following his success in tapping into the online games market in 2003. He is the richest man because of the current Shanda share price. Also, the search engines industry is gaining ground. For example, Baidu.com and 3721.com also reported escaping from the red in the second quarter of 2003.[28] The sharp rises in stock prices for the three NASDAQ-listed Chinese internet portals are luring their peers to follow suit in order to catch the tide of recovery. On 7 November 2003, the prices of Sina, Netease and Sohu stocks on the NASDAQ had risen eleven, six and seven times respectively over the previous 12 months, whilst continuing increases are mainly supported by the growth of their revenues and profits. The performance of major internet companies on the NASDAQ is quite bullish, but it is not a bad idea to take advantage of the trend. The three biggest portals made profits as follows:[29]

1. Sina's third quarter revenues in 2003 rose by an annualized 208 per cent to US$31.9 million, whilst its profits reached US$11.7 million, compared with the net losses of around US$559,000 in 2002.

2. Netease's 2003 revenues and profits also grew to US$17.7 million and US$9.2 million respectively, in contrast with US$9 million and a negative US$1.3 million for the same period in 2002.

3. Meanwhile, Sohu notched up US$22.1 million in revenues and US$49.2 million in profits, compared with US$7.5 million and US$112,000 in the third quarter of 2002.

Multiple channels for exiting

Substantial business growth, outlined in the Chinese dotcoms' financial reports, indicates that many Chinese websites have found their respective niches rather than blindly copying foreign companies. Such utilization of information technology is contributing to business growth, the rapidly increasing number of 'netizens', the increased popularity of broadband technology and a greater array of internet-based applications. With 78 million netizens and official statistics indicating that this number will rise to 150 million by 2005, China-focused web operators are looking to cash in on the explosive growth of web users.

---

[28] The Profit Road of China's Internet Industry, *China Telecom Information News*, 4 September 2003
[29] Wang Yichao (2002) The Benefit Way for Three Portal Websites Following Chinese Characteristics, *Caijing Magazine*, 29 August

The venture capitalists backing Chinese internet companies are also pushing for IPO listings. Since foreign capital is strictly regulated in China's capital market, overseas IPOs are more frequently pursued and represent the best exit channel for venture capitalists. With the robust growth trend of the NASDAQ composite index recently, good times seem to be returning for the internet industry. In addition to catching a ride on this favourable wave, the threat of competition is another factor motivating companies to seek listings. Most Chinese internet companies which are taking up overseas IPOs are operating on a small scale and their businesses are quite weak. It is difficult, given the market trends, to envisage the future of competition in their sectors. Embarking on a rash IPO listing, they may fail to meet the requirements of both the market and investors, thus exposing themselves to greater risks. On the other hand, when big companies want to enter a market, they can easily gain access through acquisitions thanks to their huge cash reserves.

History often repeats itself. A tide of initial public offering is now surging through China's internet sector suggesting yet another case of *deja vu*. In 2000, at the peak of the internet boom, more than 20 dotcoms in China set their sights on listing on overseas stock markets, but only Sina, Sohu and Netease have realized such a dream.

However, just four years later overseas public offerings have once again become a hot topic among Chinese internet companies. Justin Tang, chairman of Beijing-based travel and entertainment information provider eLong.com, expressed a strong desire to launch an IPO on NASDAQ. The reason for this was that he considered that an IPO is an important and necessary step in the development of an enterprise, and eLong would seriously consider the possibility under the appropriate conditions. Presently, both internal and external circumstances for IPOs are favourable; thus eLong has the opportunity to actively pursue flotation.

E-trading company china.alibaba.com, job-hunting company ChinaHR.com, search engine baidu.com, along with 3721's real name business are expected to list between 2005 and 2006.[30] There are already strong indications that websites offering online games, advertisements and technological services will be among those most preferred by investors. Set up in 1999 in California's Silicon Valley, Beijing based Baidu is Mainland China's most popular search engine (the name 'Baidu' comes from a Song dynasty poem about a man searching for his lover). There are on average 30 million text searches a day in Chinese alone, a seventh of Google's 200 million worldwide total.[31] Robin Li, a multimillionaire at 36, the co-founder of China's self-styled

---

[30] Baidu's IPO Road Met the Obstacle, Yesky Online, www.yesky.com, 16 June 2004

Google, is one of a new generation of western trained entrepreneurs who have returned to China to seek their fortunes in the country's blossoming hi-tech sector. He was named China's joint 11th richest IT businessman in 2003 by *Asiamoney* magazine, with personal wealth estimated at up to US$60 million.

As a consequence of issuing a total of US$265 million in no-interest bonds on the NASDAQ market in July 2003, the top three Chinese internet companies, Sina, Netease and Sohu have more capital to allocate towards acquisitions. At the same time, Yahoo's acquisition of 3721.com has stoked fears among the smaller internet firms who are now looking for a shortcut to quick expansion. The timing of the new boom in China's internet economy depends largely on the global economy. Some analysts forecast that the prosperity will last several years, and will involve greater business growth within a larger geographical area compared with the sector's last boom. Whilst during the last boom portals such as Sina.com and Sohu.com were the focus of attention, websites that provide professional services will propel the growth this time.

Some of those dotcom firms may become involved in M&As. Yahoo-HK acquired Hong Kong-based 3721, in a deal that marked the first time that a foreign-based portal had acquired a Chinese website. Also late in November 2003, Sohu.com acquired two domestic websites. One website specialized in online gaming, 17173.com; the other, real estate focus.cn, founded in 1999, maintains 1.1 million registered users and has become the most influential real estate website in Bejing.[32] Experts predict that more M&As will occur. Only the sector's leading players have listed, while less-competitive firms have begun turning towards M&As to expand their operations. As Lu Benfu, director of the Chinese Academy of Social Sciences' Internet Economy Research Centre commented in an interview: 'a listed company faces greater pressure to be profitable, and it must convince investors it will not disappoint them'. M&As are beneficial for firms looking to expand their businesses without taking on the risks that accompany listing on the stock market, and 'hasty listings' he cautioned 'are likely to occur in the next few years'.

---

[31] Xiao Niao (2004) It is not the suitable time for Baidu's flotation, Search Engine Rank Research Online, www.google123.net, 30 April

[32] Sohu Decided to Purchase the Real Estate Website Focus.cn, ChinaByte Real Estate News Online, www.chinabyte.com, 21 November 2003

Soaring ahead

An ever increasing number of internet users have laid the foundation for the growth of the Chinese internet sector. Currently, wireless data services, including SMS, multimedia messaging services and WAP, online gaming and advertising are the main growth engines that are driving China's internet industry. SMS has already undergone an explosive period of growth, and service providers in the SMS business sector will continue to advance at a growth rate of more than 30 per cent for the next three or four years before gradually slowing.[33] A recent announcement by China Mobile to stop the 'SMS Union' between service providers and personal websites is only a minor policy change. Some SP, WAP and K-JAVA businesses have experienced sudden and sharp increases over the past couple of months, recording a monthly revenue growth rate in excess of 100 per cent and signalling the advent of a new wireless data services market, including wireless application protocol (WAP), K-JAVA (J2ME/Java 2 Micro Edition) and multimedia messaging service (MMS).

In the field of SP mobile value-added service (VAS) Market, estimated at RMB1.7 billion in 2002, SMS was the main beneficiary.[34] In 2003, at the same time as the rapid increase of SMS, 2.5G VAS started up. Overall, the general scale of the SP Mobile VAS market was RMB4.56 billion. It is estimated that the Mobile VAS market was around RMB7 billion in 2004. In 2005, the SP VAS market will reach around RMB11.1 billion, including RMB4.74 billion in SMS, RMB1.15 billion in WAP, RMB1.8 billion in MMS, RMB1.2 billion in wireless games and RMB2.18 billion in interactive voice response (IVR).[35]

According to *iResearch's* report, between 2003 and 2005, the wireless data services market for SPs should progress from a reported US$332 million to US$551 million (2004) and US$909 million (2005), respectively, registering successive annual growth rates of 249 per cent, 66 per cent and 65 per cent. Research indicates that the Chinese online games market earned approximately US$216 million in 2002, whilst the number of fee-paying game players fell just short of 4 million, making up 6.3 per cent of all internet users. In 2005, the Chinese online games market is expected to generate US$920 million, with 13 million paying users, or more than ten per cent of the total number of internet users. The market's average annual growth, meanwhile, should exceed 60 per cent. In 2004, 'Legend of Mir II', 'MU' and

---

[33] Yin Yijian (2003) Investors Are Too Sensitive In The Dropping of Three Portal Websites, eNet Online, www.enet.com.cn, 23 October

[34] *China Mobile VAS Market Annual Report* (2004)

[35] 2004 China Mobile VAS Market Research Report, iResearch Inc., July 2004

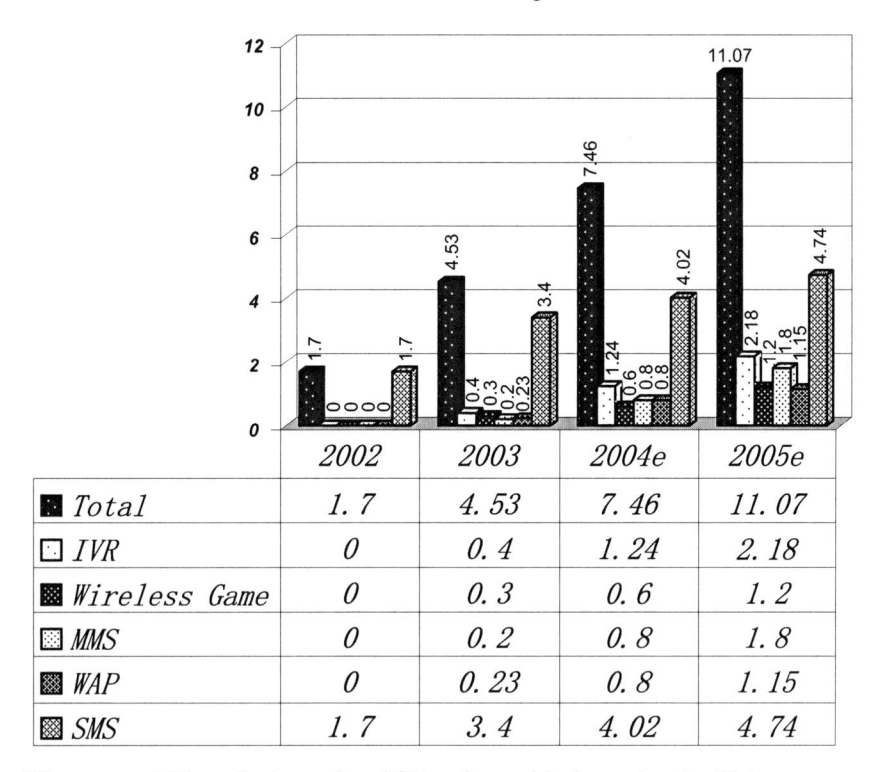

	2002	2003	2004e	2005e
■ Total	1.7	4.53	7.46	11.07
☐ IVR	0	0.4	1.24	2.18
▨ Wireless Game	0	0.3	0.6	1.2
▦ MMS	0	0.2	0.8	1.8
▨ WAP	0	0.23	0.8	1.15
▦ SMS	1.7	3.4	4.02	4.74

Figure 5.3 The whole scale of SP value added market in China (RMB1 billion)
Source: iResearch Inc 2004; China Mobile VAS Market Research Report 2004

'Dream of West Journey' are the three most popular online games in China. Netease's 'Dream of West Journey' benefited particularly from good market promotion as well as the summer holidays of 2003. Up to 30 June 2004, Netease's daily average number of 'hits' per day reached 390 million. The number of peak time concurrent users was close to 290,000, and will continue to increase.[36]

China's online advertising market includes both the web page advertising market and the paid search market. In 2002, both advertising segments began to experience accelerated growth, with web page advertising increasing by 50 per cent annually whilst the paid search market growth exceeded 100 per cent.[37] China's online advertising

---
[36] The Good News for Breaking Through 290,000 Concurrent Users, Dream of West Journey Online, http://xyq.163.com, 8 November 2004
[37] Chinese Websites Stop Using Pop-Up Advertisements, *China Tech News*, 4 August 2004

market reached US$131 million in 2003 and is expected to rise to US$310 million in 2005.[38] Adding together all the sub-sectors of the internet service industry, with the exception of internet service providers and e-commerce, China's overall internet service market registered US$451 million in 2002, rose to US$975 million in 2003, an estimated US$1.58 billion in 2004 and is forecast to reach US$2.63 billion in 2005.[39] With an annual growth rate of 116 per cent, China is one of the fastest growing internet markets in the world.[40] Huge user numbers, page hits and other advantages will ensure that the three main Chinese portals: Sina, Sohu and Netease, will achieve a combined average growth rate no lower than that of the entire industry in the next two to three years.

Kingdee and UFSoft: Different IPO exit choices for Chinese domestic SMEs

In February 2001, Kingdee Group, a leader in accounting software and ERP in China made its IPO in GEM at a price of HK$1.03 per share.[41] Kingdee raised about HK$100 million, opening at HK$1.06 and closing at HK$0.69. Its price dropped 35 per cent on its first day.[42]

UFSoft, also one of the leaders in accounting software and ERP, told a totally different story when it made its IPO debut on the SSE. In May of the same year, just two days after Kingdee's flotation, UFSoft was listed at a price of RMB36.68, HK$34.6, per share and raised about RMB917 million, HK$865 million. UFSoft opened at RMB76 and closed at RMB92, its price having risen 250 per cent.[43] UFSoft provides a variety of enterprise software, including applications for enterprise resource planning, accounting, and customer relationship management. The company is one of the largest independent software vendors in China.[44] In 2002 its sales reached a figure of US$40 million. In total, UFSoft achieved a RMB890 million stock exchange market capitalization.[45]

---

[38] *China Online Advertising Market Size Will Reach 1 Billion in 2003*, iResearch Inc., 14 January 2004
[39] ibid
[40] Chinese internet firms line up for IPOs, *China Daily HK Edition*, 18 November 2003
[41] Xu Shaochun's Plan of Kingdee Global Competition, *Securities Times*, 29 June 2001
[42] ibid
[43] Qing Qing (2002) Wang Wenjin: Spring Starts from UFSoft, Makes Chinese Bill Gates Centre of Computer World, www.ccw.com.cn, 23 May
[44] UFSoft Online, www.ufsoft.com.cn
[45] How to Spend the RMB890 million yuans, *Beijing Youth*, 9 January 2002

Kingdee and UFSoft are the two leaders of accounting software and ERP in China. Together they control about 70 per cent of China's US$150 million accounting software market.[46] UFSoft and Kingdee, the only two Chinese companies among the overall top ten software companies in China, hoped to build on their success in accounting software by diversifying into ERP and CRM systems, with the goal of taking their products to the global market by 2005. In 2001, the core business of Kingdee was transferred from accounting to ERP software, which accounted for 60 per cent of its entire profits. UFSoft's selling achievement in accounting software was even higher than in ERP, accounting for 47.75 per cent and 38.44 per cent respectively of total sales. In 2001 and 2002, UFSoft reached the peak of management software provison when it ranked No.1 with a 20.9 per cent market share of accounting software. In the ERP market, UFSoft's share was lower than that of the foreign brand SAP but it became the No.1 domestic brand with a 16.2 per cent market share in ERP (including accounting software applications). In the 2002 ERP market, UFSoft and Kingdee completed RMB128 million and RMB114 million sales respectively.[47] In 1999 UFSoft's and Kingdee's shares of the Chinese market in accounting software had been 40.1 per cent 32.8 per cent respectively. UFSoft's market shares in ERP was 6.2 per cent against Kingdee's market shares of up to 4.4 per cent.[48] Both UFSoft and Kingdee are private companies, so why did they select different markets in which to make their IPOs and achieve such different results?

Kingdee's road to IPO

Kingdee was founded by Xu Shaochun in 1991 with RMB300,000 in Shenzhen, one of the five economic special regions in China. In 1993, a public insurance company of Shenzhen Shekou industrial zone and a private investor invested in Kingdee. In 1997, Kingdee repurchased the shares of the insurance company because public insurance companies were not permitted to invest in 'high risk' industries such as software.[49] By 1997, Kingdee was starved for development capital. Typically, Chinese companies raise funds by three means:

- bank loan;

---

[46] *China Enterprise Resource Planning Software Market Research Report*, International Data Corporation, 18 June 2003
[47] *2001–2002 China Software Market Research Annual Report*, CCID Consulting Ltd., 11 March 2002
[48] 1999 *China Software Market Research Report*, CCID Consulting Ltd
[49] Kingdee Online, www.kingdee.com.hk

- shareholders loan; or

- listing on stock exchanges.

China's state-owned banks rarely offer loans to SMEs such as Kingdee, which was then a small private company. The insurance company had to withdraw from Kingdee and Xu was no longer able to rely on support from insurance companies. As to a stock exchange listing, Xu faced the same difficulties as Wang Wenjin did with UFSoft because Kingdee was a private company, making it impossible to list on Mainboard China. Fortunately, Xu was introduced to IDG by officials of the Science Department of China. In 1998 IDG invested RMB20 million into Kingdee and took a 25 per cent interest.[50] After investment, IDG restructured Kingdee, making it a foreign invested company.

According to China's listing rules, the founders' shares are not allowed to trade on the stock exchange. Therefore IDG could not exit its investment even though Kingdee was listed on China's stock exchange. Furthermore, if Kingdee listed in China, it could not reserve options for its senior management, which Xu very much wanted to do. However, if Kingdee were to list on the Hong Kong GEM, Kingdee could carry out its option plan. If Kingdee could only make its IPO in capital markets outside Mainland China, then IDG planned to apply for Kingdee listings on NASDAQ and GEM. In 2000, the NASDAQ nose-dive caused IDG to change its plans and make the IPO on Hong Kong's GEM.

UFSoft's road to IPO

In 1988, Wang Wenjin borrowed RMB50,000 to found UFSoft. In 1989, UFSoft made its first software product and in 1996, sales revenues reached RMB100 million. By 1999 its revenue had increased to over RMB500 million and UFSoft began to plan an IPO as early as 1997.[51] At that time, China's Main Board was the only choice for UFSoft because the Hong Kong GEM had not opened. The Second Board of China was still in development. As in the case of Kingdee it was very difficult for private companies like UFSoft to list on the Main Board of China, since the Main Board market was set up only to solve the funding problems of SOEs. In addition, only those enterprises recommended by local government could be candidates for listing on the Main Board of China.

---

[50] Kingdee Online, www.kingdee.com.hk
[51] UFSoft Online, www.ufsoft.com

In 1998, when the Hong Kong GEM opened, Wang wanted to list in Hong Kong, but at this time he was busy negotiating with several venture capitalists for strategic investment. When the same VCs evaluated UFSoft to be worth US$200 million,[52] Wang gave up the Hong Kong listing plan since he thought that his company would be undervalued. In the same year, China introduced new policies to promote the development of domestic high-tech ventures. The new policies stipulated that if a private high-tech venture passed the examination of the Science Department of China and the Science Academy of China, the company would be regarded as a high-tech venture. Then, the company would not be limited by quota and could be listed on a Main Board of China. In this way Wang began to prepare for UFSoft's IPO to the Main Board of China.

Before they launched the main board IPO, the attractions of listing on the Second Board made them change their minds. In 2000, the Government decided to establish a growing companies market in China, similar to NASDAQ and the Hong Kong GEM. According to the listing and trading regulation of the Second Board, all shares could be traded on the Second Board market, which was totally separate from the Main Board. In addition, listed companies could grant options. Wang was attracted by these two important factors and decided to make the UFSoft IPO on the Second Board.

However the postponement of the Second Board pushed UFSoft to a standstill again, and in March 2001 China changed the listing procedures of the Main Board, by abolishing the quota allocation system. Any company which met the requirements of the Stock Exchange and passed examination by the Security Management Committee of the State Union, could list on the Main Board of China. For the first time the door was opened to private companies, and on April 23 2001, UFSoft made its IPO on the Shanghai Stock Exchange A-share Market at a price of RMB36.68 per share. UFSoft was the first listed high-tech company after China terminated its quota policy, and with a 64 P/E ratio it was the highest rated of all IPO's on the Main board. Its price rocketed more than 150 per cent, from RMB36.68 to RMB92. The 55 per cent stake in UFSoft ('UF' stands for 'user friendly'), held by founder and chairman Wang Wenjing, was worth nearly US$600 million. This kind of performance for a technology share issue brought back memories of the NASDAQ bubble.[53]

---

[52] *How to Get the Real-Time Value*, Sina Tech News Online, http://tech.sina.com.cn, 25 May 2003
[53] Craig Watts (2001) *UFSoft seen setting the pace for industry*, BDA Analysis of BDA China Limited, 29 May

Case study 3: Pioneer in the digital age – Wang Wenjing elected as '2003 China digital figure'[54]

The awards ceremony of the 2003 China Digital Figure Selection, sponsored by the *Beijing Evening News, Talent Mag* and *China Computer World* was held in the Beijing Kunlun Hotel in lavish style. Wang Wenjing, Board Chairman of UFSoft Co Ltd was selected as the 2003 China Digital Figure from more than 100 candidates based on the high popularity, influence and the sound performance of UFSoft. Also nominated were, amongst others, Tang Jun, President of Microsoft (China) Co Ltd, Yang Xu, General Manager of Intel (China) Co Ltd, Wei Xin, Board Chairman of Beida Founder Group, Wang Mingjian, General Manager of TCL Mobile Communication Co Ltd and Zhou Shaoning, CEO of UTStarcom (China) Co Ltd.

UFSoft is the biggest management software supplier in China and has been ranked first in the financial software field for years. In the past 15 years, UFSoft has created one amazing myth after another and is influential in the history of software development in China.

Presently, UFSoft has transcended numerous competitors and has become the leading manufacturer in management software. In 2003, it gained several successes on the ERP market and expanded its business scope, as well as market share, by establishing the UFSoft Anyi Co Ltd – engaged in e-Government – and UFSoft Engineering Co Ltd, engaged in software outsourcing service. Besides delivering services to China's enterprises, UFSoft set its sights on the international market and established the UFSoft Engineering Co Ltd in 2002 to serve global clients. So far the three major services, namely UFSoft ERP, UFSoft e-Government and UFSoft outsourcing are all available and the general strategy has been formed.

Mr Wang Wenjing is the initiator and guiding hand of UFSoft, which has developed from a two-person software service agency to a software house with 3,300 employees under his guidance. Wang Wenjing has contributed much to China's management software industry development and has been named 'Excellent Private Entrepreneur in China', 'Excellent Private Technology Businessman in China', '1st Batch of Outstanding Youth in China's Software Industry', '2001 China Economic Man', '2001 China Software

---

[54] Original from *Beijing Evening News*, 5 March 2004

> Industry Leader' and 'Beijing Municipal Model Worker'. He has also been named an 'Asian Star' in American *Business Weekly*.
>
> 2003 was the last year for UFSoft's 3-year strategy of 'comprehensive upgrade, expansion and development', during which UFSoft presented an all-round growth situation through continuous adjustment. The *2002–2003 Annual Report on China's Management Software Market* issued by CCID, an authoritative IT market research organ in China, showed that UFSoft ranked as No.1 among all manufacturers in China's market, overtaking SAP, an international manufacturer, for the first time.
>
> On 17 September 2003, UFSoft formally founded a branch in Hong Kong, a milestone in UFSoft's advance towards Southeast Asia, and the expansion of its overseas market in order to become an international software house.
>
> At the 'UFSoft 2003 User Annual Meeting' in 2004, Wang Wenjing said: 'China's software industry will grow up in the world, and world-class software companies will be born in China. The mid-term objective of UFSoft is to become a world-class software company and we shall achieve this objective with the strong support of the government, users and partners, and we shall go from victory to victory.'

Different IPO choices

In 1998, IDG invested in Kingdee and took up 25 per cent of its shares. As a foreign VC, IDG could not exit on the Main Board of China. So, Kingdee can only list on the capital markets outside of China to initiate an IDG exit. Compared to Kingdee, all shareholders of UFSoft were domestic companies which mainly considered raising funds from the market.

Xu wanted Kingdee to be an international company whilst Wang attached more importance to localization. In 1998, Xu accepted the investment of IDG, which brought to Kingdee not only funds but also international business models and concepts. Kingdee wanted to be an internationalized company and the GEM of Hong Kong as an international market was a suitable option.

Conversely, Wang was the controlling shareholder, who thought of UFSoft as a domestic company, and so it was helpful for UFSoft to list on the domestic market. Wang remains confident he will continue to dominate the industry because 'Chinese-made software can more easily fit into Chinese society.'

From 1998 until its IPO, UFSoft's working capital depended on loans from the domestic commercial banks, whilst Kingdee was funded by VC and developed rapidly after investment by IDG. Kingdee used the funds to build its sales and services networks; its branches increased from 21 to 37 and the number of agents increased to 360.

Kingdee successfully raised HK$100 million from the GEM, and the funds are being used for R&D and market expansion. After listing on the GEM, Kingdee could carry out its plan of options which are very important to software companies. The GEM market is an international market; thus Kingdee could speed up its internationalization by selling its shares to international investors or companies. The P/Es of IPOs in Hong Kong are lower than on the Chinese domestic Main Board market. Usually, the P/E ratio is only 10–20 times, but on the Chinese Main Board market, the P/E ratio sometimes reached 50–60 times, ensuring that Kingdee could raise more funds than if it was listed on the Main Board of China.

Big international investors do not like to invest in the shares of a company listed on the GEM. But on the other hand, because foreign investors know less than domestic investors, Kingdee's price would be affected. In choosing a Hong Kong listing, Kingdee had its own rationale. The most important outcome is that Kingdee got what it wanted:

- Kingdee accepted the investment of international venture capitalist, IDG, which provided much help to Kingdee, not only in funds but also in the management ideas and models. It goes without saying that listing in Hong Kong is favourable to the exit of venture capitalists. IDG can cash out its funding and deal with its share option as it likes.

- From the point of views of shareholders, raising fewer funds would guarantee the relatively high return rate. Kingdee is pursuing a healthy cycle. Furthermore, the issue of a secondary public offering will be easier and more marketable than in Mainland China.

- Kingdee maintains the advantage of high internal morale through the flotation on HKGEM. The employees have the right to claim the share option, which is also a gain for Kingdee. In this way, Kingdee has retained personnel and saved cost. Currently, such a system has not been established fully and suitably in the domestic market.

- The Hong Kong Stock Exchange is a mature market in terms of monitoring and its investors, which will prompt enterprises to operate to international standards. The improvement of corporate achievement is also a challenge for Kingdee.

- Through Hong Kong GEM, the company's shares can be sold to global investors making Kingdee an international corporation.

Of course, there are still three shortcomings in listing abroad:

- Compared with domestic investors, foreign investors cannot know the enterprises as intimately, although the distance between Hong Kong and Mainland China is slight.
- Valuation abroad is relatively low. In Mainland China, the P/E Ratio will reach to 50–60 times, but in Hong Kong, it will be only 20–30 times.
- The investors' mindset is different. Large international institutions like to invest in a company whose market capitalization is large because of the easy entrance and exit.

UFSoft raised RMB800 million, which was eight times more than Kingdee raised in Hong Kong. UFSoft had enough capital in developing its new products and expand its sales network. Share options are the key to successful software companies. UFSoft could not make option for its key employees, because it was limited by domestic law. What alternative inspirational mechanism did UFSoft use to keep its management team motivated? After IPO, Wang still held directly and indirectly around a 52 per cent interest in UFSoft. Without other investors' input, will every important decision made by Wang be right? Is RMB800 million a burden for UFSoft? RMB800 million is far more than UFSoft needed. In fact, the difference of listing between Hong Kong GEM and the Mainland's stock exchange is just like the difference between an apple and egg: there is no suitable comparison. The choice of listing place should be made by enterprises and entrepreneurs themselves. The real requirements of enterprises are the most important. From a long-term perspective, the differences between the two locations will diminish. In the short term, the key question for entrepreneurs will be where to go for trading rather than where to list.

6

Successful Venture Capital-Backed SMEs in China

IPO Success on NASDAQ for Ctrip.com, the Chinese SME travel portal

The professional online travel firm

Chinese travellers will have access to cheaper and better travel services as major online travel service operators strive to promote their businesses with large amounts of capital in hand. Ctrip.com International Ltd (Ctrip), a Chinese online travel agent specializing in travel within China, known as Chinese Expedia, recently went public. Ctrip has China's largest travel service website and is a leading consolidator of hotel accommodation and airline tickets. The company aggregates information on hotels and flights, enabling customers to make informed and cost-effective hotel and flight bookings. It acts as an agent in booking transactions, and primarily targets business and leisure travellers in China who do not travel in groups. Ctrip has helped to make travel in China much more convenient, especially for business class travellers, who form a traditionally under-served yet fast-growing segment of the Chinese travel industry.[1] Ctrip was also the first local company and seventh mainland firm to list on NASDAQ and has cooperation deals with 2100 star-rated hotels in about 200 cities, mainly located in China.

Launched in 1999, Ctrip's investors included overseas venture capitalists, International Digital Group (IDG) and Softbank.[2] After purchasing the traditional room booking service centre in November 2000, it became China's largest room service seller. A year later it had started

---

[1] Ctrip Online, www.ctrip.com
[2] Zhao Haitao 'The New Upsurge of Chinese Internet Firms for NASDAQ', *E-North IT*, 9 December 2003

to report profits and set up a unified air ticket booking centre in China. Ctrip's founders, Liang Jianzhang and Shen Nanpeng, were jointly listed as the 33rd richest in the country by Rupert Hoogewerf in his 2003 China's IT rich list.[3] Carlyle Group used Carlyle Asia Venture Partners I, a US$159 million fund closed in 2000, for the Ctrip investment.[4] The fund is fully invested, although the firm still has plenty of resources remaining in two other Asia-centric funds. Combined, these two funds closed on nearly US$1 billion in commitments with more than one third of that total still available.

Ctrip has experienced substantial growth since its inception and has become one of the best-known travel brands in China. It is the largest consolidator of hotel accommodations in China in terms of the number of room nights booked and is also one of the leading consolidators of airline tickets in Beijing and Shanghai in terms of the number of airline tickets booked and sold. The company is the only airline ticket consolidator in China with a centralized reservation system and ticket fulfilment infrastructure covering all of the economically prosperous regions of China. The company offers its services through an advanced transaction and service platform consisting of its centralized toll-free, 24-hour customer service centre and bilingual websites. Ctrip's customers can book air tickets and hotels in China through its website or hotlines, via its call centre. Ctrip offers secure online and offline reservation services for hotels and airlines, as well as a vast database of travel information in both English and Chinese. It is hardly surprising that Ctrip recorded revenue of US$12 million in 2002, US$20.9 million in 2003, and US$40.3 million in 2004.[5] Pure profit was US$16.1 million in 2004.[6]

The company's goal is to create long-term shareholder value by enhancing its position as a leading hotel and airline ticket consolidator in China. Going forward, the company intends to leverage the Ctrip brand in order to attract new travel suppliers and negotiate more favourable contractual terms with its existing suppliers, whilst expanding its hotel supplier networks, room inventory, air-ticketing and other travel product offerings. The company also intends to pursue selective strategic acquisitions and expand into Hong Kong, Macau and Taiwan.

Ctrip.com International Ltd is incorporated in the Cayman Islands and conducts all of its substantial operations in China. With its operational headquarters in Shanghai, it has branches in Beijing, Guangzhou, Shenzhen and Hong Kong and also maintains a network

---

[3] *Chinese Venture Capital Say Goodbye to the Winter*, Shenzhen Online, www.szonline.net, 16 February 2004
[4] *The Carlyle Group: Ctrip.com International*, Carlyle Online, www.thecarlylegroup.com
[5] Ctrip 2004 Financial Yearbook
[6] ibid

of sales offices in about 30 cities throughout China. In addition, it has established China's largest air ticket ordering system covering 35 Chinese cities.

Ctrip bridges the gap between independent travellers and travel suppliers by helping travellers to plan and book their trips while at the same time helping travel suppliers such as hotels and airlines to improve the efficiency of their marketing and distribution channels. The company has achieved its leading position in part by establishing competitive strengths as a leading travel brand in China, with a large supplier network and nationwide coverage, a scalable platform and flexible cost structure, excellent customer service, advanced infrastructure and technology, as well as building an experienced management team.

The company's business philosophy focuses on:[7]

- **C:** Providing a guide to CUSTOMER requirements;
- **T:** Creating a seamless cooperation system between customers and partners through TEAMWORK;
- **R:** Treating customers with the utmost RESPECT;
- **I:** Cherishing INTEGRITY in its cooperation with partners; and
- **P:** Pursuing win-win cooperation with all its PARTNERS.

VC from Carlyle before listing

Ctrip is one of the Carlyle Asia Venture Partners portfolio companies. In November 2000, Carlyle invested US$8 million in Series B Preferred Stock of Ctrip. The second round of financing raised a total of more than US$11 million at a pre-investment valuation of US$16 million, providing Carlyle with an interest in the ownership of the company of approximately 29 per cent.[8] In 2002, Ctrip purchased an air ticketing counter enabling it to become a full-service provider, and in 2003–2004 Ctrip increased its revenues by more than ten times and became a profitable operation. In 2004, the company had already returned a dividend to shareholders equivalent to 12.5 per cent of investor capital.[9]

Gabriel Li, Managing Director of Carlyle Asia Venture Partners, said in an interview:

---

[7] Ctrip Online, www.ctrip.com
[8] *The Carlyle Group: Ctrip.com International*, Carlyle Online, www.thecarlylegroup.com
[9] Hirschkorn Jeffrey R, 'A New Day Has Come for IPOs', *Current Offerings Special*, 1 January 2004

Ctrip is at the forefront of the online travel services business, and is a clear market leader in China. We believe that Ctrip has a very bright future and, with Carlyle's assistance, Ctrip is evaluating partnership opportunities with global travel service providers.

Ctrip listed in December 2003 on the tech-laden NASDAQ, under the ticker symbol CTRP. Ctrip.com[10] became the seventh Chinese Internet-concept company listed on the US VC market after AsiaInfo, China.com Sina.com, Sohu.com, Netease.com etc. Its shares rallied and jumped more than 108 per cent when the stock reached a high of US$37.35 above the IPO price of US$18 on 10 December 2003, its first trading day on NASDAQ, before easing back later to close at US$33.94, with a gain of 88.56 per cent on the initial IPO offer price.[11] This was the largest first-day rise of a company on such a technology-heavy market and the highest one-day debut in New York in the previous three years. In fact, it was the highest debut on the market since Transmeta Corp. doubled its IPO price and closed 115 per cent ahead on its first day of trading on 6 November 2000. Its performance also trounced 2003's previously best first day rise of 47 per cent,[12] held by digital surround sound technology provider Digital Theatre Systems (DTSI).

When launching its IPO to raise US$75.6 million[13] for the expansion of its business, Ctrip's leading underwriter was US-based Merrill Lynch. The Ctrip IPO was a prelude to a much bigger Chinese offering – the US$2.6 billion IPO of China Life Insurance Co Ltd[14] (see Table 6.1).

While Ctrip's small float and its exposure to the heated Chinese market were two of the key drivers of its strong first day gain, its debut also demonstrates that investors are not afraid to get their feet wet in less-established, rapidly-growing enterprises. In fact, a number of high-growth, small capitalization internet names had geared up in order to complete their IPOs before 2005, including another from the Asian region. Among them were the third largest online travel portal, Orbitz (ORBZ); internet-based non-profit software provider Kintera (KNTA), online flower and fruit retailer commerce provider, Provide

---

[10] 'Rising Stars Impact Net Industry', *China Daily*, 4 February 2004
[11] Quan Libing 'The Backstage Manipulators: Best Venture Capitalists and Best Investing Bankers', *China High and New Technology Enterprises*, Issue 2, 9 May 2004
[12] 'Chinese Online Travel Portal Ctrip.com Rises 89% In Its Market Debut and Chalks Up the Biggest First Day Gain For An IPO In Three Years', *IPO Breaking News*, Renaissance Capital Corporation, 9 December 2003
[13] *This Year's Priced IPOs*, www.ipohome.com, 29 September 2004
[14] Li Qinghua, 'The Global Selling for China Life', *China Economic Times*, 8 December 2003

Table 6.1 Basic data of Ctrip after listing

Ctrip.com International (CTRP)			
Business		**Aftermarket trading**	
Business	Provides phone and online booking of hotel and airline reservations in China	Current Price	N/A
Industry	Leisure services	First Day Close	US$33.94
Employees 1420 Founded 1999		Return from IPO	N/A
Financial data (US$millions)		**IPO profile**	
Market Cap	291.9	IPO Date	12/9/03
Revenues	12	Offer Price	US$18.00
Net Income	2	Offer Shares	4.2 million
		* Increased price range: US$16-US$18 per ADS	
Corporate data		Lead Manager(s)	Merrill Lynch
Web Address	www.ctrip.com	Co Manager	USB Piper Jaffray

Commerce (PRVD); and the Korean online games developer Webzen (WZEN).[15] Looking at future possibilities, Ctrip is trying to become the Expedia of China, which shows that the economic climate in China is right to do such deals.[16]

China is one of the fastest-growing airline markets. Its three biggest carriers own a 35 per cent stake in reservations booking software firm TravelSky Technology Ltd (TTL), of which 22 per cent is owned by the Chinese government. In China, TTL is the definitive source of information for the country's airlines, airports and travel agents. TTL was formed in 2000 by 21 Chinese airlines. Through more than 20,000 client terminals in 229 domestic cities and 79 international cities, TTL provides access to its real-time data network for operational and back office areas as computer reservations, inventory control, departure control, cargo control, aviation insurance and information

---

[15] *The Best Mutual Fund Managers 2004*, Business Weekly Online, www.businessweek.com, 22 March 2004
[16] *Small Cap Focus, Live Analysis*, Briefing.com, 17 December 2003

management.[17] TTL's customers wanted access to more timely and more accurate historical data to make faster, better informed decisions, critical in China's highly competitive travel industry. TTL chose Teradata, a division of NCR Corporation, for its Teradata Warehouse and its extensive data warehousing operation. TTL received the immediate benefit of a dramatically improved system performance. With the Teradata Warehouse, data volume has grown from less than 50GB to more than 300GB as TTL now maintains three years of historical data, compared with the three months which was all that it could maintain previously. TTL can extract 100MB of data in ten seconds from its mainframe system to populate the warehouse, compared with the 1.5 hours it used to take to extract 30MB of data. Daily reports and data from the previous day that formerly took two hours to generate are now completed in 20 minutes.[18]

As an indication of the intense market interest in Chinese companies, Ctrip's IPO price of US$18 for each American Depository Share was at the top of the US$16 to US$18 preliminary range, which itself had been increased from a range of US$14 to US$16.[19] Although Ctrip has not been in existence for long, its revenues are soaring and the company is profitable. Ctrip has benefited from the growing Chinese economy and low exchange rate. The IPO was a way for investors to get in on the booming travel market in China, where Ctrip does not have a great deal of competition. According to the Securities and Exchange Commission filings for its recent reporting periods, Ctrip is profitable; in 2004 the company gained 86 per cent of its revenue from its hotel reservation business.[20]

In the November 2003 round of fundraising, Ctrip gathered US$11 million, of which US$8 million came from Carlyle in Series B preferred stock. Carlyle is the largest single shareholder in the company with 25.97 per cent of the shares. Aside from Ctrip CFO Neil Shen, who holds 10.62 per cent of the company's shares, the largest remaining shareholders all hold less than ten per cent each. Ctrip was China's first website to list overseas since 2000 – when the dotcom bubble burst – but more of China's dotcom firms are expected to follow between 2004 and 2006. While Ctrip was Carlyle's first Chinese IPO, it was the firm's second IPO in the Far East. In October 2003, Carlyle's portfolio company eAccess, a Japan-based internet access provider,

---

[17] TravelSky Technology Limited Online, www.travelsky.net
[18] ibid
[19] Willoughby J, *Giant Steps: Investors Bet On A New Bull Market in IPOs*, Barron's Cover Story, 22 December 2003
[20] Li Xiaoning, 'China Concept Appears In NASDAQ Again', *Heilongjiang Economy News*, 15 October 2004

went public. Prices skyrocketed to more than 60 per cent above the issue price on the first day of trading, tripling the value of Carlyle's original US$26 million investment.[21]

Ctrip sold 4.2 million American Depository Shares (ADSs) for the listing, including 1.5 million ADSs sold by its shareholders, which accounted for 28 per cent of its total shares.[22] The company is using the proceeds from its IPO for sales and marketing, working capital, and potential acquisitions. Merrill Lynch was the market maker for the deal and Ctrip may have to issue up to an additional 500,000 ADSs under an over-allotment option in the IPO.[23]

Investors, especially those from the US, have been increasingly interested in buying into Chinese websites. The trading volume of Chinese websites listed on NASDAQ has outperformed many leading US websites. Ctrip's excellent performance is encouraging, but not surprising.

Observers said that the fact that Ctrip was a dotcom and located in the birthplace of the SARS outbreak may have been an indicator that the Asian market was making a comeback. As a consequence of Ctrip's groundbreaking listing, US investors are expected to buy a greater number of shares in Chinese websites. What's more, Ctrip was not the only Chinese dotcom planning an IPO in 2003; others including Baidu.com, a search engine; Tom.com, a web portal; Joyo.com, an e-commerce company; and Shanda, an online games operator, all planned for IPOs on NASDAQ in 2004. Some of them realized their 'dreams'.

Activity among the online travel companies

Ctrip has decided to use the proceeds for business expansion, brand building, technological updates and strategic mergers and acquisitions. Ctrip has made some progress in acquiring a travel agency in China. At the same time, the online travel service firm is also spending more money on promotions, especially in offline business, which accounts for roughly 70 per cent of its orders. The primary target of promotions will be frequent flyers and train travellers. Ctrip has 6 million registered users, of which 600,000 are active.[24]

---

[21] *The Carlyle Group: Ctrip.com International*, Carlyle Online, www.thecarlylegroup.com
[22] *Chinese Internet Company Has Hot IPO*, Associated Press, AlwaysOn Online, www.alwayson-network.com, 9 December 2003
[23] Ctrip Online, www.ctrip.com
[24] ibid

eLong Inc, China's second-largest online travel service provider after Ctrip and its arch-rival also has ambitious plans for the next few years. eLong's Chairman Justin Tang's consistent approach to doing business is to be indifferent to weal or woe. The business, which received US$15 million worth of investment from US VC firms Tiger Technology Fund and Blueridge Capital, will raise the expansion fund with either private placements or an IPO. eLong made its IPO on the NASDAQ market late in October 2004. In the IPO, the firm raised US$62.1 million after pricing and has offered 4.6 million American Depository Receipts (ADRs), each representing two common shares, to the public. Before the IPO, eLong made another bold move by selling 30 per cent of its stake to IAC/InterActiveCorp, the world's leading multibrand interactive commerce company. After eLong's IPO, IAC's share dropped to 25 per cent. The firm's current management team, fund investors and other investors hold equal shares of the remaining 75 per cent. This shareholding structure means eLong is less affected by short-term trading, so it can maintain long-term growth.

China's biggest internet portal Sina Corp acquired Shanghai Fortune Trip Hotel Booking Website (Fortunetrip.com), a Shanghai-based online travel service provider, which mainly operates in Beijing, Shanghai, Guangzhou and Zhejiang Province with 130 employees. The acquisition will lay the foundation for Sina's development in electronic commerce.

With huge capital in hand, the online travel service market will see a lot of changes. There are many operators in the market, but their scale is very small, so the moves from Ctrip, eLong and Sina will merit much attention. Since the technological threshold for an online travel service provider is quite low, the competition will focus on network resources, such as the number of partner hotels and the discounts they can negotiate. With the intensification of the turf war, it is likely to be a win-win situation for consumers. Ctrip and eLong only account for less than five per cent of the market share of the overall travel distribution business.[25] So internet-based travel service distributors have plenty of room for further development. The market potential is quite exciting.

---

[25] Wang Yu, 'eLong Boss Always Keeps Cool', *China Business Weekly*, 9 December 2004

VC investment for a start-up enterprise[26]

Three groups investing in GTT

Located in the Zhuhai High-Tech Achievement Industrialization Demonstration Region, Zhuhai Yueke Tsinghua Electronic Ceramics Co Ltd (GTT) was formally set up on 29 April 1999. Investment in the company came from three sectors: Guangdong Technology Venture Investment Corporation (GDTVIC), Guangdong Technology Venture Capital Co Ltd (GTVC) and Tsinghua University. The company was designed to be a high-tech demonstration enterprise for transformation achievement, engaged in researching, developing, producing and selling comprehensively. The company was identified as a 'new and high technology enterprise' by the Science and Technology Bureau of Guangdong province in April 2001 and was awarded ISO9001-2000 International Quality Systems certification in December 2001. Tsinghua University contributed its proprietary electro-ceramic technology, while the two Guangdong companies contributed financial capital to the venture.

The different stages in the development of GTT illustrate how venture capital can support the growth of high-tech industries and start-up enterprises. It may also serve as a model for academic institutions to work with venture capitalists and industries to develop new products.

Establishment and management model

GTT was established in March 1999. GDTVIC and GTVC provided VC investment. Tsinghua University provided two national invention patents 'High Thermal Conductivity AIN Substrates Manufacture Technology' and 'Tape Casting Technology for Ceramic Substrates' as the consideration for its shares. The whole of the registered capital of the company is RMB72 million with Tsinghua University receiving an 18 per cent stake in the venture for its proprietary technology.

The company produces specialized ceramic materials used in the production of computer chips. Now that electronic and information technologies are becoming more and more integrated in micro-automation and multifunction, so the production of electronic technology should also be developed as smaller, lighter and thinner products with higher stability, higher speed and more functions to meet the needs of Surface Mounting Technology (SMT) and the trend towards using multilayer,

---

[26] All data statistics are from GTT Online, www.gtt-zhh.com

microchip, integration, module and multifunction in functional ceramic devices.

GTT now produces high performance alumina and high thermal conductivity AIN ceramic substrates to all specifications and will produce other microchip and multilayer functional ceramic devices in the future. The main characteristics of the high performance 96 alumina and high thermal conductivity AIN ceramic substrates are:

1. To prepare tape casting slurry using a none-toluene mixed solvent, which can reduce environment pollution, can help to control the tape casting moulding easily and improve the flan quality.

2. To develop AIN ceramic substrates with thermal conductivity higher than 180W/mK, using the <1700° low-temperature sintering process, which can help to control flatness and roughness, reduce the grain size and improve the substrate's flexible strength and thermal shock resistance.

High performance alumina ceramics substrates are mainly used in all specifications of high precision applications of HIC, chip resistance, network resistance, potentiometer assembly, semiconductor refrigerator and power modules. High thermal conductivity AIN ceramic substrates are used in the applications of high density HIC and encapsulation, power modules and highly effective radiators.

The company invested RMB336 million in fixed assets in the areas of equipment and infrastructure. The shipshape factory is equipped with high-efficiency automatic facilities which are among the top-ranking facilities of the global substrate industry. GTT can offer manufacturing and machining substrates to all customized specifications with advanced equipment imported from Japan and the US. After nearly five years of laborious efforts, the company has already achieved a good complement of equipment, personnel and technologies and has established a stable foundation for reproducible high performance, high consistency and high stability products. At the same time, the company operates in the best interests of its shareholders with a board of directors, an audit committee and professional management in place.

The company received its ISO 9001-2000 management certificate at the end of 2001. It currently has 100 employees engaging in research and development, production and management. Through the whole development process, the science and technology venture investment was used to facilitate the implementation of this cooperative project. It includes the phases of transferring the research results from laboratory to interim in-company experimentation and finally extending to mass production, accumulating valuable experience at every stage.

The company has successfully demonstrated the effective running of a new high-tech enterprise together with the operation of a venture investment organization during its different stages: from the beginning of the establishment stage through the growing stage and then to the expansion and maturity stage of entering the market. GTT's experiences show very well how to facilitate the commercialization of innovation from a top research university such as Peking University, Tsinghua University, Renmin University, Fudan University, Huazhong University of Science and Technology, and so on.

Characteristics and outlook

Supported by Tsinghua University research, the technical source of manufacturing high performance 96 alumina and high thermal conductivity AIN ceramic substrates is the result of research by the State Key Laboratory of New Ceramics and Fine Processing. Tsinghua University is an important nationally funded research centre for natural science, which enjoys a high reputation at home and abroad for teaching, research and innovative technology development.

With the technology which was transferred from the State Key Laboratory of New Ceramics and Fine Processing, Tsinghua University is at an advanced domestic world level and is the subject of independent intellectual property rights. GTT owns independent intellectual property rights in some of the high-tech research achievements which were transferred from the Laboratory. The industrialized development project of 'High Thermal Conductivity AIN Substrates Manufacturing Technology' was awarded formal technical authentication by the Science and Technology Bureau of Guangdong Province in March 2002. The authentication committee experts were unanimous in their view that it is an innovative achievement with appropriate intellectual property.

The two provincial venture investment corporations provided funding support for the high-tech enterprise to accelerate completion of its establishment and growth phase. At the same time, they also provided a good development environment and management consulting service for the enterprise and made active use of the VC mechanism to accelerate the high-tech enterprise's further expansion and maturity phase. This support has greatly helped the engagement with capital investment to speed up the investment return and efforts to obtain significant economic benefit.

There is a growing market for electronic components due to the rapid development of the electronic and computer industries in China. The company's technical products are closely connected to high-tech industries such as information techniques, microelectronics, telecommunications, power and automobile electronics. This industry is very large and prosperous, and focused especially on exploring the international market. The products are designed to promote GTT's competitive capability following China's WTO membership and can be used to replace many imported products.

Looking ahead to the exit mechanism, the GTT board of directors has considered four channels:

1. IPO. As the company enters its expansion stage, it is preparing for a public offering of its shares or part of its operation.
2. The venture capitalist companies will consider selling off their stakes to potential strategic investors after the company has entered into its expansion stage.
3. Restructuring. The company can be restructured according to its various product lines.
4. M&A. The company may engage in M&A activities to increase its capital base.

At present, the bulk of the company's market is in Mainland China. However, it has begun to receive orders from Hong Kong and Taiwan. The company is currently negotiating with other companies to develop new products. The development of GTT is tracked in Table 6.2.

Table 6.2 Stages of development of GTT

Date	Stage	Main task
April 1999	Initial stage	Establishment
June to September 1999	Initial stage	Choice of facilities. Acquired production equipment from Japan, the US and Great Britain.
End 1999	Initial stage	Finished all assembly lines
April 2000	Start-up stage	Completed the construction of its plant and the installation of equipment
October 1999 to March 2000	Start-up stage	Hired its first batch of 30 employees, then began its technological training
August 2000	Start-up stage	Production commenced, established a handful of customers as sales base
2001 to present	Growth stage	Passed its start-up period and entered the expansion stage. Seeking better management, raising liquid funds, increasing economies of scale and reducing costs through high efficiency.

Date	Stage	Main task
Present	Growth stage	Current term operating goals: completed installation of new production lines and developing new products for the market.

Sustainability of development

Five factors support the long-term development of GTT. First of all, GTT cooperates with Tsinghua University and the two VC companies to develop new products. The general manager of GTT is Professor Zhou Heping, who is the inventor of the appropriate technology and an advisor to the PhD programme at Tsinghua University. His experiences in the development of advanced technology and the ability to manage a modern high-tech enterprise have resulted in the successful achievement of all Tsinghua University's goals of commercialization and innovative activities. The professional high quality administration and production team which GTT installed was an essential condition for constructing the production line and entering normal production within a short period of time. In addition, the plan for setting up a research centre and an R&D team was carried out smoothly. The centre can offer the company a continuous flow of innovative products and technology through its R&D activities. This capability greatly strengthens GTT's competitiveness in the market.

The second factor in GTT's development is the establishment and perfection of the R&D centre's system and structure. The Guangdong Research & Development Centre for Functional Ceramics project is authorized by the Science and Technology Bureau of Guangdong Province and sponsored by both the Bureau and the Venture Capital Group of Guangdong Province (VCGGP). It is also supported by GTT. The amount of planned investment in the project is RMB10 million, of which the Science and Technology Bureau and FVCGGP each provide half. GTT supports the construction of the Research & Development Centre with Professor Zhou as head. A large group of doctors and Masters Degree candidates are working on research and development supervised by Professor Zhou. Advanced instruments and facilities for the analysis and examination of ceramics and electronic devices have been installed. The Centre has a close relationship with the State Key Laboratory of New Ceramics and Fine Processing, Tsinghua University. The research achievements of the laboratory will be transferred to the centre to facilitate their industrialization and commercialization.

The Centre is based in Guangdong Province, and gains great advantages from the excellent economic, geographic and corporate environments and local personalities of the area. By cooperating with many local research institutions and industrial corporations, the Centre has accelerated the development of high technical industry, improved the research level of functional ceramics and devices and helped the progress of sunrise industries in Guangdong Province. The Centre will always meet the requirements of the new high technologies and national economic development, and will continue to focus on the research, development, experimentation and industrialization of advanced functional ceramics and devices.

In particular, to meet the needs of Surface Mounting Technology (SMT) and the trend towards using multilayers, microchips, integration, modules and multifunctions, the centre concentrates its research and development on the high-performance electronic ceramics and development of high-tech industries such as information, telecommunications, electricity sources etc.

GTT also needs to maintain the quality performance of its products. The company uses a no-pollution slurry system in its Tape Casting process to produce $A_{12}O_3$ ceramics and AIN ceramic substrates. The annual output is 60,000 square metres. The products have passed the tests of national statutory testing organizations and have reached national standards throughout, with parts of the GTT specifications exceeding national standards. The quality of GTT's products is fully competitive with that of advanced foreign products. The products have many excellent features such as high density, high precision dimensions, smooth and flat surfaces and good anti-corrosion properties. Positive endorsement for the products is frequently given by GTT's customers who consider that they are good substitutes for imported products. Therefore, they are highly competitive in the market. The company's RMB8 million investment in modern scientific equipment has been well spent.

Fourthly, the personnel structure should be outstanding. The company plans to attract the best human resources from China and overseas to further develop its products. The company has employed more than 100 people, 40 per cent of whom hold doctor, master and bachelor degrees; 85 per cent of the production line workers have technical secondary school diplomas. The company is managed with a computer network system which helps to make up an integrated high-tech unit encompassing research and development, production operations, quality control and marketing activities.

Finally, the company has applied for funds from various government bodies for its research and development projects, such as 'The Science and Technology Office Fund of Technological Innovation for Middle/Small Enterprises' and the 'National Key Project of New Products'.

Investing in ventures at the early development stage

GTT's case is a typical early stage project investment. Research statistics show that the early development or pre-growth stage accounts for a significant proportion of VC investment in Mainland China, due to its special economic circumstances, although there are still only a few academic theorists researching this kind of investment. Summarized below is an analysis of the necessity, feasibility, basic characteristics, experience and lessons learned from investment in these ventures at such an early stage. There are four factors behind the necessity for and feasibility of this kind of investment. Firstly, as China is undergoing a process in which the Chinese planned economy is being transformed into a market economy, the booming market economy has created a lot of initial stage projects. Secondly, the investment cost at this early stage is relatively low. Thirdly, there is very great growth potential for such investment projects. Fourthly, due to the imperfections of the exit mechanism in China, small-scale investments enable venture capitalists to exit more easily in the private equity market. There are three basic characteristics of early stage investments in China:

1. Due to its early stage of development, there is often little information or data available on the investment project with which to analyze and make judgements.
2. Exiting is easy because of the small scale of investment.
3. It is necessary to provide more value-added services to ventures in their early stages of development.

The following three lessons can be gained from experience of investing in early ventures:

- Pick a large number of projects with a purpose and focus in mind.
- Perform stringent investigation and evaluation of the projects.
- Provide all-round value-added services for the projects.

The software manufacturing market in China

Developing step by step

The software market in China has grown steadily and gradually since the early 1990s, mostly in connection with the growth in PC ownership among both consumers and businesses. By 2004, China's software market had reached approximately RMB220 billion in sales revenue, growing nearly eleven-fold from RMB20.64 billion in 2000.[27]

Research and development in software and system integration has grown rapidly in the past few years. According to MII statistics, China now boasts 8,582 software enterprises with 18,000 kinds of products and has also set up six software bases including sites in Beijing and Shanghai. Chinese companies account for 32 per cent of total software sales. Some 590,000 people worked in the software industry in 2002.[28]

By the end of 2002, software companies in China had generated RMB110 billion of revenue, including income from hardware system integration, which saw an 87.3 per cent increase in revenue, amounting to RMB43.95 billion.[29] Many large and middle sized cities have set up their own software parks following the structure of Silicon Valley, where the government provides a favourable business environment for software companies. Some multinational companies like Microsoft and Motorola, for example, have set up their own software R&D centres in China, which has been a big challenge to local software companies.

IDC Research Analyze the Future expects this market to grow at a compound annual growth rate (CAGR) of 25.8 per cent between 2002 and 2007, driven by steady economic growth, improvements in IT infrastructure and increasing demand from business. According to MII's data, the sales of the electronic IT sector, which includes software, hit RMB2680 billion (US$22.3 billion). Sales in 2003 were up 45 per cent year on year, showing an average annual increase of 36 per cent from 2000 to 2003. China's software exports rose to US$2.8 billion in 2004, which was an increase of more than 40 per cent on 2003.[30]

In 2003, Chinese domestic software companies, such as UFSoft and Genersoft, switched from financial management software to the high-end of the market. The current market leader, Oracle, depends on its advantage in the database markets to expand its application software and application server market. Neusoft and TongTech, the local brands, became leaders respectively in the firewall and middleware market by right of their own long-term technology accumulation. TurboCRM made profits in the field of customer relationship management (CRM), whilst in the burgeoning application software

---

[27] Fan Zhegao and Zhou Xian, 'Chinese Software Sectors Run For RMB 10 Billion Yuans Profit', *China Electroncs News* 14 June 2004; 'The Sales Revenue of Software Will Access RMB300 billion in Chinese Market', *Science Times*, 4 April 2005

[28] Hu Kunshan, 'The Development Situation and Human Resource Requirement of China Software Industry', *China Computer News*, 1 September 2003

[29] ibid

[30] 'The Sales Revenue of Software Will Access RMB300 billion in Chinese Market', *Science Times*, 4 April 2005

field, UFGov registered a rapid increase in the electronic government affairs market.

The growth target in China's tenth Five Year Plan for the software and IT industry is more than 30 per cent per annum[31]. Such growth will bring market sales up to nearly RMB250 billion by 2005.[32] China also expects to build 20 large software companies with revenues each exceeding RMB1 billion (US$120 million), more than 100 'famous software brands', and software exports of at least US$1.5–2 billion by 2005.[33]

Among software sectors, accounting and enterprise resource planning (ERP) software have been the most 'mature' (in that they have developed very well and gained much experience through R&D, exploring the market and competing with rivals) when compared with other general management software. In 2002, for the first time ERP's market share at 46.54 percent[34] exceeded that of accounting software. It is estimated that around 80 per cent of companies and government units still do not use a computerized accounting system, which means a major growth opportunity for accounting software. China's entry into the WTO has also strengthened the need for accounting systems that are compatible with general international practice. The famous software producers include BEA, Computer Associates, IBM, Kingdee, Microsoft, Oracle, Dutch SAP, KingSoft, Beida Founder and UFSoft.

In the high-end large system market, the five largest local accounting software developers, including UFSoft, Kingdee, Anyi, NewGrand and Langchao, took a majority share of about 85 per cent of the market in 2000.[35] In the first half of 2003, the commercial management software sector reached RMB1.68 billion, an increase of 26.1 per cent over the same period in 2002. From Table 6.3 it can be seen that accounting and ERP are the mainstream products which accounted for 80 per cent. These companies will compete by product differentiation, specialist applications, network applications and services. Some of them are moving into the area of ERP solutions but for the lower-end accounting software, a differentiation strategy is difficult and a price war will be unavoidable. There are more than 50 software companies competing

---

[31] *The Tenth Five-Year Plan of Wuxi's National Economy and Society Development*, Chapter 5: Informationalization, Wuxi City Office of Information, 18 December 2003

[32] Lou Qinjian, *How To Accelerate The Development of China's Software Industry*, China News Agency, 11 November 2002

[33] ibid

[34] *2002–2003 China Software Industry Development Research Annual Report*, CCID Consulting, 24 March 2003.

[35] Accounting Software Has the Great Potential, *Finance and Accounting World Magazine*, 28 December

in ERP, including the world's top five ERP software developers – SAP, PeopleSoft, Oracle, Microsoft and Sage at the high end of the market. ERP software business is more profitable than that of the accounting software business sector. The success rate in applying ERP systems has been very low due to the fact that business process reengineering is a tough job in China. CRM and software configuration management (SCM) software was introduced to the market in 2000. The growth rate of the two sectors is much faster than that of accounting software and ERP. With the opening of the financial market and banking industry to foreign investors, financial institutions need to upgrade their computer software systems to compete with international players, which will generate many business opportunities.

Table 6.3 China's commercial management software products distribution shares in the first half of 2003 (RMB100 million)

Commercial management software	Accounting	EPP	CRM	Business management	Other	Total
Recorded sales	5.91	7.48	0.69	0.91	1.81	16.8
Percentage	35	45	4	5	11	100
Growth rate (%)	21	29	28	27	25	26.1

Source: *2003 China Mainland's Software Product Market Research Report* Hui Cong Research, July 2003.

Also in the first half of 2003, UFSoft and Kingdee were still leading the commercial management software sectors, with market shares of more than ten per cent each. Langcao, NewGrand and SAP gained six per cent market shares, but remained in the second league. They were followed by Oracle and DigitalChina. In 2003 the main changes in the commercial management software sector were:

1. Mainland China domestic firms expanded through M&A or joint ventures and used the new products strategies to attract market share.
2. Foreign companies entered the Chinese market more noticeably.
3. SMEs became the focus of the market.

Telecoms software is another profitable sector, because additional business operation support systems are needed following the split of China telecom. Call centres for customer support and operating decision support systems are big markets to be explored. China has the world's largest mobile customer base and new business support systems, as well as value-added services by mobile operators, will generate heavy demand for mobile operations software. There has been a price war in the virus control software sector since 2002. The domestic virus control software firms are Rising, Kingsoft, and JiangminTech.

Table 6.4 The brand shares of China's commercial management software products distributed in the first half of 2003

Brand	Turnover (RMB100 million)	Proportion (%)
UFSoft	2.55	15.2
Kingdee	1.70	10.1
SAP	1.31	7.8
Langcao	1.23	7.3
NewGrand	1.09	6.5
Oracle	0.82	4.9
DigitalChina	0.62	3.7
Hejia Soft	0.49	2.9
Britc	0.32	1.9
BokeSoft	0.29	1.7
SNSoft	0.25	1.5
Other	6.13	36.5
Total	16.8	100

Source: *2003 Mainland China's Software Product Market Research Report* Hui Cong Research, July 2003

Pirated intellectual property has been a big headache for the software industry in China. Pirated software is still the first choice for the majority of Chinese users. To solve this problem, it is necessary to consider the various factors that influence the issue including government support, price, distribution channels and customer education; it can be expected that the situation will improve but it will take time.

The new law for government procurement[36]

The government has begun a strategy of virtually supporting the Chinese domestic sector. On 1 January 2003, China's new Government Procurement Law (GPL) came into effect to help regulate overall government procurement. The tenth article stipulates clearly that 'government procurement should buy domestic goods, engineering projects and services'. There are five recommendations to help foreign suppliers' understanding of the law:

1. Consult with relevant industries, including foreign participants, prior to formalizing implementation rules in order to gain expert advice regarding industry specifics and to avoid unnecessary policy misunderstandings and ambiguities.
2. Clearly and broadly define 'domestic goods, engineering projects, and services' and institute regulatory and procurement process transparency.
3. Grant regional governments the flexibility to implement procurement rules in accordance with the GPL while actively monitoring compliance.
4. Adopt international best training practices to enhance procurement professionals' knowledge and experience.
5. Establish compliance monitoring systems to combat local protectionism, as well as mechanisms for redress for affected parties.

China allocated US$500 million of central government funds to support the growth of the domestic software industry up to 2005. The purchases of domestic software by Chinese local governments has created a huge software market within the field of government authority information management. The data show that government procurement of software will reach some RMB150–200 billion in the five years after 2004, including a dozen billion RMB in the field of information. The scale of the Chinese electronic government business will reach about RMB175 billion within the next five years.[37] Domestic software firms are permitted to open foreign currency accounts in a bid to help boost their exports and receive support to establish research and sales

---

[36] All the regulations cited are from Government Procurement Law P.R.C.
[37] Ren Xiaoyuan, 'Electronic Government Helps the Domestic Brands', *Beijing Youth News*, February 2003

units overseas. Software firms are also encouraged to establish research joint ventures with multinationals.

Domestic software firms are winning more and more bids in tenders for government software provision. The biggest winner is KingSoft, having signed a contract to supply around 5,000 'WPS office 2003' with the People's Bank of China in December 2003.[38] Although WPS office has a big price advantage against Microsoft Office, KingSoft will not find it easy to penetrate Microsoft's market monopoly by price advantage alone. If there had been no support strategy from the government, WPS would have been unable to survive in the market.

China's Government Procurement Rules for Software will be enacted at the end of 2005 or the beginning of 2006. This document focuses on the following five main topics:

- the general rules regulating the duties and rights of the Ministry of Finance and the Ministry of Information Industry;

- the purchase of eligible domestic products and identification of domestic software, which includes the process from application, acceptability, first trial, examination and approval, licence to the final proclamation;

- preference procurement catalogue for non-domestic software, which prescribes the priority selective range for purchasers to buy the non-domestic software. Software providers can apply for their non-domestic software to be listed into the special catalogue for one year of the period of validity if they are satisfied with the requirement of investment, ratepaying, research, transferring core technology and senior personnel training;

- the approval of purchasing non-domestic software, which regulates the period limit for Ministry of Finance, Ministry of Information Industry, and local governments;

- supervising and examining the management of software supply, which confirms the execution of domestic and non-domestic software procurement and the right of appeal for software providers.

Furthermore, the office of the Procurement Centre of the State Council has added a new mandatory term to the Government Procurement Law: 'government departments should purchase genuine original software when purchasing hardware'. Such policies show that government procurement will firmly favour the domestic software industry. In

---

[38] Li Feng, *Focus on the Procurement of Software*, ENet Online, www.enet.com, 11 February 2004

2001, the scale of government software procurement was RMB4 billion, which accounted for 14 per cent of the software market, growing to about RMB9 billion in 2004. Without doubt, the 2005 figures will be even bigger.[39] Following the rules, the Chinese government hopes to cast off the limitations of foreign enterprises in the computer industry field. Whether from research into CPUs or the increased focus on Linux or the domestic bias in the government's domestic software provision, it is clear that China would like to maintain a totally independent IT industry system.

Several factors, such as the encouraging macroeconomic situation, escalation of environmental policy and further concentration on information building, will ensure that the software market in China maintains its high rate of development. CCID Consulting has predicted that the compound annual average growth rate from 2004 to 2009 will be 19.5 per cent: a market value of about RMB97.57 billion in 2003. While rising rapidly, the Chinese software market will display the following trends:

1. Network development will be driven by the popularization of network applications.

2. The booming digital industry will accelerate the growth of consumable software.

3. The overarching ability to explore channels will become the base for putting regional strategy into effect.

4. Application service providers (ASP) will become more and more popular in the SMEs and non-business market sectors.

5. The development of industry applications will enhance the demand for high quality applications software.

6. The strategy of 'Rejuvenation of the Northeast' and the 'Go-West Campaign' will present a new opportunity for continuous development of the software market.

Telecommunications in China

The fastest growth market

China has become the world largest telecom network with more than 600 million users and the second largest number of internet citizens

---

[39] Huang Jixin, 'Microsoft Became the Final Winner In The Government Procurement "War"', *Economy Observer*, 2 February 2005

(netizens).[40] In an international context, Mainland China's four largest telecom operators: China Telecom, China Netcom, China Unicom and China Mobile can be classed as world-standard large telecom operators. There are two further developing telecom operators – China Railway Telecom and Jitong Telecom – to be considered. In 2004 there were more than 300 million people using mobile phone technology in China, which has become the biggest global market of mobile consumers. MII's reports stated that mobile users had increased to 305.28 million in the first half of 2004,[41] which means there is at least one mobile phone to every five people in Mainland China.

The average long-term growth rate of the Chinese GDP is eight per cent. Despite downturns in the world telecom industry, the Chinese market for telecommunications will keep on growing. It is expected that growth in this industry will be at least the same as, or up to twice as much as, the rate of GDP growth in the next five years. The reorganization of the state-owned telecom companies will continue, bringing fresh opportunities to suppliers. More competition is expected which will bring many further opportunities to the telecom equipment suppliers and software developers. Operations support systems and business support systems instead of infrastructure investment will be the focus of attention in the next few years. A disaster contingency system with extra-large volume, integration, expandability, and remote copying functions is badly needed by many local telecom operators. Telecom software is in strong demand after intensive investment in hardware infrastructure. Network security has become a big concern for Chinese telecom operators and is expected to attract more investment.

While there is no doubt that China is the fastest growing telecom market, it will also be the most competitive. The Chinese telecom industry has experienced several splits in the past, first the hive-off from the postal service, then the split of mobile services, and now the division of North (China Netcom) from South (China Telecom). On each occasion that a split has happened, bigger growth and more investment have followed. The split and restructure of state-owned telecom companies was in preparation for intense competition from foreign investors entering the market.

Chinese telecom companies had only three years to prepare for the competition challenge of foreign telecom giants after WTO entry. It is expected that more M&A will take place among domestic telecom operators in order to stay competitive after the market entry of foreign

---

[40] Zhang Yanchuan and Liu Gaofeng, 'The Summary of 2004 China Telecommunication Carriers and Market Development', *Communication World Magazine*, Telecom Layout Research Institute of MII, 21 October 2004
[41] ibid

telecom service providers. Three to five giant telecom operators with licences for all telecom services are expected to emerge. The radio and television broadcasting network could be merged into one of these giants. Furthermore, it will be possible to become an independent telecom services provider with additional telecom service licences.

Observing its commitment to WTO rules, there will be more telecom-related operators as well as equipment and service providers to invest in the world's most populous market. The Mainland China government has promised that it will stick to its WTO commitments and introduce better and more transparent policies. The MII will keep a close eye on the WTO's appraisal of this commitment so as to optimize market economy rules in the domestic market. Lured by this lucrative market, overseas telecom players such as SK Telecom, Vodafone, AT&T, HK's PCCW and Hutchison Whampoa, have shown increasing enthusiasm for participating in the Chinese telecom market. SK Telecom, for example, linked a cooperation pact with China Unicom in 2003 to provide telecom value-added services for China's CDMA subscribers. SK Telecom (China) believes telecom services such as wireless data and multiple media will see an explosive increase in future years. Vodafone continues to seek investment opportunities in Mainland China following its agreement on roaming and technology with China Unicom.

With the gradual lifting of restrictions on foreign participation, overseas penetration into the telecom industry is to be accelerated in the coming years. However, a sounder environment characterized by transparent policies and a good legal environment should be hammered out to attract more foreign investment. Telecom value-added services are not yet very attractive to those big telecom operators as it is still a tiny market in China.

Many foreign telecom players are adopting a wait-and-see attitude towards the domestic telecom market at the moment while considering their strategies. The favourable momentum is conducive to expanding exports, attracting more foreign investment, going public overseas and seeking overseas expansion. The number of telephone subscribers, the tele-density, sales of electronic and informative products and exports of electronic products all achieved their targets outlined in the tenth Five Year Plan (2001–2005) by the end of 2003, two years ahead of time.

Currently, the whole telecom equipment industry is experiencing a period of combined 'push' and 'pull'. 'Pull' means that the industry is at a stage of increasing lower-end investment demand. Rising demand pulls the telecom equipment industry to add to its yield and to steady rises in price. 'Push' refers to the pressure of the upstream products of each sector of the telecom equipment industry for price increases to match the sectors' own rising product costs. If the manufacturers can partly digest the cost increases resulting from the rising prices of raw and processed materials, whilst upstream product prices also advance, then their profit margins will be greater. Therefore, the effect of these influencing factors will be to improve the profitability of the telecom equipment industry step by step.

Size, trends and opportunity in the wireless market

Here, it should be noted that the charge for mobile phone calls in Mainland China is double, meaning that the holder and the caller both pay irrespective of whether he/she is receiving or calling, which differs from the UK's single charge regime. In terms of the level of maturity of its competitive atmosphere, the Chinese telecom market still belongs to the category of moderate competition but is still in its infancy. As the market leaders, China Telecom and China Mobile accounted for 62 per cent and 66 per cent of market shares respectively up to the first half of 2004.[42] Besides these two companies, China Unicom, a listed company, held a 12 per cent market share in 2003. China Netcom is a superior state-owned enterprise, reporting directly to the central government of China. It was formed by merging the ten northern provincial corporations (Beijing, Tianjin, Hebei, Shanxi, Inner Mongolia, Liaoning, Jilin, Heilongjiang, Henan and Shandong) of the former China Telecom, China Netcom and Jitong Telecom. Approved by the State Council, the experiment involved state-owned enterprises acquiring investments from the outside world, with China Netcom taking the direct benefit from its assets. China Netcom accounts for 16 per cent of the fixed line market in China. The turnover is forecast to increase to US$35 billion in 2006 from US$22 billion in 2002. Up to October 2003, there were 255 million fixed line users and there will be at least 342 million in 2006. However, the most important market is in wireless telecom where the 263 million users at the end of December 2003 exceeded the fixed line participants.[43]

The dominant wireless telecom operators are China Mobile and China Unicom. China Mobile is the biggest wireless telecom operator in the world, with more than 188.35 million customers. User numbers like China Mobile's are only a dream for other international telecom operators, such as Vodafone, which has an ambition to acquire a share of one of the largest Chinese mobile carriers.

Copying imported products by reverse engineering has been a major R&D method for many domestic telecom equipment manufacturers.

---

[42] Zhang Yanchuan and Liu Gaofeng, 'The Summary of 2004 China Telecommunication Carriers and Market Development', *Communication World Magazine*, Telecom Layout Research Institute of MII, 21 October 2004
[43] ibid

Because this practice is now forbidden, WTO entry is having a big influence on telecom equipment manufacturers. On the other hand, more and more foreign competitors will be selling their products and services to China or even setting up R&D centres in China, which will give domestic manufacturers a chance to learn from the foreign competition. Indeed the market share of foreign telecom equipment manufacturers increased sharply after 2002's fall. In the first half of 2002, Motorola, Siemens and Nokia still accounted for 70 per cent, but Chinese domestic manufacturers, such as Birds, TCL, Amoisonic and other Chinese local brands accounted for 66 per cent of the market by the end of 2002. However in the first half of 2004, foreign mobiles had driven the share of domestic mobile manufacturers down to 48.1 per cent.[44]

While Chinese telecom equipment manufacturers will lose further market share to foreign competitors in high-end products, in low to mid-end equipment they will have a better chance to grow because imported components will be cheaper and they will gain more export opportunities.

The mobile communication market orientation may very soon move from voice transfer to digital data transfer, which means more business in short messaging, electronic games, interactive entertainment and mobile banking services. The volume of wireless digital data will reach today's volume of wired internet data within five years. This fast-growing market provides many opportunities for VC investment.

Frequency resource has been limited in many Chinese cities, and the shortage will continue as high speed digital data transmission services increase. Mobile telecommunication service providers are planning to upgrade their network to 3G. There is still a big argument about which 3G technologies to adopt. Whatever the outcome, the business opportunity from 3G will arrive in Mainland China within three years. In China Mobile's total capital budget for the next two years, expenditure on 2.5G (GPRS) accounts for only 4.7 per cent of the budget total of US$1.036 billion.[45] At the same time, China Unicom has adopted the CDMA plan to compete with China Mobile. Value-added service for CDMA and GPRS mobile users should now be under consideration. This business is expected to be big but will also be a very competitive market. It is said that there are some 400 content providers who have developed more than 6000 wireless applications including traffic news, news broadcasting, weather report, travel service, mobile banking and online games.

---

[44] Huang Rong, Foreign Mobiles Increase the Competition With Domestic Mobile, *Eastern Morning News*, 3 November 2004
[45] Zhu Wei *The Quanqiutong's Worry*, BlogChina.com, 27 August 2004

With the confidence of future Chinese market growth, international investors picked China as their favourite location. Ericsson planned to invest US$5 billion in China in the five-year time frame from 2001. Sony Ericsson raised an additional US$15 million for its Beijing-based factory.[46] Siemens Information and Communication Mobile (IC Mobile) has planned to invest 60 million euros each year in Chinese firms and to explore the Chinese market for 3G.[47] In the field of wireless communication equipment, Ericsson, Siemens, Nokia, and Nortel are the dominant suppliers with 85 per cent of the market, but Alcatel is catching up having bought out Shanghai Bell.[48]

The issuing of new licences and deregulation will lead to more intense competition. As the market moves forward, the growth rate of subscribers should gradually slow down, but value-added services will increase.

As competition among China's telecom carriers becomes fiercer, more new services will drive up the demand for billing software. With the break-up of China Telecom into two companies, China's telecoms market is experiencing dramatic changes, and billing software will have a larger role to play.

The splitting of China Telecom into two companies covering the northern and southern regions has resulted in no major differences in network capacity. Service is their only competitive weapon. More services require the support of more complicated billing software. Demand from mobile telecoms carriers is even greater, as competition in that field is fiercer. China Mobile and China Unicom are bound to install more billing software to sharpen their competitive edge. According to industry insiders, China's billing software market is growing at a rate of more than 30 per cent year-on-year and reached around RMB10 billion (US$1.2 billion) in 2003.[49]

The adoption of 3G mobile phone technology will bring significant changes to the business models of mobile operators in China. While consumers now deal directly with China's two mobile operators, in the future they are also likely to deal with application providers and service providers. Licensing such operators could dramatically boost competition in China's mobile market, which is now split between China

---

[46] Zhao Lei 'Sony Ericsson Increased Investment in China', *China Business Times*, 7 July 2004

[47] Xiao Cheng tr. 'Simenz Planned to Invest in China Annually', *Netease IT*, 11 August 2003

[48] Li Lina 'The Difficulty of Ericsson's Transformation', *Internet Weekly*, 17 February 2003

[49] Henry J et al 'Telecommunications and Information Technology in China: Market Opportunities for Small and Medium-sized Enterprises', *Export America, News From Commerce*, June 2003

Mobile and China Unicom. These two companies both offer mobile data services using their current 2G networks, but are expected dramatically to expand such offerings when they adopt the faster 3G technology. For the same data applications, 3G will be cheaper than 2G, just as today's digital phones are cheaper than analogue phones. In the past, Mainland China's telecom operators targeted white-collar customers but now they need to redefine their customers.

A good message for SMS[50]

Short-messaging services (SMS) will enjoy another great period of growth, due largely to the booming local mobile market. China's mobile phone users are reported to have sent a thumb-aching 300 billion short messages in 2004, a figure which is likely to increase sharply in the next few years since this represents a 50 per cent increase over 2003. By limbering up their thumbs to type short messages, Chinese mobile phone users have created a 'thumb economy' worth billions of US dollars. The explosion of short messages during holidays, such as the traditional Chinese New Year, has caused network traffic jams. A staggering 7 billion short messages were sent during the first week of the 2003 lunar New Year, nearly ten times more than the previous year.

MII statistics show that approximately 200 billion short messages were sent in China in 2003. The SMS market will continue to enjoy explosive growth in 2005 over the development in 2003 and 2004 but might show signs of flatter growth in 2007. The same MII statistics also indicated that China had 263.478 million mobile phone users at the end of November 2003 and predicted that China would have 92 million new mobile phone subscribers in 2004. Asians have been obsessed with sending text messages.

The low-price charging system will continue to buoy the SMS boom. Sending a text message costs a meagre RMB0.1 (US$0.012) in China. The SMS market still offers huge potential, as a great number of low-end mobile phone users began to use the system in 2004. Cost-conscious mobile phone users in recent years have found SMS a more convenient and inexpensive way to stay in touch than lengthy and costly conversations.

Despite China's huge population of nearly 1.3 billion people, mobile phone penetration remains low. The SMS boom is largely due to a successful model developed by mobile operators. Currently, web portals offer SMS downloads, mainly music, greetings and jokes, to mobile

---

[50] Li Weitao '2004: A good message for SMS' *China Business Weekly*, 13 January 2004; 'Message Services to Be Connected', *China Daily*, 12 January 2005

phone users, who then send the messages to others. Mobile operators and web portals, known as service providers (SPs), share the revenues. The interconnection of SMS with mobile and Xiaolingtong networks will also boost the SMS boom. Xiaolingtong, also known in the industry as 'Little Smart', PHS (personal handy service) or PAS (personal access system), is a limited mobility service that has been aggressively promoted by fixed-line carriers China Telecom and China Netcom. Xiaolingtong adopts a one-way charging system, which costs less than the mobile services offered by the mobile duopoly China Mobile and China Unicom. There were an estimated 65 million Xiaolingtong subscribers at the end of 2004 and there is no doubt that the Xiaolingtong market will continue to grow in the next few years. By the end of November 2004, the Little Smart phone service was operating in 355 cities in the country's 31 provinces, municipalities and autonomous regions.

The interoperability of SMS between 'Xiaolingtong' wireless phones and GSM (global system for mobile communications) or CDMA (code division multiple access) mobile phones was launched in the first month of 2005. The cost of sending short messages will differ from region to region. In Beijing, Xiaolingtong users have to pay 0.08 yuan (0.96 US cents) to send a short message, while China Mobile users have to pay 0.15 yuan (1.8 US cents) for every short message to Xiaolingtong phones. The inter-service SMS connection between Xiaolingtong and GSM phones will be conducive to the popularity of Xiaolingtong services. The service will also help boost the ARPU (average revenue per user) for both fixed-line and mobile operators. However, some analysts are concerned that the upcoming third generation (3G) of mobile telecommunications will gradually phase out the Xiaolingtong service as 3G offers faster wireless internet connection and speedier data transmission as well as a full range of value-added telecoms services. Nevertheless, there is still a market for the development of the Xiaolingtong service because Xiaolingtong will continue to play an important role in driving revenue growth for both China Netcom and China Telecom as the market demand for traditional fixed-line services has shrunk in the face of stiff competition from cellular service providers.

In fact, to consolidate its market share, China Netcom signed a US$40 million contract with UTStarcom to expand its Xiaolingtong network in Beijing and in Shandong and Henan provinces in 2004. Simultaneously, China Telecom signed contracts valued at about US$120 million with UTStarcom to boost its Xiaolingtong network in Jiangsu, Zhejiang and Sichuan provinces.

7

Best Practices in Products and Services for M&A Operations in China

Mergers and acquisitions in Mainland China[1]

The current situation

In April 2004, Chinese M&A activity had increased by 55 per cent compared with the same period in 2003. According to data compiled by M&A Asia, the aggregate value of Chinese deals announced in the first quarter of 2004 was US$8.7 billion compared with the same period in the previous year (US$3.1 billion). In terms of Asia-Pacific as a whole, aggregate deal values were 11 per cent higher at US$47.4 billion, compared with US$42.7 billion in the earlier period.[2]

M&A deals occur in various ways: deals between two Chinese companies; between two foreign companies in China or between a foreign company and a Chinese company. Foreign investors who wish to acquire or increase an equity interest in a target company within Mainland China would commonly do so in one of the following ways:

- direct acquisition;
- offshore or indirect acquisition;
- asset acquisition.

---

[1] Some paragraphs in this chapter are from a) *2003 Guide to Mergers & Acquisitions, China*, Baker & McKenzie; b) Kathleen A. Flaherty, Associate White & Case - China Practice, Figure: New M&A Rules for Foreign Investors in China, *China Legal News*, November 2003; c) Sheng Lijun *et al* (2003) *Investment in China: Opportunities in Private Equity and Venture Capital,* Tsinghua University Press, June.

[2] China M&A up 55% in the first quarter of 2004, compared with the corresponding period in 2003, PricewaterhouseCoopers (Hong Kong), 26 April 2004.

Generally speaking, there are two ways of effecting a merger in China. One is merger by 'reestablishment', whereby a new company is established and the pre-merger entities are automatically dissolved by law. The other is a merger by 'absorption' whereby existing entities are merged into a surviving entity and the entities absorbed by the surviving entity are also automatically dissolved. Such acquisitions can be accomplished by either a share or asset deal.

M&A is becoming increasingly important for foreign enterprises and investors trying to gain 'strategic' access into the Chinese market. The 2002 World Investment Report of the United Nations Conference on Trade and Development (UNCTD) shows that the value of equity bought by overseas companies in Chinese companies reached almost US$15 billion in 2002, a sharp increase from less than US$5 billion in 2001. This trend will certainly continue and gain further momentum as the increasing transparency of Chinese businesses attracts foreign investors wanting to catch up with competitors that may have been 'early birds' in China.

In an effort to catch up, technology acquisition (TA) played a very important role. In 1997 and 1998, China spent US$15.9 billion and US$16.3 billion on technology, in acquiring sets of equipment and key equipment items respectively.[3] TA can be defined as a process of planned, selective, focused importation of advanced technology which the enterprise does not have or could not master, or a new appliance of imported technology which can bring expected economic benefits to new users. TA is also one way of transforming the ability to understand and develop acquired technology.

The Chinese M&A market is very dissimilar to western markets and is more complicated in terms of law, ownership structure, government involvement and human behaviour. Foreign investors wanting to enter China by M&A need to set up their China business strategies and choose proper business models which will better enable them to exploit opportunities. Investors should acquire sufficient information on the law, government policy and the target company before making any decisions. Although comparable to 'Greenfield Investment' (the alternative choice a firm has to face when entering a foreign market via FDI of setting up an entirely new plant), M&A seems to be a better and faster way to enter China. There are numerous reasons for this:

1. Investors always choose a target company with an excellent financial track record, a market-proven product range and a well developed distribution system. Investors can bypass the dangers

---

[3] Wu Xiaobo et al, *The Factor Analysis on China's Manufacturing Enterprises' Technology Acquisition Performance*, Zhejiang University, PRC.

involved in setting up a new company, reducing risks when investing in China.

2. The local acquired company will provide foreign investors with skilled local employees who know the local market and business environment well, making it easier for the foreign investors to adapt to the local business environment and to serve the local market.

3. M&A does not immediately require new material or human resources, but may instantly increase the parent company's sales and cashflow from the acquired company.

4. M&A is the fastest way to enter a new market. If international competitors want to enter the same market, M&A will help investors to gain market share. This is important if a market is sensitive to brand name and market share. The competition between two Taiwanese instant noodle producers, the Master Kong and Uni-president are good examples which attest to this point.

China imposes strict controls on all types of foreign exchange transactions across its borders and its official currency, the Renminbi (RMB), is not freely convertible in the international foreign exchange market. The State Administration of Foreign Exchange (SAFE), the authority in charge of foreign exchange in China, regulates the following four types of transaction involving the movement or conversion of foreign exchange:

- inward remittance of foreign exchange;
- settlement of foreign exchange;
- sale of foreign exchange;
- outward remittance of foreign exchange to an overseas party.

Under the relevant rules, mergers do not entail any taxation of capital gains corresponding to the difference between the market value of the assets, liabilities transferred and their tax bases. Assets, liabilities and shareholder's equity interest of companies to be dissolved are transferred to the surviving or newly created company at their book values at the time of the merger. No asset re-evaluation is therefore authorized for tax purposes upon such mergers. If the post-merger entity adjusted the book value of certain assets in the course of the merger, it is required to make relevant adjustments to the accounting profits for the calculation of its tax payable to negate any changes in tax allowable depreciation or amortization which may result from the revaluation of assets.

In China there is no strict legal requirement for a preliminary/framework agreement between the parties, such as a letter of intent (LOI) or memorandum of understanding (MOU), for M&A transactions. It could be said that LOIs or MOUs are important tools by which the partners or parties can agree at an early stage on the principles, basic terms and contemplated procedures of a proposed transaction, and they are usually prepared in major transactions. The Chinese side always expect that all the terms contained in the LOI/MOU will finally appear in the formal agreements, although LOIs and MOUs are generally stated to be non-binding in nature.

Usually, aside from the specific issues with which either side is concerned and expects to include in the document, an LOI/MOU would include the following 12 key terms of the transaction:

- identities of the parties or partners;

- total purchase price, timing and method of payment;

- total investment, registered capital and business scope of the target company post acquisition;

- equity percentages and form of capital contribution by the investors (if any);

- land use arrangement;

- labour arrangement;

- new management arrangements;

- trademark, brand, technology licensing, and other ancillary agreements;

- conditions precedent that must be satisfied in order for the transaction to proceed;

- exclusivity and confidentiality obligations (this part should be expressly legally binding on the parties or partners);

- buyer's right to due diligence and vendor's undertaking to cooperate and participate;

- further steps to be undertaken by the parties in order to proceed with the proposed transaction.

Due diligence investigations remain an essential tool for reducing the risks of any M&A transaction in China. In the absence of complete knowledge of the operations, the scope of the assets and the extent of the liabilities of the target company, due diligence investigations afford the prospective purchaser an opportunity to assess the legal and financial state of affairs of the target company, and the parties will be able to consider structuring the proposed transaction on the basis of the results of the pre-acquisition review. Accordingly, due diligence is vital in almost all mergers and acquisitions in China.

From 2004, more multinational M&A express channels have been launched to lure more investment into China, such as cooperation with the China Beijing Equity Exchange (CBEE) and Beijing Investment Promotion Bureau (BIPB). CBEE, one of the major exchanges for the trading of state-owned assets and assets with other types of ownership, has joined the BIPB to launch the so-called 'Multinational Merger and Acquisition Express Channel'. The move is a major step towards further improving Beijing's investment environment for domestic and overseas investors.

The purpose of the cooperation is to better serve investors looking for M&As of state-owned assets listed on the exchange, thus helping to attract FDI to the Chinese capital. The exchange and bureau will make use of their advantages to share project and member information, jointly launch project promotional activities at home and abroad, provide policy consultation and guidance services to international investors and coordinate links between international investors and government organizations. They will also accelerate the process of examination and approval, and assist investors in handling the procedures of M&A deals, according to an agreement signed by both sides. CBEE is the only platform for equity trading in the Chinese capital. According to earlier BIPB reports, the total volume of equity trading in Beijing hit RMB72.4 billion (US$8.74 billion) in 2003. In the coming three to five years, the figure is expected to hit RMB200–300 billion (US$24.16 to US$36.24 billion).[4]

In Beijing, the ratio of state-owned to total equity amounts to over 50 per cent while in East China's Zhejiang Province, where the non-state economy is developing very quickly, the ratio of state-owned equity only accounts for about ten per cent. The situation leaves great potential for the future development of trading in state-owned assets. The Chinese government is making efforts to encourage the development of the non-state sector and downsize state-owned assets in many sectors. Therefore, an increasing number of state-owned companies and projects are expected to be listed on domestic equity exchanges for M&As by domestic and international investors. There is no question

---

[4] Multinational M&A Express Channel Launched to Lure More Investment, *China Daily*, 15 March 2004

that equity exchange has a very bright future in China. The favourable cooperation between CBEE and BIPB will better serve investors and promote FDI in Beijing.

New M&A rules for foreign investors

In 2003, China unveiled a new framework governing the M&A of SOEs and other domestic enterprises (excluding foreign investment enterprises, or FIEs) by foreign investors. A series of new regulations provides foreign investors with broader opportunities, at least in principle, to acquire shares within SOEs, domestic enterprises, state-owned and legal person shares of listed companies. In very exceptional circumstances, foreign investors accredited as Qualified Foreign Institutional Investors (QFII) are permitted to invest in shares. However, new approvals and additional requirements that appear in many of the new regulations only seem to reiterate and in some cases expand the scope of government control over M&A transactions involving foreign investors.

Two important new regulations in particular govern the acquisition of assets and/or shares of Chinese domestic enterprises by foreign investors. While these new regulations offer few new opportunities with respect to the acquisition of assets by foreign investors, they do provide regulatory guidance for foreign investors to acquire shares in domestic enterprises.

The *Provisional Regulations on Utilizing Foreign Investment in Restructuring State-owned Enterprises,* the 'State Restructuring Regulations', set forth a framework for foreign investors to restructure SOEs using foreign capital in a manner consistent with government policy.

The *Interim Provisions on the Acquisition of Domestic Enterprises by Foreign Investors*, the 'M&A Regulations', ostensibly govern only the acquisition of private domestic enterprises by foreign investors, and may be viewed as an effort by the Ministry of Commerce (MOFCOM) to reassert its approval and regulatory authority following the promulgation of the State Restructuring Regulations. While it appears, on the face of these regulations, that there will be no overlap as to their application, all equity acquisition transactions under both regulations require foreign investors to restructure their investments into FIEs upon completion of an acquisition, regardless of the nature of the domestic target company being acquired. Thus, it is clear from these new regulations that the restructuring of SOEs under the State Restructuring Regulations will require MOFCOM's approval, and that some degree of overlap of these new regulations is inevitable.

Moreover, the reorganization of ministries and reshuffling of responsibilities for foreign investment which occurred shortly after the promulgation of the M&A Regulations in 2003, has added to the confusion surrounding the application of these new regulations and their ability to coexist. The State Economic and Trade Commission (SETC) and MOFTEC were dissolved, and various departments below them were merged with other ministries, including the new Ministry of Commerce (MOFCOM) and the State-owned Assets Supervision and Administration Commission (SASAC), as well as the reorganized and renamed State Development and Reform Commission (SDRC), formerly known as the State Development and Planning Commission (SDPC). It is still not altogether clear how these new and reorganized ministries will implement these new regulations.

The State Restructuring Regulations were issued jointly by the SETC, the Ministry of Finance (MOF), the State Administration of Industry and Commerce (SAIC) and the State Administration for Foreign Exchange (SAFE), and became effective on 1 January 2003. The State Restructuring Regulations set forth the requirements and procedures for the approval of the restructuring of SOEs into FIEs. Pursuant to these regulations, foreign investors may participate in the restructuring of SOEs, other than financial institutions or listed companies, provided that such SOEs do not fall within the prohibited category of the *Catalogue for Guiding Foreign Investment in Industries*. In addition, if the SOE target is one in which the Chinese party must have a controlling interest, the Chinese party must maintain a controlling interest after the acquisition in the FIE. There are five methods of using foreign capital to restructure SOEs:

1. Foreign investors may restructure an SOE into an FIE by acquiring all or part of the state interest in an SOE;

2. Foreign investors may restructure a 'company with state interests' into an FIE by acquiring all or part of the state shares in that company;

3. Foreign investors may acquire from domestic creditors debt owed to them by the SOE and restructure such an enterprise into an FIE;

4. Foreign investors may acquire all or the majority of the assets of an SOE and subsequently establish an FIE;

5. Foreign investors may purchase an equity stake and become shareholders in a SOE and convert such an SOE into an FIE.

A reorganization plan, in many respects similar to the 'feasibility study report' required for all FIEs, must be submitted by the reorganizing party of the SOE, highlighting information about the foreign investor, its financial status, its business scope and equity structure, and a plan for the settlement of staff. In addition, it appears from the State Restructuring Regulations that in permitting foreign investment in the restructuring of SOEs, one of the state's main requirements is the introduction of sound corporate governance to the target SOE. Article 5 of the State Restructuring Regulations specifically requires foreign investors to provide plans to improve the enterprise's corporate governance structure and promote sustained growth of the SOE. Such a restructuring plan must also include measures for strengthening corporate management and an investment plan, and provide for the introduction and development of new products and technology. The submission of such a reorganization plan is a new requirement for foreign investors.

The M&A Regulations were issued on 7 March 2003 by MOFTEC, the State Administration of Taxation (SAT), the SAIC and SAFE, and became the final regulatory piece of legislation to be issued by MOFTEC prior to it being dissolved and merged into MOFCOM. The M&A Regulations are somewhat less clear in their drafting than the State Restructuring Regulations. While the State Restructuring Regulations apply only to the acquisition of interests in SOEs, the M&A Regulations set forth a framework for foreign investors' acquisition of interests in domestic enterprises and the restructuring of such enterprises upon acquisition, including SOEs. Thus, the M&A Regulations will also apply to the acquisition of SOEs, and conflicts may arise between the two new regulations. The M&A Regulations expand MOFCOM's regulatory control over asset acquisitions, mandating that MOFCOM shall regulate and approve all asset acquisitions, including the acquisition of non-state-owned assets. Prior to the issuance of the M&A Regulations, the acquisition of non-state-owned assets was not normally regulated and no approvals were necessary, provided that the industry was not restricted and creditors' rights were taken into account.

MOFCOM's regulatory control over share acquisition has also been expanded under the M&A Regulations. Foreign investors who acquire less than 25 per cent of a domestic enterprise must obtain MOFCOM or its local counterpart's approval and register with the SAIC or its local counterpart as an FIE.

As in the case of the State Restructuring Regulations, the M&A Regulations require foreign investors to adhere to the *Catalogue for Guiding Foreign Investment in Industries*. However, no specific qualifications for foreign investors have been incorporated in the M&A Regulations. While China has never had a merger control regime, these new regulations indicate that an antitrust regime will be introduced. Both the State Restructuring Regulations and the M&A Regulations incorporate antitrust provisions aimed at curing and controlling the new opportunities presented to foreign investors if the relevant approval authorities see them as a threat to domestic enterprises seeking to gain a foothold in the market ahead of foreign competition. The State Restructuring Regulations require foreign investors to declare in their reorganization plan their percentage of market share in the same industry in China, and permit the SDRC to hold a hearing in the event that it determines that the restructuring would have an anticompetitive effect or result in a monopoly. The M&A Regulations take it a step further, expressly providing thresholds that will trigger MOFCOM scrutiny of proposed transactions, introducing reporting requirements and even permitting domestic enterprises in competition with the target to request a hearing in the event that such enterprises fear anticompetitive effects will result from an acquisition.

The maximum total investment of FIEs established as a result of equity acquisition by foreign investors should comply with the schedule shown in Table 7.1.

Table 7.1 Maximum total investment of FIEs in equity acquisitions

Registered capital	Maximum total investment
<US$2.1 million	1.43 times the registered capital
US$2.1–5 million	2 times the registered capital
US$5–12 million	2.5 times the registered capital
>US$12 million	3 times the registered capital

As for asset acquisitions by foreign investors, the total investment in the FIE to be established should be determined according to the asset transaction price and scale of production and operation. The ratio of registered capital to total investment should comply with the relevant regulations. Moreover, the foreign investor must not operate the assets of the domestic enterprise to be acquired before the FIE is established.

The plethora of recently issued legislation in the M&A sector within China should provide foreign investors with new opportunities to enter the domestic Chinese market, particularly with the ability now to purchase the shares of SOEs and other domestic enterprises. However, neither of these regulations offers any new corporate forms of business for foreign investors in China, and it is unlikely that the current foreign investment regime will be replaced with a unified corporate regulatory framework in the foreseeable future. Moreover, there are several new approvals and additional requirements that now apply to acquisitions by foreign investors. It remains to be seen whether the benefits of these new regulations will outweigh the additional requirements that

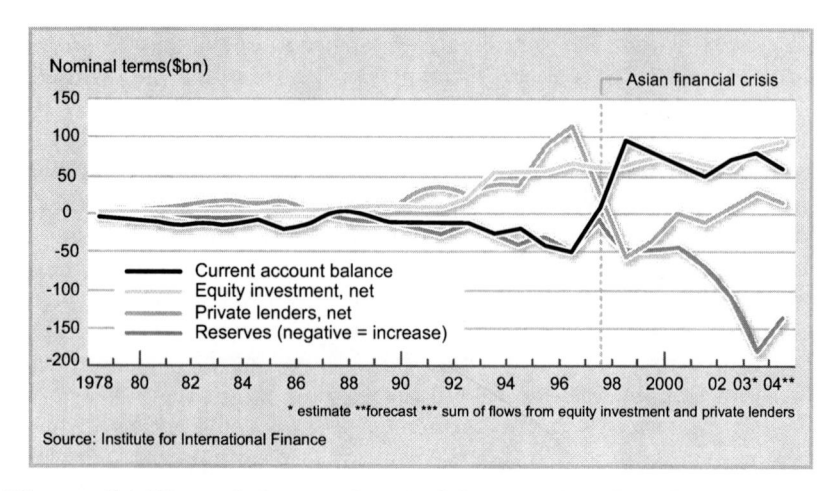

Figure 7.1 Ups and downs of capital flows to Asia/Pacific emerging market economies

they impose, and how the reorganized government ministries will implement these new regulations.

China's M&A market expects to bloom in five years

The history of capital flows to the dynamic emerging economies of the Asia-Pacific region (or, more precisely, to China, India, Indonesia, Malaysia, the Philippines, South Korea and Thailand) is shown in charts sourced from the Washington-based Institute for International Finance and reproduced as Figures 7.1 and 7.2.

From the figures displayed above, it can be seen that until 1996 these economies ran aggregate current account deficits. But after the Asian financial crisis, their current accounts shifted into substantial surplus. Between 1996 and 1998, the shift amounted to US$150 billion. The Institute of International Finance (IIF) forecast that the cumulative current account surplus of these economies between 1998 and 2004 would be US$495 billion. Over the same period, the cumulative rise in foreign currency reserves is forecast to be US$647 billion. It follows that, in addition to the current account surplus, the region is forecast to be a net recipient (after allowance for capital outflows) of US$152 billion in private capital. There have been stable and rising net inflows of equity finance, largely in the form of direct investment. Between 1998 and 2004 the net equity inflow is estimated to be a healthy US$516 billion; and the net lending is estimated to be minus US$58 billion (a net repatriation of capital by foreigners).

In August 2004, Martin Wolf, Associate Editor and Chief Economics Commentator at *The Financial Times* offered three reasons why

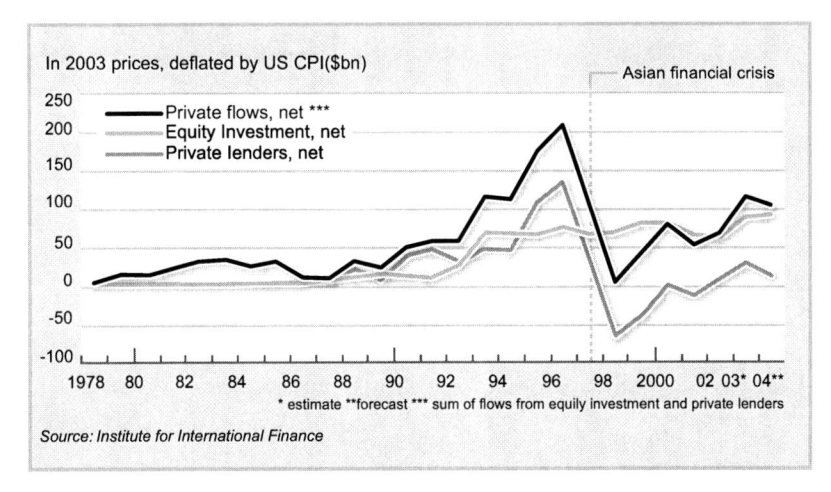

Figure 7.2 Ups and downs of private capital flows to Asia/Pacific emerging market economies

Asia-Pacific countries have been net exporters of capital for so long: the precautionary motive, economic structure and mercantilism. In his opinion, the precautionary motive states that a country that cannot borrow internationally in its own currency must act to curb aggregate currency mismatches in the economy. It can do so by restricting its own or private sector foreign currency borrowing. Alternatively, it can offset private sector borrowing by its own official lending. Either way, the risk of crises over which the authorities have little or no control is greatly reduced.

Ronald McKinnon of Stanford University has also discussed the economic structure. In 2002, the economies of East Asia and the Pacific registered gross domestic savings rates of 37 per cent of GDP, compared with 14 per cent in the US. China's savings rate was 43 per cent. Given these high savings rates, quite modest curbs over spending on investment will generate a strong current account, provided the real exchange rate can be kept sufficiently competitive (as it can be). Against this background, argues Professor McKinnon, in important cases of dollar pegging such as China, hard currency pegging against the dollar facilitates hedging against exchange risk, stabilizes competitiveness across the region and provides a domestic anchor for inflationary expectations. In this way, trade is promoted and stability enhanced.

The most sophisticated version of the mercantilist explanation has been expounded by three economists who work for Deutsche Bank. In essence, the argument is that China, the region's pivotal economy, has a huge pool of labour to bring into the modern labour force. The government's aim, however, is to bring this surplus into efficient employment

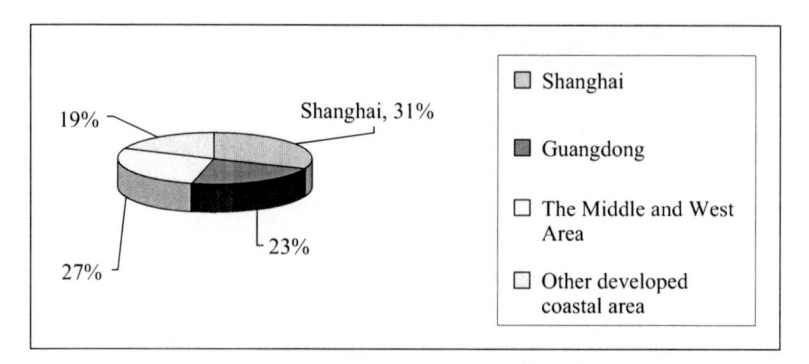

Figure 7.3 Regional M&A from foreign investment

Pie chart values: Shanghai, 31%; 23%; 27%; 19%
Legend: Shanghai; Guangdong; The Middle and West Area; Other developed coastal area

by encouraging both inward direct investment and exports. But to succeed, it must find accommodating markets and willing inward investors. They also mention that the US is the most accommodating final market because it is prepared to adjust to rising imports of manufactures from the Asian economies. Very low real wages (and so a highly competitive real exchange rate) generate excess profits for the inward investors, thus giving China a motive both to make the investment and to lobby to keep Mainland China's home market open.

Undoubtedly, M&A is a very important way for foreign investors to invest in Mainland China. JP Morgan's information showed that foreign investors who have been outside of the M&A market in Asia – especially China – for a number of years are beginning to return. M&A activity in the pipeline in China will be dominated by the restructuring of SOEs. A lot of assets need much repackaging and some of the deals will take time. In the next few years the majority of assets will come to the market. Mainland Chinese banks are limited to selling only a small stake to foreign investors and therefore candidates for M&A deals will be found in industrial and manufacturing sectors, including consumer products. M&A targets will have to offer foreign investors attractive human resources as well as scale and pricing power from controlling a dominant domestic market position. They will also need to demonstrate the support of the Chinese government and access to ongoing working capital provided by the state-directed banking system. The sale of Chinese government assets will be the driver behind M&A activity. The Chinese government's mentality has changed; it no longer wants to own assets, rather it wants the tax revenues. Statistics published by *China Business Post* show the current regional distribution and listed enterprises in which foreign funds are invested, profiled in Figures 7.3 to 7.5.

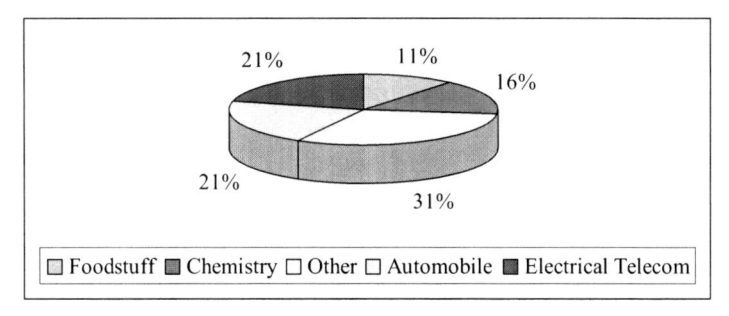

Best Practices in Products and Services for M&A Operations in China 221

[Pie chart: 21%, 11%, 16%, 31%, 21%]

☐ Foodstuff ■ Chemistry ☐ Other ☐ Automobile ■ Electrical Telecom

Figure 7.4 M&A listing industries by foreign investment

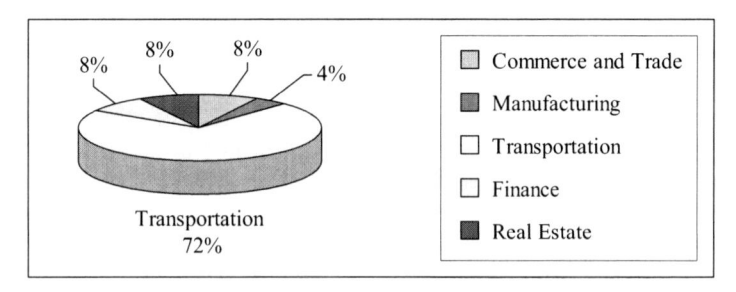

[Pie chart: Transportation 72%, 8%, 8%, 8%, 4%]

☐ Commerce and Trade
■ Manufacturing
☐ Transportation
☐ Finance
■ Real Estate

Figure 7.5 M&A listing enterprises by foreign investment

There are three factors which can explain why the developed southeastern coastal areas of Mainland China account for 75 per cent of foreign investment:

1. Most listed enterprises are concentrated in those economically developed regions, such as Shanghai Municipality and Guangdong Province. Foreign funds favour listed enterprises located in coastal areas because these companies tend to have mature operations and maintain a sound and transparent financial condition;

2. It is also important for foreign funders to acquire corporate information when venture capitalists choose domestic target companies. Generally, when investing initially in China, foreign investment companies will locate in the developed areas due to a lack of knowledge about the venture backed enterprises elsewhere.

3. Economically developed cities lead the way in the extent to which markets are open, government is managed efficiently and elements of the infrastructure and corresponding industry systems are established, although the middle and western areas of China hold abundant natural resources. Investment and M&A policy will

only be directed there if the venture capitalist's main goal is in those special natural resources.

In China, there are two key factors influencing foreign funding for M&A:

- The market potential and the stage of industry development;
- Industrial policy for foreign investment. As the 'global factory', China has a leading cost advantage in the manufacturing industry.

Internal linkage between sectors is obvious, such as in the automobile and electrical telecom sectors. Average automobile and electrical telecom domestic personnel expense in China is much lower in comparison with other countries, so foreign investment is focused on these two industries. However, there are still many industries where fragmented competition may be found, such as the milk industry, where there is really no favourable opportunity for foreign M&A entry. M&A in industries which receive limited foreign investment, such as finance, insurance, electric power, coal, gas, water, wholesale and retail selling, are driven by the Chinese authorities' policy. The banking industry in Mainland China is well known for its bad debts, yet international finance capitalists still cast a covetous eye on profits in the banking sector. New Bridge Capital and Citi Bank are two such pioneering examples. The new version of the *Catalogue for Guiding Foreign Investment in Industries* lists the new open industries, in which foreign investments were not previously allowed, such as the telecom, gas, heating and water supply sectors. After M&A in water supply factories, foreign funded M&A in gas and electric power will soon follow.

For US investment bankers, China represents a largely untapped market where the vast population and evolving corporate structure are expected to propel growth. Bankers may swap fees for promises, but the future of M&A in China rests largely on the Chinese government's support of deal-making. Achieving the kind of growth that investment bankers envision could take many years, so the immediate payback from M&A activity does not currently justify the commitment of significant resources and personnel. Nevertheless, investment banks clamouring for the attention of Chinese companies are often willing to waive fees in exchange for the promise of more business down the road. The question is how long it will take for relationship-building to translate into the kind of profits needed by the investment banks.[5]

---

[5] Chris Cockerill (2003) China: The New Frontier For M&A, The Next Big M&A Story, *Euromoney*, pp 129-132, April

Limits and control deter acquisitions. China's regulations limit foreign buyers, as fund managers involved in joint ventures can own only 33 per cent of the equity, whilst foreigners cannot own more than a 15 per cent stake in any Chinese bank. Issues of control often arise during negotiations because of this limitation, since acquirers rarely relish the role of being a passive shareholder. Hoping for change, Citigroup has shareholder agreements in place, which would allow it to buy a controlling stake by 2006 if the regulations change. Among the other areas of concern cited by the author is the lack of transparency or adequate controls in the financial sector, communications breakdowns, inexperienced negotiators, culture clashes and the high price tags of proven deal winners. Yet, despite the obstacles, large US banks are starting to reap rewards in the regions. Both the size and the frequency of deals are increasing as the Chinese realize the benefit of shedding some assets. The trend should continue, given the Chinese government's shift in focus to regulating companies rather than owning them.

Banking and oil/gas industries are the most popular sectors. With China's huge population and the incredible potential for expansion in credit cards, mortgages, consumer finance, and mutual funds, it is not surprising that the financial area is attracting the most interest from acquisitive investors. Recent buyers include Citigroup, which purchased a five per cent stake in a Shanghai development bank, and HSBC, which bought an eight per cent stake in the Bank of Shanghai. Fund management companies, seeking to capitalize on pension reform that could add US$400 billion to mutual funds by 2010, are also jumping on the acquisition bandwagon. ABN Amro Asset Management purchased a 33 per cent share of a Shanghai-based fund management company in February 2003. The M&A fever is not all one-sided, driven by dwindling resources and expanding needs. Chinese acquirers have shown a particular interest in overseas oil and gas companies, but with their limited expertise in global management, convincing foreign companies to sell could prove difficult.[6]

China could generate 10,000 big M&A deals over the coming five years and should enhance the enforcement of laws and regulations to speed up the M&A of SOEs. From 1995 to 2002, the number of Chinese SOEs in the industrial sector was reduced from 77,600 to about 42,000. Furthermore, total profits surged by 163.6 per cent to RMB 221billion (US$26.6 billion) and the number of small and medium-sized SOEs fell from 245,000 to 149,000, as figures from SASAC show.[7]

---

[6] ibid
[7] China to have 10,000 big merger deals in five years, *Xinhua News Agency*, 20 November 2003.

China has become a growing market for international M&As. The transition can be seen in every field of the country's financial markets. One of the most important characteristics of current economic globalization is the soaring growth of transnational M&A activity: it is notable that more than 80 per cent of international direct investment all over the world arises through M&A. Transnational M&A, especially those involving large-scale multinationals, huge investments and significant restructuring have become the most distinct characteristic of economic globalization. China is regarded as one of the hottest spots for international investment, but foreign investment in China introduced by means of enterprise purchases constitutes only five per cent of the total. Transnational purchase will become one of the most important methods to attract foreign investment.

Cooperation between Chinese and transnational companies has greatly improved, evolving from the simple acceptance of production investment to the establishment of Chinese headquarters and research and development centres as well as supporting purchasing organizations. Between April and September 2003, the State-owned Assets Supervision and Administration Commission of the State Council (SASAC) gave approval to 48 enterprises to transfer property rights or assets, involving a total of RMB22.5 billion (US$2.56 billion) in state-owned capital and equities. Chinese local governments were assigned more autonomy for disposition of assets.[8] M&A trends among local SOEs became rather predictable under the newly established management system of state-owned assets. As a result, it is quite reasonable to assume that China will soon be embracing a climax in M&A activity, whilst all the participants, from investors to agencies, are sure to find enormous new opportunities.

AsiaInfo: From venture-backed company to an M&A player

> *China needs a really great enterprise which has not just had five years of success but success for 50 years. Going public is only a new point on the hard road for AsiaInfo.*
>
> Suning Edward Tian[9]
> (Former President and CEO of AsiaInfo,
> Present CEO and Vice-president of China Netcom)

---

[8] *China Newsletter*, Confederation of India Industry, Vol 1, No 2, 16 February 2004.
[9] Su Xiaohua (2001) AsiaInfo, Born from The Golden Egg by Venture Capital, *Yang Cheng Wan Bao*, 4 January

Ten-year growth

The AsiaInfo Technologies Co Ltd (AsiaInfo) is based both in Beijing and at Santa Clara, California, in the heart of Silicon Valley. It builds customer billing and call-handling software for China Telecom and China Netcom, China's biggest telephone operators.[10]

AsiaInfo, the architect of China's internet infrastructure, and the backbone of the Chinese internet, was established in the mid-1990s by a group of returning Chinese students to address a major market void, namely the lack of professional domestic IT solution providers capable of helping Chinese telecom carriers to construct the backbone of the country's internet. Figure 7.6 outlines a brief history of AsiaInfo's development.

Since its inception in 1993, AsiaInfo has grown from a small Texas-based company with a handful of employees into a global, Chinese-based company with more than 1000 employees and clients in 32 of China's provinces and administrative regions. AsiaInfo has grown along with China's internet infrastructure and gained a reputation as 'the Engineer of China', setting numerous precedents:[11]

- First national commercial internet backbone designed, constructed and operated in China;
- First large-scale TCP/IP data network covering all mainland provinces;
- First WAN providing public services;
- First network system providing nationwide roaming capability.

AsiaInfo shares, with the trading symbol ASIA, ended 315 per cent above the US$24 offering price in March 2000, rating the sixth-best first-day rise. AsiaInfo placed five million shares at US$24 with Morgan Stanley Dean Witter as the lead underwriter and raised US$138 million of capital,[12] a highly successful share price compared with Sohu and Sina. Up to 2000, AsiaInfo had sold 1.8 million customer management and billing software licences, 9 million licences of its messaging software, and 7 million licences of its wireless telephony billing and customer management software.[13]

---

[10] AsiaInfo Online, www.asiainfo.com.cn
[11] ibid
[12] Morgan Stanley Named Best Investment Bank in China, Morgan Stanley Online, www.morganstanley.com
[13] AsiaInfo Online, www.asiainfo.com.cn

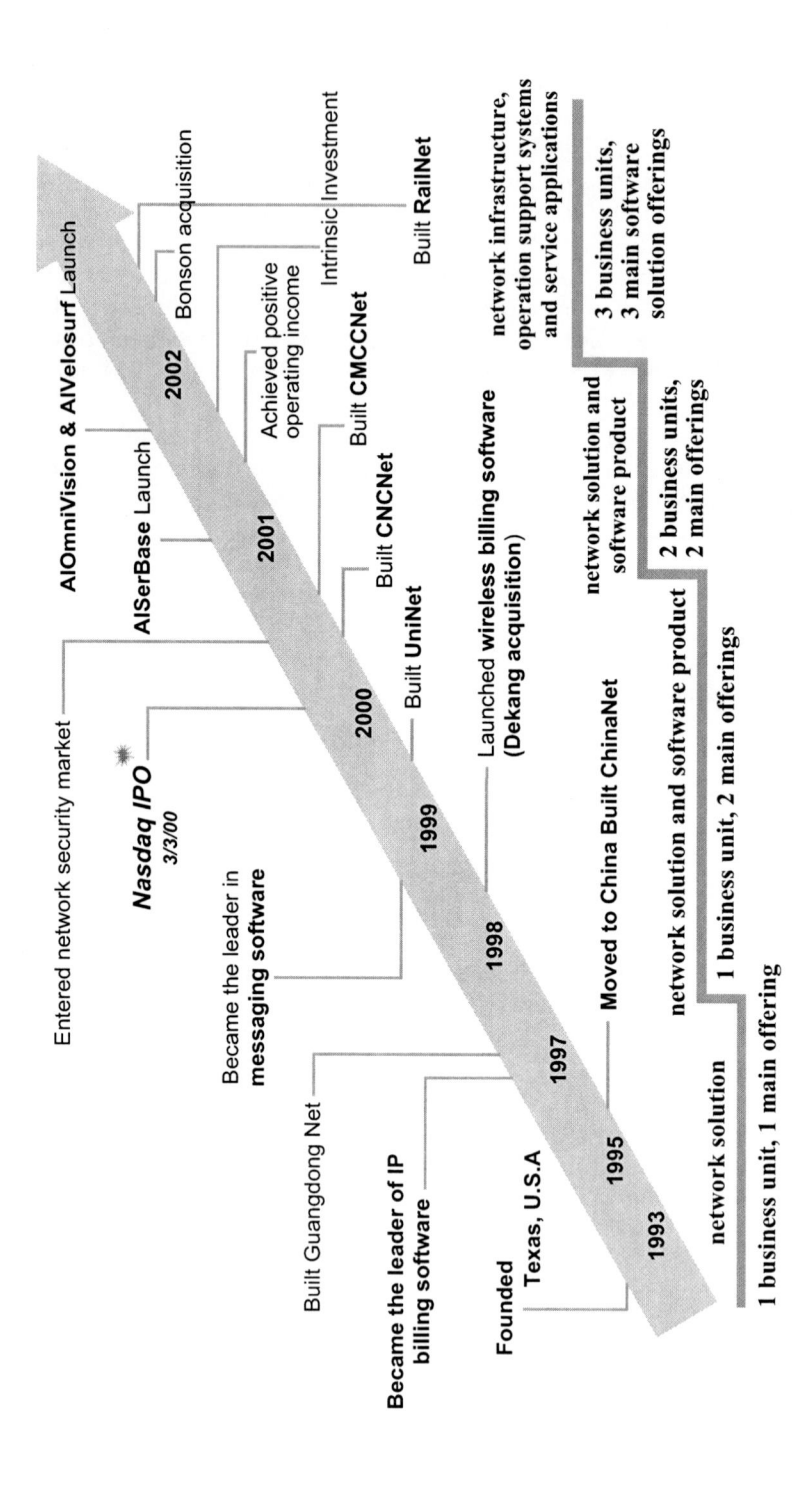

226   Investing in China: The Emerging Venture Capital Industry

Figure 7.6 The brief history of AsiaInfo up to 2002

Source: AsiaInfo-Online, 2003

Timeline events:
- 1993: Founded Texas, U.S.A; 1 business unit, 1 main offering; network solution
- 1995: Built Guangdong Net
- 1997: Became the leader of IP billing software
- 1998: Entered network security market; Became the leader in messaging software; Moved to China Built ChinaNet; 1 business unit, 2 main offerings; network solution and software product
- 1999: Launched wireless billing software (Dekang acquisition)
- 2000: Nasdaq IPO 3/3/00; Built UniNet; 2 business units, 2 main offerings; network solution and software product
- 2001: AISerBase Launch; Built CNCNet
- 2002: AIOmniVision & AIVelosurf Launch; Bonson acquisition; Achieved positive operating income; Intrinsic Investment; Built CMCCNet; Built RailNet; 3 business units, 3 main software solution offerings; network infrastructure, operation support systems and service applications

Today, AsiaInfo has firmly established itself as a leading provider of telecom network integration and software solutions in China, offering total network solutions and proprietary software products to meet the complete internet and telecommunication infrastructure and operating needs of Chinese carriers. AsiaInfo has strong relationships with all of China's major telecom carriers. Moreover, it aims to further upgrade and standardize its proprietary software applications to exploit new opportunities in China's fast growing IT industry.

AsiaInfo's 2001 net revenue was up at US$71.4 million, giving earnings per share (EPS) of US$0.28. In 2003, AsiaInfo's gross revenue was US$116 million and net revenue was US$57.5 million. Net revenue is expected to be approximately US$66–70 million in fiscal year 2004, representing an increase of 15–21 per cent on 2003. Net income for the fiscal year 2004 is expected to be in the range of US$5–7 million, or US$0.12 to $US0.16 per basic share.[14]

Venture capital invested

The founders' initial concept was to build an information services company with the intention to expand throughout Asia and China. The first VC investment for AsiaInfo was US$500,000 from Mr Louis Lau, a venture capital angel and an overseas Chinese businessman engaged in the real estate sector in the United States. Mr Lau was Chairman of the Board until 2003 and currently holds the position of Director.[15] There were two requirements that Mr Lau stipulated when making his investment in the 1990s:

1. All employees should work in China in the future;
2. AsiaInfo must not be connected to real estate business.

In 1995, AsiaInfo began looking for further VC investment because the management team was aware that it was not in AsiaInfo's best interests for the founders to hold 100 per cent of the share capital. They also needed the support of abundant capital. AsiaInfo's key criterion for choosing the right venture capitalists for the company was that they could enhance the value of its management, reputation, and technology. In December 1997, Warburg Pincus, ChinaVest, and Fidelity Ventures introduced significant expansion VC of US$18 million in

---

[14] Liu Wei (2004) *AsiaInfo's Road for NASDAQ*, SP Online, www.spn.com.cn, 19 March
[15] *The Story Between AsiaInfo and Venture Capitalists*, China Science and Technology Online, www.chinatech.com.cn, 19 September 2003.

exchange for 30 per cent of the issued share capital. AsiaInfo's first action after gained this injection of VC was to acquire Dekang.[16]

Warburg Pincus is one of the leading and largest private equity investment firms in the world and has been a leading private equity investor since 1971. Over the last 30 years, the firm has invested approximately US$14 billion into more than 466 companies in 29 countries around the world. When Warburg Pincus met the founding management team in July 1997, AsiaInfo had already been involved in over 70 per cent of the key internet backbone projects in China but was still an early-stage company experiencing growing pains and in need of strategic and operational guidance. Since 1997, Warburg Pincus has worked closely with the company in assembling and continuously strengthening a world-class professional management team, developing operational and strategic plans and executing acquisitions. Over its brief operating history, AsiaInfo has been able to establish the de facto industry design standards for the internet framework in China, develop strong relationships with all major Chinese telecommunications companies, and secure a dominant market share in all of its product categories.[17]

Fidelity Ventures is backed by Fidelity Investments, the leading global money management firm. With Fidelity and its affiliates as Fidelity Ventures' core source of capital and total commitments in excess of US$500 million, Fidelity Ventures has greater flexibility in the strategy, as well as a long-term investment horizon. In the website sector, Fidelity Ventures maintains that it brings more than capital to the companies in which it invests. In order to bring greater understanding and experience to their portfolio companies, they focus on Enterprise Information Technology and Communications and AsiaInfo which holds one of their portfolios in the field of communications.[18]

ChinaVest was the first independent American VC firm to be established in Mainland China and is among the oldest venture capital firms operating in the region. Founded in 1983, its mission is to provide long-term investment capital and management expertise to growing companies doing business in or with the economies of Mainland China, Hong Kong and Taiwan. It invests in four sectors of the Greater Chinese economy (precision manufacturing, branded consumer services, logistics and supply chain services) as well as telecommunications and IT. AsiaInfo is a select member of ChinaVest's current investments portfolio.[19]

---

[16] Craig Watts (2004) *Stable Growth Opportunities in China's Telecom Sector*, Norson Telecom Consulting, 5 October
[17] Warburg Pincus Online, www.warburgpincus.com.
[18] Fidelity Ventures Online, www.fidelityventures.com
[19] ChinaVest Online, www.chinavest.com

The benefits received from the three chosen venture capitalists

AsiaInfo got not only its capital fund but also the 'resources' it required, via the investment of US$18 million in 1997 from the three US venture capitalists – Warburg Pincus, ChinaVest and Fidelity – the largest high-tech VC investment in Asia in that year. AsiaInfo took into account the additional value received from investors, bringing in advanced and developed management resources, business operation network resources and social resources. In respect of these resources AsiaInfo built a long-term cooperation agreement with the three funds that was not related to any investment exit issue.

From the management resource point of view, the three famous venture capitalists have wide-ranging and successful experience in managing high-speed growth enterprises, especially in the high-tech sector. They clearly understood what kind of management measurement and development strategy policies should be taken. Following the VC investment, AsiaInfo reorganized its board of directors, reconstituted decision-making procedures, defined its human resource policy, and finally formed a management system suitable for high-speed development and high-calibre management. Management is a core element for high-speed growth firms. Poor management will damage a good business opportunity but good management will accelerate the enterprise's healthy development. The venture capitalists brought the precious resource of world-class management into AsiaInfo.

In business network resources, the venture capitalists had accumulated a wide range of business customers in their networks through investment in familiar sectors. The three venture capitalists investing in AsiaInfo were all familiar with the IT sector. Their experience assisted AsiaInfo in adopting a suitable operational strategy, choosing the right direction for R&D, and establishing logical strategic goals that guaranteed a sound capability.

With regard to social resources, each venture capitalist had its own special characteristics. The strategic alliance encouraged AsiaInfo to improve its competitiveness and achieve stable development, as well as to realise its strategic goals. Warburg Pincus had already invested in more than ten enterprises in the IT field in China up to 1997 and AsiaInfo became a member of this 'family' which provided mutual support wherever the technology lay. ChinaVest has a strong relationship with the Chinese government and is familiar with the investment environment, economy and politics of China. Fidelity is one of the largest scale investment funds which was able to provide steady and unceasing funding support. The high profile of the three venture capitalist funds established the social reputation of AsiaInfo, consequently boosting its name and swelling the confidence of customers and employees. Due to the investment of these world-class VC funds, AsiaInfo can be ranked against world-class top level standards in management, business operations and R&D. The takeover of Dekang was a case of successful cooperation for AsiaInfo and its three venture capitalists.

The road to M&A

From 1998 to 2002, AsiaInfo undertook three key M&As and strategy investments which resulted in the company expanding into the wireless internet and mobile sectors from the internet sector. AsiaInfo is now one of the biggest telecom solution providers covering IP, mobile and fixed networks in China.

Acquisition of Dekang
In 1998 AsiaInfo, together with its investors Warburg Pincus, Fidelity Ventures and ChinaVest, acquired Dekang Communications Technology Co Ltd (Dekang) for US$5 million in cash and US$5 million in AsiaInfo stock. Dekang, founded in 1994, was the first Chinese company to develop a Billing System. By 1997, Dekang had become the biggest provider of wireless and fixed-line service billing software.[20]

After acquiring Dekang, AsiaInfo appointed three vice presidents in charge of R&D, finance and human resource to Dekang, while the 11 software technicians, general manager and heads of sales, engineering and R&D remained in place. In fact, almost all Dekang's employees continued working for the new company. When AsiaInfo gave a training course to all Dekang colleagues, the content was related to AsiaInfo's management concept and business model.

Rationale for the Dekang acquisition
Acquiring Dekang was a win-win situation for AsiaInfo, which had started its business in China in 1995 by helping China to construct the backbone of its internet network. By 1998, AsiaInfo had become the biggest internet systems integration provider in China. The development of China's telecom market caused AsiaInfo to notice that wireless and digital data would be the next two important fields of telecommunications. After occupying a monopoly position in the infrastructure of China's internet, AsiaInfo then placed itself as a future solution provider for wireless, long distance and local telephone, as well as the internet and mobile sectors.

---

[20] Ding Jian, the Candidate of China's Economic Leaders for Tomorrow 2003, by *Caijing Magazine*, the *World Economic Forum* and the programme *Dialogue*, presented by CCTV (China Central Television), 20 October 2003.

With the rapidly growing population of Chinese mobile users, it was clear that the billing system would become a fast-growing market. AsiaInfo really wanted to enter this field, but had neither experience nor R&D in billing systems even if it had advantages in IP billing systems. It was not easy to enter such a new field, and it was estimated that it would take at least two or three years for AsiaInfo to complete its own R&D. The acquisition of Dekang was a prudent choice which gave AsiaInfo access to the billing system market within the shortest possible period. Before 1998, in order to protect its domestic manufacturers China did not allow foreign companies to enter the field of billing systems. Under this protection policy, Dekang had developed fast and became one of the biggest providers of billing systems. In 1998, China lifted the barrier blocking foreign competitor entry and allowed them to sell billing systems to Chinese carriers. Dekang faced severe competition without the protection policy, however the ever-increasing numbers of China's mobile users forced the carriers to use the new system to provide high capacity and performance. Dekang needed to put more funds into R&D, improve its management skills and optimize its sales and marketing strategy so that it could upgrade its products. All of this seemed to be a task for Dekang. However, the investment by AsiaInfo solved this problem.

By joining AsiaInfo, Dekang could gain funding support, good management experience, technology, sales and marketing strategy. Post-acquisition, Dekang's revenue increased six-fold in 1999, equivalent to the total revenue from 1995 to 1998. AsiaInfo's revenue also improved. In March 2000, AsiaInfo completed its IPO on NASDAQ.

Strategic investment in Intrinsic Technology
On 8 May 2001, AsiaInfo acquired a strategic equity stake in Intrinsic Technology, a leading provider of wireless internet infrastructure software products and solutions. Under the terms of the agreement, AsiaInfo and its partner, Fidelity Ventures, invested US$8.2 million into Intrinsic Technology in order to acquire a significant minority stake in the company. The structure of the agreement allowed AsiaInfo to see whether the technology would become as profitable as projected, and then to use its option to invest additional capital and increase ownership up to 51 per cent, thereby consolidating Intrinsic's revenues with its own over the following two years. Existing shareholders of Intrinsic Technology included Acer Technology Ventures and Icon Medialab Asia. Credit Suisse First Boston advised AsiaInfo and Goldman Sachs advised Intrinsic on the deal.[21]

---

[21] *Intrinsic Technology: A Chinese wireless data software company transforms itself,* ChinaOnline, www.chinaonline.com, 17 May 2001

Intrinsic was founded in mid-1999 in Shanghai by CEO Wu Jun, who returned to China after a long career in Stockholm, where he had worked for the mobile phone messaging company Sendit, which was bought in 1999 by Microsoft. The iDAP (Intrinsic Data Application Platform), Intrinsic Technology's flagship product, is a carrier-grade wireless internet service provisioning and management system. As part of the strategic alliance, AsiaInfo and Intrinsic are integrating iDAP with AsiaInfo's Convergent Billing Solution (AICBS) software and co-developing future product offerings.[22]

Daniel Auerbach, Managing Director of Fidelity Ventures, stated at that time after completion of the investment in Intrinsic:

> As a global venture investor in the telecommunications services and technology sector, we see the provision of robust wireless data platforms as a major opportunity area, and regard China as a rapidly emerging key wireless market. We are very excited to be supporting this partnership, as it brings together Intrinsic Technology, the leading wireless team in China, with AsiaInfo's unparalleled position and reputation as the leading provider of carrier class solutions to China's telecom industry.

This action has allowed both companies jointly to market turnkey solutions that meet the emerging needs of mobile network operators, mobile service providers and mobile virtual network operators both within China and globally. Increasing wireless internet usage has created a tremendous need for enabling technologies, as mobile operators introduce value-added services and upgrade their networks. AsiaInfo and Intrinsic's products address the access and billing requirements for revenue-sharing initiatives and other services currently under development. Rapidly increasing SMS offerings, particularly under China Mobile's Monternet initiative, and the rollout of GPRS (General Packet Radio Service, or '2.5G'), scheduled for late 2001, were just two examples of the market opportunities that Intrinsic and AsiaInfo targeted jointly.

Will the relationship with AsiaInfo prove beneficial for Intrinsic? AsiaInfo at that time of investment was upgrading the billing systems at various telecoms across China and replacing their legacy systems. AsiaInfo's huge salesforce gives Intrinsic the ability to spread its products across China. AsiaInfo also has ambitions to set up an international sales-force. In fact, the company's link with AsiaInfo was not only an endorsement and funding, but also provided Intrinsic with a distribution platform. The software company has offices in six major

---

[22] Intrinsic Online, www.intrint.com

cities in China and is now using those offices to handle installation jobs for Intrinsic.

Acquisition of Bonson
On 23 January 2002, AsiaInfo acquired 100 per cent of Bonson Information Technology Ltd (Bonson). Bonson was a leading provider of telecom operation support system solutions in China. The transaction, valued at approximately US$47.3 million, comprised US$28.9 million in cash and US$18.4 million in AsiaInfo stock. The management shareholders received US$18.5 million cash and US$11.3 million stock with a one-year lock-up prohibiting the sale of AsiaInfo shares received for 12 months. Other shareholders received US$10.4 million cash and US$7.1 million stock with a three-month lock-up.[23]

BOSS is an integrated software platform to optimize the provincial carrier's business processes, improve network efficiency and enhance customer satisfaction and is a Bonson main product line. The solution encompasses a range of mission critical functions including data collection, billing, accounting, settlement, comprehensive reporting, customer service, and decision support systems.

Founded in 1994, Bonson is 61 per cent owned by the management and 39 per cent owned by an affiliate of IDG and other private investors. Bonson was a top provider of BOSS solutions, and the company's other product lines include mobile network monitoring systems, network management and wireless data applications.

In 2001,[24] Mobile BOSS accounted for approximately 85 per cent of Bonson's net revenue and employed approximately two thirds of Bonson's workforce. Bonson's main customer is China Mobile. The company provides interconnect and roaming settlement systems for the China Mobile Group and BOSS solutions to provincial operators including Guangxi Mobile, Guizhou Mobile, Gansu Mobile and Tibet Mobile. In addition to BOSS, Bonson markets and sells other products and solutions to more than 20 provincial operators of China Mobile and China Unicom.

The acquisition allowed AsiaInfo to capitalize fully on the tremendous growth opportunity of the operation support systems market, expected to be one of the fastest growing areas of telecom investment over the next few years. This acquisition also increased AsiaInfo's market share significantly, vaulting AsiaInfo into undisputed number one position in the wireless BOSS market in China. Bonson's industry expertise, large installation base, and proven profitability complemented

---

[23] AsiaInfo to Acquire Bonson Technology for US$47 Million; AsiaInfo Vaulted to No.1 Position in Key Wireless Market, *Business Wire*, 22 January 2002
[24] ibid

AsiaInfo's strengths as a leading provider of telecom software and solutions.

While tariffs in China have been decreed by government mandate, China's telecom service prices will eventually be determined by the market. Liberalizing tariffs will further drive carrier investment in supporting software. Getting into the mobile BOSS market early is important because provincial carriers tend to stick with a single solution provider, building upgrades and additional capabilities on top of an established platform to avoid risk and obtain a better return on investment. In 1999, China Mobile began to build BOSS; each of its provincial branches would invest more than RMB100 million in BOSS. Some 20 per cent of the investment would be in software: the fastest growing market. In 2002, China Mobile alone was set to invest over RMB3 billion on BOSS solutions.

Though AsiaInfo was the bellwether in IP, it was very difficult for AsiaInfo to expand from its IP billing and accounting system to wireless BOSS. AsiaInfo had previously tried to enter this field in 2000 when it acquired Dekang, who had signed contracts with the carriers of five provinces of China. In 2001, AsiaInfo secured contracts from only two provinces in BOSS. A more important factor was that AsiaInfo's experience in IP did not help it to gain a share in the BOSS market. Compared with AsiaInfo, Bonson had been the second largest provider of BOSS and had signed contracts with four provinces. Therefore, acquisition of Bonson was the best solution. Although AsiaInfo paid a premium price for the acquisition, the purchase of Bonson, which had secured a number of key national and provincial contracts with China Mobile, established AsiaInfo as the sector leader. There was a significant increase in customers for AsiaInfo after the acquisition.

An overview of Bonson's customers is provided first by Figure 7.7. Bonson's major customers include the headquarters and over 20 provincial operators of China Mobile. The points in the map in Figure 7.8 provide a clear picture of AsiaInfo's expanding customers. The acquisition of Bonson confirmed AsiaInfo's position as a clear leader in telecom operation support systems (OSS) solutions. A number of new contracts with a particular interest in OSS were announced in the first quarter of 2002, including contracts with China Netcom, a China Mobile subsidiary, and Guangxi Mobile, China Railcom, Shanghai Mobile, and Shanxi Mobile. The acquisition leapfrogged AsiaInfo to an undisputed number one position in the wireless BOSS market in China, already identified as one of the fastest growing areas of telecom investment over the next few years. The acquisition was also highly beneficial to AsiaInfo's financial situation, adding approximately eight to ten per cent to its net income in 2002 with increased contributions over the next few years.

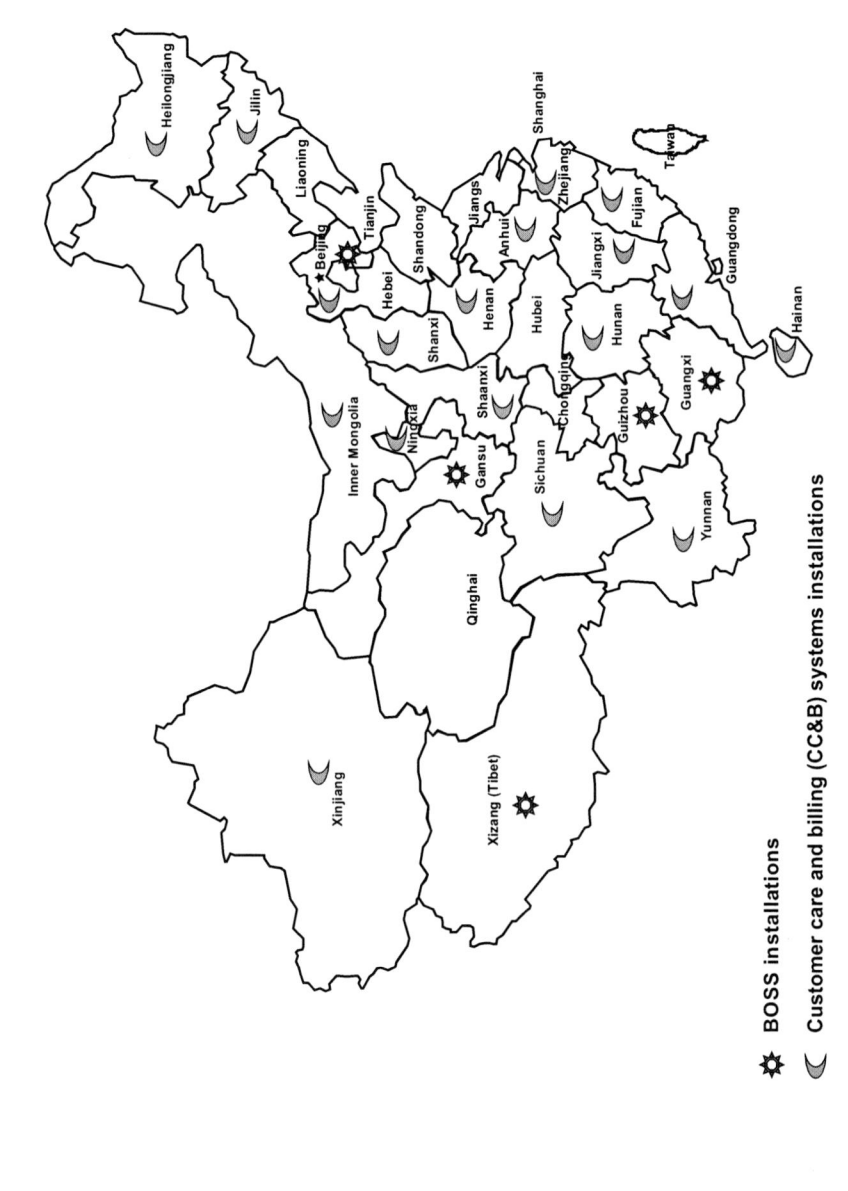

Source: AsiaInfo-Online, 2003

Figure 7.7 Bonson's customers

236   Investing in China: The Emerging Venture Capital Industry

✸ BOSS installations
︶ Customer care and billing (CC&B) systems installations
⊕ Compatible unit (CU) and customer care and billing (CC&B) installations

Source: AsiaInfo-Online, 2003

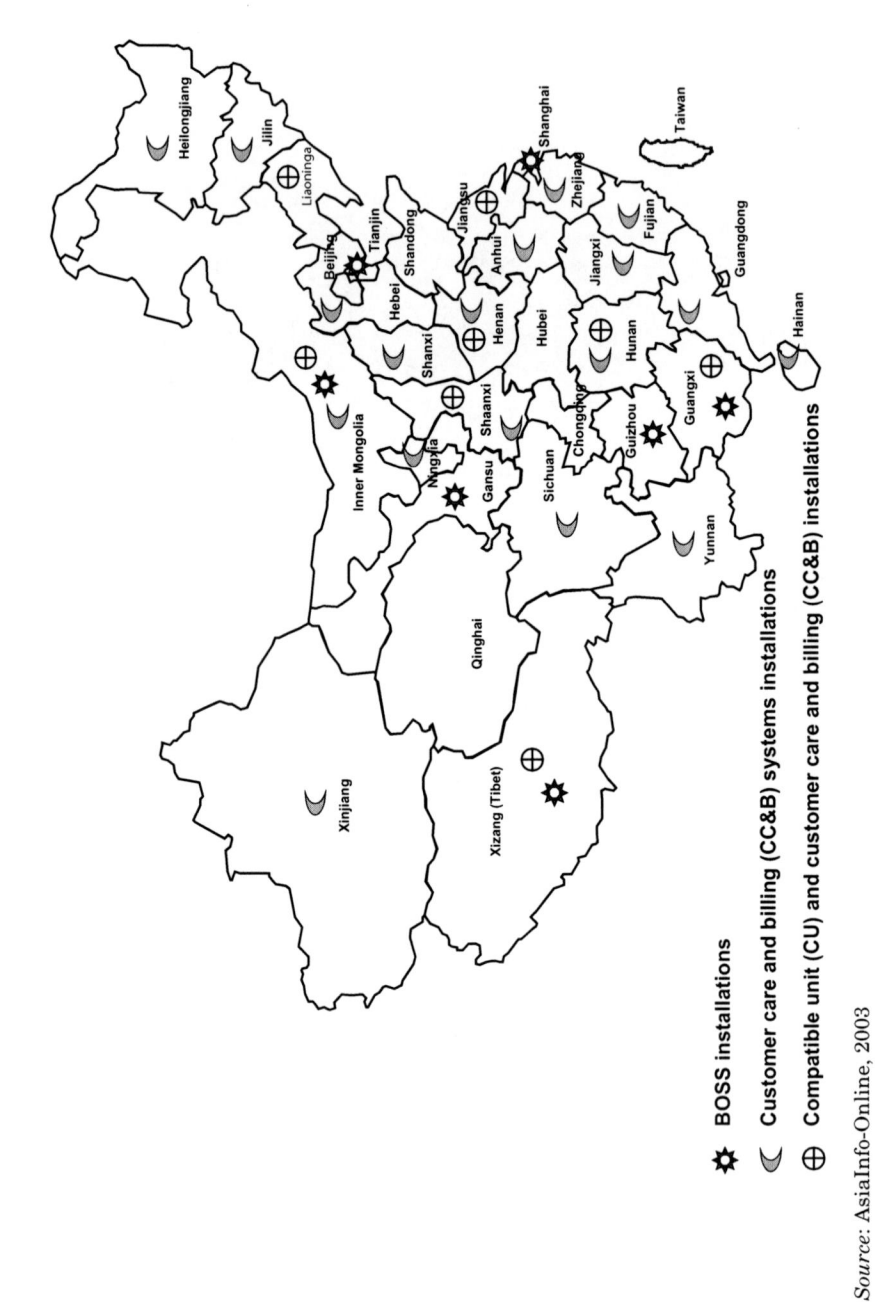

Figure 7.8 AsiaInfo's installation after acquisition

Strategic issues following M&A

From these three deals, the strategies behind AsiaInfo's acquisitions are evident:

1. A tendency to use a combination of cash and stock for acquisitions. In acquiring Dekang and Bonson, AsiaInfo used cash and issued new shares;
2. Preference for joint acquisition and investment. In all three cases, AsiaInfo teamed up with its VC partners to carry out the acquisitions;
3. Cooperation with professional financial advisors. Credit First Boston acted as AsiaInfo's advisor in its Intrinsic strategic investment;
4. Acquiring targets to be the leading competitors in their fields;
5. Company management usually unchanged post-acquisition. After acquisition, Bonson continued to operate independently for a long time and management was not merged into AsiaInfo's BOSS team.

When discussing the M&A strategies of AsiaInfo, it should be remembered firstly that there are few financing routes for SMEs in China. When high-tech venture-backed SMEs are funded by venture capitalists, their only effective choice is M&A. M&A is especially important in China, because failure to invest in the related field means that funds and finance are invested in vain. No M&A, no second chance.

Secondly, as a technology-based SME, maintaining competitiveness and being the strongest firm in the market, while still a relatively small enterprise, is very important. In such an environment, those who do not plan to acquire another when they are in funds will be acquired themselves. It is good to acquire, if only to avoid the risk of being acquired.

Thirdly, only a few SMEs can raise sufficient financing from venture capitalists. To seize the opportunity and deploy funds in the market, rather than in the bank to earn interest, the best method is M&A. In China, firms that are funded have the right to speak. Capital is everything.

Fourthly, unlike AOL Time Warner, for example, AsiaInfo belongs to the SME category. The stage of development, characteristics and company goals differ between the SME and the mega-enterprise.

Fifthly, integration of the management board should be carried out carefully because it is always poses a dilemma in the post-M&A period.

AsiaInfo took a fancy to Bonson because of the latter's large domestic market share: around one third of the BOSS systems in China Mobile are sourced from Bonson. After acquisition, the original management team of Bonson were kept in place and remained located at Guangzhou, its original headquarters. The former president, Li Jian, joined the Board of Directors as Senior Vice President. The loose integration of management structure concealed the problems arising from cultural integration. While AsiaInfo focused on operational criteria in its corporate culture, Bonson paid attention to capital cost and efficiency. The middle-rank employees of the former two firms still like to speak and analyze as two firms but not as one. It is embarrassing that there are two separate systems of business management. By contrast, the acquisition of Dekang passed through a long period of quietly adapting to and accommodating each other. It is necessary for domestic enterprises to undergo this period.

The AsiaInfo experience can provide many lessons for other Chinese domestic enterprises. Firstly, VC has contributed the most towards AsiaInfo's development. The successful IPO on NASDAQ means that AsiaInfo, a technology-based enterprise of Chinese background, was admitted to the international capital market. Secondly, in addition to the economic and technological background factors, an essential key to success was that the founders were able to grasp the 'pulse of the era', find a niche opportunity in the market and create and guide market demand, according to the situation at the time China was preparing to developing its internet infrastructure. Thirdly, AsiaInfo attaches importance to the pursuit of basic and practical issues and takes a tight grip on its core technology business. Finally, the management team has a mature financing approach with an emphasis on long-term development.

SWOT analysis for AsiaInfo

SWOT analysis is a commonly used planning tool for formulating business strategy in terms of its strengths, weaknesses, opportunities and threats. Focusing on both internal and external environments, it serves to highlight a firm's distinctive competencies, which will enable it to gain competitive advantage.

Strengths analysis
AsiaInfo has a number of general strengths over systems integrators:

1. *Established customer relationships.* AsiaInfo has established close business relationships with almost all the key national telecom carriers in China through handling their internet-backbone projects over the last ten years. This has given the company a detailed understanding of its customers' requirements and

makes it more likely to capture additional telecoms-applications contracts;

2. *Strong development team at a competitive cost.* AsiaInfo has recruited more than 200 software engineers locally at very attractive rates. Monthly salaries range from RMB5000 to RMB8000 (US$605 to US$967),[25] substantially lower than its competitors which have based only a part of their software teams in China;

3. *Local touch in mainland market.* Top management is comprised of western educated but home-grown personnel who have extensive experience of doing business in China. At the operational level, AsiaInfo has a strong local customer support team to respond quickly to customer needs;

4. *Strong financial resources.* AsiaInfo tapped the capital market in a timely fashion in early 2000, raising more than US$130 million from its IPO. The cash reserve should enable AsiaInfo to acquire local companies to complement its existing business lines.

Weaknesses needing resolution
A few issues could damage AsiaInfo's ability to sustain long-term profitability and competitiveness:

1. *Cyclical business.* AsiaInfo's network solution business is project-based and is therefore cyclical. Any slowdown in internet-backbone spending could have a direct impact on the company;

2. *Staff turnover.* IT companies in China also face competition from rivals for experienced IT personnel. This might lead to higher pay packages to retain key personnel, thus diminishing AsiaInfo's cost advantage. However, staff turnover in 1999 was 12 per cent, in line with market norms;

3. *Pricing power.* AsiaInfo is mainly focused on the top national carriers. Pricing power is therefore relatively weak unless it can offer higher value-added and proprietary services to the principals;

4. *The dotcom bubble.* Following its US$138 million IPO in March 2000, the company suffered the consequence of the internet slump, and its share price fell from a high of over US$100 to a low of just over US$3 in March 2002. Since then, however, the stock has kicked back up to almost US$11 before falling on news that the company made a SARS-induced loss of US$1.1 million in the

---

[25] AsiaInfo Online, www.asiainfo.com.cn

second quarter of 2003.[26] But through appropriate operation of the enterprise, the weakness could be another strength factor for AsiaInfo. The dotcom bubble made AsiaInfo insist on the road of technology amalgamation and not only invention. Whatever from the content or the infrastructure, the future internet development would lean to another telecommunication network. Internet is three sectors' integration: telecommunication, computer and media. The news content has been done very well for many portal websites. In the following 10–15 years, the internet will focus on the wireless and broadband equipment. The application of broadband will bring new explosion to the internet and the new wheel of impact to the traditional modern media, such as TV. The year 2000's internet crisis did not change AsiaInfo's development but made it care about the internet more. The combinations for internet technology and market demand, internet and telecommunication are the key for AsiaInfo to cast off the weakness and transfer it into a strength.

Opportunities from the telecom market
As China's telecom market shifts towards competition, rigid state-mandated spending plans in hardware and infrastructure are giving way to flexible, market-based investment meant to attract and retain consumers. Reflecting this shift, operator investment in developed markets will be strong in areas such as BOSS, broadband access (ADSL, LAN), VPN, call centres, and intelligent networks. Conditions are right for companies such as Harbour and Linkage that rely on operator spending for the latest low-priced products and services.

Mobile is a growth area in the telecom sector. According to telecom department statistics, there are more than 160 million mobile users with five million new users continuing to be added each month. The potential marketing power should not be ignored. In 2001, Chinese users sent nearly 20 billion SMS messages. Primitive peer-to-peer SMS has been an important profit source similar to value-added services such as ringtone and picture download games, and information services offered by private third-party service providers. Although China's three listed portals have already asserted a dominant position in SMS services, the sector remains a largely new greenfield opportunity populated by growth companies such as AsiaInfo.[27]

---

[26] AsiaInfo Online, www.asiainfo.com.cn
[27] Craig Watts (2004) *Stable Growth Opportunities in China's Telecom Sector*, Norson Telecom Consulting, 5 October

Virtual operation is another area of interest. Following the split of China's fixed-line monopoly into China Telecom and China Netcom, the two giants are likely to rely on virtual operators to garner customers in areas where they lack infrastructure and entrenched sales forces. AsiaInfo has focused attention on 'rebuilding' the infrastructure of the new two carriers.

Threats from local and overseas competitors in the same trade
By late 2002, improved handsets and new technologies such as MMS, GPRS, and CDMAIX were enabling the provision of more sophisticated value-added services. Under WTO conditions, minority foreign investment is now approved for value-added service providers in China's telecom sector. Major competitors for systems integration include local players Suntek and Aotian as well as US IT powerhouses such as IBM and Hewlett-Packard. For billing software, AsiaInfo cites Portal Software as its main competition. On the messaging front, AsiaInfo competes with Software.com and Netease.

Benefits from M&A

The three main acquisitions mentioned above provide a clear picture of AsiaInfo's strategy. As a systems integrator of internet to software and solution provider, its target is to be a provider of software and solutions for all telecom fields. In 1998, AsiaInfo had helped to establish the backbone of China's internet. AsiaInfo needs to find new fields, whilst mobile telecom and wireless internet are the next two hot areas. AsiaInfo thought that 90 per cent of the investment would go into mobile and local networks and that only 10 per cent would be made in IP. By acquiring Dekang and making its strategic investment in Intrinsic, AsiaInfo quickly entered the field of mobile telecom and wireless telecom. In 2002, after acquiring Bonson, AsiaInfo penetrated the field of BOSS. As Figure 7.9 demonstrates, AsiaInfo always follows the telecom infrastructure value chain to strive for high growth and high profitability and to develop multiple offerings of high-end software and solutions.

Through acquisitions, AsiaInfo transformed itself into a software provider. In the mobile field, having completed massive infrastructure build-ups to keep pace with the rapid growth in telecom subscribers, China's carriers are now turning their attention to software and services. Nascent competition is driving China's mobile carriers to offer more sophisticated services and to track information on customers/ projects that require software support. Most of the investment will flow into software and services; thus AsiaInfo must change into a provider of software and solutions. But AsiaInfo did not have any advantages in software so the best choice was to acquire the leading

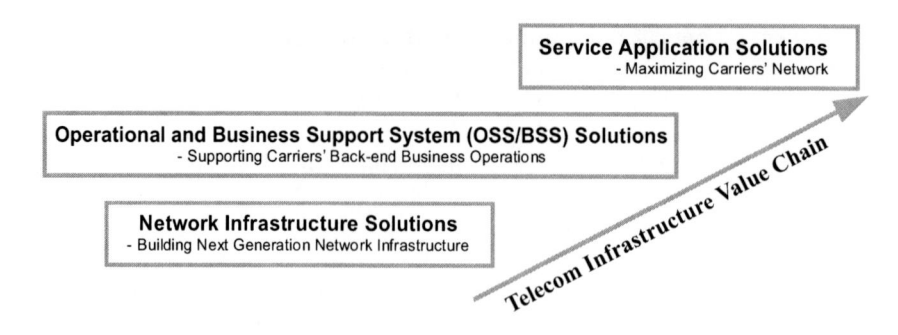

```
                                    ┌─────────────────────────────┐
                                    │ Service Application Solutions│
                                    │ - Maximizing Carriers' Network│
                                    └─────────────────────────────┘
        ┌──────────────────────────────────────────────┐
        │ Operational and Business Support System (OSS/BSS) Solutions │
        │ - Supporting Carriers' Back-end Business Operations │
        └──────────────────────────────────────────────┘
              ┌────────────────────────────────┐
              │ Network Infrastructure Solutions│
              │ - Building Next Generation Network Infrastructure │
              └────────────────────────────────┘
```

Figure 7.9 Telecom infrastructure value chain

software providers. After acquiring Dekang, AsiaInfo's net profit after tax in 2001 hit US$16 million, with 39 per cent of its net income (US$27.9 million) coming from software. In 2002, half its profit came from software, while a third were derived from BOSS. In later years most of its profit would come from software.

Through acquisitions, AsiaInfo has also increased its sales return and profits. Although AsiaInfo became the biggest internet systems integration provider in China and listed on NASDAQ in 2000, it did not break into profit until 2001. Making profit was AsiaInfo's Achilles heel. Before 1999, its core business had been systems integration, but the profits generated from this activity were slim. For example, in the first nine months of 2000, the revenue generated from internet solutions was US$120 million, the cost of sales US$110 million. AsiaInfo needed to penetrate other telecom fields to realize profit. After acquiring Dekang, its return on sales in software increased six times. Bonson has been consistently profitable since 1999. Based on Bonson's management accounts for 2000, Bonson registered approximately US$6.9 million, US$2.4 million and US$2.2 million in net revenue, operating profit and net income respectively. For the first nine months of 2001, it recorded US$6.2 million, US$1.6 million and US$1.5 million in the same areas. After acquiring Bonson, AsiaInfo's revenue and profit figures greatly improved. For the first quarter of 2002, AsiaInfo posted a higher than expected operating profit of US$1.1 million, a significant improvement on the company's loss of US$23,000 in the same period the previous year. AsiaInfo's first quarter operating profit of 2002 was driven by high-margin software and services. After adjusting for the cost of hardware, net revenue rose 20 per cent over the previous year's quarter to US$17.1 million. The net sales backlog rose 16 per cent over the previous year and continued to be steady despite a traditionally slow first quarter.

Conclusion

The AsiaInfo business model signals a new trend for high-tech venture-backed SMEs and is worth studying as a benchmark. Dealing with management conflict was very important in the post-acquisition period. It ensured that AsiaInfo grasped its market opportunity. The market is the deciding factor in the development of a company. If you are unable to follow the movement of the market and have no good products in related fields, business in the sector will decline, resulting in a price war and eventually elimination of the sector. AsiaInfo operates well in terms of share performance, competition and the provision of a VC exit. AsiaInfo also focuses clearly on its aim to be a provider of software solutions in all telecom fields. AsiaInfo can be proud of its record in timely IPO and M&A. Of course, there are some key differences between AsiaInfo and local Chinese SMEs whose management boards are normally drawn from technology departments:

1. AsiaInfo was founded by overseas Chinese students who had acquired advanced western learning;

2. The excellent management board has thorough experience of investment and financing;

3. AsiaInfo operates successfully through a 'cocktail' of Chinese enterprise and western corporate cultures.

8
Insight into the Potential and Traditional Sectors

The financial miracle of online gaming

From RMB500,000 to RMB5 million in four years

Nintendo's Chinese strategy brings with it problems such as pirating and difficulties with return payment for goods etc; this, together with the propensity for online gaming, has caused the company to lose its advantage of 20 years. While Nintendo is still following a hard road for its Chinese strategy and Sony is currently hesitating to clarify its development plans in China, Shanda has expanded rapidly and now has the biggest share of Mainland China's online gaming market.

Founded in Pudong, Shanghai and having RMB500,000 registered capital on December 1999, Shanda Interactive Entertainment Ltd (Shanda) is China's leading online gaming operator, also known as the current 'games giant'. With a professional management team and advanced network technologies, Shanda helps its customers to enjoy the many pleasures of online gaming. Its portfolio of games, played over the internet, includes traditional and role-playing games, many of which allow large numbers of people to compete against each other simultaneously. Shanda has 170 million registered users and 30 million active users, according to its website. The number of concurrent users has exceeded 1 million, across 29 provinces, 60 major cities and over 1000 clusters of servers, as well as over 500,000 end outlets.[1] These figures constitute a significant record in the online gaming industry in Mainland China.

The founder of the company, Tianqiao Timothy Chen, 31, was ranked by Forbes magazine as China's sixth-richest individual in

---

[1] Shanda Online, www.shanda.com.cn; 'Shangda's Management Skill', *China Investment Guide*, 1 February 2004

2003 and the third-richest in 2004 with a net fortune of US$490 million[2] and US$1.3 billion respectively.[3] This valuation was based on the predicted post-IPO valuation of the company at US$1–2 billion. Timothy founded Shanda when he was 27 years old and owns about 70 per cent of the registered capital. Shanda entered China's online gaming market by initiating open testing of 'The Legend of Mir II', a massive multiplayer online role-playing game (MMORPG) in September 2001.[4] Shanda then launched 'The Legend of Mir II' commercially in November 2001. The company's enormous success to date gives it complete confidence in its ability to maintain a leading role in the online gaming industry and to evolve into China's most successful online entertainment operation. The operational philosophy for Shanda is:

- to strengthen its position as the leading online game operator in China;
- to become the most influential online entertainment provider in China;
- to develop an outstanding corporate culture; and
- to stand out as a model for other companies in the gaming industry.

Softbank Asia Infrastructure Fund (SAIF), a private equity fund affiliated to Japan's Softbank Corp, with US networking giant Cisco Systems Inc, invested US$40 million in Shanda in March 2003.[5] The fund invests in broadband, wireless, media and IT firms in the Asia Pacific region and the US. In addition to financial resources, the SAIF investment also introduced international management concepts to Shanda. The successful financing marks not only a key milestone in Shanda's journey into the global market but also recognition of China's online game industry by international capital markets.

Shanda used the funds to develop new businesses, increase core competencies and prepare for future challenges. The boom time for online games is approaching. The value of the online gaming industry in China exceeded RMB2.47 billion in 2004 (a growth of 47.9 per cent on 2003) and RMB1.32 billion in 2003 (a growth of 45.8 per cent on

---

[2] *China's 100 Richest (2003)*, Forbes Online, www.forbes.com, 30 October 2003
[3] *China's Richest 200 (2004)*, Forbes Online, www.forbes.com, edited by Russell Flannery, 4 November 2004
[4] Shanda Online, www.shanda.com.cn
[5] Paul Denlinger 'Shanda Networking Heads For Nasdaq Listing' *China Business Strategy*, 11 November 2003

2002).⁶ Sales of more than RMB6.7 million are forecast for 2007.⁷ According to Deloitte Touche Tohmatsu, Shanda was the mainland's fastest-growing company in the telecommunications, media and technology (TMT) industry in 2003.

Shanda's leading programme is the South Korean multiplayer fantasy game, 'Legend'. Players pay a flat fee of RMB35 (US$4.25) for 120 hours of playing time.⁸ The five-year-old company is already profitable, earning profits of US$25 million in 2002 on sales revenue of US$50 million, and it estimates that revenues will reach US$900 million within two years, and with more than 12.6 million paying players, it will continue to grow at a rapid pace.⁹ Before Shanda's listing, it announced that cash income/receipts were US$33 million and net income was US$72 million in 2003. The rate of profit is around an amazing 45 per cent.¹⁰

Shanda's major cooperative partners are pivotal to its successful business development strategy. The company is constantly looking at ways to improve and expand its product offerings within the context of its growth as an online entertainment operator. Shanda's service is of international quality and makes it a most attractive cooperative partner. Table 8.1 identifies Shanda's partners according to their different industry sectors.

Table 8.1 Shanda's partners

Category	Introduction	Partners
Telecom and network companies	Shanda actively works to expand its business channels, and has established stable long-term cooperative relations with major Chinese telecom and network companies	China Telecom, China Unicom, Great Wall Broadband Network, China Mobile, China Network, Tianfu Hotline, Shanghai line, 263, OPTISP

---

⁶ *2004 China Online Game Survey*, The General Administration of Press and Publication P.R.C, The First China Game Industry Conference, 21 January 2005; *2003 China Online Game Survey*, The General Administration of Press and Publication P.R.C, *The Forum of Copyright Protection Under the Internet*, Copyright Society of China, 4 September 2004

⁷ *2003 China Online Game Survey*, The General Administration of Press and Publication P.R.C; *The Forum of Copyright Protection Under the Internet*, Copyright Society of China, 4 September 2004

⁸ Shanda Online, www.shanda.com.cn

⁹ Yang Cheng Wan Bao 'Shanda's IPO Goal Is US$1 billion' 12 November 2003

¹⁰ Quakeyudi 'The Dividend Before IPO of Shanda' *Sina Online Game*, 10 May 2004

Category	Introduction	Partners
Game software distributors	Shanda is on good terms with major domestic software distributors	Federal Soft, Softstar, MLSoft, AomeiSoft and King-Hope
Web hosts	Shanda maintains cooperative relations with well-known portals and works with these companies to promote online games.	Sina.com, China.com, 163.com, Sohu.com, Lycos.com and 21cn.com
International partners	Shanda has close relations with famous game producers from Europe, the United States, Japan and South Korea. Shanda works with these companies to identify products likely to succeed in the Chinese market.	Wemade Entertainment, CCR, Actoz Soft and Taewool.

Sources: Shanda Online, www.shanda.com.cn

On 12 February 2004, Tang Jun joined Shanda as its new president. Timothy Chen resigned from the post of president, but continues to hold the positions of Chairman of the Board and Chief Executive Officer.

Prior to joining Shanda, Mr Tang served as the President of Microsoft China from March 2002 to January 2004 and as General Manager of Microsoft Asia Product Support and Service and Microsoft Global Technical Engineering Centre from January 1998 to March 2002. Tang remains Honorary President of Microsoft China, and received the Bill Gates Award in 1998 as well as Microsoft's Top Honour Award in 2002. In 2002, Tang founded Intertex Company, a software and entertainment company in California. His arrival at Shanda strengthened the management organization and will help Shanda to achieve its development goals.[11]

Investment ventures and business strategy

One of Shanda's rivals, founded in 2001, Beijing-based Matrix Interactive Software Technology Ltd (Matrix), which distributes and

---

[11] Shanda Online, www.shanda.com.cn

operates online games, faced bankruptcy in December 2003. Before ceasing business, Matrix held talks on a possible acquisition by Shanda, but the talks broke down because Shanda felt that the online games offered by Matrix were not popular enough.

Matrix was established in early 2001 as a successful PC game distributor. It then launched an online game called Shadowbane, which ran into technical difficulties. According to an Interfax report, the peak number of simultaneous users for Shadowbane never exceeded 5,000. Matrix was the first company of Shanda's competition to run short of funds and investment. Shanda was smart to avoid acquiring Matrix.[12]

However, in January 2003, Shanda did acquire a 51 per cent holding in Shenzhen Fenglin Huoshan Computer Technology Co Ltd, a company that develops mobile phone-based wireless games.[13] A succession of further investments followed.

On 20 February 2003, Shanda entered into a cooperation agreement with Bothtech, a Japanese personal computer game developer. Pursuant to the terms of the agreement, Shanda purchased an 11.2 per cent interest in Bothtech and would become the exclusive distributor in China for Ginga Eiyuu Densetsu VII, an online game that Bothtech is developing. Ginga Eiyuu Densetsu is based on a popular science fiction story that captured the attention of readers in Japan, Mainland China, Korea and Taiwan, selling approximately 560,000 copies.[14] Shanda's investment in Bothtech is its first step into the Japanese online game market and it has secured the distribution rights for a very promising online game.

In April 2003, Shanda acquired a 90 per cent ownership interest in Shanghai Shulong Technology Development Co Ltd, a company that provides SMS in cooperation with the mobile telecommunications operators in China. In June 2003, Shanda and Xinhua Holdings co-founded Shanghai Shanda Xinhua Network Development Co Ltd, a company that develops and distributes online game publications and peripheral products. In September 2003, Shanda acquired a 90 per cent controlling interest in Chendu Jisheng Technology Co Ltd, a company that develops and distributes management software for internet cafes. In October 2003, Shanda established and retained a 51 per cent majority interest in Shanghai Shengjin Software Development Co Ltd, an online game development company.

In January 2004, Shanda acquired a 35 per cent minority interest in Beijing Digital-Red Software Application Technology Co Ltd, a

---

[12] 'Xiao Shui, Matrix Will Be The First Bankrupter In the Field of Online Games in China', *Netease Business Report*, 20 December 2003
[13] Shanda Online, www.shanda.com.cn
[14] ibid

company that focuses on wireless game development. In the same month, Shanda acquired all of the assets of Zona Inc, an American company that develops server infrastructure platforms for online game developers and operators.

In August 2004, Shanda decided to purchase for cash a stake in Shanghai Haofang Online Information Technology Co Ltd (Haofang), a privately-owned company that develops and operates the largest network PC game platform in China. Pursuant to the terms of the agreement, Shanda will acquire a majority interest in Haofang in 2006 with a combination of cash and ordinary shares in Shanda. Haofang operates a network PC game platform which, according to data provided by Haofang's management, had over 320,000 peak concurrent users and 200,000 average concurrent users in June 2004. Haofang's network game platform, which operates through more than 200 servers located throughout China, allows users to find and connect easily with thousands of other players of the same PC game via the internet.[15] This contrasts with typical PC games, which can only connect users in a local area network (LAN) environment, and allow only a limited number of players to play at one time. Haofang's platform is compatible with most of the popular multiplayer network games in China. The platform is especially appealing to home users because it is otherwise rather inconvenient for them to find other gamers with whom to play together at the same time.

In addition to the network game platform, Haofang established and operated the first online-arena portal in China, www.cga.com.cn which organizes large competition events among PC game users and provides news and information about various kinds of multiplayer games and events. According to information provided by Haofang's management, this portal currently has over 30 million daily page views and is ranked by Alexa among the top 50 websites in China in terms of traffic. The strategic investment in Haofang will help Shanda to add a third games segment to its current line of massive multiplayer online role-playing games (MMORPGs) and casual games. Through close cooperation, Shanda can leverage its extensive nationwide distribution network and Haofang's network game platform to expand its user base and increase user loyalty by providing more game options. In addition, this investment further strengthens Shanda's strategy of penetrating the fast growing home-based game user market.

In August 2004, Shanda acquired Hangzhou Bianfeng Software Technology Co Ltd (Bianfeng), a leading developer and operator of chess and board games in China.[16] The upfront consideration was paid

---

[15] ibid
[16] Shanda Online, www.shanda.com.cn

in cash upon acquisition with the remaining consideration to be paid in cash in mid-2005 on an earn-out basis. Bianfeng's www.gameabc.com portal provides users with a variety of casual games, including card games, board games, mahjong and simple arcade games. Currently, Bianfeng offers over 50 different games, which attracted over 200,000 peak concurrent users in July 2004, according to data provided by Bianfeng's management. Chess and board games are deeply rooted in Chinese culture and have a large and loyal user following, especially among the more mature age groups. The acquisition of Bianfeng adds another important segment to Shanda's casual games platform and further broadens user base demographics.

Shanda opened a Seoul branch in October 2003. The function of the Korean office is to secure content from local games companies on behalf of Shanda headquarters for distribution in China. Shanda is allocating a budget of at least US$10 million for imports of foreign online game content, although a portion will be spent in the United States and Europe.[17] Shanda realized significant profits by servicing 'Legend of Mir II', an immensely popular online programme from Korea's Actoz Soft. Over 700,000 users are said to have logged onto the game at once, thus helping to lift the company to the top of China's list of successful online game distributors, with a monthly income totalling about US$6 million.[18]

Shanda recently settled a dispute with Actoz, the Korean games company, which had accused Shanda of copying its content. Shanda, which started out as the Chinese distributor for Actoz's game, the 'Legend of Mir', is now actively developing its own games, and will switch to offering its own products through its gaming network.

Chinese firms, including Shanda, still have much to learn from the online gaming products of Korea and the US, especially Korean products because of the two countries' similar culture and customs. And it is well known that online gaming in Korea has gained a lot of experience, which repays study by Chinese gaming developers. However, the Korean market is not at all comparable to that of Mainland China because of the population difference. Chinese players are now gradually getting used to paying. So long as the number of fee-paying players increases sharply, the Chinese market will definitely exceed those of Korea and the US.

---

[17] FinanceAsia & IRG 'A Week in Tech', *Finance Technology*, 21 May 2004
[18] *Online-game contract prolonged*, Eastday News Online, www.eastday.com.cn, 22 August 2003

Big appetite for an IPO but some wishful thinking

In 2003, to tap into the demand for fantasy role playing in the world's most populous nation, Shanda filed an application for an IPO on NASDAQ in 2004, and planned to raise US$300–500million. The Shanghai-based firm, which had an estimated value of more than US$1 billion, would sell between 20 and 25 per cent of its share capital, declared Andrew Yan, president of SAIF. 'We plan to IPO in Q1 2004' he said in a 2003 telephone interview. 'It's the largest online gaming operator, not only in China but also in the world in terms of both users and revenue.' It was believed that Shanda would have Goldman Sachs as the lead underwriter for the listing, which could take place as early as the beginning of 2004. Compared with Asian markets, companies listed on the US NASDAQ command a premium valuation. In March 2003, Shanda had attracted a US$40 million investment from SAIF. Presumably the IPO would give SAIF a chance to cash in on some of its investment.

The optimistic plans were derived from the good performance of the three NASDAQ-listed Chinese internet media firms, Sina, Sohu and NetEase, which rose several hundred per cent in 2002 as all became profitable through advertising, SMS and online games.

At the end of November 2003, Chinese truck and sport utility vehicle maker Great Wall Automobile priced its IPO at the top end of an indicated range, raising HK$1.516 billion (US$194 million) from an issue that was vastly oversubscribed.[19] In December 2003, online travel agent Ctrip made a US$76 million public offering in New York and saw its stock gain 88.56 per cent on its first trading day, the biggest first-day gain in New York for three years.

As the current market share leader, Shanda has many competitors. Its continuing lawsuit with Wemade, a South Korean game developer, was a cause for concern over the IPO plans and in the event, the lawsuit did impede Shanda's listing plans. Wemade sued Shanda in a Beijing court over intellectual property rights infringement regarding its rights over a game called 'The World of Legend'. If Shanda lists, it will join a handful of publicly traded online gaming firms such as South Korea's NCSoft Corp. There is a possibility of losing the lawsuit with Wemade, which Shanda doesn't deny. In Shanda's opinion for investors, the fine will not exceed US$500,000.

But Shanda's proposed IPO listing came at a difficult time for Chinese concept internet companies. The share prices of five NASDAQ-listed Chinese internet companies, bright stars in the market during

---

[19] 'Great Wall IPO Nets US$194m on Hot Buy', *People's Daily Online*, www.people.com.cn, 10 December 2003

2003, stumbled in the first quarter of 2004, with Sohu shares even dropping by about 40 per cent. This situation led to a delay in the IPO of Beijing-based wireless service provider Mtone, which had already made an IPO filing to the NASDAQ, but had not yet decided on the pricing and the IPO date. These falls were mainly due to US investors' fears over the overheating of some parts of the Chinese economy. The decline in wireless revenues for companies like Sohu and Netease increased investors' concerns about these companies' prospects.

However, the internet sector should be viewed in a different light from other overheating sectors such as steel, real estate and cement, because there are currently about 80 million internet users among the population of 1.3 billion. The internet sector cannot be cited as a case of overheating but as a growing business.

On 13 May 2004, Shanda announced its initial public offering of 13.8 million American Depository Shares (ADSs) (down from an original offering plan of over 17.31 million ADS), consisting of 9.6 million ADSs offered by Shanda and 4.2 ADSs offered by its shareholders and priced at US$11 per ADS. Shanda and the selling shareholders granted the underwriters an option to purchase up to an additional 2.1 million ADSs, for a total IPO take of around US$151.8 million.[20] The ADSs were scheduled under the trading symbol 'SNDA'. Goldman Sachs, Bear Stearns, CLSA/CIBC World Markets, HSBC and Piper Jaffray were underwriters to the IPO, according to a regulatory filing with the Securities and Exchange Commission. Goldman Sachs (Asia) LLC served as the global coordinator and sole market maker for the offering.[21]

Online games are all the rage in China

With the temperature in online gaming continuing to rise, the international finance, media, and industry sectors are attracted to this field. The Chinese phenomenon has been the subject of a co-research project for international investors, scholars and the media. Based on the outstanding achievements in return on investment and profit-making, foreign venture capitalists have started to think that many 'young' Chinese online gaming SMEs could probably be bred into new world-class Chinese enterprises.

Now that the online gaming industry has the support of the Chinese government as a strategic industry, more players, such as Netease, an

---

[20] Shanda Online, www.shanda.com.cn
[21] Greg Pilarowski 'Shanda Listed on NASDAQ' Shanda Interactive Entertainment Company, 13 May 2004

internet portal, and Kingsoft, a maker of anti-virus and English dictionary software, have entered this rapidly emerging field. The result is a highly volatile and competitive market with many players. Ultimately, the winners will be the companies that can generate the most popular titles on a long-term basis. In many ways, the internet market in China is now similar to that of the US in 1999. The biggest difference is that the Chinese companies have substantive revenues and earnings.

Sudden market changes cannot cause deviation from the industry's long-term trend. With the fast development of technology and national policy support, there are more and more sectors taking part in the internet gaming business. Following the emergence of listed companies, online games are following a standard development route of self-R&D, agency operation, better service, extended industry chains, sector relationships and wider distribution networks. Currently, the business model of online gaming has changed from simple 'point accumulating account and card buying accounting models' to a more sophisticated, more appropriate new style of collective website portals. Generally, investors in domestic online gaming shares are not very satisfied with the scale of products, the operating situation and corporate and employee structures. Furthermore, the whole strength of the industry must be increased. There are more than 30 shares of companies engaged in and owning internet gaming, which together form the online game board. According to corporate function, all the online game concept listing companies in Mainland China can be classified as:

- operators;

- channels and distributors;

- server providers;

- content providers.

Soaring revenues win industry respect

The *People's Daily* has estimated that there are over 70 Chinese enterprises in the online games industry. The companies are riding the surging popularity of online games among an estimated 40 million of China's 78 million internet users. The industry's games generate a further US$1.4 billion in business for telecoms and other industries. According to MII statistics, in 2002 the market value of China's online game business, which was only around US$37 million in 2001, rose to about US$110 million with an increasing growth rate as high as 187.6 per cent. The industry in China was then estimated at over US$250 million for 2003 and was expected to more than double in 2004, earning respectability for an industry that was once 'despised and scorned'.[22]

In April 2004, a Ministry of Information Industry statistic showed that 20.605 million consumers in China had subscribed to broadband access in order to play online games and other rapid requirement programmes. The growing demand is fuelling not just game software developers but also internet cafes, ISPs and hardware vendors. The local companies hope to close the gap with new products and training programmes for gaming professionals in Beijing and elsewhere. Among Chinese success stories, the current market leader and largest operator in China is Shanda. The internet game business will boost the development of the media, IT, telecommunications, publishing, retailing and other sectors.

China's first domestically developed game, 'Legend of Knights Online' hit 80,000 simultaneous paid players in the first week of December 2003, a positive sign for the growing Chinese software industry in a Korean-dominated market.[23] Kingsoft, the Beijing-based company behind 'Legend of Knights Online', needed several hundred internet servers in order to meet demand from venture capitalists. Kingsoft has updated 30 versions of the game during the two months of the market test period.[24] Overseas companies could not have responded so quickly to 'Legend of Knights Online' which is based on popular Chinese martial arts and Chinese-style love affairs. The 'Xia', Chinese warriors, draws on local mythology rather than western-myth monsters and soldiers. Kingsoft plans to challenge South Korean giants with 'JXOnline', a game that combines 'Chinese martial arts and modern love'. After three years of development at a cost of US$1.8 million, the company planned to begin offering the game online. In a 2003 interview, Kingsoft's CEO Lei Jun said that the company had plans but no definite timeframe to promote the game internationally, and hoped to follow the success of China's international blockbuster film *Crouching Tiger, Hidden Dragon*.[25]

---

[22] 'China promotes home-made online game business', *People's Daily Online*, www.people.com.cn, 8 December 2003
[23] 'Made-in-China played in China', CNETAsia Online, http://asia.cnet.com, 18 December 2003
[24] Kingsoft Online, www.kingsoft.com
[25] 'Web Games All The Rage In China', MMIII The Associated Press, CBS News Online, www.cbsnews.com, 8 December 2003

Piracy hampers China online game sector

Software piracy has hampered commercial sales of PC games. Game console makers such as Nintendo and Sony have shunned the Chinese market for fear that their games will be pirated. Online gaming is especially effective at preventing piracy, and makes money in China because it requires payment to play, usually with a prepaid billing card, which can be ordered on the internet or bought from the corner shop. The local consumers are opening their wallets and internet cafes are often filled until the early hours with gamers competing against each other on linked computers or against scores of other competitors online. Once, it was thought that piracy would disappear within the China online game sector without the CD or floppy disc as the intermedium, but in fact software pirates are gouging China's online games industry. They offer identical games for free. Such acts are undermining planned NASDAQ listings by companies long thought to be immune to copyright abuse. A visit to any internet cafe in Beijing, the strictest city in the country, reveals groups of glassy-eyed gamers hunched over computers fighting fantasy enemies, mostly without paying for the privilege.

According to conservative estimates, there are literally hundreds, maybe thousands of pirate servers where the gamers can play their favourite games for free. For example www.17ez.com lists illegal servers offering the popular game Mu in China. Piracy in the online game industry is rampant in China. How to deal with 17ez has been a problem to be solved with the authority of the law. Downloadable cheating software that allows people to make faster progress through the official games takes out an additional bite. The existence of 'server piracy', such as 17ez, is bad news for the Chinese online game industry. It's difficult to quantify exactly how much knock-off sites hack into market sales, but the rip-offs are thought to be worth at least US$400 million in one year. The targets of Chinese piracy include the 'Legend of Mir' series distributed by Shanda.

Foreign investors have invested hundreds of millions of US dollars in China's young internet game SMEs. It is anticipated that the gradually improving laws will enable foreigners to sidestep the piracy curse and assimilate the lessons of charging, learned from western software firms like Microsoft and Sony.

Promoting home-made business

The value brought by the online game business to other industries is even greater, ten times that produced by the online game business itself. In 2002, the direct contribution of China's online game industry to the telecom, IT and publishing industries was RMB6.83 billion, RMB3.28 billion and RMB1.82 billion respectively.[28]

The online game is now a part of China's national science and technology programme and the government offers creators tax breaks and other support. China will boast more domestic-made online games in the near future, as further efforts by the Chinese government and enterprises are being made to boost this market's high potential. The government hopes to encourage more domestically developed online games. In the summer of 2003, two projects on online game technology development projects were listed in the '863' High-Tech Programme, the national science and technology development programme of China initiated in March 1986, which indicates official support. Yet Chinese game makers' profits have been limited because this large market is mostly held by foreign companies. With just ten per cent held by made-in-China games, foreign companies have developed about 80 per cent, especially those from South Korea, which have more than 70 per cent of the game software industry. However, the Chinese government hopes to change that soon.[27] Without the ownership of intellectual property, most of China's market profits are lost.

In an interview, Lei Jun said that he regarded it as a strong positive signal that China's online gaming industry, which had been 'despised and scorned' as a regular industry, has now achieved the support of the Chinese government. The move was driven by the great potential shown by China's online game market. Despite bans on online gambling and pornography, as well as monitoring of the web for dissident political commentary, the industry's growth parallels China's surging internet use. According to the Internet Society of China, China has about 500,000 web sites and 30 million computers connected to the internet. In addition to online gaming in the internet market, intellectual property is seen as a way to retain market profits in China.

Since its arrival in China in 1999, online games have won over 300 million users. But the personnel specifically engaged in online game development totalled only 1000 in 2001 and the gap in numbers between users and programmers has continued to grow since then. An official from the internet department of the Ministry of Culture has stated that China plans more preferential policies for domestic online games development, as well as government research and development. In October 2003, in response to the demand for online game professionals and the dearth of game software programmers, Sichuan

---

[26] 'China promotes home-made online game business', People's Daily Online, www.people.com.cn, 8 December 2003

[27] *Web Games All The Rage In China*, MMIII The Associated Press, CBS News Online, www.cbsnews.com, 8 December 2003

University in Chengdu, capital of southwestern China's Sichuan province, set up a department of game software, the first of its kind in China. Lessons in literature, the arts, English and software are all considered to be necessary in the curriculum of the new department as online game programming requires personnel with encyclopaedic knowledge. It is believed that the training programmes and projects for the professionals who design games software, which includes online gaming and mobile gaming, has started and will soon be developed by the Chinese domestic personnel.

In Beijing, China's IT industry hub, an online game personnel training system has been established, another significant move by the Chinese government to boost China's online game industry. Combining advanced technology and specific Chinese culture, China's home-made online games have begun to achieve remarkable things.

Web game firms top Asia tech revenues survey[28]

According to a survey released by Deloitte Touche Tohmatsu in December 2003, Asia's three fastest growing high-tech firms in 2003 all came from the online game sector, fuelled by the region's rapid development of high-speed phone and internet access.

Taiwanese online game developer Chinese Gamer International Corp topped the list, with 20,402 per cent revenue growth over the last three years in the annually-compiled surveys. Chinese Gamer posted 2002 revenues of TW$667.85 million (US$19.6 million), or nearly double its 2001 total.

Shanda finished second with 10,342 per cent growth over the period, followed by Japan's G-Mode Co Ltd, a developer of games for mobile phones, with 5,624 per cent growth. Revenue figures were not available for unlisted Shanda, but G-Mode posted 2.5 billion yen (US$23 million) in revenues for its fiscal year ended March 2003. The company spokesman said that their fast growth was facilitated by the rapid development of high-speed data services in their markets, via broadband internet in Taiwan and Mainland China and next-generation mobile (NGM) phone services in Japan. Thanks to the popularization of broadband, the development of online gaming in China has accelerated. According to Deloitte, Shanda's revenue growth far outpaced TCL Mobile Communications, which registered growth of 2,964 per cent in the same three-year period. Deloitte recognized TCL as the mainland's fastest-growing TMT Company for 2002. Another mainland internet

---

[28] Peter Cheng, *Online Gaming Craze Continues To Sizzle As Asian Providers Scramble For Market Share*, Government Information Office Online, http://publish.gio.gov.tw, 2 July 2004

company, Baidu.com, had a revenue growth rate of 1,300 per cent. At the end of June 2003, Asia had about 30 million broadband users, with 10.5 million in Japan, 4 million in Mainland China and 2.4 million in Taiwan, according to Media Partners Asia. In Japan, the country's 12.8 million users of high-speed NGM phone services from KDDI Corp and NTT DoCoMo Inc have also proven fertile ground for online games. The rise of online games also owes something to the region's growing wealth. The level of disposable income is rising all over the world, particularly in China.

The first media venture capital experience

A famous Chinese saying likens a person with a sense of adventure to the first person who ate a crab. Lu Xingdong, in the field of Media VC, is this person.

Lu became a famous industry insider because of the cooperation between his own Tanglong International Media Ltd (Tanglong) and the international media giant Viacom. Viacom, whose 2003 revenues amounted to US$26.6 billion, was ranked 171 in the 2003 Fortune 500.[29] In his fourth visit to China, Sumner M Redstone, Chairman & CEO of Viacom, announced that its offspring channel Nickelodeon of MTV Global Networks, one of the subsidiaries of Viacom, had begun to broadcast successfully through the 1000 plus city TV channels of Mainland China through the agency of Tanglong from 1 May 2001. The mainspring for Viacom's cooperation with Tanglong was the fancy that Viacom took to Tanglong's channels in the circulation of China's domestic TV programmes and Tanglong's ability to provide content.

Since its inception in 1994, Tanglong has clung tightly to its aspirations of cultural diffusion, and to its four business principles of social responsibility, media regulation compliance, advocacy of broadcasting system reform and mutual benefit through cooperation. Tanglong currently controls Tanglong Culture Development Co Ltd, Innovation Advertisement Co Ltd, and Beijing PROCN E-commerce Co Ltd, employing a total of 350 staff. Tanglong programmes feature three fields of interest – international news updates, leisure and entertainment, culture and science – encompassing 17 categories. It nurtures coverage over the mainstream TV channels among 300 mid-to-large cities, and supports 100 per cent coverage of the 80 million cable users. On the basis of its cooperation with foreign partners, such as Viacom, Tanglong has designed a toll-bridge and content-supply

---

[29] *The 2003 Fortune 500 (Rank 1-100) The Biggest Companies 2003*, cyList Online, www.cylist.com

platform between local media companies and foreign media markets. At the end of 2004, Tanglong's own-made programmes exceeded four hours per day, spread around 16 special-made programmes and taking up more than 600 TV channels in Mainland China.[30]

Redstone bought the Chinese private TV producer, Tanglong, initially in a condition of 'lying fallow at the bottom of the stream under the surface of the water'. Under the umbrella of Viacom and Redstone, Lu, formerly always cautious and taking a slow approach to development, changed his approach and embarked on a series of new activities. From 2000, Tanglong sooner or later brought forward many well-known and profitable operations and modes, such as the toll-bridge, media venture capital (MVC) investment, TV trade sales union, professional production channel platforms, licence production and exploration management, and so on, especially to stimulate cooperation between domestic and foreign TV programmes. A series of actions from Lu enthused media practitioners and his name appeared frequently in the newspapers.

Lu's home city is Shanghai: he graduated from Zhejiang University, a key Chinese university, in 1990. Lu set up Tanglong in 1994, investing in and co-producing the TV series 'Lu Xingdong's Personal Profile: Love in Moscow'. As a result of the TV series, Lu is known as the first domestic folk independent TV producer in Mainland China. On 27 October 2004, Tanglong was awarded the 2004 China Culture Industry Year-Innovation Enterprise.[31]

MVC investment

From the initial TV series production to dealing in TV programmes, Lu conceived the idea of building his own platform through buying TV station advertisement time. His theory of MVC on periods of advertisement time attracted the attention of industry insiders and became a beacon for private media enterprises to look for opportunities under the Chinese media monopolization policy.

In 2002, Lu issued an invitation to industry groups, 'We have advertisement time valued at RMB2 billion and have decided to invite public bidding. To enjoy a fancy Ad Meal, enterprises don't have to pay any money'.[32] The new ad running mode pushed by Tanglong was named MVC.

---

[30] Tanglong International Media Group Online, www.tanglong.com
[31] Zhang Mengyin 'Lu Xingdong: The Media Manager's Real Road', *The Economic Observer*, 23 March 2004
[32] ibid

Simply put, Tanglong uses the value-added ad time in exchange for capital investment in companies. Tanglong converts the enterprises' distribution profits into its accounts receivable. The traditional relationship between TV stations and enterprises for advertisements has been changed. The phases of this change are described in Table 8.2 below.

Table 8.2 Tanglong's MVC process

Phase	Action
Phase 1	Tanglong provides TV programmes to TV stations.
Phase 2	In exchange, TV stations provide periods of ad time to Tanglong. The periods of ad time have a total value of RMB2 billion or more.
Phase 3	Tanglong uses the 'free' ad time to attract the enterprises.
Phase 4	In exchange, the free ad time is converted into capital investment by the enterprises.
Phase 5	The negotiated investment return will be a percentage of enterprises' sales value and profit or in some other form.
Phase 6	At the end of each financial year, the enterprises pay Tanglong its profit share.
Phase 7	Tanglong uses the profit for the further development.

Through RMB2 billion of ad time, Tanglong secures investment in an indirect form, which could be described as another kind of VC investment. Such an operation favours a long line of engagement, large investment and a large cycle. Tanglong focuses on future profits after propping up the advertisers with the supply of advertisement periods, which is attractive compared with a simple cash transaction between the advertisers, agencies and TV stations.

The 'free lunch' impression of the deal is most attractive to SME ad time customers. Under pressure to expand their customer awareness through TV advertising in order to increase sales results, Tanglong's deal is a good choice for SMEs, and is particularly suitable for those companies with little cash liquidity.

Besides SMEs, the proposal is also attractive to those large enterprises that pay more than RMB500 million for their advertising slots each year.[33] In the case of the Gaizhonggai Calcium tablet produced by

---

[33] 'The Sector Standard Is Waiting for the New Phase', *China Industry News*, 19 November 2004

Haerbin Pharmaceutical Group, for example, its advertisements could be said to 'blot out the sky and cover up the earth'. Whenever you switch on the TV in China at any hour on any channel, you will see the Gaizhonggai ad. According to the new PRC Rules for Before Tax Bargain Deduction of Enterprise Income Tax, advertising fees in excess of two per cent of production sales revenue will not qualify as expenses for deduction before tax, which means that most of Gaizhonggai's advertisement fees – amounting to about RMB1 billion annually – are a charge against post-income tax earnings.[34] Tanglong's approach can help enterprises to avoid the tax restriction. Enterprises can place their TV ads as usual but no payment for the advertisement period is recorded in the account statement. The principle is simple. The expense is changed into an investment by Tanglong through a cooperation contract on which a return equal to the advertisement fee is derived from the resultant sales of the enterprise representing real capital on which no tax is payable. There is no reason for large advertisers, Tanglong's potential clients, to be solicitous about the huge tax cost for advertisement expense because Tanglong's investment replaces the advertisement cost in the financial statement, so that those groups will make it easy for the formal tax avoidance.

The operation of MVC

Eventually, the operation of Tanglong's MVC became an actual venture capitalist activity. One of its significant characteristics is participation in the management of enterprises. At first, Tanglong *invested* in around ten enterprises. From the point of resource consumption per se, there were not many problems. But in the course of cooperation, problems arose when Tanglong encountered many different results, because the sales and marketing of products were not only driven by the media, which is just one aspect of a marketing campaign, but also involved other operational aspects, such as funding and cash, brand strategy, marketing decisions by the enterprise's management, and so on. A series of problems caused different effects on different products. And so, Tanglong started to regulate its own involvement. On the one hand, Tanglong considered how to perfect use of the media resource. On the other hand, Tanglong increased the quality of its decision-making in the choice of products and involved itself fully as a management expert in each enterprise's day-to-day operations.

Except for the manufacturing link in the production chain, Tanglong now involves itself in all other links in the cycle such as advice,

---

[34] Zheng Guobiao 'Gaizhonggai's Successful Marketing Strategy', *China Enterprises Planning Online*, www.cnqihua.com, 6 November 2004

marketing, team building and planning. If Tanglong wants further profit, it must consider undertaking more for the enterprise. After Tanglong addresses the key points in its investment and follows up on service delivery, the project will be pushed through more quickly and will guarantee a greater return.

An entrepreneurs' mentality was unavoidable. Before cooperation, enterprises thought that they controlled the products and brands and therefore there was no self-motivation to urge entrepreneurs on. Once Tanglong participates in corporate management, the demands on brands and teams will be higher but legal guarantees of profit such as share options will also be tighter. Tanglong will claim control over or hold a percentage of the shares. As always, the entrepreneurs cannot be afraid of the shareholders. The use of shares brings a co-win for Tanglong and the enterprises. For Tanglong, it has enhanced its service consciousness since it will actively create the media resource of an integrated network to its own advantage when it feels that new products and teams have performed well.

Diversification has changed the initial MVC model developed by Tanglong. The reasons for change are based on the exchange of TV programmes and ad time between Tanglong and TV stations. Firstly, the offer of periods of advertisement time has been changed. Under the current conditions of more and more ad time, TV stations are afraid of Tanglong engaging in low-price trade dumping in case such action adversely affects the TV stations' mainstream price system. But if TV channels gave off-peak ad time rather than peak viewing time to Tanglong, it would be difficult for Tanglong to support a brand using such ad periods. Secondly, Tanglong operated the MVC as a kind of ad promotion because too much ad time was wasted and it was difficult to secure customers and difficult to get the cash from them. Business promotion is quite different from doing business, and this caused Tanglong to change its ideas.

The biggest problem of running MVC arises from the media itself, whose ad times are inflexible. For example, if the exchanged ad time is at 10 o'clock, the ad should be broadcast at the exact time, and there is no provision for variation. For the product, especially for a new brand, it is necessary to broadcast at a defined degree of density. Only through a high-frequency rate of broadcasting could the ad possibly produce results allowing for only three months for people to get to know the brand. But Tanglong's adverts may only be shown twice in one night. Tanglong's strategy is to provide more than one year's exposure, which can be a long period of support for a famous brand. Because of different enterprises' performance and business characters, there is no standard for Tanglong to select its advertisers' customer in exchange for a percentage of the enterprises' profit. Finally, Tanglong has changed its initial way of thinking and now selects suitable companies, depending on the ongoing media situation.

In general, entrepreneurs perceive at least eight advantages from MVC:

- relief from corporate funding pressure, supporting rapid corporate growth, enabling enterprises with limited funds to address a large market;
- promoting and guaranteeing market expansion, regional filter, and an effective territory through professional media operation and management involvement;
- helping the management of corporate capital and the effective improvement of corporate social and economic benefits;
- appropriate and reasonable avoidance of corporate income tax in exchange for VC investment;
- saving and using corporate funds effectively;
- rapid build-up of distribution network and new product promotion in the market;
- breaking through bottle-necks while canvassing business orders;
- containing the risks of promotional investment.

The future of the media industry

The operation of MVC can be described as the effective use of media resources. At present, there is much waste in Mainland China's media resources which could be converted into cash or further capital resources, especially ad time periods. The only issue to be solved is the cooperation model between agencies and enterprises. Foreign media groups may not be satisfied on points such as few channels or programmes. Global media competition does not accommodate a monopoly situation.

During the four years following China's accession to the WTO, the world has witnessed the opening up of a number of PRC industries which were previously off-limits to foreign investment. But a handful of industries are still closed to foreign investors and the media industry is one of the more notable examples. Central government has been slowly easing the restrictions on foreign broadcasters and publishers entering the mainland market, though they remain tightly controlled. However, one step towards the liberalization of the mainland's tightly controlled media industry was taken in August 2003 when the State Administration of Radio, Film and Television (SARFT) agreed to grant

television production licences to eight privately owned Chinese companies. These new measures were a first sign of growing pressure on China to produce high quality TV, beneficial as much for Chinese TV consumers as for international companies trying to enter this vast market.

Foreign investors have been keeping an eye on the Chinese media industry for some time. According to the *Media Industry Reform Plan* (the 'Reform Plan') drafted by The General Administration of Press and Publication of the PRC, the limit on private investment in the equity capital newspaper business deal is set at 40 per cent, no matter whether the investor is domestic or foreign.[35]

Another major liberalization measure allows the distribution of more foreign cable channels than before. The number of TV production viewing hours does not even meet a quarter of the need. About 30 foreign channels have been approved for mainland broadcasting, but since they are beamed by satellite, they reach only a limited audience of foreign residence compounds and luxury hotels.[36]

Beijing People's Broadcasting Station (BPBS) and Phoenix Satellite Television Holding (Phoenix) signed a deal for strategic collaboration in broadcasting and advertising in October 2004 during the Eighth Beijing-Hong Kong Economic Cooperation Symposium in Hong Kong. The plan calls for Phoenix, a Hong Kong-based affiliate of Rupert Murdoch's News Corp, and BPBS, a leading domestic broadcaster, to set up a joint venture, Simul Cast (Beijing) Co Ltd.[37] Wang Qiu, vice-president of BPBS, was appointed chairman of the new company. BPBS will invest RMB30 million for a 55 per cent stake in the company and Phoenix will take the remaining 45 per cent share.[38] A report from an AC Nielson media company issued in July 2004 said that China was the world's second largest radio market after the United States. Initial investment in the Simul Cast venture will be RMB30 million (HK$28.28 million). Phoenix supplies the Mandarin InfoNews Channel and Chinese Channel to selected pay-TV operators on the mainland. Simul Cast will not undertake advertising agency work for Phoenix and BPBS. Instead, it will explore business opportunities in other provinces, such as Henan, Shandong, Yunnang and Shaanxi.[39]

---

[35] 'The Media Industry Reform', *Caijing Magazine*, 6 August 2003
[36] Collier Andrew K 'China Opens TV Production Sector', *SCMP*, 3 September 2003
[37] Wei Annie 'Phoenix Joins Beijing Radio in Local Airwaves', *Beijing Today Online*, www.bjtoday.ynet.com, 9 October 2004
[38] 'Phoenix Satellite TV in Beijing radio venture', *Xinhua News Agency*, 6 September 2004
[39] Tran Anthony 'Phoenix For National Radio Ad Agency', *The Standard*, 6 September 2004

The operations model of Tanglong's MVC

Media choices
Decisions on the choice of media are taken by both parties. There are 600 channels among 300 cities in the national range. During peak viewing times, the maximum advertising time for each station is no more than ten minutes and the minimum is 15 seconds. The total value of each project ranges from RMB20 million to RMB200 million.

Investment accounting
Accounting for the golden peak viewing ad time of province and city media is calculated at a preferential price. Complementary ad times are not calculated into the investment value.

Investment modes

Mode 1: Deducting a percentage from investment
The investor makes a bargain investment through the TV advertisement and deducts the venture profits from the products' sales income.

After deducting the operating costs, the residual part of gross sales will be the return on Tanglong's investment as the media venture capitalist. If the incremental profit does not balance the amount of the investment, both parties bear the risk according to their investment percentages.

After recovering the investment, a certain percentage of the incremental gross sales should be distributed as the earnings yield for both parties. The media venture capitalist receives its profit according to its ad time investment percentage.

Any enterprise can propose other models for negotiation with Tanglong.

Mode 2: Becoming a shareholder after investment
Media venture capitalists convert the investment capital into shares in the registered capital, which should be valued according to an enterprise's assets.

Combination of Modes 1 and 2
The investor takes part of its return from the gross sales and buys shares with the rest, which should be valued according to the assets of the enterprise.

Supervising the broadcasting
The media broadcaster confirms CCTV (China Centre Television) or another appointed organization to supervise the accounting report on broadcasting.

Cooperating and monitoring
Both parties construct a team to take part in defining the marketing project, implementing a media plan and auditing the sales financial statements.

The MVC operations process

The MVC investment process can be broken down into the following 11 phases, identified in Figure 8.1.

Phase 1: Customer evaluation

- product: life cycle, function, components, usage, price, make-up, novelty features etc;
- corporation: history, brand resources, credit, operating condition, human resource management etc;
- market base: distribution network, strengths, advertising, public relations, sales promotion etc;
- competition: similar products, rival evaluation, focus etc;
- environment: customer attitudes, relevant rules of law and regulation, industry trends etc;

Phase 2: Report drafting

- product evaluation and results;
- corporate evaluation and results;

Figure 8.1 The MVC investment process

- market base evaluation and results;
- competitive situation evaluation and results;
- market environment evaluation and results;
- superiority complementary evaluation and results;
- investment risk evaluation and results.

Phase 3: Internal decision-making

- investment advice;
- whether to invest;
- mode of investment;
- share of investment.

Phase 4: Sign contract

- negotiation and outline agreement;
- decide on cooperation mode;
- rights and duties for both parties;
- contract signature.

Phase 5: Establish project team

- investment team;
- business strategy team;
- media team;
- public relations team;
- resources sharing team;
- advertisement creativity team;
- execution team.

Phases 6 and 7: Marketing research and marketing promotion project

- competitors;

- customers;
- channels (by both parties);
- marketing promotion blueprint;
- orientation of market, product and positioning;
- scheduling;
- channels strategy;
- advertisement strategy;
- public relations strategy;
- promotional strategy (by both parties).

Phase 8: Operating preparations

- salesperson training;
- establishment of distribution network;
- unclog circulation channels;
- advertisement originality;
- advertisement execution;
- design of the product for sales promotion.

Phase 9: Start-up market

- enforce contract clauses.

Phase 10: Promoting marketing fully

- monitor marketing promotion;
- impact evaluation;
- adjust policy and strategy;
- grasp the target customers.

Phase 11: Confirm investment return

- summarize the results;

- look for the further cooperation opportunities.

VC investment in traditional industries[40]

VC does not merely pursue sudden, overnight wealth but also seeks stable investment opportunities. There is no reason for traditional industry to follow the fashionistas. VC can be understood simply as high risk and high return. From the end of the last century, by virtue of the upsurge in internet investment, VC has pushed forward Mainland China's industry and capital market with high technology but immediately after the internet bubble burst, foreign venture capitalists began to pay more attention to more traditional sectors. For example:

- Hambrecht & Quist Group Asia Pacific (H&Q Asia Pacific) invested US$11 million to bring Starbucks Coffee to locations in China.
- The US-based Warburg Pincus LLC pumped US$22 million into Zhejiang Kasen Industrial Corporation Ltd, a leather manufacturer, to become one of the latter's major shareholders.
- Morgan Stanley, CDH China (China Ding Hui, formerly Direct Investment Department of CICC, China International Capital Co Ltd), and CGU-CDC China (CGU-CDC China Investment Co, a joint venture under CGU Insurance and British CDC Capital) invested US$61.2 million in Mengniu Dairy.

Do venture capitalists change the direction of their investment? Can VC investment in traditional sectors be pure 'venture capital'? In fact, investment companies' projections depend on the project itself. VC firms focus on high growth rather the nature of a venture. So it cannot be said that VC firms have changed their investment field if they invest in the traditional sectors. And, conversely, it cannot be said that investment in the traditional sectors is not VC investment.

Investing in traditional industries is not new

In fact, whether from overseas or domestic areas, VC firms often invest in both traditional and high-tech industries simultaneously. In Mainland China, VC investment projects were launched in traditional

---

[40] Some paragraphs of this part are from Wang Qi 'Can a Venture In The Field of Traditional Industry Be a Venture Capital Investment?', *China Entrepreneur Magazine*, 19 August 2004

fields earlier than those in high-tech fields. In 1995, when most Chinese people did not know what VC was, domestic venture capitalists led by the government always focused on traditional industries, even in traditional manufacture. For example, a Guangzhou-based investment firm, which is not well known in the market because of its local nature and limited funds, has not stopped investing in traditional industries and recently invested in a company named Xiada in Dongguan which produces toy automobiles and was listed on NASDAQ.

Offshore VC firms that entered the mainland at the earliest point initially invested in traditional industries. H&Q Asia Pacific entered the mainland in 1994, when there were few high-tech projects and no concept of the internet, and they invested in traditional industries such as Beijing Yansha Emporium at an average of US$10 million per project. Even at the time of peak internet investment, ChinaVest invested in TGI Friday's (the famous American style casual dining chain); Walden International invested in Henan Kelong, Jiangsu Littleswan and Cygnet, and many VCs invested funds into the housing market, leading to an upsurge in the real estate industry. Even in the hottest internet period when all venture capitalists were pursuing high returns from internet companies, VC firms never stopped investing in traditional industries. But they were all concealed by the internet focus.

Traditional industries contain high growth potential

During this time when China is beginning to evolve as the global centre of machining and manufacturer, most traditional industries transferred from developed western countries still offer high growth potential by reason of their long-term lower labour costs. The value of such manufacturing bases will be doubled when they have overseas markets and their own distribution channels.

CGU-CDC China gives priority to traditional projects which offer larger share options. However, when investing in Xiamen-based North Pole China Ltd (Jinxiong), CGU-CDC acquired 80 per cent of its registered capital. The exception in this case was made on the basis of Xiamen Jinxiong's overseas market and customer channels. Jinxiong manufactures items of outdoor camping equipment, essentials for European and US families. Unquestionably, Jinxiong's products command a huge market. In fact, Jinxiong itself had owned many big customer outlets and efficient distribution channels and offered an optimal development process to industry insiders before CGU-CDC China considered and finally acquired its majority shareholding.

In Mainland China, a product sells with difficulty in the remoter regions, but it can sell well in the hinterland. VC firms investing in traditional Chinese industries follow the same principle. The traditional projects in which VC firms invest are not the sunset industries in the conventional sense, but enterprises that experienced a high early growth stage, have entered a new period of increasing activity and possess high growth capabilities. The most important feature is that such kinds and categories of product can be accepted and consumed by Mainland China's emerging middle classes. Some VC firms have categorized these traditional industries as 'Brand-name Consumption Goods'.

With the continuous growth of GDP and personal disposable income, Mainland China's broad market makes many industry sectors sparkle, such as coffee shops, restaurants, dairy products, fruit juices and even private housing and automobiles, which are all enjoying periods of robust growth. CGU-CDC China is particularly satisfied with its investment in Mengniu Dairy, which is the project with the highest profit rate of all its mainland ventures. In the United States or Europe, it would be hard to imagine the dairy industry could have annual growth near even 50 per cent, but Mengniu has maintained a 229 per cent growth rate for four consecutive years. In fact, even in the so-called high-tech industries, it is hard to achieve such a miracle.

Other types of traditional industry that are favoured by venture capitalists are those with high-tech components which qualitatively transform products or processing. The modernization of Chinese traditional herbal medicines, medical healthcare treatment, and Ctrip, which listed on NASDAQ at the end of 2003, are all such examples. Ctrip carries on the traditional business of booking hotel rooms and flight tickets, which is difficult to connect with high technology or as an internet firm. However, through making use of an internet e-commerce sales process, Ctrip gained recognition from venture capitalists and NASADQ investors.

Canton Venture Capital Co Ltd (C-VCC) was established by the Guangzhou municipal government to support the development of high-tech enterprises. Its investment field especially targets high-tech products, but C-VCC still invests in traditional industries, such as participation in Guangzhou Baolong Special Automobile Co Ltd (Baolong). The reason for Baolong becoming a C-VCC investment target is that its additional high-tech components make it outstanding within the traditional auto industry.

Compared with investment in high-tech sectors, investment in traditional industries carries the advantages of long development periods, broad markets, stable technology and foreseeable revenues. In conventional investment terms, the stability that traditional industries offer is certainly attractive. As many of the examples quoted have shown and in the breakdown of the internet legend, though VC investments in traditional industries are less glamorous than their internet counterparts, they can be just as lucrative.

Legendary Mengniu: An exercise in capital restructure

As Mainland China's fastest growing domestic dairy manufacturer, the capital development path of Mengniu Dairy Group (Mengniu) is a saga of praise or blame. Why did Mengniu choose the expedient of 'capital midwifery'? What are the original and special points in Mengniu's capital design? How was the realization of maximum benefit balanced between highly mature venture capitalists and highly experienced founders? Is there any hidden calculation behind Mengniu's careful capital design? Mengniu's president, Niu Gensheng, once said that Mengniu's capital exceeded the level which other enterprises would want or dare to think about. Mengniu's quantum leap was built on the magic of capital.

Ranked 1,116th in 1999, and from a RMB13.98 million start-up fund in 1997 to RMB45.98 million registered capital in 2002, Mengniu is now one of China's leading dairy product manufacturers and was rated by the Chinese General Chamber of Commerce (CGCC) as the top liquid milk producer in China by sales volume in 2003.[41] Statistics released by CGCC showed that it had overtaken another milk manufacturing giant, Yili (China's largest state-owned dairy) with a 16.67 per cent share of sales, against Yili's market share of 16.18 per cent. Founded in 1999 by three former employees of Yili, Mengniu's main products are liquid milk (UHT milk, milk beverages and yoghurt), ice cream and milk powder. Increasing levels of disposable income, awareness of dietary nutrition and changes in dietary behaviour coupled with a proactive dairy programme by the Chinese government have all led to rapidly accelerating rates of growth in dairy consumption.[42] The Chinese investment bank, China International Capital Corporation Limited (CICC) estimates that the annual growth rate jumped from 5.4 per cent to 14.4 per cent between 1998 and 2002. In urban areas the growth rate in liquid milk consumption has been as high as 30 per cent.[43]

On 10 June 2004, Mengniu made its debut on the Hong Kong Stock Exchange (HKSE). The listed 'H' share on HKSE is called Mengniu Dairy (code: 2319).[44] Mengniu dramatically increased its IPO price in a bid to raise HK$1.37 billion (US$164 million).[45] Mengniu decided

---

[41] 'The Investment Philosophy of CDH China', *Zero2IPO Venture Capital Monthly Journal*, 2 May 2003
[42] Jiang Jingjing 'Yili, Mengniu Fighting for No 1' *China Business Weekly*, 27 April 2004
[43] *Case Study of Mengniu Dairy*, Actis Online, www.act.is
[44] 'Mengniu Dairy Raises Offering Price In HK', *Shenzhen Daily*, 3 June 2004
[45] 'Mengniu Dairy Listed In HK', *People's Daily*, 11 June 2004

to offer 350 million shares and attracted investors by paying out 25 per cent of 2004's profits as dividends. Finally, Mengniu's IPO was priced at HK$3.925 per share, or 19 times its 2004 expected earnings.[46] Bankers had raised the indicative range about 10 per cent to between HK$3.315 and HK$3.925 per share after the market recovery.[47] Retail investors placed orders for over 200 times the shares available to them. Because the retail portion of the deal was covered more than 100 times, under Hong Kong rules 50 per cent of the share issue will be planned. The institutional portion of the deal was covered about 30 times. Such IPO response was good despite a volatile market and proved that investors still fancy retail plays and are interested in good quality IPOs.[48]

By obtaining capital from the public capital markets, Mengniu will be able to capitalize on favourable market conditions to build upon the Mengniu brand and develop existing and new markets to further strengthen its market leadership position. Ninety per cent, or 315 million of the new shares were initially offered to institutional and professional investors, and the remaining 35 million shares were offered through the Hong Kong public offer.

Corresponding with the good feedback from the stock exchange, the biggest miracle was created by Mengniu itself. Mengniu's sales revenues, which only amounted to RMB37.3 million in 1999, had increased sharply up to RMB4.072 billion at the end of 2003, an increment of about 108,155.5 per cent.[49] The average annual growth rate was an amazing 450 per cent[50] and Mengniu was ranked market leader in Mainland China. Mengniu's operating profit after tax for the first half of 2004 was reported at RMB293 million.[51]

Supporting Mengniu to exceed general industry performance and to develop so rapidly is a prime example of the power of 'capital midwifery'. Through the continuous changes in the proportions of shareholdings, the differentiated categories and character of its share options, and through the operation of financial instruments, Mengniu's fast growth story is one of skilful and careful achievement. This story rewrote history for Chinese private enterprises connecting with mature foreign VC firms.

Niu has coined a metaphor, 'Mengniu follows a law of aviation. If Mengniu could not grow up at high speed, it would be destroyed at

---

[46] *Mengniu Dairy Raises $176m From IPO* Reuters, 16 June 2004
[47] Eli Lau and Bloomberg 'Mengniu Raises IPO Price', *The Standard*, 2 June 2004
[48] *Mengniu Dairy Raises $176m From IPO* Reuters, 16 June 2004
[49] Jiang Desong 'Mengniu's Capital Running', *21st Century Business Review*, 14 October 2004
[50] 'The Different Yili', *Global Business and Finance*, 3 August 2004
[51] Mengniu Online, www.mengniu.com.cn

the same speed. If it is not possible to reach flying speed, an aircraft will drop down. Only by surpassing its own flying speed, can Mengniu achieve permanent development'. However, the problem of how Mengniu keeps up speed and rate of growth remains. Other than dependence on capital, will Mengniu be able to find a second source of acceleration in order to continue this dairy industry legend and myth?

In fact, Mengniu's real development only started from its listing in June 2004.

Reputation is the most important capital - Niu Gensheng and Xie Qiuxu

All the questions and answers come from the personal experience of Niu, the founder of Mengniu. Niu has never admitted the development of Mengniu is in any way legendary. Niu has been engaged in the dairy business for 25 years from milk bottle cleaner to senior executive, with an interval of five years in the ox breeding field and ten years as the deputy president of product operations in Yili. The Mengniu team includes about 500 professionals, who originally worked for Yili in dairy operations for more than ten years.[52]

In 1999, following a difference of opinion, Niu was sacked by Yili, currently Mengniu's biggest rival. Niu walked away with several colleagues from Yili and decided to set up a new dairy product company. The immediate problem was to source funds. Through innumerable trials and hardships, Niu and his colleagues raised RMB9 million from relatives and friends before starting a new company in the arid plains of Hohhot, the capital of northern Inner Mongolia Autonomous Region. In practice, the RMB9 million was insufficient for Niu to build a complete dairy complex.[53]

During Mengniu's start-up stage in 1999, there was a 'three no situation'; no milk source, no plant and no market. However, Mengniu adopted the audacious strategy of 'building marketing first, and then establishing the factory'. Niu seemed undeterred by the absence of sources of milk, factories and end users in this initial stage. Through a dummy joint venture, Mengniu devoted its brand, management, technology and expert direction to cooperation with eight local milk producers in Inner Mongolia, also signing sales contracts. Niu made the most of his longtime management expertise and even introduced an

---

[52] 'How Mengniu Becomes Legendary', *Nanfang Daily*, 20 October 2004
[53] Jiang Desong 'Mengniu's Capital Running', *21st Century Business Review*, 14 October 2004

original equipment manufacturer (OEM) model which was used in industrial manufacturing in dairy production operations.

Niu's personal charm appears to have been an important asset at Mengniu's birth. People familiar with him are convinced by his personal image, which later turned out to be a critical selling point for Mengniu. He always gives priority to business credibility and to the building of an extensive public relations network. For an industry such as the dairy business, dependence on a splendid founding concept or idea and a visionary, effective management team is not enough to attract venture capitalists. Furthermore, it is equally difficult for privately-owned firms to gain the necessary funding support from the state banks. So the best way to raise funds is to attract partners to participate in the business operation, which requires good networking. Not only did Niu take many professionals from Yili, building a human resource nucleus, and finalize product design quickly, but he also won the trust of clients and suppliers by right of his past relationships when he was at Yili. In this way, the first key start-up funding came from Xie Qiuxu, the general manager of Chaozhou Sun & Sky Printing Ltd, a Guangdong-based firm, and from Niu's colleagues, customers and suppliers.

Niu and Xie became good friends when Niu was responsible for back-orders and the manufacture of packaged goods in Yili. When Niu was doing business with him, Xie likened him to a secure money box, and gave great financial support. By way of a simple option on a proportion of the shares, Xie was Mengniu's first biggest shareholder.

In addition to supporting the formation of Mengniu and continuous funding, Xie also helped Mengniu to complete the capital bridging process. Xie generously drew cash from his typography business which he injected into the start-up of Mengniu and freely donated share options on almost 95 per cent of the shares in a trust formed for the benefit of Mengniu's management team, employees, and other beneficiaries. Furthermore, Xie transferred the voting rights in Yinniu Milk Industry Ltd (Yinniu), which holds 50 per cent of the stock of Mengniu, totally to Niu, without any intervention in the management, daily operations, and decision-making of Mengniu.

Xie performed an important role in Mengniu's further growth. The Mengniu management team's benefits were skilfully grafted onto Xie's trust. Xie controls only 2829 shares in Yinniu under his own name. Legal ownership of the remaining 39,378 shares is difficult to determine, but Xie's status in Mengniu is as holder of the balance. Eventually, Xie gained a high return from his investment of RMB3.8 million – a profitable deployment of his seed money since now Xie's shareholding is valued at up to RMB1 billion.[54] In effect, Xie can be regarded as the VC angel in Mengniu's development.

Niu's start-up fundraising for Mengniu highlights the importance of personal charm and reputation.

Creating a shell and the first round of fundraising[55]

Cooperation with Xie was just the beginning of the story and brought a human touch to the Mengniu legend. But Niu's plans were not fully satisfied by a few millions dollars/yuan for Mengniu. Niu's view had expanded to including external strategic VC investors. At the 2002 Spring Festival Art Gala Party held by CCTV, Niu had a confidential discussion with the investment head of the Wall Street firm Morgan Stanley, providing a taste of a new round of more eye-catching capital base expansion. Ten months later, the capital expansion story of Mengniu began.

From 17 October 2002, Mengniu began its first round of fundraising. Unlike GOME Electrical Appliances, China's top consumer-electronics chain which had listed directly on an overseas stock exchange without private equity investment, Mengniu attached importance to raising venture capital funding. The main aim during the first round of fundraising was to provide interim funding before approaching latter stage funders.

The first round of fundraising involved three ways of guaranteeing Mengniu's further development:

1. Getting an external investor to provide continuing funds for expansion and an external restriction mechanism;

2. Twice-restructuring the corporate ownership framework to strengthen the capacity for expanding the business;

3. Using financial instruments to build an internal mechanism for corporate motivation and to strengthen internal cohesion by way of awarding options and other incentives.

The Chinese media wrote a number of stories in connection with Mengniu's fundraising, but they reversed the real logic. On June 2002, Mengniu and three foreign investors (Morgan Stanley, CDH China and CGU-CDC) subscribed RMB216 million for 32 per cent of the stock.

---

[54] Li Tong 'How To Live With Angel: Mengniu's Financing Road', *Economics Professional*, 17 August 2004

[55] Some paragraphs of this part are from Jiang Desong 'Mengniu's Capital Running', *21st Century Business Review*, 14 October 2004

Pre-investment there were more than 40 million shares in issue. Post-financing the issue share capital increased by fewer than 20 million shares. The cost to the foreign VCs was RMB10.1 per share. It was no wonder that Niu, the government, and the original shareholders felt comfortable with the share option because the investment price rose from RMB8.8 per share (the negotiated price with Morgan Stanley) to RMB10.1 per share for adding CDH China and CGU-CD. According to a Chinese commentator, Morgan Stanley was prepared to pay more now to be Mengniu's shareholder. The cost of foreign financing can be calculated as above. However, the future IPO's principal entity was not intended to be Mengniu Dairy Group (Mengniu), but rather China Dairy Holdings (Mengniu Cayman Islands), a Cayman Islands registered company. Mengniu is merely the subsidiary company of Mengniu Cayman Islands. Having completed the offshore capital structure, Mengniu's price per share will be insignificant compared with the investment of China Dairy Holdings. This story illustrates the difference between the use of funding by a Chinese and western company.

On 6 June 2002, Mengniu Cayman Islands was established. The number of registered shares at US$1 per share was 1000 with a par value of US$0.001. Eight days later, on 14 June Mengniu Cayman Islands set up a wholly-owned subsidiary called China Dairy (Mauritius) Ltd (Mengniu Mauritius). In the Mengniu Prospectus, this series of events was described as follows: 'On 5 June 2002, Mengniu Cayman Islands was established…Beforehand, the three VC investors, Jinniu Milk Industry Ltd (Jinniu) and Yinniu Milk Industry Ltd (Yinniu) together owned 50 per cent of Mengniu Cayman Islands' issued stock.' Although the sequence of establishing the offshore companies is not clearly described, readers would be wrong to conclude that China Dairy Holdings (Mengniu Cayman Islands) was established by Jinniu and Yinniu. The real data shows that the timing of the registration of Jinniu and Yinniu was three months later than the formation of Mengniu Cayman Islands. How could the 'baby' have been born if the 'parents' had not yet been born?

Let's examine one more detail. At the same time that Mengniu Cayman Islands was established, Morgan Stanley set up another wholly-owned subsidiary in the Cayman Islands, MS Dairy Holdings, which became the shareholder's main vehicle to invest in Mengniu. Now it becomes clear that Morgan Stanley was the 'baby's father'. Mengniu Cayman Islands's name, China Dairy Holdings, shows no relationship with Mengniu but is similar to MS Dairy Holdings…

In practice, Mengniu and the three VCs adopted a three-step approach, as follows.

The first step was to restructure Mengniu and establish an expandable ownership structure. On 5 June 2002, Morgan Stanley set up two shell companies, China Dairy Holdings (Mengniu Cayman Islands) and MS Dairy Holdings. The first is meant to be the accounting company for receipt of the funds invested by Morgan Stanley. The other is the shareholder company for investment in Mengniu. On 14 June 2002, Mengniu Mauritius was set up. Mengniu Cayman Islands and Mengniu Mauritius became two typical overseas shell companies to act as a secondary ownership rights platform, convenient for dealing with stock allocations and transfers.[56] On 23 September 2002, Mengniu formed two investment holding companies in the British Virgin Islands, Jinniu Milk Industry Ltd (Jinniu) and Yinniu Milk Industry Ltd (Yinniu) as the company's de facto controlling shareholders. Jinniu and Yinniu were shell investment companies formed for Mengniu's shareholders and positioned at the top of the ownership structure. The registered share capital of each company is US$50,000 in 50,000 shares of US$1 par value. With these two-tier ownership platforms Megniu could readily accommodate external capital according to varying future situations.

The second step was for Mengniu to use each kind of financial instrument to build an internal employee motivation scheme. At another level, the real purpose of establishing the two investment holding companies Jinniu and Yinniu was to use them as incentive benefit vehicles for Mengniu's management team, employees, other investors and business associates, through financial arrangements such as transfers of stock, direct allocation of shares and shares held in trust. Through Jinniu and Yinniu corporate shareholdings, the management team of Mengniu became ultimate indirect shareholders in Mengniu.

Jinniu was owned by 15 natural persons working for Mengniu, with Niu and other six senior executives, Zheng Jiuqiang, Lu Jun, Sun Yubin, Yang Wenjun, Sun Xianhong, and Qiu Lianjun, together holding an 87.4 per cent stake. Meanwhile, Yinniu was 63.5 per cent owned by Xie, with 15 other shareholders including mid-level or senior managers at Mengniu's associated companies except De Jiuqiang.[57] Not only would the two investment firms ensure a consistency of interests and operational targets inside the dairy kingdom but the arrangement also aimed to promote a stable external market environment. After their establishment, Jinniu and Yinniu immediately took up the full share option over 1000 shares of China Dairy Holdings as the par value. The price was US$1 and the shares were distributed 50 per cent each to Jinniu and Yinniu. Under the control of Jinniu and

---

[56] Mengniu Online, www.mengniu.com.cn
[57] 'Announcement Completion of The Subscription of Shares In Inner Mongolia Mengniu Milk Industry (Group) Co Ltd' *South China Morning Post*, 19 October 2004

Yinniu, Mengniu's share capital could be injected into the foreign IPO entity, China Dairy Holdings.

In fact, Mengniu did not make its huge market breakthrough until 2002. Mengniu had become the champion of corporate growth among all non state-owned, non-public companies in China as a result of its annual growth of up to 1947.31 per cent in 1999–2001 during which years annual sales totalled RMB43 million, RMB290 million and RMB850 million respectively. Sales for 2002 were a stunning RMB2.1 billion.

For the privately-owned Mengniu, it was a good decision to instil the share option spirit during the process of corporate assets reorganization. Jinniu and Yinniu clearly identify with the corporate ownership structure and the boundaries of everyone's advantage in Mengniu's development. It should be noted that Niu did not have an excessive personal interest in Mengniu.

The third step was to attract investment from strategic venture capitalists. Under the Company Articles of the Cayman Islands, the company's share capital could be separated into A-shares and B-shares. A-shares have the right of ten votes per share. B-shares, however, only have the right of one vote per share. On 24 September 2002, Mengniu Cayman Islands carried out a stock split whereby 1000 shares were converted into 100 billion shares, which included A-shares (5,200 shares, valued at US$1 per share) and B-shares (99,999,994,800 shares, valued at US$0.001 per share). The original 1000 shares were folded into the 5200 A-shares. The proportions were therefore 51:49 (Jinniu and Yinniu: three investors) for the voting rights of the two parties.

On 17 October 2002, Jinniu and Yinniu respectively purchased 1,134 shares (at a cost of US$1,134) and 2,968 shares (at a cost of US$2,968) of the A-shares of Mengniu Cayman Islands. Adding the previous respective holdings of 500 shares each, Jinniu and Yinniu now held 5,102 shares in total.

Holdings of 32,685 shares, 10,372 shares, and 5,923 shares in B-shares of Mengniu Cayman Islands were bought respectively by MS Dairy (Morgan Stanley), CDH China and CGU-CDC China, spending US$17,332,705, US$5,500,000 and US$3,141,007 respectively at the price of US$530 per share. In this way Mengniu completed its first round of fundraising. These three venture capitalists were successfully brought into Mengniu. Overseas capital was eager to ride on Mengniu's robust growth potential and professional management standards. Mengniu's clear-cut ownership structure was also a factor of pivotal significance for investors.

Although three venture capitalists controlled 90.6 per cent (9.4 per cent was controlled by Jinniu and Yinniu) of Mengniu's share options at the initial stage, they did not participate in its corporate management. The contracts signed between the three VC firms and Mengniu's management team provided that the B-shares held by the three VC firms had rights at one vote per share, while the management team had rights at ten votes per share in their holding of A-shares through Jinniu and Yinniu. In this way, the management team actually owned 51 per cent of the voting rights of Mengniu Cayman Islands.

Of special interest here was the management team's incentive to enhance business achievement, whereby both sides agreed that the management team had the right to convert its holding of A-shares into B-shares, on the basis of ten B-shares for one A-share, if the team achieved defined outstanding results.

After accepting the capital injection, Mengniu Cayman Islands bought all the shares of Mengniu Mauritius for US$25,973,712. Mengniu Mauritius then used these funds to purchase 66.7 per cent of stock from Mengniu's corporate legal-person shareholders and some of the natural person shareholders. Thus, Mengniu's first round of capital injection and share option restructuring was completed. At first sight the benefits of Mengniu's original shareholders appeared lost in the process; however all the benefits were actually transferred into Yinniu, which made suitable arrangements for every original shareholder.

But the first round of financing required Mengniu to increase sales dramatically. If not, the three VCs would control Mengniu and Niu would lose his job. By way of 'punishment', the remaining investment cash for Mengniu Cayman Islands and its subsidiary Mengniu Mauritius would be controlled by the three VCs so that investors would have absolute control over 60.4 per cent of the share options of Mengniu (90.6 per cent internal share option of Mengniu Cayman Islands multiplied by 66.7 per cent of Mengniu's share option controlled by Mengniu Cayman Islands), which would give the three VCs the power to replace the management team of Mengniu at any moment. The three VCs recognized the 1:10 percentage from A-share to B-share only when the 'task' was completed by the management team. Only when the management team of Mengniu was able to increase sales significantly would RMB216 million be converted into a 32 per cent share option. Otherwise, RMB216 million investments would fully control Mengniu, which could make the profit after tax more than RMB77.86 million.

Figure 8.2 and Figure 8.3 below illustrate the first round of Mengniu's finance.

The second round of mature equity capital subscription

After Mengniu's first round of fundraising, its annual sales revenue increased 1.5 times from RMB1.6687 billion at the end of 2002 to RMB4.0715 billion at the end of 2003. The management team's

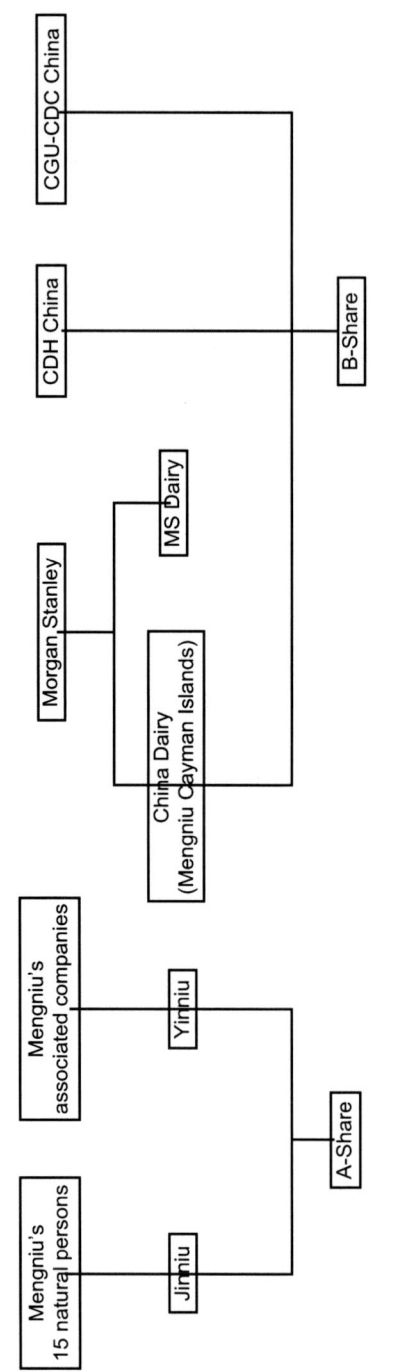

Figure 8.2 The first round of Mengniu's finance (investors and investees)

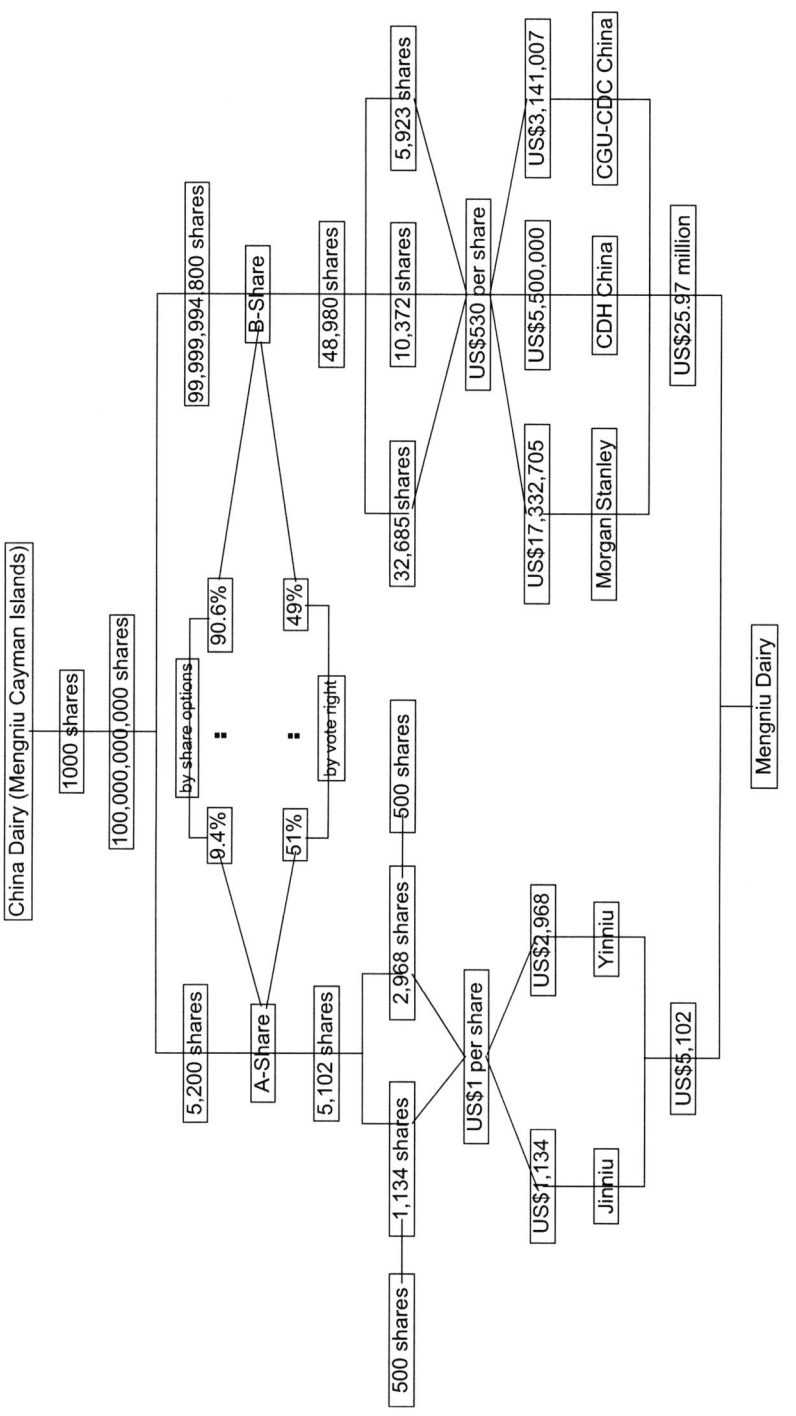

Figure 8.3 The first round of Mengniu's finance (share and price)

outstanding performance won recognition from the three foreign venture capitalists.

By August 2003, Niu had completed the task. The financial statement of Mengniu shows that the profit after tax increased 194 per cent from RMB77.86 million to RMB230 million. Therefore, on 19 September 2003, Jinniu's 1,634 A-shares in Mengniu Cayman Islands (formed by combining the 500 shares brought by Jinniu when Mengniu Cayman Islands was set up with 1,134 shares brought by the management team of Mengniu during the first round of capital funding) were transferred into 16,340 B-shares in Mengniu Cayman Islands. At the same time, Yinniu's 3,468 A-shares in Mengniu Cayman Islands (formed by combining the 500 shares brought by Yinniu when Mengniu Cayman Islands was set up with 2,968 shares brought by the management team of Mengniu during the first round of capital funding) were transferred into 34,680 B-shares in Mengniu Cayman Islands and so the management team's share option proportions became the same as their voting rights at 51 per cent.[58]

To promote a second increase of equity capital from the three venture capitalists, Mengniu (Cayman Islands) reclassified its stock and redeemed the A-shares and B-shares in exchange for 90 billion ordinary shares and 10 billion convertible securities, with a face-value of US$0.001 per share.[59] The B-shares originally held by Jinniu, Yinniu, MS Dairy (Morgan Stanley), CDH, CGU-CDC transferred into ordinary shares according to the relative par value.

In October 2003, the three venture capitalists purchased the convertible securities issued by Mengniu Cayman Islands and invested US$35.23 million a second time. One question that emerged was how investors could be sure of the increased equity capital in the second round of fundraising from the investment value. Mengniu's operating profit after tax had reached RMB184.1 million in 2003 and the three investors realized a profit on their first round investment. The balanced outcome for both sides was that the three investors invested RMB500 million twice and took up 34 per cent of the stock, which meant that their valuation of Mengniu was about RMB1.4 billion. The price-earnings ratio (P/E ratio) decreased by 7.3 times, which was less than the previous 10 times. Previously, the three investors had obtained 49 per cent of Mengniu's parent company stock, which meant they accepted a RMB400 million valuation of Mengniu at a P/E ratio equal to 10 times.[60] The secondary fundraising arrangement reflected

---

[58] Li Tong 'How To Live With Angel: Mengniu's Financing Road', *Economics Professional*, 17 August 2004
[59] Mengniu Online, www.mengniu.com.cn
[60] Jiang Desong 'Mengniu's Capital Running', *21st Century Business Review*, 14 October 2004

the investors' feeling that the accumulated risk would be driven down if they put more eggs in Mengniu's basket.

Mengniu Mauritius acquired 80,010,000 shares of Mengniu in advance at US$2.1775 per share on 18 September 2003. On 20 October 2003, Mengniu Mauritius acquired a further 96 million shares of Mengniu at US$3.038 per share and increased its shareholding up to 81.1 per cent.[61] These funds were from the second round of capital increase.

The most interesting feature of the second round of fundraising was the issue of convertible securities, which were not convertible bonds in a generic sense. Mengniu's convertible securities were more like extendable share-exchange certificates, which reflected the ability of investors to control Mengniu's operating risks. Having regard to the absence of any increase in the scale of corporate capital at the time of issue, the scheme designed by Mengniu and the three investors was based on three factors and illustrated the maturity of Mengniu's capital structure:

1. Leaving the management team's percentage shareholding undiluted in order to safeguard the management's absolute control and leadership;

2. Guaranteeing a stable increase in the corporate earnings per share record in order to prepare for the financial statements before listing;

3. Limiting the investors' investment cost, under clauses of the convertible securities agreement document, to limit its investment risk in case Mengniu's performance declined.

The sprint for IPO

As 2004 arrived, Mengniu fine-tuned several blueprints for its listing and made final preparations for an IPO. On 15 January 2004, Niu purchased 18,100,920 shares from Xie, representing 8.2 per cent of the issued capital[62] and made his first appearance at the forefront of Mengniu's ownership structure.

On 22 March 2004, several Yinniu shareholders transferred 3,244 shares to two internal staff. On the same day, Jinniu and Yinniu issued and allotted 32,392 shares and 32,184 shares respectively to several other shareholders. At the time, Yinniu's largest shareholder, Xie, acquired 20,446 shares of Yinniu, increasing XIE's shareholding to

---

[61] ibid
[62] 'The Mature of Capital', *21st Century Business Review*, 20 October 2004

63.5 per cent. Before listing, the numbers of shares held by Mengniu's current investor group were sharply increased. On the same day, Jinniu and Yinniu adjusted the Plan of Corporate Rights and Interests further to show appreciation of the contribution made by executives, non-executives, service providers and other investors to Mengniu Group. The number of shares in the Plan differed but the share price remained the same at US$1. The transfer prices for exchange of the Jinniu and Yinniu share options were US$238 and US$112 respectively.

On 23 March 2004, Niu's trust was crystallized. The purpose of Niu's trust was to inspire and reward the main employees, business related persons and associates. In this way, Mengniu brought all the persons it could contact into its own strategic alliance and locked those unrelated to the corporate share options into long-term corporate profit development through the medium of the trust. The beneficiaries of Niu's trust can enjoy the benefit of Mengniu's development but don't have voting rights in Jinniu or Yinniu.

The IPO and issue of shares

In the five years since Mengniu entered the Chinese dairy market, it has become a household name in the world's most populous nation. Through a combination of strong management, a powerful distribution network, stringent quality control standards and a steady supply of high-quality raw milk, Mengniu expects to continue to enjoy exceptional growth. 2004 also signalled a milestone for the dairy giant, whose nationwide market share of 16.67 per cent has left Yili Group behind at 16.18 per cent, according to statistics from the China General Chamber of Commerce. In 2004, liquid milk products contributed 85.9 per cent of Mengniu's revenue, while ice cream and other dairy products contributed 11.7 per cent and 2.4 per cent respectively.[63]

On 10 June 2004, Mengniu's 'H' shares were listed on the Hong Kong Stock Exchange as Mengniu Dairy (code: 2319).

Mengniu successfully raised a total of HK$1.37 billion (US$164 million) from the initial offering at the issue price of US$0.50 per share. Morgan Stanley as sponsor and BNP Paribas Peregrine as co-sponsor were the joint global coordinators and joint market makers of the IPO.[64] The offer of 350 million shares, or 35 per cent of the enlarged share capital, was oversubscribed 205 times; thus half of the IPO was sold to retail investors instead of the former ten per cent, under the 'green shoe' over-allotment option. The move, which involved raising

---

[63] Foster Wong 'Mengniu Leaps 24% on debut', *The Standard*, 11 June 2004
[64] Ma Wei 'Mengniu Debut Soars 24%', *China Daily*, 11 June 2004

the original IPO price range by 16 per cent, flew in the face of current trends.[65] As sentiment for HK stocks continued to drift down on fears of interest rate increases, rising oil prices and tightened economic policies, several companies had slashed the size their IPO plans.

Mengniu's three overseas investors cashed in US$50 million from their sale of 100 million shares. This successful IPO is the result of the fast and steady growth of Mengniu. Funds raised from the capital market will be used to further improve its production and extend its product line. According to the Mengniu Prospectus, RMB494 million (US$60 million) of the funds raised will be used to expand liquid milk production facilities, RMB190 million to expand ice cream production facilities and RM46 million to expand other dairy production facilities. Table 8.3 tracks the progress of Mengniu's IPO.

Mengniu's main listing body is Mengniu Cayman Islands. The authorized share capital is 3 billion in shares of HK$0.1 each. There are still 2 billion unissued blank shares. Adopting the skills of international investment bankers, Mengniu only issued 35 million shares and set up multilevel compensatory plans. The funds raised would be injected into Mengniu, increasing the foreign proportion of shareholdings from 81.1 per cent to 84.3 per cent. But the increased foreign share requires authorization and confirmation by MOFCOM and the gap between first and second fund raising should not be less than 12 months.[66] The last capital increase of Mengniu happened on September 2003, so the funds raised from the IPO had to wait abroad until at least September 2004. In the end, the immediate effect of the IPO was not as good as that of a bank loan.

The foreshadowing of capital

On 23 March 2004, the purchase by Niu of 5,816 shares from MS Dairy (Morgan Stanley), 1,846 shares from CDH and 1,054 shares from CGU-CDC of Mengniu Cayman Islands, at the symbolic price of US$1 per share was approved, giving Niu direct control of 6.1 per cent of the stock of Mengniu Cayman Islands. The share sales can be viewed as an affirmation and encouragement by the three investors of NIU's management achievement through which MS Dairy (Morgan Stanley), CDH, and CGU-CDC gained more from their capital investment. In summary, the three international investors invested US$25.97 million in Mengniu in the first round of fund-raising in June 2002 and invested US$35.23 million in the secondary fundraising round. Their total

---

[65] ibid
[66] Jiang Desong 'Mengniu's Capital Running', *21st Century Business Review*, 14 October 2004

Table 8.3 The IPO of China Mengniu Dairy Company Limited

Listing data

Stock Code	2391	Sector		Food & Beverage	
Exchange	Hong Kong	Market		Main Board	
Board lot	1,000	Company Website		www.mengniu.com.cn	

Company profile

China Mengniu is one of the leading dairy product manufacturers in China. Its principal product categories are liquid milk, ice cream and other dairy products, such as milk powder, milk tea powder and milk tablets. The company markets the majority of its products under its primary MENGNIU trademark.

The share offer

Total amount raised	HK$1,093.75 million* – HK$1,373.75 million*
Total no. of shares to offer	350,000,000 shares (excluding the exercise of over-allotment option)
No. of international offer shares	315,000,000 shares (subject to the exercise of over-allotment option and reallocation)
No. of Hong Kong public offer shares	35,000,000 shares (subject to reallocation)
Offer price	HK$3.125 per share – HK$3.925 per share
Over-allotment option	Yes
No. of over-allotment shares	52,500,000 shares

* excluding the exercise of over-allotment option

Share offer statistics

Prospective P/E	Basic - 13.3 times (based on an offer price of HK$3.925 per share) - 10.6 times (based on an offer price of HK$3.125) Fully diluted - 19.0 times (based on an offer price of HK$3.925 per share) - 15.1 times (based on an offer price of HK$3.125 per share)	Dividend Yield	n/a
Adjusted net tangible asset value per share	Maximum HK$1.17 ^ Minimum HK$1.03 ^	Market capitalization	Maximum HK$3,925 million Minimum HK$3,125 million

^ Based on an exchange rate of HK$1 for RMB 1.061 yuans

Timetable

Lodging applications	12 noon on 4 June 2004
Announcement of the offer price and allotment results	8 June 2004
Despatch of share certificates	8 June 2004
Despatch of refund cheques	8 June 2004
Listing date	10 June 2004

Parties involved in share offer

Sponsor	BNP Paribas Peregrine Capital Limited
Joint lead managers	BNP Paribas Peregrine Capital Limited, Morgan Stanley Dean Witter Asia Limited
Receiving banker	Bank of China (Hong Kong)

Source: HSBC Broking Services (Asia) Limited

investment was US$61.2 million (HK$477 million). Three investors sold 100 million shares in the IPO and cashed out HK$392.5 million, leaving a shortfall of only about HK$100 million from its total investment. After exercising the huge amount of convertible securities options 12 months after the IPO in June 2005, the three investors' shareholding will stand at 31.1 per cent. On the assumption that net profit will amount to HK$300 million and at a 20 times P/E ratio, the capitalization of Mengniu would be HK$6 billion. At that time, the share value of three investors would be about HK$1.9 billion. From 2002 to 2005, the initial HK$477 million investment would have risen by 374 per cent.

The Evaluation Adjustment Agreement signed by the three investors and Mengniu's management team regulates that Jinniu should make equity carve-outs, which means Jinniu can be forced to transfer freely 783 million shares (accounting for 5.7 per cent of the total stock) to the three investors. MS Dairy (Morgan Stanley), CDH, and CGU-CDC would then hold 36.8 per cent of the issued stock. This clause predicates the net profit of Mengniu should be more than HK$550 million in 2006. If the net profit rate can be maintained at around 4.5 per cent, a 2006 turnover of more than HK$12 billion would be required. Furthermore, the three investors can grasp additional share subscription opportunities. They can purchase shares of Mengniu Cayman Islands at a price of HK$1.24 per share before dilution within ten years in one or more tranches. Compared with the investors, Niu only received stock valued at less than HK$200 million and cannot cash out within five years. Niu's personal shareholding represents only 4.6 per cent and will decrease to 3.3 per cent after the exercise of convertible securities options in 2005. If Mengniu cannot deliver the miracle of the increased sales achievement, MS Dairy (Morgan Stanley), CDH and CGU-CDC might discard Niu's team. The future Mengniu ownership structure is uncertain.

Morgan Stanley is a world-class investment bank. It bases its conclusions on the principle that the stockholders' benefits are paramount. In investors' eyes, entrepreneurs are the representatives of the investors and the necessaily energetic managers. The management team has only one choice, which is to work harder, harder and harder.

Potential risks

There are still some obstacles in Mengniu's way. The high cost of Mengniu's media advertising is the first risk. On 18 November 2003, Mengniu was the winning bidder in the CCTV Annual Golden Time Ad Auction. Thus Mengniu must pay RMB310 million for CCTV advertising time, which amounts to about RMB850,000 per day.[67] When counted as an addition to fixed costs, no one can calculate the equivalent value in the volume of dairy products.

However, Mengniu's marketing strategy always attracts industry approval. After the launch of the Shenzhou-5 manned spacecraft, Mengniu advertised Chinese Astronauts' Special Milk everywhere for a short period of time, which cost Mengniu more than RMB15 million. However, Mengniu is not the exception. The whole dairy products industry does not hesitate to advertise in its marketing. Although Shanghai Bright Dairy & Food Co Ltd (Bright Dairy), a joint venture set up by six enterprises including Shanghai Dairy (Group) Co Ltd, Shanghai Industry Food Co Ltd and Danone Co Ltd (Asia) didn't feature in CCTV's annual bidding, the ad fees of Bright Dairy were determined to be RMB98 million.

There is no alternative to appearing in peak marketing time following the dairy industry's most recent round of expansion and competition. Since 2002, the capital investment war has continued in the dairy market. The old overlords extended their corporate scope through M&A. The new participants have invested largely in this industry with their sensitive market trend instinct. From 2000 to 2002, Bright Dairy acquired 30 companies. According to the statistics of AFX European Focus, the French food giant Danone's Asian offshoot has signed an agreement to purchase an additional two per cent stake in Bright Dairy. Danone will pay roughly US$9.5 million for 20.84 million shares. Upon completion of the deal, Danone's stake in Bright Dairy will reach 5.85 per cent; in 2003, in a separate deal for which government approval is still pending, Danone purchased a 3.85 per cent shareholding in the company. Currently, Danone owns 9.7 per cent of the shares in Bright Dairy.[68]

In 2002, Beijing Sanyuan Foods Co Ltd offered US$9.3 million for the Beijing dairy operations of New York-based Kraft Food International and went to southern China to acquire Shanghai Best Milk Products Co Ltd.[69] On 9 December 2002, the New Hope Group shattered the ownership dream of Nestlé Alimentana of Switzerland and Bright Dairy by acquiring a 91.8 per cent shareholding in Dengchuan Diequan Dairy Co (Diequan) with an investment of RMB55 million (US$6.65 million) in Yunnan's largest dairy producer, located in Eryuan County, the Bai Autonomous Prefecture of Dali.[70] In addition, New

---

[67] Xiao Xiao 'Can Exchange the Audi A6 from Santana', *Sichuan News Online*, www.newssc.net, 4 December 2003
[68] Zuo Zhijian et al 'Danone's Chinese Dilemma', *21st Century Economy Report*, 22 November 2004
[69] Jia Ke 'Sanyuan Acquired Kafu', *Southern Weekend*, 5 January 2001
[70] Ruan Juying 'New Hope Defeated Nestle', *South News*, 12 December 2002

Hope Group expanded its influence to the provinces of Sichuan, Anhui, Jilin, Zhejiang, Hebei, Shangdong, and Yunnan.

At the start of 2003, Master Kong set up a farm of 200 hectares in Hangzhou city, Anji Province, and invested US$12.5 million to establish a dairy products factory in Guangzhou, Guangdong Province.[71]

The secret of Mengniu's rapid development is to acquire small local companies and introduce superior original equipment into local enterprises. Mengniu has to sell its products fully across the spread of the market in order to avoid corporate risk. In order to sell their products and expand the scope of their business, enterprises have to jump into advertising. Firms have to be able to afford the heavy cost pressure of advertising to build their markets. Conversely, in order to reduce product costs, companies have to expand their product scales. By working through this cycle, the dairy industry turns round in an astonishing circle.

The second obstacle is in milk sourcing. As a consequence of the territorial spread, the dairy industry is facing a milk source crisis. Competition accompanies expansion. According to official statistics, annual growth in the quantity of raw milk is about 120,000 tons, while annual growth in the quantity of fresh milk is 360,000 tons. The increase of raw milk cannot be reconciled with market demand. Baotou, the well known Chinese milch cow breeder has a total of 150,000 milch cows that produce no more than 0.35 tons each per year. Against Mengniu's 2003 sales of US$4 billion, its milk resource purchases amounted to RMB1.6 billion, representing 40 per cent of sales. Assuming a purchase price of RMB1700 per ton, the demand quantity for raw milk would be 1 million tons. The shortfall in the ability to provide raw milk is more than 0.6 million tons, and that is only to satisfy the requirement of Mengniu.[72]

If market expansion and construction of milk source capability are uncoordinated, or the increasing rates of both demand and supply exceed actual growth rates, the only result will be the appearance of a Bubble Dairy Economy, with overproduction, unused production lines and a low quality of milk resource.

The capital invested in Mengniu could not solve the problems of milk sourcing, because the supply of raw milk is restricted by natural phenomena. Capital cannot milk. In the Mengniu blueprint, sales should be RMB10 billion to maintain its leading status. But for Mengniu alone, the demand quantity for raw milk will be about 2.5 million tons, which is equivalent to the output of at least 8 million milch cows.

---

[71] Tang Yuan, 'Master Kong Entered the Dairy Market', *Global Food Industry Magazine*, 20 April 2004
[72] Xiao Xiao, 'Mengniu's Risk', *The Economic Observer*, 4 December 2003

Milk is a rare resource and the problem requires deep consideration by all enterprises. One approach to solving the problem is investment, investment and investment again.

Finally, this advance warning to the financing chain poses another important potential risk for Mengniu. Buying farms, competing for milk resources, media advertising etc are all finally a matter of money. Mengniu's ratio of debts to assets (RDA) is 54 per cent. In general, RDA of less than 50 per cent is categorized as relatively moderate although RDA around 50 per cent implies some gearing.[73] Therefore, the rapid pace of Mengniu's development will be affected by hidden troubles including the fields of management and cash provision.

The value of the Chinese dairy market in 2003 was around RMB35 billion.[74] Growth in customer demand over the next ten years will be around 20–30 per cent.[75] In line with Mengniu's current development, sales of RMB10 billion in 2006 is not an impossible goal but capital will be required to meet it. But whatever the requirement may be, the HKSE listing has relaxed Mengniu's tight financing chain.

---

[73] Gao Guangzhi and Bao Shenghua, The State Management Account Xinhua News Agency, 5 June 2003
[74] 'International Fund Invested In Chinese Dairy', *China Economy Times*, 13 October 2003
[75] 'There Will Be Big Development for Chinese Dairy Industry Within Ten Years', *Beijing Business Today*, 25 October 2004

Appendix A

Regulations on Administration of Foreign Invested Venture Capital Investment Enterprises

Jointly issued by the Ministry of Foreign Trade and Economic Cooperation, the Ministry of Science and Technology, the State Administration for Industry and Commerce, the State Administration of Taxation and the State Administration of Foreign Exchange on 30 January 2003, and effective as of 1 March 2003.

Part One: General provisions

Article 1: These Regulations have been formulated in accordance with the PRC Sino-foreign Cooperative Joint Venture Law, the PRC Sino-foreign Equity Joint Venture Law, the PRC Wholly Foreign-owned Enterprise Law, the Company Law and other relevant laws and regulations in order to encourage foreign companies, enterprises and other economic organizations or individuals (the foreign investors) to make venture capital investments in China and to establish and perfect the venture capital investment mechanism of China.

Article 2: 'Foreign-invested venture capital investment enterprise' (FIVCIE), as used in these Regulations, means a foreign-invested enterprise established within the territory of China by foreign investors, or by foreign investors together with companies, enterprises or other economic organizations registered and established under Chinese law (the Chinese investors), in accordance with these Regulations to be engaged in venture capital investment business.

Article 3: 'Venture capital investment', as used in these Regulations, means a type of investment activity pursuant to which equity investments are injected mainly into hi- and new-tech enterprises that have not been publicly listed (the investee enterprises) and venture capital management services are provided in order to obtain capital appreciation benefits.

Article 4: A FIVCIE may take the form of a non-legal person entity or the form of a company. Investors of a FIVCIE in the form of a non-legal person entity (non-legal person FIVCIE) shall be jointly and severally liable for such FIVCIE's debts. Alternatively, such investors may also agree in the contract of the FIVCIE that the requisite investor, as provided under Article 7, will be jointly and severally liable for the FIVCIE's debts where the assets of the FIVCIE are insufficient to discharge such debts while the liability of each other investor will be limited to the amount of its respective capital contribution subscribed for. The liability of each investor of a FIVCIE in the form of a company (corporate FIVCIE) shall be limited to the amount of its respective capital contribution subscribed for. The liability of each investor of a FIVCIE in the form of a company (corporate FIVCIE) shall be limited to the amount of its respective capital contribution subscribed for.

Article 5: FIVCIEs shall observe relevant Chinese laws and regulations, shall comply with the foreign investment industrial policies, and shall not harm the public interest of China. The legitimate business activities and the lawful rights and interests of FIVCIEs are protected by Chinese law.

Part Two: Establishment and registration

Article 6: The following requirements shall be met in order for a FIVCIE to be established:

1. It has at least two but at most 50 investors and shall have at least one requisite investor qualified under Article 7.

2. The minimum amount of the total capital contribution subscribed for from all investors shall be US$10 million for each non-legal person FIVCIE and US$5 million for each corporate FIVCIE. Except for the requisite investors provided under Article 7, each other investor's minimum capital contribution subscribed for shall not be less than US$1 million. Foreign investors shall make their capital contributions in freely convertible currencies and Chinese investors in RMB.

3. It has a clear organizational structure.

4. It has a clear and legitimate investment direction.

5. Except for situations where a FIVCIE has contracted with a venture capital investment management company to manage its activities, each FIVCIE shall have at least three professional personnel who possess venture capital investment experience.

6. Other conditions that may be required by laws and administrative regulations.

Article 7: A requisite investor shall meet the following requirements:

1. Venture capital investment is its main line of business.

2. In the 3 years before the application it has had cumulative capital under its management of not less than US$100 million, of which at least US$50 million have been used for venture capital investments. In the case of the requisite investor being a Chinese investor, the aforementioned cumulative capital shall be RMB100 million of which at least RMB50 million has been used for venture capital investments.

3. It has at least three professional management personnel who possess at least 3 years' experience in the venture capital investment area.

4. An investor may also apply to become a requisite investor if its affiliated entity satisfies the requirements set forth above under this Article. As used in this paragraph, an 'affiliated entity' means an entity that controls, is controlled by or is under common control with the investor concerned and a party is 'controlled' by another party if the controlling party owns more than 50 per cent voting power of the controlled party.

5. Neither the requisite investor nor its aforementioned affiliated entity shall have been prohibited from being engaged in venture capital investment or investment consultancy business or been subject to penalty for commitment of fraud by the judicial authority or any other relevant regulatory authority in its home country.

6. In the case of a non-legal person FIVCIE, at least 1 per cent of the total capital contribution subscribed for by all investors to the FIVCIE and at least 1 per cent of the total actual capital contribution from all investors to the FIVCIE shall be made by its requisite investor(s) and such requisite investor(s) shall be jointly and severally liable for the debts of such FIVCIE. In the case of a corporate FIVCIE, at least 30 per cent of the total capital contribution subscribed for by all investors to the FIVCIE and at least

30 per cent of the total actual capital contribution from all investors to the FIVCIE shall be made by its requisite investor(s).

Article 8: The following procedures shall be followed when applying to establish a FIVCIE:

1. Investors shall submit to the provincial-level department in charge of foreign trade and economic cooperation of the place where the FIVCIE is proposed to be established an application for establishment and relevant documents.

2. The provincial-level department in charge of foreign trade and economic cooperation shall, within 15 days after receipt of all materials submitted, complete its initial review and submit the materials to the Ministry of Foreign Trade and Economic Cooperation (hereafter, the Examination and Approval Authority).

3. The Examination and Approval Authority will, within 45 days of its receipt of all application materials submitted to it and upon consultation with and consent by the Ministry of Science and Technology, make a written decision as to whether the application is approved or not. If the application is approved, a Foreign-invested Enterprise Approval Certificate will be issued.

4. Within 1 month of receipt from the Examination and Approval Authority of the Foreign Invested Enterprise Approval Certificate, the approved FIVCIE shall apply to register, on the strength of the certificate, with the State Administration for Industry and Commerce or its provincial-level office where the proposed FIVCIE is to be located having administrative authority over registration of foreign-invested enterprises (the Registration Authority).

Article 9: The following documents shall be submitted to the Examination and Approval Authority when applying to establish a FIVCIE:

1. the application for establishment signed by the requisite investor(s);

2. the contract of the FIVCIE and the articles of association of the FIVCIE signed by all investors;

3. a written declaration from the requisite investor(s) (on its or their satisfaction of the qualification requirements under Article 7 hereof, the authenticity of all materials submitted, and its or their willingness to strictly comply with these Regulations and the requirements of other relevant Chinese laws and regulations);

4. a legal opinion issued by a law firm on the legal existence of the requisite investor(s) and as to the above-referenced declaration having been duly authorized and executed;

5. descriptions of the requisite investors' venture capital investment business, the capital under management for the past 3 years, the capital actually invested by such investor(s), and the résumés of such investors' venture capital investment management professionals;

6. a copy of each investor's certificate of registration and a copy of its legal representative's authority certificate;

7. the name pre-approval notice for the FIVCIE issued by the name registration authority;

8. if the qualification of a requisite investor is based on the provision of the fourth paragraph under Article 7 hereof, the relevant materials with respect to the qualified affiliated entity shall also be included; and

9. other documents relevant to the application for establishment that are requested by the Examination and Approval Authority.

Article 10: All FIVCIEs shall contain in their names the words 'venture capital investment'. Except for FIVCIEs, no foreign-invested enterprises may contain in its name the words 'venture capital investment'.

Article 11: When applying for establishment of a FIVCIE, the following documents shall be submitted to the Registration Authority and the applicant shall be responsible for the authenticity and the effectiveness of such documents:

1. the application for establishment signed by the chairman of the board or the responsible person of the joint management committee of the FIVCIE;

2. the contract and the articles of association, and the approval documents and certificates issued by the Examination and Approval Authority;

3. each investor's proof of lawful commencement of business or lawful identification;

4. each investor's proof of creditworthiness;

5. the appointment document and identification certificate of the legal representative and the filing documents for directors, managers etc of the enterprise;
6. the enterprise name pre-approval notice; and
7. the proof of the enterprise's residency or business place.

When applying for establishment on a non-legal person FIVCIE, the applicant shall also submit a copy of the articles of association or the partnership agreement of the offshore requisite investor. If the fourth paragraph of Article 7 applies to any investor in the enterprise, a letter of guarantee issued by the affiliated entity stating that it will be jointly and severally liable for such investor's capital contribution obligations shall also be submitted.

All documents described above shall be submitted in the Chinese language. Standard Chinese translation version shall be provided if any such document is prepared in a foreign language. Changes in any registered item of a FIVCIE shall be filed for modification registration with the Registration Authority that originally registered the FIVCIE.

Article 12: All Corporate FIVCIEs checked and approved by the Registration Authority will be issued an Enterprise Legal Person Business Licence and all non-legal person FIVCIEs checked and approved by the Registration Authority will be issued a Business Licence.

The Business Licence shall state the total amount of capital contributions subscribed for by all investors of such non-legal person FIVCIE and the name of the requisite investor(s).

Part Three: Capital contributions and relevant amendments

Article 13: Capital contributions by investors of a non-legal person FIVCIE and the amendments thereof shall be made pursuant to the following provisions:

1. Investors may, within a maximum period of 5 years, make their capital contributions in instalments based on the progress of the venture capital investments made by the FIVCIE. The amount of the capital contribution to be made in each instalment shall be determined independently by the FIVCIE in accordance with the contract of the FIVCIE and the agreements it signed with its investee enterprises. The investors shall agree in the contract of the FIVCIE on the liability and other related measures in connection with an investor's failure to timely contribute its capital.

2. During the existence of a FIVCIE, the investors generally may not reduce the amount of their capital contributions subscribed for. However, the investors may reduce the amount of their subscribed capital if such reduction is agreed by the investors collectively representing more than 50 per cent of the total contributed capital to the FIVCIE and the requisite investor(s), will not cause the FIVCIE to be in breach of the legal requirement of a minimum amount of US$10 million subscribed capital, and is further approved by the Examination and Approval Authority (with exception of the reduction by the investors of their contributed capital pursuant to Item (5) of this article or the cancellation upon expiry of the investment period of any unutilized subscribed capital). Investors shall agree in the contract of the FIVCIE on the conditions, procedures and specific steps for the reduction of the amount of their subscribed capital.

3. During the existence of a FIVCIE, no requisite investor may withdraw from such FIVCIE. If a requisite investor does need to withdraw in special cases, such requisite investor shall first obtain the consent of other investors collectively representing more than 50 per cent of the total contributed capital to the FIVCIE and shall transfer its interests to a new investor qualified under Article 7 hereof. In the case of such a transfer, the contract and the articles of association of the FIVCIE shall be amended accordingly and be submitted for approval by the Examination and Approval Authority. A transfer of the subscribed capital or contributed capital by any investor other than the requisite investor(s) shall be handled in accordance with the provisions of the contract of the FIVCIE and the transferee investor shall meet the applicable requirements under Article 6 hereof. In the case of such a transfer, the contract and the articles of association of the FIVCIE shall all be amended accordingly and be filed with the Examination and Approval Authority for its record.

4. After a FIVCIE has been established, additional investors may be admitted if such admission would be consistent with the provisions of these Regulations and the contract of the FIVCIE and is further consented to by the requisite investor(s). In such case, the contract and the articles of association of the FIVCIE shall be amended accordingly and be filed with the Examination and Approval Authority for its record.

5. Of the income derived by a FIVCIE from sale or other disposition of its equity investment in an investee enterprise, the amount equal to such FIVCIE's original amount of capital contribution to such investee enterprise may be distributed directly to the

investors. Such distribution will constitute a reduction by the investors of the amount of their contributed capital. A FIVCIE shall stipulate in its FIVCIE contract the specific methods for such distributions and shall, at least 30 days prior to any such distribution, submit to the Examination and Approval Authority and the local foreign exchange administration for their record a statement requesting for a corresponding reduction in the total amount of capital contribution, together with its certification that the remaining uncontributed subscribed capital of the FIVCIE investors and any available funds held by the FIVCIE are at least equal to all investment obligation of the FIVCIE then outstanding. However, no such distribution shall operate as a defence to any claim against such FIVCIE that it breached any of its investment obligations.

Article 14: When a non-legal person FIVCIE applies to the Registration Authority for a modification registration, the aforementioned filing registration certificate issued by the Examination and Approval Authority may be submitted as the corresponding approval document.

Article 15: Following each capital contribution by investors of a non-legal person FIVCIE according to the progress of the venture capital investments made by the FIVCIE, the investors shall take the relevant capital contribution verification report and register their capital contributions with the original Registration Authority. The Registration Authority will note in the 'amount of capital contributed' column of the Business Licence the actual amount of capital contributed based on the actual amount contributed. Any non-legal person FIVCIE that has failed to pay or fully pay in the capital subscribed for by its investors within the maximum investment period will be penalized by the Registration Authority in accordance with existing provisions.

Article 16: The capital contributions and the relevant amendments with respect to investors of a corporate FIVCIE shall be handled in accordance with existing provisions.

Part Four: Organizational structure

Article 17: A non-legal person FIVCIE shall establish a joint management committee. A corporate FIVCIE shall establish a board of directors. The joint management committee or the board of directors shall be constituted as provided by investors in the contract and the articles of association of the FIVCIE and shall manage the FIVCIE on behalf of the investors.

Article 18: Management and operating structure shall be established under the joint management committee or the board of directors and shall, within the authority set forth in the contract and the articles of association of the FIVCIE, be responsible for the day-to-day management and operations of the FIVCIE and execute the investment decisions made by the joint management committee or the board of directors.

Article 19: The responsible person(s) of the management and operating structure shall meet the following requirements:

1. possess full capacity for civil acts;

2. have no criminal records;

3. have no record of bad business practices;

4. have work experience in the area of venture capital investment and have no record of violations of rules governing operations; and

5. other requirements relating to their management qualifications required by the Examination and Approval Authority.

Article 20: The management and operating personnel shall periodically report to the board of directors (or the joint management committee) on the following matters:

1. authorized major investment activities;

2. interim and annual operating performance reports and financial reports;

3. other matters required by laws and regulations; and

4. other relevant matters provided in the contract and the articles of association of the FIVCIE.

Article 21: The joint management committee or the board of directors may elect not to establish any management and operating structure, but to contract with a venture capital investment management enterprise or another FIVCIE so that all day-to-day management and operating authority of the FIVCIE will be carried out by such management enterprise or such other FIVCIE. The venture capital investment management enterprise may be a domestic Chinese-funded, a foreign-invested or an offshore venture capital investment management enterprise. Where a venture capital investment management enterprise is engaged, the FIVCIE and the venture capital investment management enterprise shall enter into a management contract pursuant to which the parties will stipulate their respective rights and obligations. Such management contract will become effective only if it has been consented to by all investors and approved by the Examination and Approval Authority.

Article 22: Investors of a FIVCIE may agree in the contract of the FIVCIE, in accordance with customary international practice, on an internal profit allocation mechanism and a performance-based compensation system.

Part Five: Venture capital investment management enterprises

Article 23: The venture capital investment management enterprise engaged to manage a FIVCIE shall meet the following requirements:

1. Its main line of business shall be the management of business invested by the engaging FIVCIE.
2. It has at least three professional management personnel who possess at least 3 years' experience in the venture capital investment area.
3. Its registered capital or total amount of capital contribution is no less than RMB1 million or its equivalent in foreign exchange.
4. It has a sound internal control system.

Article 24: A venture capital investment management enterprise may take the form of a company or the form of a partnership.

Article 25: A venture capital investment management enterprise may be engaged to manage more than one FIVCIE.

Article 26: The venture capital investment management enterprise shall periodically report to the joint management committee or the board of directors of the engaging FIVCIE on all items provided in Article 20 hereof.

Article 27: When applying to establish a foreign-invested venture capital investment management enterprise, the requirements set forth in Article 23 hereof shall be met. The application shall be submitted to the Examination and Approval Authority for approval through the provincial-level department in charge of foreign trade and economic cooperation at the place where the proposed foreign-invested venture capital investment management enterprise will be located. The Examination and Approval Authority will, within 45 days of its receipt of all application materials submitted to it, make a written decision as to whether the application is approved or not. If the application is approved, a Foreign-invested Enterprise Approval Certificate will be issued. Within 1 month of receipt of the Foreign-invested Enterprise Approval Certificate, the approved foreign-invested venture capital investment management enterprise shall apply to register with the Registration Authority on the strength of such Approval Certificate.

Article 28: When applying for establishment of a foreign-invested venture capital investment management enterprise, the following documents shall be submitted to the Examination and Approval Authority:

1. the application for establishment;
2. the contract and articles of association of the foreign-invested venture capital investment management enterprise;
3. a copy of each investor's registration certificate and a copy of its legal representative's certificate; and
4. other relevant documents in support of the application that may be requested by the Examination and Approval Authority.

Article 29: All foreign-invested venture capital investment management enterprises shall contain in their names the words 'venture capital management'. Except for foreign-invested venture capital investment management enterprises, no foreign-invested enterprise may contain in its name the words 'venture capital management'.

Article 30: Within 30 days of the approval date of the management contract, an offshore venture capital investment management enterprise authorized to be engaged in venture capital investment management business within China for FIVCIEs shall apply to the Registration Authority for business registration. When applying for such business registration, the following documents shall be submitted and the offshore venture capital investment management enterprise shall be responsible for the authenticity and the effectiveness of such documents:

1. the registration application signed by the chairman of the board of the offshore venture capital investment management enterprise or the person having the authority to sign on behalf of such offshore venture capital investment management enterprise;
2. the management contract and the approval document issued by the Examination and Approval Authority;

3. the articles of association or the partnership agreement of the offshore venture capital investment management enterprise;
4. the proof of lawful commencement of business of the offshore venture capital investment management enterprise;
5. the certificate of creditworthiness of the offshore venture capital investment management enterprise;
6. the power of attorney for, the résumé and the identification certificate of the person responsible for China projects appointed by the offshore venture capital investment management enterprise; and
7. the proof of the offshore venture capital investment management enterprise's business place in China.

All documents described above shall be submitted in the Chinese language. Standard Chinese translation version shall be provided if any such document is prepared in a foreign language.

Part Six: Operation management

Article 31: FIVCIEs may be engaged in the following businesses:

1. using all of its own capital to make equity investments including in the form of setting up new enterprises, making investment into existing enterprises, acquiring equity interests from transferring investors in existing enterprises and any other form of investment permitted by applicable State laws and regulations;
2. providing consulting services relating to venture capital investment;
3. providing management consulting services to their investee enterprises; and
4. conducting other businesses approved by the Examination and Approval Authority.

Funds of FIVCIEs shall be used primarily to make equity investments in their Investee Enterprises.

Article 32: FIVCIEs may not be engaged in the following activities:

1. investing in areas that are prohibited by the State to be invested by foreign entities;

2. investing, directly or indirectly, in publicly traded stocks and corporate bonds, however, after an investee enterprise becomes publicly listed, shares previously acquired by the FIVCIE concerned shall not be subject to this restriction;

3. investing, directly or indirectly, in real estate not for its self-use;

4. borrowing to make investments;

5. using funds of people other than its investors to make investment;

6. extending loans or guarantees, except for corporate bonds with at least 1 year's maturity and convertible bonds, in each case issued by an investee enterprise of the FIVCIE (this provision however takes no position on whether an investee enterprise may under Chinese law issue such convertible bonds); and

7. any other activity prohibited to be engaged by laws, regulations or provisions of the FIVCIE contract.

Article 33: Investors shall agree on an investment period in their FIVCIE contract during which the FIVCIE may make portfolio investments.

Article 34: A FIVCIE derives its income primarily from the successful sale or other disposition of its equity investments in investee enterprises. When a FIVCIE sells or otherwise disposes of an equity investment in an investee enterprise, it may choose appropriate exit mechanisms in accordance with the law. Such exit mechanisms include:

1. transferring to other investors all or any part of its equity interest in an investee enterprise;

2. entering into an equity interest repurchase agreement pursuant to which the investee enterprise will, in accordance with the law, buy back the equity interest held by the FIVCIE on certain terms and conditions;

3. the investee enterprise going public on domestic or foreign stock exchanges when it meets the listing conditions under laws and administrative regulations. The FIVCIE will then be able to transfer its equity interest in the investee enterprise on the stock market; and

4. other mechanisms permitted by Chinese laws and administrative regulations.

The specific procedures of how an investee enterprise could buy back its equity interest held by a FIVCIE will be separately formulated by the Examination and Approval Authority together with the Registration Authority.

Article 35: FIVCIEs shall declare their income and pay taxes pursuant to State tax law. In the case of a non-legal person FIVCIE, each investor may declare its income and pay its enterprise income tax separately pursuant to relevant provisions of State tax law. Alternatively, the non-legal person FIVCIE may, by application and upon approval, elect to jointly calculate and pay income tax for all investors pursuant to tax laws. The specific administrative procedures on collection of enterprise income tax of a non-legal person FIVCIE will be separately issued by the State Administration of Taxation.

Article 36: Profits and other gains that the foreign investors of a FIVCIE are entitled to receive may be remitted offshore by the FIVCIE using funds deposited in its foreign exchange account or foreign exchange funds purchased from designated foreign exchange banks based on a profit distribution resolution adopted by the joint management committee or the board of directors, auditor's report issued by an accounting firm, foreign investors' proof of inflow of investment funds and capital contribution verification reports, evidence of payment of taxes and the related tax returns (where tax exemption or reduction treatment is applicable, or certification documents issued by relevant tax departments to such effect shall also be provided). Return of the original capital contributions received by foreign investors from a FIVCIE may be remitted out of China by purchase of foreign exchange by application in accordance with the law. The opening and use of foreign exchange accounts, capital adjustments, and other foreign exchange receipts and payments of a corporate FIVCIE shall be handled in accordance with existing provisions on foreign exchange administration. Provisions on foreign exchange administration concerning non-legal person FIVCIEs will be formulated separately by the State Administration of Foreign Exchange.

Article 37: Investors shall agree on a term for the FIVCIE in the contract and the articles of association of the FIVCIE, which generally shall not exceed 12 years. Upon expiration, the term may be extended if approved by the Examination and Approval Authority.

Upon approval by the Examination and Approval Authority, a FIVCIE may be dissolved before its term expires and its contract and articles of association will be terminated early. No such approval is required, however, if all investments of a non-legal person FIVCIE have been sold or otherwise disposed of, the debts of such FIVCIE have been discharged and the remaining assets of such FIVCIE have been distributed to its investors, but a written notice of any such dissolution shall be given to the Examination and Approval Authority for its record by such FIVCIE at least 30 days before the dissolution is to become effective.

All dissolving FIVCIEs shall be liquidated in accordance with relevant regulations.

Article 38: A FIVCIE shall apply to the original Registration Authority for cancellation registration within 30 days after completion of its liquidation. When applying for cancellation registration, the following documents shall be submitted and the FIVCIE shall be responsible for the authenticity and the effectiveness of such documents:

1. the application for cancellation registration signed by chairman of the board, the responsible person of the joint management committee, or the responsible person of the liquidation committee;

2. a resolution of the board of directors or the joint management committee;

3. the liquidation report;

4. the certificates for cancellation registration issued by tax authority and customs;

5. the approval documents or the filing registration certificates issued by the Examination and Approval Authority; and

6. other documents required to be submitted pursuant to the provisions of laws and administrative regulations.

A FIVCIE will terminate upon check and approval by the Registration Authority of its cancellation registration. The joint and several liability assumed by the requisite investor(s) of a non-legal person FIVCIE shall not be exempted as a result of termination of such FIVCIE.

Part Seven: Examination and regulation

Article 39: Investment activities by FIVCIEs within China shall be handled with reference to the provisions of *Guiding the Direction of Foreign Investment Provisions and the Foreign Investment Industrial Guidance Catalogue.*

Article 40: When investing in any investee enterprise that falls into the encouraged or permitted industry category, a FIVCIE shall file a report for record with the authorized department in charge of foreign trade and economic cooperation of the place where such investee enterprise is located. The authorized local department in charge of foreign trade and economic cooperation shall complete a filing and verification procedure and issue to such investee enterprise a Foreign-invested Enterprise Approval Certificate within 15 days of receipt of the materials filed with it. The investee enterprise will then apply to register with the Registration Authority on the strength of such Approval Certificate. The Registration Authority will decide whether it will register or refuse to register in accordance with relevant laws and administrative regulations. Upon approval for registration, a Foreign-invested Enterprise Legal Person Business Licence will be issued.

Article 41: When investing in any investee enterprise that falls into the restricted industry category, a FIVCIE shall apply to the provincial department in charge of foreign trade and economic cooperation where the proposed investee enterprise is located and submit the following documents:

1. a declaration from the FIVCIE that it has adequate amount of funds for the proposed investment;
2. a copy of the FIVCIE's approval certificate and business licence; and
3. the contract and articles of association of the proposed investee enterprise that the FIVCIE has signed with other investors in the proposed investee enterprise.

The provincial-level department in charge of foreign trade and economic cooperation shall, within 45 days of receipt of such application, decide by a written response whether or not it approves the proposed investment. If the investment is approved, a Foreign-invested Enterprise Approval Certificate will be issued. The investee enterprise shall then apply for registration with the Registration Authority based on such written response and the Foreign-invested Enterprise Approval Certificate. The Registration Authority will decide whether it will register or refuse to register in accordance with relevant laws and administrative regulations. For any investment authorized for registration, a Foreign-invested Enterprise Legal Person Business Licence will be issued.

Article 42: Investments by FIVCIEs within China in service areas that are gradually liberalized for foreign investments shall be examined and approved in accordance with relevant State regulations.

Article 43: Any increase or transfer by a FIVCIE of its investments in any investee enterprise shall also be handled in accordance with the procedures set forth under Articles 40, 41 and 42.

Article 44: A FIVCIE shall file a report with the Examination and Approval Authority for its record within 1 month after its completion of the applicable procedures set forth under Articles 40, 41, 42 and 43.

Article 45: Each FIVCIE shall in addition file a report in each March on its fund raising and utilization information for the last year with the Examination and Approval Authority for its record. The Examination and Approval Authority shall, within 5 working days after receipt of such documents filed by a FIVCIE for its record, issue to the FIVCIE a filing registration certificate which will constitute one of the mandatory documents when the FIVCIE is called for the joint annual inspection. Failure to comply with the filing requirements set forth in this article will be penalized accordingly by the Examination and Approval Authority after consultation with relevant departments of the State Council.

Article 46: An investee enterprise will be entitled to the preferential treatments available to foreign-invested enterprises if the actual capital contribution held by foreign investors of the investing FIVCIE or the combined equity percentage of foreign investors of such FIVCIE and all other foreign investors is at least 25 per cent of the investee enterprise's registered capital. Otherwise, the investee enterprise will not be entitled to the preferential treatments available to foreign-invested enterprises.

Article 47: If an established domestic enterprise has Chinese natural person investor(s) and is converted into a foreign-invested enterprise as a result of a FIVCIE's investment, such Chinese natural person(s) may continue to keep its or their shareholder(s)' status as Chinese natural person(s) in such enterprise.

Article 48: If any responsible person of the management and operating structure of a FIVCIE or any responsible person of a venture capital investment management enterprise is engaged in illegal practice, liability will be pursued in accordance with the law; and in serious cases, such persons shall also be prohibited from conducting venture capital investments and the related investment management activities.

Part Eight: Supplementary provisions

Article 49: Establishment of FIVCIEs in mainland China by investors from Hong Kong Special Administrative Region, Macao Special Administrative Region and Taiwan area shall be handled with reference to these Regulations.

Article 50: The Ministry of Foreign Trade and Economic Cooperation, the Ministry of Science and Technology, the State Administration of Industry and Commerce, the State Administration of Taxation and the State Administration of Foreign Exchange shall be responsible for the interpretation of these Regulations.

Article 51: These Regulations shall take effect as of 1 March 2003. The Tentative Rules on Establishment of Foreign-invested Venture Capital Investment Enterprises jointly issued by the Ministry of Foreign Trade and Economic Cooperation, the Ministry of Science and Technology and the State Administration for Industry and Commerce on 28 August 2001 shall be repealed simultaneously.

Appendix B

Interim Provisions on the Acquisition of Domestic Enterprises by Foreign Investors

Order No 3 of 2003 of the Ministry of Foreign Trade and Economic Cooperation, the State Administration of Taxation, the State Administration for Industry and Commerce and the State Administration of Foreign Exchange.

The Interim Provisions on the Acquisition of Domestic Enterprises by Foreign Investors, considered and adopted at the First Ministerial Meeting of the Ministry of Foreign Trade and Economic Cooperation of the People's Republic of China on 2 January 2003, are hereby promulgated and shall be implemented from 12 April 2003.

Ministry of Foreign Trade and Economic Cooperation (now Ministry of Commerce)
State Administration of Taxation (SAT)
State Administration for Industry and Commerce (SAIC)
State Administration of Foreign Exchange (SAFE)
7 March 2003

Article 1: These Provisions are formulated in accordance with the laws and administrative regulations on foreign-invested enterprises and other related laws and administrative regulations to promote and standardize investment in China by foreign investors, introduce advanced technology and management experience from outside China, raise the level of utilization of foreign investment, achieve rational allocation of resources, guarantee employment, and maintain fair competition and national economic security.

Article 2: The acquisition of a domestic enterprise by a foreign investor as referred to in these Provisions means a foreign investor, by agreement, purchasing the equity interest of a shareholder in a non-foreign-invested enterprise in China (hereinafter referred to as a 'domestic company') or subscribing for an increase in the registered capital of a domestic company, resulting in the conversion of the domestic company into a foreign-invested enterprise (hereinafter referred to as a 'share acquisition'); or a foreign investor establishing a foreign-invested enterprise that, by agreement, purchases assets of a domestic enterprise and operates such assets, or a foreign investor, by agreement, purchasing assets of a domestic enterprise and investing such assets in the establishment of a foreign-invested enterprise that operates such assets (hereinafter referred to as an 'asset acquisition').

Article 3: The acquisition of domestic enterprises by foreign investors shall comply with the laws, administrative regulations and departmental regulations of China, adhere to the principles of fairness and reasonableness, equal consideration and good faith, and not cause excessive concentration, eliminate or restrict competition, disrupt social or economic order or harm the public interest.

Article 4: The acquisition of a domestic enterprise by a foreign investor shall comply with the requirements of the laws, administrative regulations and departmental regulations of China regarding investor qualifications and industrial policies.

Pursuant to the *Catalogue for Guiding Foreign Investment in Industry*, in industries where foreign investors are not permitted to establish wholly foreign-owned enterprises, an acquisition must not result in a foreign investor holding all of the equity in an enterprise; in industries where the Chinese party is required to have a controlling interest or a relative controlling interest, the Chinese party shall retain the controlling interest or relative controlling interest in the enterprise following the acquisition; and in industries where foreign investors are prohibited from operating, foreign investors must not acquire enterprises.

Article 5: A foreign-invested enterprise established upon acquisition of a domestic enterprise by a foreign investor must be approved by the approval authority and either change its registration or register with the registration authority pursuant to these Provisions. The proportion of capital contributions by foreign investors to the registered capital of a postacquisition foreign-invested enterprise generally must be no lower than 25 per cent.

Where the proportion of capital contributions by foreign investors is lower than 25 per cent, examination, approval and registration must be carried out pursuant to the current examination and approval and registration procedures for establishing foreign-invested enterprises, except where laws or administrative regulations provide otherwise. When the approval authority issues the foreign-invested enterprise approval certificate, it shall mark the words 'foreign investment proportion lower than 25 per cent' thereon. When the registration authority issues the foreign-invested enterprise business licence, it shall mark the words 'foreign investment proportion lower than 25 per cent' thereon.

Article 6: The approval authority hereunder shall be the Ministry of Foreign Trade and Economic Cooperation of the People's Republic of China (MOFTEC) or the authority in charge of foreign trade and economic relations at the provincial level (the 'Provincial-level Approval Authority'). The registration authority shall be the State Administration for Industry and Commerce of the People's Republic of China or its authorized local administrations for industry and commerce.

Where, pursuant to laws, administrative regulations and departmental regulations, a postacquisition foreign-invested enterprise is in a specially designated category or industry requiring examination and approval by MOFTEC, the Provincial-level Approval Authority shall transfer the application documents to MOFTEC and MOFTEC shall decide whether or not to grant approval pursuant to law.

Article 7: In the case of a share acquisition by a foreign investor, the post-acquisition foreign-invested enterprise shall succeed to the obligatory rights and liabilities of the acquired domestic company.

In the case of an asset acquisition by a foreign investor, the domestic enterprise that sells its assets shall undertake its original obligatory rights and liabilities. The foreign investor, the acquired domestic enterprise, its creditors and other relevant parties may reach a separate agreement with respect to the disposition of the obligatory rights and liabilities of the acquired domestic enterprise. However, such agreement shall not harm the rights and interests of third parties or the public interest. The agreement for disposition of the obligatory rights and liabilities must be submitted to the approval authority.

A domestic enterprise that sells its assets shall issue a notice to its creditors and post an announcement in a nationally-distributed newspaper of provincial level or higher within ten days of the date on which the resolution concerning the sale of assets is made. Creditors shall have the right, within ten days of the date of receipt of such notice or the date on which the announcement is posted, to request the domestic enterprise whose assets will be sold to provide corresponding security.

Article 8: The parties to the acquisition shall determine the transaction price on the basis of the results of an appraisal by an asset appraisal institution of the value of the equity interest to be assigned or the assets proposed to be sold. The parties to the acquisition may agree on an asset appraisal institution established in China in accordance with law. Generally applied international appraisal methods shall be adopted for the asset appraisal.

When the acquisition of a domestic enterprise by a foreign investor results in a change in an equity interest created by the investment of state-owned assets or a transfer of state-owned assets or property, appraisal shall be carried out in accordance with the regulations concerning state-owned assets administration to determine the transaction price.

It is prohibited for equity interests to be assigned or assets to be sold at a price clearly lower than the appraisal results or for capital to be covertly transferred outside of China.

Article 9: Where a foreign-invested enterprise is established upon acquisition of a domestic enterprise by a foreign investor, the foreign investor must pay the full consideration to the shareholders assigning equity interests or to the domestic enterprise selling its assets within three months of the date on which the foreign-invested enterprise business licence is issued. Where it is necessary to make an extension under special circumstances, following approval by the approval authority, 60 per cent or more of the full consideration must be paid within six months and the full price must be paid within one year of the date on which the foreign-invested enterprise business licence is issued. Benefits shall be distributed in accordance with the ratios of actual paid-up capital contributions.

In the case of a share acquisition by a foreign investor, where there will be an increase in the registered capital of a post-acquisition foreign-invested enterprise, the investors shall stipulate the period for making capital contributions in the contract and articles of association of the proposed foreign-invested enterprise. Where lump sum payment of the capital contributions is stipulated, the investors shall pay in full within six months of the date on which the foreign-invested enterprise business licence is issued. Where payment of capital contributions by instalments is stipulated, the first instalment by the investors must not be lower than 15 per cent of their respective subscribed capital contributions and must be paid within three months of the date on which the foreign-invested enterprise business licence is issued.

In the case of an asset acquisition by a foreign investor, the investor shall stipulate the period for making capital contributions in the contract and articles of association of the proposed foreign-invested enterprise. Where a foreign-invested enterprise is established, and such foreign-invested enterprise, by agreement, purchases the assets of a domestic enterprise and operates such assets, the investor shall pay the portion of the capital contribution equal to the asset price within the price payment period stipulated in the first paragraph of this Article.

The period for paying the remaining portion of the capital contribution shall be agreed in conformity with the manner stipulated in the second paragraph of this Article.

When a foreign investor acquires a domestic enterprise and establishes a foreign-invested enterprise, and the foreign investor's proportion of capital contributions is lower than 25 per cent, then where the investor contributes cash, the capital contribution must be paid in full within three months of the date on which the foreign-invested enterprise business licence is issued; and where the investor contributes in kind or in industrial property rights etc, the capital contribution must be paid in full within six months of the date on which the foreign-invested enterprise business licence is issued.

The means of payment shall conform to relevant state laws and administrative regulations. Where a foreign investor pays in shares for which it has the right of disposal or in lawfully held Renminbi assets, it must obtain approval from the State Administration of Foreign Exchange.

Article 10: Where a foreign investor, by agreement, purchases the equity interest of a shareholder in a domestic company, then after the domestic company is converted into a foreign-invested enterprise, the registered capital of such foreign-invested enterprise shall be the registered capital of the original domestic company, and the foreign investor's proportion of capital contributions shall be the proportion of the original registered capital represented by the equity interest that it purchased.

Where the registered capital of a domestic company in which an equity interest is acquired is also increased, the registered capital of the post-acquisition foreign-invested enterprise shall be the sum of the registered capital of the original domestic company and the increased amount of registered capital. The foreign investor and the original investors in the acquired domestic company shall determine their respective proportions of contributions to registered capital on the basis of the appraisal of the domestic company's assets.

Where a foreign investor subscribes for an increase in the registered capital of a domestic company, then after the domestic company is converted into a foreign-invested enterprise, the registered capital of such foreign-invested enterprise shall be the sum of the registered capital of the original domestic company and the increased amount of registered capital.

The foreign investor and the original shareholders in the acquired domestic company shall determine their respective proportions of contributions to the registered capital of the foreign-invested enterprise on the basis of the appraisal of the domestic company's assets.

Where the Chinese natural persons are shareholders in a domestic company in which an equity interest has been acquired and they have enjoyed shareholder status in the original company for one year or more, they may, with approval, continue as Chinese investors in the foreign-invested enterprise established following the conversion.

Article 11: In the case of a share acquisition by a foreign investor, the maximum total amount of investment of the post-acquisition foreign-invested enterprise shall be determined on the basis of the following ratios: (1) where the registered capital is less than US$2.1 million, the total amount of investment must not exceed 70 per cent of the registered capital; (2) where the registered capital is between US$2.1 million and US$5 million, the total amount of investment must not exceed twice the registered capital; (3) where the registered capital is between US$5 million and US$12 million, the total amount of investment must not exceed 2.5 times the registered capital; (4) and where the registered capital is US$12 million or more, the total amount of investment must not exceed three times the registered capital.

Article 12: In the case of a share acquisition by a foreign investor, the investor shall submit the following documents to the approval authority that, based on the total amount of investment of the post-acquisition foreign-invested enterprise, has the corresponding authority to approve:

1. a unanimous resolution of the shareholders of the domestic limited liability company to be acquired, agreeing to the share acquisition by the foreign investor, or a resolution of a general meeting of shareholders of the domestic joint stock limited company to be acquired, agreeing to the share acquisition by the foreign investor;

2. an application letter for the conversion of the domestic company to be acquired into a foreign-invested enterprise pursuant to law;

3. the contract and articles of association of the post-acquisition foreign-invested enterprise;

4. the agreement for the foreign investor to purchase an equity interest from a shareholder in the domestic company or to subscribe for an increase in the registered capital of the domestic company;

5. the financial audit report for the latest financial year of the domestic company to be acquired;

6. the identification documents or licence to do business and a certification of creditworthiness of the investor(s);

7. an explanation of the particulars of the enterprises in which the domestic company to be acquired has invested;

8. the business licence (duplicate) of the domestic company to be acquired and the enterprises in which it has invested;

9. the plan for placement of the employees of the domestic company to be acquired;

10. the documents required to be submitted under Articles 7 and 19 hereof.

Where the business scope, scale or acquisition of land use rights of the post-acquisition foreign-invested enterprise involve permits from other relevant government departments, the relevant permit documents must also be submitted.

The business scopes of the companies in which the domestic company to be acquired has invested shall comply with the requirements of relevant foreign investment industrial polices, and where they do not comply, shall be adjusted.

Article 13: The law of China shall govern the equity purchase agreement and the agreement to increase the registered capital of a domestic company as specified in Article 12 hereof. Such agreements shall include the following main content:

1. the particulars of each party to the agreement, including its name and place of domicile and the name, position, nationality etc of its legal representative;

2. the share and price of the equity interest to be purchased or of the subscribed increase in registered capital;

3. the term and manner for performance of the agreement;

4. the rights and obligations of each party to the agreement;

5. liability for breach of contract and dispute resolution;

6. the time and location of signature of the agreement.

Article 14: In the case of an asset acquisition by a foreign investor, the total amount of investment of the proposed foreign-invested enterprise shall be determined based on the transaction price for the purchased assets and the actual scale of production and operations.

The ratio of registered capital to total amount of investment of the proposed foreign-invested enterprise shall comply with relevant regulations.

Article 15: In the case of an asset acquisition by a foreign investor, the investor shall submit the following documents to the approval authority that, based on the total amount of investment, enterprise form and industry of the proposed foreign-invested enterprise, and pursuant to the laws, administrative regulations and departmental regulations on the establishment of foreign-invested enterprises, has the corresponding authority to approve:

1. a resolution by the person who holds the property rights in the domestic enterprise or by the authoritative body of the domestic enterprise agreeing to the sale of assets;
2. an application letter for establishment of the foreign-invested enterprise;
3. the contract and articles of association of the proposed foreign-invested enterprise;
4. the asset purchase agreement signed by the proposed foreign-invested enterprise and the domestic enterprise, or the asset purchase agreement signed by the foreign investor and the domestic enterprise;
5. the articles of association and business licence (duplicate) of the domestic enterprise to be acquired;
6. proof that the acquired domestic enterprise has notified and made a public announcement to creditors;
7. the identification documents or licence to do business and a certification of creditworthiness of the investor(s);
8. the plan for placement of the employees of the domestic enterprise to be acquired;
9. the documents required to be submitted under Articles 7 and 19 hereof.

Where the purchase and operation of the assets of a domestic enterprise pursuant to the foregoing provisions involve permits from other relevant government departments, the relevant permit documents must also be submitted.

Where a foreign investor, by agreement, purchases the assets of a domestic enterprise and invests such assets in the establishment of a foreign-invested enterprise, such assets must not be used to carry out business activities prior to the establishment of the foreign-invested enterprise.

Article 16: The law of China shall govern the asset purchase agreement specified in Article 15 hereof. Such agreement shall include the following main content:

1. the particulars of each party to the agreement including its name and place of domicile and the name, position, nationality etc of its legal representative;
2. a list and the prices of the assets to be purchased;
3. the term and manner for performance of the agreement;
4. the rights and obligations of each party to the agreement;
5. liability for breach of contract and dispute resolution;
6. the time and location of signature of the agreement.

Article 17: Where a foreign-invested enterprise is established upon acquisition of a domestic enterprise by a foreign investor, the approval authority shall decide whether or not to grant approval within 30 days of receiving all the documents that are required to be submitted, except where Article 20 hereof stipulates otherwise. Where the approval authority decides to grant approval, it shall issue a foreign-invested enterprise approval certificate.

Where a foreign investor, by agreement, purchases the equity interest of a shareholder in a domestic company and the approval authority decides to grant approval, it shall simultaneously copy the relevant approval documents to the local foreign exchange administration authorities of the assignor and the domestic company. The local foreign exchange administration authority of the assignor shall handle the procedures for the receipt of foreign exchange from foreign investment by the assignor, and shall issue a foreign investment foreign exchange registration certificate to show that the foreign investor has paid in full the consideration for the share acquisition.

Article 18: In the case of an asset acquisition by a foreign investor, the investor shall apply to register with the registration authorities within 30 days of the date on which it receives the foreign-invested enterprise approval certificate, and shall obtain a foreign-invested enterprise business licence.

In the case of a share acquisition by a foreign investor, the acquired domestic company shall apply to its original registration authority to change its registration and obtain a foreign-invested enterprise business licence in accordance with these Provisions. Where the original registration authority does not have registration jurisdiction, it shall transfer the application documents, together with the domestic company's registration files, to the registration authority with jurisdiction within ten days of the date of receiving the documents. When the acquired domestic company applies to change its registration, it shall submit the following documents, and shall be responsible for the authenticity and validity thereof:

1. an application for a change in registration;
2. a resolution of the shareholders' meeting (general meeting) of the acquired domestic company, made pursuant to the Company Law of the People's Republic of China and the company's articles of association, concerning the assignment of equity interest or increase in registered capital;
3. the agreement for the foreign investor to purchase the equity interest of a shareholder in the domestic company or to subscribe for an increase in the registered capital of the domestic company;
4. the company's amended articles of association or a document amending the original articles of association and, where required by law, the foreign-invested enterprise contract;
5. the foreign-invested enterprise approval certificate;
6. the identification documents or licence to do business and a certification of creditworthiness of the foreign investor(s);
7. the amended name list of the board of directors, a document recording the names and places of domicile of the new directors and the documents for appointing the new directors;
8. other relevant documents and certificates as stipulated by the State Administration for Industry and Commerce.

Where state-owned equity interests are assigned or a foreign investor subscribes for an increase in the registered capital of a company the equity of which is state-owned, the approval documents shall also be submitted to the department in charge of economics and trade.

The investor shall carry out registration procedures at the tax, customs and management, foreign exchange control and other relevant departments within 30 days of the date on which the foreign-invested enterprise business licence is issued.

Article 19: Where a foreign-invested enterprise acquires a domestic enterprise and any of the following circumstances are present, the investor shall report such circumstances to MOFTEC and the State Administration for Industry and Commerce:

1. any party to the acquisition has operating revenue from the Chinese market in excess of RMB1.5 billion in that year;

2. it has acquired a total of more than ten enterprises in the same or related industries in the past year;

3. any party to the acquisition has a market share in China of 20 per cent or more; or

4. as a result of the acquisition, any party to the acquisition would achieve a market share in China of 25 per cent or more.

If the above conditions are not met, MOFTEC or the State Administration for Industry and Commerce, in response to a request by a domestic enterprise with a competitive relationship, a related functional department or an industry association, may nonetheless require the foreign investor to file a report where they believe that the market share related to the acquisition by the foreign investor is excessively large or that there exist other key factors which seriously affect market competition or the people's livelihood and national economic security etc.

The above-mentioned parties to the acquisition include affiliates of the foreign investor.

Article 20: Where the acquisition of a domestic enterprise by a foreign investor involves one of the circumstances set out in Article 19 hereof, and MOFTEC and the State Administration for Industry and Commerce believe that it may cause excessive concentration, impair fair competition or harm the interests of consumers, then within 90 days of the date on which they have received all the documents that are required to be submitted, they shall jointly or, after consultation, independently convene a hearing with the relevant departments, organs, enterprises and other interested parties, and decide in accordance with law whether or not to grant approval.

Article 21: Under any of the following circumstances, a party to a foreign acquisition shall submit an acquisition plan to MOFTEC and the State Administration for Industry and Commerce prior to the public announcement of the acquisition plan or at the same time as submitting it to the competent bodies in their own countries. MOFTEC and the State Administration for Industry and Commerce shall examine whether or not the acquisition will cause excessive concentration in the domestic market, impair domestic fair competition or damage the interests of domestic consumers, and make a decision on whether or not to consent.

1. The foreign acquirer has assets in China of RMB3 billion or more.
2. The foreign acquirer has operating revenue from the China market of RMB1.5 billion or more that year.
3. The foreign acquirer and its affiliates have a market share in China of 20 per cent or more.
4. As a result of the foreign acquisition, the foreign acquirer and its affiliates would achieve a market share in China of 25 per cent or more.
5. As a result of the foreign acquisition, the foreign acquirer would directly or indirectly have equity interests in more than 15 foreign-invested enterprises in the same or related industries in China.

Article 22: Where one of the following circumstances is present in an acquisition, the parties to the acquisition may apply to MOFTEC or the State Administration for Industry and Commerce to examine whether they are eligible for an exemption:

1. Improvement of the conditions for fair competition in the market.
2. Restructuring of loss-making enterprises and guaranteeing employment.
3. Introduction of advanced technology and management talent and enabling the enterprise to raise its international competitiveness.
4. Improvement of the environment.

Article 23: The documents submitted by the investor shall be categorized and have a table of contents attached in accordance with regulations. All the documents that are required to be submitted shall be written in Chinese.

Article 24: These Provisions shall apply to the acquisition of domestic enterprises by investment holding companies established by foreign investors in China in accordance with law.

The current laws and administrative regulations on foreign-invested enterprises and the Several Provisions on Changes in the Equity Interests of Shareholders of Foreign-Invested Enterprises shall apply to share acquisitions of foreign-invested enterprises in China by foreign investors. Where such laws and regulations are silent, reference shall be made to these Provisions.

Article 25: The acquisition of enterprises in other regions of China by investors from the Hong Kong Special Administrative Region, the Macao Special Administrative Region and the Taiwan region shall be handled with reference to these Provisions.

Article 26: These Provisions shall be implemented from 12 April 2003.

Appendix C

Chinese Overseas Students[1]

In spite of the frosty winter in China and the global economic winter, different regions in China are putting out the welcome mat to win overseas students back to China. Recruitment conferences, exhibitions showing off the fruits of returnees' research projects, seminars on preferential policies, are all being conducted especially for these returnees in the new year. Chinese overseas students are finding themselves wooed by the motherland. In today's market analysis, we will take a look at how China is providing a sound all-round environment for these returnees.

VIPs from both political and business circles, congratulate each other on their business success and award prizes for efficient management of companies. This is not an ordinary new year party. The Overseas Students Pioneer Park of Zhongguancun Haidian Science Park is celebrating its fifth birthday. The park mainly aims at providing a platform for overseas Chinese students to start their own business and incubates them for bigger and greater things.

Wang Shiqi, Deputy Director of the Zhongguancun Overseas Students Pioneer Park, stated that 'the Zhongguancun district is in urgent need for talents, who have both advanced technologies and new management concepts. It's obvious that Chinese overseas students have grasped both. The country and government are hoping they can come back, and use their knowledge to benefit the country's development'.

After five years of operation, the Zhongguancun Overseas Students Pioneer Park has embraced over 260 returnees, who have set up more than 260 enterprises in the area of 50,000 square metres. So far, 22 enterprises have been successfully incubated. In addition, the park construction also got a helping hand from the local government who poured in around US$4 million. The municipality also issued preferential policies to establish a sound business environment for overseas students.

---

[1] Source: China Central Television (CCTV)

Zhao Feng, Director of the Beijing Municipal Service Center for Scholarly Exchange, explained that 'to enact policies for the start-ups and to construct a healthy business environment is our main task. In 2000, the Beijing municipality issued a regulation on how to encourage overseas students to come to Beijing starting up companies. The announcement tried to solve problems overseas students encountered in setting up business. Some of these initiatives are carried out for the first time throughout the country'.

The Government has had a keen eye on these returnees. So far, more than 60 overseas student pioneer parks have been set up around China. The number of enterprises established by these returnees reached 4000 with an annual output exceeding US$1 billion. Their success has also attracted overseas companies' attention. Chinese talents are well known for their business acumen. Many overseas students are attracted back to the country because China's economy is in the stage of rapid growth. Many international companies, in this case, choose these returnees to bring their international investments to China.

Lai Seckk Khui, President of the Times Publishing Ltd, Singapore, said that 'Chinese talents in business are very famous around the world. The Chinese students increasingly find China an attractive place to return to after their education overseas, because China is a very big market, and it's a market which will eventually become very strong in many other manufacturing [sectors]'.

The tide of returning Chinese overseas students has also roused the competition among human resource service companies. Many worldwide recruitment companies also put Chinese overseas 'talent hunting' as their top priority. According to statistics, so far, over 400,000 Chinese have gone abroad for further education. Over 90 per cent have been granted masters degree or doctorate. Among them, 80 per cent want to return. Over 140,000 students have come back and many have achieved success. The talent flow has undoubtedly provides opportunities for headhunting companies.

Paul C Reilly, Chairman of Korn/Ferry International, stated that these graduates 'come back to China, bringing their international experiences to local companies. What's been a big issue is that some [settle in] very well, but some [have] adapt[ed] to the western style [and] have to handle the operation in Chinese companies. So it's not a perfect fact for all. But for many companies, it's a great way to [encourage] talents'.

The returning of Chinese overseas students has got much support from so many circles. Is it right or not? This special phenomenon has evoked controversy. Returnees' activities and ideas have also met with disagreement from some experts. Under such circumstances, the China Investment Press initiated a discussion, aiming at boosting society's understanding of these returnees. In their chief editor, Guo Hong's opinion, the key problem is how to correctly utilize these returnees' skills and let them fully contribute to the country. Guo explained that 'through this activity, we can introduce some successful returnees to the society, and let the society know their advanced international experiences. Especially at this moment when economies in America and Japan are in recession, many overseas students have come back. These returnees know little about the current conditions in the country. As media, we are under the charge of the nation's economic departments. It's up to us to introduce them to the country's investment environment and polices'.

Although controversies exist, many overseas students have insisted on coming back, not only because there is great business potential ahead, but also because they are Chinese. For the returnees, their beloved motherland is their main reason to choose the road back home. As outlined by Daniel Xu, a returnee with Blue Asset Canada international Inc: 'I've been in Canada for five years. During that period, we've developed a lot of new products, technologies. Our Canadian partners wanted to invest huge amount of money to set new business. The products are good, but we belong to China, we are Chinese, we should put this product in China, not in [an]other country'.

Perhaps that's one of the main reasons why so many overseas students are aspired to return. Actually, at the same time that they bring back the knowledge and culture of other nations, and they have already instilled elements of China's knowledge and culture into these foreign areas. The talents exchange has brought benefits for both China and the world. Frederick C Dubee, Global Compact of the Executive Office of Secretary General UN agrees: 'It's good for the world and for China. Of course Chinese students return with very interesting knowledge and very interesting experiences. They are even creating bridges between their friends and knowledge they have learned outside China to bring that to China. At the same time, they create bridges the other way, help a lot of Chinese ideas, influence and culture go to the rest of the world. What I think is we have to do more of this'.

The Chinese government is putting much emphasis on setting up this win-win environment. An investment market with a standardized management and transparent legal system will be gradually formed. This can provide more development space for overseas students coming back to China. During the transitional period of China's global integration, these returnees are becoming a necessary part of China's human talent pool. Fan Hengshan, Director of the Economy System Reform Office, clarified that 'if we have a healthy environment for starting up companies, many overseas Chinese students will be glad to return. At this time, the country is in urgent need for talents and investment, especially those who have deep understanding of both global market rules and China's characteristics. Returnees' coming back can benefit both themselves and the country. By serving the country, they can find the best model of generating profits. Thus, we can get a win-win situation'.

Entering the 21st century, the lure of China as an investment destination grows in the eyes of international investors, especially as the country becomes a member of the World Trade Organization. In the years to come, there are still many areas in both the economy and society that need to be developed. This is a golden time for overseas students to return and find a platform to start new careers or expand existing businesses. China is embracing more and more returnees and these engineers of the future will play a key role in changing the social and economic landscape.

Appendix D

President Calls on Students Abroad to Contribute More to Nation[1]

On Wednesday, Chinese President Hu Jintao called on Chinese students abroad to contribute more wisdom and strength to the all-round construction of a better-off society in their motherland.

Hu, also general secretary of the Communist Party of China (CPC) Central Committee, said students studying abroad should link their fate with that of the CPC and the Chinese nation, keep pace with the times, study harder still and work whole-heartedly for the service of their country.

Hu made these remarks while addressing a ceremony marking the 90th anniversary of the Western Returned Students Association (WRSA) in the Great Hall of the People.

The WRSA boasts more than 11,000 members across the globe and the event attracted high-ranking officials like Jia Qinglin, Zeng Qinghong and Huang Ju, all members of the Standing Committee of the Political Bureau of the CPC Central Committee, the CPC's top decision-making body.

Speaking highly of the tremendous contributions made by returned students through China's history, the president said practice had proved that students returning from overseas had lofty ambitions to contribute to the motherland, to the people and to the Chinese nation.

Students returning from overseas were China's valuable assets, an important component part of China's human resources and a vital force propelling China's social development and rejuvenation, Hu acknowledged.

---

[1] *People's Daily* 10 October 2003.

The Chinese government encouraged its young people to go abroad for education and learn advanced science and technology from other countries as an important way to foster qualified personnel.

The Chinese central government had decided to implement the strategy of building up and invigorating the country through training more gifted people, he said, adding this would create more opportunities for returned students to explore their careers.

Hu also urged CPC committees and governments at all levels to realize the major significance of helping returned students, calling on them to conscientiously implement the relevant policies and attract more students to participate in domestic construction or to serve the country in a variety of ways.

The ceremony, attracting more than 3000 members of the WRSA, was presided over by WRSA president, Ding Shisun, who is also vice-chairman of the Standing Committee of the Chinese National People Congress (NPC).

WRSA vice-president Han Qide, vice-chairman of the NPC Standing Committee, delivered a working report, saying that the WRSA would organize more students studying abroad to return to serve their country in varied ways and contribute more to the building of a better-off society in their motherland.

On Wednesday, the WRSA also sponsored a forum on career prospects for students abroad.

Appendix E

Term Sheet Sample

24 July 2000

The intent of this Term Sheet is to describe some key terms of the proposed agreement between XX Capital and XX Inc. (the 'Company')

This Term Sheet is not a legally binding agreement between XX Capital and the Company with respect to the subject matter hereof, except for the paragraph immediately below under the heading, 'Confidentiality'. A legally binding agreement between the parties will not occur unless and until all necessary corporate approvals have been obtained by both of the parties, and the parties have negotiated, approved, executed and delivered the appropriate definitive agreements. Until execution and delivery of such definitive agreements, both parties shall have the absolute right to terminate all negotiations for any reason without liability thereof.

Confidentiality

The terms and conditions described in this Term Sheet, including its existence shall be confidential information and shall not be disclosed to any third party, unless required by applicable law. In addition, during the closing period of this contemplating investment by XX Capital into the Company, except for any potential co-investors that will follow this Term Sheet, the Company warrants that it will not solicit external offers from any third parties for an exclusive period of 30 days.

Amount of Financing:	Up to US$1 million from XX Capital as part of an integrated financing round that would include up to US$4 million from other investors mutually acceptable to XX Capital and the Company.
Types of Securities:	Up to Series A Preferred Shares ('Series A Preferred Shares'), initially convertible into an equal number of the Company's Common Shares, par value US$0.001 each (the 'Common Shares'). The Common Shares issuable upon conversion of the Series A Preferred Shares shall

represent 20 per cent of the Company's total issued share capital (inclusive of the Common Shares issuable upon conversion of the Series A Preferred Shares), including all outstanding options and warrants on an as-exercised basis.

Purchase Price: Series A Preferred Shares: US$1.667 per share (the 'Purchase Price'). This represents a fully diluted pre-money valuation of US$20 million for the Company.

Closing Date: Before 20 August 2000, or as soon as practicable (the 'Closing Date').

Closing Condition:
(i) Completion of legal and financial due diligence;

(ii) Completion of satisfactory documentation;

(iii) All required approvals and consents including but not limited to the approval from the investment committee of XX Capital have been obtained;

(iv) All required approvals and consents including but not limited to the approval from the investment committee of have been obtained;

(v) Execution of Service Contract by key employees;

(vi) Other customary closing conditions.

Rights and Preferences of Series A Preferred:

Dividend rights: No dividend, whether in cash, in property or in shares of the capital of the Company, would be allowed to be paid on any other class or series of shares of the Company unless and until a dividend in like amount was first paid in full on the Series A Preferred Shares (on an as-converted basis). The Series A Preferred also would be entitled to participate fully in any non-cash distributions declared by the Board, on an as-converted basis.

Liquidation preference: In the event of any liquidation, dissolution or winding up of the Company, the holders of the Series A Preferred Shares would be entitled to receive, prior to any distribution to the holders of the Common Shares or any other class or series of shares, an amount per Series A Preferred Share equal to US$1.667 plus an annual interest of 6 per cent (the 'Preference Amount'). All remaining assets, if any shall be distributed to the holders of the Common Stock and Preferred Stock pro rata (on an as if converted basis). If the Company had insufficient assets to permit payment of the Preference Amount in full to all holders of Series A Preferred Shares, then the assets of the Company would be distributed ratably to the holders of the Series A Preferred Shares in proportion to the

Preference Amount each such holder of Series A Preferred Shares would otherwise be entitled to receive.

A merger or consolidation of the Company in which its shareholders did not retain a majority of the voting power in the surviving entity, or a sale of all or substantially all the Company's assets, would each be deemed a liquidation, dissolution or winding up of the Company.

Redemption: Subject to any applicable legal restrictions on the Company's redemption of its share capital, beginning on a date five years from the Closing Date, the holders of a majority of the then outstanding Series A Preferred Shares may require the Company to redeem all of the outstanding Series A Preferred Shares. The redemption price for each Series A Preferred Share would be US $1.667 plus an accrued annual interest of 6 per cent there on to the date of redemption (the 'Redemption Price'). The Redemption Price would be proportionally adjusted for share splits, share dividends, recapitalizations and the like. If on the redemption date, the number of Series A Preferred Shares that may then be legally redeemed by the Company is less than the number of such Series A Preferred Shares to be redeemed, then such excess number of Series A Preferred Shares would be carried forward and redeemed as soon as the Company had legally available funds therefor.

Conversion rights: The holders of the Series A Preferred Shares would have the right, at their sole discretion, to convert all or any portion of the Series A Preferred Shares into Common Shares at any time after the Closing Date. The initial conversion price for the Series A Preferred Shares would be equal to the Purchase Price, resulting in an initial conversion ratio of 1:1, but the conversion price and rate would be adjusted as described below, effective 31 December 2001. Said adjustment shall be made as follows: the conversion price in effect immediately prior to the adjustment shall be adjusted downward to equal the price obtained by multiplying: (i) the conversion price immediately prior to the adjustment by (ii) the consolidated gross revenues actually recognized by the Company from 1 July 2000 until 31 December 2001 (as determined by the Company's independent auditors), expressed as a percentage of US$20 million; *provided that* if the consolidated gross revenues actually realized by the Company during the period are US$15 million or less, the percentage calculated under clause (ii) shall be deemed to be 75 per cent. By way of illustration only, if the current conversion price and conversion ratio immediately prior to the adjustment are US$1.667 and 1:1 and the Company recognizes consolidated gross revenues of US$19 million during the period ending 31 December 2001, the adjusted conversion price would be US$1.584 (the figure obtained by multiplying (i) the pre-adjustment conversion price of US$1.667 by (ii) 95 per cent or US$19 million expressed as a percentage of US$20 million); and the resulting adjusted conversion ratio would be 1.05:1, or the original conversion price of US$1.667 divided by the adjusted conversion price of US$1.584. For the avoidance of doubt, there are no upward adjustments.

Automatic conversion: The Series A Preferred Shares would automatically be converted into Common Shares, at the then applicable conversion rate, upon the closing of an underwritten public offering of Common Shares or depositary receipts evidencing Common Shares in the US that has been registered under the Securities Act of 1933, as amended, at a public offering price of at least US$5 per share and gross proceeds to the Company in excess of US$15 million or in a similar public offering of Common Shares in a jurisdiction and on a recognized securities exchange outside of the US, provided such public offering in terms of price, offering proceeds and regulatory approval is reasonably equivalent to the aforementioned public offering in the US (a 'Qualified IPO').

Anti-dilution provisions: The conversion price of the Series A Preferred Shares would be subject to adjustment on a full ratchet basis for issuances of any securities of the Company at a purchase price less than the then-effective conversion price with a carve-out for issuances of Common Shares to employees, officers or directors of the Company pursuant to share purchase or share option plans or agreements or other incentive share arrangements approved by the Board, which shall not exceed 20 per cent of all outstanding shares of the Company on a fully-diluted basis immediately subsequent to the completion of the financing contemplated hereby. The Series A Preferred Shares shall be entitled to proportional anti-dilution protection for share splits, share dividends, recapitalizations and the like.

Voting rights: Each Series A Preferred Share would carry a number of votes equal to the number of Common Shares then issuable upon its conversion into Common Shares. The Series A Preferred Shares would generally vote together with the Common Shares and not as a separate class, except as provided below under the heading 'Protective provisions'.

- Protective provisions:	Consent of the holders of at least 66 per cent (two-thirds) of the outstanding Series A Preferred Shares would be required for: (i) any amendment or change of the rights, preferences, privileges or powers of, or the restrictions provided for the benefit of, the Series A Preferred Shares; (ii) any action that authorized, created or issued any class of the Company's securities having preferences superior to or on a parity with the Series A Preferred Shares or any other securities of the Company; (iii) any action that reclassified any outstanding shares into shares having preferences or priority as to dividends or assets senior to or on a parity with the preference of the Series A Preferred Shares; (iv) any action that repurchases, redeems or retires any of the Company's voting shares other than pursuant to contractual rights to repurchase Common Shares or Preferred Shares by employees, directors or consultants of the Company or its subsidiaries upon termination of their employment or services or pursuant to the exercise of a contractual right of first refusal held by the Company; (v) any material amendment of the Company's constitutional documents that adversely affected the rights of the Series A Preferred Shares; (vi) consolidation or merger with or into any other business entity or the sale of all or substantially all the Company's assets; (vii) the liquidation or dissolution of the Company; (viii) the declaration or payment of a dividend on the Common Shares (other than a dividend payable solely in shares of Common Shares); (ix) incurrence of indebtedness in excess of US$100,000; (x) any loans by the Company to any director, officer or employee; (xi) the purchase or lease by the Company of any asset valued in excess of US$50,000; (xii) the purchase by the Company of any securities of any other company in excess of US$100,000 in a twelve (12) month period; (xiii) the increase in compensation of any of the five (5) most highly compensated employees of the Company and/or any of the Company's subsidiaries by more than 15 per cent in a twelve (12) month period; (xiv) any transaction or series of transactions between the Company and any holder of Common Shares, director, office or employee of the Company and any director, officer or employee of the Company' subsidiaries that is not in the ordinary course of business or for which the aggregate

value exceeds US$25,000; (xv) other than in the ordinary course of business, any transaction that results in a pledge of any assets of the security interest, lien or other encumbrances or any assets of, or the Company's; (xvi) any material change in the Company's business plan; (xvii) the appointment by the Company of any directors of any of its subsidiaries; (xviii) the hiring of any management member with annual remuneration of over US $80,000.

In addition, the Company will not, without prior consent of the holders of at least 66 per cent (two-thirds) of the outstanding Series A Preferred Shares, (a) directly or indirectly transfer or pledge any economic interest in any of its several Subsidiaries or their respective businesses; or (b) cause or permit any of its several Subsidiaries to take any of the following actions: (i) any amendment to such Subsidiary's Articles of Association or the Joint Venture Contract or other constitutional document; (ii) any liquidation, termination or dissolution of such Subsidiary; (iii) any change in the capital structure of such Subsidiary, either by increase or decrease of its registered capital or issuance of stock or otherwise; (iv) any sale of substantially all the assets of such Subsidiary or reorganization, merger or consolidation of such Subsidiary with any other economic organization; or (v) any change in the business scope or plan of such Subsidiary.

Terms of the Share Purchase Agreement and Rights Agreement: The purchase of Series A Preferred Shares would be made pursuant to a Share Purchase Agreement and a Rights Agreement reasonably acceptable to the Company and Series A Preferred Shareholders, which agreement would contain, among other things, customary representations and warranties of the Company, its Subsidiaries and the existing shareholders of the Company, covenants of the Company reflecting the provisions set forth herein, and appropriate conditions of closing, including a legal opinion of the Company's counsel.

Board of directors: The Company's Memorandum and Articles of Association would provide for a Board of Directors (the 'Board') consisting of six (6) directors. The number of directors may not be changed except by amendment in accordance with the terms hereof.

With respect to the election of the directors to the Board, so long as at least 10 per cent Series A Preferred Shares remain outstanding, the holders of Series A Preferred Shares would be entitled to elect two members of the Board or, at the sole election of such holders, to

	appoint a representative to attend all meetings of the Board and committees thereof as an observer. Board meetings shall be held every two months with 7 days' advanced notice from the management.
Use of proceeds:	The Company would use the proceeds from the sale of the Series A Preferred Shares for research and development, business expansion, acquisitions of multimedia and wireless communication related businesses and technology, capital expenditures, marketing and general working capital to its business of providing application solutions and services.
Rights of first offer:	Each holder of Series A Preferred Shares would have a right of first offer to purchase up to its pro rata share (based on its percentage of the outstanding Common Shares, calculated on a fully-diluted as-converted basis) of any equity securities offered by the Company (other than in a Qualified IPO), on the same price and terms and conditions as the Company offers such securities to other potential investors. This right would not apply to the issuance by the Company of Common Shares (or options therefor) issued to employees, officers or directors of the Company pursuant to purchase or share option plans approved by the Board, which shall not exceed 20 per cent of all shares of the Company on a fully-diluted basis immediately subsequent to the completion of the financing contemplated hereby.
Right of first refusal and co-sale agreement:	The Company, each holder of Series A Preferred Shares, Dr Li, Mr Kang and Dr Huang (the latter three individuals the 'Founders') and key shareholders of the Company designated by Series A Preferred Shareholders would enter into a Co-Sale Agreement, which would give the holders of the Series A Preferred Shares first refusal rights and co-sale rights providing that any Founder or key shareholder who proposed to sell all or a portion of his shares to a third party must first permit the holders of the Series A Preferred Shares at their option (i) to purchase such shares on the same terms as the proposed transferee or (ii) sell a proportionate part of their shares on the same terms offered by the proposed transferee. The rights set forth in the Co-Sale Agreement would terminate upon the closing of a Qualified IPO. In addition, the Founders will undertake not to sell more than 20 per cent of their current shareholdings in the period before pre IPO or within two years after the closing of the document, without the consent of the Series A Preferred Shareholders.

Change in control:	Prior to entering into any transaction that would result in a change of control of the Company or a sale of all or substantially all of the Company's assets (a 'Corporate Event'), the Company would give Series A Preferred Shareholders notice of such event. For a period of 45 days following receipt of such notice, Series A Preferred Shareholders would have the right to enter into an agreement to acquire the Company or its assets on substantially the terms set forth in the notice. The rights set forth in this paragraph would terminate upon the closing of a Qualified IPO. Such notice is not necessary in case of an acquisition of the company with a purchase price of more than three times the original costs of Preferred Series A Shares.
Information rights:	So long as any Series A Preferred Shares were outstanding, the Company would deliver to each holder of the Series A Preferred Shares the following (relating to itself and all its subsidiaries): (i) audited annual financial statements within 90 days after the end of each fiscal year, audited by a 'Big 5' accounting firm of the Company's choice; (ii) unaudited quarterly financial statements within 45 days after the end of each fiscal quarter; (iii) unaudited monthly financial statements within 30 days after the end of each month; (iv) copies of all documents or other information sent to any shareholder; and (v) an annual budget and a revision within 30 days prior to the end of each half fiscal year. All such financial statements are to be prepared in conformance with US Generally Accepted Accounting Principles (GAAP). For as long as any Series A Preferred Shares were outstanding, holders of Series A Preferred Shares would have standard inspection rights of the facilities of the Company and any of its subsidiaries (including all its subsidiaries), including, without limitation, discussing the business, operations and conditions of the Company and any subsidiaries with its directors, officers, employees, accountants, legal counsel and investment bankers. These information and inspection rights would terminate upon a Qualified IPO. Following an initial public offering, the Company would deliver to each holder of Series A Preferred Shares or Common Shares issued upon conversion of Series A Preferred Shares, promptly after filing, copies of the Company's annual reports, interim reports and/or quarterly reports to shareholders and all other filings required to be made with the SEC or other relevant securities exchange, regulatory authority or governmental agency.

Registration/Offering rights:	(1) *Demand, F-3 (or Equivalent) and Piggyback Rights:* The holders of the Series A Preferred Shares would have registration rights with respect to potential offerings in the US, and the equivalent rights with respect to similar offerings in other jurisdictions, that are customary in financings of this nature. The specific terms of such rights would include at least the following: (i) after a Qualified IPO, three (3) demand registrations, or their equivalent, upon the request of holders of 25 per cent of the registrable securities; (ii) unlimited registrations on Form F-3 or equivalent transactions; (iii) unlimited piggyback registrations, or their equivalent, in connection with registrations and sales of shares for the account of the Company or selling shareholders exercising demand rights subject to customary underwriters' cutbacks; and (iv) cut-back provisions providing that registrations or other similar sales of shares, other than a Qualified IPO, must include at least 25 per cent of the shares requested to be included by the holders of registrable or eligible securities and employees, directors etc must be cut back before the holders of such securities would be cut back.
	(2) *Expenses:* The Company would bear the expenses (excluding underwriting discounts and commissions but including all other expenses related to the registration or equivalent transaction) of all such registrations or equivalent transactions.
	(3) *Transfer of rights:* The registration/offering rights may be transferred.
	(4) *Termination:* The registration/offering rights would terminate seven (7) years after the Closing Date.
Confidentiality and invention assignment agreement:	Each key officer and employee of the Company and the Subsidiaries would have entered into an acceptable confidentiality and invention assignment agreement. The Company would use its best efforts to have the remainder of the employees and officers sign such an agreement.
Administrative fee:	The Company will pay up to US$25,000 fee to cover Series A Preferred Shareholders' due diligence and legal expenses, should the financing contemplated hereby be consummated. Such fee would be paid by the Company concurrently with the Closing Date.

Employee Vesting: Additional shares of the Company's capital issued to employees, directors and consultants would be subject to vesting/repurchase over four years.

Appendix F

The Winners of 2003's Best Companies Survey in China

FinanceAsia (www.financeasia.com) congratulates the winners of 2003's best companies survey. Here we present the results for China.

This survey covers the performance of the top companies in ten countries in Asia. We polled institutional investors and equity analysts and received a total of 296 votes. The results are given in more detail in the April 2005 edition of FinanceAsia Magazine.

Table A.F.1 Best managed company

Position	Company	Votes
1	CNOOC	47
2	China mobile	41
2	TCL	41
3	Petrochina	28
4	Legend	26
5	Denway Motors	17
6	Sinopec	15
7	China Oilfield Services	11
8	Beijing Datang Power	10
8	Zhejiang Expressway	10

Table A.F.2 Best investor relations

Position	Company	Votes
1	Legend	43
2	TCL	41
3	China Mobile	36
4	Sinopec	31
5	CNOOC	27
6	Petrochina	18
6	China Resources Enterprises	18
7	Beijing Datang	15
8	Denway Motors	10
9	Asiainfo	9

Table A.F.3 Most committed to creating to shareholder value

Position	Company	Votes
1	CNOOC	43
2	China Mobile	37
3	Petrochina	29
4	Legend	28
5	TCL	20
6	Netease	19
7	Cosco Pacific	15
8	Zhejiang Expressway	14
9	Denway Motors	10
9	Sinopec	10

Table A.F.4 Best corporate governance

Position	Company	Votes
1	Legend	41
2	China Mobile	37
3	TCL	31
4	CNOOC	24
5	Petrochina	17
6	China Resources	16
7	Sinopec	13
8	Cosco Pacific	10
9	Asiainfo	9
9	Denway Motors	9

Table A.F.5 Best financial management

Position	Company	Votes
1	China Mobile	43
2	CNOOC	35
3	Legend	34
4	TCL	20
5	Cosco Pacific	15
6	Petrochina	14
7	Beijing Datang	12
7	China Unicom	12
9	Denway Motors	9
10	Zhejiang Expressway	8

Bibliography

21st Century Online (2003) *The Exiting Point for Foreign M&A in China: Consumable, Finance and Insurance*. Available at http://finance.21cn.com/news/2003-04-25/1022036.html (accessed 28 April 2003).

Adelman C, Jenkins D and Kemmis S (1977) 'Re-thinking case study: notes from the Second Cambridge Conference' *Cambridge Journal of Education* 6:3.

Ahuja G and Katila R (2001) 'Technological acquisitions and the innovation performance of acquiring firms: a longitudinal study' *Strategic Management Journal* 22(3): 197–220.

Arnold G (2002) *Corporate Financial Management* 7th edition, London: Prentice Hall.

Baker & McKenzie Online (2003) *China – Guide to Mergers & Acquisitions 2003*. Available at: www.bakernet.com (accessed 5 May 2004).

Barry C (1994) 'New directions in research on venture capital finance' *Financial Management* 23(3): 3–15.

Barry C, Muscarella C, Peavy J and Vetsuypens M (1990) 'The role of venture capitalists in the creation of public companies: evidence from the going public process' *Journal of Financial Economics* 27: 447–71.

Beckerling L 'Asian M&A starts to lure back foreign investors', *The Standard* 25 March 2004.

Beijing Normal University Online (2001) *The Story between AsiaInfo and Venture Capital*. Available at: www.academic.net.cn/innovation/examp/doc_001.htm (accessed 16 June 2003).

Brutona GD and Ahlstromb D (2003) 'An institutional view of China's venture capital industry Explaining the differences between China and the West', *Journal of Business Venturing* 18: 233–259.

Burgess R (1991) *In the Field: An Introduction to Field Research*, London: Routledge.

Burton D (ed) (2000) *Research Training for Social Scientists: A Handbook for Postgraduate Researchers*, London: Sage Publications.

Business Alert - China Online (2003) *Provisional M&A Rules Take Effect in April* Available at: www.tdctrade.com/alert/cba-e0304a-1.htm (accessed 21 June 2003).

British Venture Capital Association (1992) *A Guide to Venture Capital*, London: Price Waterhouse.

Calif 'AsiaInfo to acquire Bonson Technology for US$47 million; AsiaInfo vaulted to No.1 position in key wireless market', *Business Wire* 22 January 2002, Beijing.

Capener CR 'M&A in China comes of age', *The China Business Review* 26 June 1998.

Casinoman Online (2003) *China's Online Game Makers Reportedly Bring in US$250 million* Associated Press. Available at: www.casinoman.net/Content/casino_gambling_news/gambling_news_article.asp?arti d=2387 (accessed 10 December 2003).

Chen YX (2002) 'Venture capital innovations and policy recommendations for the development of China's venture capital industry' *China Venture Capital* 1(2): 20.

Chen ZG and Gu T 'Four models for foreign investment in Chinese M&A', *China Business Post* 29 June 2003.

Chen ZY (2002) 'An analysis of the development and operating conditions of the venture capital industry in Taiwan' *China Venture Capital* 1(4): 38.

Cheng SW (2002) 'Venture capital investment and the fictitious economy' *China Venture Capital* 1(1): 1.

China Daily Online (2003) *China will be Asian Leader in Foreign Direct Investment.* Available at: www1.chinadaily.com.cn/news/2002-01-22/53221.html (accessed 16 November 2002).

China Daily Online (2003) *A Lot on the Plate for Sino-EU Summit.* Available at: www.chinadaily.com.cn/en/doc/2003-10/28/content_275986.htm (accessed 8 December 2003).

China Daily Online (2004) *Chinese Internet Firms Line up for IPOs.* Available at: www.chinadaily.com.cn/en/doc/2003-11/18/content_282449.htm (accessed 30 October 2003).

Dresdner Kleinwort Benson (2000) *Building China's e-Infrastructure* Industry report, September 2000, Available at: www.ctil.com/

investor_relations/analysis_reports/download/DKB_Sept 2000.pdf (accessed 5 June 2003).

Cockerill C (2003) 'The next big M&A story', *Euromoney* April: 129–132.

Coopers & Lybrand (1992) *Making A Success of Acquisitions*. London: Coopers & Lybrand.

Cowton CJ (1998) 'The use of secondary data in business ethics research', *Journal of Business Ethics* 17(4): 423–34.

Dale A, Arber S and Proctor M (1988) *Doing Secondary Analysis* London: Unwin Hyman.

De Ramos A and Cesar B (2003*)* *A Better Field of Play: CFO Asia's Fourth Annual Deals of the Year* CFO Asia. Available at: www.cfo.com/article.cfm/3011347?f=archives (accessed 29 December 2003).

Dehesa G de la (2002) *Venture Capital in the United States and Europe*, Washington DC: Group of Thirdy.

Denlinger P 'Shanda files for Nasdaq IPO; lowers expectations' *China Business Strategy* 19 April 2004.

Department of PD English Edit '10,000 big merger deals expected in five years in China' *People's Daily* 20 November 2003.

Department of PD English Edit 'China – rising market for transnational M&A' *People's Daily* 11 November 2003.

Dignan L (2000) *AsiaInfo, UTStarcom IPOs Surge*. Available at: www.news.com (accessed 18 March 2003).

Dignan L (2000) *The Day Ahead: AsiaInfo, UTStarcom Cash In On China's Growth Prospects*. Available at: www.news.com (accessed 20 April 2003).

Drucker PF 'Five rules for successful acquisition' *Wall Street Journal* 15 October 1981.

Donews Online (2004) *Shanda Listed on Nasdaq*. Available at: www.donews.com/donews/article/6/62658.html (accessed 18 May 2004).

Dooley M, Folkerts-Landau D and Garber P *Direct Investment, Rising Real Wages and the Absorption of Excess Labour in the Periphery*, NBER Working Paper 10626. NBER Conference on G7 Current Account Imbalances: Sustainability and Adjustment, Bureau of Economic Research Inc, 1–2 June 2005, Newport, Rhode Island.

Easterby-Smith M, Thorpe R and Lowe A (1991) *Management Research – An Introduction*, London: Sage Publications.

Etgen B (2003) 'Mergers and acquisitions' *Asian News* March, Beijing: Beiten Burkhardt.

Evan FC and Bishop DM (2001) *Valuation of M&A: Building Value in Private Companies*, New York: John Wiley & Sons.

EVCA and Coopers & Lybrand (1996) *The Economic Impact of Venture Capital in Europe*. Belgium: EVCA.

Flaherty KA (2003) 'New M&A rules for foreign investors in China' *China Legal News* November: 15–19.

Folta HP (1999) 'The rise of venture capital in China' *The China Business Review* November/December: 6–15.

Fried VH and Hisrich RD (1994) 'Toward a model of venture capital investment decision making' *Financial Management* 23(3): 28–37.

Ghauri P, Grønhaugh K and Kristianslund I (1995) *Research Methods in Business Studies: A Practical Guide* London: Prentice Hall.

Guide to Venture Capital in Asia (2000) *Guide to Venture Capital in Asia* Hong Kong: Asian Venture Capital Association.

Habeck MM, Kröger F and Träm MR (2000) *After the Merger: Seven Strategies for Successful Post-merger Integration* London: Prentice Hall.

Hakim C (1982) *Secondary Analysis in Social Research* London: Allen & Unwin.

He GJ (2002) 'Zhuhai Yueke Tsinghua Electro-Ceramic Company Limited case study' *China Venture Capital* 1(1): 49.

Healey MJ (1991) 'Obtaining information from businesses'. In: Healey MJ (ed) *Economic Activity and Land Use* Harlow: Longman.

Healey MJ and Rawlinson MB (1993) 'Interviewing business owners and managers: a review of methods and techniques' *Geoforum* 24(3): 339–355.

Healey MJ and Rawlinson MB (1994) 'Interview techniques in business and management research'. In: Wass VJ and Wells PE *Principles and Practice in Business and Management Research* Aldershot: Dartmouth.

Hennessey R 'Losers outpace gainers in IPO market by margin of 2-1' *The Wall Street Journal* 4 December 2000.

Hsieh B and Jen D 'Investors beware in China' *China Economic Review* May 2001.

Hyman HH (1972) *Secondary Analysis of Sample Surveys* New York: Wiley.

ICXO World Business Online (2004) *Big Appetite of M&A*. Available at: http://digest.icxo.com/htmlnews/2004/03/19/106068.htm (accessed 21 March 2004).

iResearch (2004) *China Online Game Research Report 2003* (Simple Version) Shanghai iResearch Co Ltd.

Irvine S (2001) *An M&A Deal in China*. Available at: www.FinanceAsia.com (accessed 21 November 2001).

Jones T (2003) *Regulating M&A activity in China* Hong Kong: Freshfields Bruckhaus Deringer.

Kanth R (2002) *UN Sees 27% Fall in Global FDI Inflows*. Available at: http://business-times.asia1.com.sg/news/story/0,2276,61610,00.html (accessed 22 October 2002).

Ko T (2003) 'Why China's new M&A rules need a second look' *International Financial Law Review* 21(11): 33–35.

Kortum S and Lerner J (1998) *Does Venture Capital Spur Innovation?* NBER Working Paper 6846, December, New York.

Kracht J (2002) *Mergers and Acquisitions in China: A New Generation of Investment Opportunities* Fiducia Management Consultants/CDI. Available at: http://www.amcham-shanghai.org/contents/amchat-article.aspx?doc_id=133 (accessed 8 January 2003).

Lan SR (2002) 'On establishing perfect legal circumstance for venture capital' *China Venture Capital* 1(1): 33.

Lees S (1992) 'Auditing mergers and acquisitions: Caveat Emptor' *Managerial Auditing Journal* 17(4): 6–11.

Lees S (2003) *Global Acquisitions: Strategic Integration and Human Factor* London: Palgrave Macmillan.

Li L (2004) 'Li Yinan's Harbour' *CEO & CIO in China* 4: 33.

Li WN 'Shanda's difficult decision for listing' *Caijing Magazine* 25 May 2004.

LightReading-Online (2003) *AsiaInfo Names CEO, Chairman*. Available at: www.lightreading.com/document.asp?doc_id=28892 (accessed 22 March 2003).

Liu JJ (2002) 'Framework of the Special Regulation on Venture Capital Firm' *China Venture Capital* 1(4): 35.

MacMillan I, Zemann L and Subbanarasimha P (1987) 'Criteria distinguishing successful from unsuccessful ventures in the venture screening process'. *Journal of Business Venturing* 2(2): 123–137.

Manigart S and Sapienza HJ (2000) 'Venture capital and growth' In: Sexton NL and Landstrom H (eds) *The Blackwell Handbook of Entrepreneurship* Oxford: Blackwell Publishers.

Mayer C, Schoors K and Yafeh Y (2001) *Sources of funds and Investments Strategies of Venture Capital Funds: Evidence from Germany, Israel, Japan and the UK* Working Paper. Oxford: Oxford Financial Research Centre.

Mills G (2000) 'Post-acquisition management' In: Davis A *Tolley's Company Acquisitions Handbook* 6th edition, London: Tolley.

Morris T and Wood S (1991) 'Testing the survey method: continuity and change in British industrial relations' *Work Employment and Society* 5(2): 259–282.

Morrison J (2002) *The International Business Environment: Diversity and the Global Economy* London: Palgrave Macmillan.

Muzyka D, Birley S, and Leleux B (1996) 'Trade-offs in the investment decisions of European venture capitalists' *Journal of Business Venturing* 11(1): 273–287.

Nisbt J and Watt J (1980) *Case Study Ediguide 26* Nottingham: University of Nottingham School of Education.

National Venture Capital Association (2001) *Research Conducted for the Association by DRI-WEFA* Washington DC: NVCA.

Qin R 'All eyes are in the listing of China Netcom' *People Info News* 11 February 2004.

Ormerod J and Burns I (1988) *Raising Venture Capital in the UK* London: Butterworths.

Osnabrugge MV and Robinson RJ (2000) *Angel Investing: Matching Start-up Funds with Start-up Companies – The Guide for Entrepreneurs, Individual Investors, and Venture Capitalists* San Francisco: Jossey-Bass.

Peng M 'The new era for China Online Gaming in 2004' *The Beijing News* 11 February 2004.

Peng MW (2000) *Business Strategies in Transition Economies.* Thousand Oaks: Sage Publications.

People Daily Online (2003) *10,000 Big Merger Deals Expected in Five Years in China*. Available at: http://english.peopledaily.com.cn/200311/20/eng20031120_128674.shtml (accessed 12 December 2003).

People Daily Online (2003) *China Reforms State-owned Enterprises through M&A*. Available at: http://english.peopledaily.com.cn/200312/09/eng20031209_129948.shtml (accessed 12 December 2003).

People Daily Online (2003) *China - Rising Market for Transnational M&A*. Available at: http://english.peopledaily.com.cn/200311/11/eng20031111_128058.shtml (accessed 12 November 2004).

People Daily Online (2003) *Economists: Conditions Favorable for China to Boost Transnational Merger, Acquisition*. Available at: http://english.peopledaily.com.cn/200311/20/eng20031120_128619.shtml (accessed 22 November 2003),

People Daily Online (2003) *Fledgling M&A Market to Bloom in Five Years*. Available at: http://english.peopledaily.com.cn/200311/24/eng20031124_128877.shtml (accessed 26 November 2003).

Pike R and Neale B (2003) *Corporate Finance and Investment: Decistions and Strategies* 4th edition, London: Prentice Hall.

Ping L 'The theory and positive study of technological diffusion' *Shanxi Economy Press* March 1999.

Platt J (1996) 'Has funding made a difference to research methods?' *Sociological Research Online* 1(1) Available at: www.socresonline.org.uk/socresonline/1/1/5.html (accessed 10 October 2002).

Poterba JM (1989) *Venture Capital and Capital Gains Taxation*, NBER Working Paper 2832, Cambridge: NBER.

Ragin CC (1992) 'Introduction: cases of what is a case?' In: Ragin CC and Becker HS (eds) *What is a Case?* Cambridge: Cambridge University Press.

Reuters (2003) *AsiaInfo names ex-Ericsson China exec as CEO* (Online) Available at: http://asia.news.yahoo.com/030224/3/setq.html (accessed 26 February 2003).

Reuters (2004) *Shanda Interactive Prices IPO at USD 11/share* (Online) Available at: www.forbes.com/reuters/newswire/2004/05/12/rtr1369591.html (accessed 18 May 2004).

Riquelme H and Xu L (2001) *Venture Capital, Venture Capitalists' Decision Criteria, and Implications for China* International Conference on the Chinese Economy, 4–6 July 2001, Beijing.

Robson C (1993) *Real World Research* Oxford: Blackwell.

Sahlman WA (1988) 'Aspects of financial contracting in venture capital' *J Appl Corp Finance* 1: 23–36 (Summer).

Saunders M, Lewis P and Thornhill A (2000) *Research Methods for Business Students* 2nd edition, London: Prentice Hall.

Shanda Online (2004) *Microsoft's Tang Jun Joins Shanda as President* Available at: www.shandaentertainment.com/en/news/news.jsp?id=10 (accessed 18 May 2004).

Shen LL (2004) *The Review and Consideration for 2003's Internet Market in China*, Beijing: Qianlong Academe Ltd. Available at: www.ahtt.net.cn/artview.php?num=868 (accessed 16 March 2004).

Shepherd D (1999) 'Venture capitalists' introspection: a comparison of "in use" and "espoused" decision policies' *Journal of Small Business Management* 27(2): 76–87.

Strategic-Online (2003) *AsiaInfo to Acquire Bonson Technology for US$47 Million* (Online) Available at: www.strategic.com.hk/media_release/media_clientid.asp?media_id=839 (accessed 16 January 2003).

Su XH 'AsiaInfo got the gold egg from venture capital' *Guangzhou Evening Newspaper* 4 January 2001.

Taulli T (2003) 'Ethics and due diligence' *Corporate Governance Advisor* 11(3): 19–21.

Tony Lorenz Memorial Trust (1994) *The Role of Venture Capital* London: BVCA.

Wang SQ and Wang GG (2002) *China Venture Capital Investment Development Report 2002*, Beijing: China Finance and Economy Press.

Watts C (2003) *Stable Growth Opportunities in China's Telecom Sector* (Online) Available at: www.adhitech.com/menu_48/menu_56/ (accessed 16 June 2003).

Weston JF and Weaver SC (2001) *Mergers and Acquisitions* Columbus: McGraw-Hill.

Wolf M 'Asia's game with America is a long way from ending' *Financial Times* 11 August 2004.

Wong SK (2001) *Major Reforms of China's Laws and Legal System in the Run-up to her Accession to the World Trade Organisation*

Conference on Investment in China and the WTO, 17 October 2001, Hong Kong.

Wright M and Robbie K (eds) (1999) *Management Buy-outs and Venture Capital Into the Next Millennium* Cheltenham: Edward Elgar.

Wu X, Ni Y and Cao ZG (2002) *The Factor Analysis on China's Manufacturing Enterprises Technology Acquisition Performance* Beijing: NSF China & NSF Zhejiang.

Xiang JX (2004) *The Six Trends for Chinese Software Market in 2004* CBIQ On-line, Available at: www.cbiq.com/news/newshtml/guangcha/20040218152336.htm (accessed 20 February 2004).

Xie QS (2004) 'Chinese software market will access to RMB90 billion in 4 years' *Guanzhou Daily* Available at: www.southcn.com/it/itinternet/200402272102.htm (accessed 14 February 2004).

Xu L (2000) *Financial Development and Mobilisation of Household Savings in China* Shanghai: Shanghai Academy of Social Sciences Publishing House.

Xu LP, Wang B and Wang LL (2002) 'Complements and cooperation in the development of growth enterprise markets in Hong Kong and Shenzhen' *China Venture Capital* 1(4): 41.,

Yan SM 'Harbour copied the romaunt of HuaWei?' *21st Century Business Post* 6 February 2004.

Yan Tai 'Foreign media has eyes for China' *Space Daily* 10 March 2004.

Yi DD 'Foreign investment for M&A in China: cake is big but difficult to eat' *China News Agent* 25 November 2003.

Yin RK (1994) *Case Study Research: Design and Methods* 2nd edition, London: Sage Publications.

Yu H 'Four trenders, top ten persons and top ten events in Chinese M&A' *Xinhua News Agent* 2 January 2004.

Zacharakis A and Meyer D (1998) 'A lack of insight: Do venture capitalists really understand their own decision process?' *Journal of Business Venturing* 13(1): 57–76.

Zeng M 'M&A hit China cyber business' *Shanghai Star* 11 July 2000.

Zerega B (2000) 'What would Mao think?' *Red Herring Magazine*, October (Online) Available at: www.redherring.com/mag/issue83/mag-china-83.html (accessed 6 December 2002).

Zhang DS and Liu JJ (2002) 'On the transformation of China's venture capital system' *China Venture Capital* 1(1): 36.

Internet references

http://asia.cnet.com
http://hightechmagazine.com/FrontPage.asp
http://hk.yahoo.com
http://it.sohu.com
http://soft.winzheng.com
www.3721.com
www.allegronetworks.com
www.asiainfo.com
www.brodeur.com
www.caijingshibao.com (China Business Post On-line)
www.cbinews.com
www.cbronline.com/index.htm
www.cbsnews.com
www.channelnewsasia.com
www.china.gov.cn
www.china-ready.com
www.chinabyte.com/
www.chinadaily.com.cn
www.chinainternetupdate.com
www.chinanews.com.cn
www.chinavest.com
www.cnradio.com.cn/
www.cs.com.cn
www.cvca.com.hk
www.domainsmagazine.com
www.eastday.com
english.ctrip.com/index.asp
www.donews.com
www.fidelityventures.com
www.forbes.com
www.gtt-zhh.com
www.gtvc.com/index.htm
www.hindustantimes.com
www.hostingtech.com
www.icxo.com
www.ipohome.com/default.asp
www.ipwireless.com
www.internetnews.com
www.intrint.com

www.investorab.com
www.magisnetworks.com
www.nasdaq.com
www.p5w.net
www.pacificepoch.com/index.php
www.pconline.com.cn
www.people.com.cn
www.reuters.com
www.shanda.com.cn/english/homepage/index.php
www.shanghai-star.com.cn
www.siliconvalley.com
www.sina.com.cn
www.sinoculture.com/
www.southcn.com
www.stock2000.com.cn
www.tclhk.com
www.techcentralstation.com
www.theasianinvestor.com/index.html
www.thecarlylegroup.com/eng/index.html
www.thestar.com
www.thestreet.com
www.tom.com
www.ventureeconomics.com
www.wangandwang.com
www.xinhuanet.com
www.yahoo.com
www.zh-web.com
www1.chinadaily.com.cn/en/bw/in China

Index

NB: page numbers in italic indicate figures or tables

3721 Technology Co Ltd   106–13, 167
  Chinese language service/keywords   106–09
  technology standard   106–08
  venture capital investment   108–10
  Yahoo!/Yahoo-HK   110–13

airline market   183–84
Alibaba/Alibaba.com   14, 16, 89–90, 113–16, 166
anti-cancer drugs,   74, 75 see also gene therapy
AsiaInfo   xvii, 182, 224–43
  benefits from M&A   241, *242*, 242
  benefits from venture capitalists   229–30
  mergers and acquisitions (M&A)   230–34, *235, 236*
  strategic issues following M&A   237–38
  SWOT analysis   238–41
  ten-year growth   225, *226*, 227
  venture capital invested   227–28
Assets Supervision and Administration Commission (SASAC)   215, 224

banking industry   222–23
Beijing   10–11, 59, 67, 213–14, 258
  Beijing Investment Promotion Bureau (BIPB)   213
  China Beijing Equity Exchange (CBEE)   213
Best Companies Surveys Winners in China (2003)   341–43
best practices in products and services for M&A operations see mergers and acquisitions
biotechnology R&D   70–76, *76–77*, 77–79
  biotech opportunities in China   72–75
  Chinese Academy of Science   70–71
  Chinese biotechnology research institute (SEBC)   71–72
  gene therapy and venture capital   75–76
  product life cycle   74–75
business to business (B2B)   113–16

capital restructure: Mengniu   272, 273–92
  foreshadowing of capital   287, 289
  fundraising: first round   277–81
  IPO and issue of shares   286–87, *288*
  IPO preparations   285–86
  mature equity capital subscription: second round   281, *282, 283*, 284–85
  potential risks   289–92
  reputation as capital   275–77

case studies   20, 113–16, 116–18, 118–20, 120–22, 147–48, 163, 174–75
  Chinese SME Board   147–48
  digital age pioneer: Wang Wenjing   174–75
  factors affecting stock markets (2004–2005)   20
Catalogue for Guiding Foreign Investment in Industries   215, 216, 222
ceramics and substrates   188–92
  AIN ceramic substrates   188–89
  surface mounting technology (SMT)   192
China and
  GDP growth   19
  multilayered capital market system   150
  venture capital see venture capital
China Internet Network Information Centre (CNNIC)   81, 83, 90, 113
China Mobile   103, 201, 203, 204, 205–06, 207, 234
China Netcom   201, 207, 234, 241
China Securities Regulatory Commission (CSRC)   32, 147, 148, 155
China Telecom   86, 98, 102–03, 201, 203, 241
  Vnet Instant Messenger (VIM)   102–03
China Unicom   201, 203, 204, 205–06, 207
China Venture Capital Development Research Report (2004)   11
Chinese General Chamber of Commerce (CGCC)   273
Chinese Government   26–29, 112, 183, 200, 219–20 see also legislation *and* venture capital
  controlled venture capital funds   2
  Ministry of Commerce (MOFCOM)   214, 215, 216–17, 287
  Ministry of Finance   199, 215
  Ministry of Information (MII)   59, 113, 199, 202, 206, 254, 255
  Ministry of Science and Technology   2–3
  Procurement Centre of the State Council   199
  Procurement Rules for Software   199
  rules for registrar companies man internet addresses   112–13
  State Administration for Industry and Commerce (SAIC)   132, 215
  State Council of China   155
  State Planning Committee   59

tenth five-year plan   xv, 195, 202
Chinese market, investing in   1–52 *see also* legislation (China) *and* venture capital
   establishing perfect legal circumstances   23–26
   foreign investment: new provisions/rules   26–29
   investment system reform   30–31
   milestones of VC industry   33–52
   SME Board   31–32
Chinese overseas students (Appendix C)   325–28 *see also* overseas/local Chinese students
Chinese State Food and Drug Administration (SFDA)   75, 76
Communist Party of China, Central Committee of CCCPC   150
creative products and markets   81–122
   3721 Technology Co Ltd   106–13 *see also main entry*
   B2B in China: case study   113–16 *see also* Alibaba.com
   e-tailing and bicycle deliveries: case study   120–22
   EVD and home-viewing: case study   118–20
   instant messaging   93–106 *see also main entry*
   internet and e-commerce   81–93 *see also main entry*
   small electric appliances: case study   116–18
criteria for investments   53–79
   aspects of successful investment   53, *54*
   biotechnology research and development (R&D) *see main entry*
   functions of management teams in VC projects   54–55
   operation of founders of Harbour *see* Harbour Networks Limited
   overseas/local Chinese students   56–57 *see also main entry*
Ctrip.com   179–86
   business philosophy   181
   IPO success on NASDAQ   179–82, *183*, 183
   venture capital investment: Carlyle Asia Venture Partners   181–85

due diligence and investment monitoring   123–37, 212–13
   fraudulent accounting: Penshibao *see main entry*   123–25, *125*, 126–31
   venture capitalists, considerations for   131–37 *see also main entry*
DVDs and EVDs   118–20

e-commerce   86, *86–87 see also* internet and e-commerce
   venture capital backing for   88–91
e-tailing and bicycle deliveries   120–22
eBay   84–85, 90, 91
electronic technology   187–89

foreign direct investment (FDI)   15, 210, 213, 214
Foreign Exchange, State Administration of (SAFE)   211, 215, 216
foreign-invested venture capital investment enterprises (FIVCIEs)   28–29, 293–310
foreign investment   221–23
foreign investment enterprises (FIEs)   214, *217*, 217
Foreign Trade and Economic Cooperation, Ministry of   114
Foreign Trade and Economics, China University of   114
foreign VC investment: new provisions   26–29
foreign VC organizations   14–15
foreign venture capitalists   15, 75
fraudulent accounting: Penshibao   123–31
   discovery of   127–29
   overseas financing   129–31
   restructure and financing   123–25, *125*, 126–27

gene engineering adenovirus injection (H101)   74
gene therapy   76, *76–77*, 77–79
   and venture capitalism   75–76
   Gendicine™   75
GTT and VC investment   187–93
   characteristics and outlook   189–90, *190–91*
   establishment and management model   187–89
   groups investing in GTT   187
   investing at early development stage   193
   sustainability of development   191–92

Harbour Networks Limited   58–60, *61*, 61–70
   build-up of   59
   business model and native entrepreneurs   69–70
   exit strategy and VC firms' investment   67–69
   funding   58–59
   internal management   64–65
   Li Yinan (founder)   59–60, 61–62, 64, 67–69
   market prospects   62–64
   mergers and acquisitions   65–67
   Warburg Pincus   59, 60, 62, 63, 67–68, 132

Industry and Commerce, State Administration of (SAIC)   215, 216
information and communication technology (ICT)   10, 227
initial public offering (IPO)   9, 10, 55, 94, 139–42, 163–77, 179–86, 231, 238, 243, 287
insight into potential and traditional sectors   245–92
   capital restructure: Mengniu   273–92 *see also main entry*
   finance and online gaming   245–53 *see also* online games

media venture capital experience 259–70 *see also* media industry
online gaming 253–54 *see also* online games
revenues 254–59 *see also* online games
venture capital investment in traditional industries 270–72 *see also main entry*
instant messaging 93–106 *see also* Tencent Technology Limited
  IPO on Hong Kong Stock Exchange 99–100, *101*, 101–02
  new business model 96–98
  Real Time eXpert and IBM 98–99
  Tencent and QQ 93–98
  threat from competitors 102–05
  value-added service and online games 105–06
  venture capitalist financing 95–96
intellectual property (IP) 3, 58
  legislation 74
  protection 73
  rights 71
  Trade-Related Aspects of Intellectual Property Rights (TRIPS) 74
Interim Provisions on the Acquisition of Domestic Enterprises by Foreign Investors (M&A Regulations) 214, 215, 216–17, 311–23
International Finance, Institute of (IIF) 218
International Finance Cooperation 73
internet and e-commerce 81–93
  in the 21st century 83–86, *86–87*, 87, *88, 89*
  internet development 91–93
  market growth and current trends 81, *81, 82*, 83
  regulations 113
  venture capital backing 88–91
Internet Corporation for Assigned Names and Numbers 107
internet development and investment 163–65 *see also* IPO exits
Internet Economy Research Centre: Chinese Academy of Social Sciences 157
investment system reform 30–31
  State Council Decision on 30
IPO as main exit route for capital investment 139–42
  international venture capitalists 140–42, *142*
  stock exchange listing 140, *141*
IPO exits 139–42, 163–65
  growth of internet sector 168, *169*, 169–70
  internet development, investment enthusiasm for 163–65
  IPO and Chinese internet firms: case study 163
  IPO as main exit route for capital investment *see main entry*
  Kingdee and UFsoft: IPO exit choices 170–73, 175–77 *see also* Kingdee *and* UFsoft
  multiple channels for exiting 165–67

  value-added market 168, *169*
IPO exits and the Stock Exchange *see* IPO exits *and* stock exchanges

Kingdee 170–72, 175–77, 195, 196, 197

legal and IP protection 58
legislation (China)
  Company Law 25
  Government Procurement Law 2003 (GPL) 198, 199
  implementation of laws and regulations 74
  Interim Regulations on the Establishment of Foreign-invested Venture Investment Enterprises (IREFVIE) 26–27
  Partnership Law 25
  policy recommendations for VC industry development 8–9
  Regulations on the Administration of Foreign-invested Venture Investment Enterprises (RFIVCIE) 3, 27, 28, 29
  steps to take 24–26
  venture capital 23–26
legislation (US) 23–24
  Employee Retirement Income Security Act (ERISA) Prudentman rule 23–24
  Limited Partnership Act (1974) 23
  Small Business Investment Act (1980) 24
  venture capital 23–24

media industry 259–70
  future of 264–65
  media venture capital (MVC) investment 259–61, *261*, 262
  MVC operations process 267, *267*, 268–70
  operation model of Tanglong's MVC 266–67
  operation of MVC 262–64
Media Industry Reform Plan 265
Mengniu Dairy Group *see* capital restructure: Mengniu
mergers and acquisitions (M&As) 55, 84, 105, 156, 167, 190, 201, 209–43, 290
  Asia.Info 224–43 *see also main entry*
  Harbour 65–67 *see also* Harbour Networks Limited
  Mainland China *see* mergers and acquisitions: Mainland China
mergers and acquisitions: Mainland China 209–24
  current situation 209–14
  foreign investors: new M&A rules 214–17, *217, 218*, 218
  future prospects 218, *219*, 219, *220*, 220, *221*, 221–24
milestones of VC industry, Mainland China 33–52
multimedia messaging service (MMS) 83
multiservice transport platform (MSTP) 65

NASDAQ (National Association of Securities Dealers Automatic Quotation) xvi, 9, 16–17, 32, 58, 67, 73, 83, 100, 115, 139, 153,

155, 165, 166, 167, 172, 173, 179–86, 231, 238, 242, 252–53, 256, 271, 272
National Bureau of Statistics of China 15
National Committee of the Economy and Trade 86
next generation networks (NGNs) 59

online games 83, 99, 105–06, 245–54
  and finance 245–47, *247–48*, 249–53
  China's online game industry 256–58
  investment ventures and business strategy 248–51
  IPO listing plans 252–53
  piracy 256
  popularity of 253–54
  revenue from 254–59
overseas/local Chinese students 3, 56–57
  and foreign VC companies 56–57
  Chinese overseas students (Appendix C) 325–28
  industrial and technological parks 56
  President's call for contribution to nation (Appendix D) 329–30
  SMEs 56
  work experience 57

piracy, software 197, 245, 256

qualified foreign institutional investors (QFII) 147, 214

Radio, Film and Television, State Administration of (SARFT) 264
research and development (R&D) 32, 65, 71–72, 119, 133, 191, 194, 203, 204, 229, 230, 231, 254 *see also* biotechnology R&D management
research/surveys 11, 15, 116, 144, 168, 258
Rules on Administration of Foreign Invested Venture Capital Investment Enterprises (Appendix A) 293–310

Securities and Exchange Commission (SEC) 100, 184, 253
Shenzhen Stock Exchange (SZSE) 20, 31–32, 143–47, 148–57
  and SSE 143–47, 148–57
  SME Board 31–32, 58, 148
  VC Board 149, 155–57
short-messaging services (SMS) 206–07, 240
small and medium-sized enterprises (SMEs) xiv, xv–xvi, 2–3, 32, 55, 56, 64–65, 83, 84, 85, 107, 110, 111, 115, 130, 149, 154, 155, 156, 170–73, 168, 200, 253, 261
  government policies and measures for 2
  internet SMEs 88, 91–92
  venture-backed 10, 18, 237, 243 *see also* venture capital-backed SMEs in China
small electric appliances 116–18
  inferior technology 118
  lack of competition 118

poor management strategy 118
SME Board *see* Shenzhen Stock Exchange (SZSE) *and* stock exchanges in Mainland China
software and telecom enterprises 10–11
software manufacturing market 193–200
  accounting and enterprise resource planning (ERP) 195–96
  CRM and software configuration management (SC) 196
  development of 193–96, *196*, 197, *197*
  Government Procurement Rules for Software 199
  legislation on government procurement 198–200
  piracy 197
  telecoms software 196–97
Standing Committee of National People's Congress of China 23
State Development and Reform Commission (SDRC) 215
state-owned enterprises (SOEs) 1, 2, 214–17, 223
State Restructuring Regulations (Provisional Regulations on Utilizing Foreign Investment in Restructuring State-owned Enterprises) 214, 216
stock exchanges in Mainland China 142–44, *144*, 145, *145*, 146–62, 177
  AIM 155–56
  Chinese SME Board: case study 147–48
  chronology (1990–2004) *157–62*
  HKGEM and SZSE's VC board 152–54, *154*
  multitier capital market development 152
  Shenzhen Stock Exchange (SZSE) *see main entry*
  SME Board 148–51, 152
stock exchanges *see also* UK Stock Exchange *and* US Stock Exchange
  case study 20
  Hong Kong 17, 18, 67, 94, 100, 110, 176, 273–74, 286, 292
  Hong Kong Growth Enterprise Market (GEM) 127, 140, 152–54, 172–73, 176, 177
  Mainland China *see* stock exchanges in Mainland China
  Singapore 17, 110
  Singapore Dealing and Automated Quotation System (SESDAQ) 139
students *see* overseas/local Chinese students
SWOT analysis: AsiaInfo 238–41

Taxation, State Administration of (SAT) 216
telecommunications market 58, 62–63, 200–07, 234–35, 241
  broadband network 62
  fastest growth of 200–03
  short-messaging services (SMS) 206–07
  size, trends and opportunity 203–06
  third generation 3G technology 204, 205, 207

Tencent Technology Limited   93–106 *see also* instant messaging
  and QQ   93–98
  competitors   102–05
  financing from venture capitalists   95–96, 98
  floating on Stock Exchange   99–100, *101*, 101–02
  online games   99, 105–06
  projects and profits   96–98
  value-added service   105–06
term sheet sample (Appendix E)   331–40
Trade and Development, United Nations Conference on (UNCTD)   210
travel service market   179–86 *see also* Ctrip.com

UFSoft   170–71, 172–75, 177, 194, 195, 196
  Wang Wenjing: 2003 China digital figure   174–75
UK Stock Exchange   151
  Alternative Investment Market (AIM)   140, 155
  London (LSE)   151, 155
US Stock Exchange   151
  electronic NASDAQ   151–52
  New York (NYSE)   73, 151, 152

value-added service (VAS) market   168
venture-backed companies: stages in investment   21–23
venture capital   xv–xvi, 1–2, 166, 222, 227–33 *see also* foreign VC investment
  activity   2–4, *5–8*, 8–9
  activity rise   9–11
  and biotech products   74–75
  domestic and foreign VC firms   17–19
  factors affecting stock markets in 2004–2005: case study   20
  legislation   23–26 *see also* legislation (China)
  milestones of Mainland China's VC industry   33–52
  projects and management teams   54–55
  technology-based VC communities   4
  transition and forward trend   11, *11*, 2, *12–13*, 14–17
Venture Capital Association, British (BVCA)   22, 23
venture capital industry development: policy recommendations   8–9
venture capital investment
  global transfer   10
  management enterprise (VCIME)   28, 29
  management organizations   11
venture capital investment in traditional industries   270–72
  high growth potential   271–72
venture capital-backed SMEs in China   179–207
  Ctrip.com: IPO success on NASDAQ   179–86 *see also* Ctrip.com
  software manufacturing market   193–200 *see also main entry*
  telecommunications in China   200–07 *see also* telecommunications market
  VC investment for start-up enterprise   187–93 *see also* GTT and VC investment
venture capitalists, considerations for   131–37, 157
  agency problems and solutions   133–37
  agreement   *134*
  companies, obtaining information about   131–33
  exit strategy   157
  legal contract   *135–37*
venture funds sourced from foreign capital   18

Warburg Pincus   59, 60, 62, 63, 67–68, 132, 227–28, 229–30
World Trade Organization (WTO)   xiv, xv, 17, 73, 74, 87, 114, 117, 145, 147, 151, 190, 195, 201, 202, 204, 241, 264, 328

Yahoo!   90, 91, 94, 96, 104, 105, 107
  Yahoo-HK   110–13, 167